THE FIFTH QUARTER

MIKE DAWSON

:01

First Second
New York

:01

First Second

Published by First Second
First Second is an imprint of Roaring Brook Press,
a division of Holtzbrinck Publishing Holdings Limited Partnership
120 Broadway, New York, NY 10271
firstsecondbooks.com
mackids.com

Library of Congress Control Number: 2020919611

Our books may be purchased in bulk for promotional, educational, or business use.
Please contact your local bookseller or the Macmillan Corporate and Premium Sales
Department at (800) 221-7945 ext. 5442 or by email at
MacmillanSpecialMarkets@macmillan.com.

FIRST

EDITION

First edition, 2021
Edited by Mark Siegel and Samia Fakih, with assistance from Rachel Stark
Cover design by Kirk Benshoff
Interior book design by Mike Dawson and Sunny Lee
Printed in China by 1010 Printing International Limited, North Point, Hong Kong

Drawn digitally using a Wacom Cintiq tablet, colored digitally in Photoshop

ISBN 978-1-250-24418-5 (paperback)
10 9 8 7 6 5 4 3 2 1

ISBN 978-1-250-24417-8 (hardcover)
10 9 8 7 6 5 4 3 2 1

Don't miss your next favorite book from First Second!
For the latest updates go to firstsecondnewsletter.com and sign up for our enewsletter.

BY ART
WE LIVE

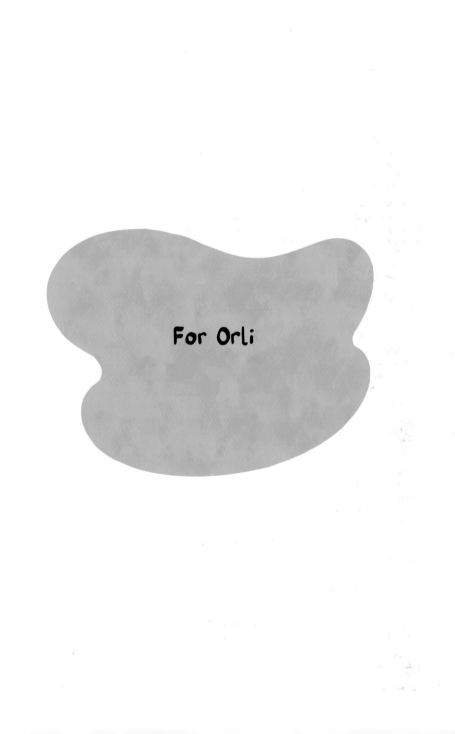

For Orli

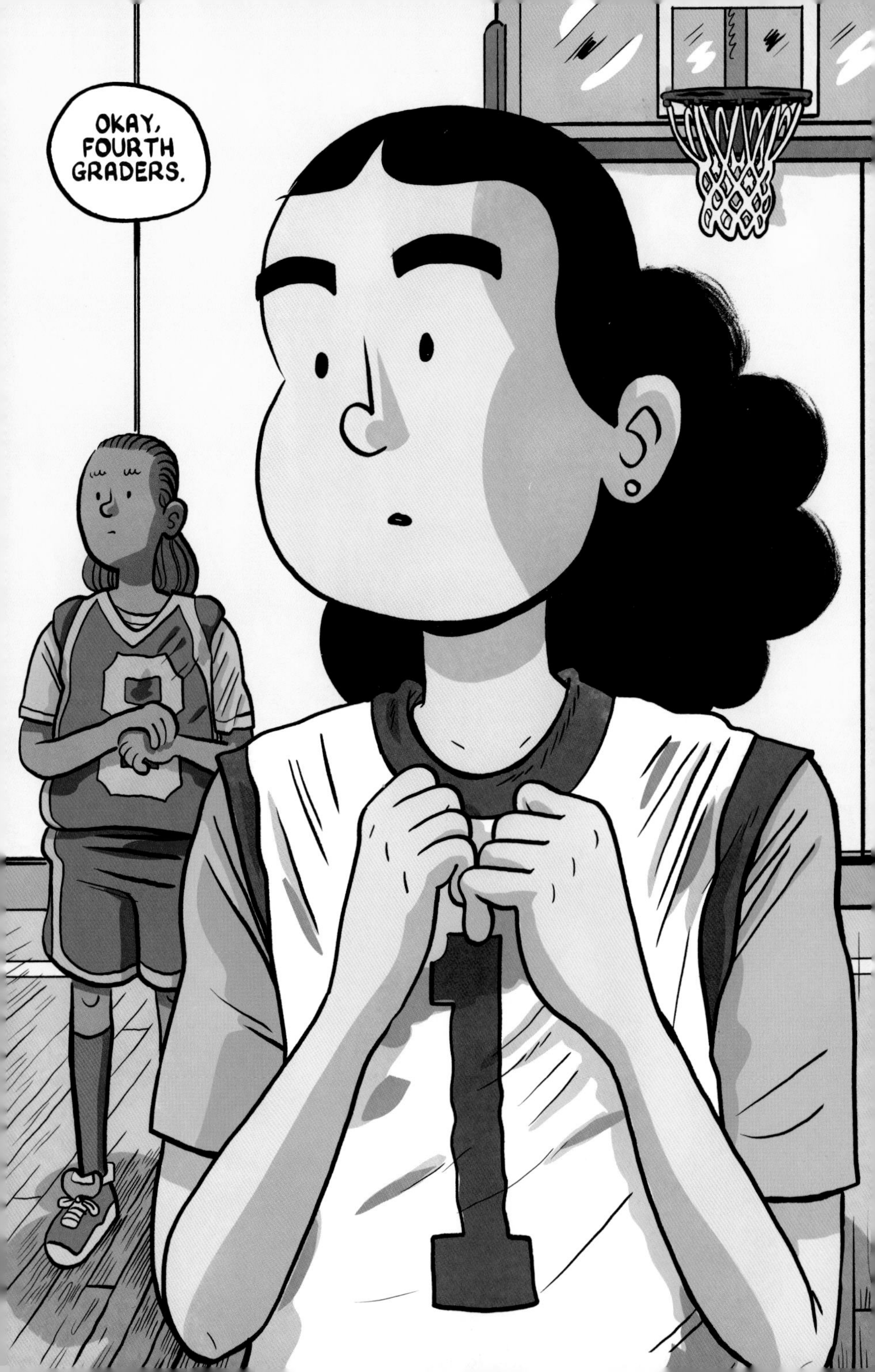
OKAY, FOURTH GRADERS.

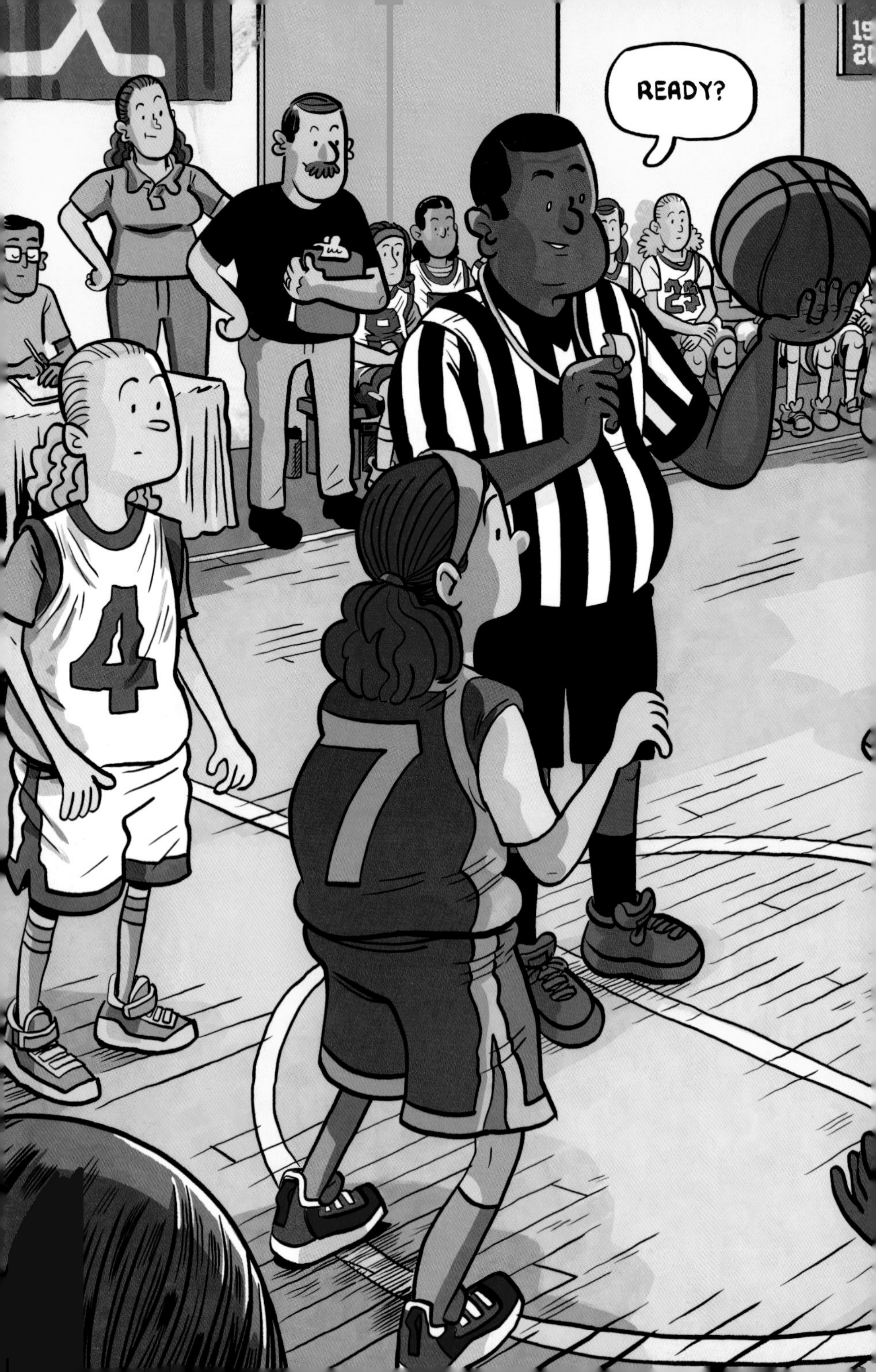
READY?

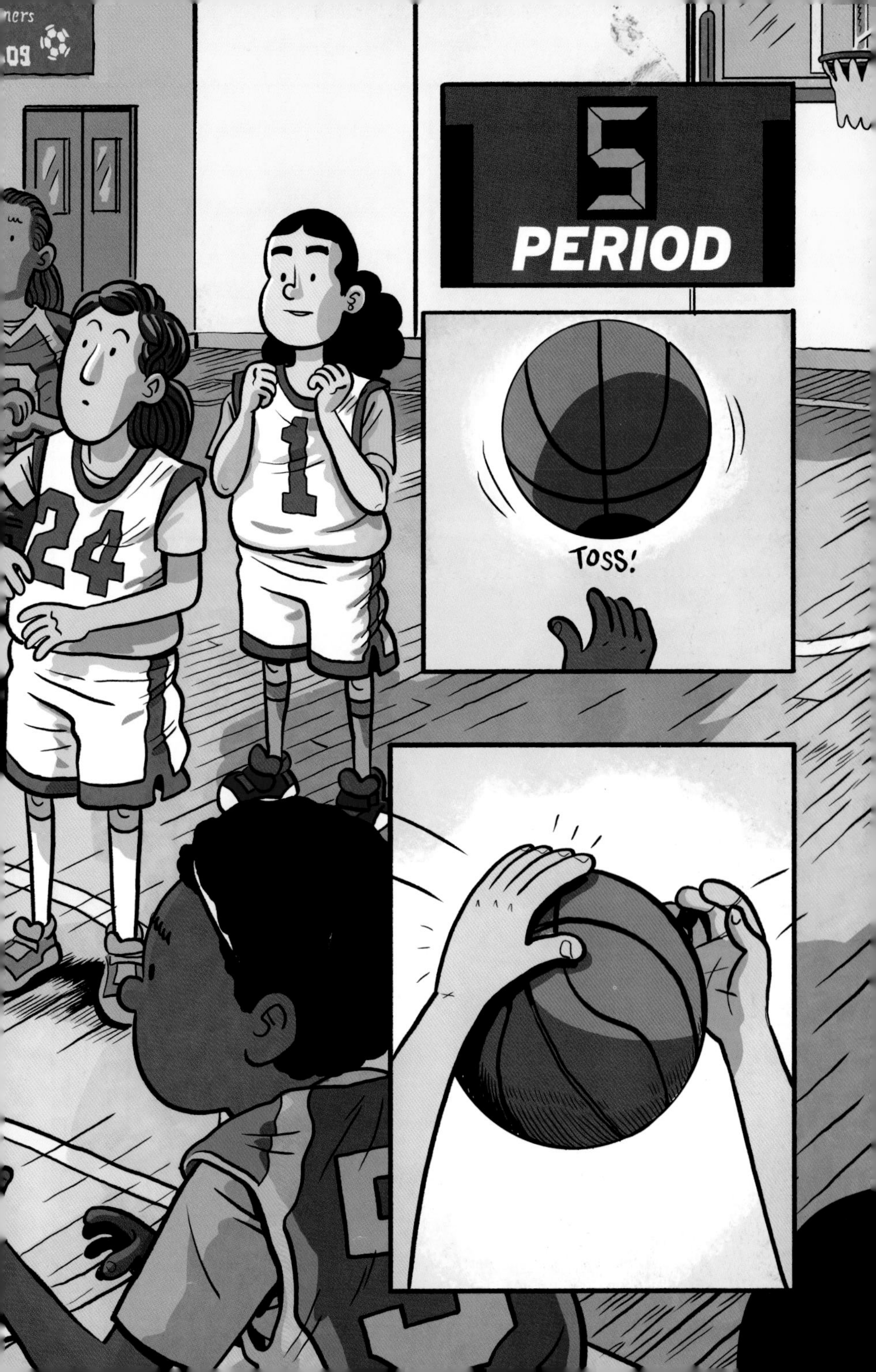
ners
09
5
PERIOD
24
1
TOSS!

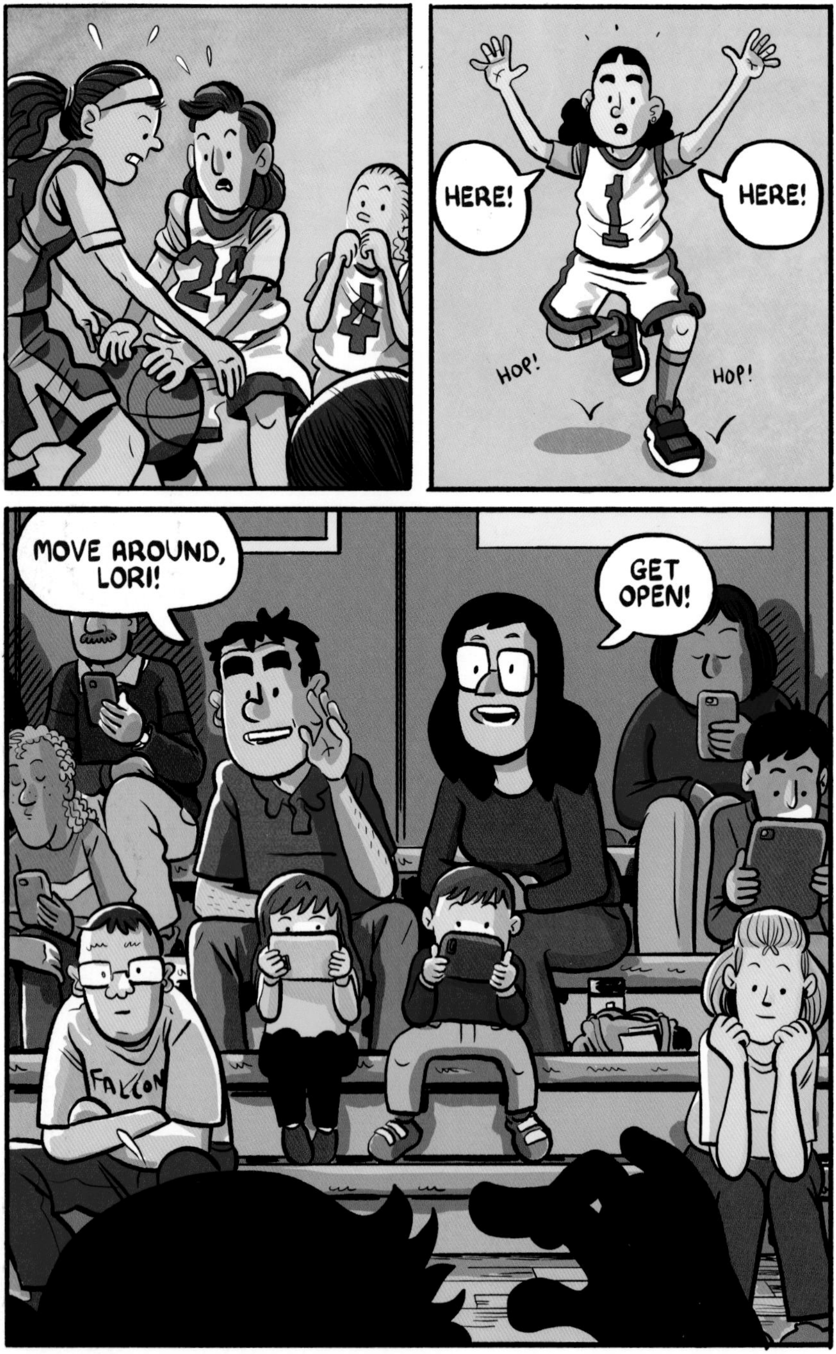
HERE!
HERE!
HOP!
HOP!
MOVE AROUND, LORI!
GET OPEN!
FALCON

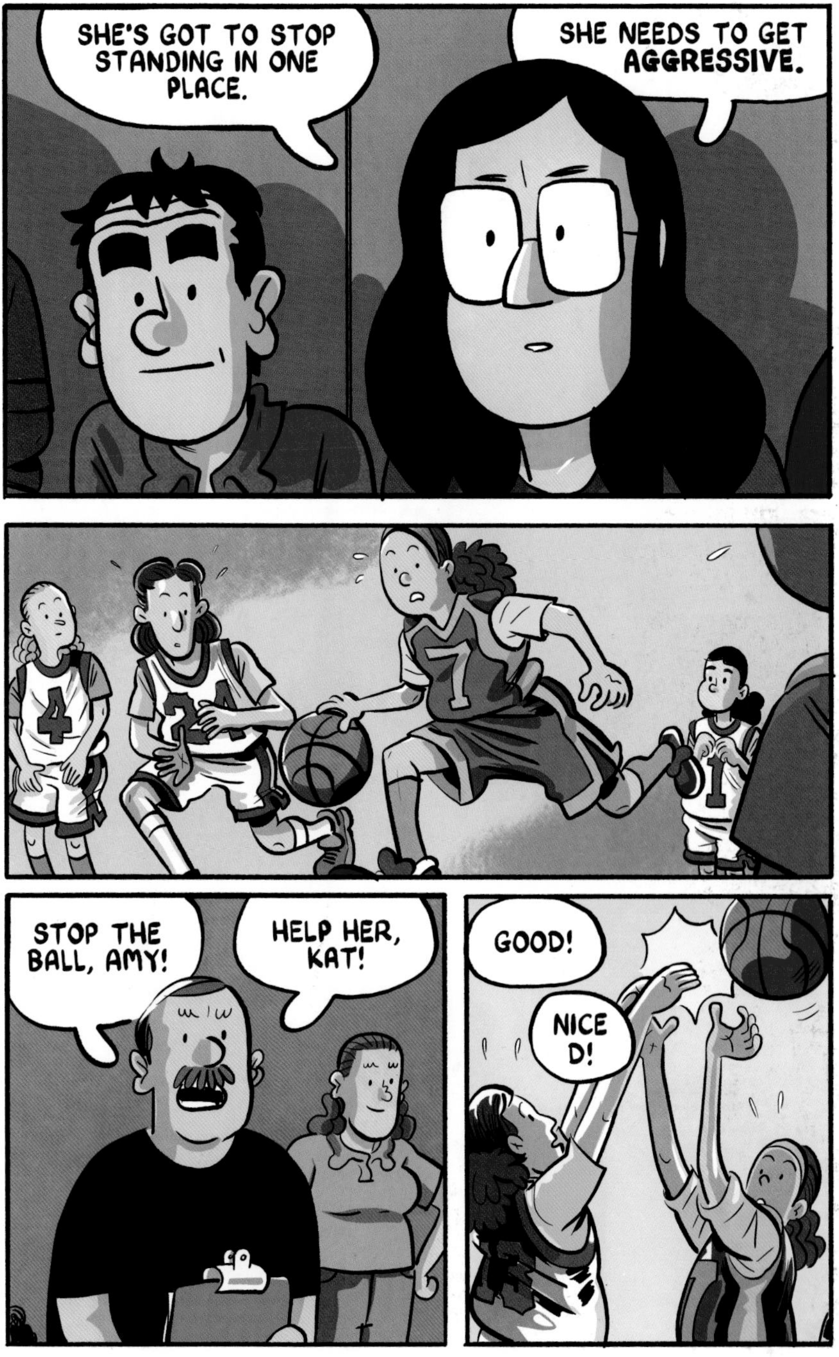
SHE'S GOT TO STOP STANDING IN ONE PLACE.
SHE NEEDS TO GET **AGGRESSIVE.**
STOP THE BALL, AMY!
HELP HER, KAT!
GOOD!
NICE D!

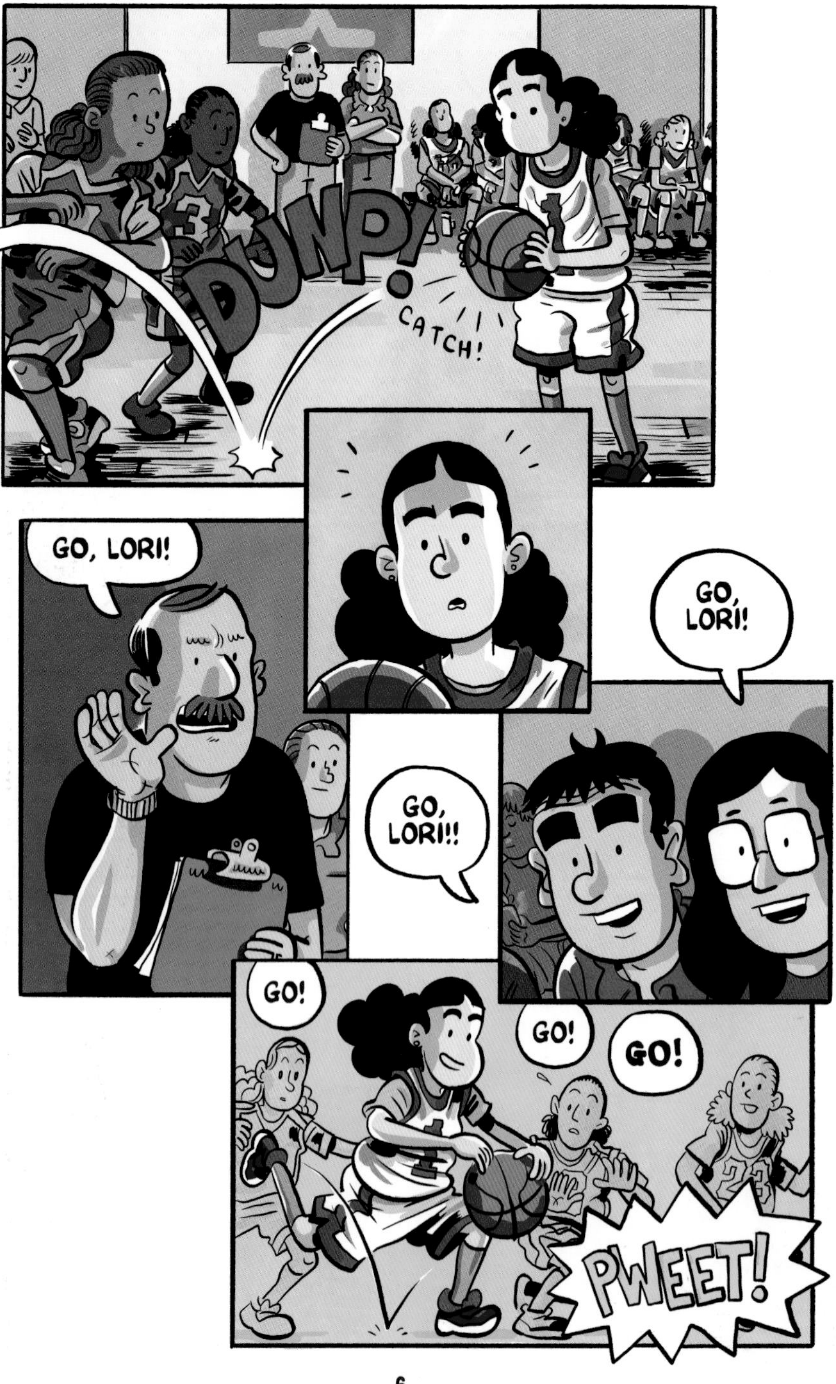
DUNP!
CATCH!
GO, LORI!
GO, LORI!
GO, LORI!!
GO!
GO!
GO!
PWEET!

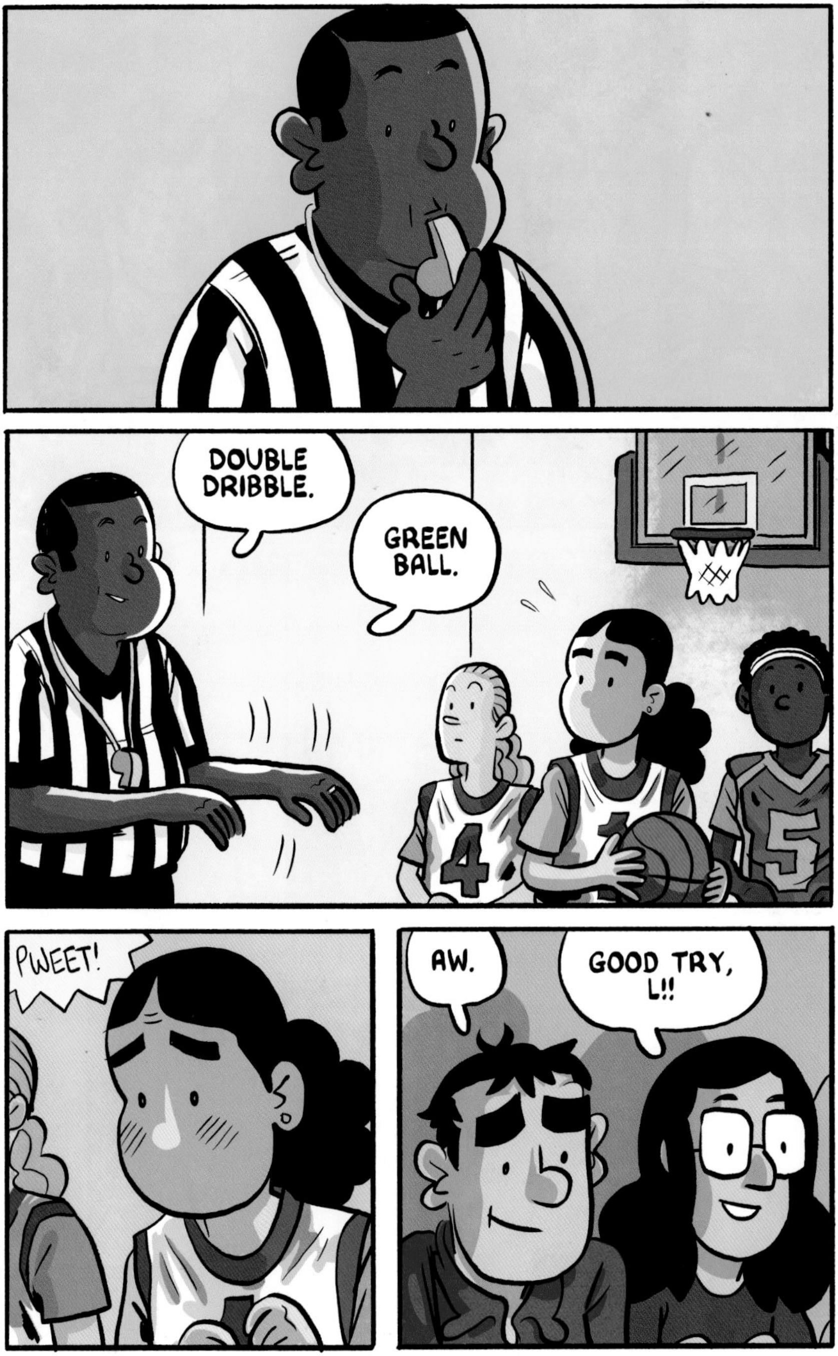
DOUBLE DRIBBLE.
GREEN BALL.
PWEET!
AW.
GOOD TRY, L!!

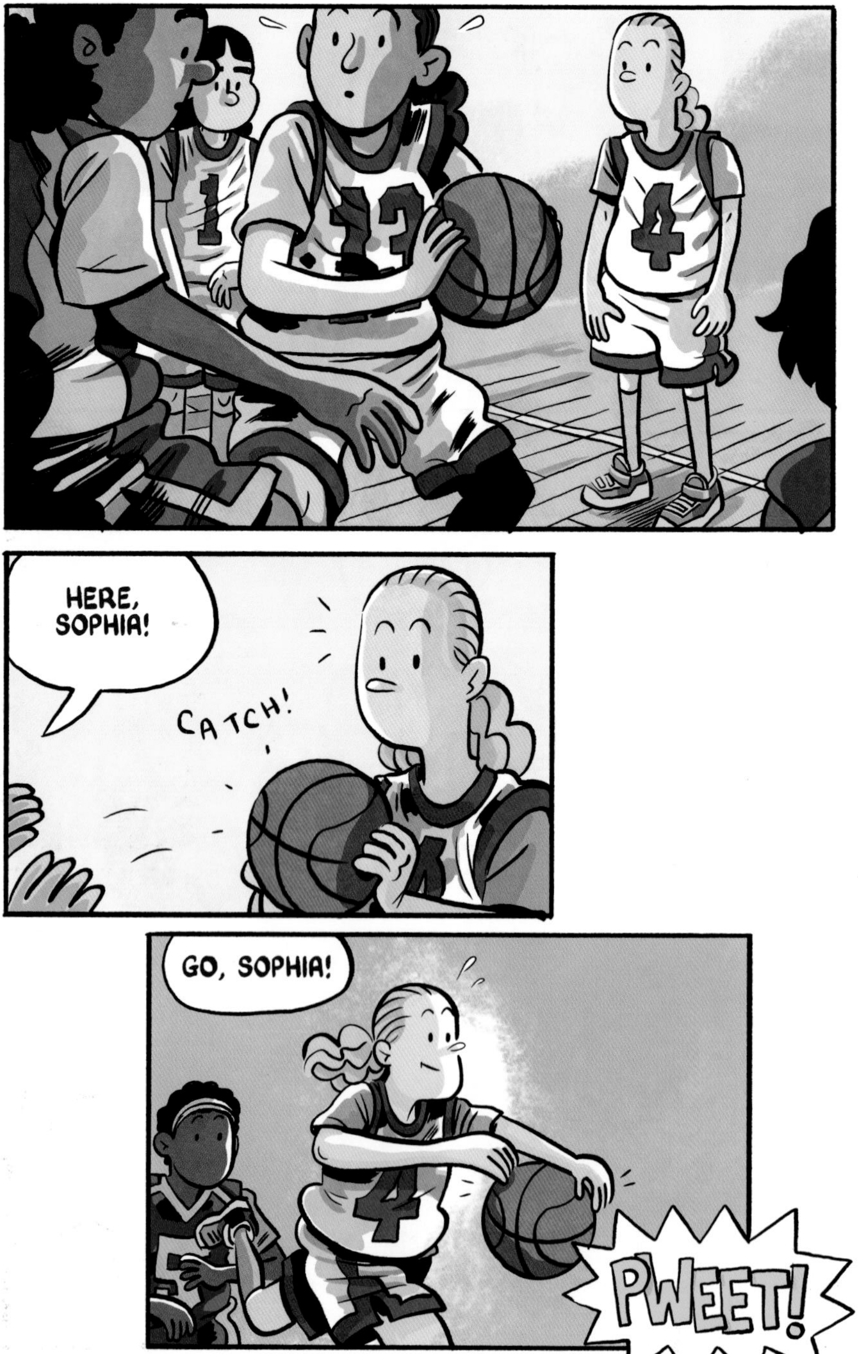
HERE, SOPHIA!
CATCH!
GO, SOPHIA!
PWEET!

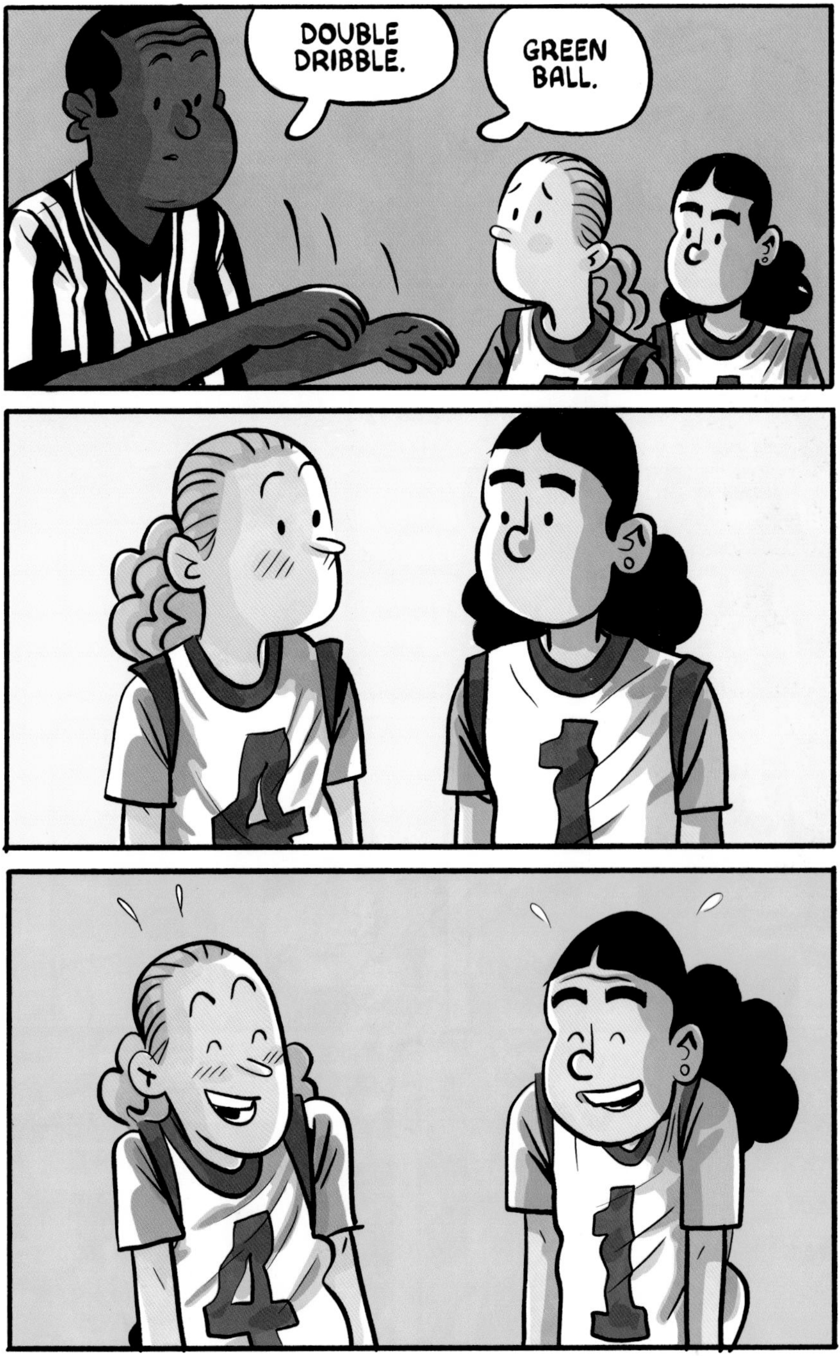
DOUBLE DRIBBLE.
GREEN BALL.

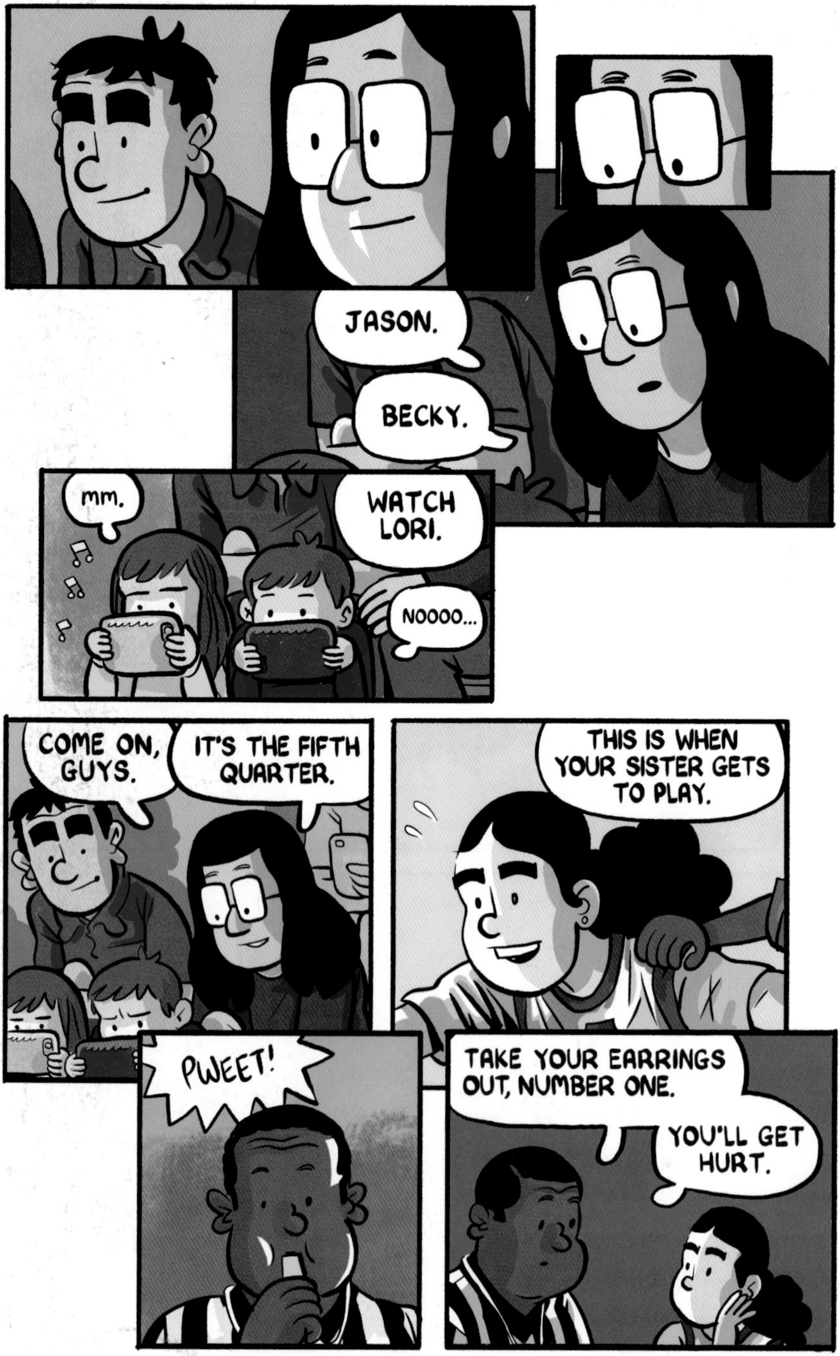
JASON.
BECKY.
mm.
WATCH LORI.
NOOOO...
COME ON, GUYS.
IT'S THE FIFTH QUARTER.
THIS IS WHEN YOUR SISTER GETS TO PLAY.
PWEET!
TAKE YOUR EARRINGS OUT, NUMBER ONE.
YOU'LL GET HURT.

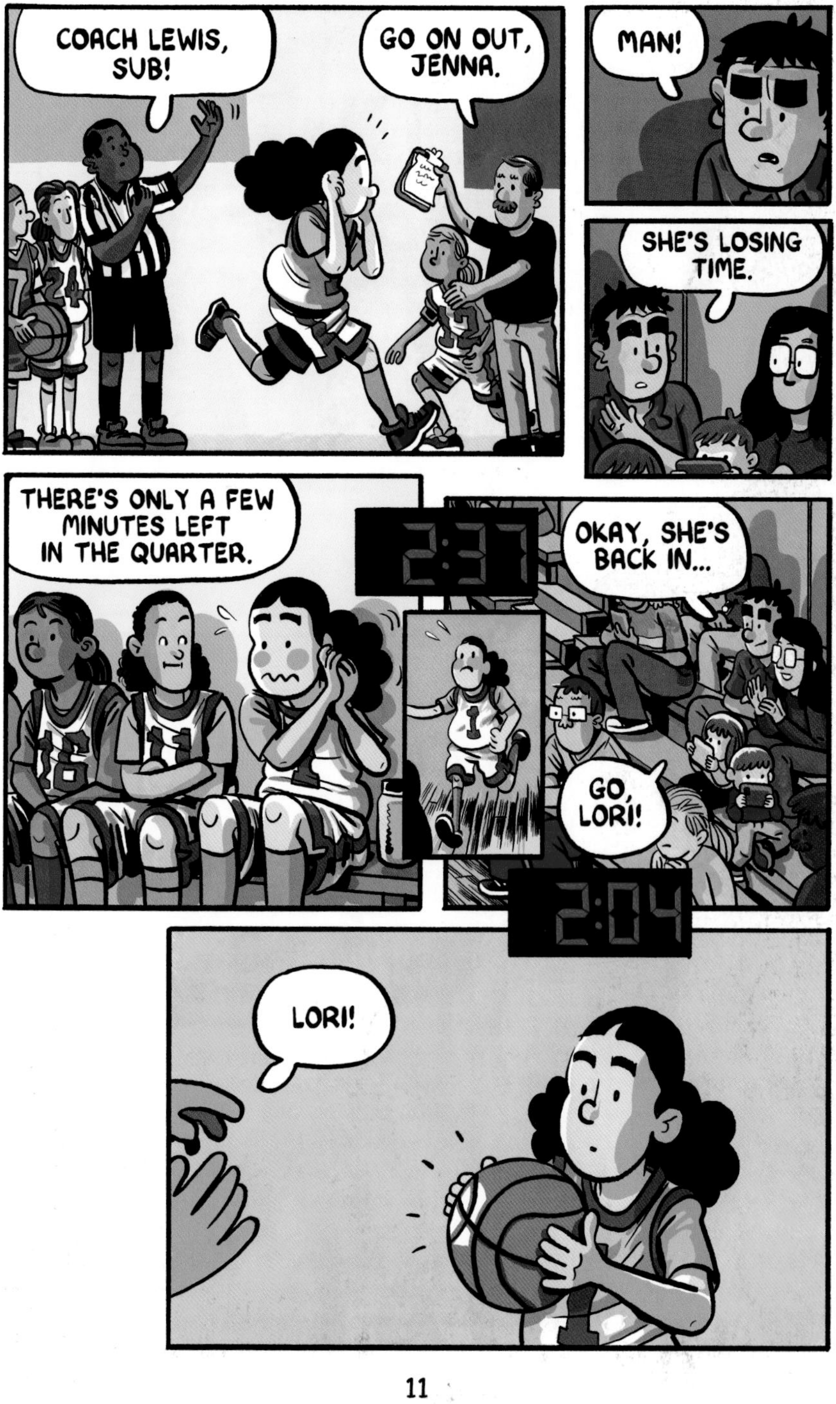
COACH LEWIS, SUB!
GO ON OUT, JENNA.
MAN!
SHE'S LOSING TIME.
THERE'S ONLY A FEW MINUTES LEFT IN THE QUARTER.
2:37
OKAY, SHE'S BACK IN...
GO, LORI!
2:04
LORI!

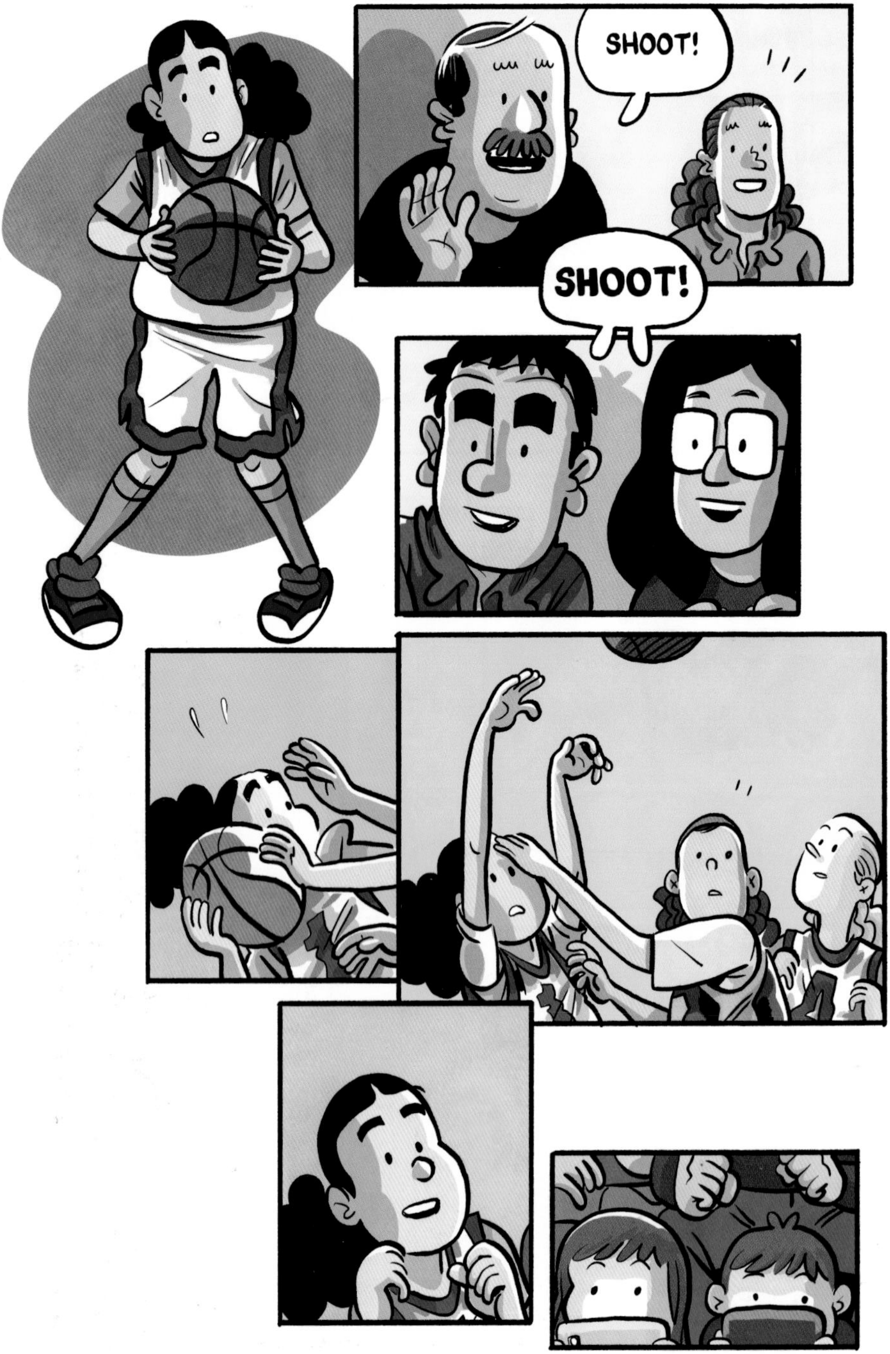
SHOOT!
SHOOT!

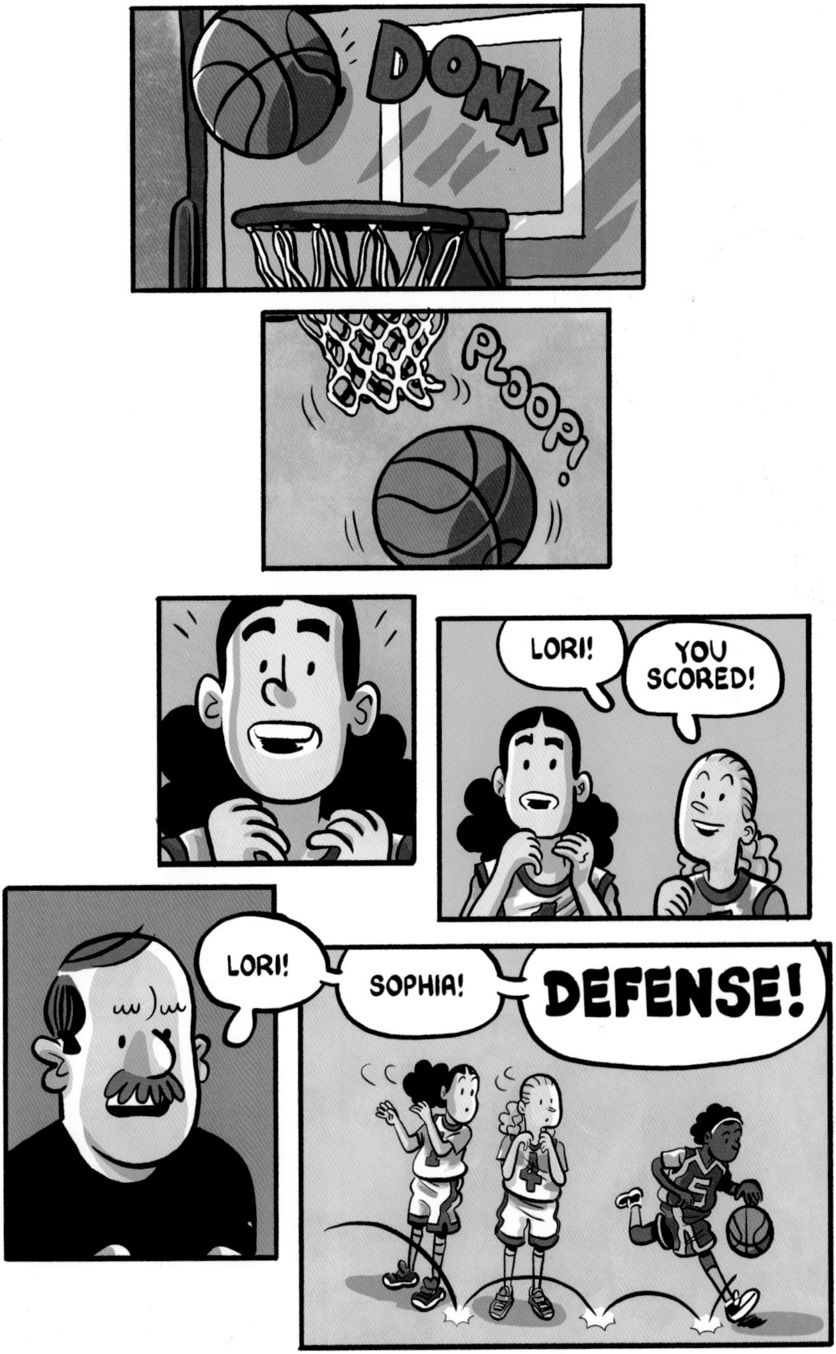
DONK
PLOOP!
LORI!
YOU SCORED!
LORI!
SOPHIA!
DEFENSE!

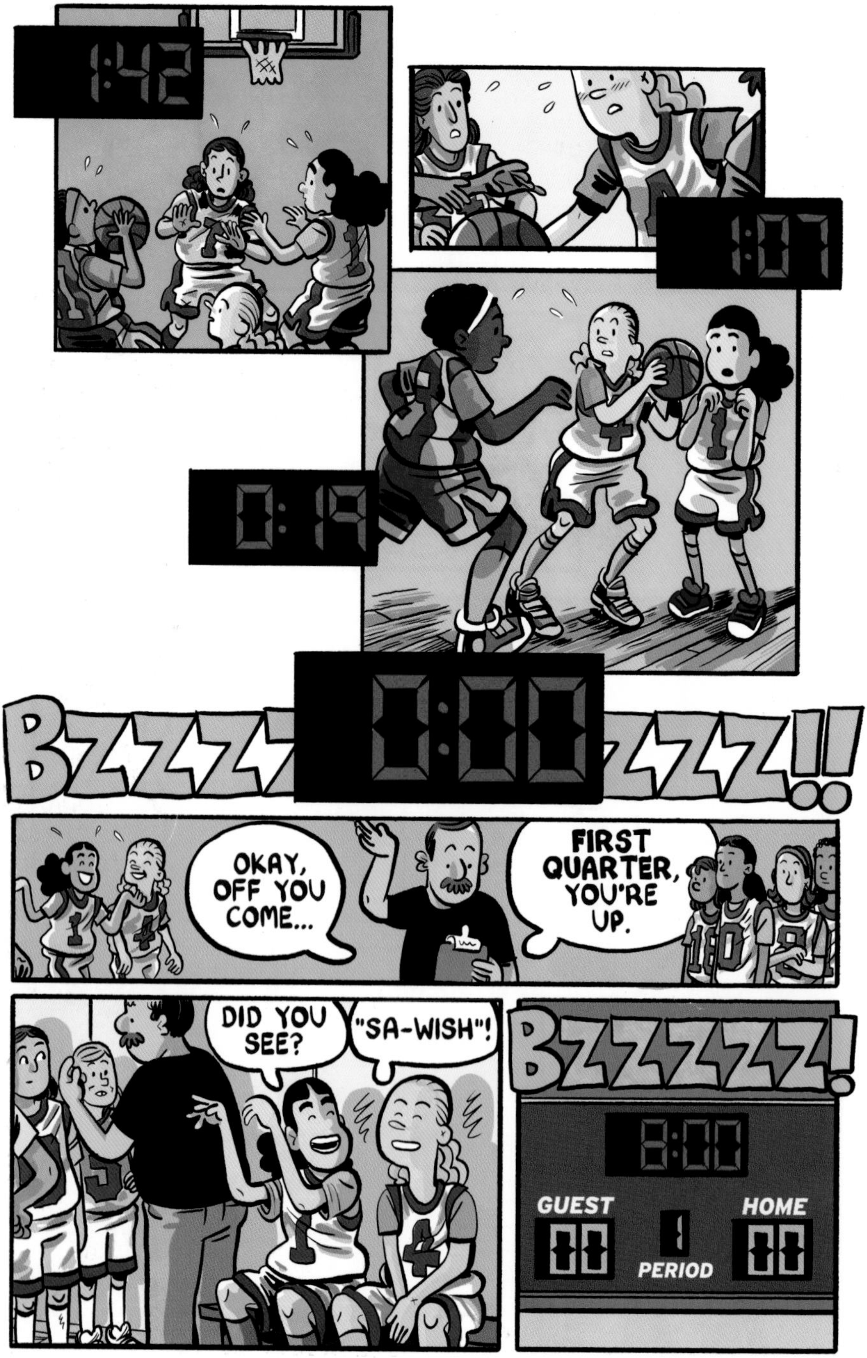
1:42
1:07
0:14
BZZZZ 0:00 ZZZZ!!
OKAY, OFF YOU COME...
FIRST QUARTER, YOU'RE UP.
DID YOU SEE?
"SA-WISH"!
BZZZZZZ!
GUEST
HOME
PERIOD

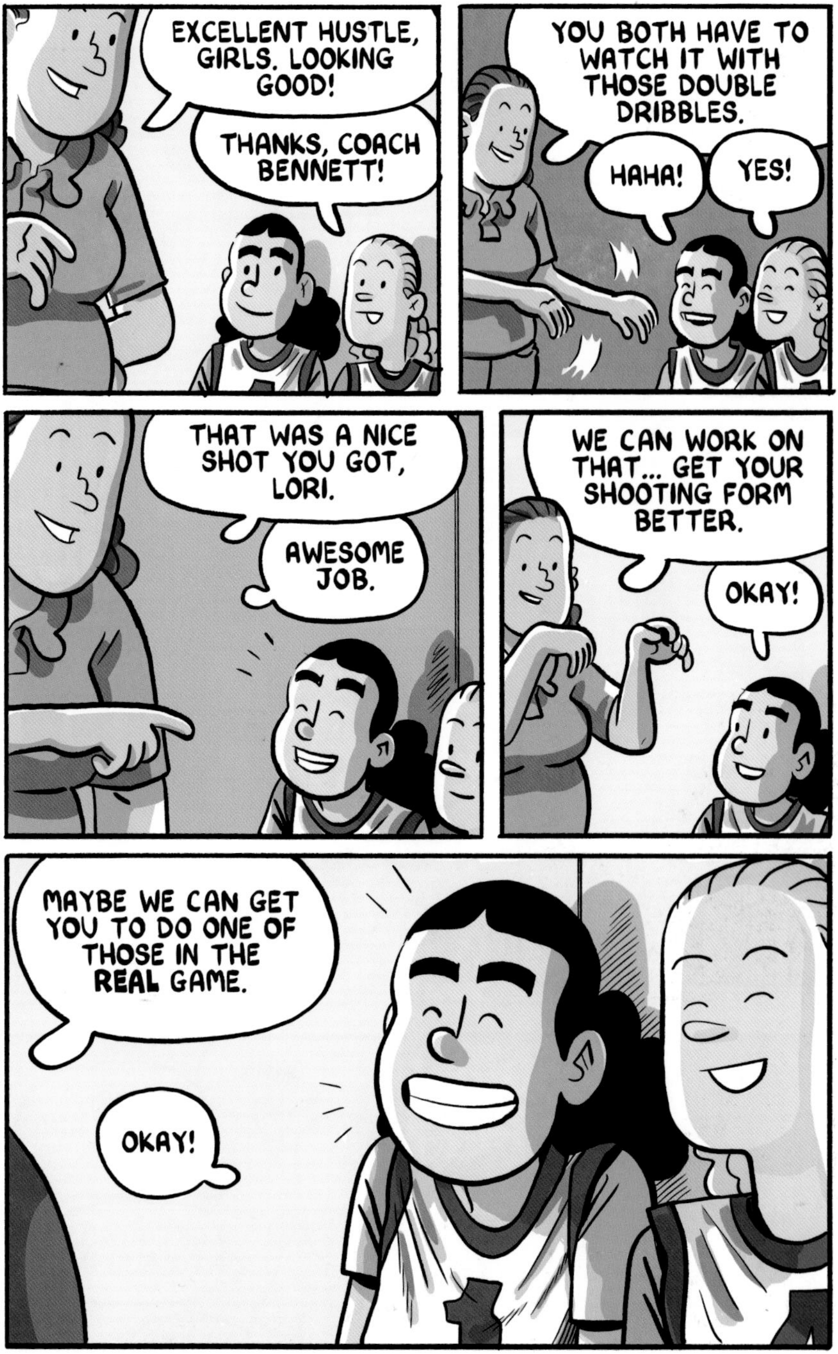
EXCELLENT HUSTLE, GIRLS. LOOKING GOOD!
THANKS, COACH BENNETT!
YOU BOTH HAVE TO WATCH IT WITH THOSE DOUBLE DRIBBLES.
HAHA!
YES!
THAT WAS A NICE SHOT YOU GOT, LORI.
AWESOME JOB.
WE CAN WORK ON THAT... GET YOUR SHOOTING FORM BETTER.
OKAY!
MAYBE WE CAN GET YOU TO DO ONE OF THOSE IN THE **REAL** GAME.
OKAY!

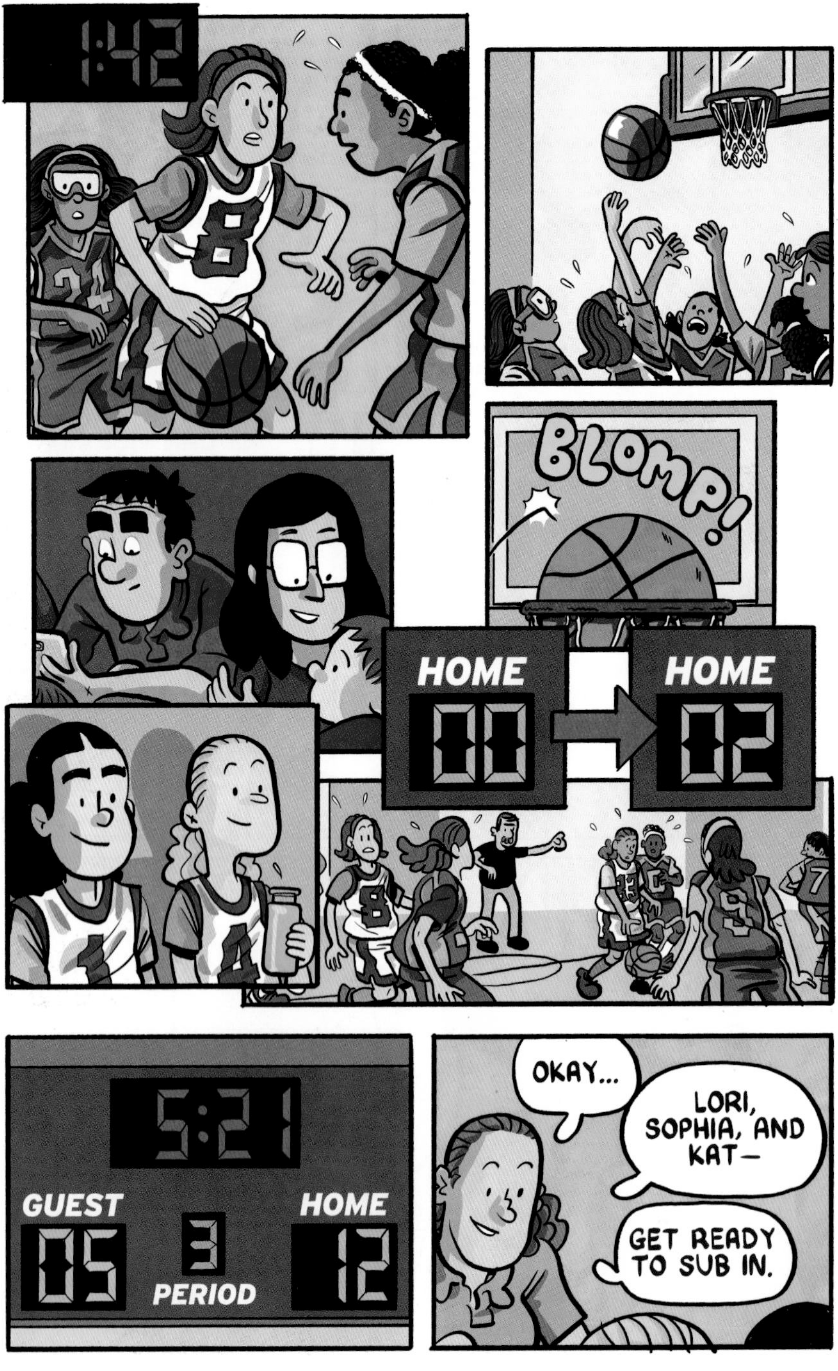
1:42
BLOMP!
HOME
00
HOME
02
5:21
GUEST
05
3
PERIOD
HOME
12
OKAY...
LORI, SOPHIA, AND KAT—
GET READY TO SUB IN.

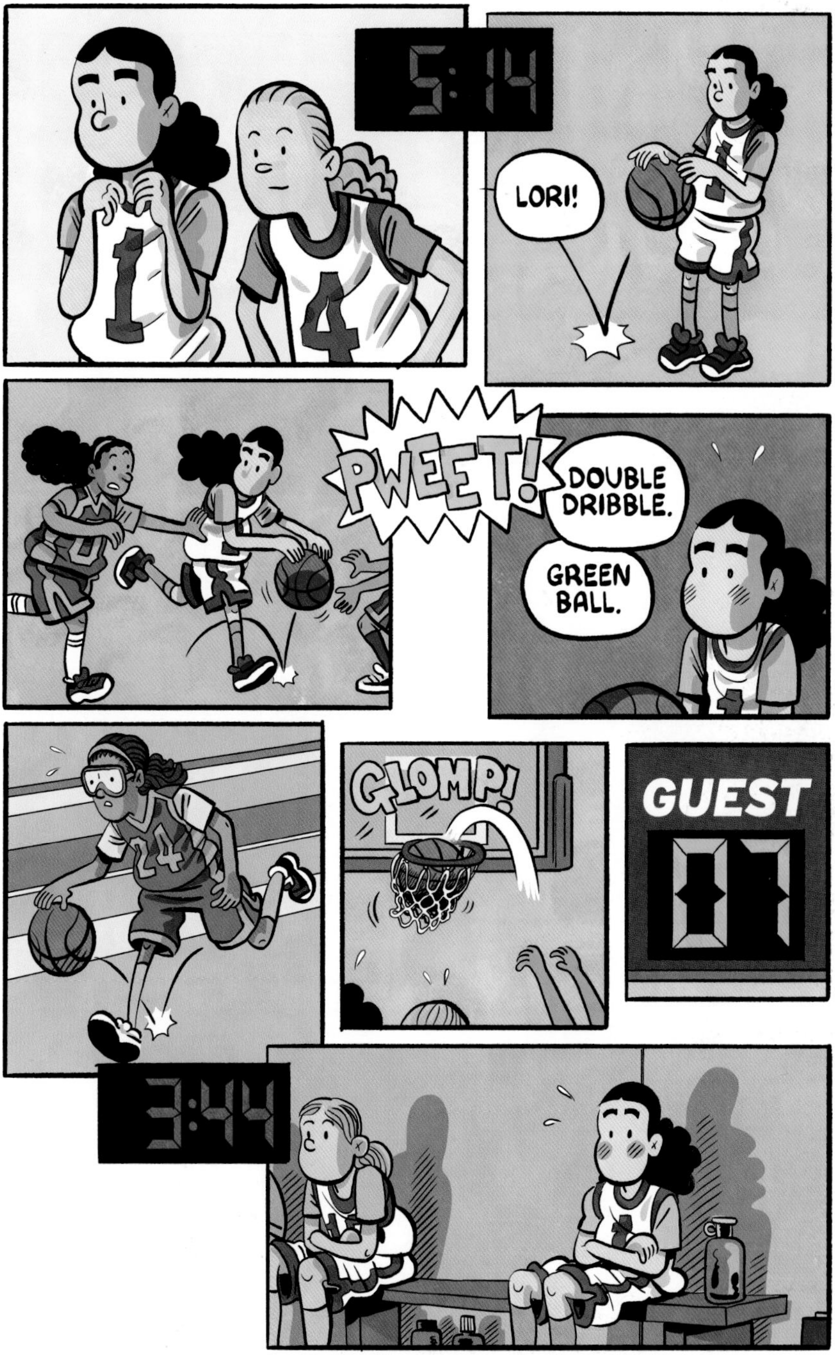
5:14
LORI!
PWEET!
DOUBLE DRIBBLE.
GREEN BALL.
GLOMP!
GUEST
3:44

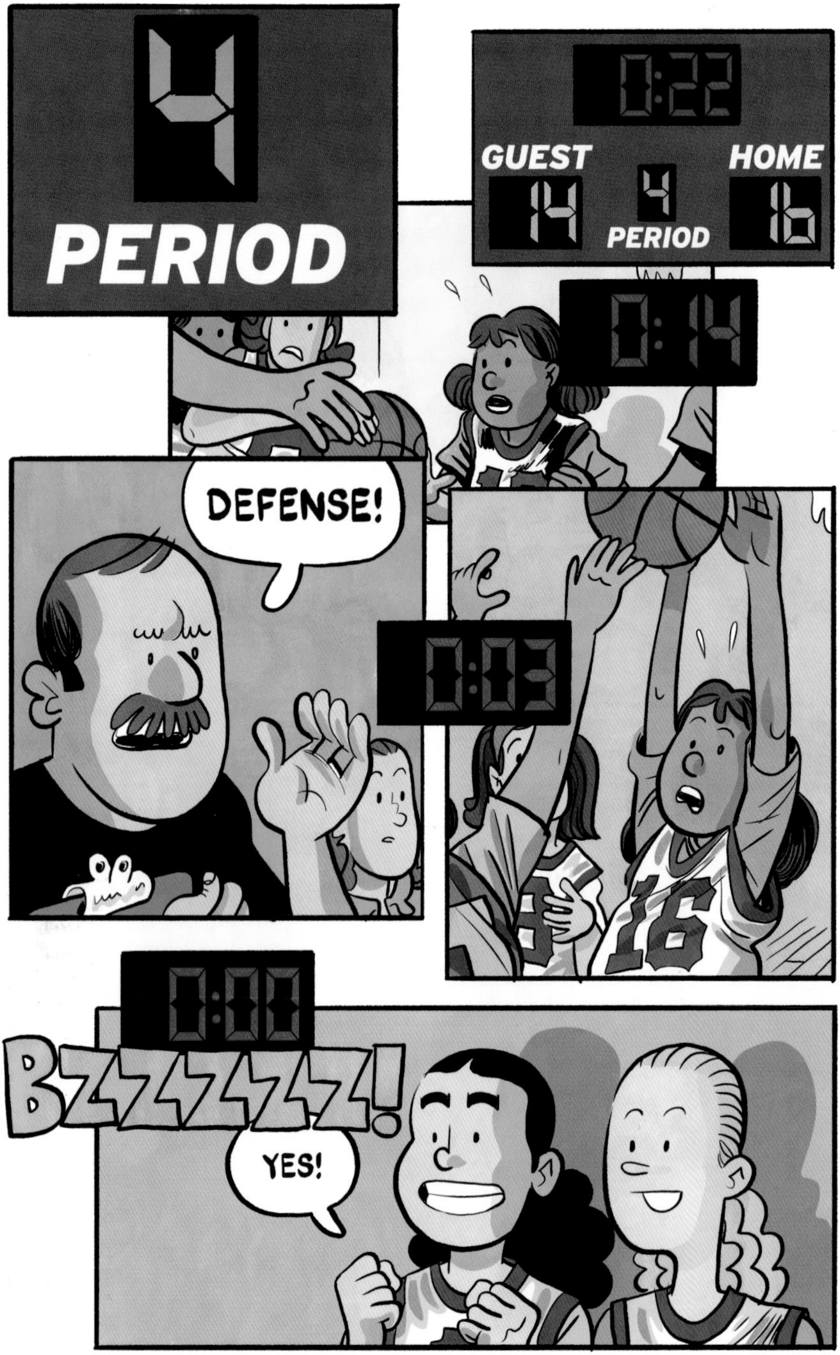
4
PERIOD
0:22
GUEST
HOME
14
4
PERIOD
16
0:14
DEFENSE!
0:03
16
0:00
BZZZZZZZ!
YES!

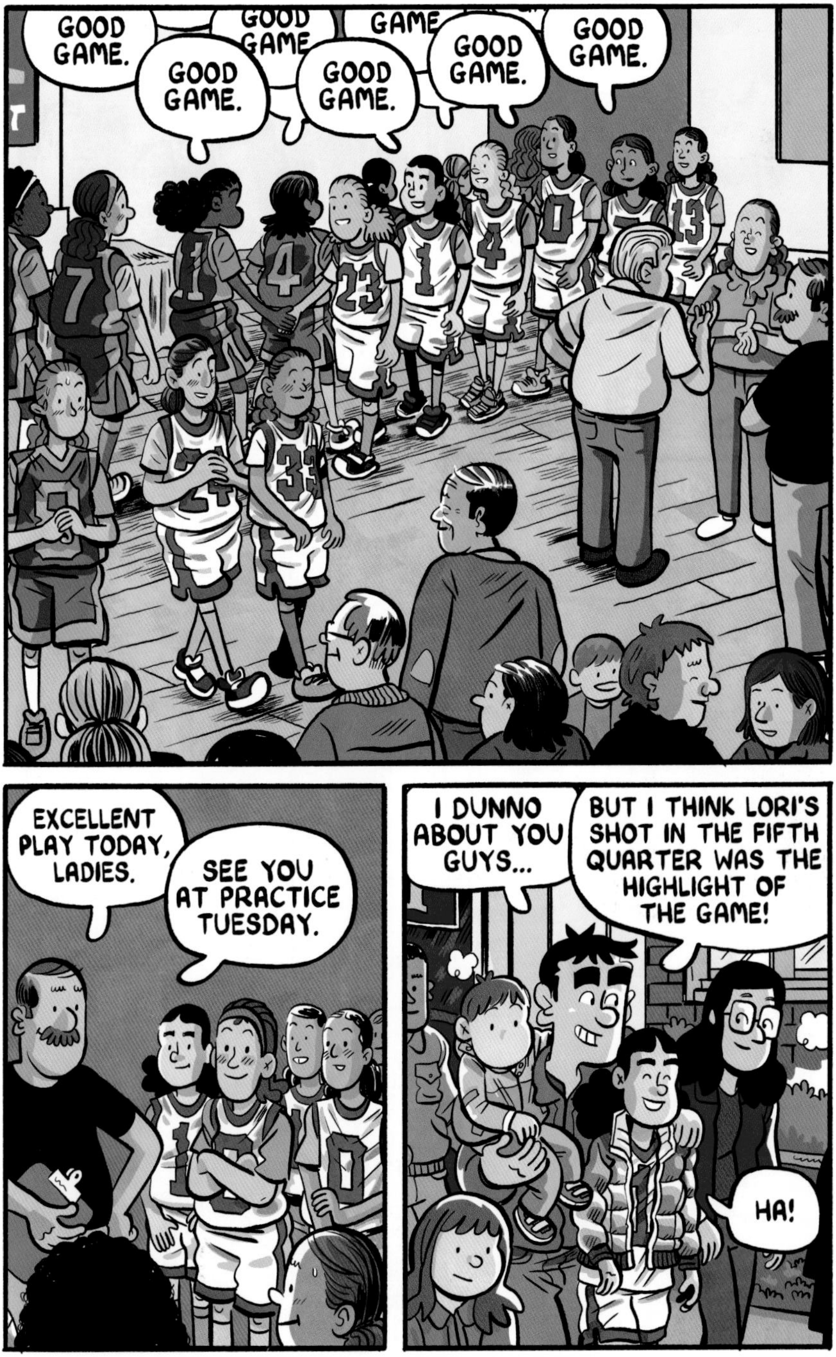
GOOD GAME.
GOOD GAME
GAME
GOOD GAME.
GOOD GAME.
GOOD GAME.
GOOD GAME.
GOOD GAME.
EXCELLENT PLAY TODAY, LADIES.
SEE YOU AT PRACTICE TUESDAY.
I DUNNO ABOUT YOU GUYS...
BUT I THINK LORI'S SHOT IN THE FIFTH QUARTER WAS THE HIGHLIGHT OF THE GAME!
HA!

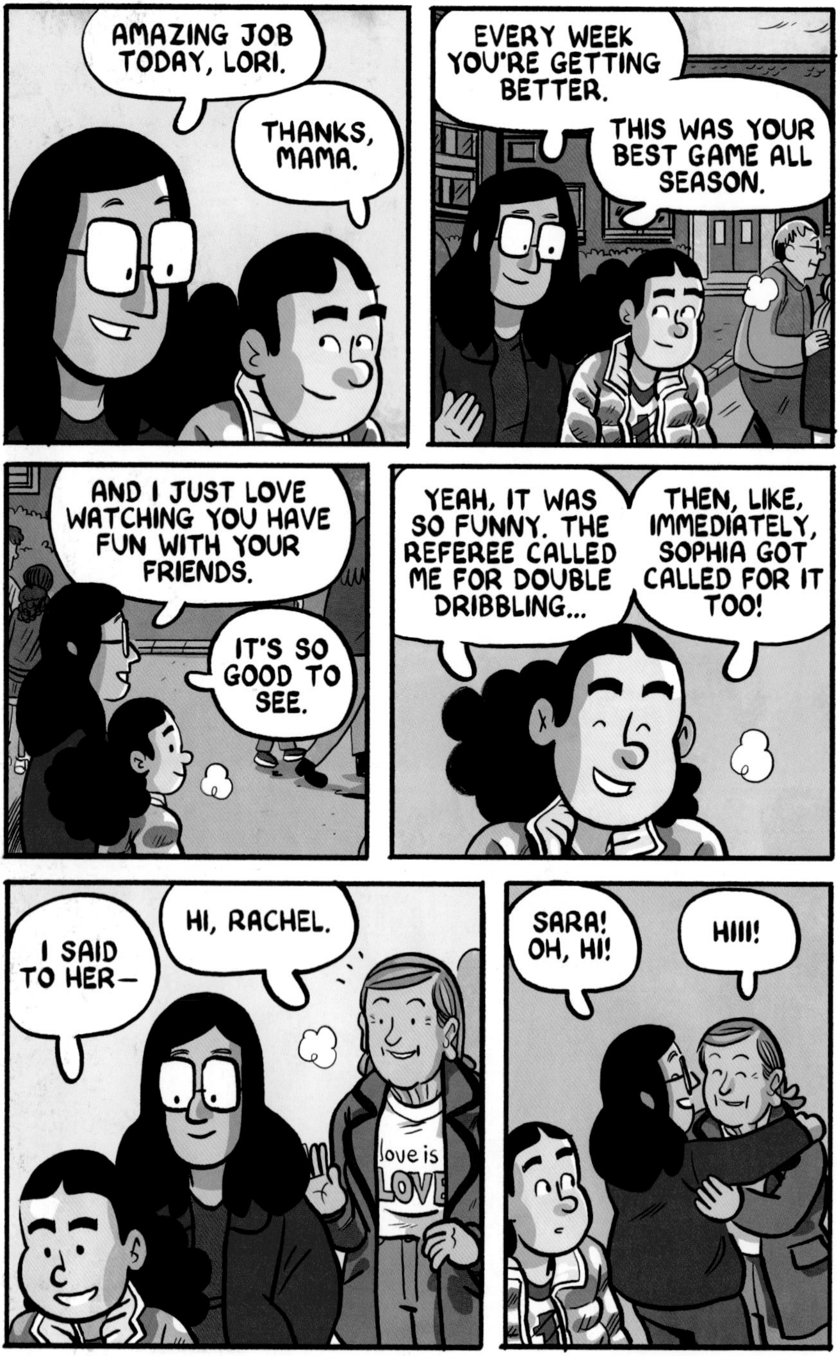
AMAZING JOB TODAY, LORI.
THANKS, MAMA.
EVERY WEEK YOU'RE GETTING BETTER.
THIS WAS YOUR BEST GAME ALL SEASON.
AND I JUST LOVE WATCHING YOU HAVE FUN WITH YOUR FRIENDS.
IT'S SO GOOD TO SEE.
YEAH, IT WAS SO FUNNY. THE REFEREE CALLED ME FOR DOUBLE DRIBBLING...
THEN, LIKE, IMMEDIATELY, SOPHIA GOT CALLED FOR IT TOO!
I SAID TO HER—
HI, RACHEL.
love is LOVE
SARA! OH, HI!
HIII!

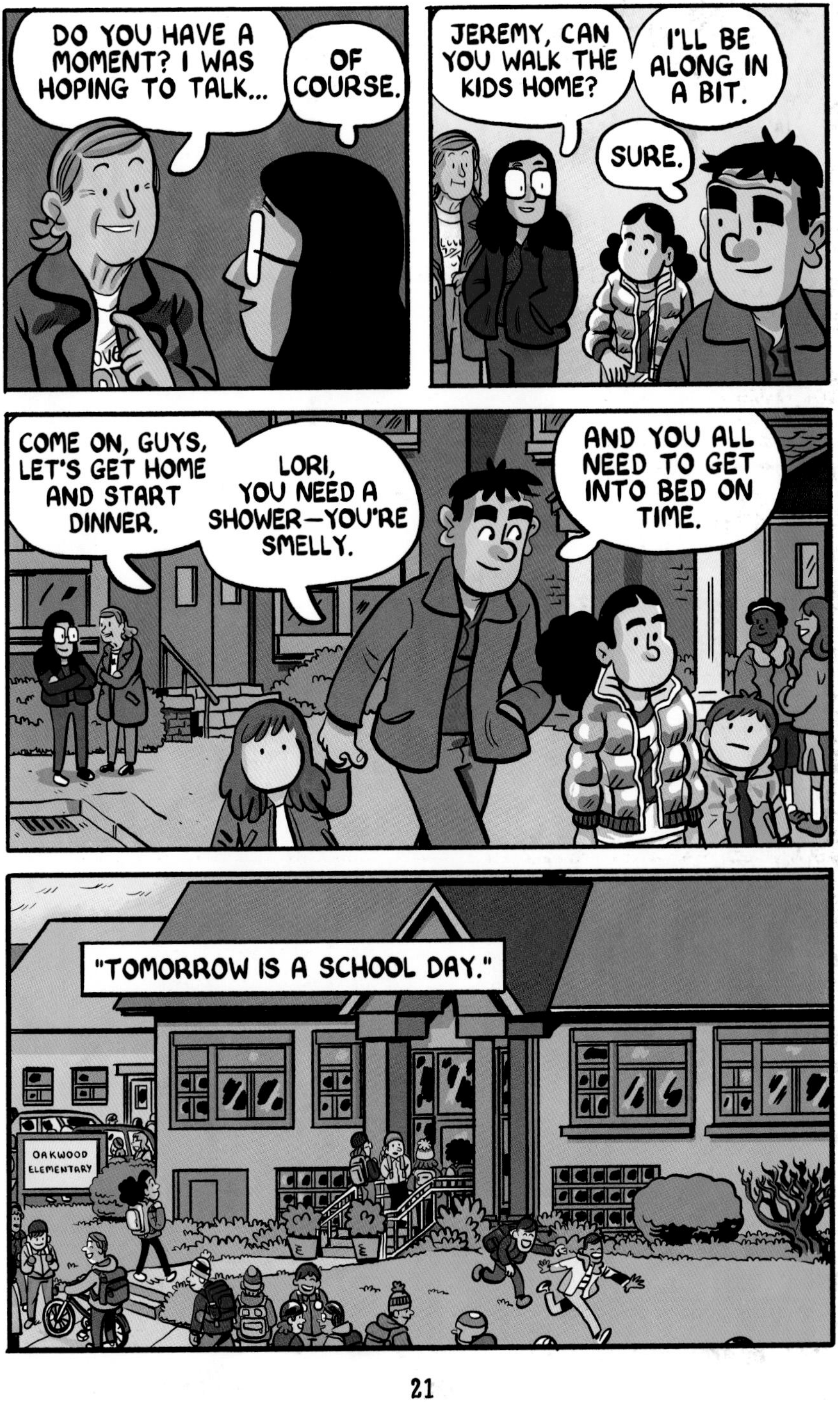
DO YOU HAVE A MOMENT? I WAS HOPING TO TALK...
OF COURSE.
JEREMY, CAN YOU WALK THE KIDS HOME?
I'LL BE ALONG IN A BIT.
SURE.
COME ON, GUYS, LET'S GET HOME AND START DINNER.
LORI, YOU NEED A SHOWER—YOU'RE SMELLY.
AND YOU ALL NEED TO GET INTO BED ON TIME.
"TOMORROW IS A SCHOOL DAY."
OAKWOOD ELEMENTARY

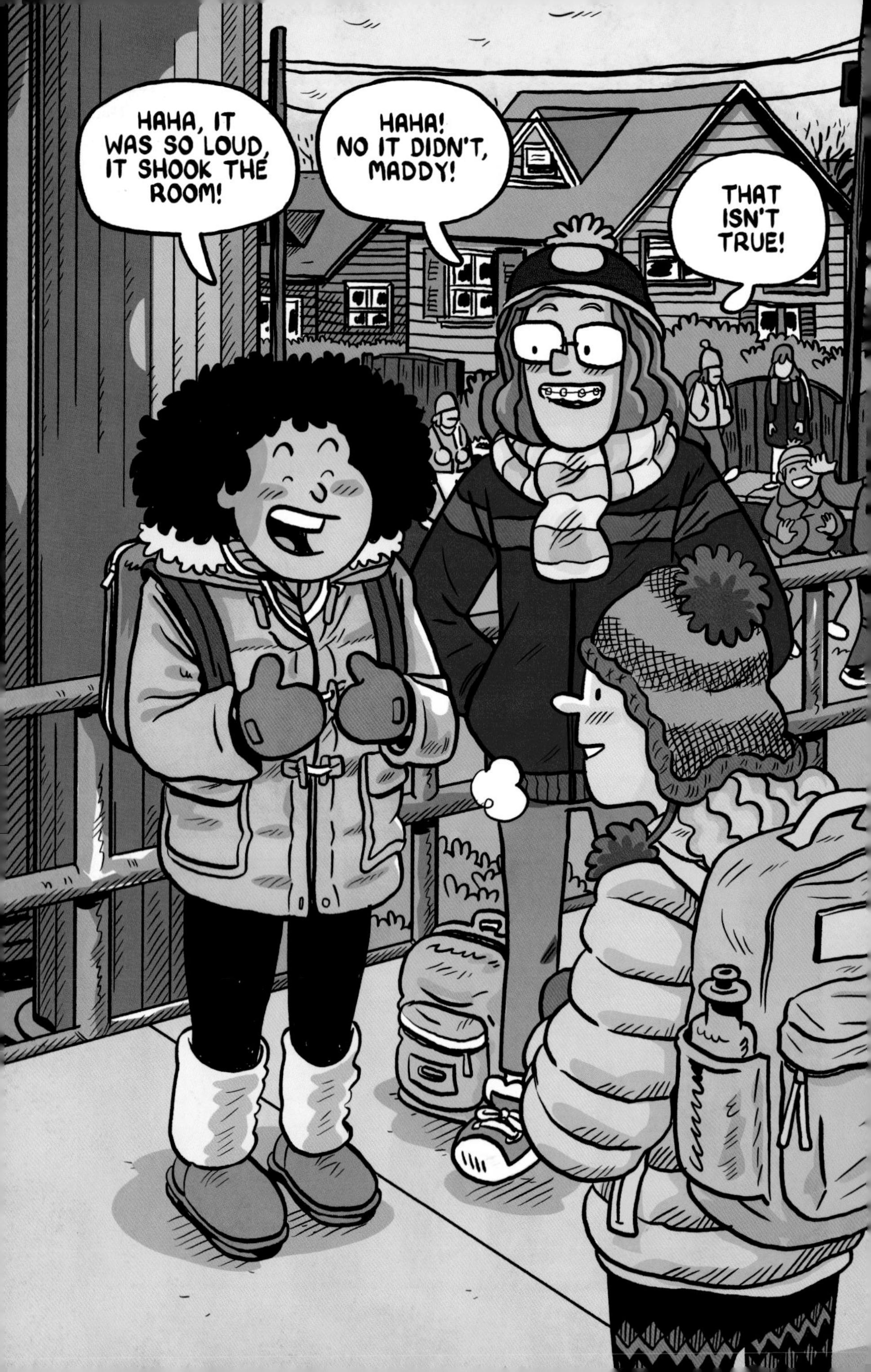
HAHA, IT WAS SO LOUD, IT SHOOK THE ROOM!
HAHA! NO IT DIDN'T, MADDY!
THAT ISN'T TRUE!

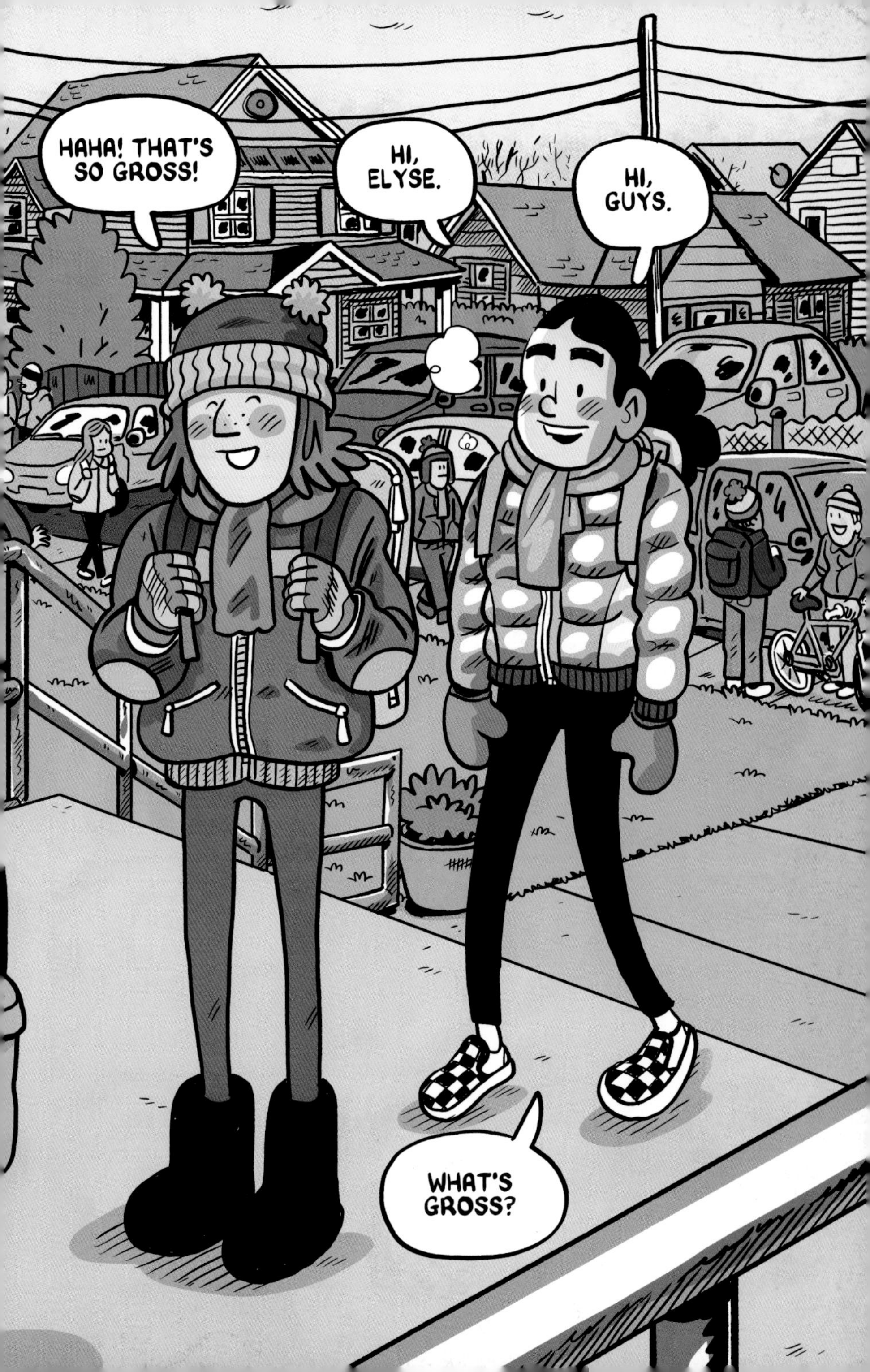
HAHA! THAT'S SO GROSS!
HI, ELYSE.
HI, GUYS.
WHAT'S GROSS?

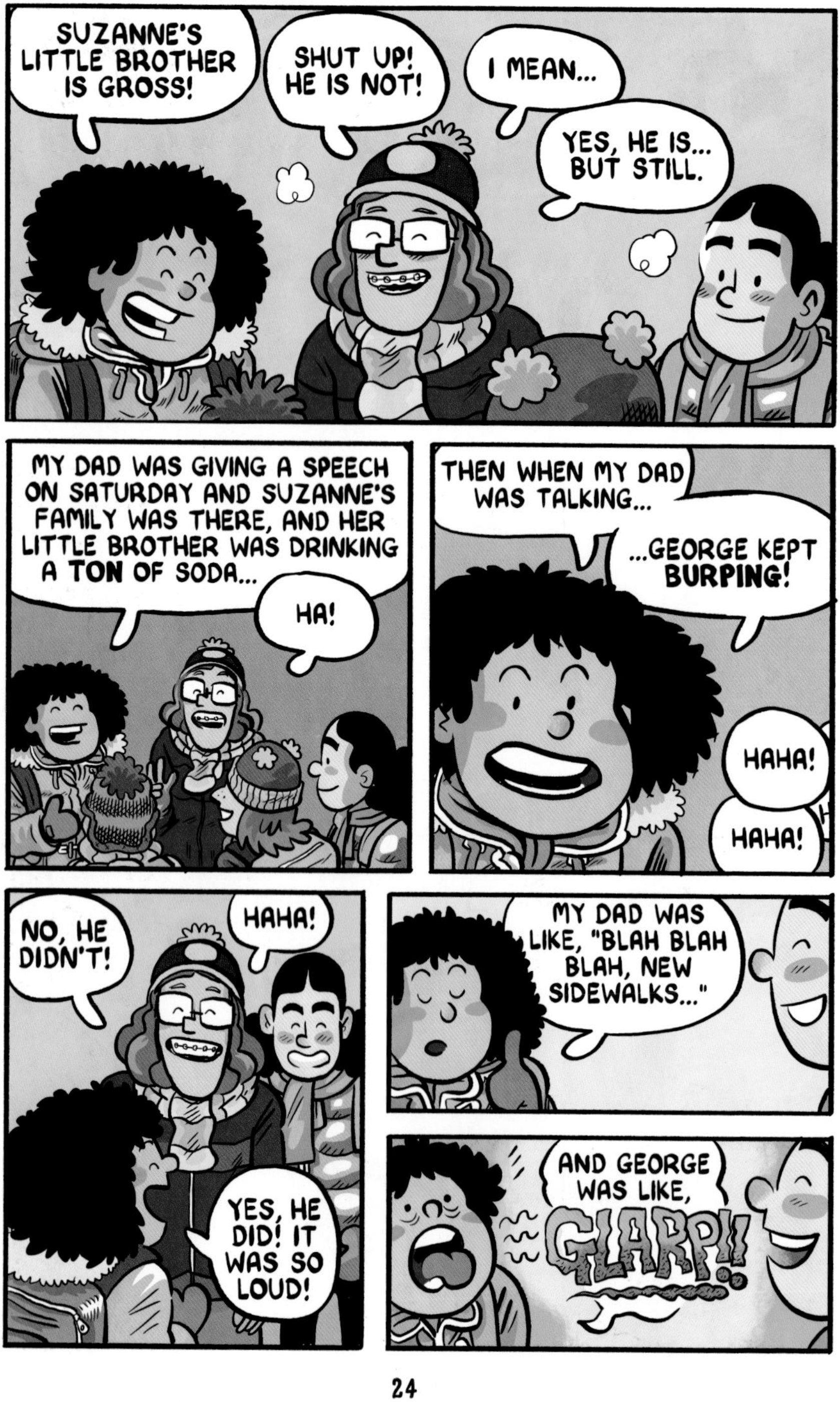
SUZANNE'S LITTLE BROTHER IS GROSS!
SHUT UP! HE IS NOT!
I MEAN...
YES, HE IS... BUT STILL.
MY DAD WAS GIVING A SPEECH ON SATURDAY AND SUZANNE'S FAMILY WAS THERE, AND HER LITTLE BROTHER WAS DRINKING A **TON** OF SODA...
HA!
THEN WHEN MY DAD WAS TALKING...
...GEORGE KEPT **BURPING**!
HAHA!
HAHA!
NO, HE DIDN'T!
HAHA!
YES, HE DID! IT WAS SO LOUD!
MY DAD WAS LIKE, "BLAH BLAH BLAH, NEW SIDEWALKS..."
AND GEORGE WAS LIKE,
GLARP!!

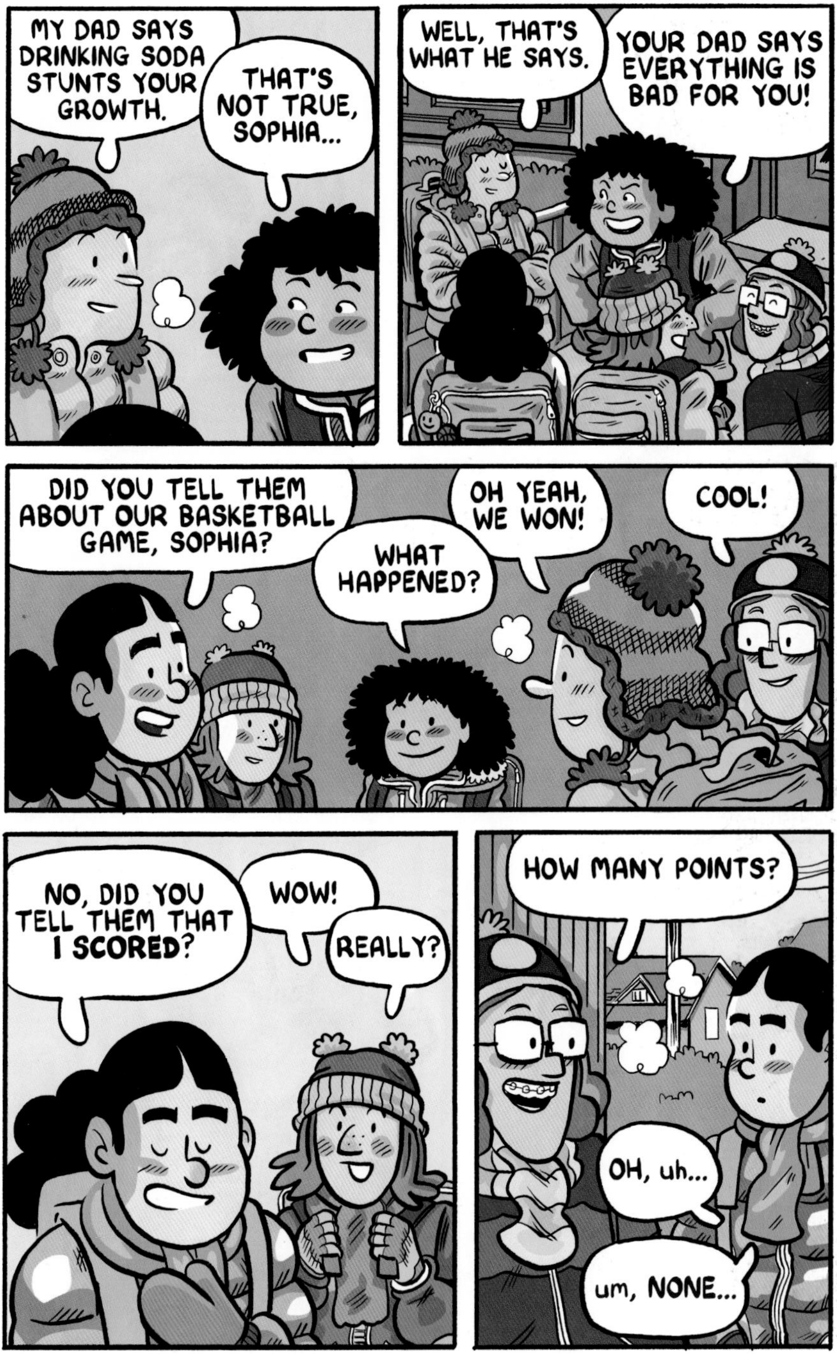
MY DAD SAYS DRINKING SODA STUNTS YOUR GROWTH.
THAT'S NOT TRUE, SOPHIA...
WELL, THAT'S WHAT HE SAYS.
YOUR DAD SAYS EVERYTHING IS BAD FOR YOU!
DID YOU TELL THEM ABOUT OUR BASKETBALL GAME, SOPHIA?
WHAT HAPPENED?
OH YEAH, WE WON!
COOL!
NO, DID YOU TELL THEM THAT I SCORED?
WOW!
REALLY?
HOW MANY POINTS?
OH, uh...
um, NONE...

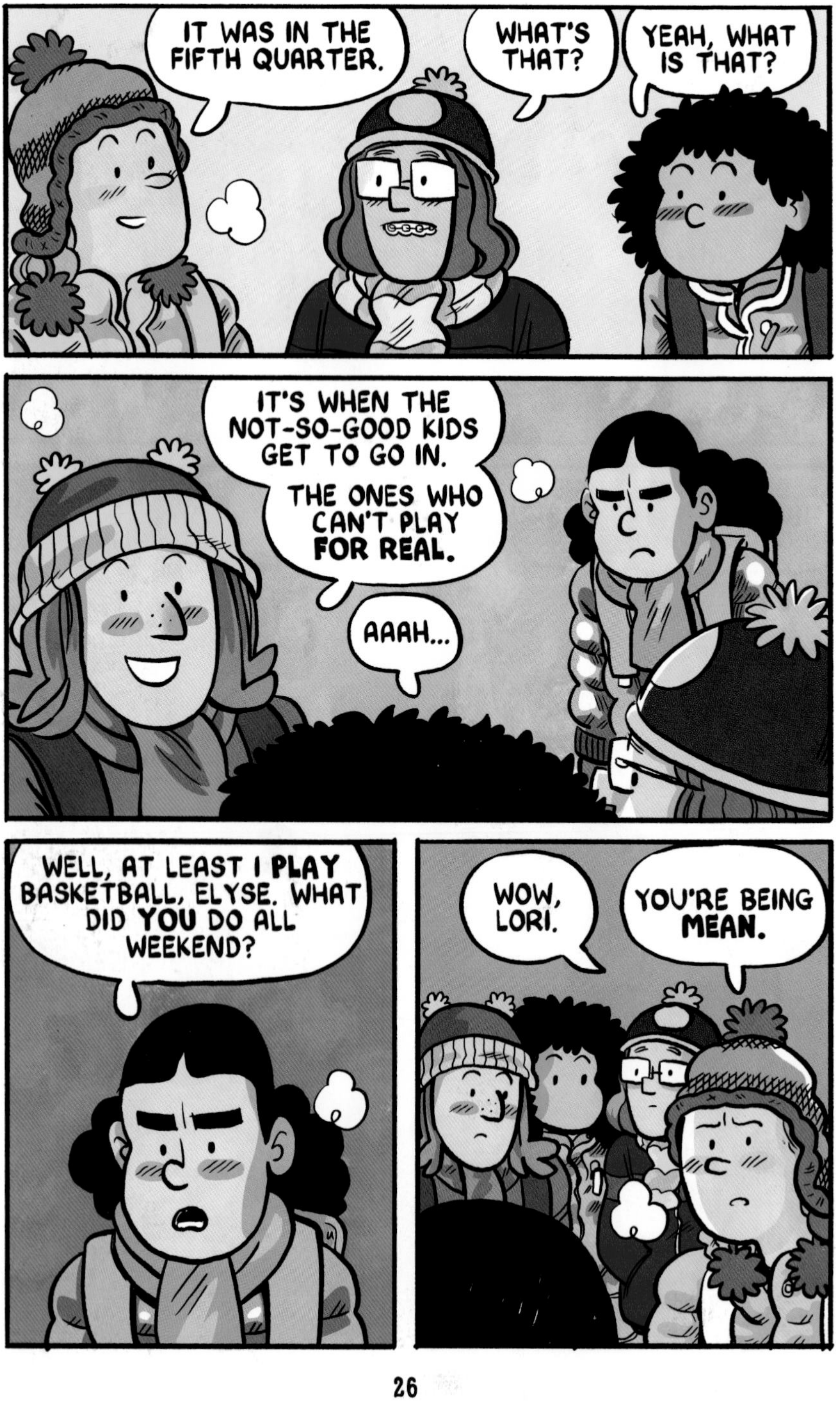
IT WAS IN THE FIFTH QUARTER.
WHAT'S THAT?
YEAH, WHAT IS THAT?
IT'S WHEN THE NOT-SO-GOOD KIDS GET TO GO IN.
THE ONES WHO CAN'T PLAY **FOR REAL.**
AAAH...
WELL, AT LEAST I **PLAY** BASKETBALL, ELYSE. WHAT DID **YOU** DO ALL WEEKEND?
WOW, LORI.
YOU'RE BEING **MEAN.**

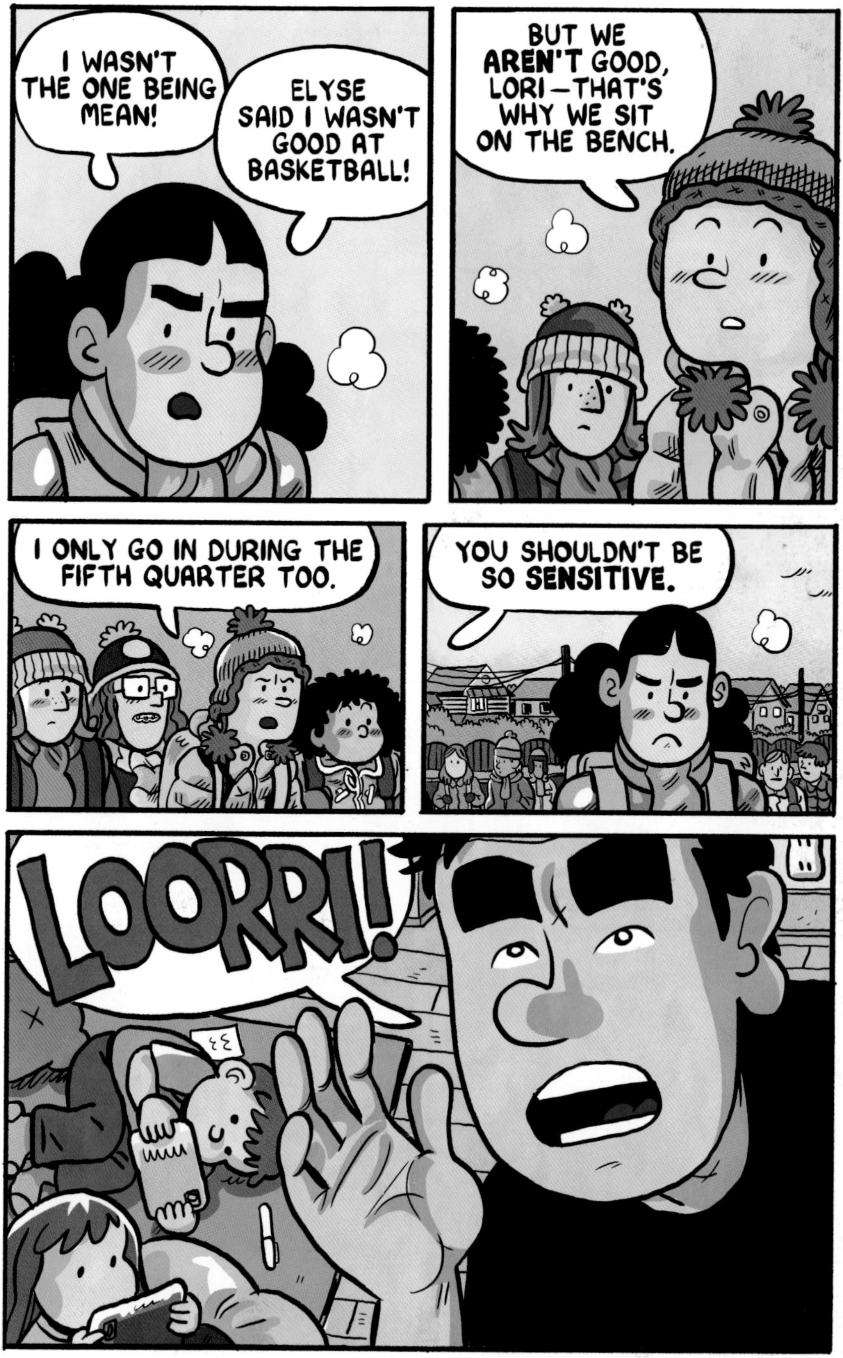
I WASN'T THE ONE BEING MEAN!
ELYSE SAID I WASN'T GOOD AT BASKETBALL!
BUT WE **AREN'T** GOOD, LORI—THAT'S WHY WE SIT ON THE BENCH.
I ONLY GO IN DURING THE FIFTH QUARTER TOO.
YOU SHOULDN'T BE SO **SENSITIVE**.
LOORRI!

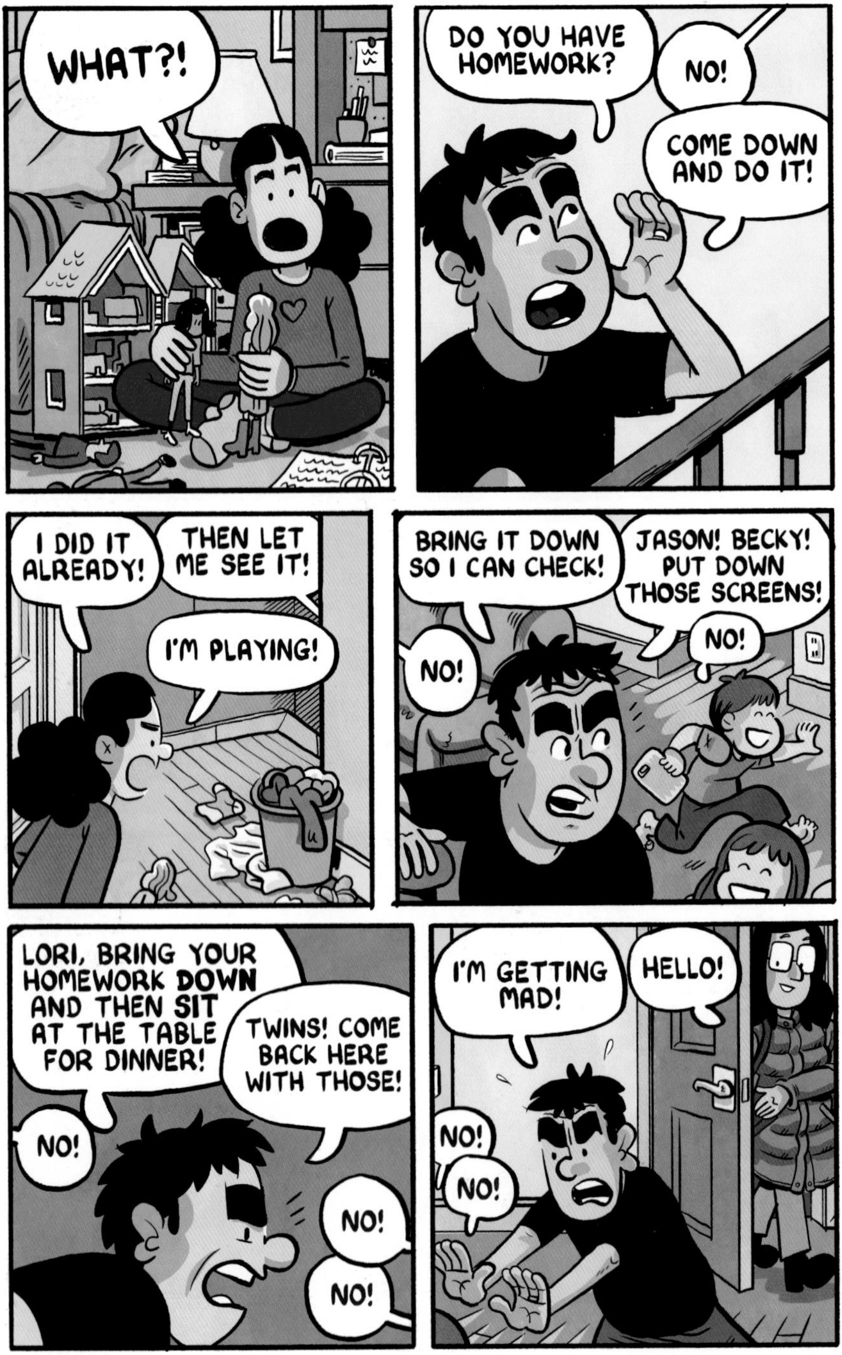
WHAT?!
DO YOU HAVE HOMEWORK?
NO!
COME DOWN AND DO IT!
I DID IT ALREADY!
THEN LET ME SEE IT!
I'M PLAYING!
BRING IT DOWN SO I CAN CHECK!
NO!
JASON! BECKY! PUT DOWN THOSE SCREENS!
NO!
LORI, BRING YOUR HOMEWORK DOWN AND THEN SIT AT THE TABLE FOR DINNER!
NO!
TWINS! COME BACK HERE WITH THOSE!
NO!
NO!
I'M GETTING MAD!
HELLO!
NO!
NO!

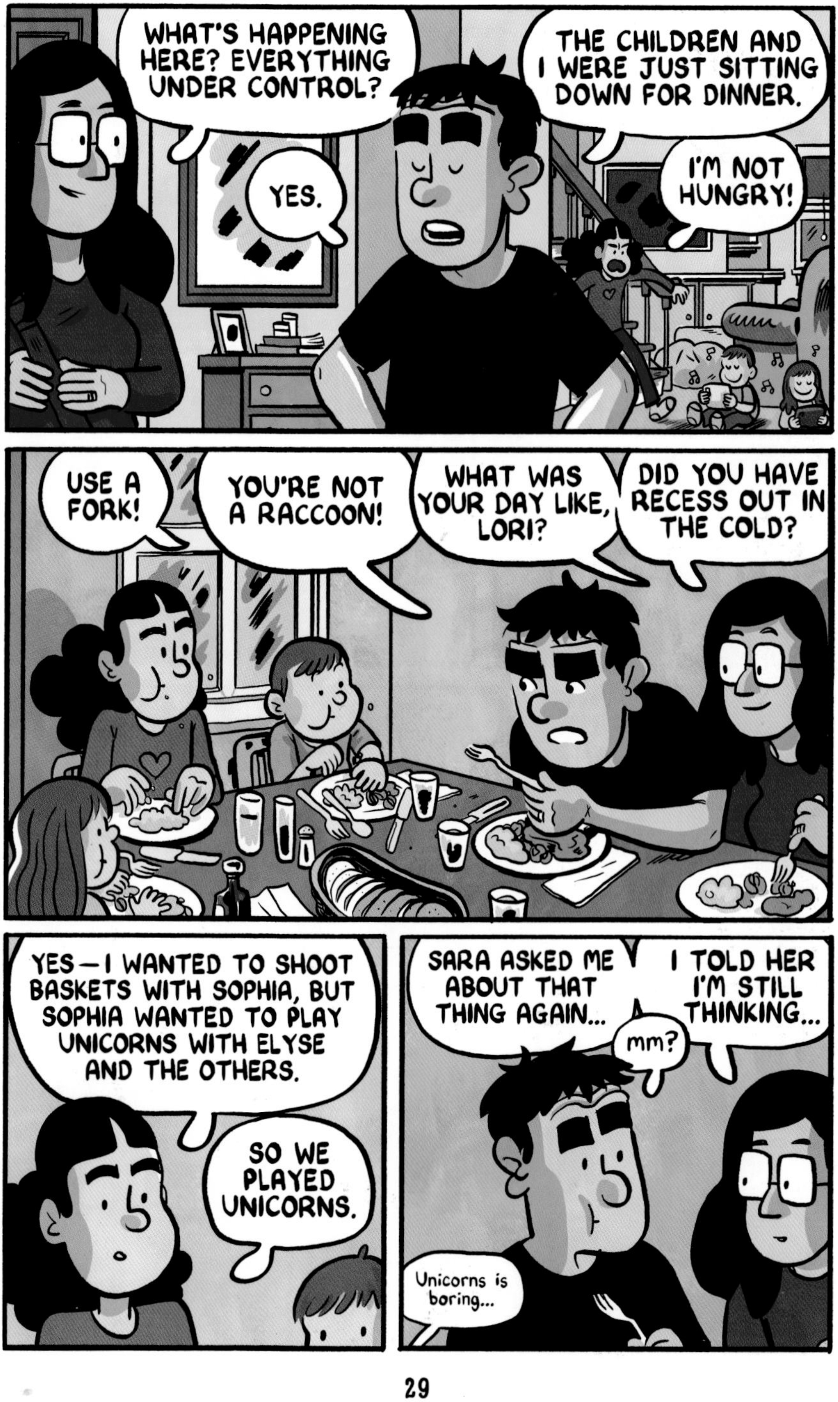
WHAT'S HAPPENING HERE? EVERYTHING UNDER CONTROL?
YES.
THE CHILDREN AND I WERE JUST SITTING DOWN FOR DINNER.
I'M NOT HUNGRY!
USE A FORK!
YOU'RE NOT A RACCOON!
WHAT WAS YOUR DAY LIKE, LORI?
DID YOU HAVE RECESS OUT IN THE COLD?
YES—I WANTED TO SHOOT BASKETS WITH SOPHIA, BUT SOPHIA WANTED TO PLAY UNICORNS WITH ELYSE AND THE OTHERS.
SO WE PLAYED UNICORNS.
SARA ASKED ME ABOUT THAT THING AGAIN...
mm?
I TOLD HER I'M STILL THINKING...
Unicorns is boring...

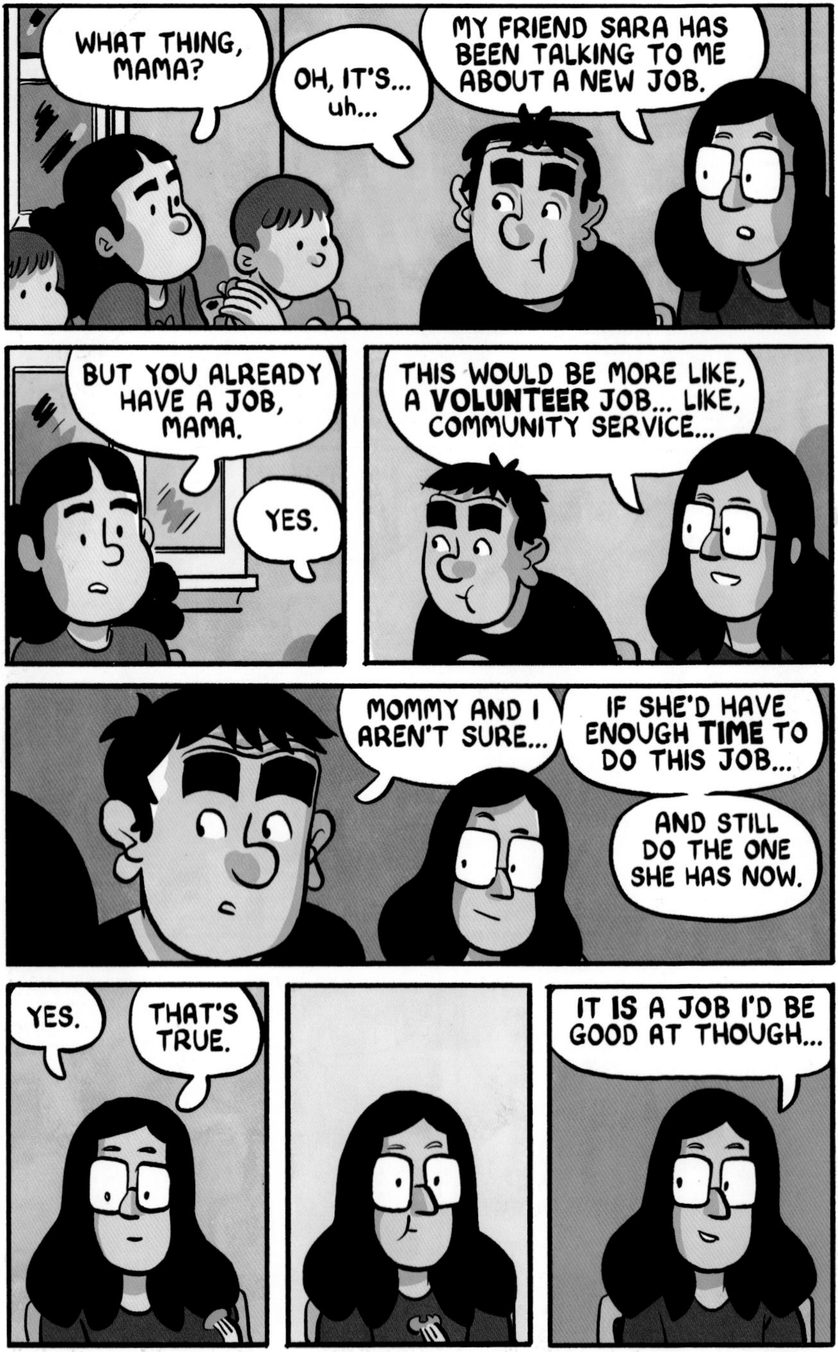
WHAT THING, MAMA?
OH, IT'S... uh...
MY FRIEND SARA HAS BEEN TALKING TO ME ABOUT A NEW JOB.
BUT YOU ALREADY HAVE A JOB, MAMA.
YES.
THIS WOULD BE MORE LIKE, A VOLUNTEER JOB... LIKE, COMMUNITY SERVICE...
MOMMY AND I AREN'T SURE...
IF SHE'D HAVE ENOUGH TIME TO DO THIS JOB...
AND STILL DO THE ONE SHE HAS NOW.
YES.
THAT'S TRUE.
IT IS A JOB I'D BE GOOD AT THOUGH...

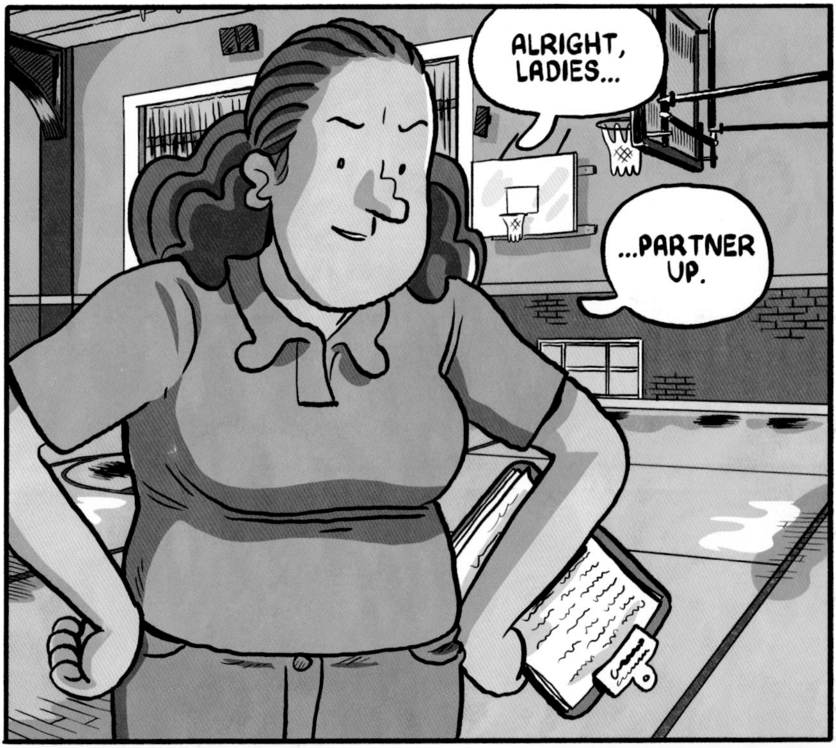
ALRIGHT, LADIES...
...PARTNER UP.

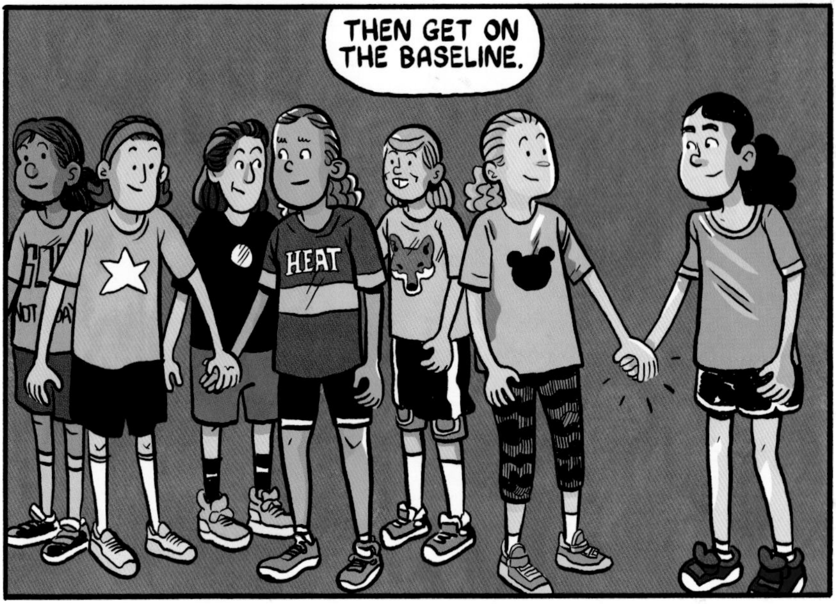
THEN GET ON THE BASELINE.
HEAT

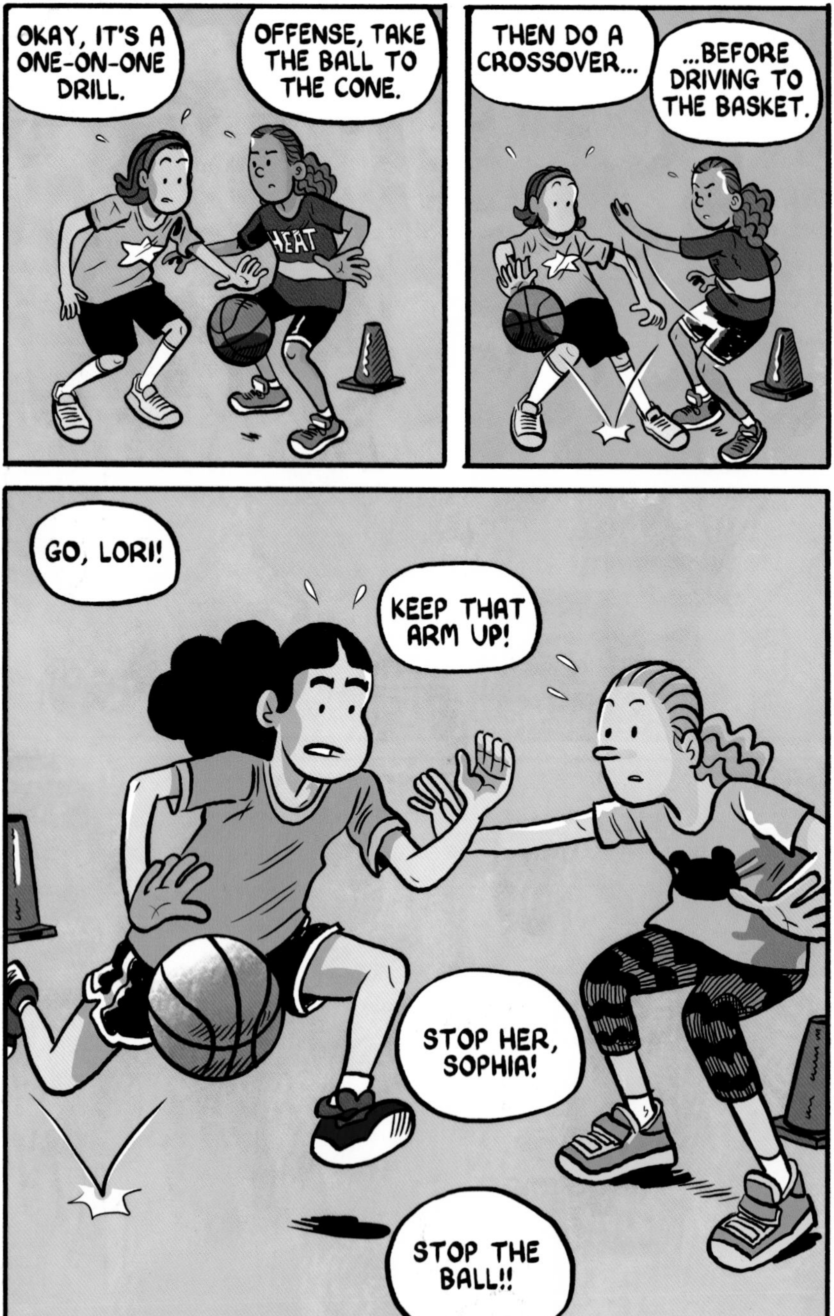
OKAY, IT'S A ONE-ON-ONE DRILL.
OFFENSE, TAKE THE BALL TO THE CONE.
THEN DO A CROSSOVER...
...BEFORE DRIVING TO THE BASKET.
GO, LORI!
KEEP THAT ARM UP!
STOP HER, SOPHIA!
STOP THE BALL!!

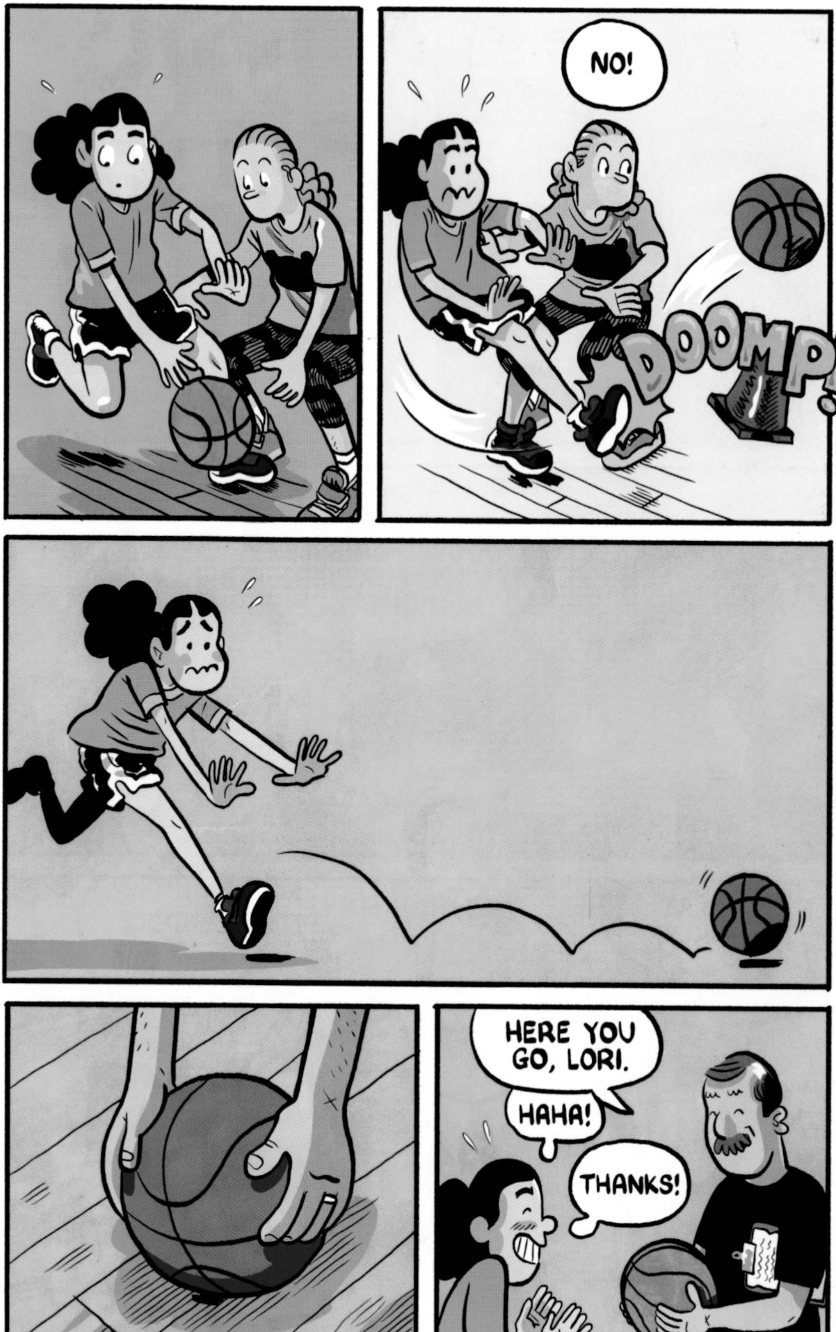
NO!
DOOMP!
HERE YOU GO, LORI.
HAHA!
THANKS!

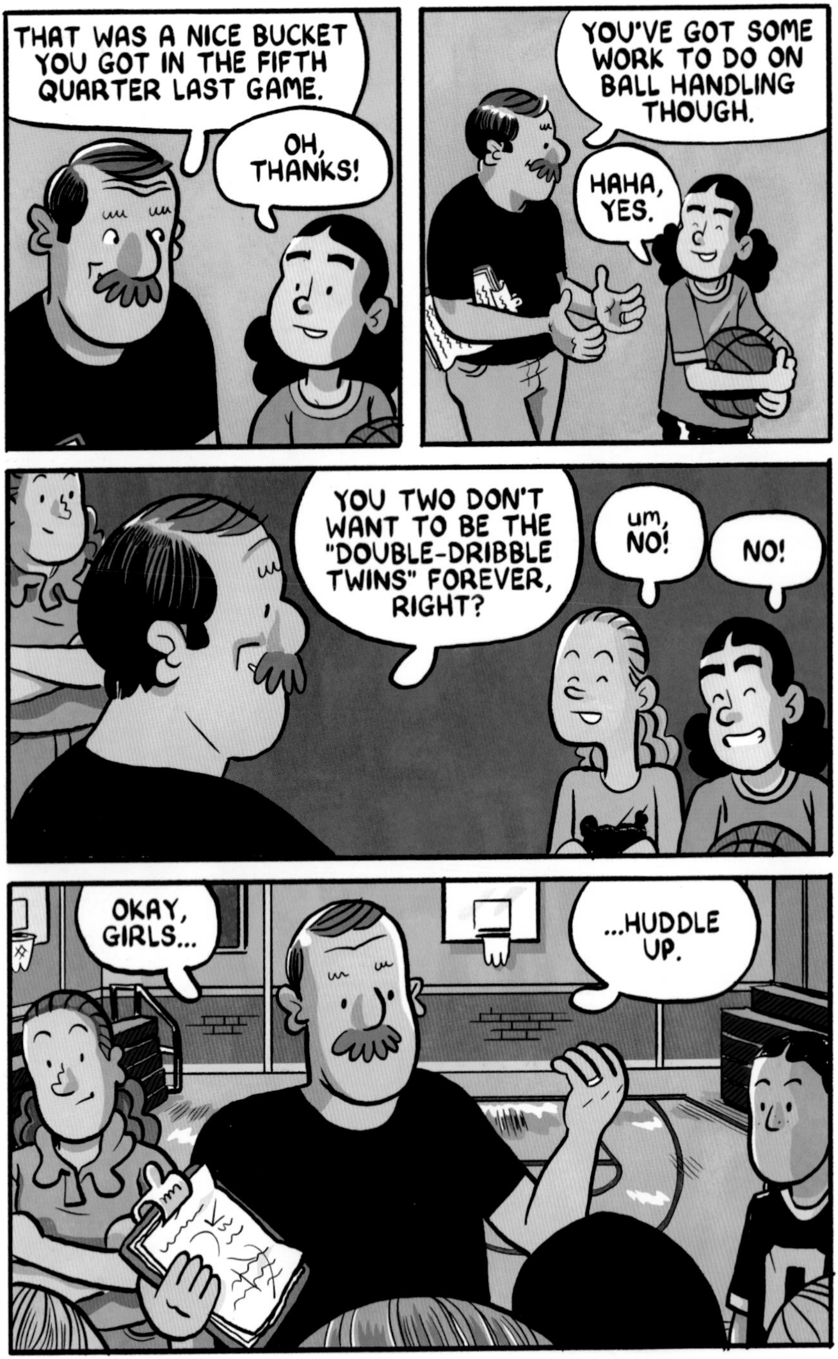
THAT WAS A NICE BUCKET YOU GOT IN THE FIFTH QUARTER LAST GAME.
OH, THANKS!
YOU'VE GOT SOME WORK TO DO ON BALL HANDLING THOUGH.
HAHA, YES.
YOU TWO DON'T WANT TO BE THE "DOUBLE-DRIBBLE TWINS" FOREVER, RIGHT?
um, NO!
NO!
OKAY, GIRLS...
...HUDDLE UP.

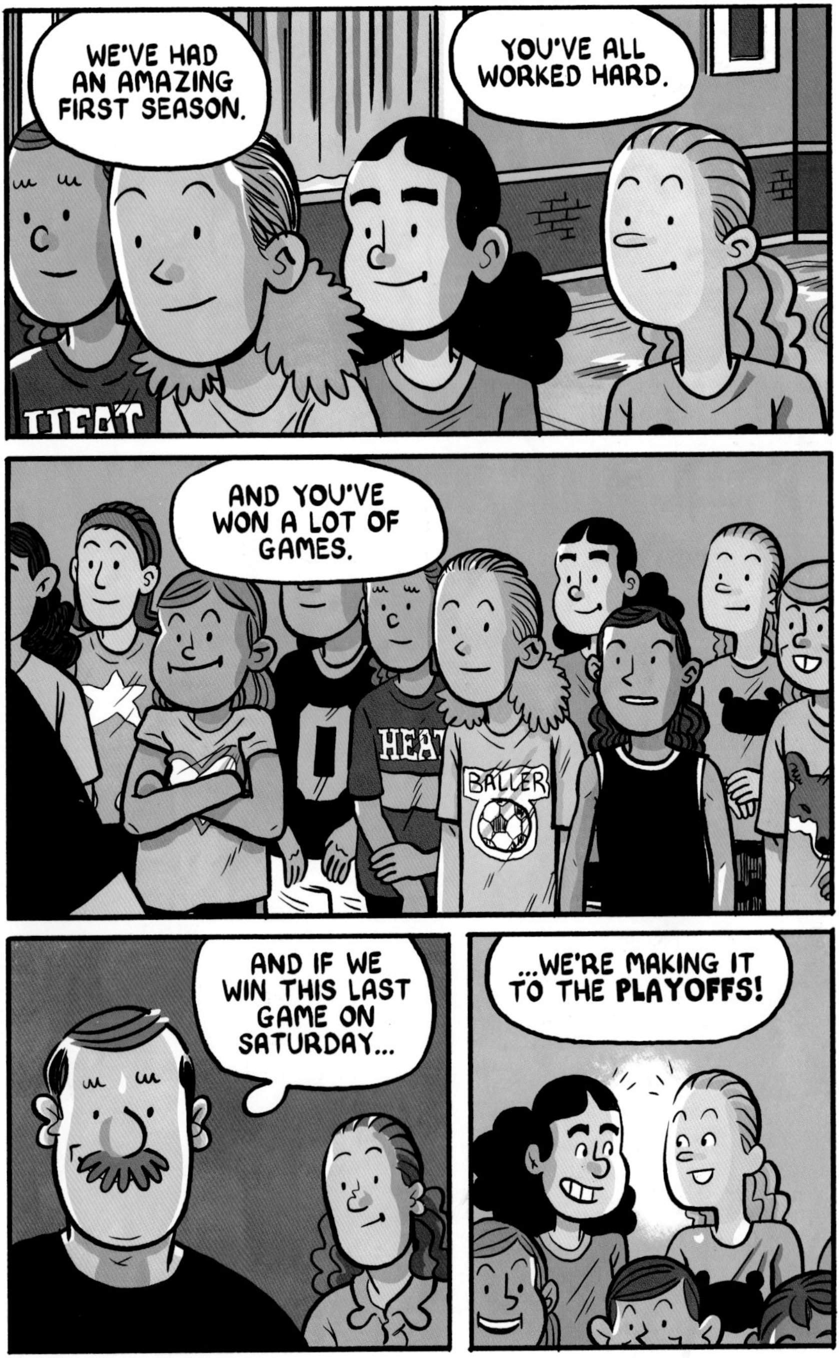
WE'VE HAD AN AMAZING FIRST SEASON.
YOU'VE ALL WORKED HARD.
AND YOU'VE WON A LOT OF GAMES.
HEAT
BALLER
AND IF WE WIN THIS LAST GAME ON SATURDAY...
...WE'RE MAKING IT TO THE **PLAYOFFS**!

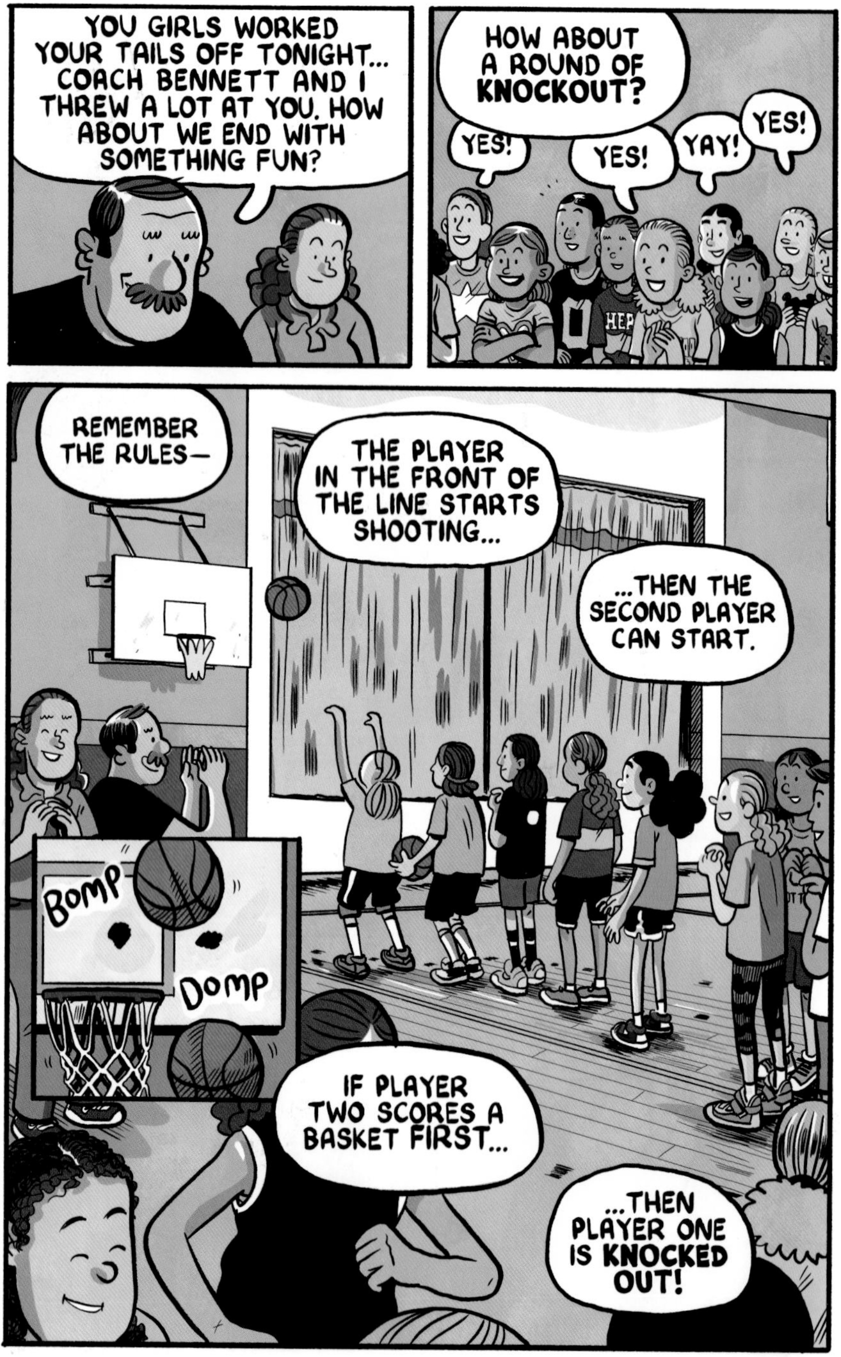
YOU GIRLS WORKED YOUR TAILS OFF TONIGHT... COACH BENNETT AND I THREW A LOT AT YOU. HOW ABOUT WE END WITH SOMETHING FUN?
HOW ABOUT A ROUND OF **KNOCKOUT?**
YES!
YES!
YAY!
YES!
REMEMBER THE RULES—
THE PLAYER IN THE FRONT OF THE LINE STARTS SHOOTING...
...THEN THE SECOND PLAYER CAN START.
BOMP
DOMP
IF PLAYER TWO SCORES A BASKET FIRST...
...THEN PLAYER ONE IS **KNOCKED OUT!**

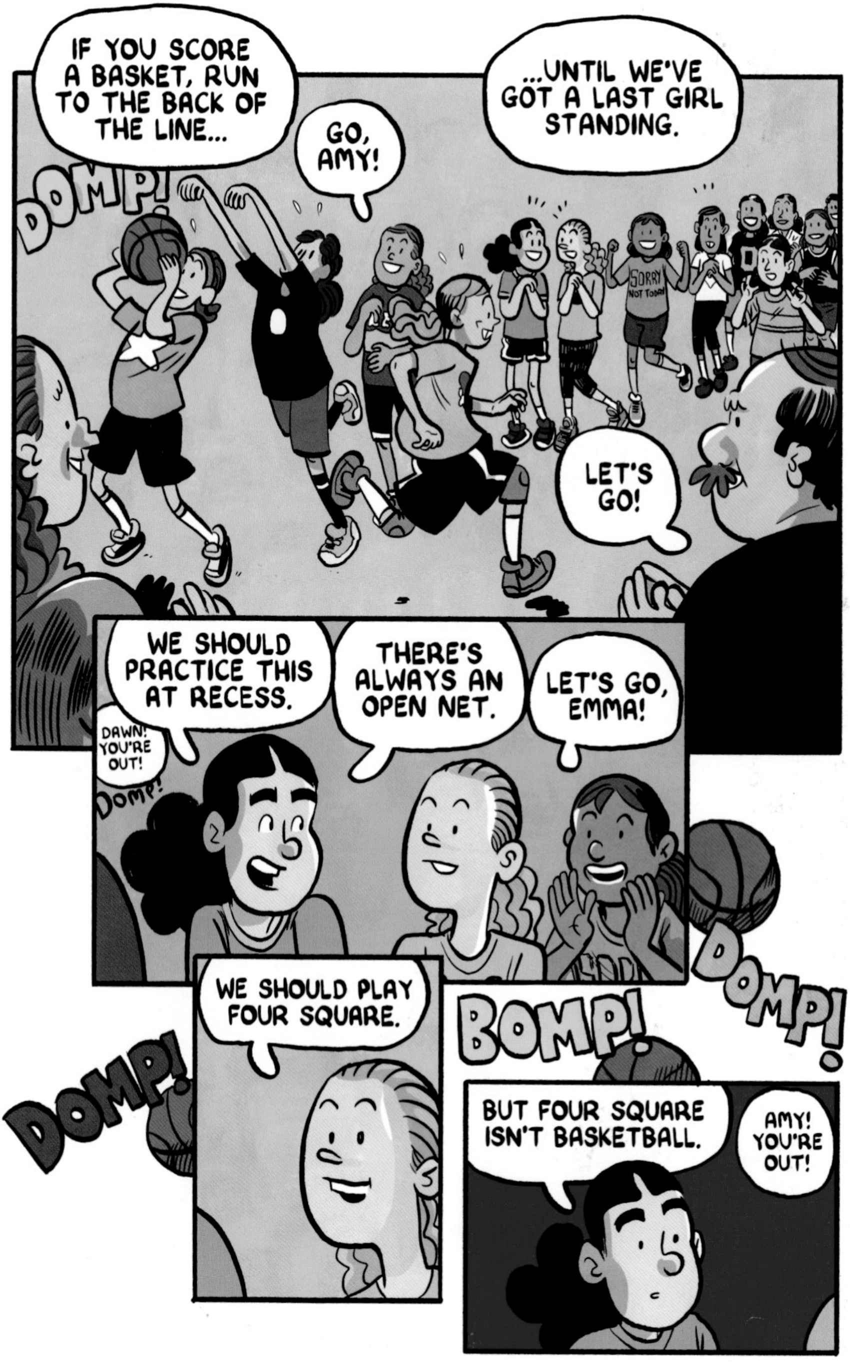
IF YOU SCORE A BASKET, RUN TO THE BACK OF THE LINE...
GO, AMY!
...UNTIL WE'VE GOT A LAST GIRL STANDING.
DOMP!
SORRY NOT TODAY
LET'S GO!
WE SHOULD PRACTICE THIS AT RECESS.
DAWN! YOU'RE OUT!
DOMP!
THERE'S ALWAYS AN OPEN NET.
LET'S GO, EMMA!
WE SHOULD PLAY FOUR SQUARE.
DOMP!
BOMP!
DOMP!
BUT FOUR SQUARE ISN'T BASKETBALL.
AMY! YOU'RE OUT!

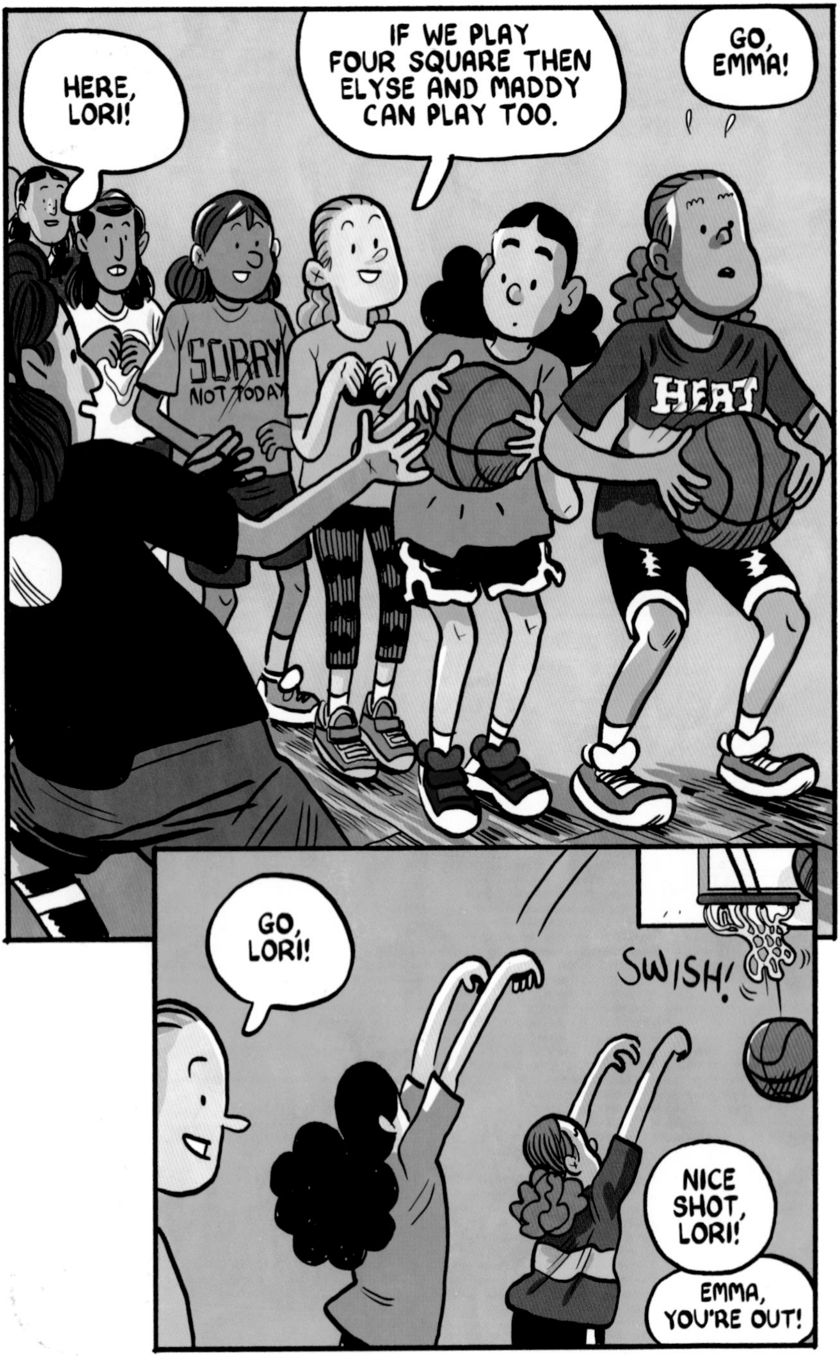
HERE, LORI!
IF WE PLAY FOUR SQUARE THEN ELYSE AND MADDY CAN PLAY TOO.
GO, EMMA!
SORRY NOT TODAY
HEAT
GO, LORI!
SWISH!
NICE SHOT, LORI!
EMMA, YOU'RE OUT!

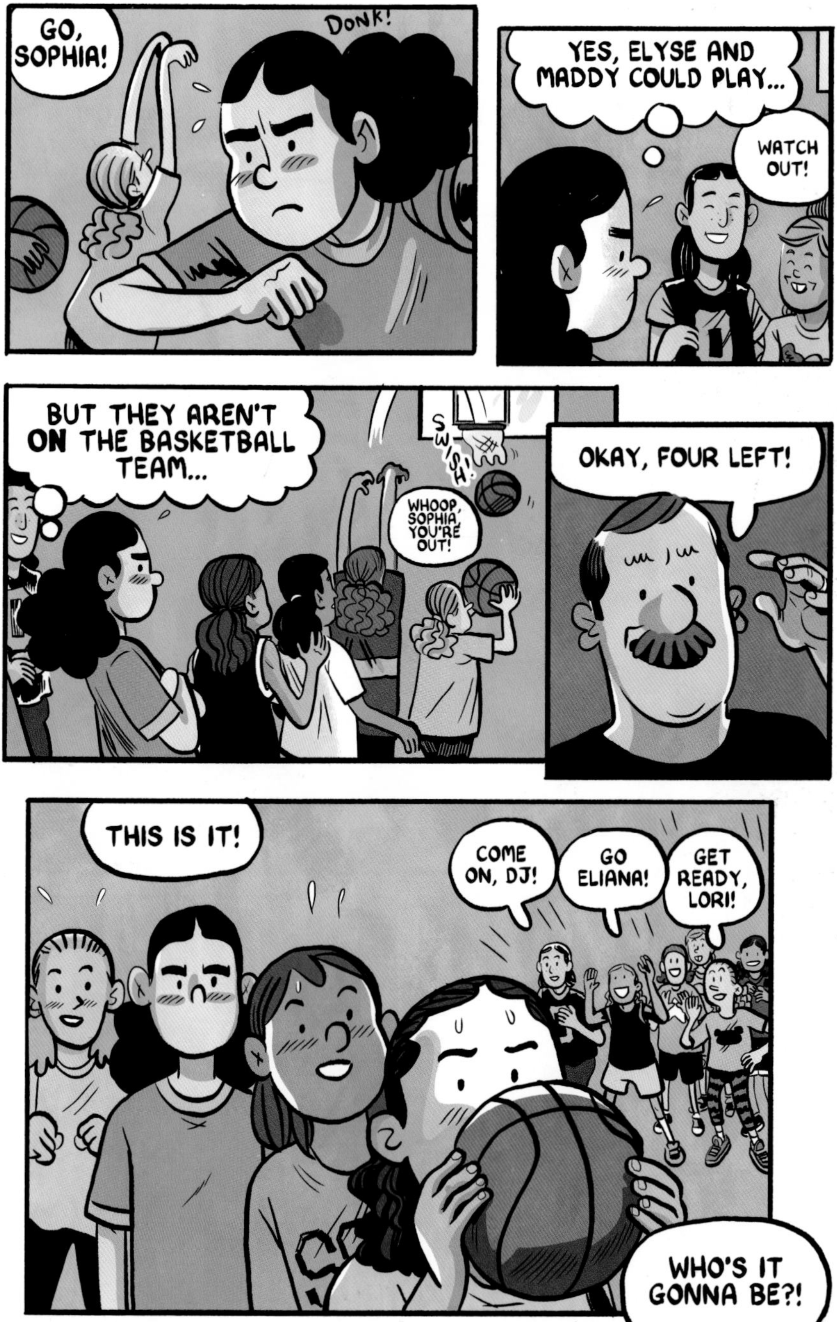
GO, SOPHIA!
DONK!
YES, ELYSE AND MADDY COULD PLAY...
WATCH OUT!
BUT THEY AREN'T **ON** THE BASKETBALL TEAM...
SWISH!
WHOOP, SOPHIA, YOU'RE OUT!
OKAY, FOUR LEFT!
THIS IS IT!
COME ON, DJ!
GO ELIANA!
GET READY, LORI!
WHO'S IT GONNA BE?!

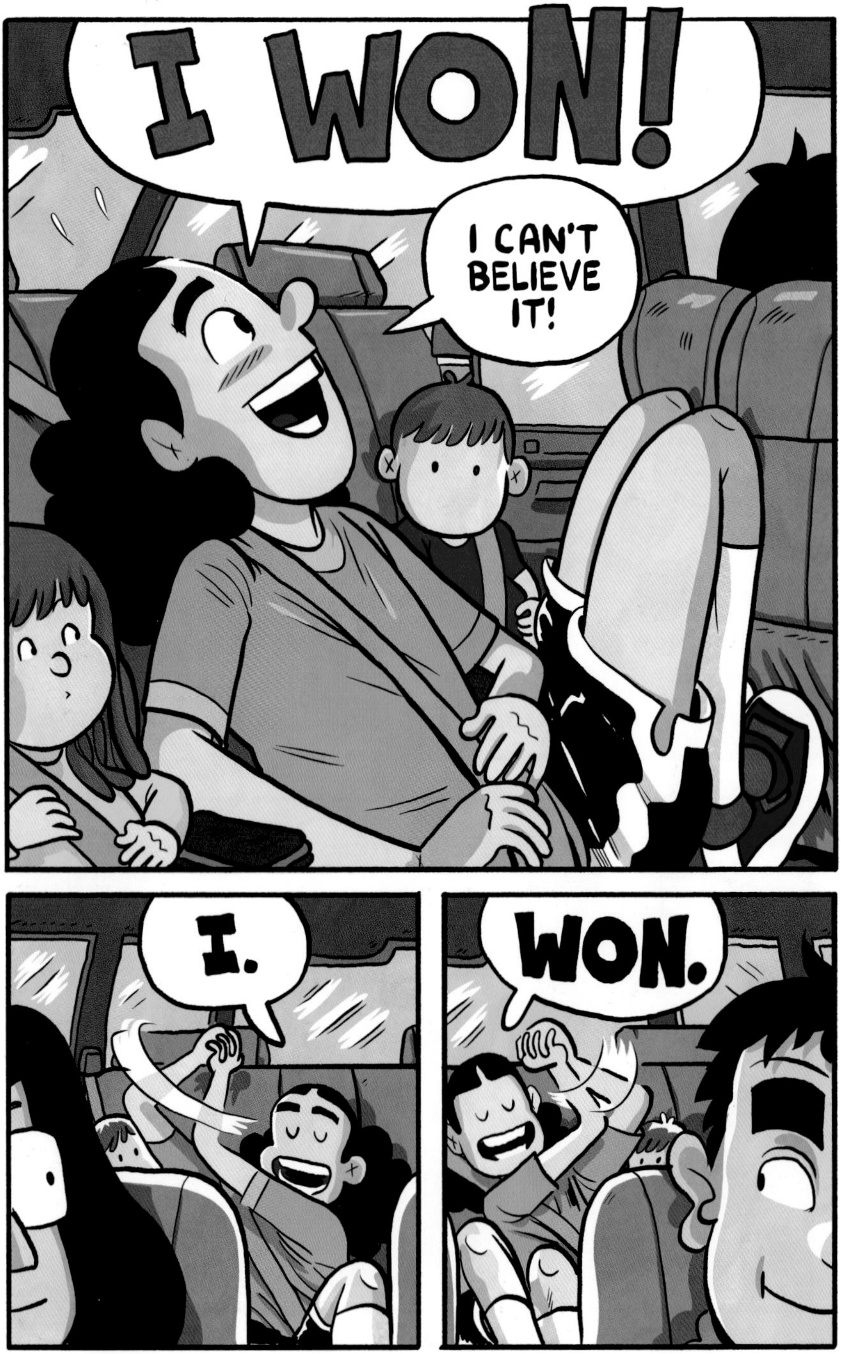
I WON!
I CAN'T BELIEVE IT!
I.
WON.

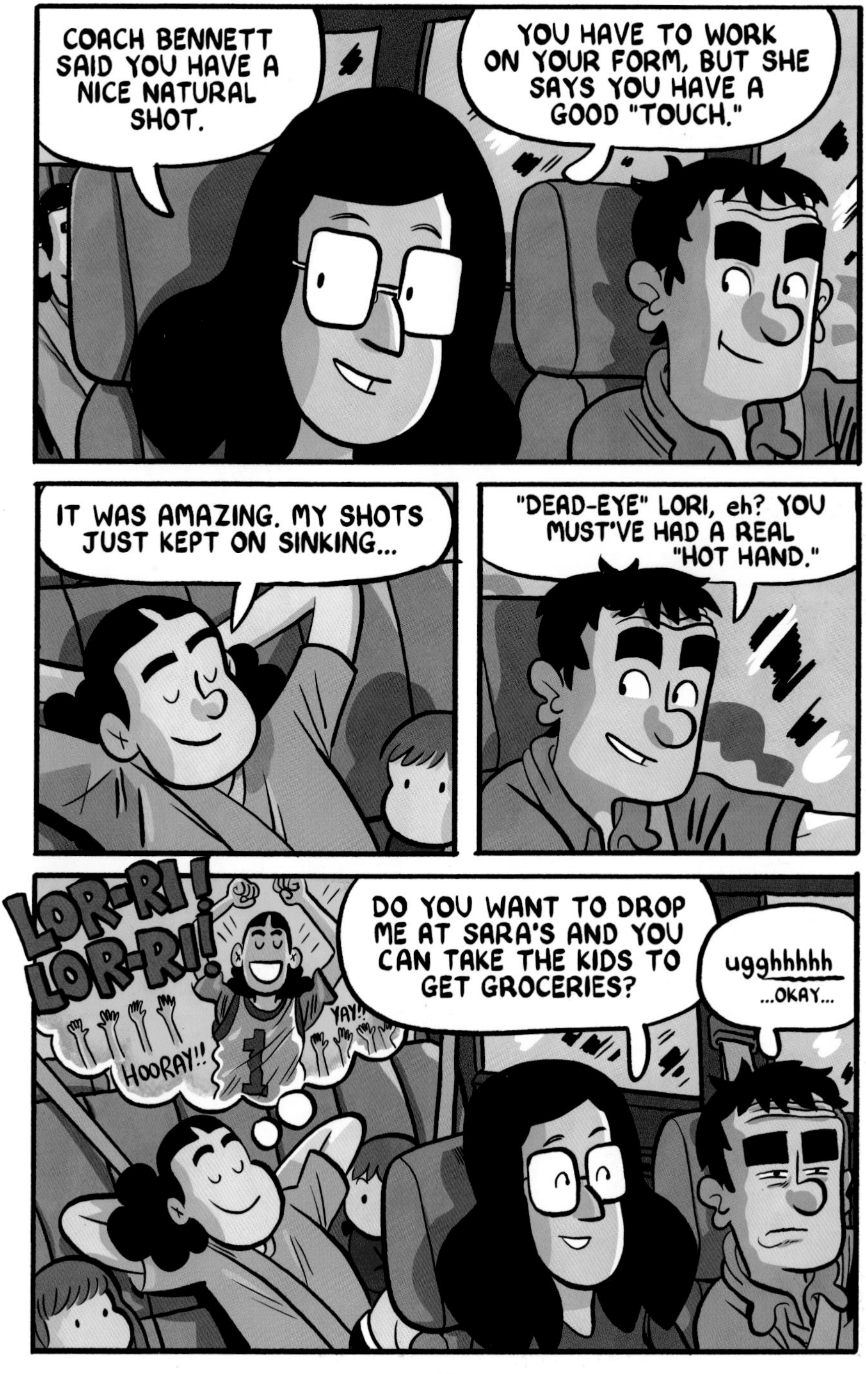

COACH BENNETT SAID YOU HAVE A NICE NATURAL SHOT.
YOU HAVE TO WORK ON YOUR FORM, BUT SHE SAYS YOU HAVE A GOOD "TOUCH."
IT WAS AMAZING. MY SHOTS JUST KEPT ON SINKING...
"DEAD-EYE" LORI, eh? YOU MUST'VE HAD A REAL "HOT HAND."
LOR-RI! LOR-RI!
YAY!!
HOORAY!!
DO YOU WANT TO DROP ME AT SARA'S AND YOU CAN TAKE THE KIDS TO GET GROCERIES?
ugghhhhh
...OKAY...

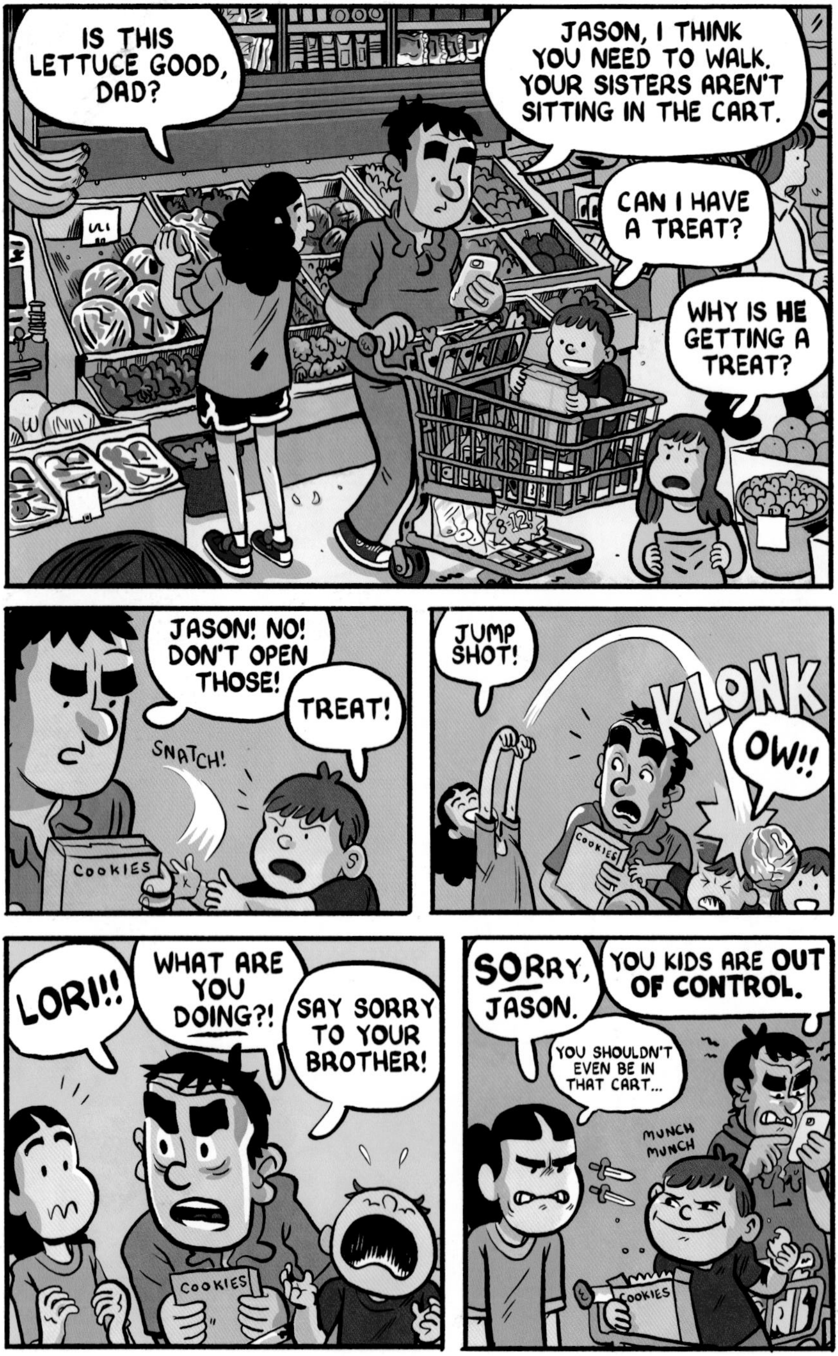
IS THIS LETTUCE GOOD, DAD?
JASON, I THINK YOU NEED TO WALK. YOUR SISTERS AREN'T SITTING IN THE CART.
CAN I HAVE A TREAT?
WHY IS HE GETTING A TREAT?
JASON! NO! DON'T OPEN THOSE!
TREAT!
SNATCH!
COOKIES
JUMP SHOT!
KLONK
OW!!
COOKIES
LORI!!
WHAT ARE YOU DOING?!
SAY SORRY TO YOUR BROTHER!
COOKIES
SORRY, JASON.
YOU KIDS ARE OUT OF CONTROL.
YOU SHOULDN'T EVEN BE IN THAT CART...
MUNCH MUNCH
COOKIES

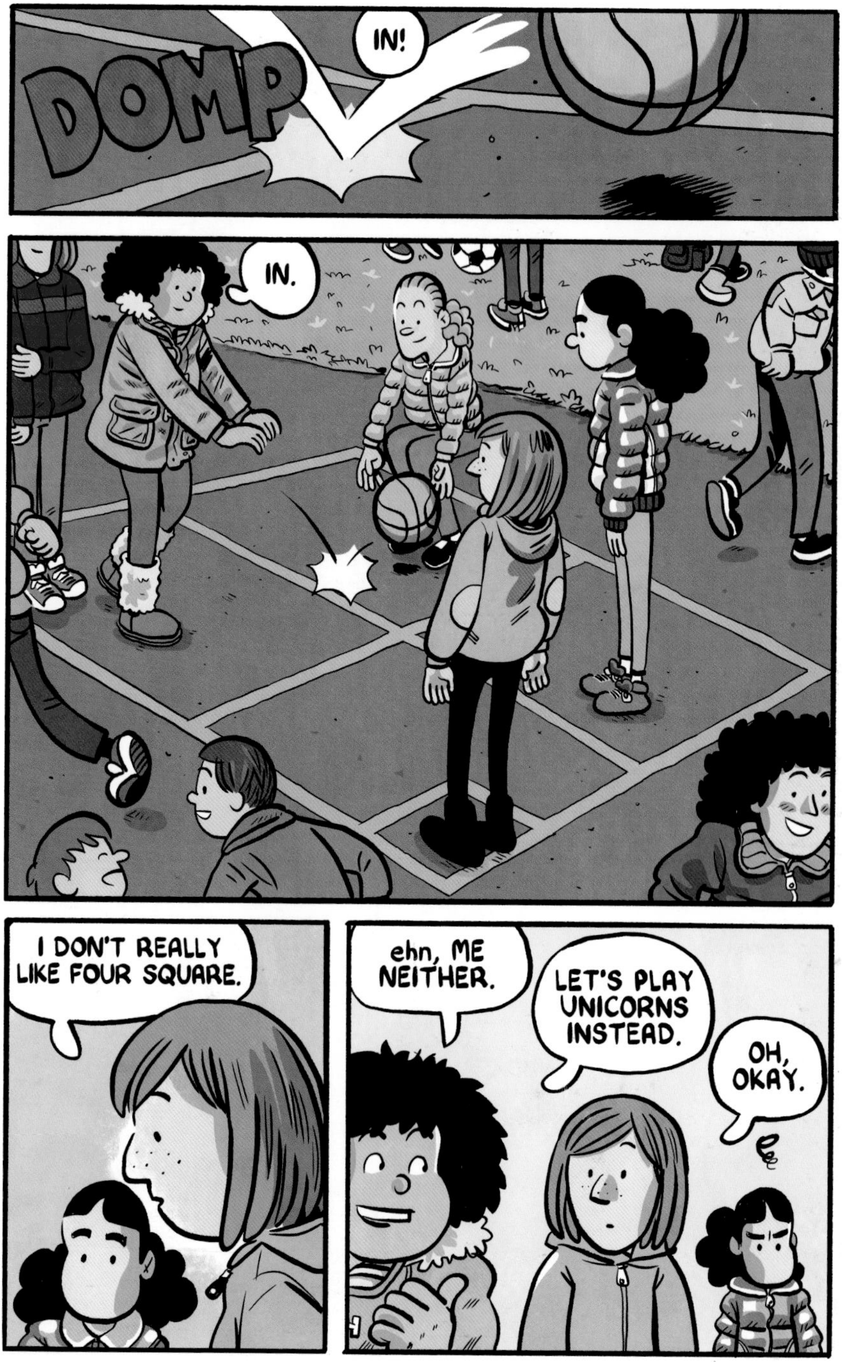
DOMP
IN!
IN.
I DON'T REALLY LIKE FOUR SQUARE.
ehn, ME NEITHER.
LET'S PLAY UNICORNS INSTEAD.
OH, OKAY.

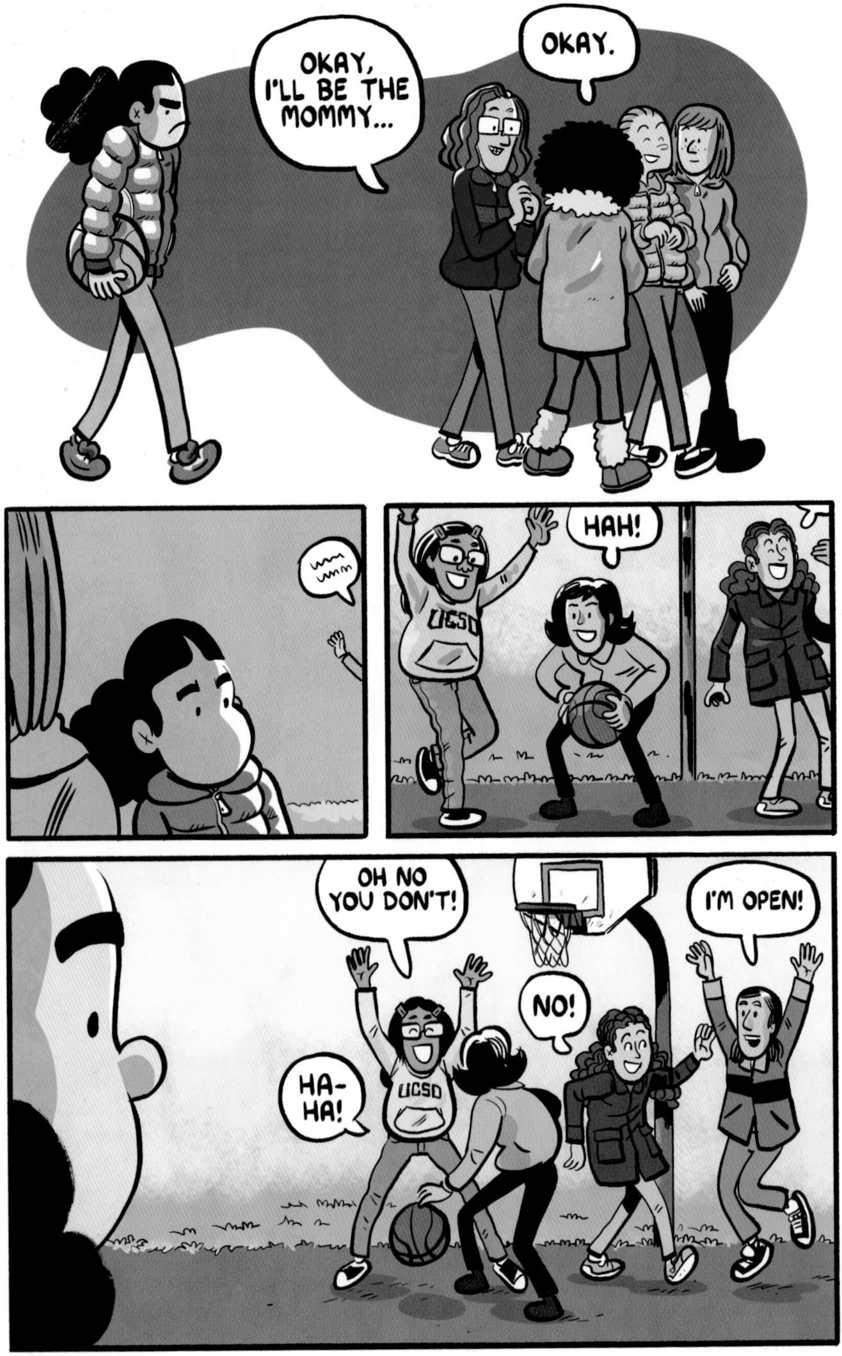
OKAY, I'LL BE THE MOMMY...
OKAY.
HAH!
UCSD
OH NO YOU DON'T!
I'M OPEN!
NO!
HA-HA!
UCSD

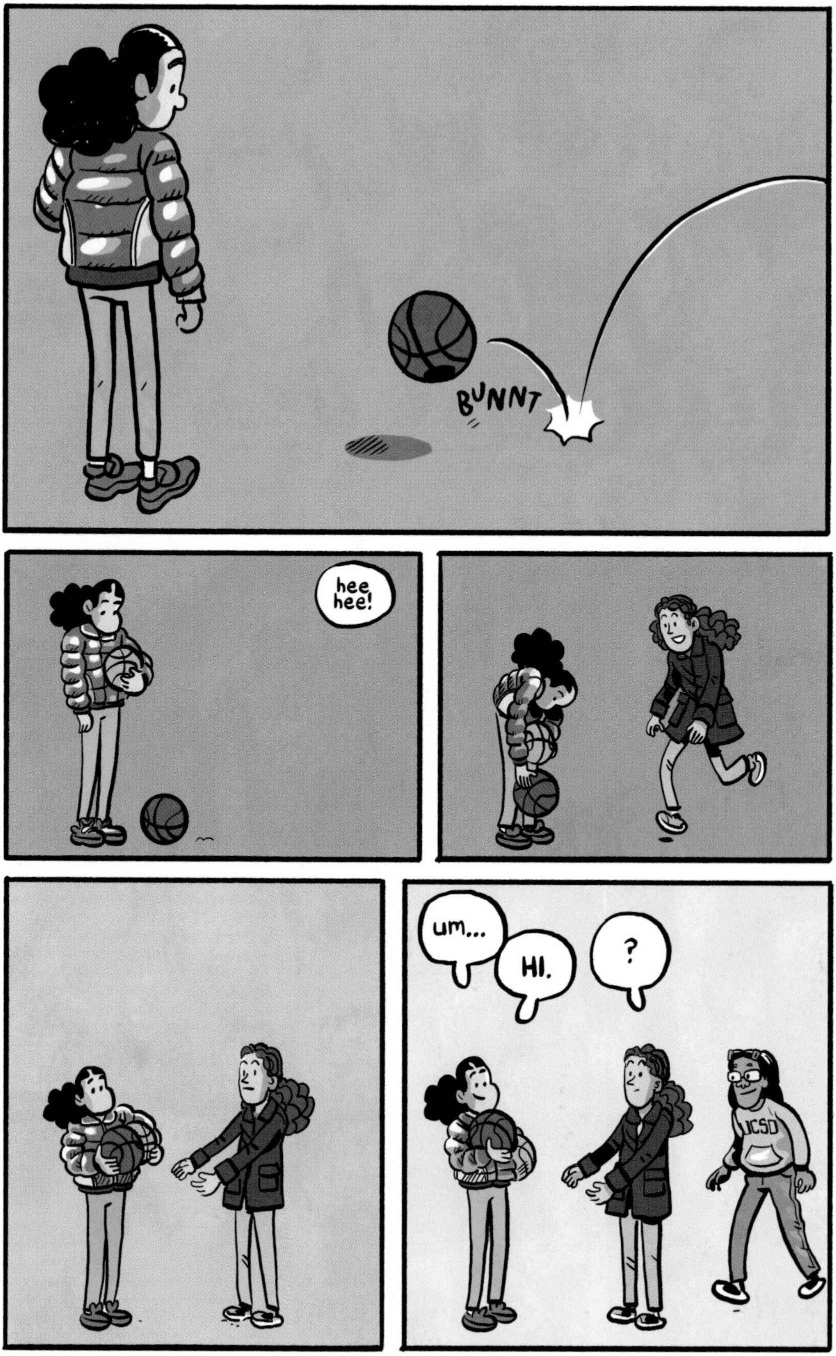
BUNNT
hee hee!
um...
HI.
?

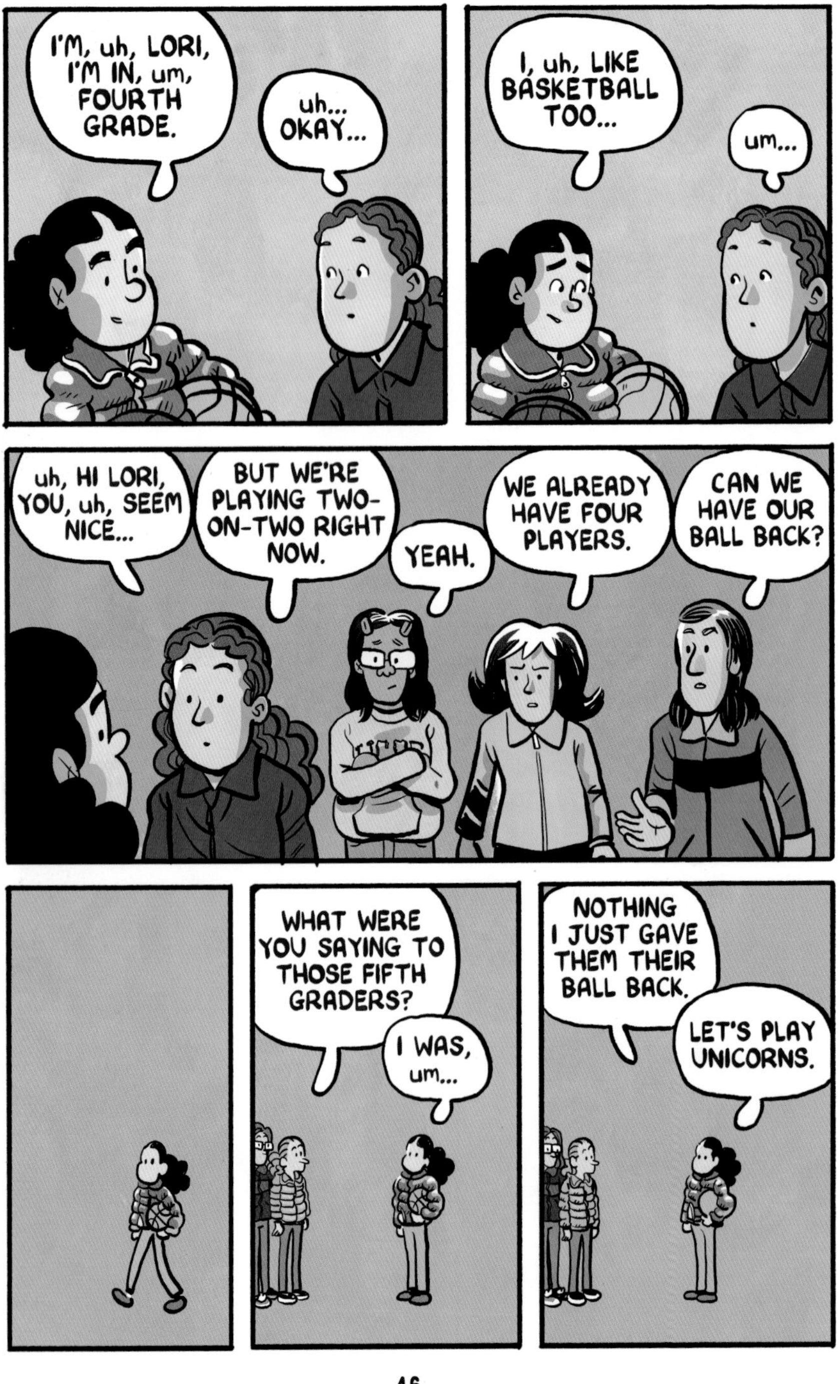
I'M, uh, LORI, I'M IN, um, FOURTH GRADE.
uh... OKAY...
I, uh, LIKE BASKETBALL TOO...
um...
uh, HI LORI, YOU, uh, SEEM NICE...
BUT WE'RE PLAYING TWO-ON-TWO RIGHT NOW.
YEAH.
WE ALREADY HAVE FOUR PLAYERS.
CAN WE HAVE OUR BALL BACK?
WHAT WERE YOU SAYING TO THOSE FIFTH GRADERS?
I WAS, um...
NOTHING I JUST GAVE THEM THEIR BALL BACK.
LET'S PLAY UNICORNS.

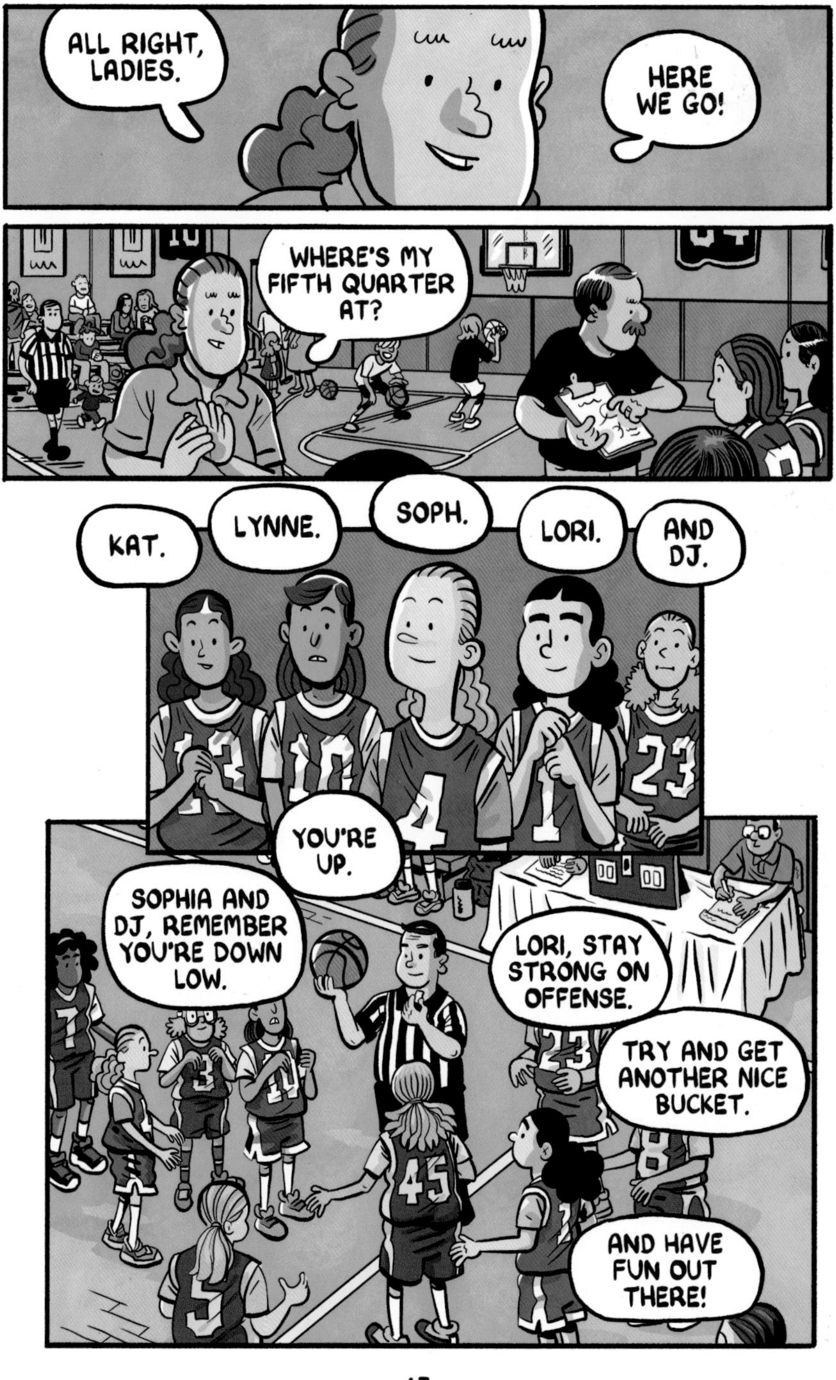
ALL RIGHT, LADIES.
HERE WE GO!
WHERE'S MY FIFTH QUARTER AT?
KAT.
LYNNE.
SOPH.
LORI.
AND DJ.
YOU'RE UP.
SOPHIA AND DJ, REMEMBER YOU'RE DOWN LOW.
LORI, STAY STRONG ON OFFENSE.
TRY AND GET ANOTHER NICE BUCKET.
AND HAVE FUN OUT THERE!

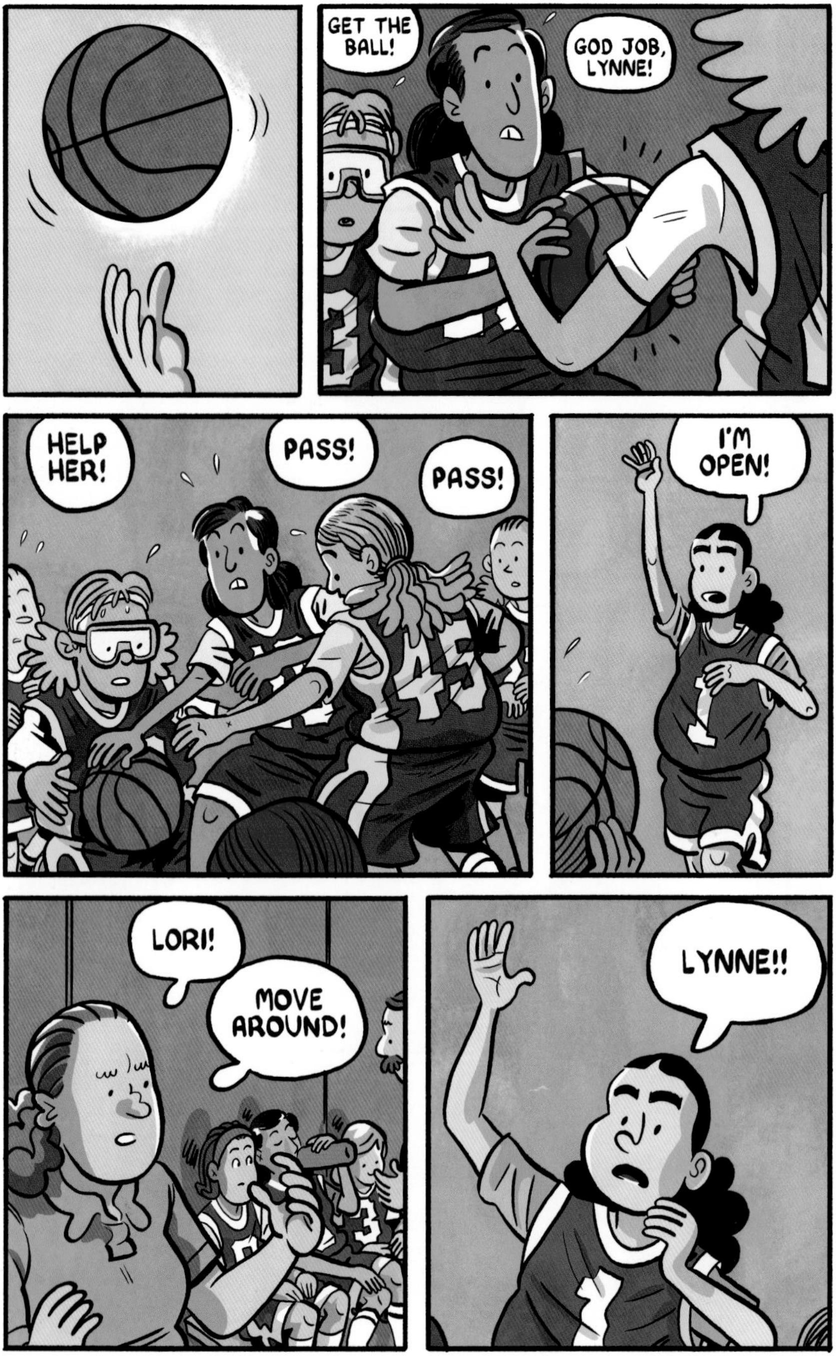
GET THE BALL!
GOD JOB, LYNNE!
HELP HER!
PASS!
PASS!
I'M OPEN!
LORI!
MOVE AROUND!
LYNNE!!

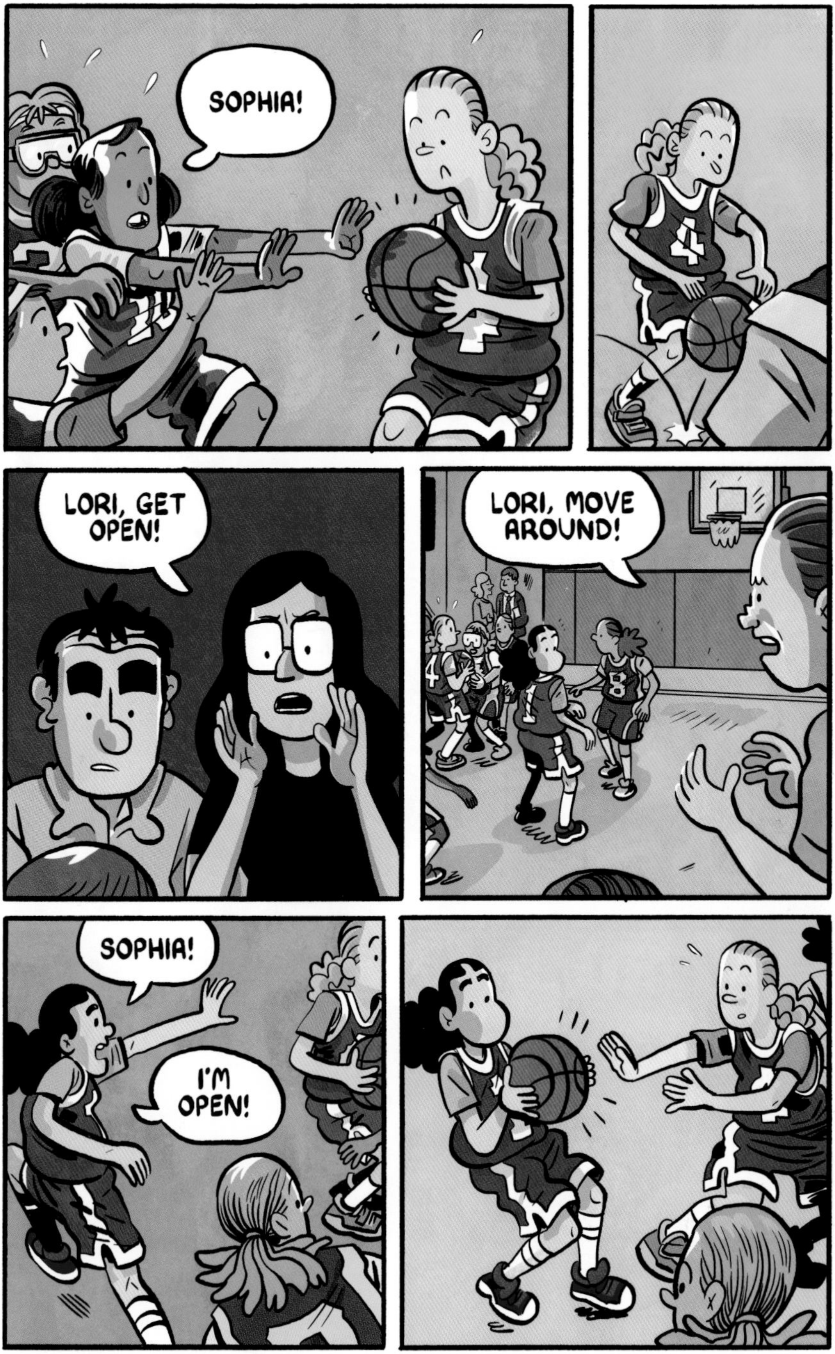
SOPHIA!
LORI, GET OPEN!
LORI, MOVE AROUND!
SOPHIA!
I'M OPEN!

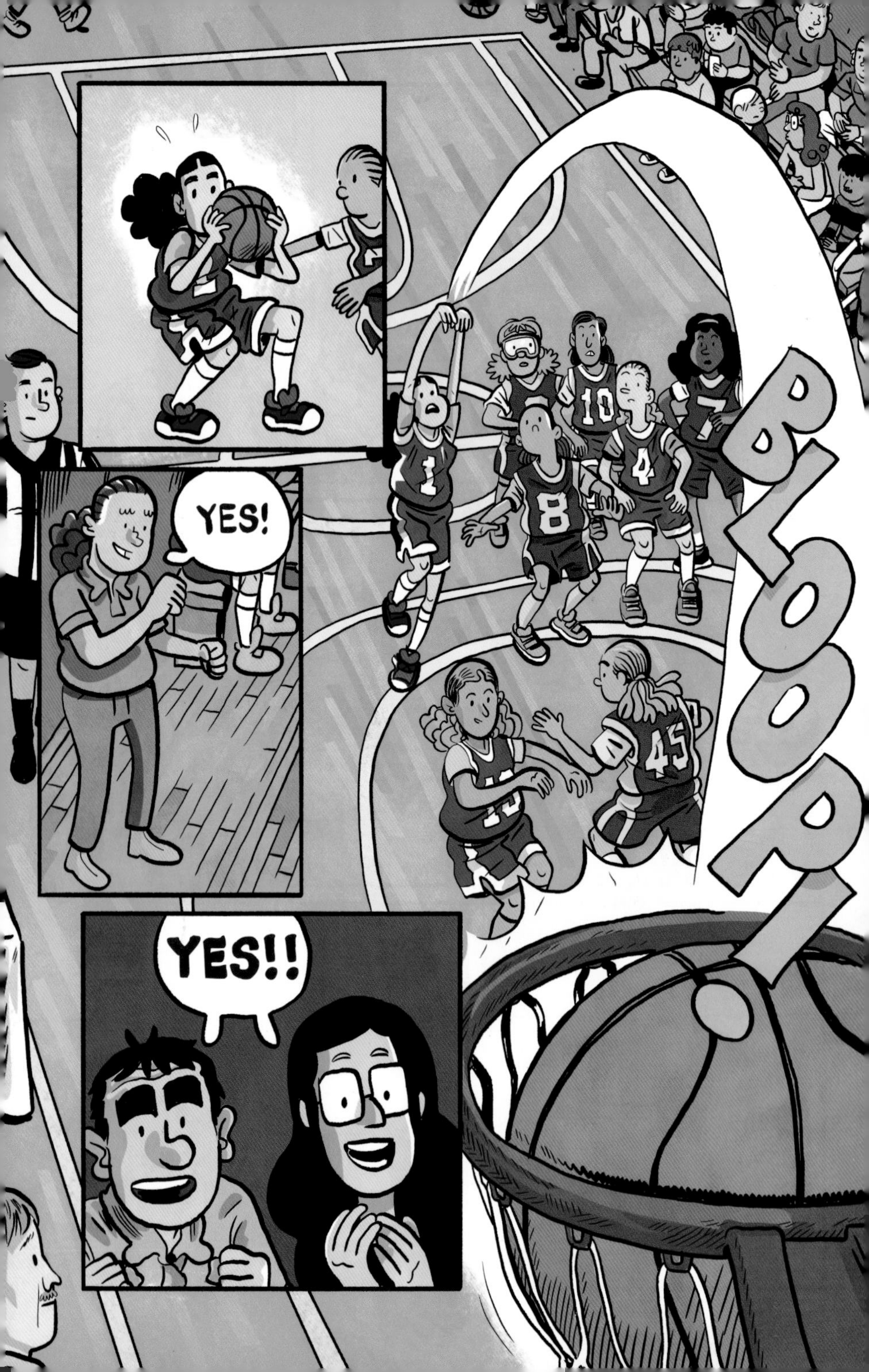
YES!
YES!!
BLOOP!

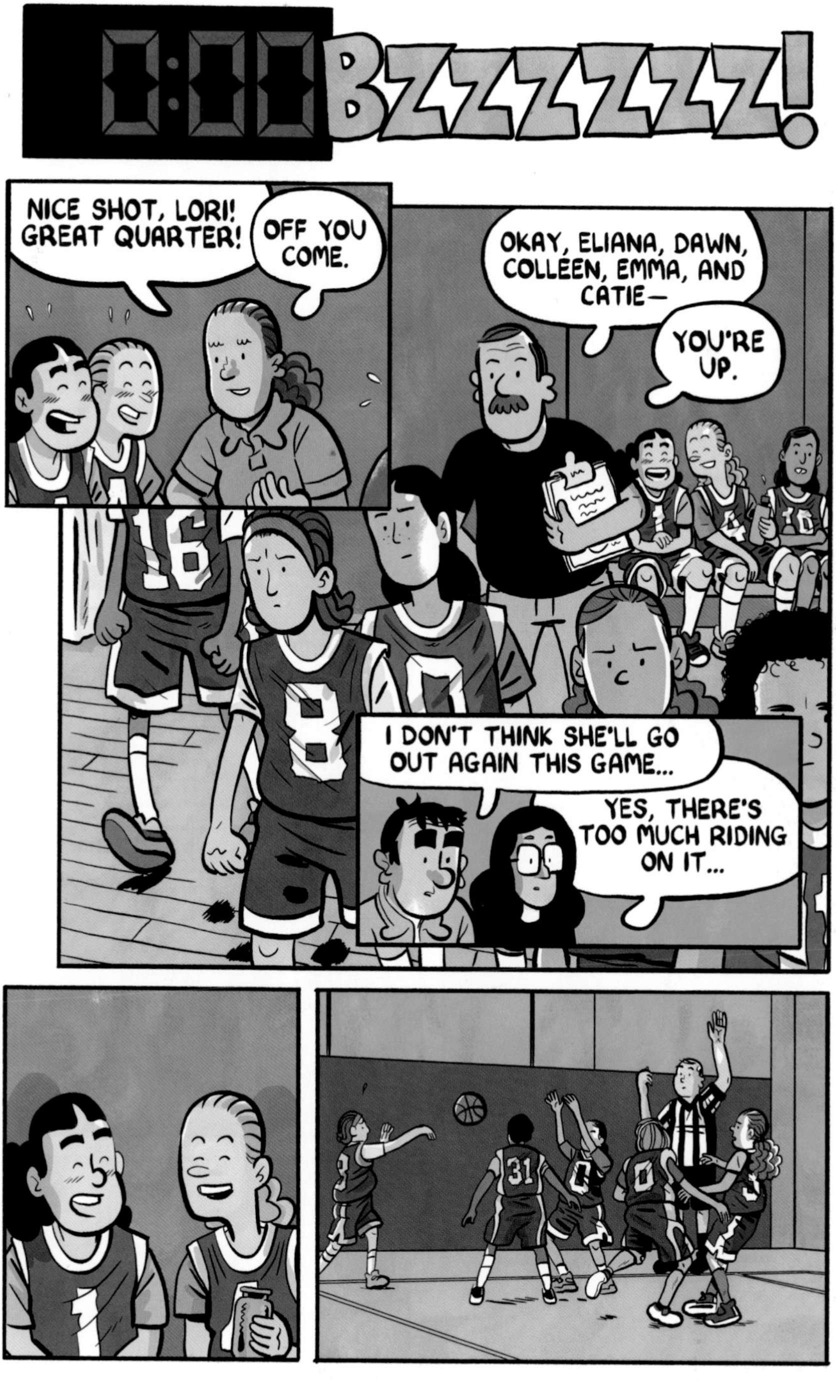

0:00
BZZZZZZZ!
NICE SHOT, LORI! GREAT QUARTER!
OFF YOU COME.
OKAY, ELIANA, DAWN, COLLEEN, EMMA, AND CATIE—
YOU'RE UP.
I DON'T THINK SHE'LL GO OUT AGAIN THIS GAME...
YES, THERE'S TOO MUCH RIDING ON IT...

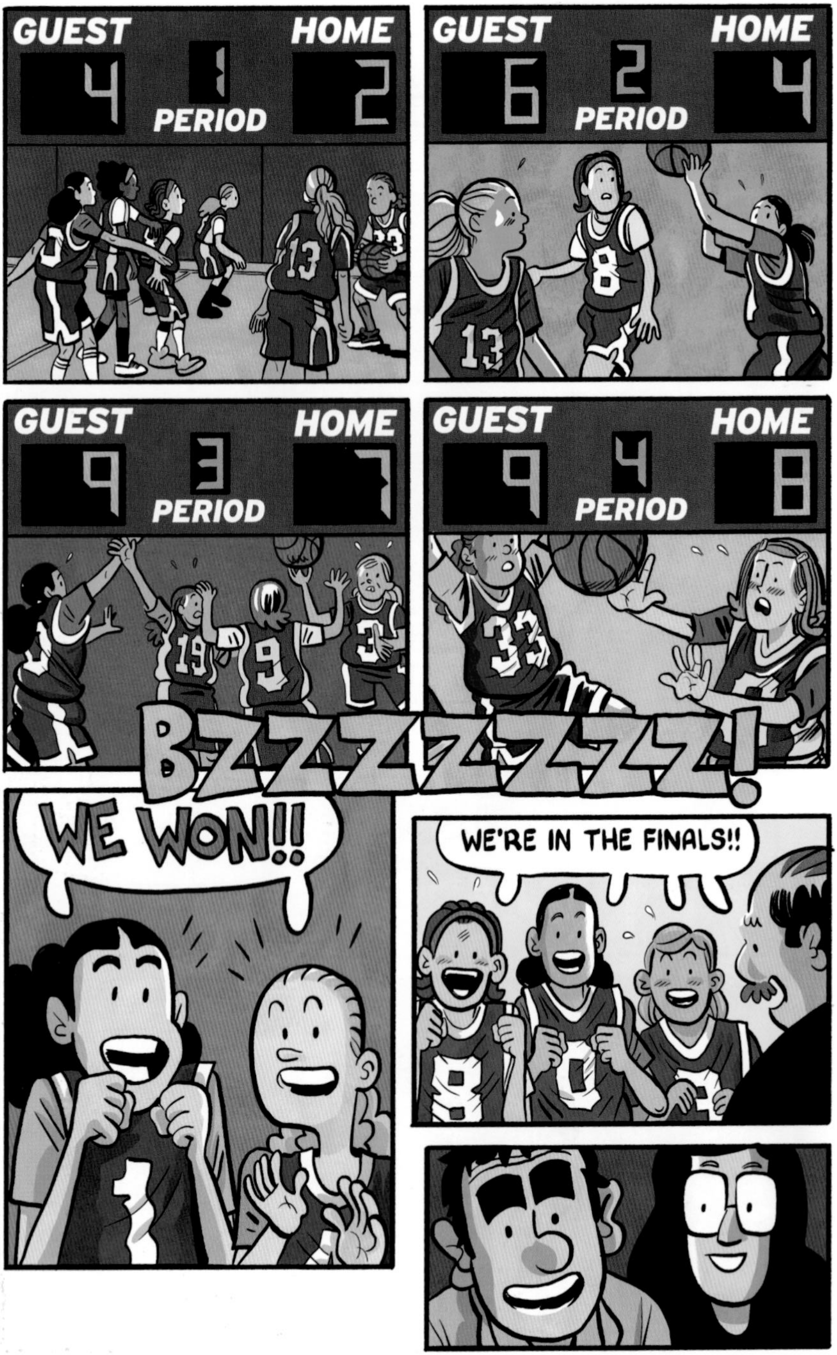
GUEST
HOME
4
1
2
PERIOD
GUEST
HOME
6
2
4
PERIOD
GUEST
HOME
9
3
7
PERIOD
GUEST
HOME
9
4
8
PERIOD
BZZZZZZZ!
WE WON!!
WE'RE IN THE FINALS!!

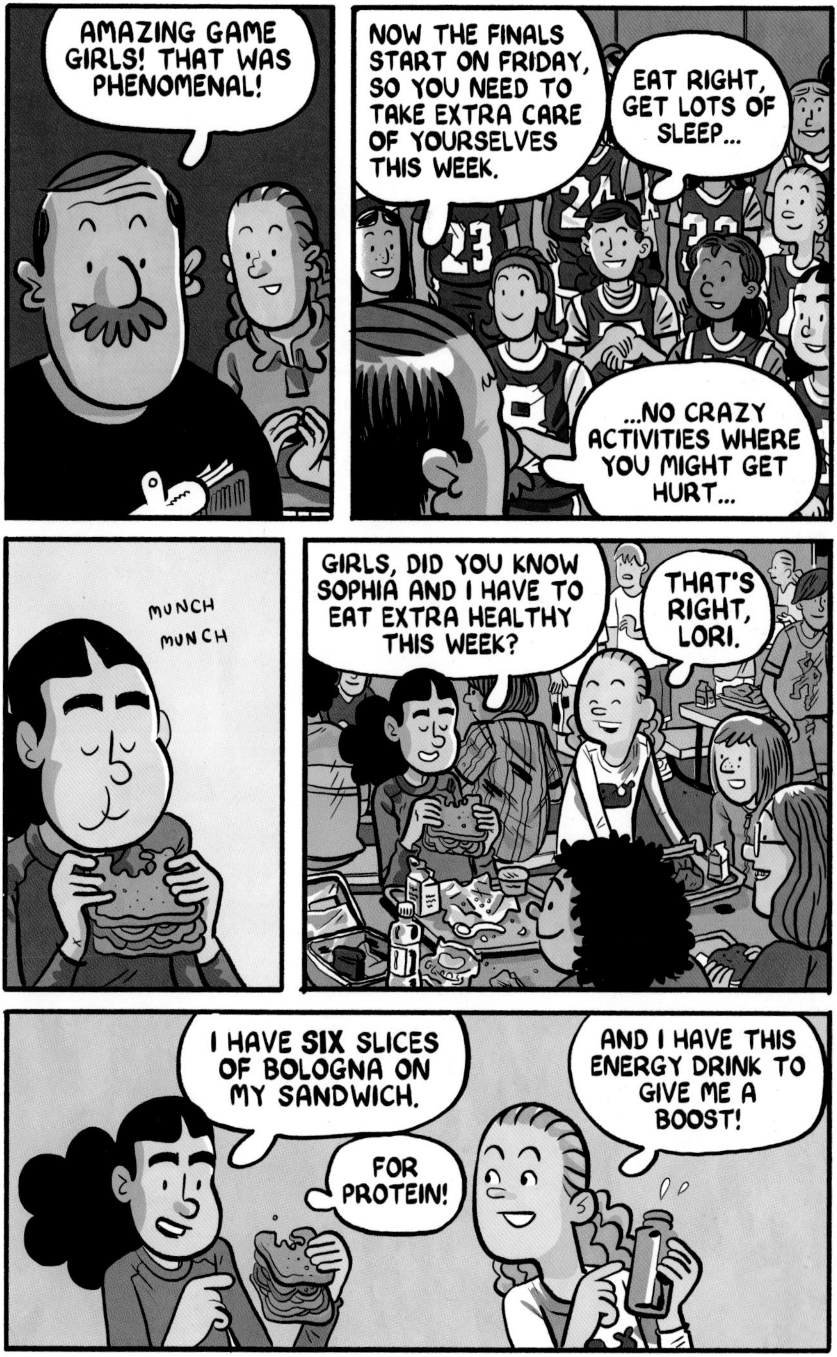
AMAZING GAME GIRLS! THAT WAS PHENOMENAL!
NOW THE FINALS START ON FRIDAY, SO YOU NEED TO TAKE EXTRA CARE OF YOURSELVES THIS WEEK.
EAT RIGHT, GET LOTS OF SLEEP...
...NO CRAZY ACTIVITIES WHERE YOU MIGHT GET HURT...
MUNCH
MUNCH
GIRLS, DID YOU KNOW SOPHIA AND I HAVE TO EAT EXTRA HEALTHY THIS WEEK?
THAT'S RIGHT, LORI.
I HAVE **SIX** SLICES OF BOLOGNA ON MY SANDWICH.
FOR PROTEIN!
AND I HAVE THIS ENERGY DRINK TO GIVE ME A BOOST!

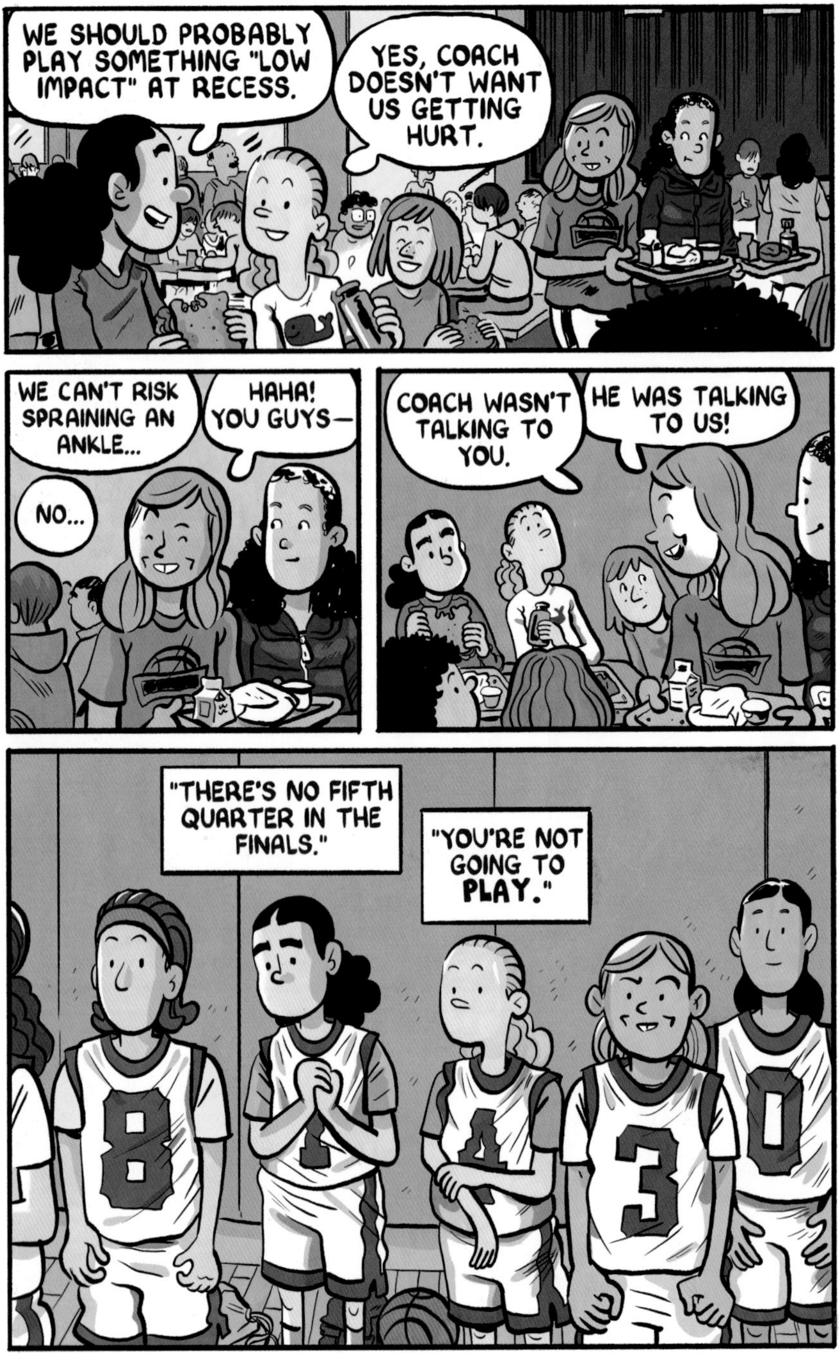
WE SHOULD PROBABLY PLAY SOMETHING "LOW IMPACT" AT RECESS.
YES, COACH DOESN'T WANT US GETTING HURT.
WE CAN'T RISK SPRAINING AN ANKLE...
HAHA! YOU GUYS—
NO...
COACH WASN'T TALKING TO YOU.
HE WAS TALKING TO US!
"THERE'S NO FIFTH QUARTER IN THE FINALS."
"YOU'RE NOT GOING TO PLAY."

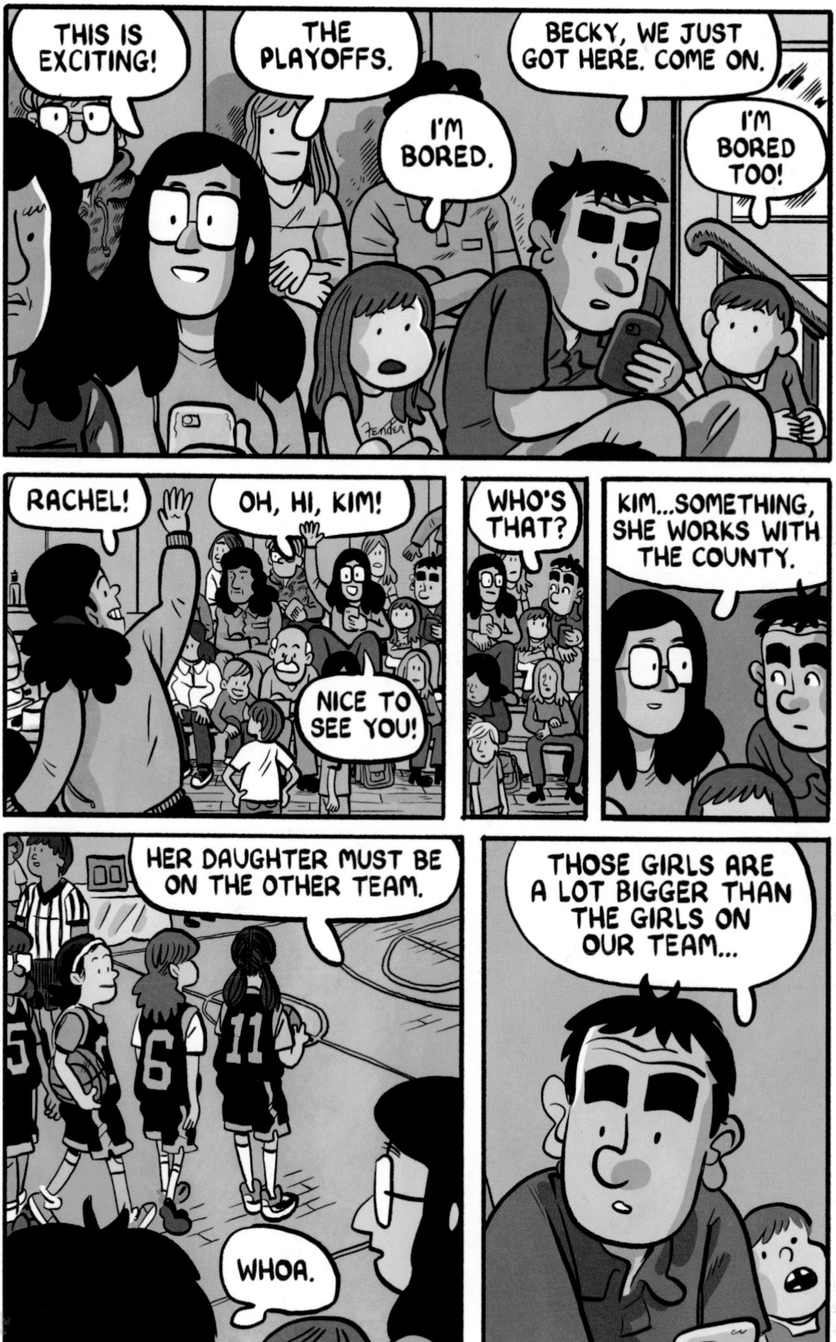
THIS IS EXCITING!
THE PLAYOFFS.
I'M BORED.
BECKY, WE JUST GOT HERE. COME ON.
I'M BORED TOO!
RACHEL!
OH, HI, KIM!
NICE TO SEE YOU!
WHO'S THAT?
KIM...SOMETHING, SHE WORKS WITH THE COUNTY.
HER DAUGHTER MUST BE ON THE OTHER TEAM.
WHOA.
THOSE GIRLS ARE A LOT BIGGER THAN THE GIRLS ON OUR TEAM...

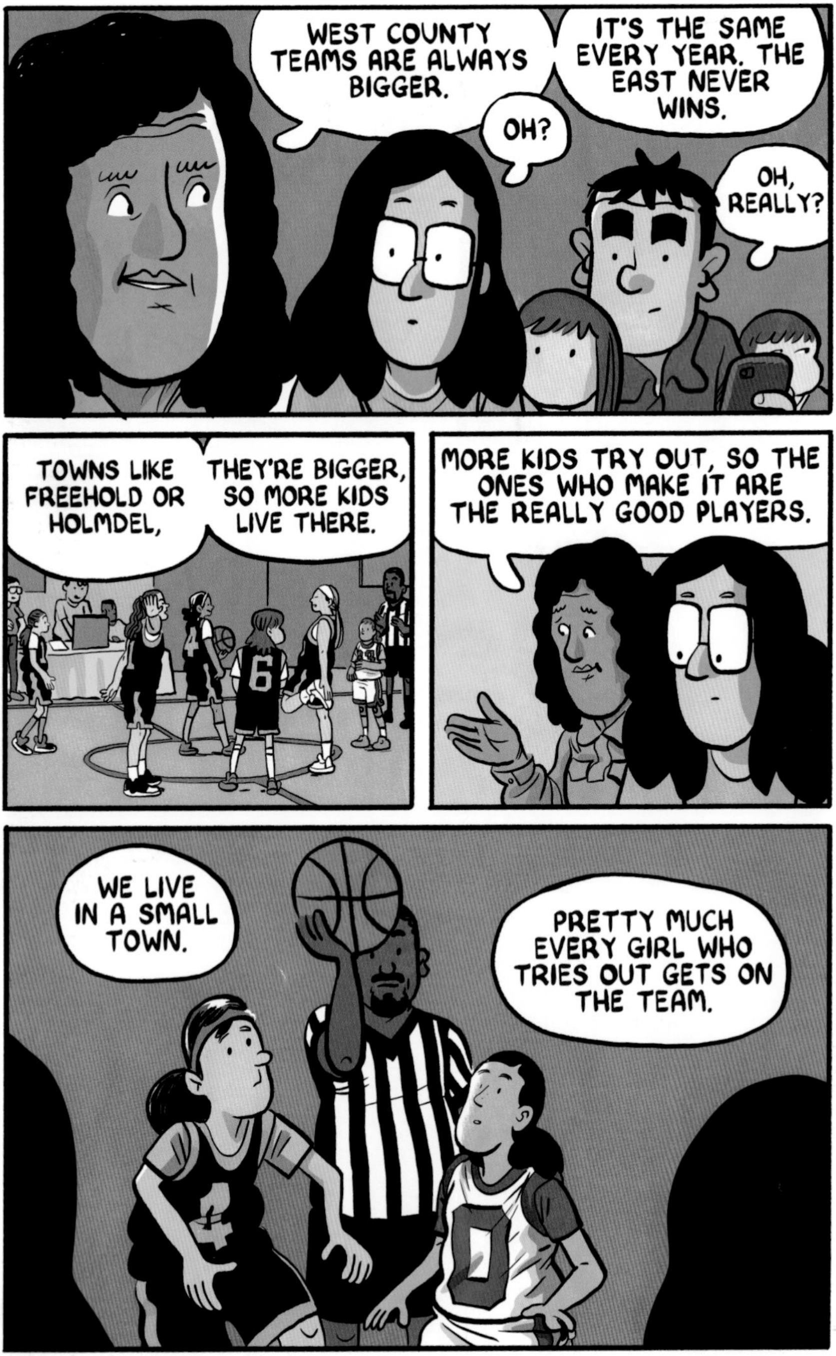
WEST COUNTY TEAMS ARE ALWAYS BIGGER.
OH?
IT'S THE SAME EVERY YEAR. THE EAST NEVER WINS.
OH, REALLY?
TOWNS LIKE FREEHOLD OR HOLMDEL,
THEY'RE BIGGER, SO MORE KIDS LIVE THERE.
MORE KIDS TRY OUT, SO THE ONES WHO MAKE IT ARE THE REALLY GOOD PLAYERS.
WE LIVE IN A SMALL TOWN.
PRETTY MUCH EVERY GIRL WHO TRIES OUT GETS ON THE TEAM.

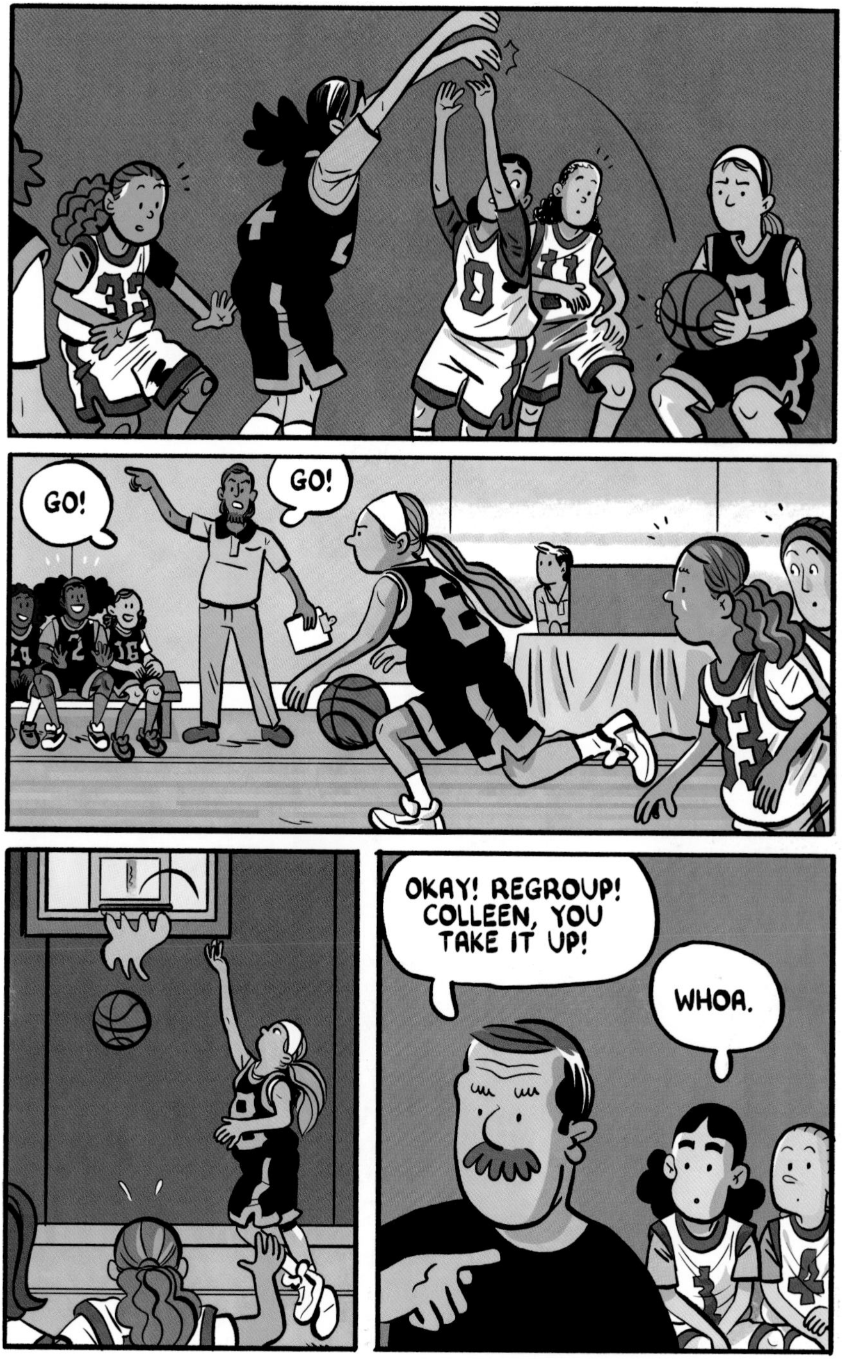
GO!
GO!
OKAY! REGROUP! COLLEEN, YOU TAKE IT UP!
WHOA.

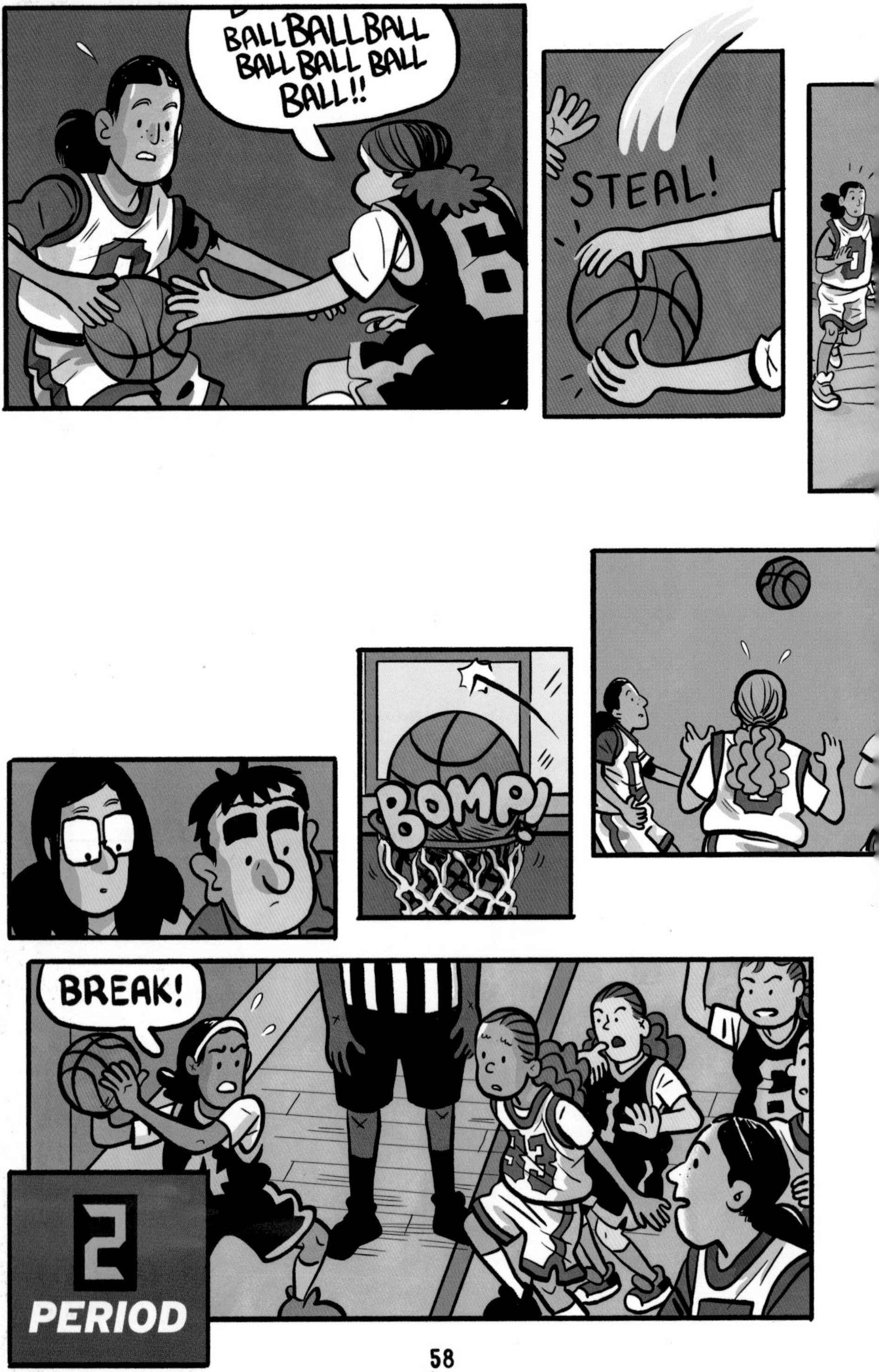
BALL BALL BALL BALL BALL BALL BALL!!
STEAL!
BOMP!
BREAK!
2
PERIOD

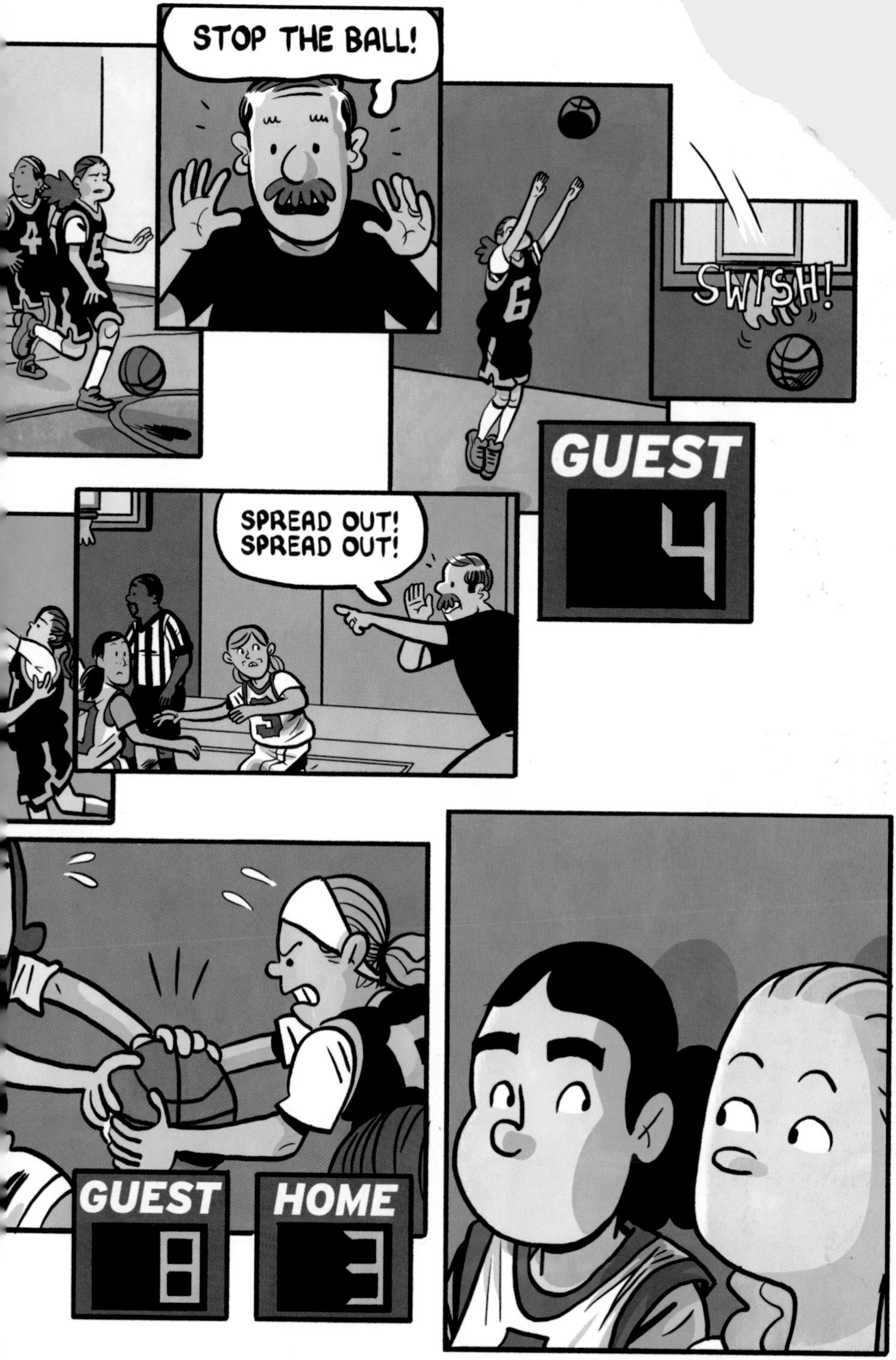
STOP THE BALL!
SWISH!
GUEST
4
SPREAD OUT! SPREAD OUT!
GUEST
8
HOME
3

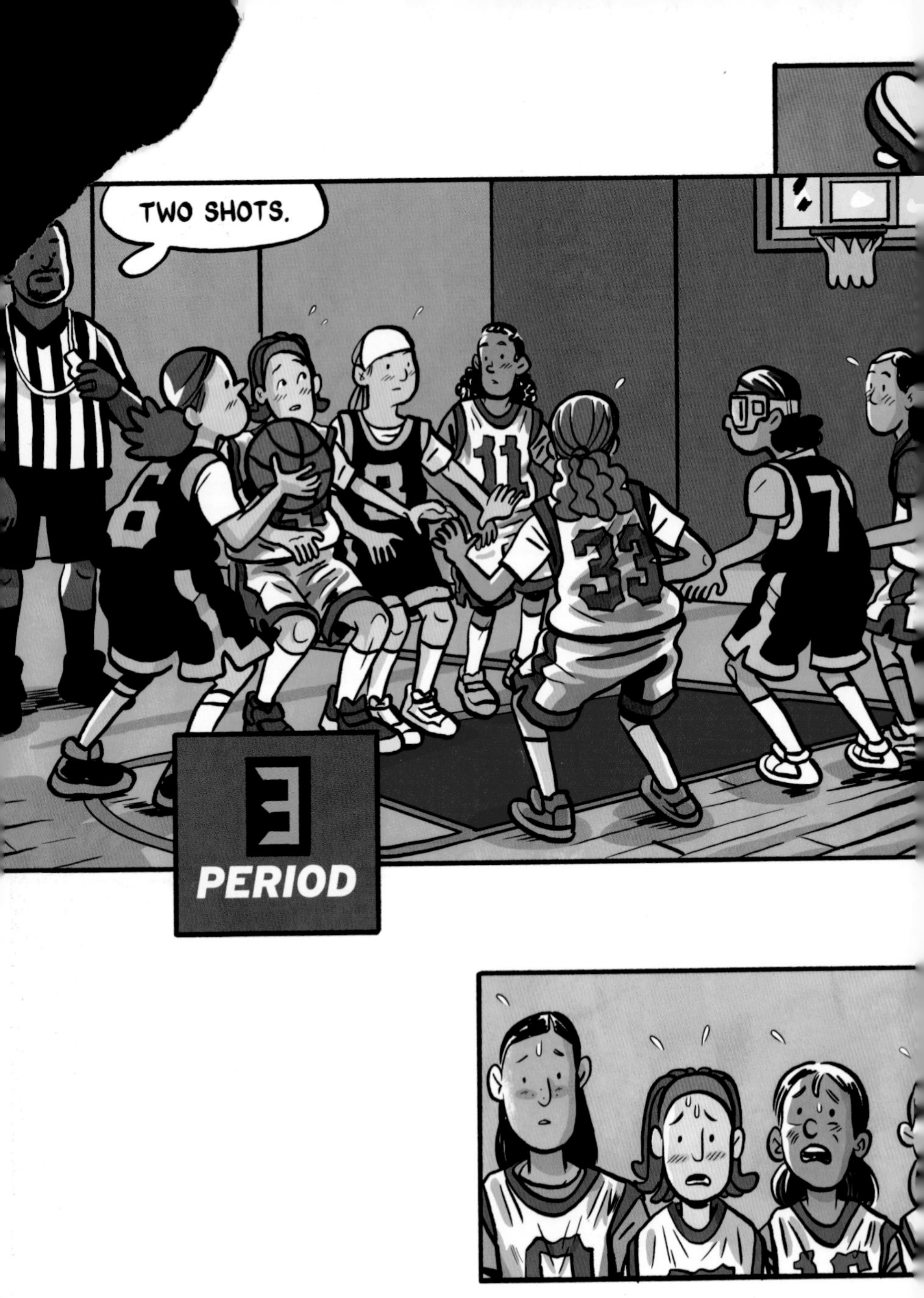
TWO SHOTS.
3
PERIOD

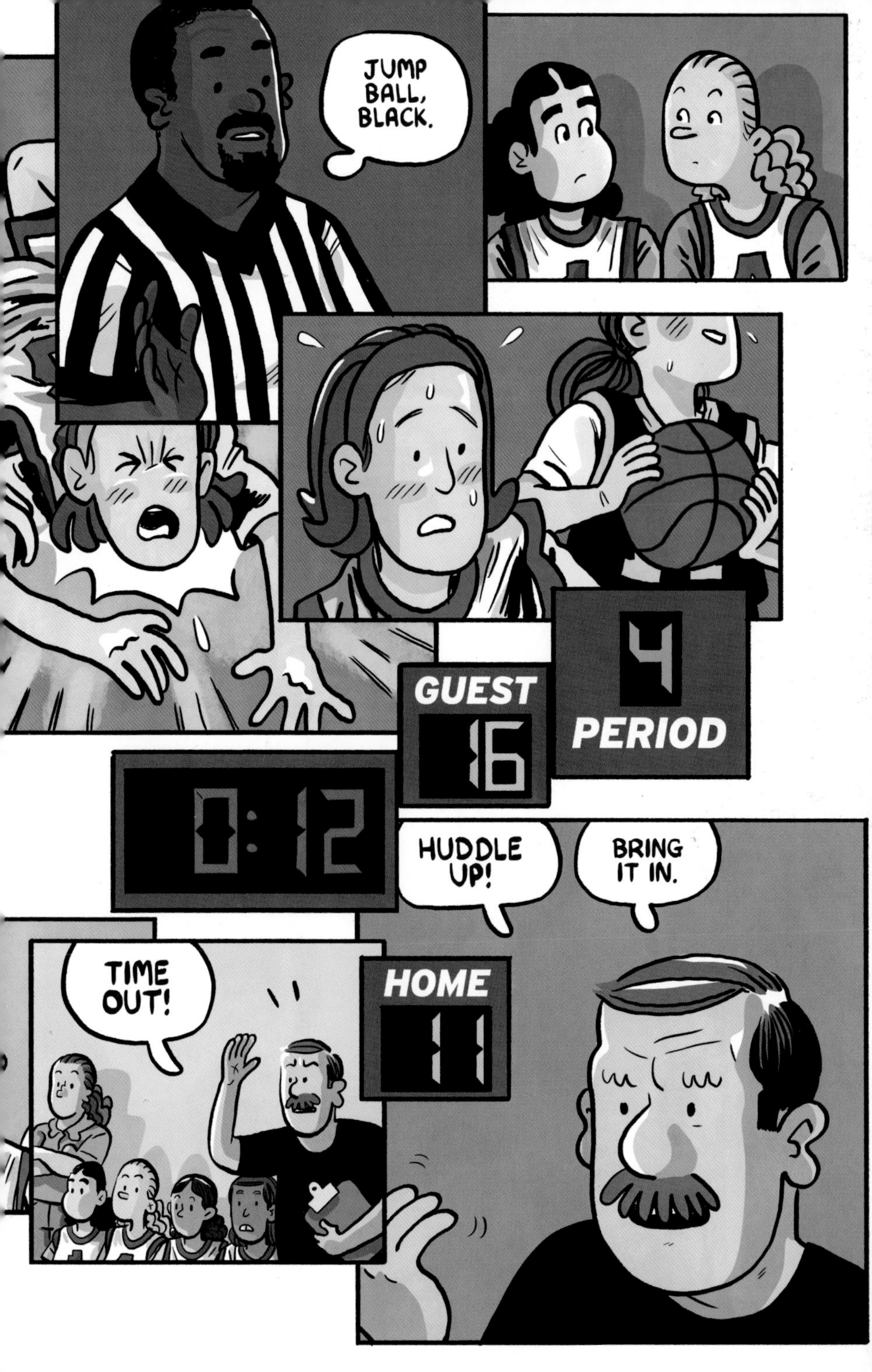
JUMP BALL, BLACK.
GUEST
16
4
PERIOD
0:12
HUDDLE UP!
BRING IT IN.
TIME OUT!
HOME
11

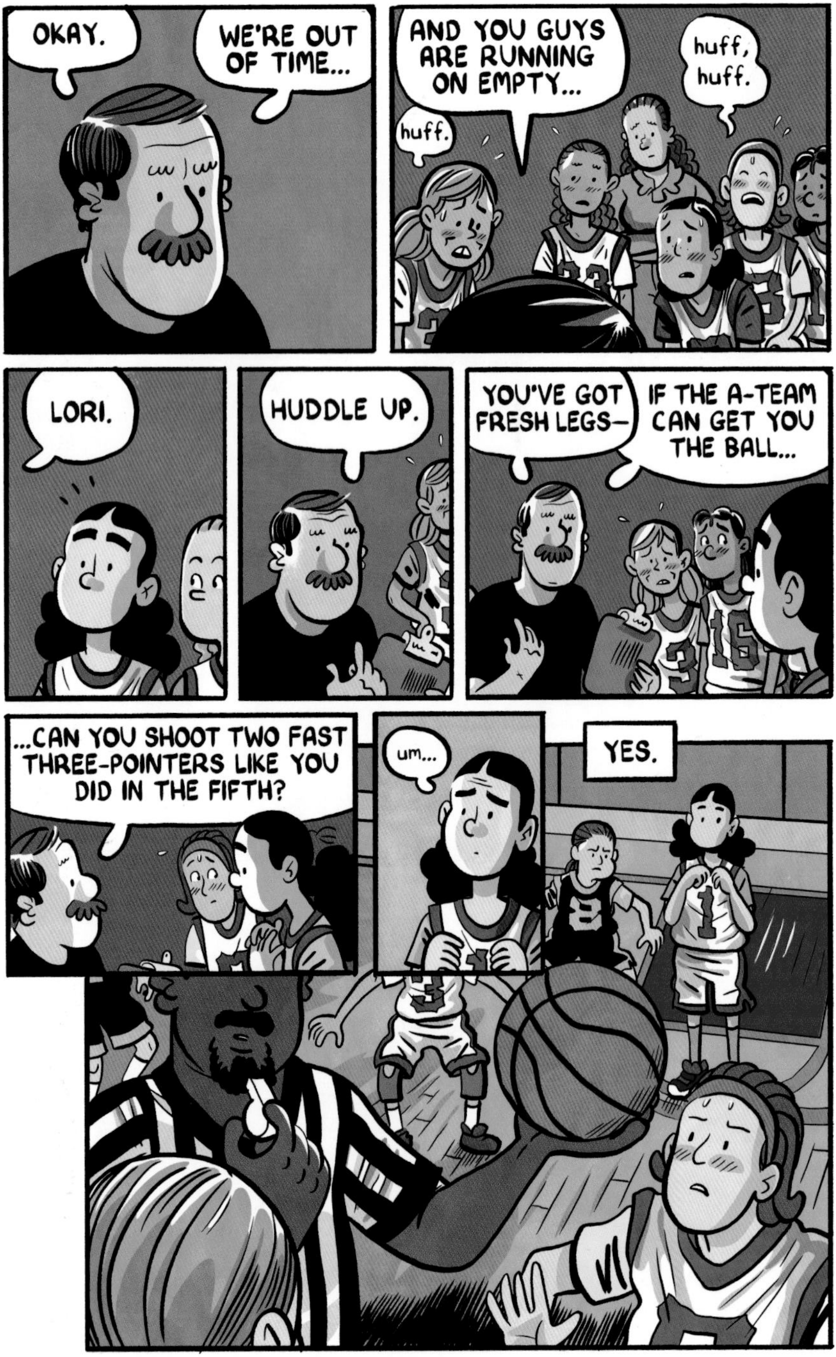
OKAY.
WE'RE OUT OF TIME...
AND YOU GUYS ARE RUNNING ON EMPTY...
huff.
huff, huff.
LORI.
HUDDLE UP.
YOU'VE GOT FRESH LEGS—
IF THE A-TEAM CAN GET YOU THE BALL...
...CAN YOU SHOOT TWO FAST THREE-POINTERS LIKE YOU DID IN THE FIFTH?
um...
YES.

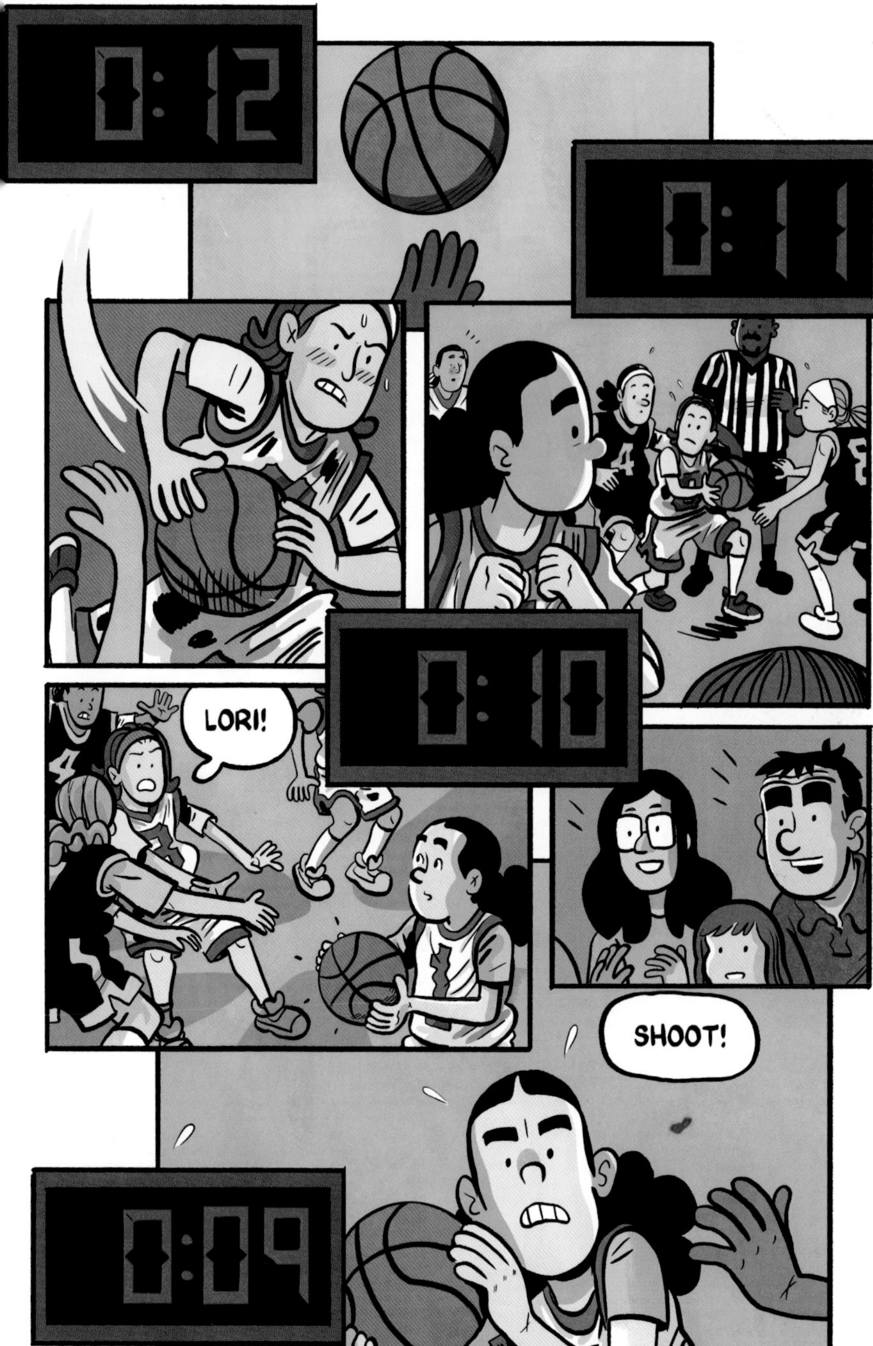
0:12
0:11
0:10
LORI!
SHOOT!
0:09

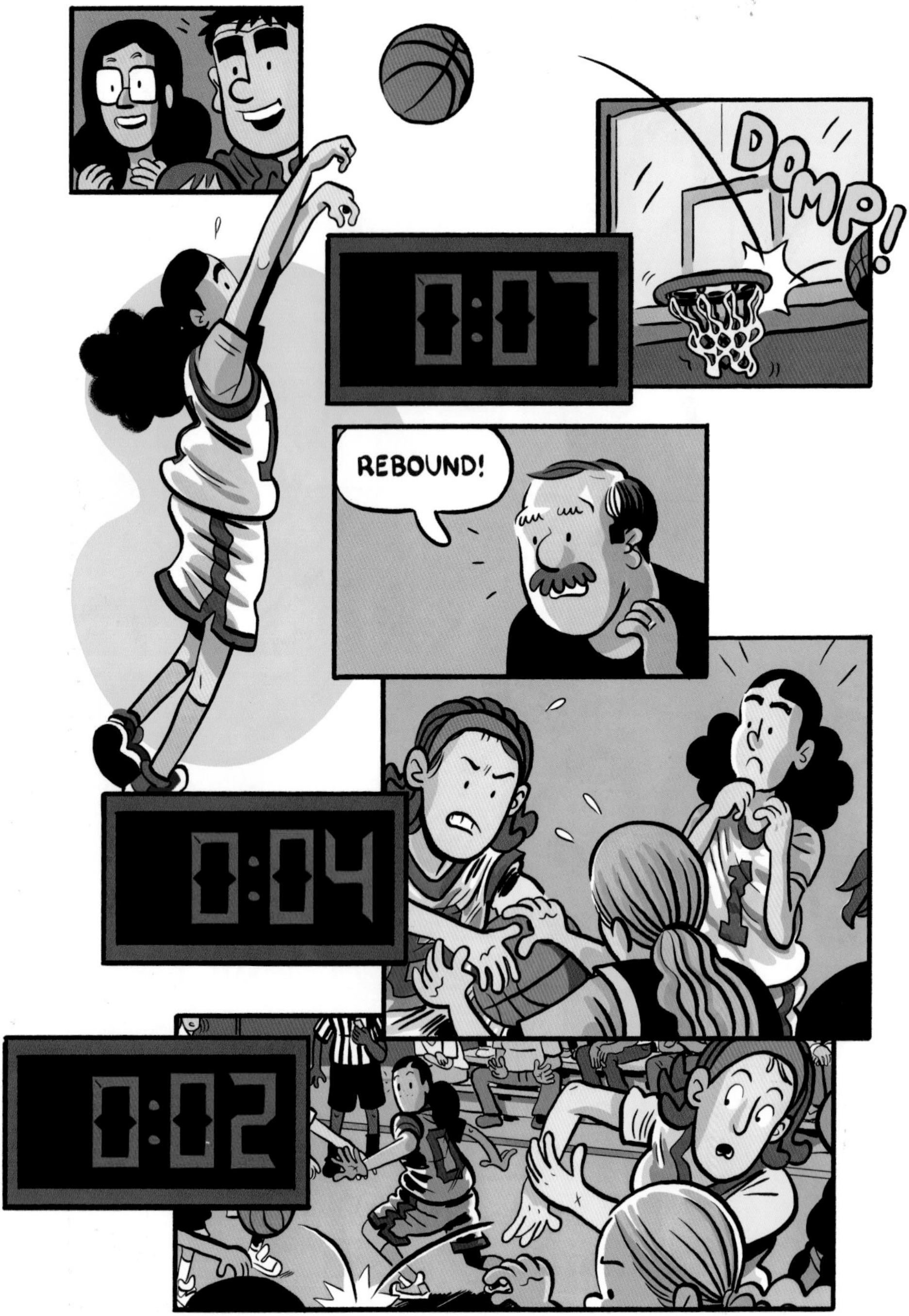
DOMP!
0:07
REBOUND!
0:04
0:02

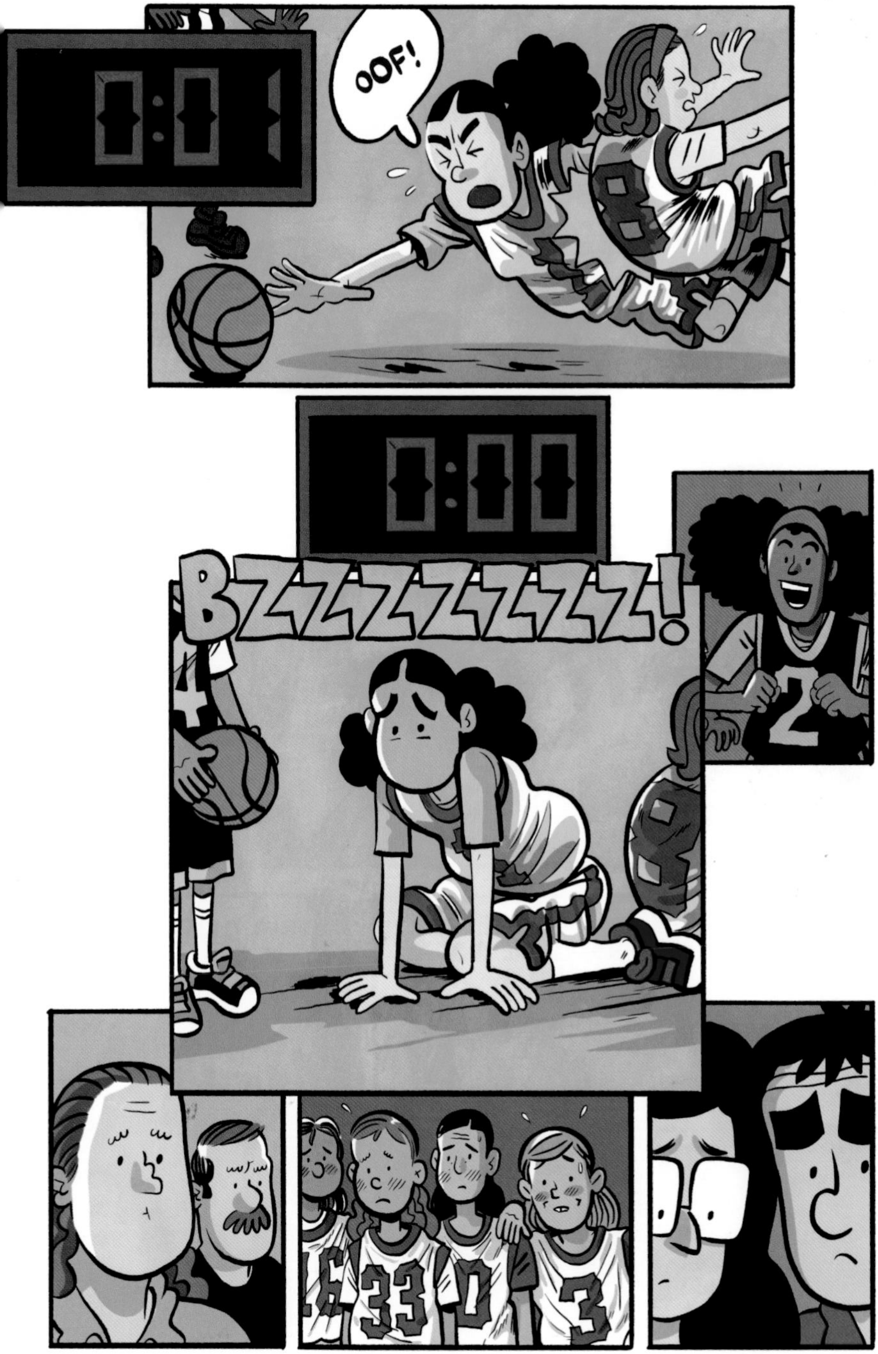
0:01
OOF!
0:00
BZZZZZZZZZ!

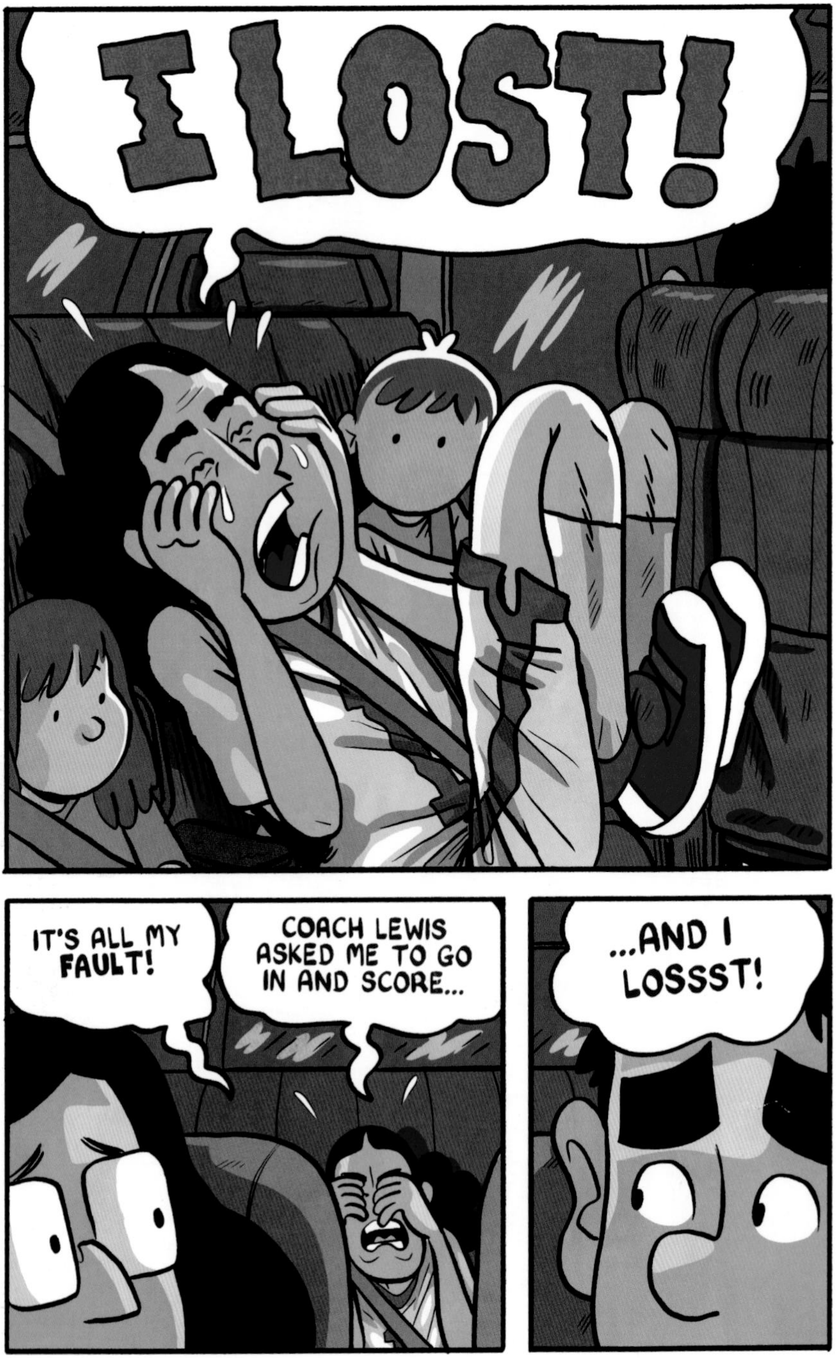
I LOST!
IT'S ALL MY FAULT!
COACH LEWIS ASKED ME TO GO IN AND SCORE...
...AND I LOSSST!

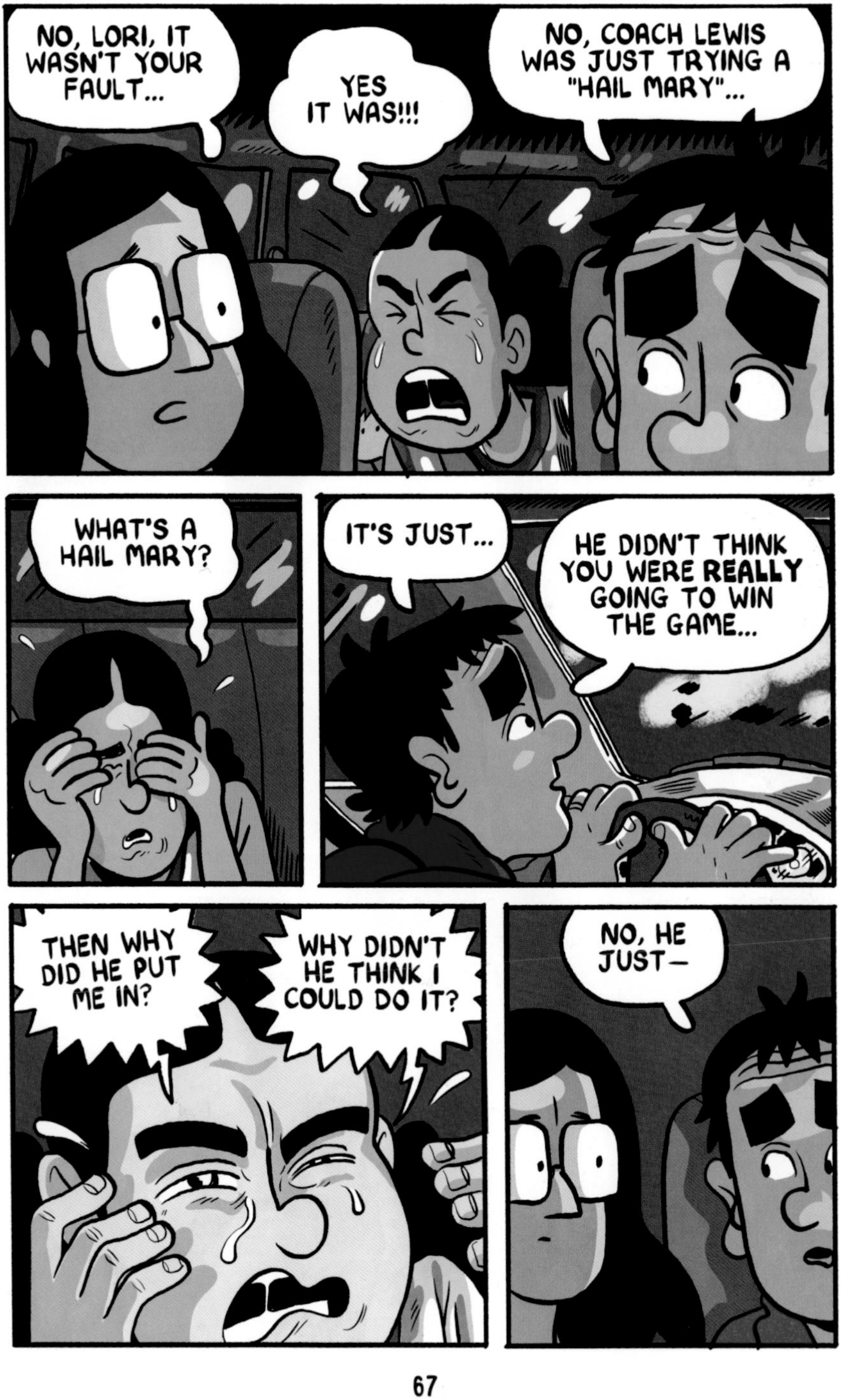
NO, LORI, IT WASN'T YOUR FAULT...
YES IT WAS!!!
NO, COACH LEWIS WAS JUST TRYING A "HAIL MARY"...
WHAT'S A HAIL MARY?
IT'S JUST...
HE DIDN'T THINK YOU WERE **REALLY** GOING TO WIN THE GAME...
THEN WHY DID HE PUT ME IN?
WHY DIDN'T HE THINK I COULD DO IT?
NO, HE JUST—

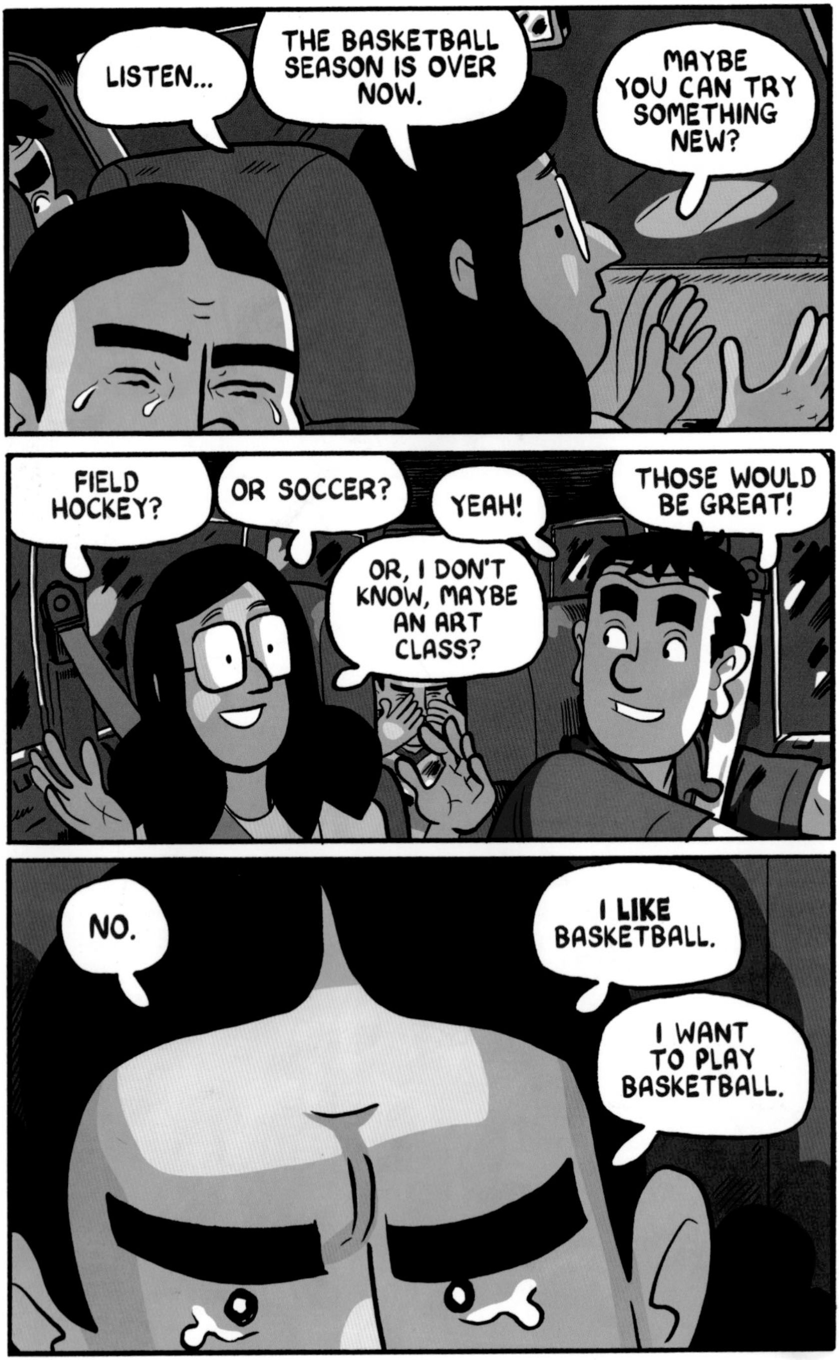
LISTEN...
THE BASKETBALL SEASON IS OVER NOW.
MAYBE YOU CAN TRY SOMETHING NEW?
FIELD HOCKEY?
OR SOCCER?
YEAH!
THOSE WOULD BE GREAT!
OR, I DON'T KNOW, MAYBE AN ART CLASS?
NO.
I LIKE BASKETBALL.
I WANT TO PLAY BASKETBALL.

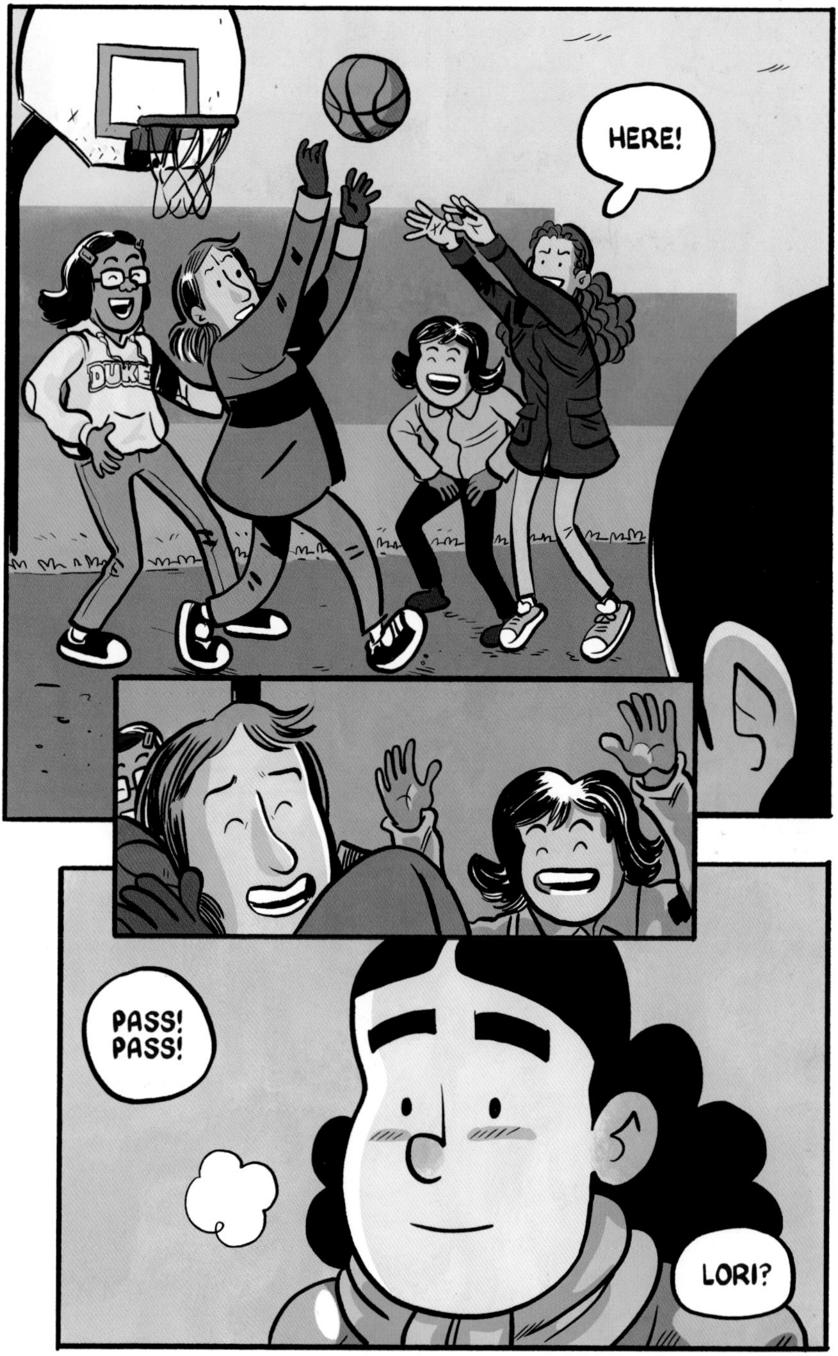
HERE!
DUKE
PASS! PASS!
LORI?

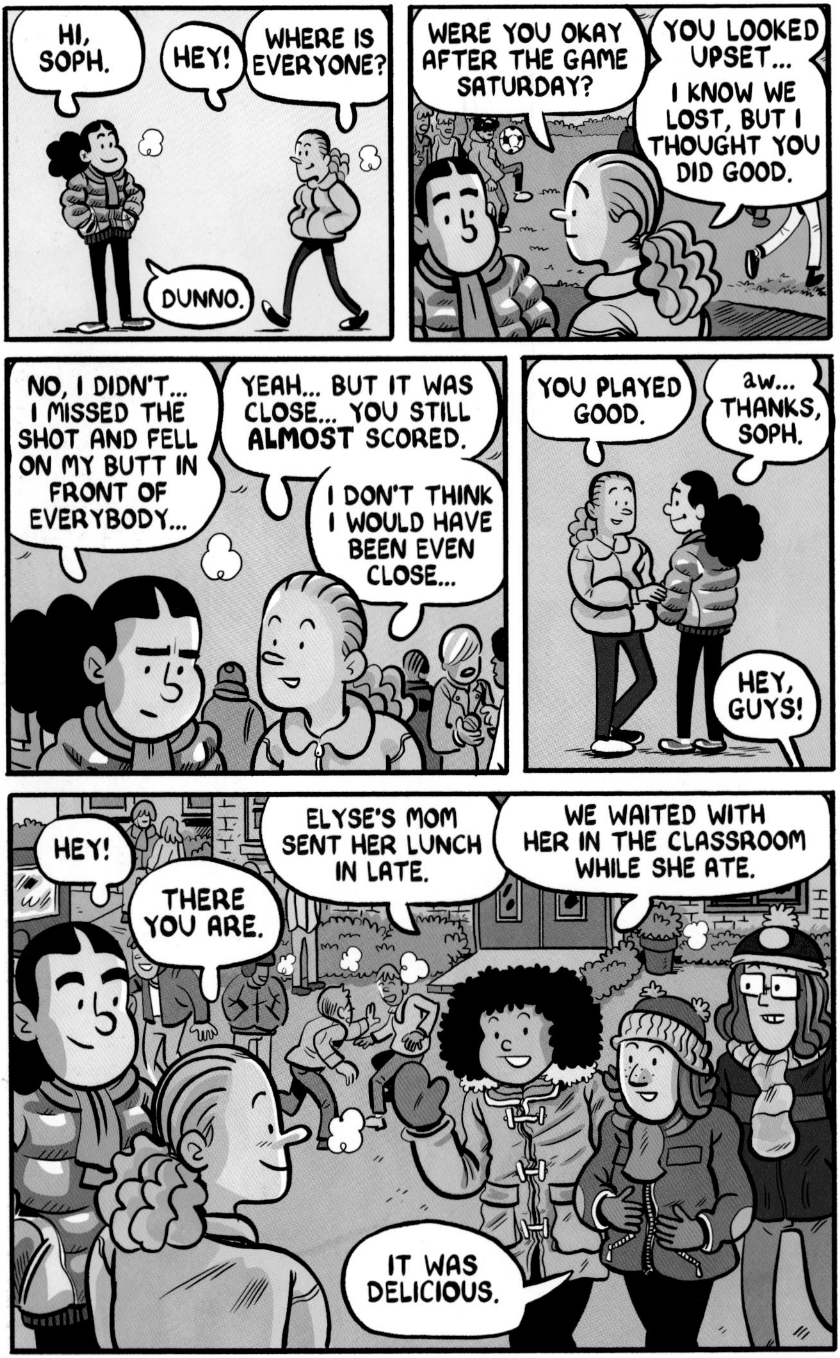
HI, SOPH.
HEY!
WHERE IS EVERYONE?
DUNNO.
WERE YOU OKAY AFTER THE GAME SATURDAY?
YOU LOOKED UPSET...
I KNOW WE LOST, BUT I THOUGHT YOU DID GOOD.
NO, I DIDN'T... I MISSED THE SHOT AND FELL ON MY BUTT IN FRONT OF EVERYBODY...
YEAH... BUT IT WAS CLOSE... YOU STILL **ALMOST** SCORED.
I DON'T THINK I WOULD HAVE BEEN EVEN CLOSE...
YOU PLAYED GOOD.
aw... THANKS, SOPH.
HEY, GUYS!
HEY!
THERE YOU ARE.
ELYSE'S MOM SENT HER LUNCH IN LATE.
WE WAITED WITH HER IN THE CLASSROOM WHILE SHE ATE.
IT WAS DELICIOUS.

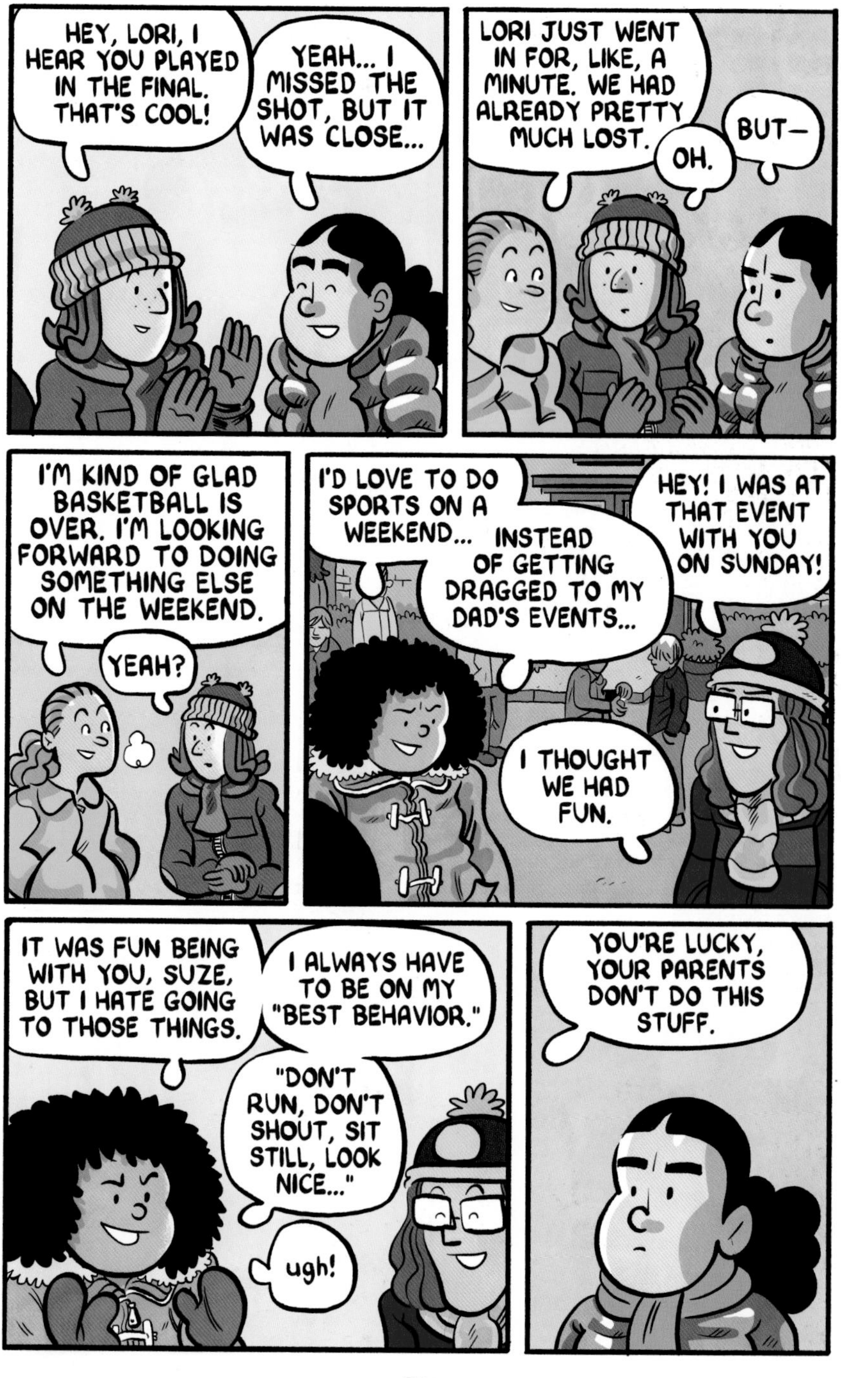
HEY, LORI, I HEAR YOU PLAYED IN THE FINAL. THAT'S COOL!
YEAH... I MISSED THE SHOT, BUT IT WAS CLOSE...
LORI JUST WENT IN FOR, LIKE, A MINUTE. WE HAD ALREADY PRETTY MUCH LOST.
OH.
BUT—
I'M KIND OF GLAD BASKETBALL IS OVER. I'M LOOKING FORWARD TO DOING SOMETHING ELSE ON THE WEEKEND.
YEAH?
I'D LOVE TO DO SPORTS ON A WEEKEND...
INSTEAD OF GETTING DRAGGED TO MY DAD'S EVENTS...
HEY! I WAS AT THAT EVENT WITH YOU ON SUNDAY!
I THOUGHT WE HAD FUN.
IT WAS FUN BEING WITH YOU, SUZE, BUT I HATE GOING TO THOSE THINGS.
I ALWAYS HAVE TO BE ON MY "BEST BEHAVIOR."
"DON'T RUN, DON'T SHOUT, SIT STILL, LOOK NICE..."
ugh!
YOU'RE LUCKY, YOUR PARENTS DON'T DO THIS STUFF.

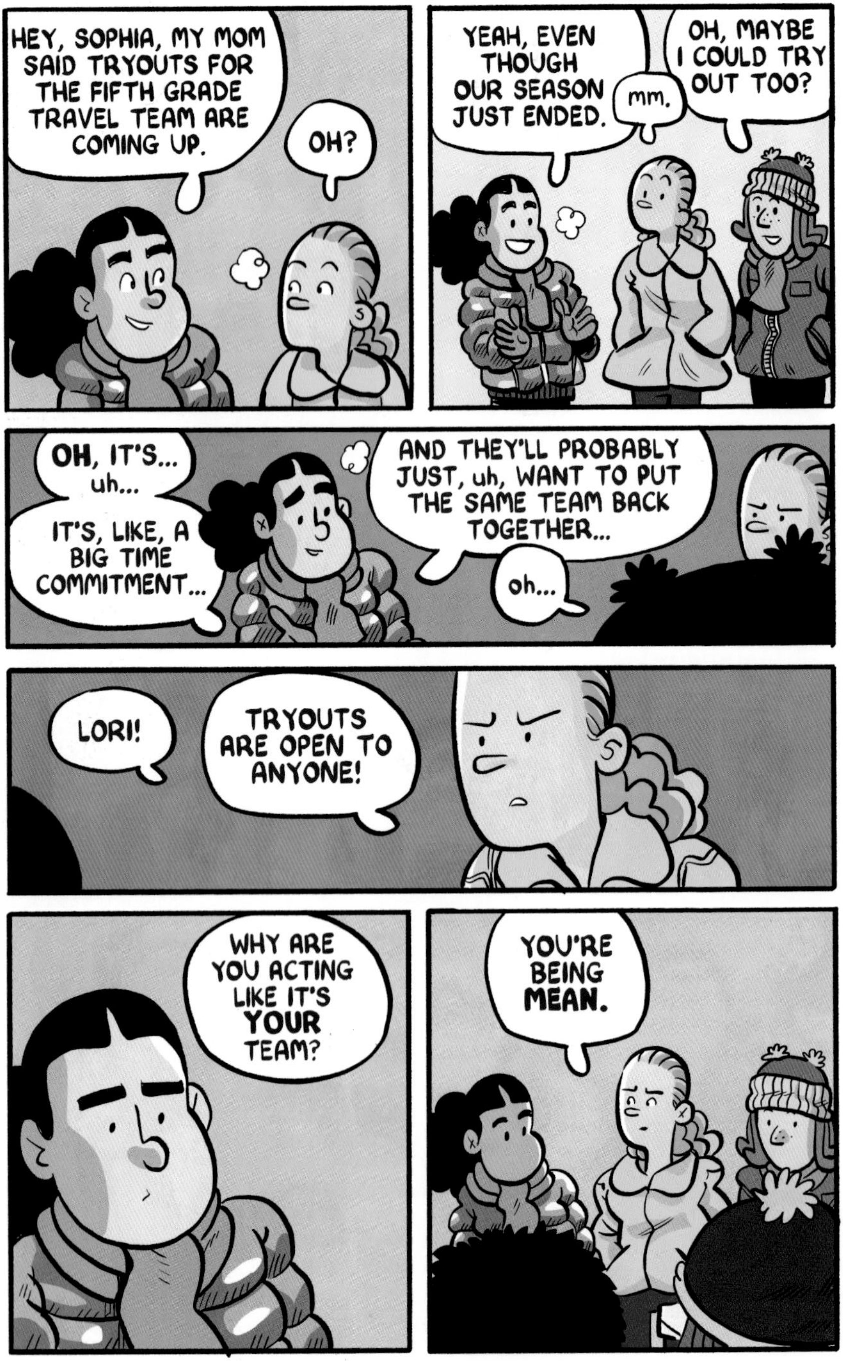
HEY, SOPHIA, MY MOM SAID TRYOUTS FOR THE FIFTH GRADE TRAVEL TEAM ARE COMING UP.
OH?
YEAH, EVEN THOUGH OUR SEASON JUST ENDED.
mm.
OH, MAYBE I COULD TRY OUT TOO?
OH, IT'S... uh...
IT'S, LIKE, A BIG TIME COMMITMENT...
AND THEY'LL PROBABLY JUST, uh, WANT TO PUT THE SAME TEAM BACK TOGETHER...
oh...
LORI!
TRYOUTS ARE OPEN TO ANYONE!
WHY ARE YOU ACTING LIKE IT'S YOUR TEAM?
YOU'RE BEING MEAN.

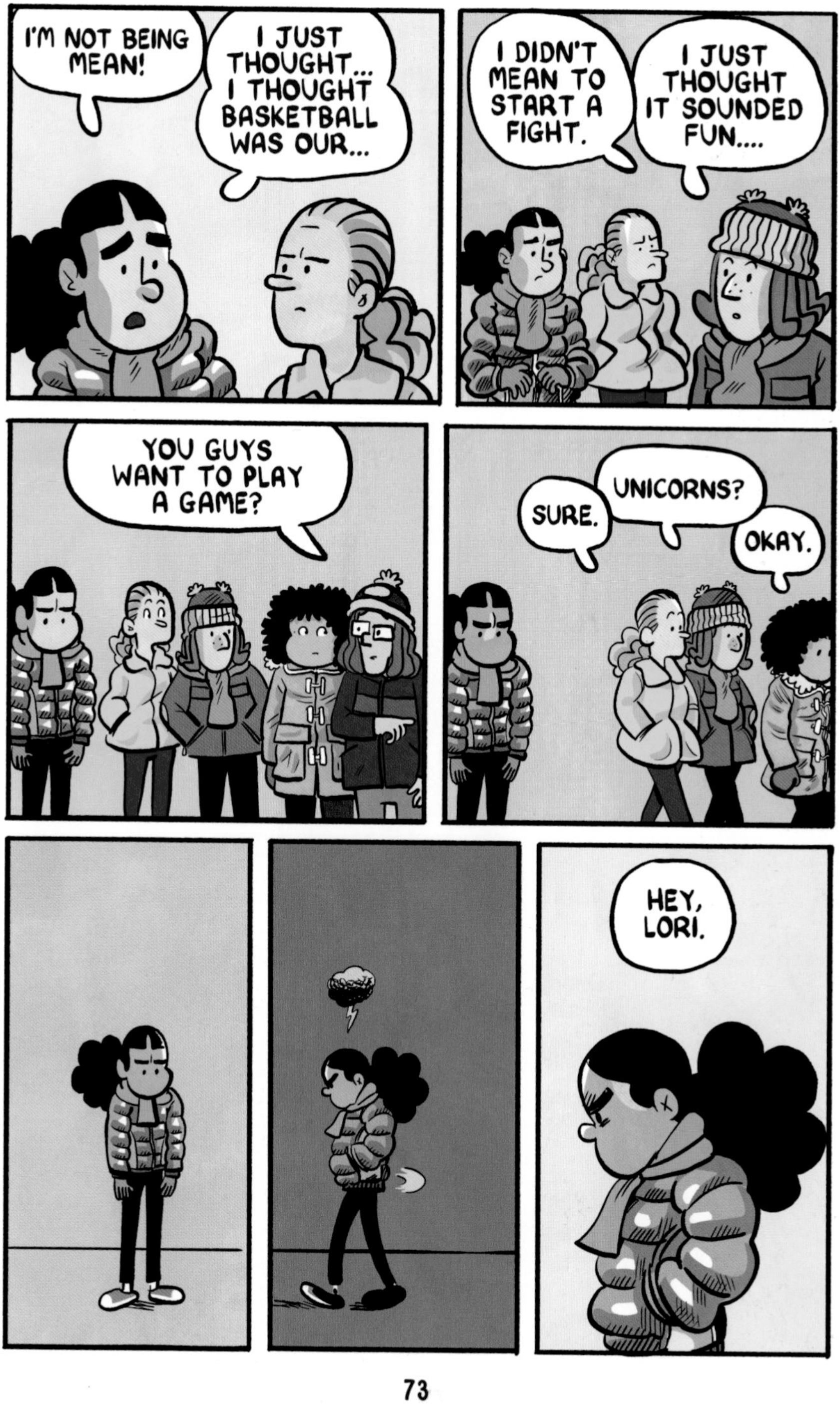
I'M NOT BEING MEAN!
I JUST THOUGHT... I THOUGHT BASKETBALL WAS OUR...
I DIDN'T MEAN TO START A FIGHT.
I JUST THOUGHT IT SOUNDED FUN....
YOU GUYS WANT TO PLAY A GAME?
SURE.
UNICORNS?
OKAY.
HEY, LORI.

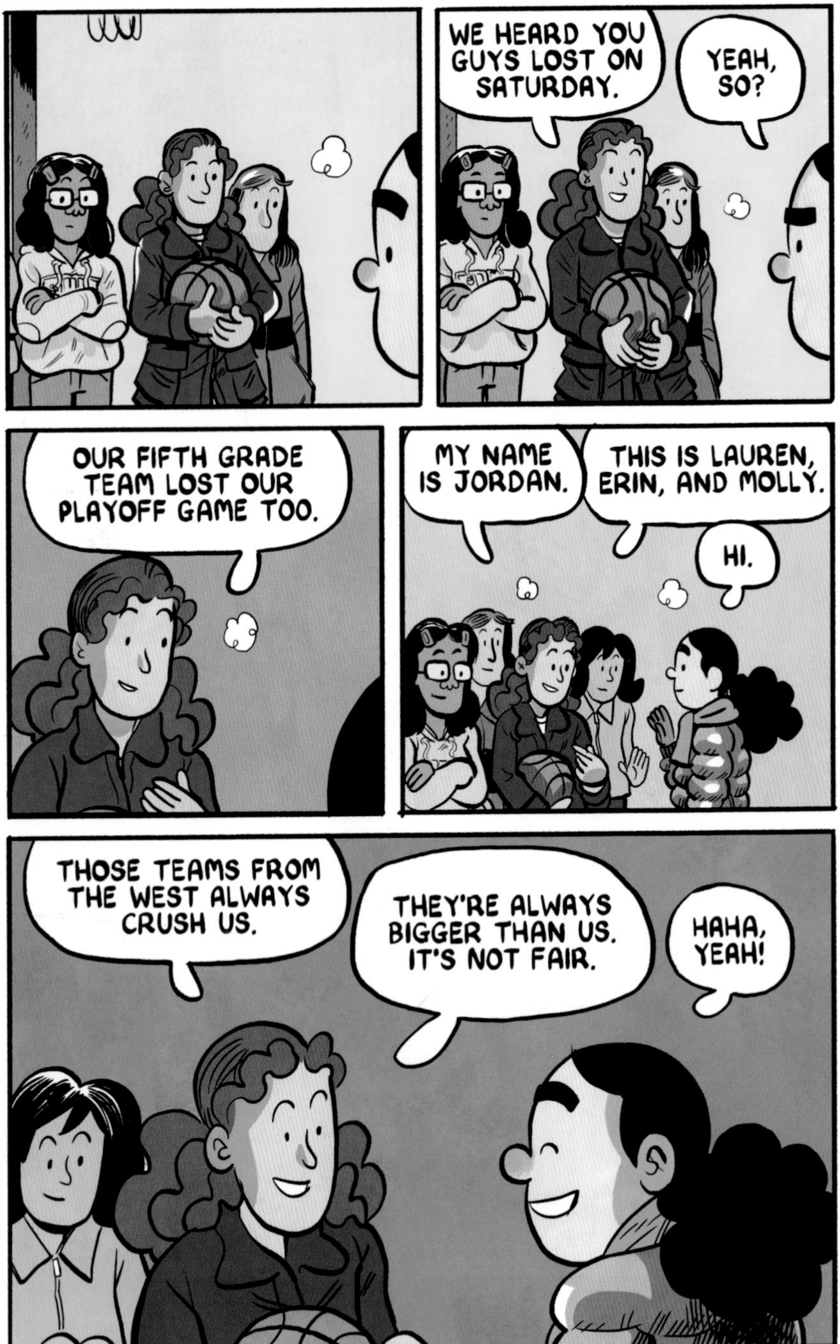
WE HEARD YOU GUYS LOST ON SATURDAY.
YEAH, SO?
OUR FIFTH GRADE TEAM LOST OUR PLAYOFF GAME TOO.
MY NAME IS JORDAN.
THIS IS LAUREN, ERIN, AND MOLLY.
HI.
THOSE TEAMS FROM THE WEST ALWAYS CRUSH US.
THEY'RE ALWAYS BIGGER THAN US. IT'S NOT FAIR.
HAHA, YEAH!

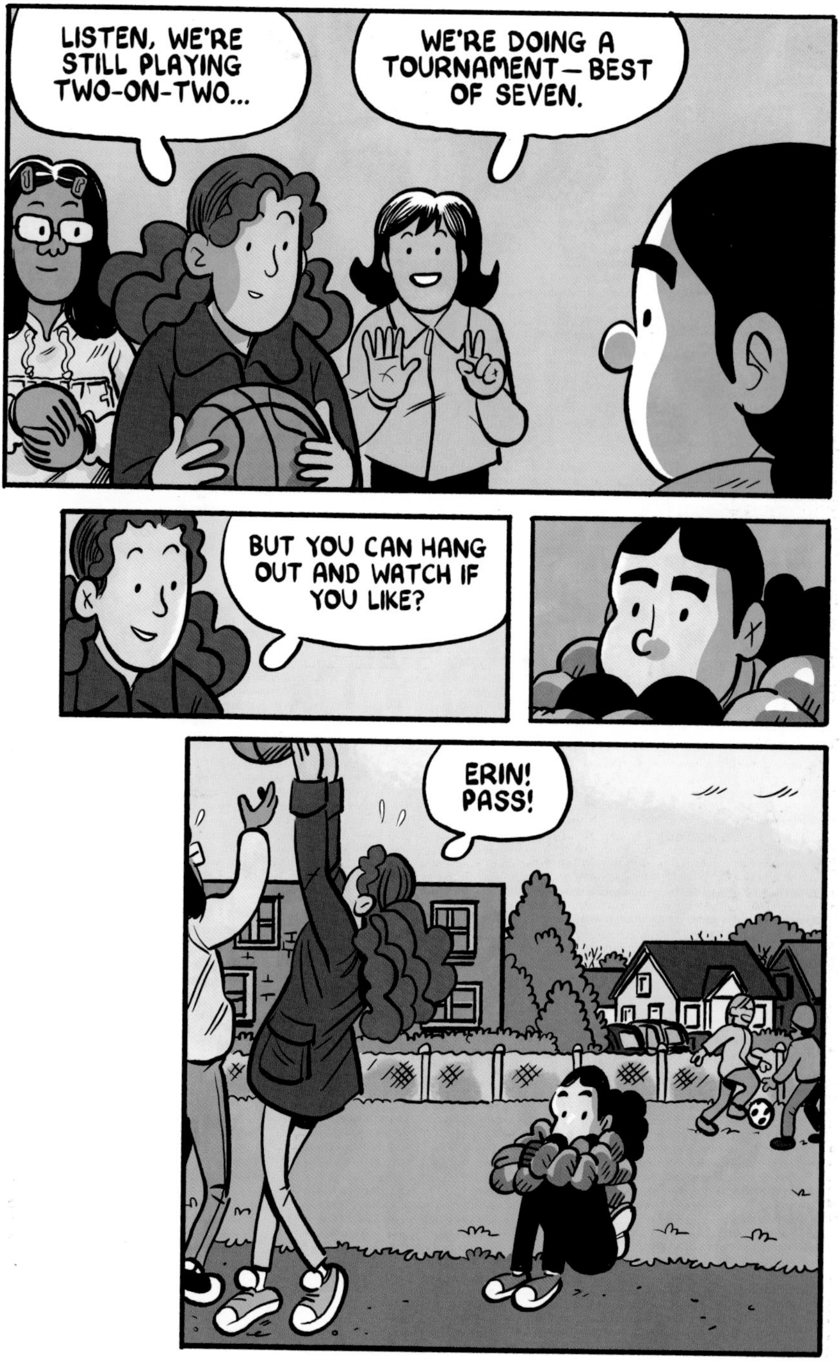
LISTEN, WE'RE STILL PLAYING TWO-ON-TWO...
WE'RE DOING A TOURNAMENT—BEST OF SEVEN.
BUT YOU CAN HANG OUT AND WATCH IF YOU LIKE?
ERIN! PASS!

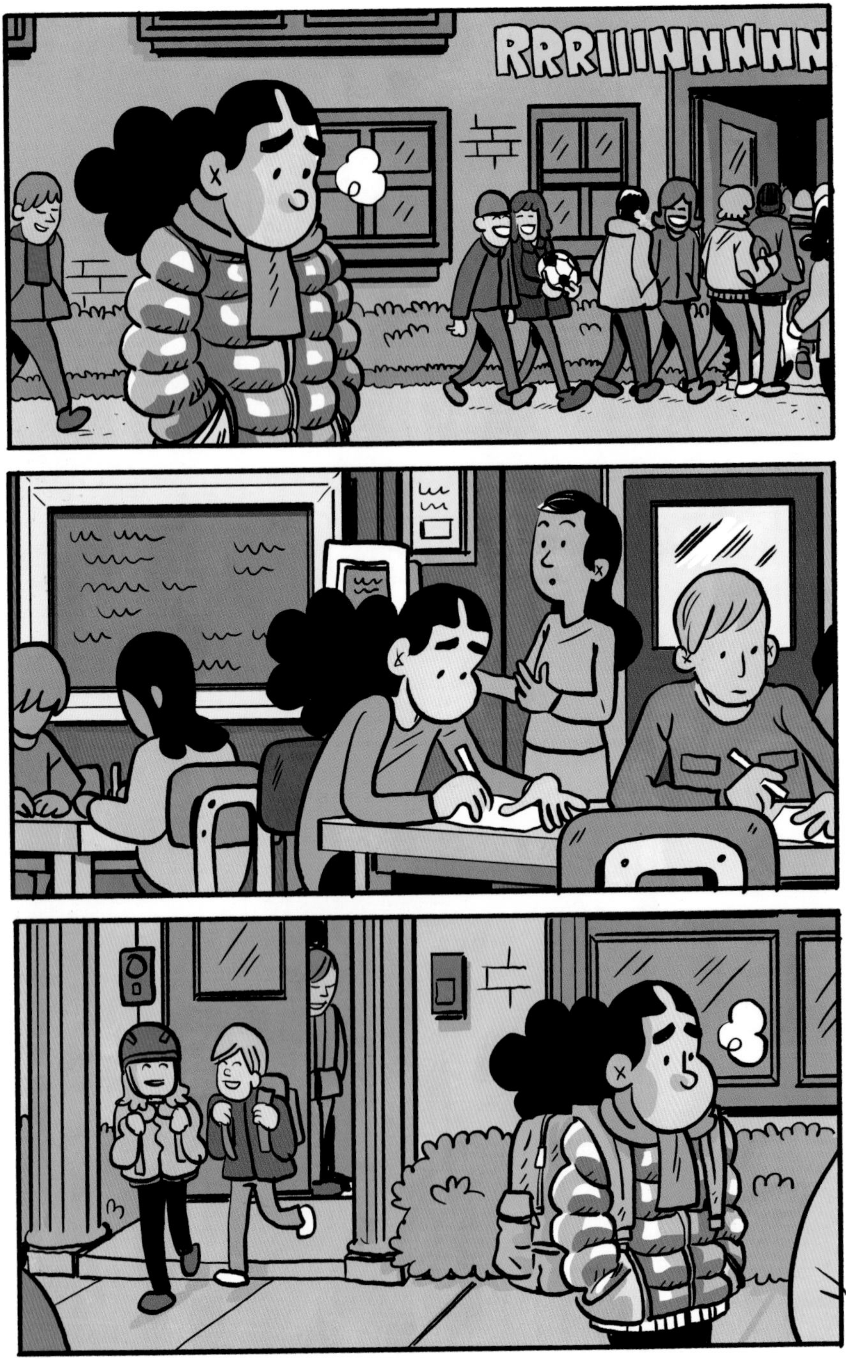
RRRIIINNNNN

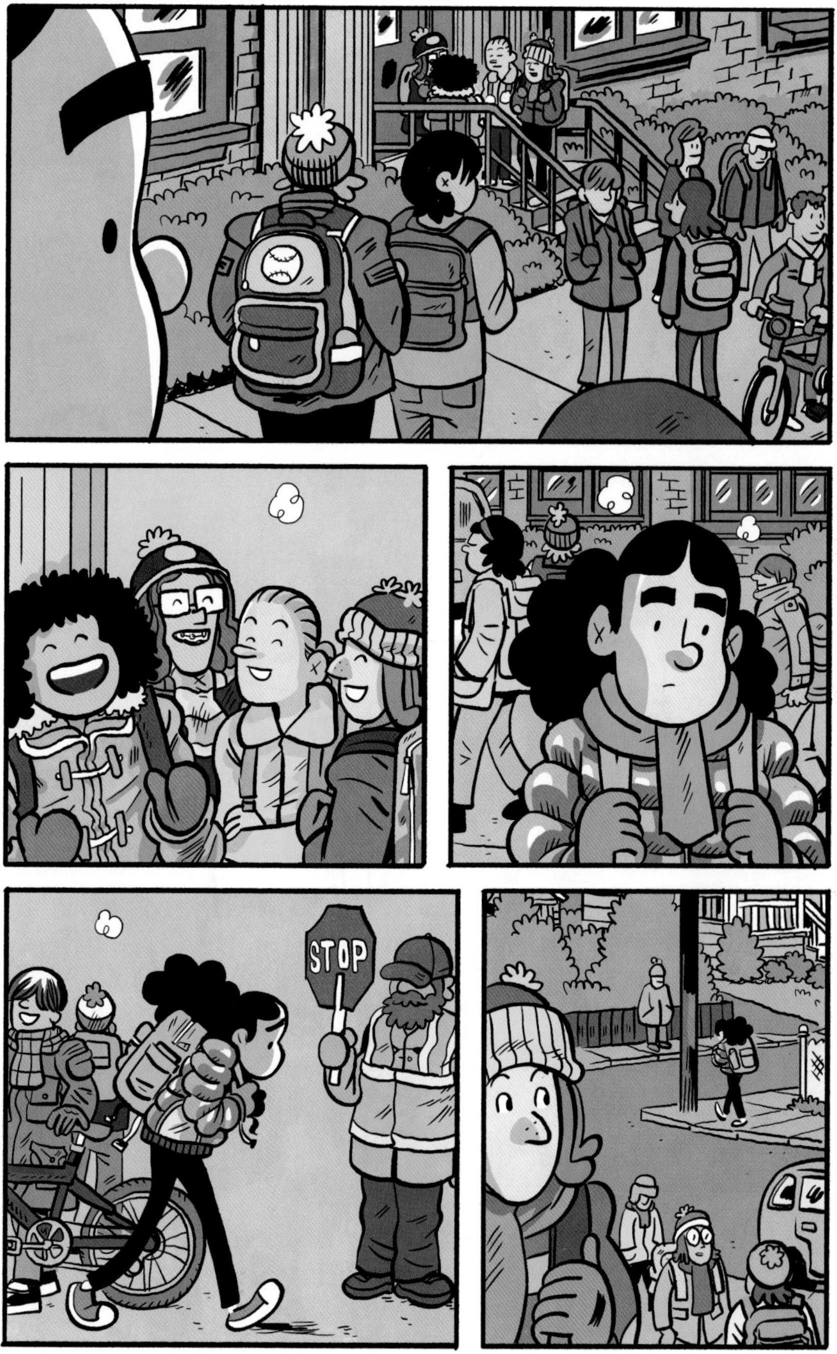
STOP

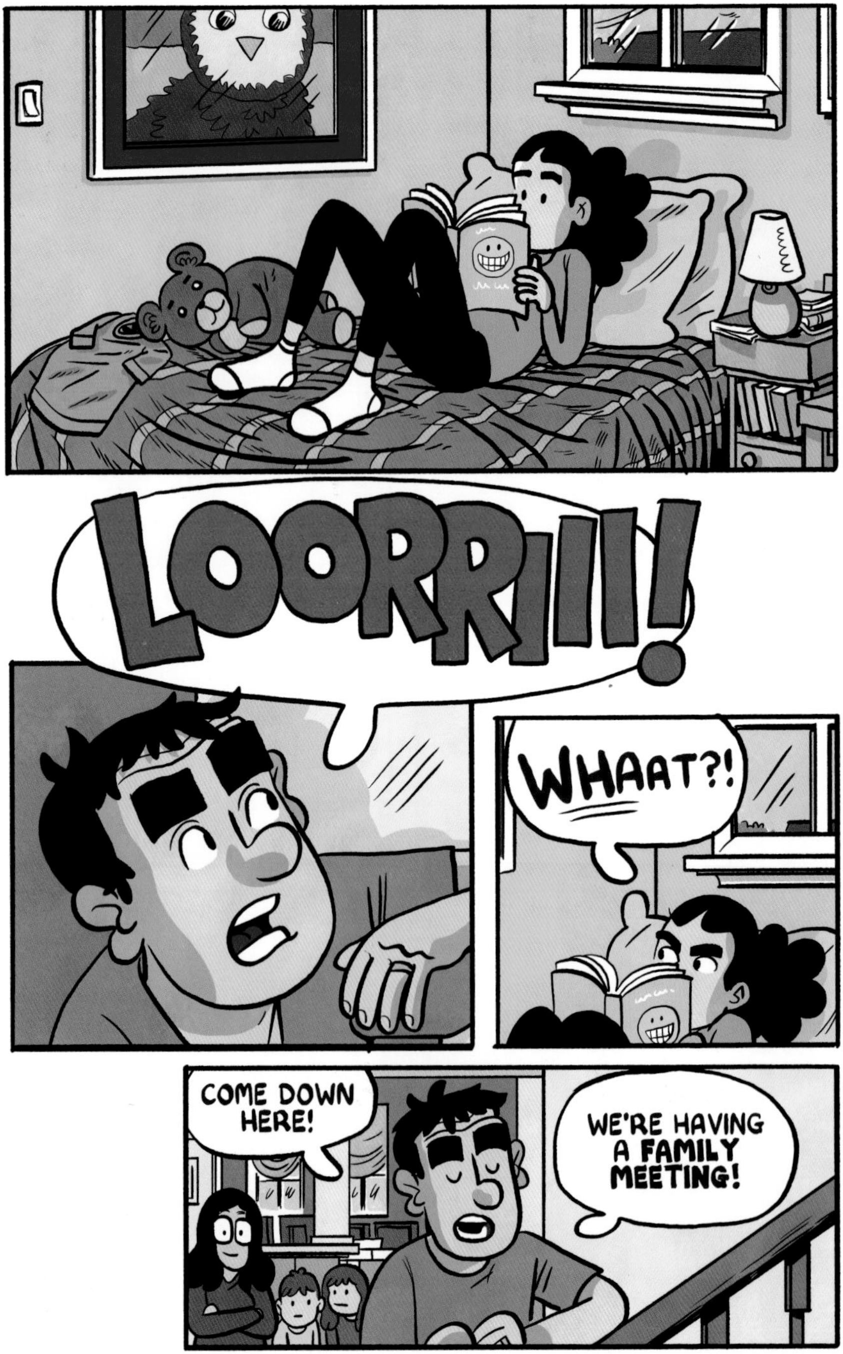
LOORRIII!
WHAAT?!
COME DOWN HERE!
WE'RE HAVING A FAMILY MEETING!

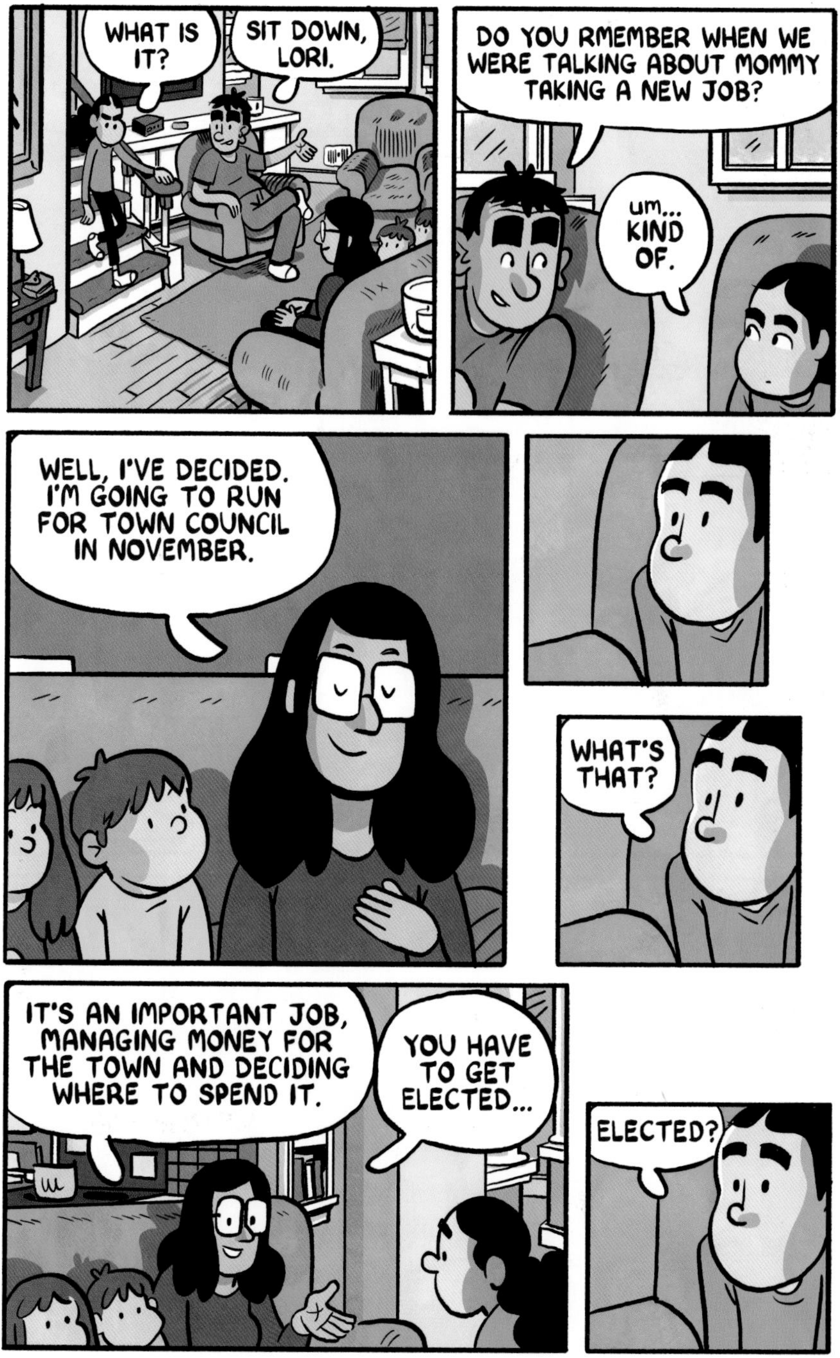
WHAT IS IT?
SIT DOWN, LORI.
DO YOU RMEMBER WHEN WE WERE TALKING ABOUT MOMMY TAKING A NEW JOB?
UM... KIND OF.
WELL, I'VE DECIDED. I'M GOING TO RUN FOR TOWN COUNCIL IN NOVEMBER.
WHAT'S THAT?
IT'S AN IMPORTANT JOB, MANAGING MONEY FOR THE TOWN AND DECIDING WHERE TO SPEND IT.
YOU HAVE TO GET ELECTED...
ELECTED?

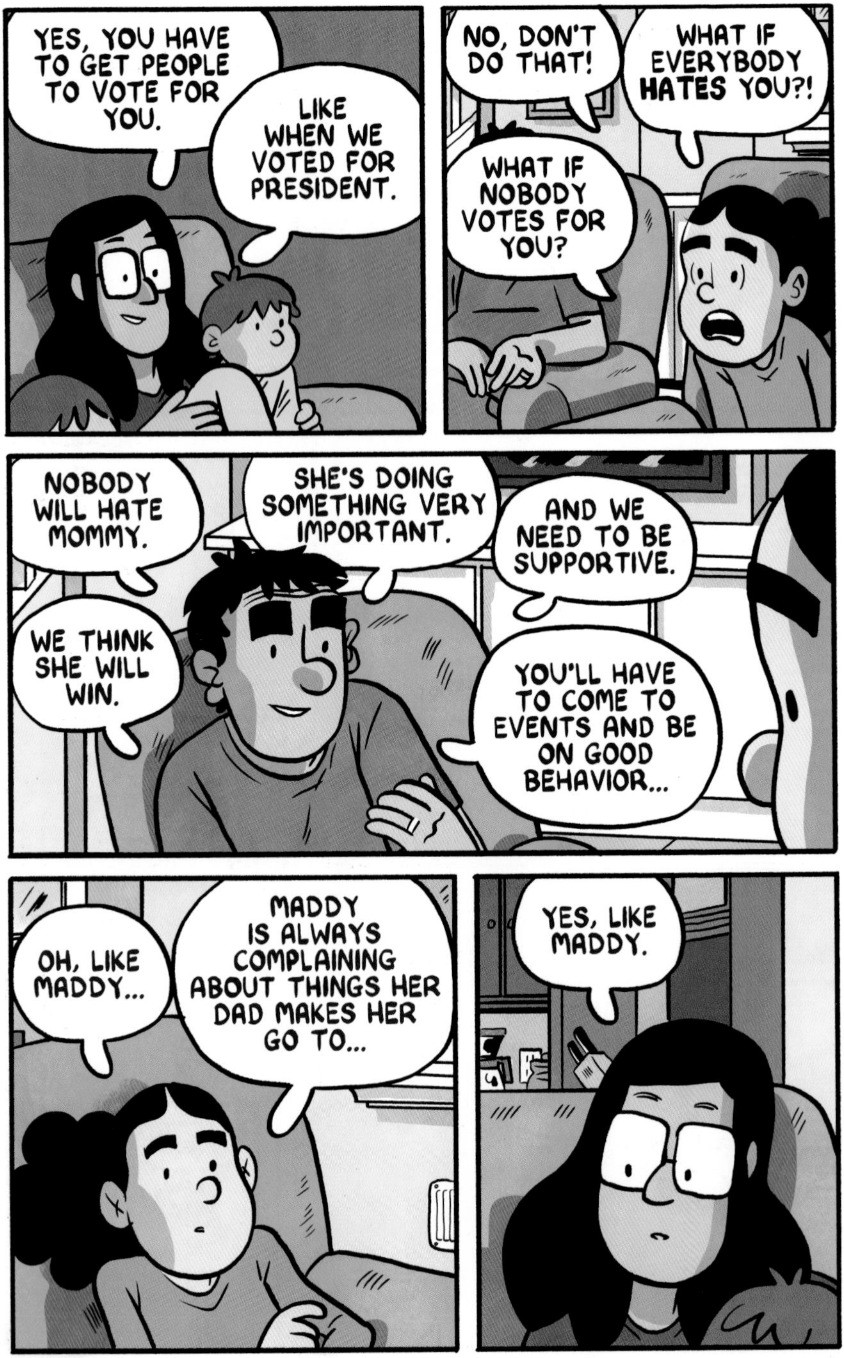
YES, YOU HAVE TO GET PEOPLE TO VOTE FOR YOU.
LIKE WHEN WE VOTED FOR PRESIDENT.
NO, DON'T DO THAT!
WHAT IF EVERYBODY **HATES** YOU?!
WHAT IF NOBODY VOTES FOR YOU?
NOBODY WILL HATE MOMMY.
SHE'S DOING SOMETHING VERY IMPORTANT.
AND WE NEED TO BE SUPPORTIVE.
WE THINK SHE WILL WIN.
YOU'LL HAVE TO COME TO EVENTS AND BE ON GOOD BEHAVIOR...
OH, LIKE MADDY...
MADDY IS ALWAYS COMPLAINING ABOUT THINGS HER DAD MAKES HER GO TO...
YES, LIKE MADDY.

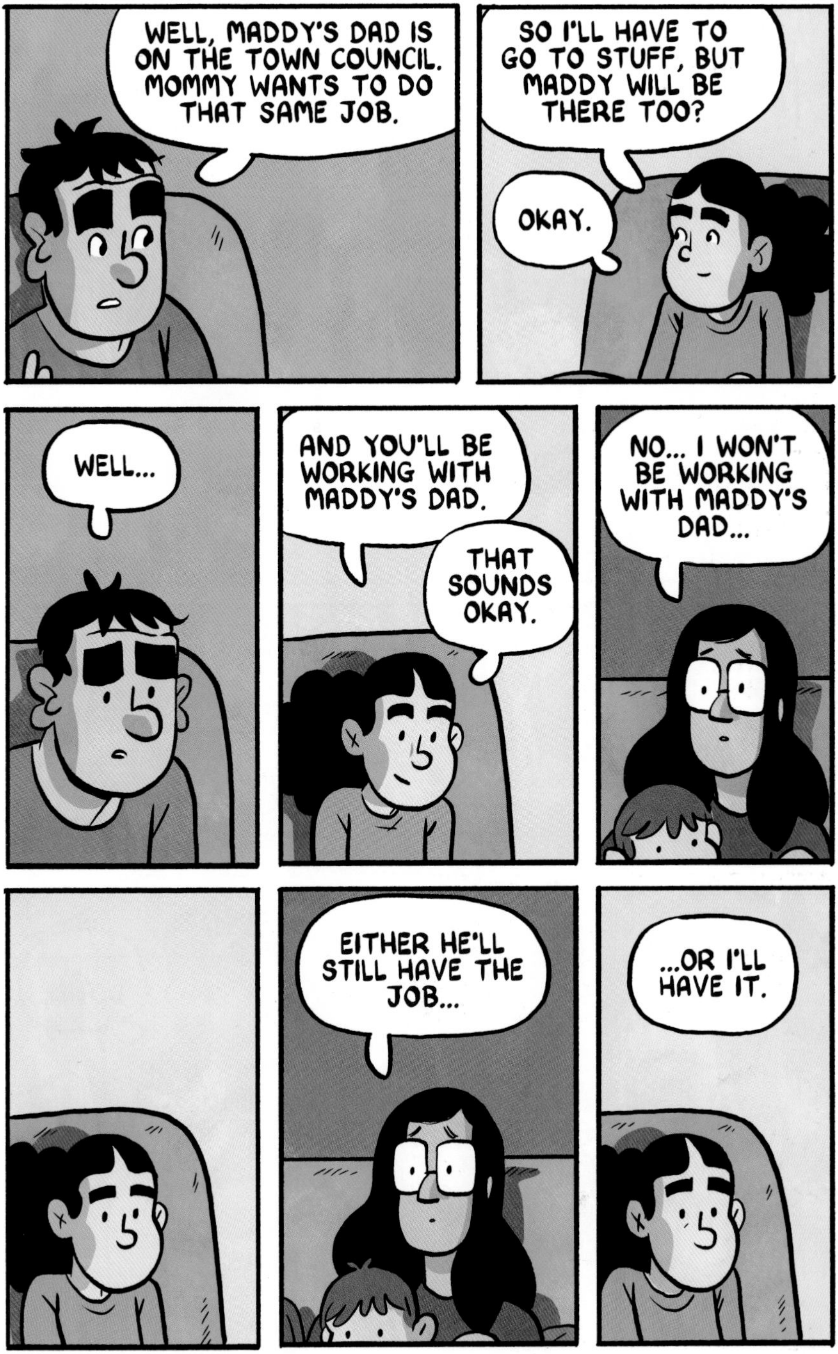
WELL, MADDY'S DAD IS ON THE TOWN COUNCIL. MOMMY WANTS TO DO THAT SAME JOB.
SO I'LL HAVE TO GO TO STUFF, BUT MADDY WILL BE THERE TOO?
OKAY.
WELL...
AND YOU'LL BE WORKING WITH MADDY'S DAD.
THAT SOUNDS OKAY.
NO... I WON'T BE WORKING WITH MADDY'S DAD...
EITHER HE'LL STILL HAVE THE JOB...
...OR I'LL HAVE IT.

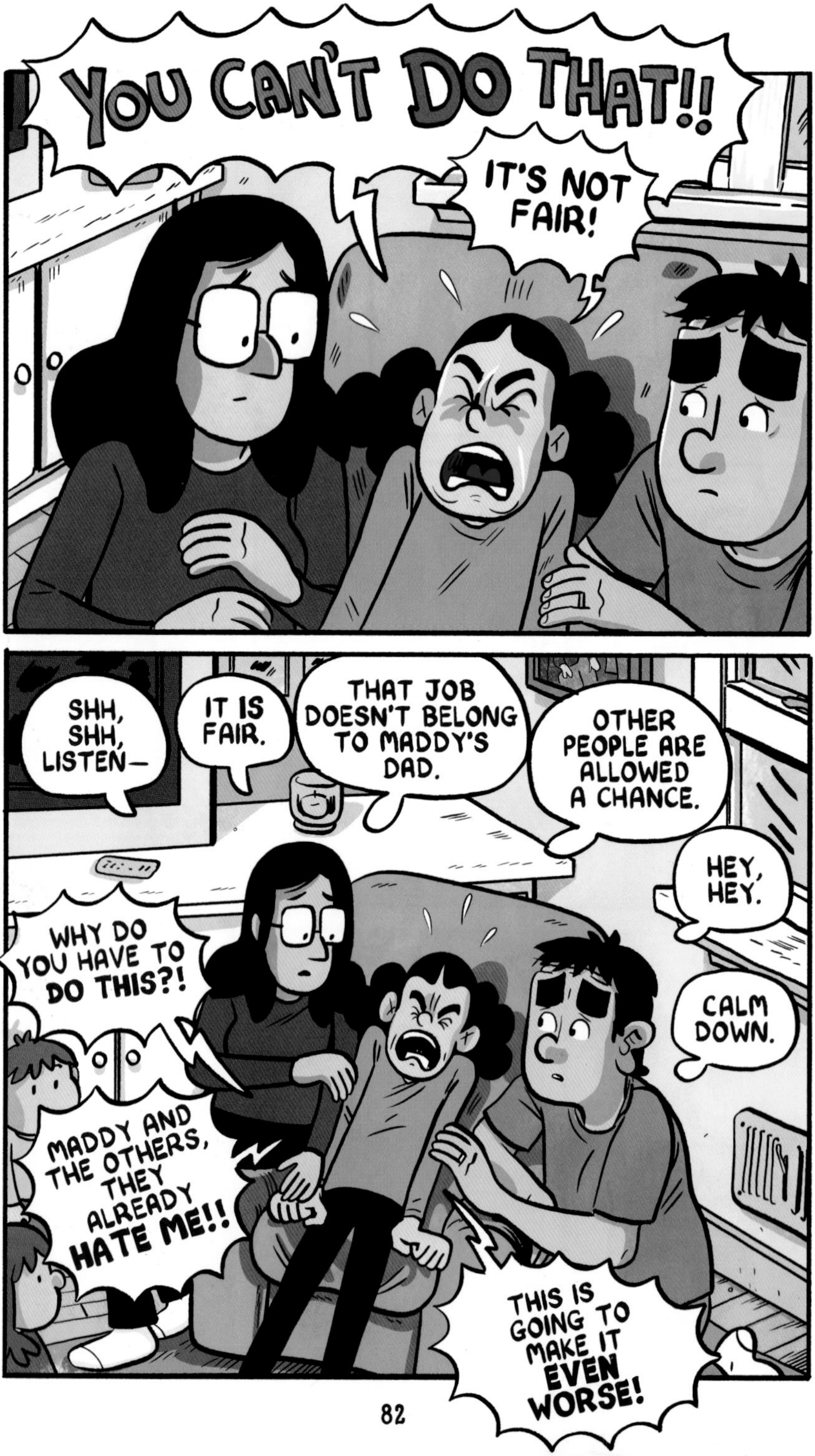
YOU CAN'T DO THAT!!
IT'S NOT FAIR!
SHH, SHH, LISTEN—
IT IS FAIR.
THAT JOB DOESN'T BELONG TO MADDY'S DAD.
OTHER PEOPLE ARE ALLOWED A CHANCE.
HEY, HEY.
WHY DO YOU HAVE TO DO THIS?!
CALM DOWN.
MADDY AND THE OTHERS, THEY ALREADY HATE ME!!
THIS IS GOING TO MAKE IT EVEN WORSE!

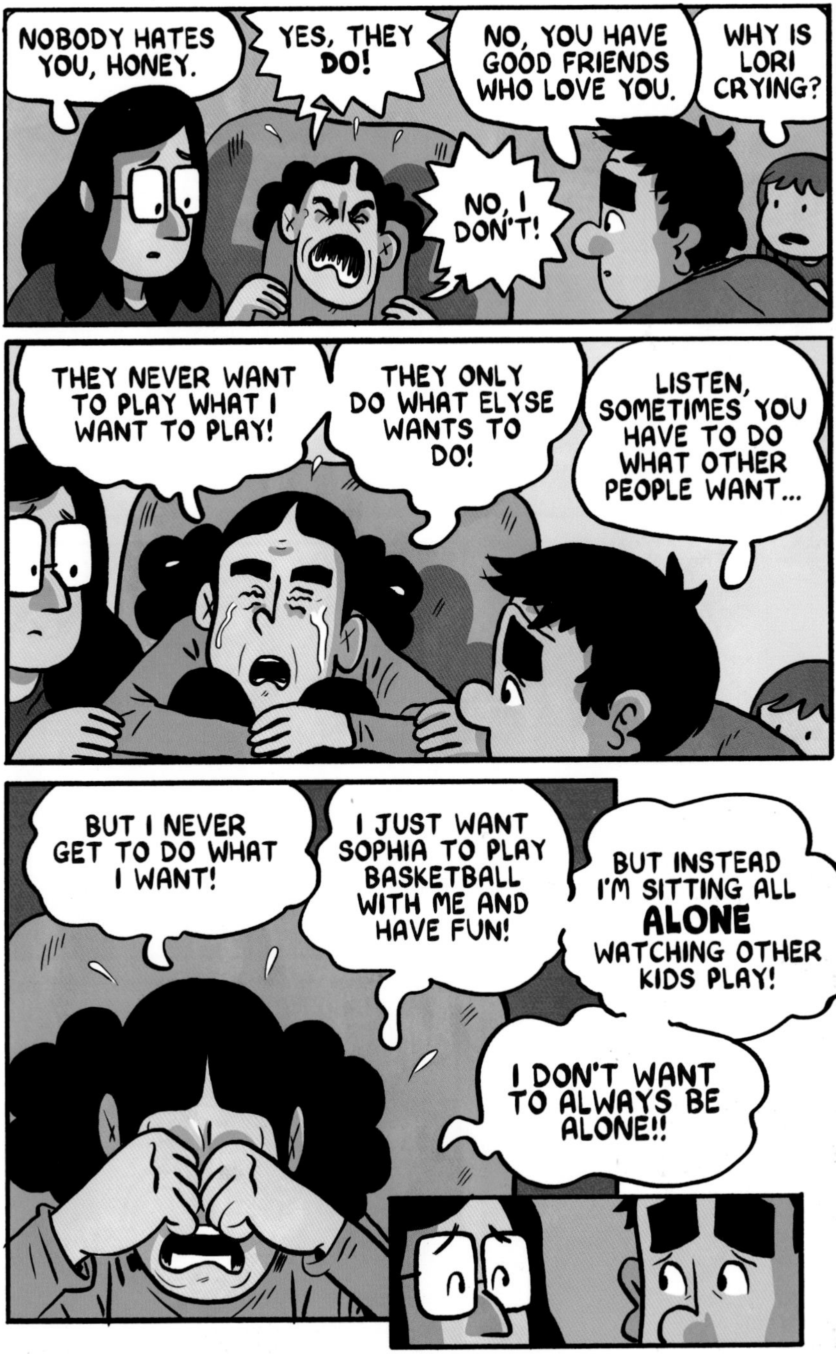
NOBODY HATES YOU, HONEY.
YES, THEY DO!
NO, YOU HAVE GOOD FRIENDS WHO LOVE YOU.
NO, I DON'T!
WHY IS LORI CRYING?
THEY NEVER WANT TO PLAY WHAT I WANT TO PLAY!
THEY ONLY DO WHAT ELYSE WANTS TO DO!
LISTEN, SOMETIMES YOU HAVE TO DO WHAT OTHER PEOPLE WANT...
BUT I NEVER GET TO DO WHAT I WANT!
I JUST WANT SOPHIA TO PLAY BASKETBALL WITH ME AND HAVE FUN!
BUT INSTEAD I'M SITTING ALL ALONE WATCHING OTHER KIDS PLAY!
I DON'T WANT TO ALWAYS BE ALONE!!

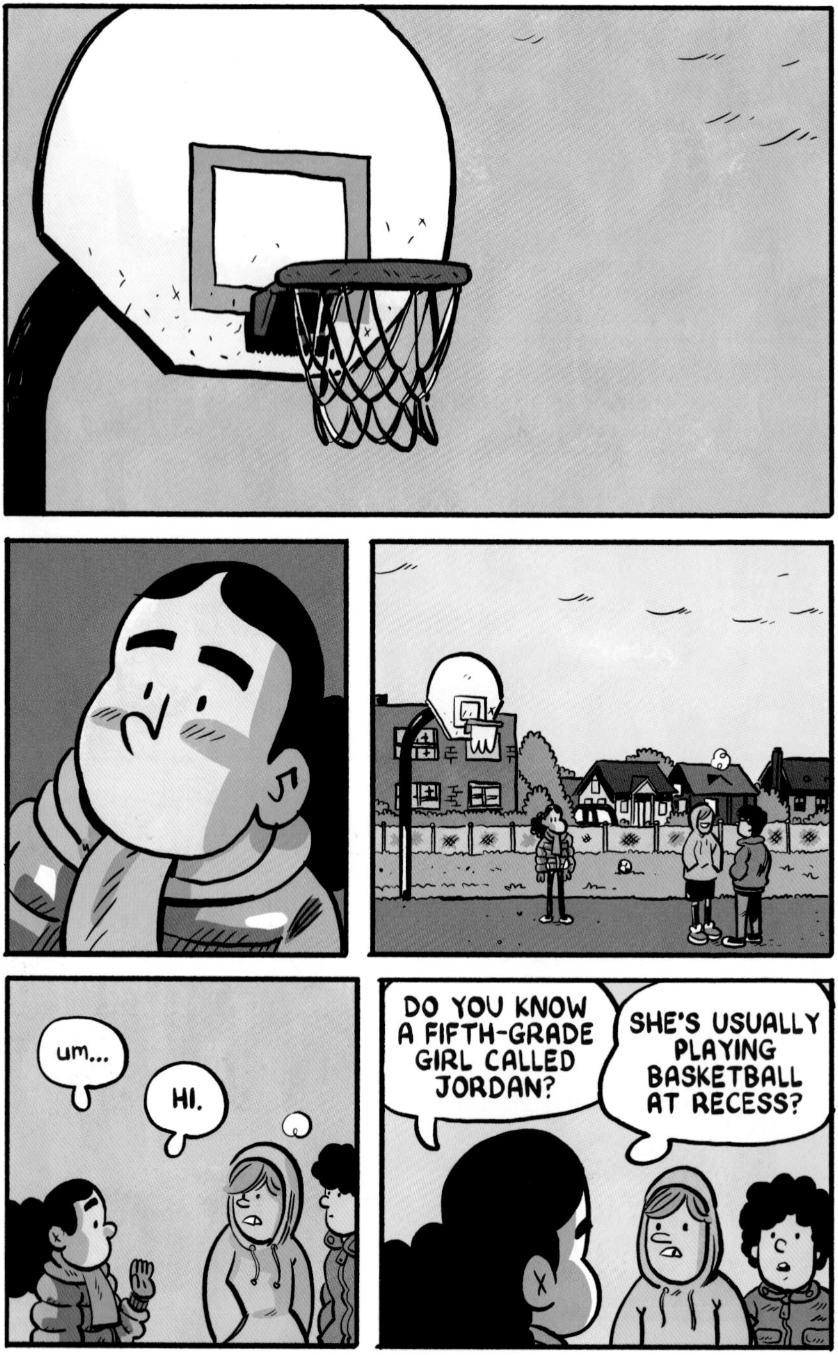
um...
HI.
DO YOU KNOW A FIFTH-GRADE GIRL CALLED JORDAN?
SHE'S USUALLY PLAYING BASKETBALL AT RECESS?

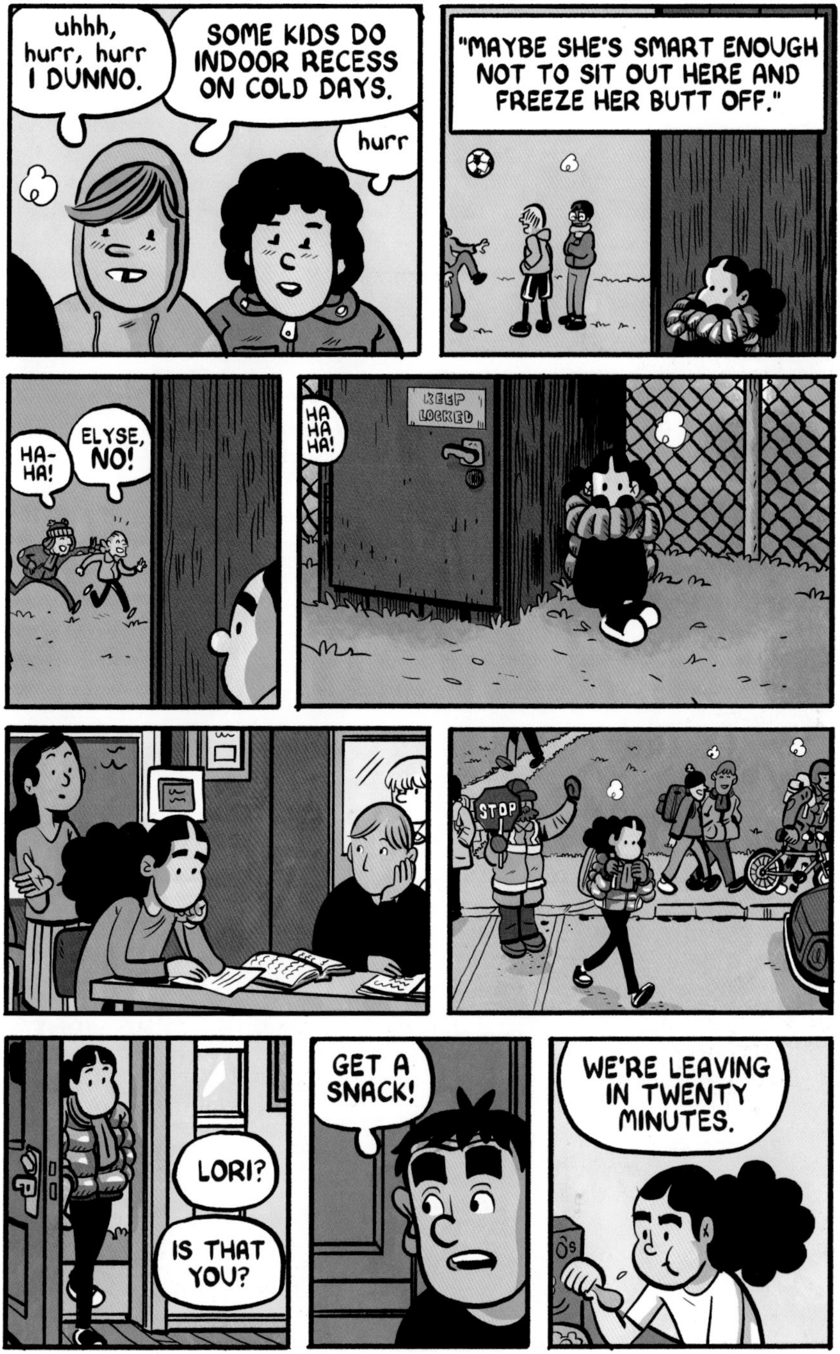
uhhh, hurr, hurr I DUNNO.
SOME KIDS DO INDOOR RECESS ON COLD DAYS.
hurr
"MAYBE SHE'S SMART ENOUGH NOT TO SIT OUT HERE AND FREEZE HER BUTT OFF."
HA-HA!
ELYSE, NO!
KEEP LOCKED
HA HA HA!
STOP
LORI?
IS THAT YOU?
GET A SNACK!
WE'RE LEAVING IN TWENTY MINUTES.

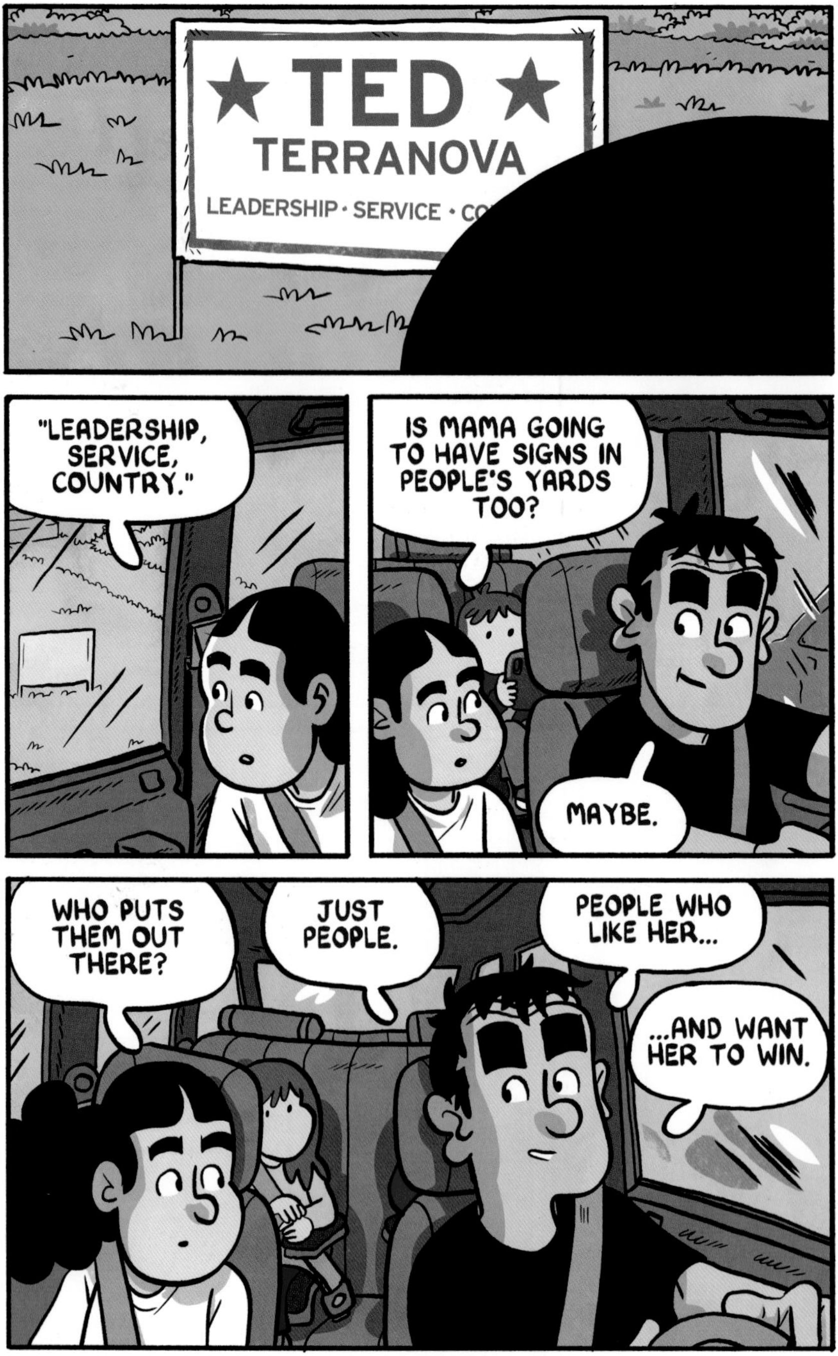
TED
TERRANOVA
LEADERSHIP · SERVICE · CO
"LEADERSHIP, SERVICE, COUNTRY."
IS MAMA GOING TO HAVE SIGNS IN PEOPLE'S YARDS TOO?
MAYBE.
WHO PUTS THEM OUT THERE?
JUST PEOPLE.
PEOPLE WHO LIKE HER...
...AND WANT HER TO WIN.

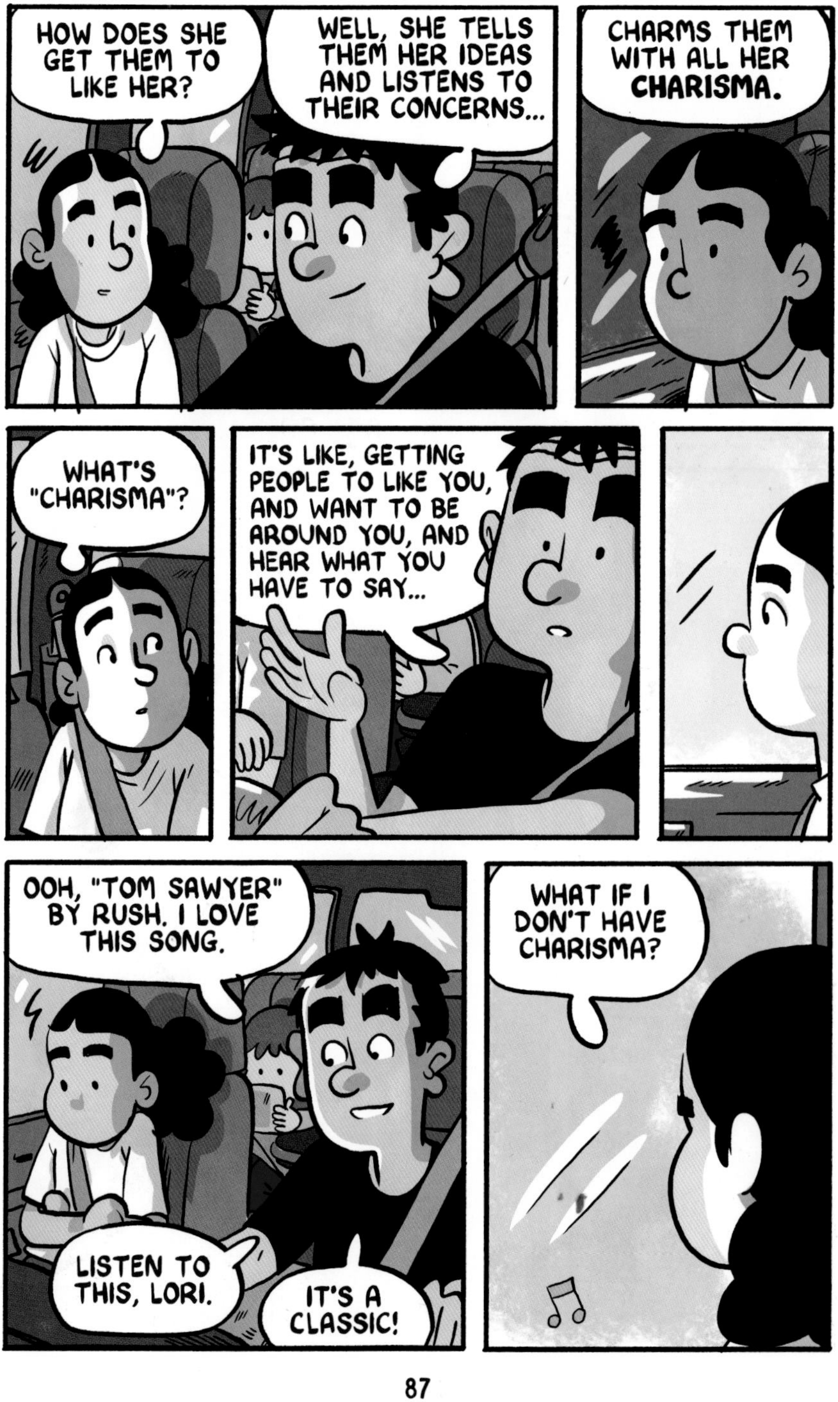
HOW DOES SHE GET THEM TO LIKE HER?
WELL, SHE TELLS THEM HER IDEAS AND LISTENS TO THEIR CONCERNS...
CHARMS THEM WITH ALL HER **CHARISMA.**
WHAT'S "CHARISMA"?
IT'S LIKE, GETTING PEOPLE TO LIKE YOU, AND WANT TO BE AROUND YOU, AND HEAR WHAT YOU HAVE TO SAY...
OOH, "TOM SAWYER" BY RUSH. I LOVE THIS SONG.
LISTEN TO THIS, LORI.
IT'S A CLASSIC!
WHAT IF I DON'T HAVE CHARISMA?

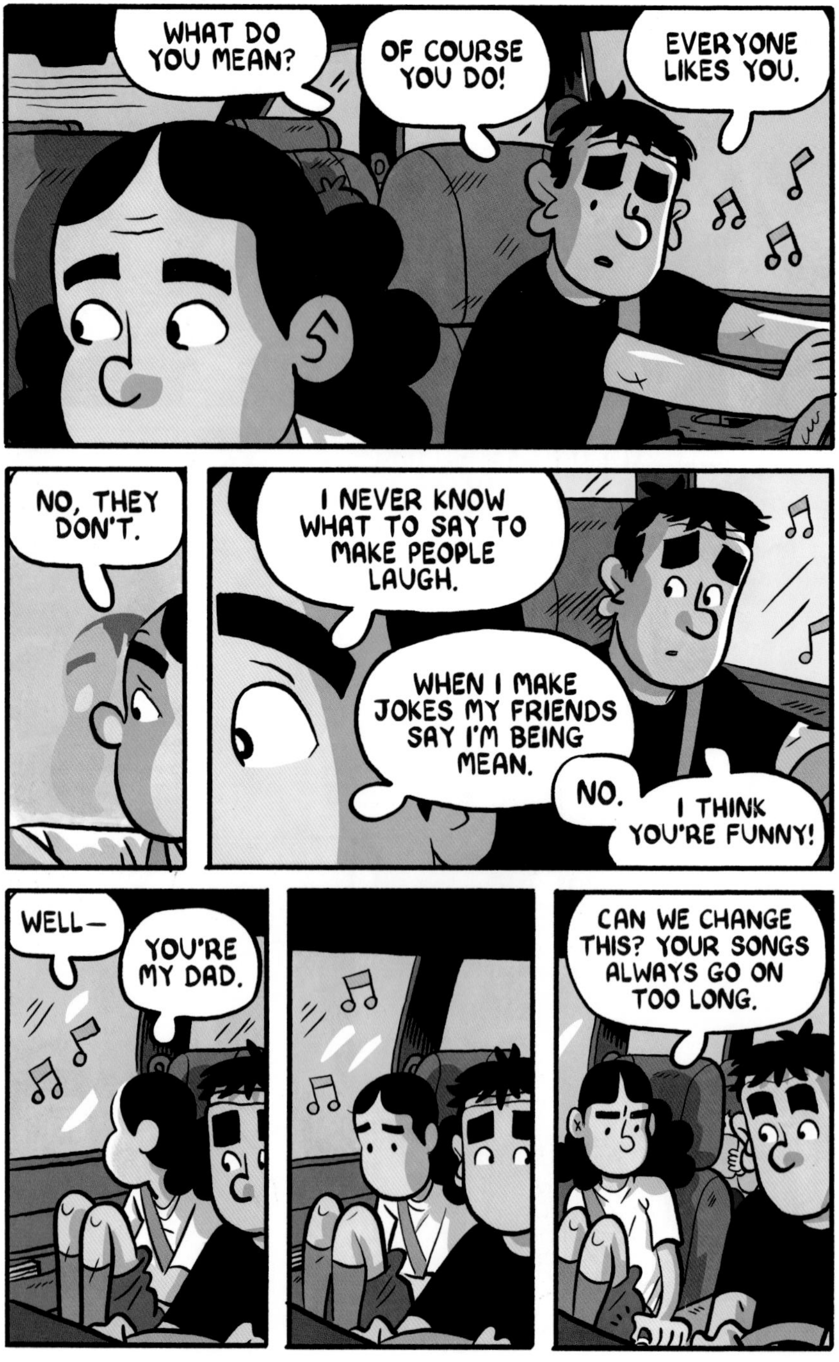
WHAT DO YOU MEAN?
OF COURSE YOU DO!
EVERYONE LIKES YOU.
NO, THEY DON'T.
I NEVER KNOW WHAT TO SAY TO MAKE PEOPLE LAUGH.
WHEN I MAKE JOKES MY FRIENDS SAY I'M BEING MEAN.
NO.
I THINK YOU'RE FUNNY!
WELL—
YOU'RE MY DAD.
CAN WE CHANGE THIS? YOUR SONGS ALWAYS GO ON TOO LONG.

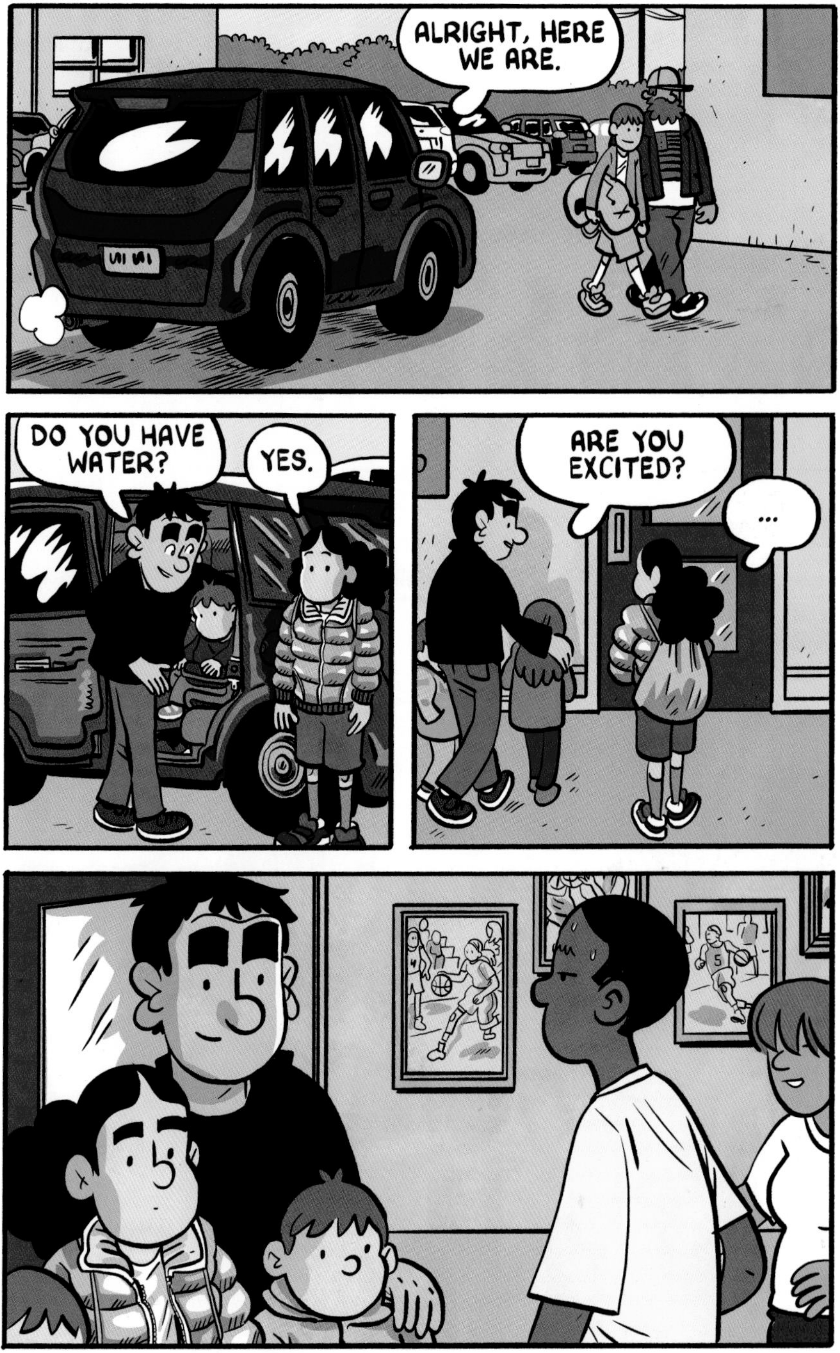
ALRIGHT, HERE WE ARE.
DO YOU HAVE WATER?
YES.
ARE YOU EXCITED?
...

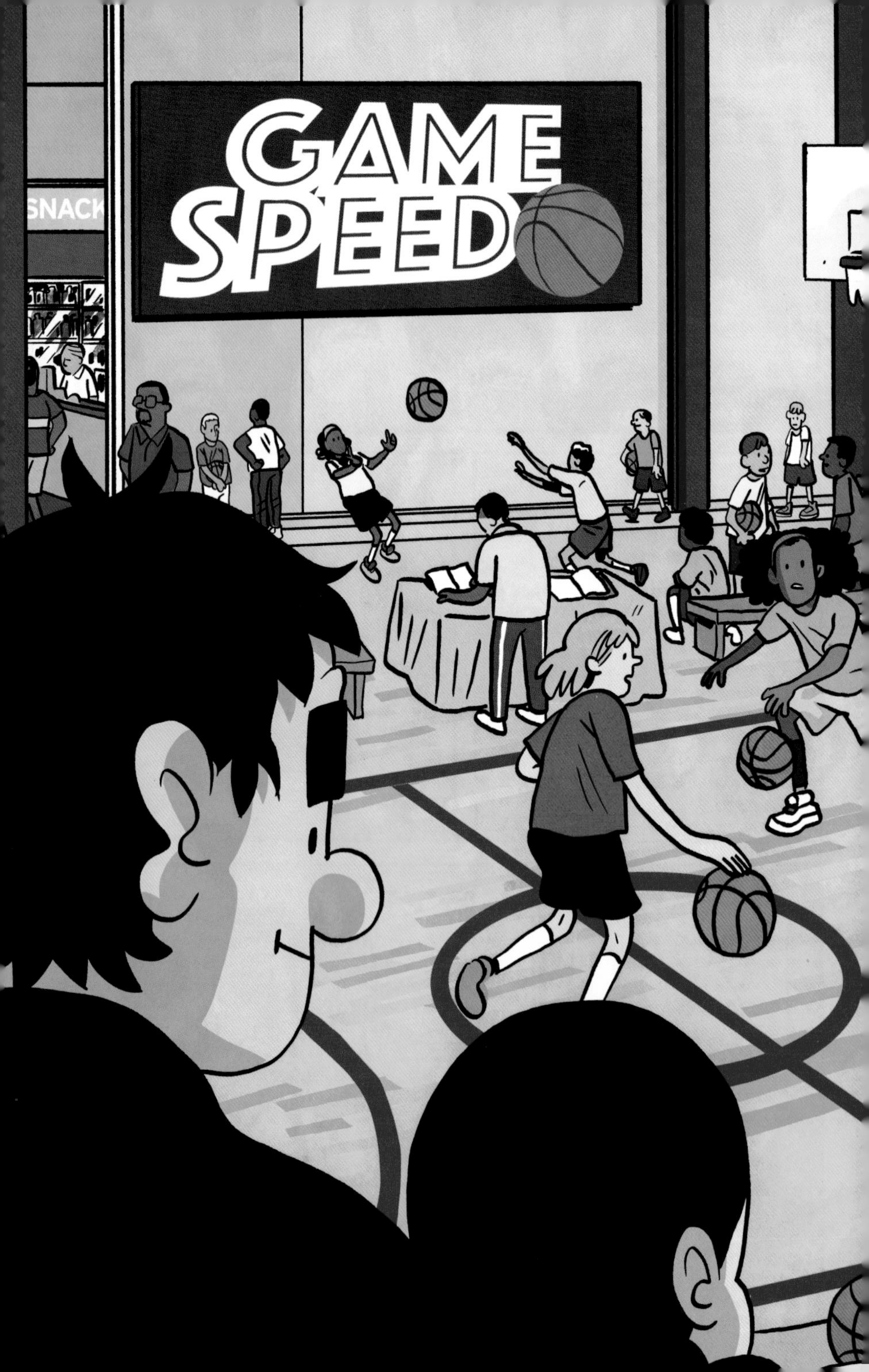
GAME SPEED
SNACK

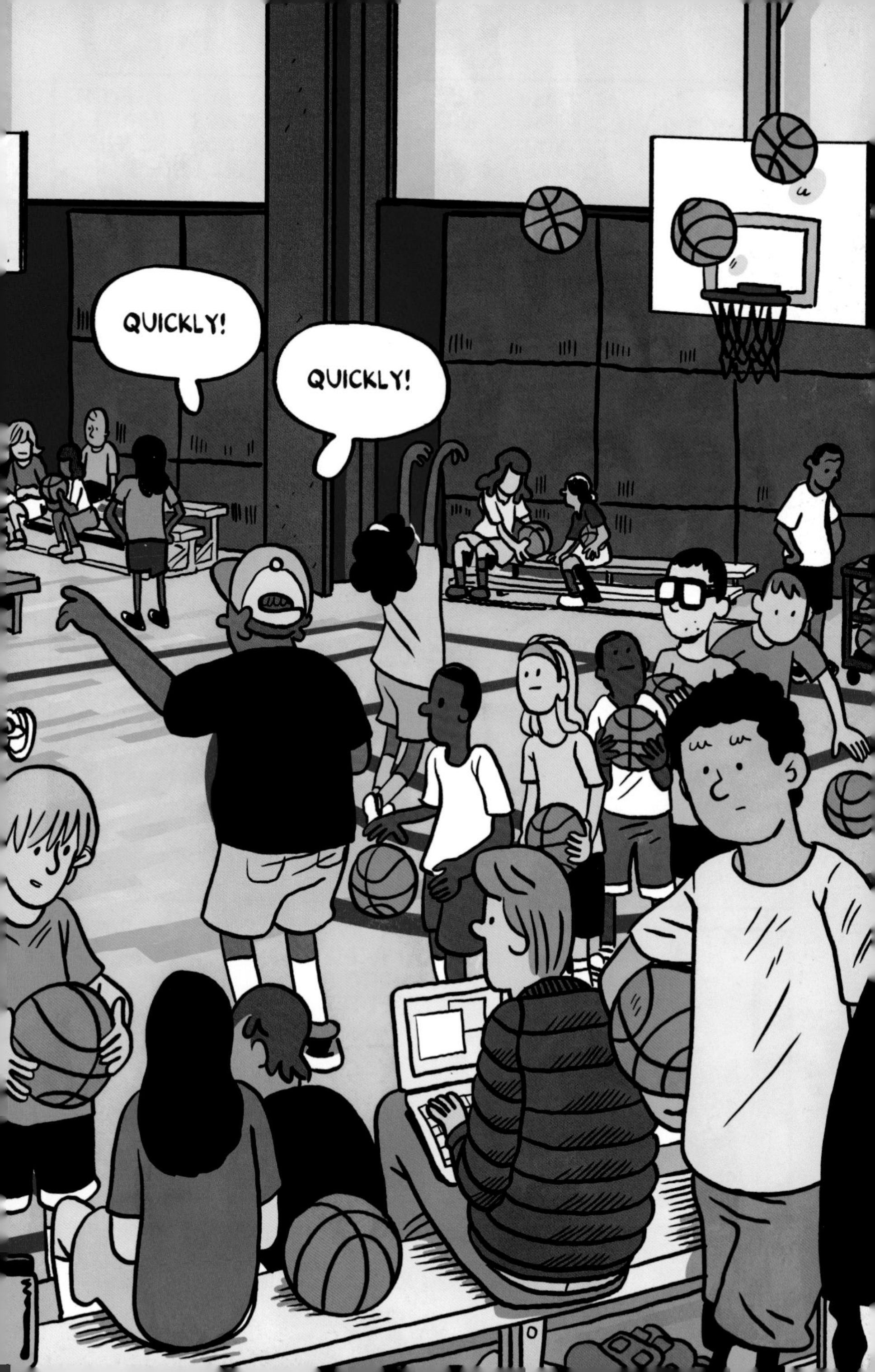
QUICKLY!
QUICKLY!

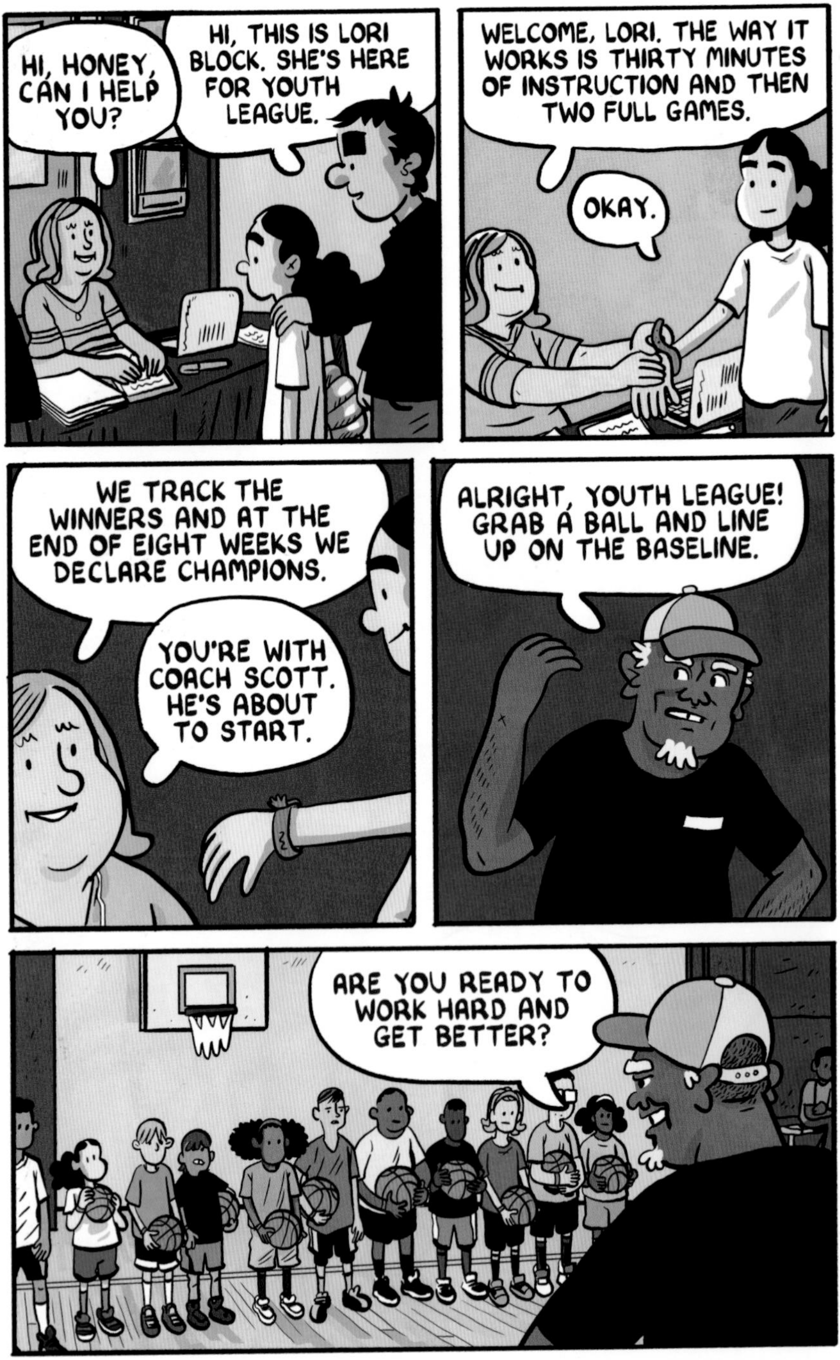
HI, HONEY, CAN I HELP YOU?
HI, THIS IS LORI BLOCK. SHE'S HERE FOR YOUTH LEAGUE.
WELCOME, LORI. THE WAY IT WORKS IS THIRTY MINUTES OF INSTRUCTION AND THEN TWO FULL GAMES.
OKAY.
WE TRACK THE WINNERS AND AT THE END OF EIGHT WEEKS WE DECLARE CHAMPIONS.
YOU'RE WITH COACH SCOTT. HE'S ABOUT TO START.
ALRIGHT, YOUTH LEAGUE! GRAB A BALL AND LINE UP ON THE BASELINE.
ARE YOU READY TO WORK HARD AND GET BETTER?

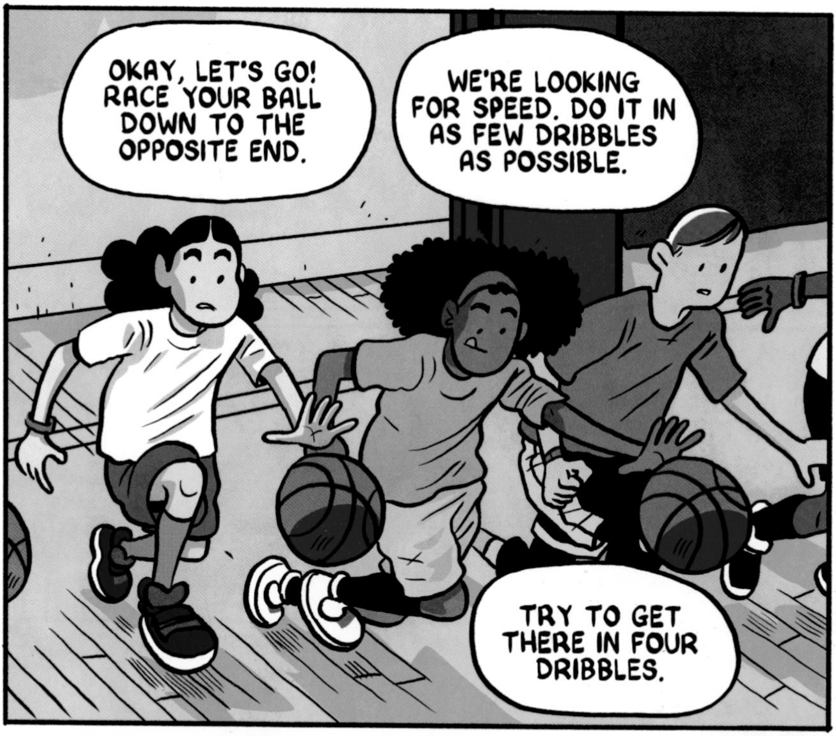
OKAY, LET'S GO! RACE YOUR BALL DOWN TO THE OPPOSITE END.
WE'RE LOOKING FOR SPEED. DO IT IN AS FEW DRIBBLES AS POSSIBLE.
TRY TO GET THERE IN FOUR DRIBBLES.

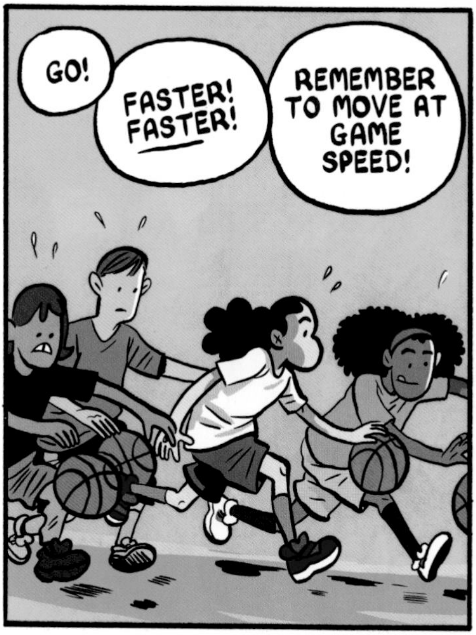
GO!
FASTER! FASTER!
REMEMBER TO MOVE AT GAME SPEED!

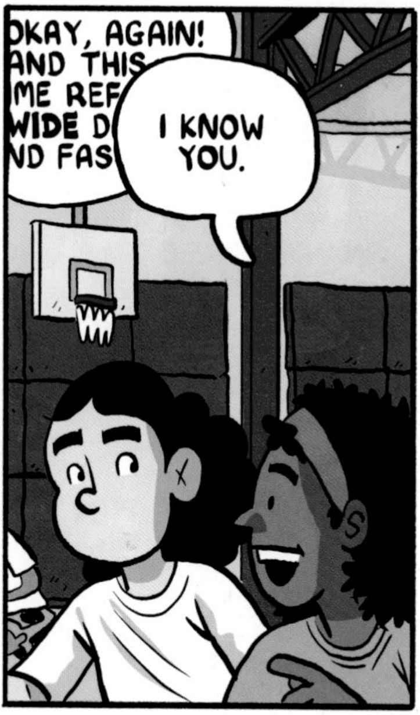
OKAY, AGAIN!
I KNOW YOU.

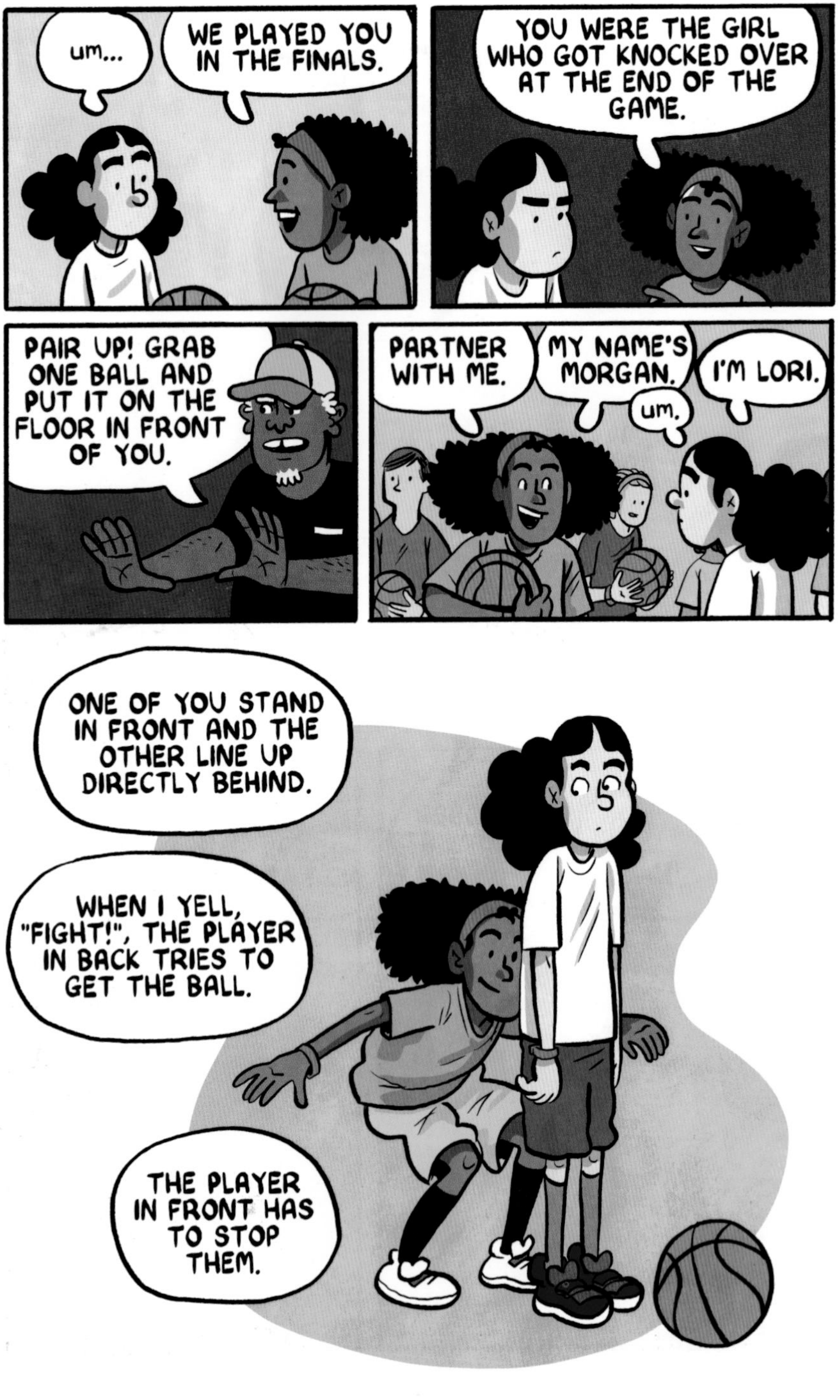
um...
WE PLAYED YOU IN THE FINALS.
YOU WERE THE GIRL WHO GOT KNOCKED OVER AT THE END OF THE GAME.
PAIR UP! GRAB ONE BALL AND PUT IT ON THE FLOOR IN FRONT OF YOU.
PARTNER WITH ME.
MY NAME'S MORGAN.
um.
I'M LORI.
ONE OF YOU STAND IN FRONT AND THE OTHER LINE UP DIRECTLY BEHIND.
WHEN I YELL, "FIGHT!", THE PLAYER IN BACK TRIES TO GET THE BALL.
THE PLAYER IN FRONT HAS TO STOP THEM.

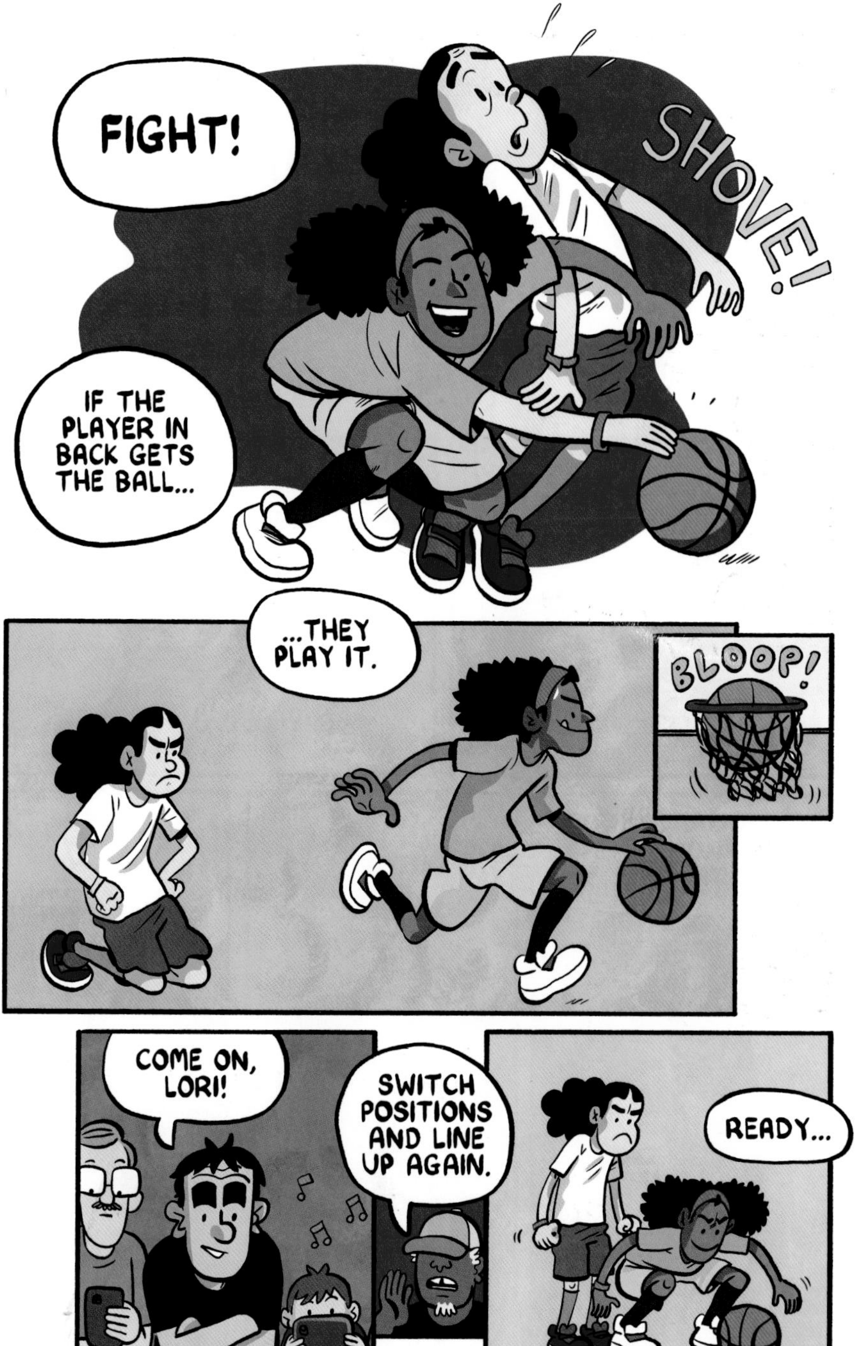
FIGHT!
SHOVE!
IF THE PLAYER IN BACK GETS THE BALL...
...THEY PLAY IT.
BLOOP!
COME ON, LORI!
SWITCH POSITIONS AND LINE UP AGAIN.
READY...

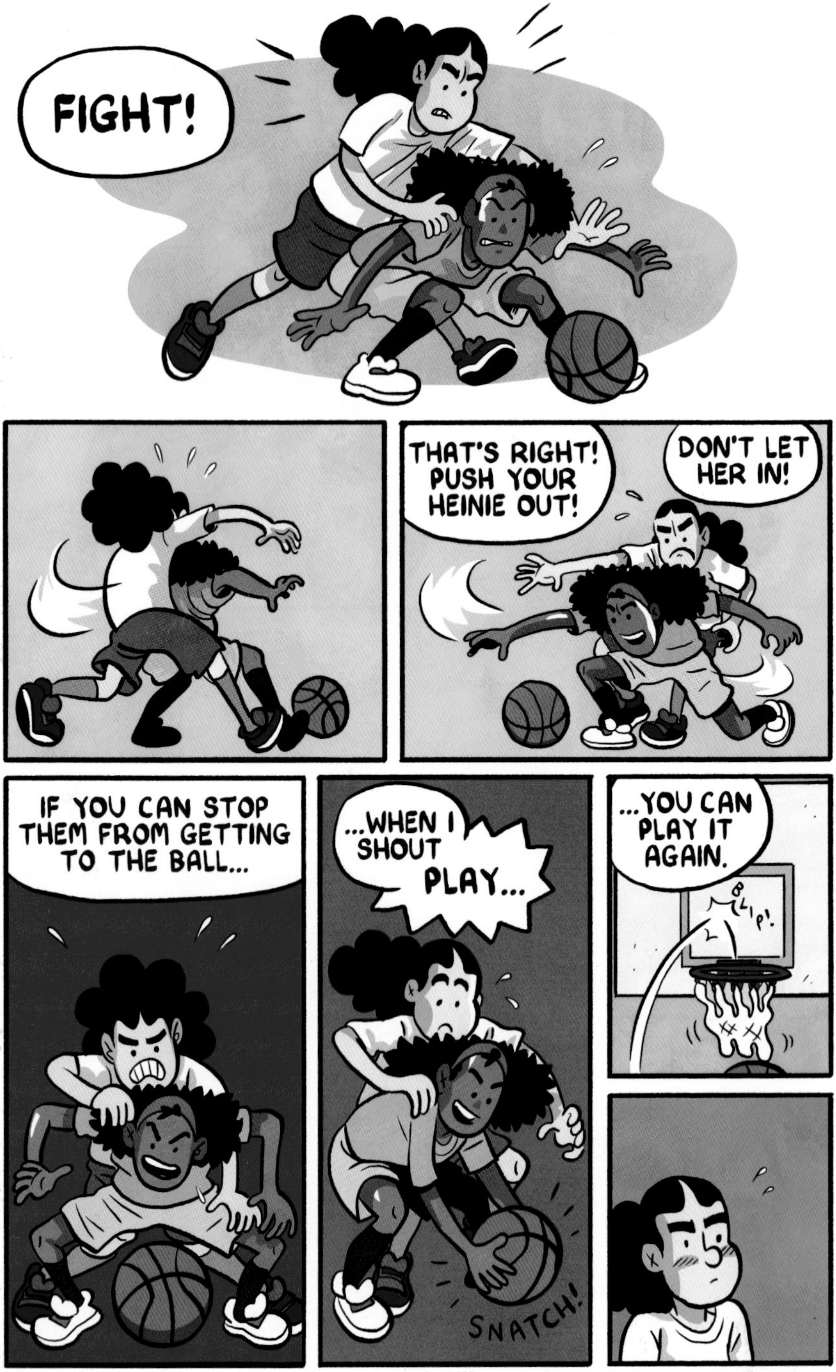
FIGHT!
THAT'S RIGHT! PUSH YOUR HEINIE OUT!
DON'T LET HER IN!
IF YOU CAN STOP THEM FROM GETTING TO THE BALL...
...WHEN I SHOUT PLAY...
SNATCH!
...YOU CAN PLAY IT AGAIN.
BLIP!

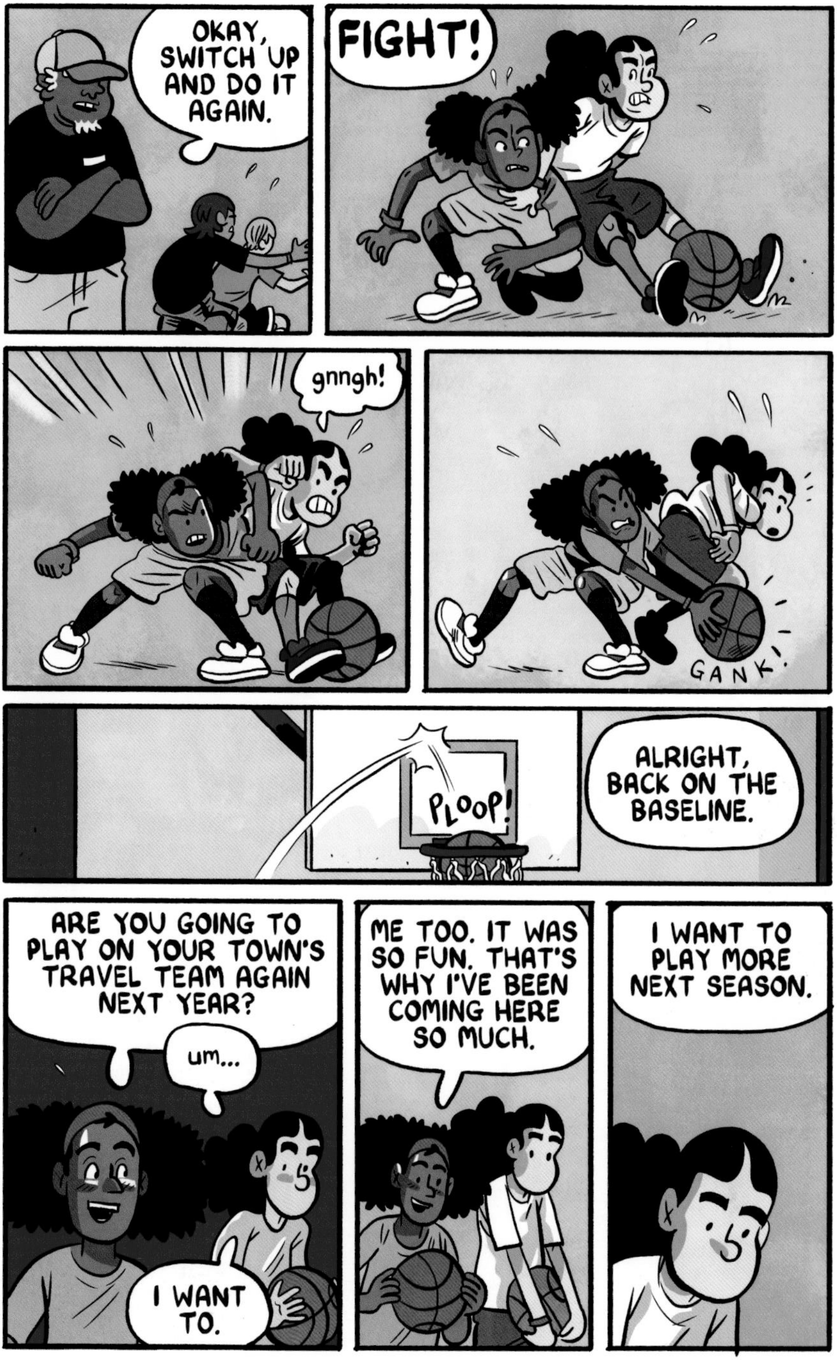
OKAY, SWITCH UP AND DO IT AGAIN.
FIGHT!
gnngh!
GANK!
PLOOP!
ALRIGHT, BACK ON THE BASELINE.
ARE YOU GOING TO PLAY ON YOUR TOWN'S TRAVEL TEAM AGAIN NEXT YEAR?
um...
I WANT TO.
ME TOO. IT WAS SO FUN. THAT'S WHY I'VE BEEN COMING HERE SO MUCH.
I WANT TO PLAY MORE NEXT SEASON.

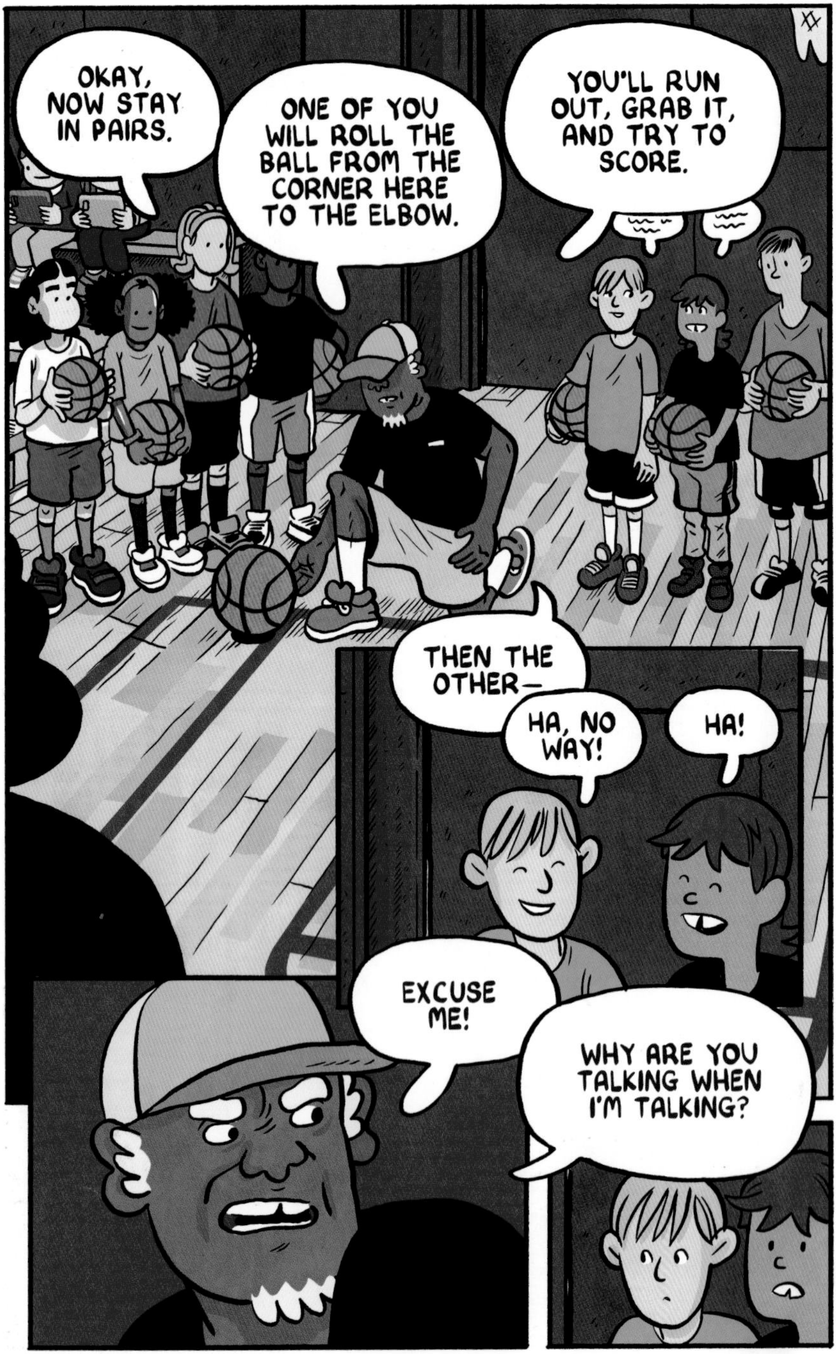
OKAY, NOW STAY IN PAIRS.
ONE OF YOU WILL ROLL THE BALL FROM THE CORNER HERE TO THE ELBOW.
YOU'LL RUN OUT, GRAB IT, AND TRY TO SCORE.
THEN THE OTHER—
HA, NO WAY!
HA!
EXCUSE ME!
WHY ARE YOU TALKING WHEN I'M TALKING?

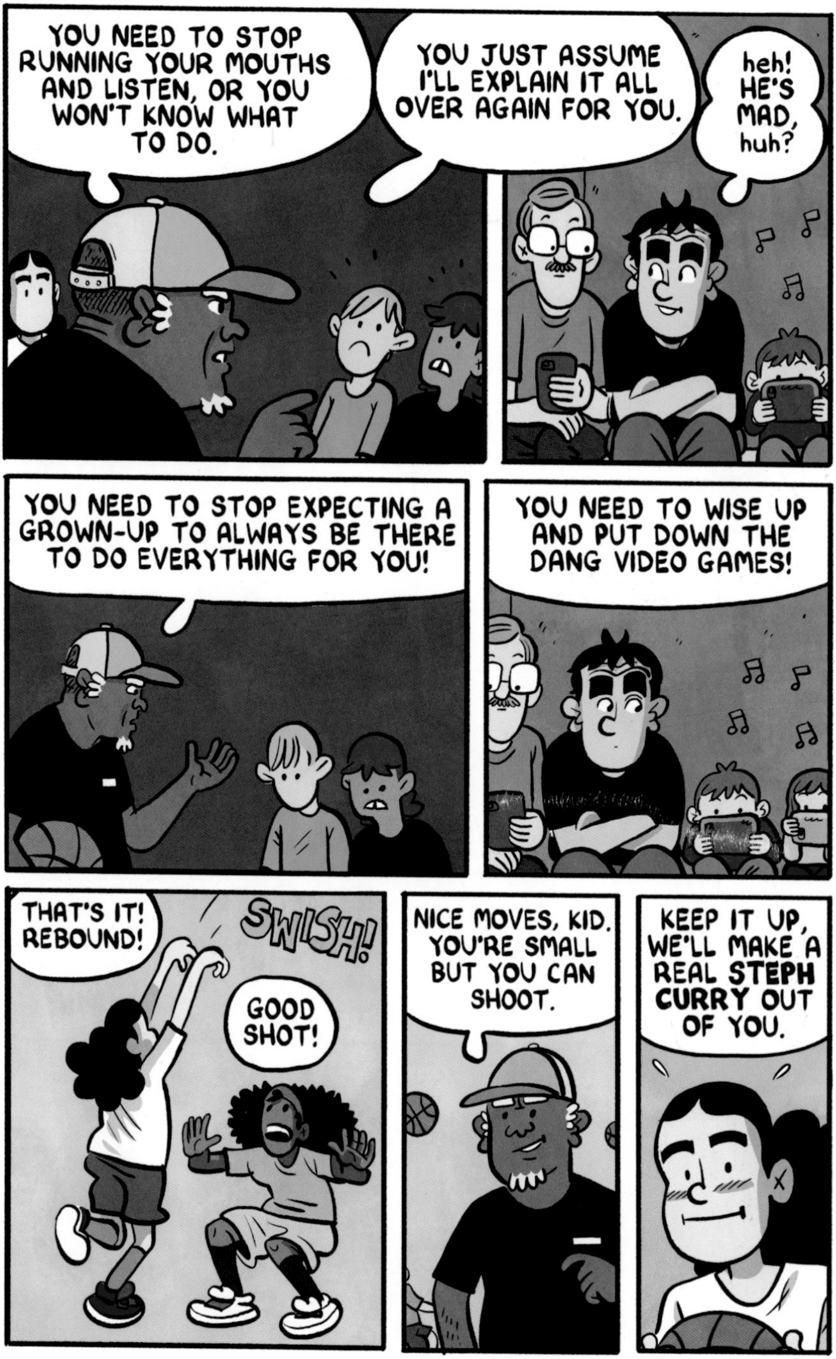
YOU NEED TO STOP RUNNING YOUR MOUTHS AND LISTEN, OR YOU WON'T KNOW WHAT TO DO.
YOU JUST ASSUME I'LL EXPLAIN IT ALL OVER AGAIN FOR YOU.
heh! HE'S MAD, huh?
YOU NEED TO STOP EXPECTING A GROWN-UP TO ALWAYS BE THERE TO DO EVERYTHING FOR YOU!
YOU NEED TO WISE UP AND PUT DOWN THE DANG VIDEO GAMES!
THAT'S IT! REBOUND!
SWISH!
GOOD SHOT!
NICE MOVES, KID. YOU'RE SMALL BUT YOU CAN SHOOT.
KEEP IT UP, WE'LL MAKE A REAL **STEPH CURRY** OUT OF YOU.

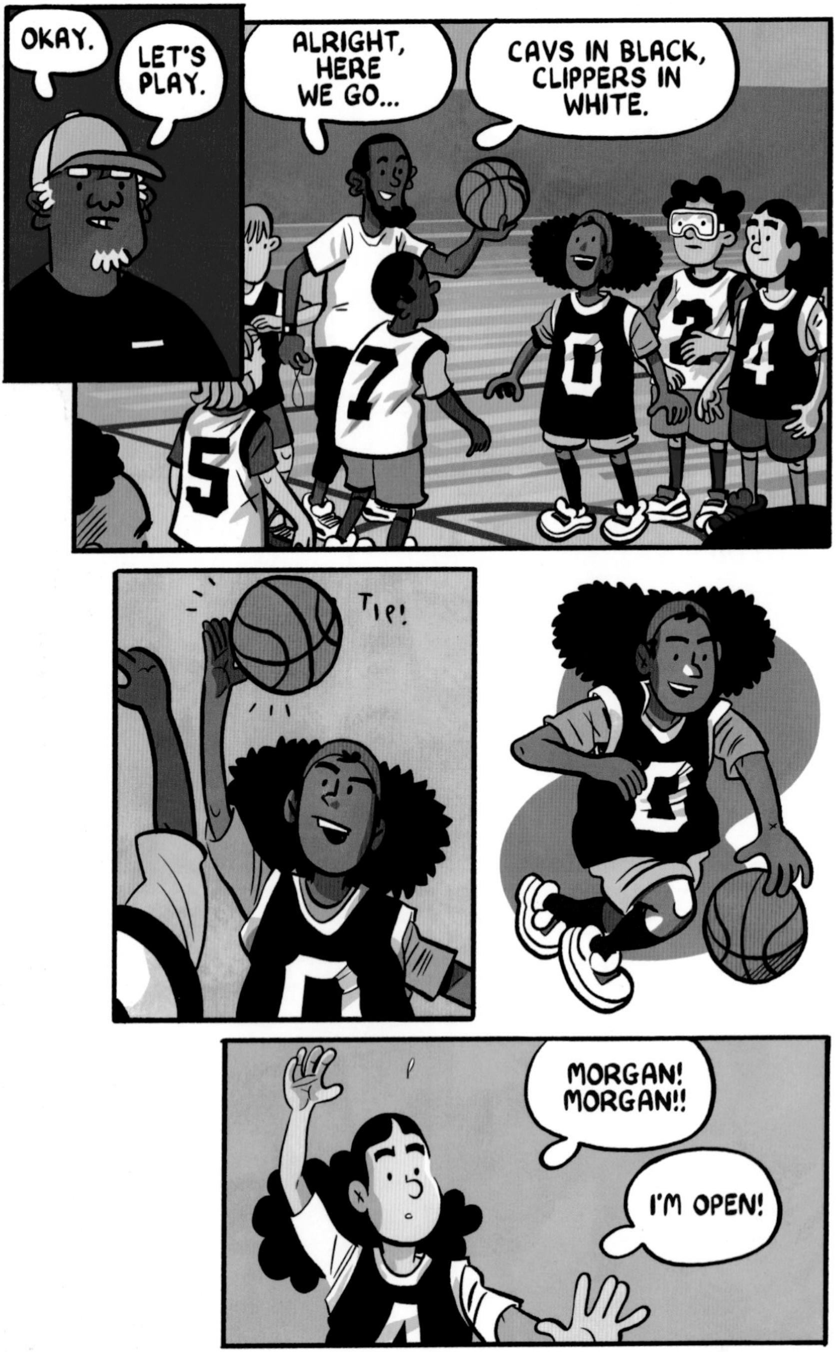
OKAY.
LET'S PLAY.
ALRIGHT, HERE WE GO...
CAVS IN BLACK, CLIPPERS IN WHITE.
TIP!
MORGAN! MORGAN!!
I'M OPEN!

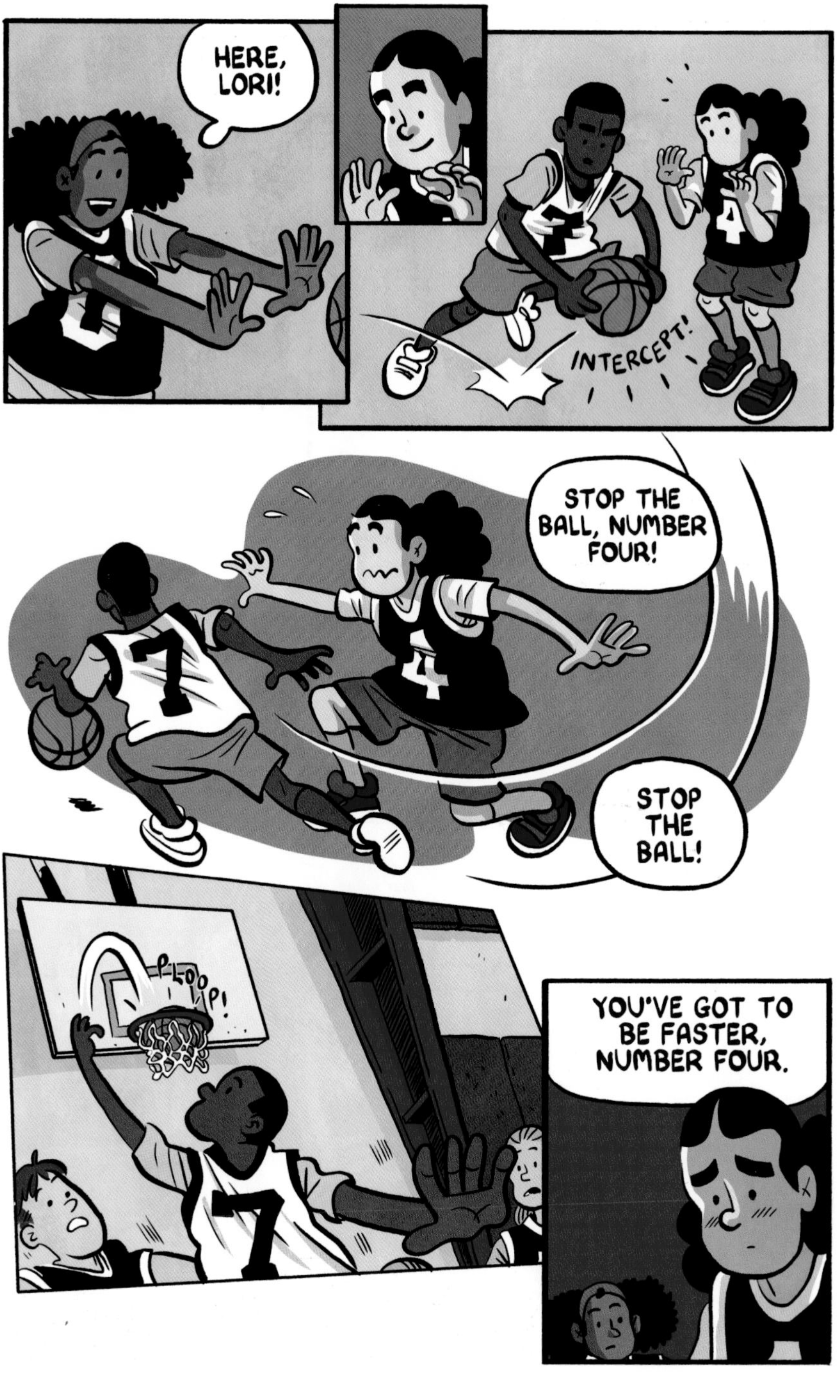
HERE, LORI!
INTERCEPT!
STOP THE BALL, NUMBER FOUR!
STOP THE BALL!
P-LOOP!
YOU'VE GOT TO BE FASTER, NUMBER FOUR.

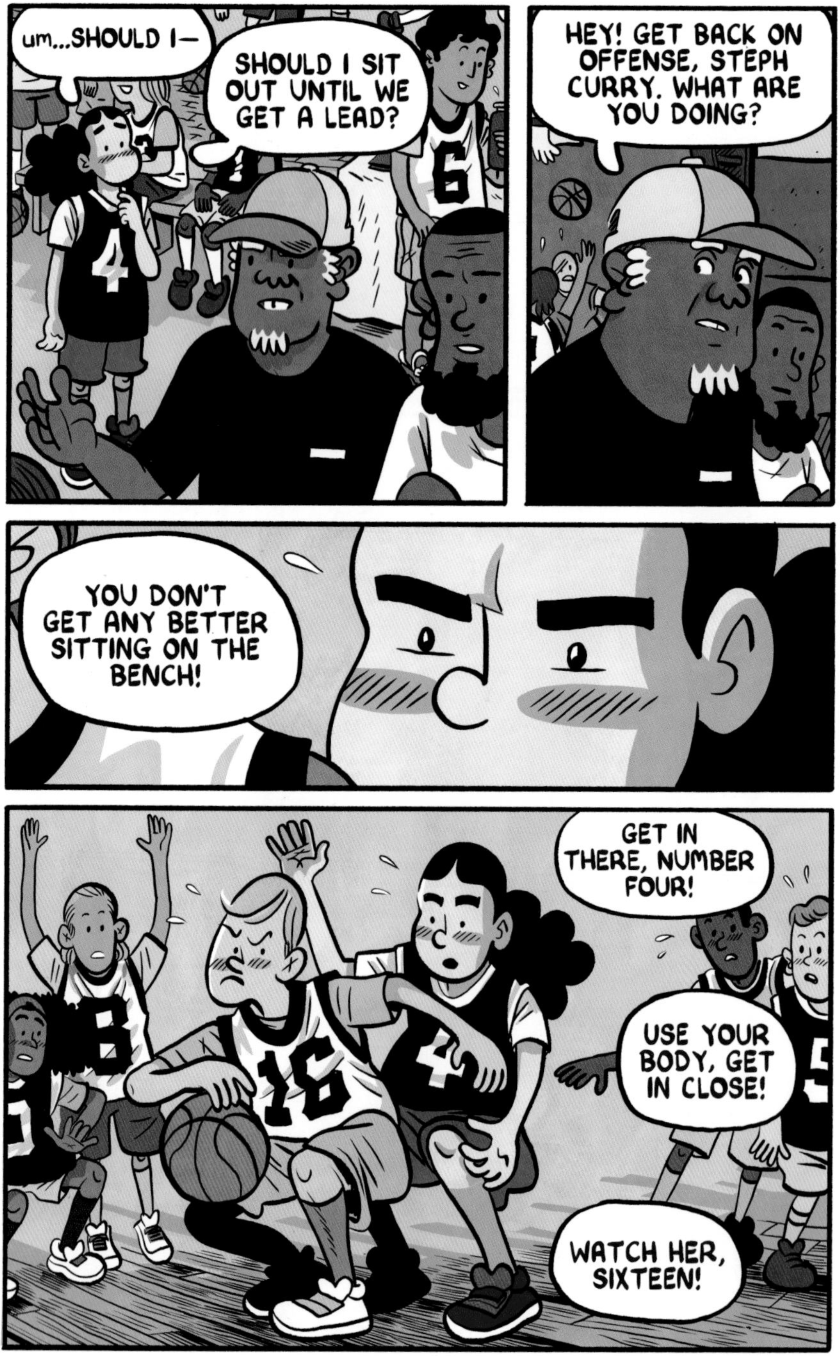
um...SHOULD I—
SHOULD I SIT OUT UNTIL WE GET A LEAD?
HEY! GET BACK ON OFFENSE, STEPH CURRY. WHAT ARE YOU DOING?
YOU DON'T GET ANY BETTER SITTING ON THE BENCH!
GET IN THERE, NUMBER FOUR!
USE YOUR BODY, GET IN CLOSE!
WATCH HER, SIXTEEN!

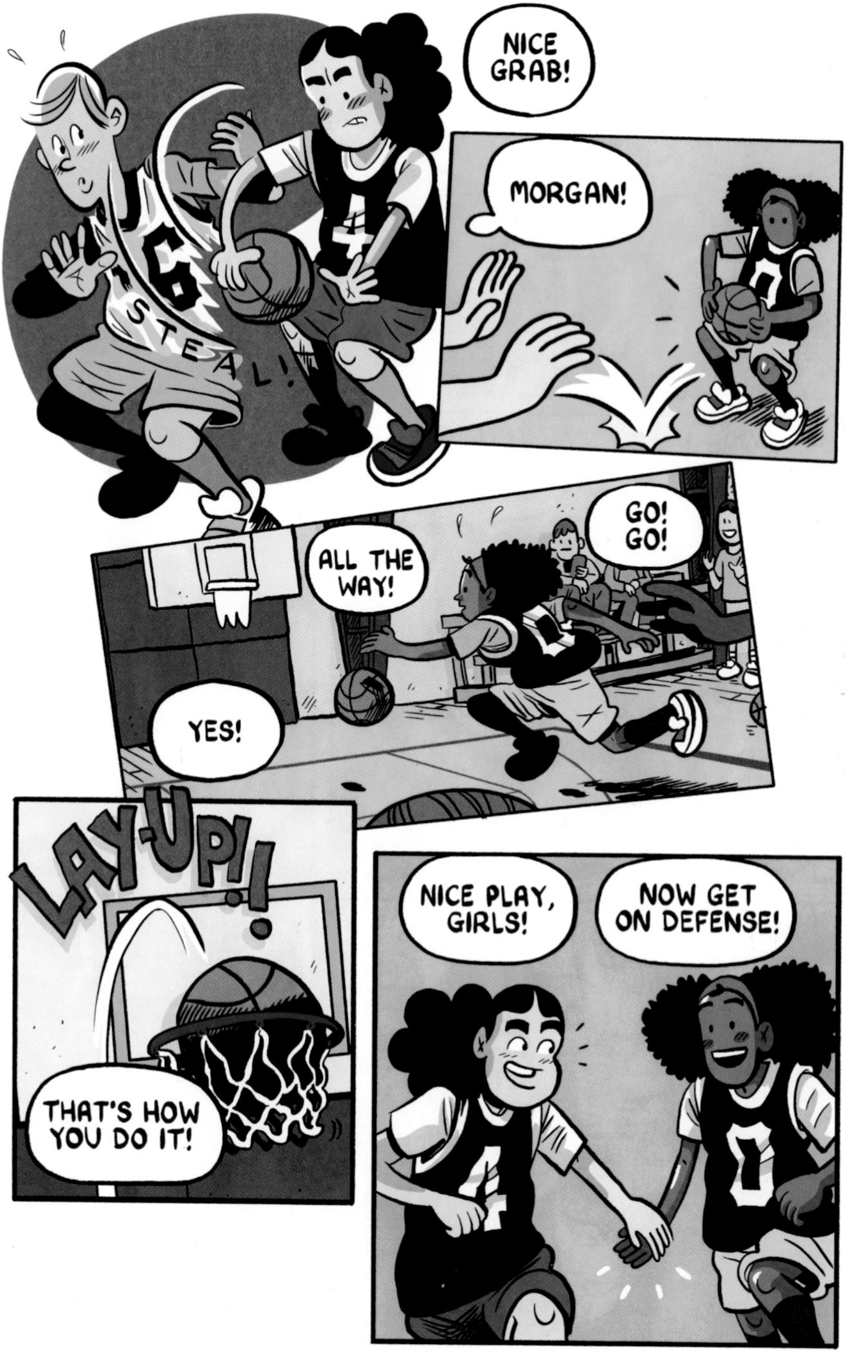
NICE GRAB!
STEAL!
MORGAN!
ALL THE WAY!
GO! GO!
YES!
LAY-UP!!
THAT'S HOW YOU DO IT!
NICE PLAY, GIRLS!
NOW GET ON DEFENSE!

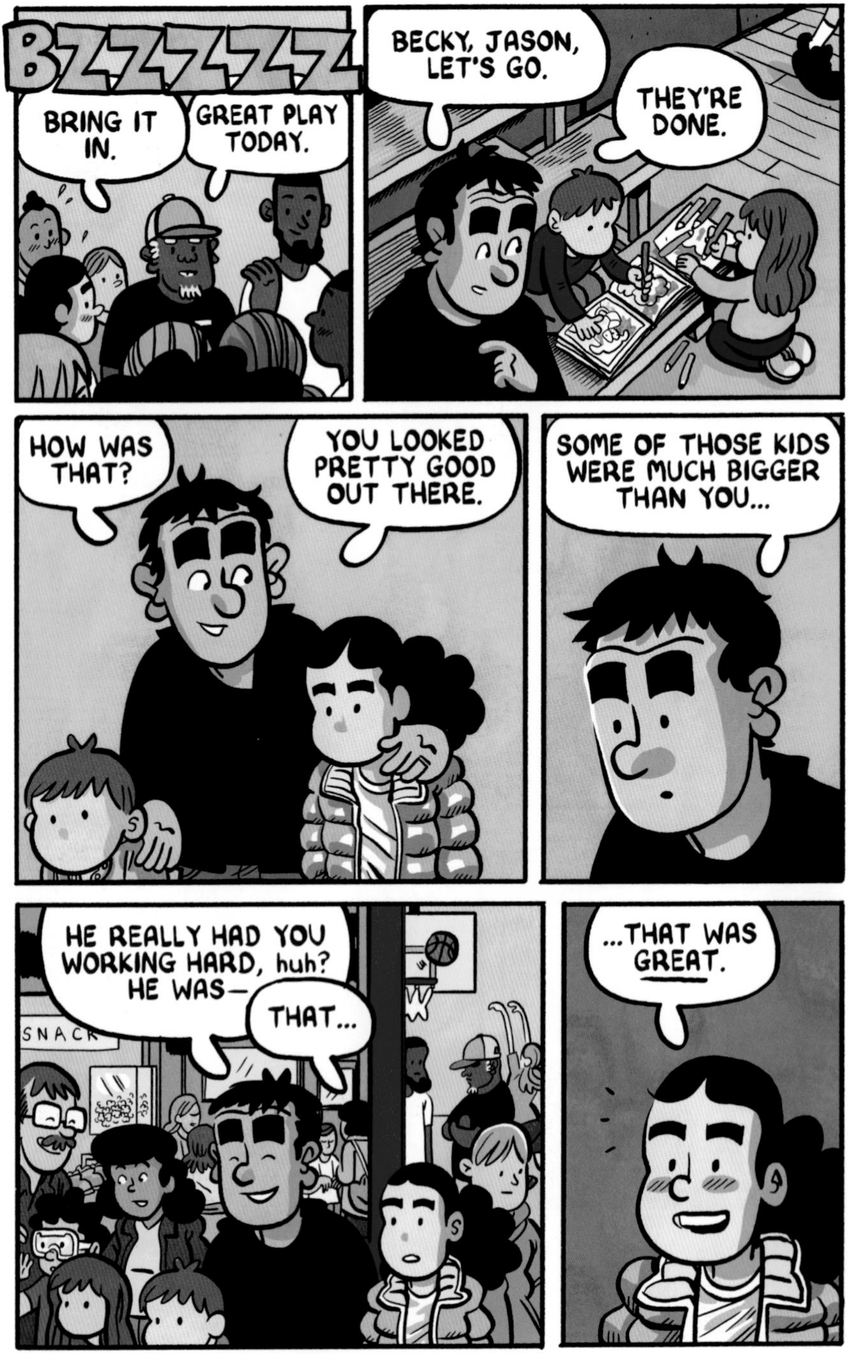
BZZZZZZZ
BRING IT IN.
GREAT PLAY TODAY.
BECKY, JASON, LET'S GO.
THEY'RE DONE.
HOW WAS THAT?
YOU LOOKED PRETTY GOOD OUT THERE.
SOME OF THOSE KIDS WERE MUCH BIGGER THAN YOU...
HE REALLY HAD YOU WORKING HARD, huh? HE WAS—
THAT...
SNACK
...THAT WAS GREAT.

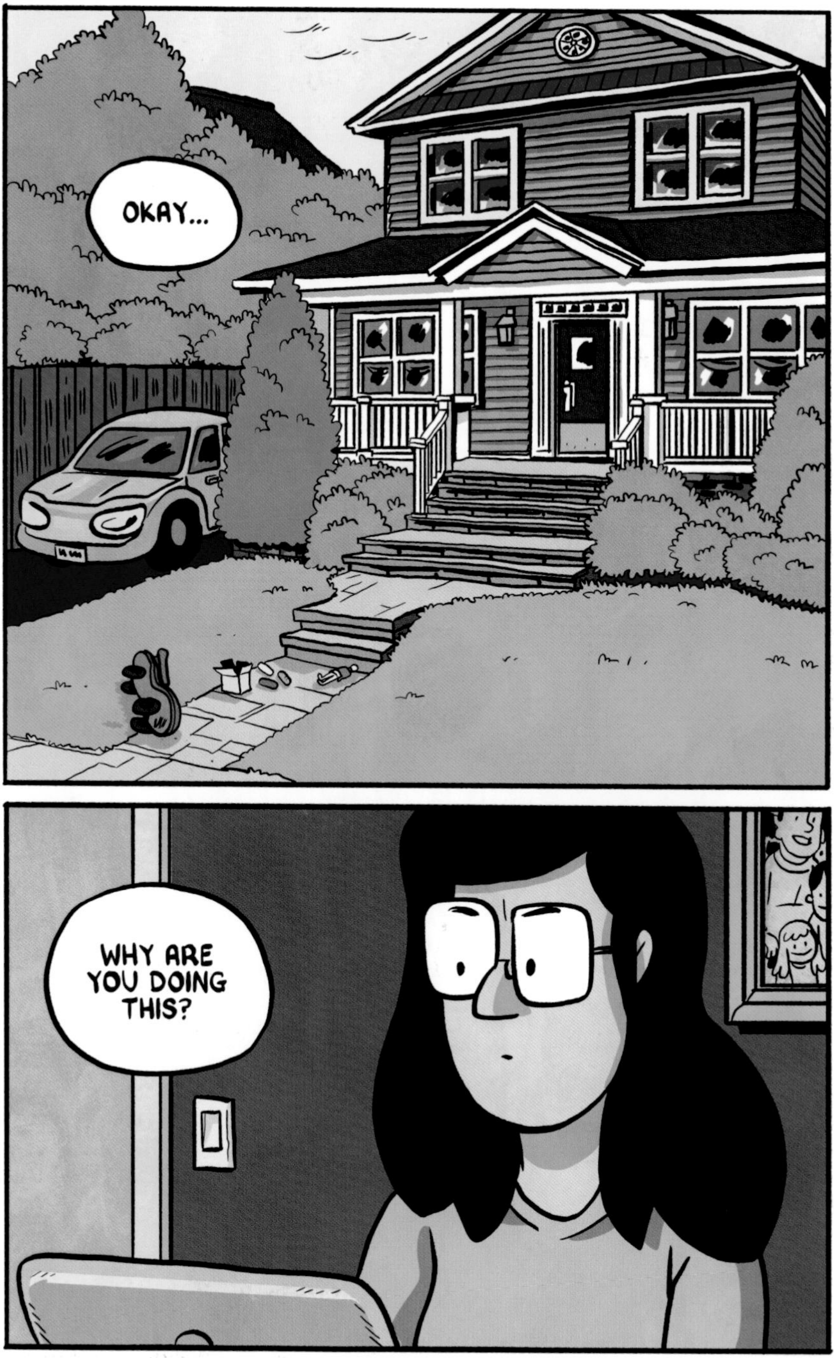
OKAY...
WHY ARE YOU DOING THIS?

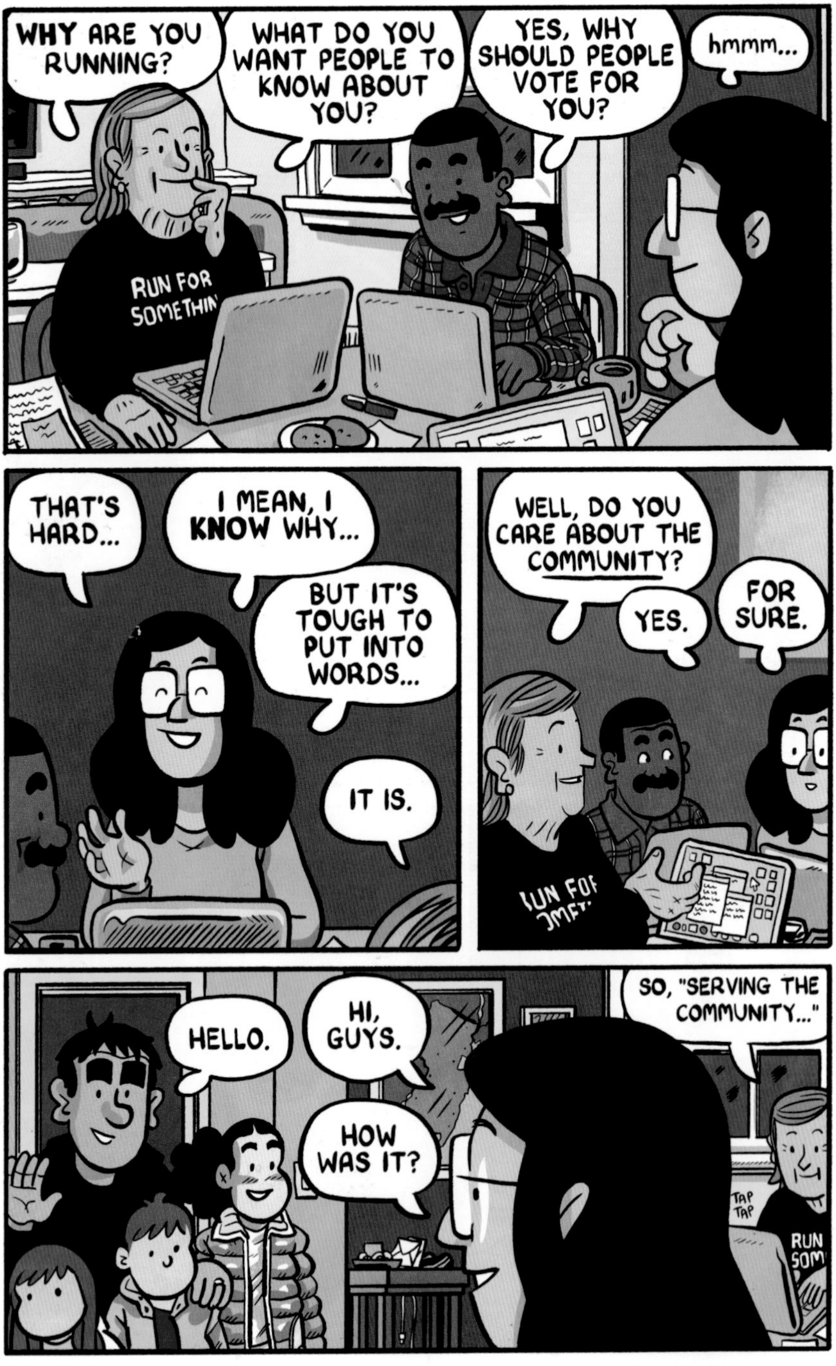
WHY ARE YOU RUNNING?
WHAT DO YOU WANT PEOPLE TO KNOW ABOUT YOU?
YES, WHY SHOULD PEOPLE VOTE FOR YOU?
hmmm...
RUN FOR SOMETHIN
THAT'S HARD...
I MEAN, I KNOW WHY...
BUT IT'S TOUGH TO PUT INTO WORDS...
IT IS.
WELL, DO YOU CARE ABOUT THE COMMUNITY?
YES.
FOR SURE.
HELLO.
HI, GUYS.
HOW WAS IT?
SO, "SERVING THE COMMUNITY..."
TAP TAP

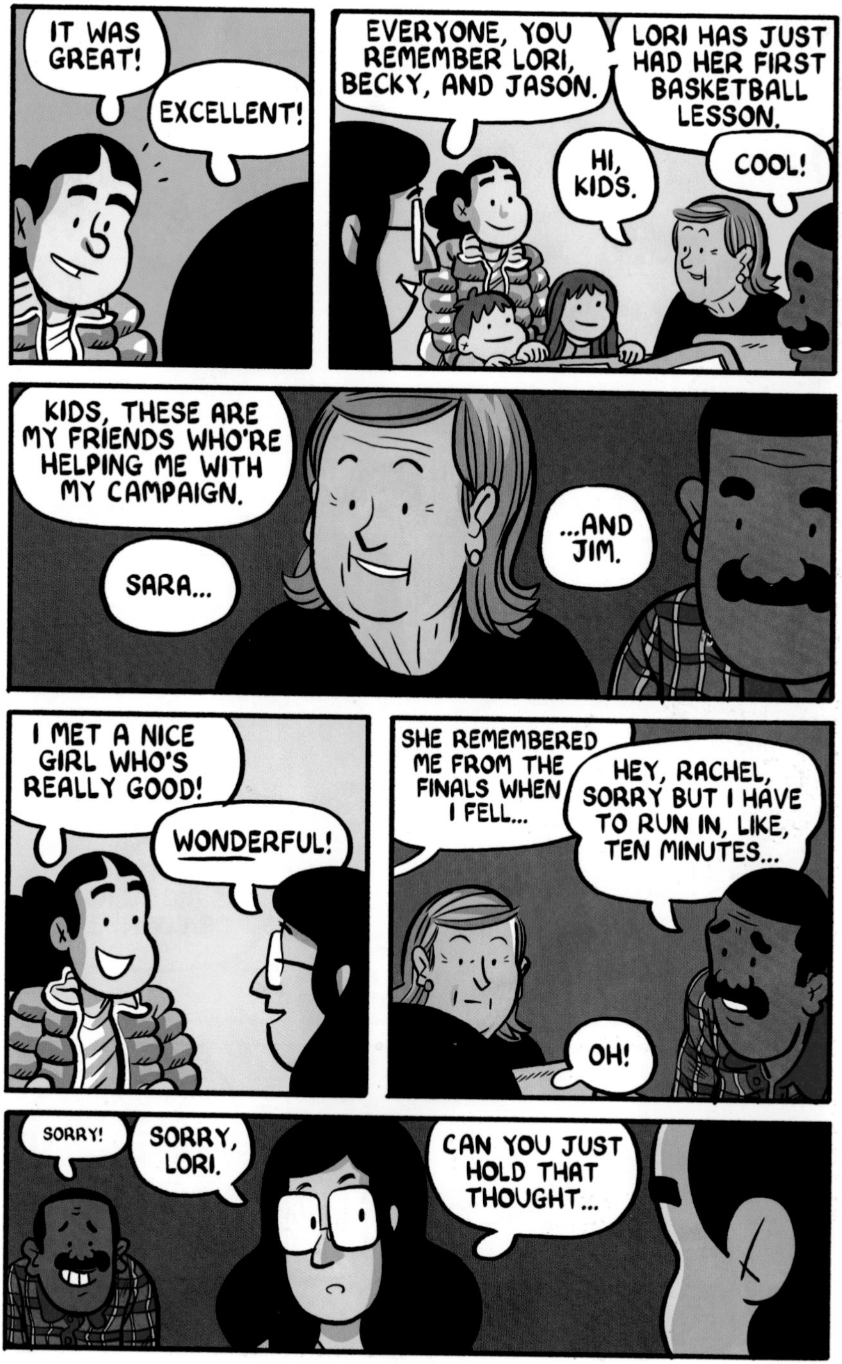
IT WAS GREAT!
EXCELLENT!
EVERYONE, YOU REMEMBER LORI, BECKY, AND JASON.
LORI HAS JUST HAD HER FIRST BASKETBALL LESSON.
HI, KIDS.
COOL!
KIDS, THESE ARE MY FRIENDS WHO'RE HELPING ME WITH MY CAMPAIGN.
SARA...
...AND JIM.
I MET A NICE GIRL WHO'S REALLY GOOD!
WONDERFUL!
SHE REMEMBERED ME FROM THE FINALS WHEN I FELL...
HEY, RACHEL, SORRY BUT I HAVE TO RUN IN, LIKE, TEN MINUTES...
OH!
SORRY!
SORRY, LORI.
CAN YOU JUST HOLD THAT THOUGHT...

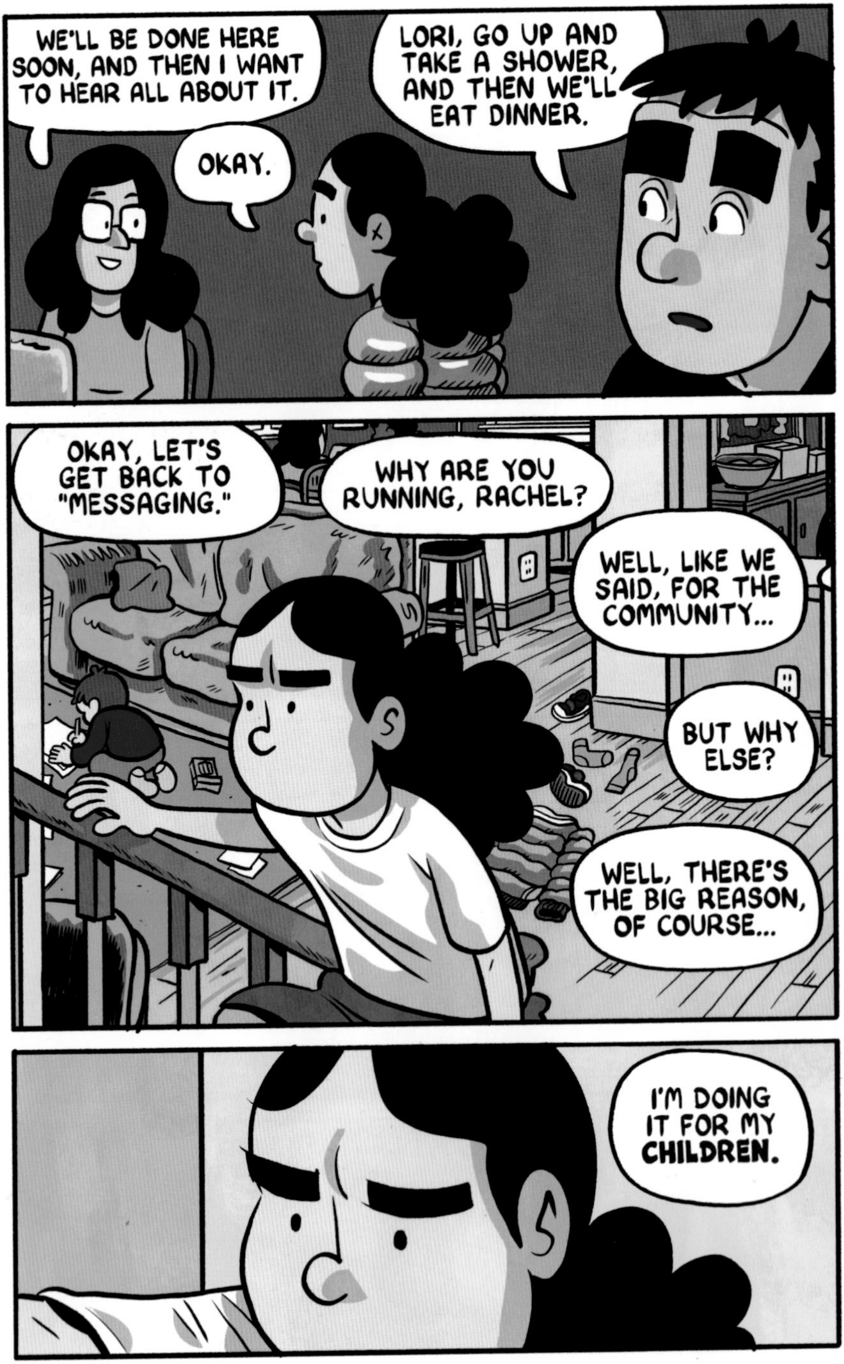
WE'LL BE DONE HERE SOON, AND THEN I WANT TO HEAR ALL ABOUT IT.
OKAY.
LORI, GO UP AND TAKE A SHOWER, AND THEN WE'LL EAT DINNER.
OKAY, LET'S GET BACK TO "MESSAGING."
WHY ARE YOU RUNNING, RACHEL?
WELL, LIKE WE SAID, FOR THE COMMUNITY...
BUT WHY ELSE?
WELL, THERE'S THE BIG REASON, OF COURSE...
I'M DOING IT FOR MY **CHILDREN.**

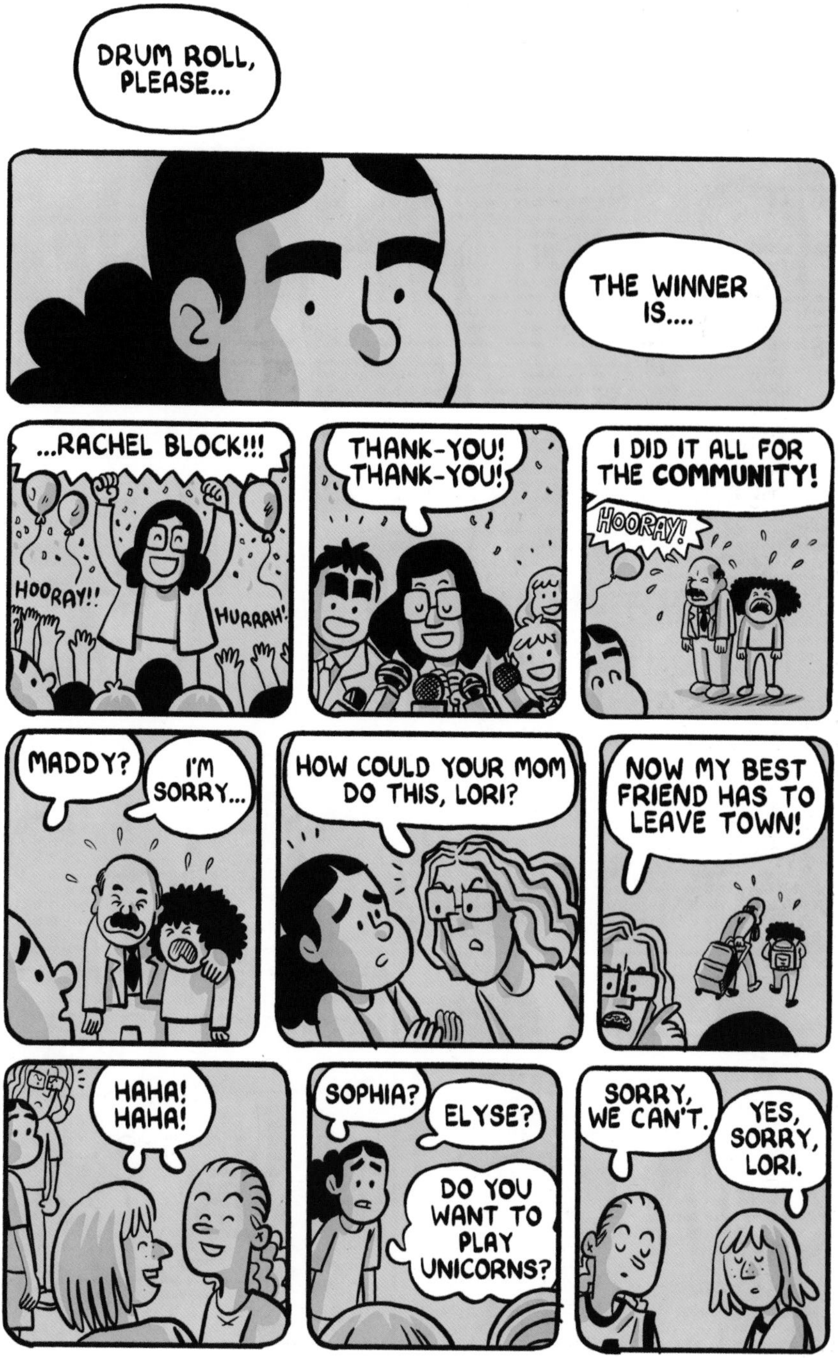
DRUM ROLL, PLEASE...
THE WINNER IS....
...RACHEL BLOCK!!!
HOORAY!!
HURRAH!
THANK-YOU! THANK-YOU!
I DID IT ALL FOR THE **COMMUNITY!**
HOORAY!
MADDY?
I'M SORRY...
HOW COULD YOUR MOM DO THIS, LORI?
NOW MY BEST FRIEND HAS TO LEAVE TOWN!
HAHA! HAHA!
SOPHIA?
ELYSE?
DO YOU WANT TO PLAY UNICORNS?
SORRY, WE CAN'T.
YES, SORRY, LORI.

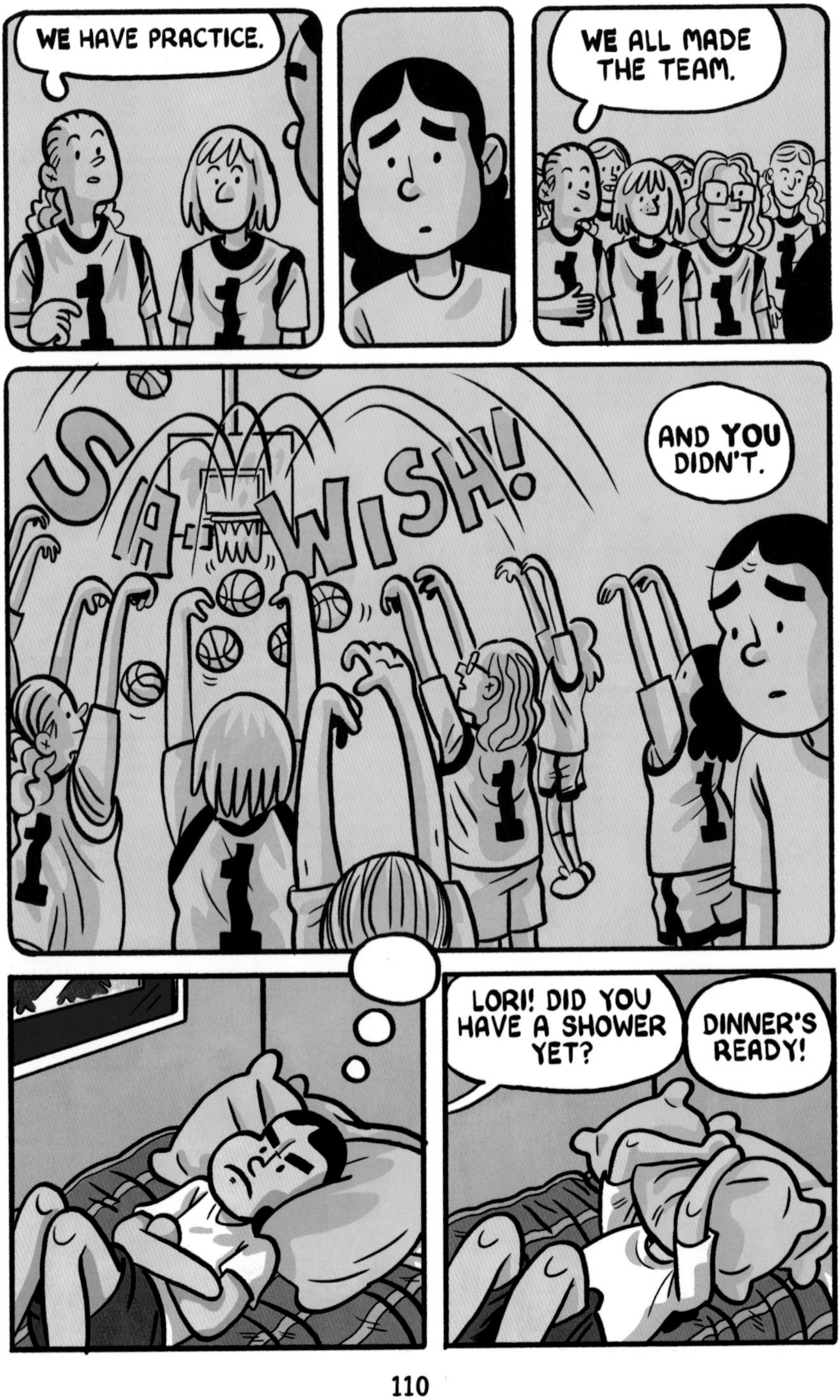
WE HAVE PRACTICE.
WE ALL MADE THE TEAM.
SA-WISH!
AND YOU DIDN'T.
LORI! DID YOU HAVE A SHOWER YET?
DINNER'S READY!

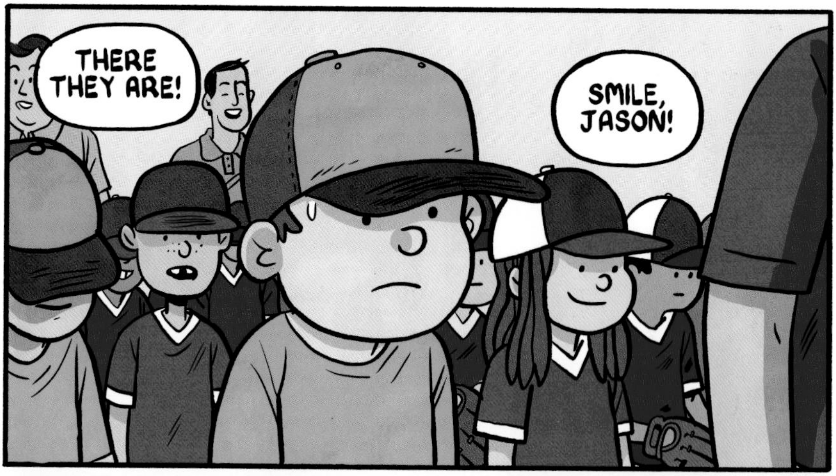
THERE THEY ARE!
SMILE, JASON!

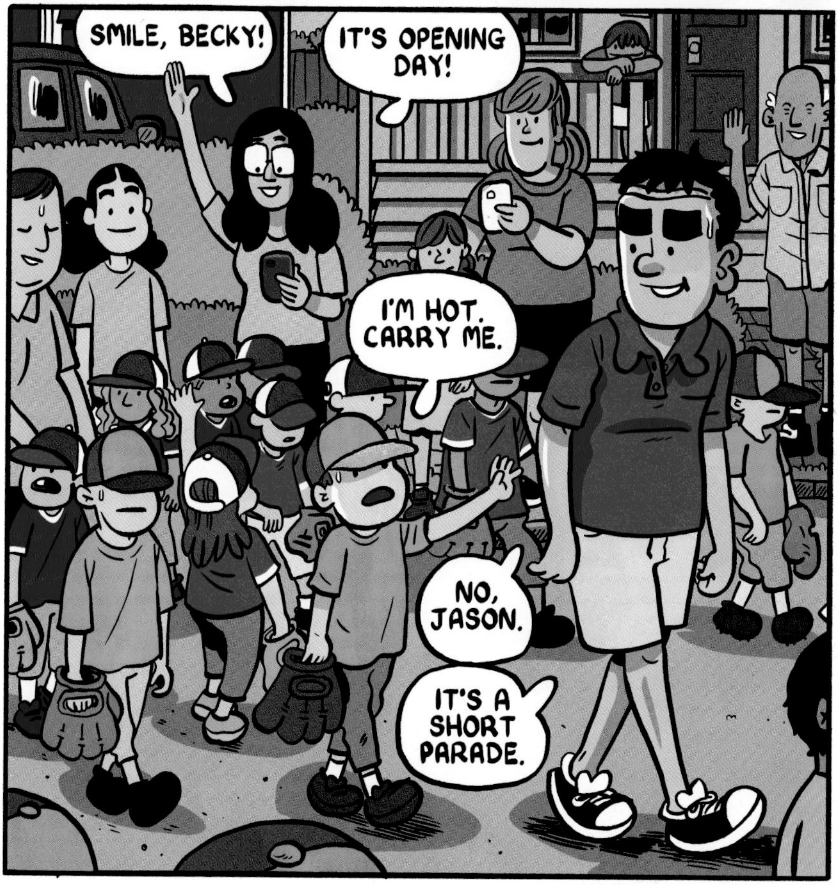
SMILE, BECKY!
IT'S OPENING DAY!
I'M HOT. CARRY ME.
NO, JASON.
IT'S A SHORT PARADE.

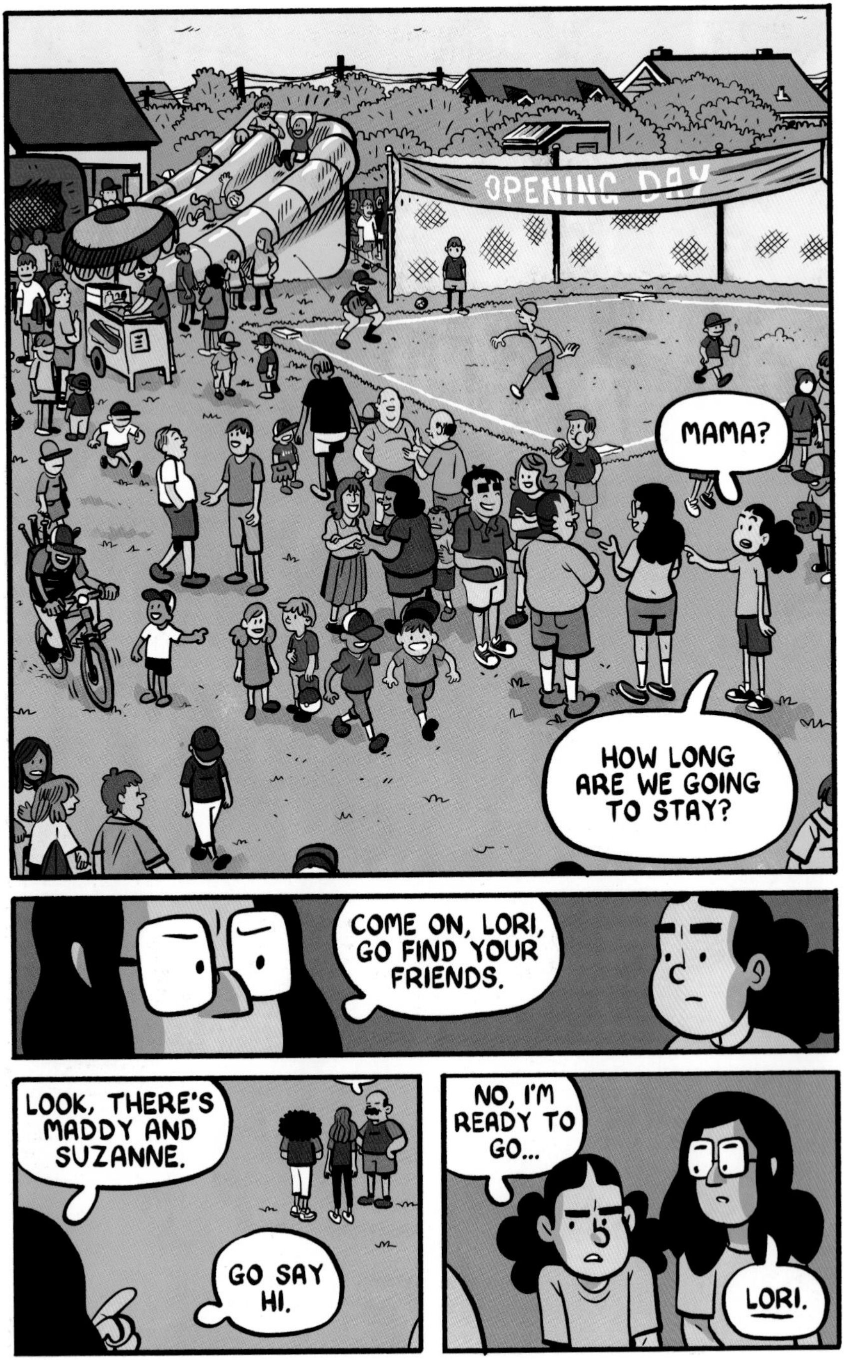
OPENING DAY
MAMA?
HOW LONG ARE WE GOING TO STAY?
COME ON, LORI, GO FIND YOUR FRIENDS.
LOOK, THERE'S MADDY AND SUZANNE.
GO SAY HI.
NO, I'M READY TO GO...
LORI.

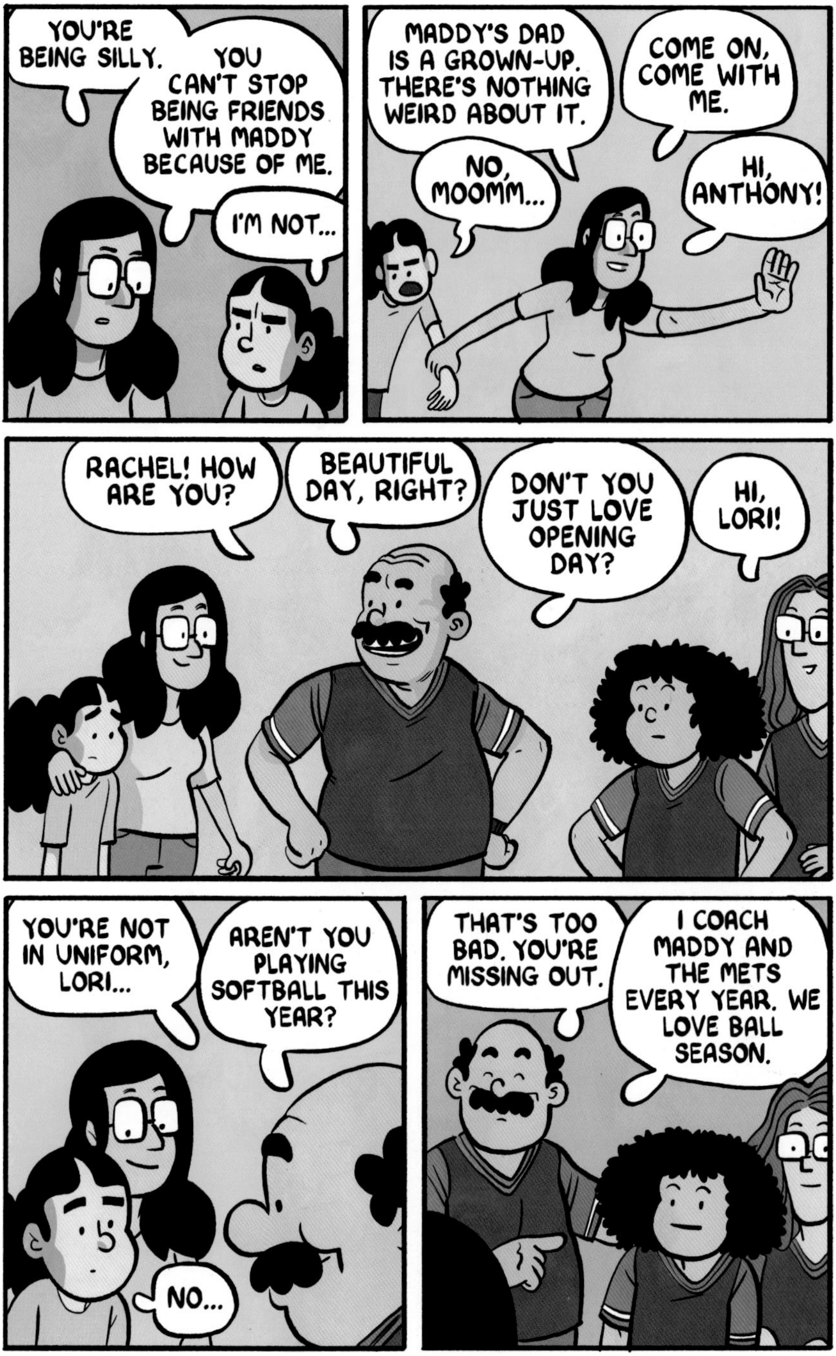
YOU'RE BEING SILLY.
YOU CAN'T STOP BEING FRIENDS WITH MADDY BECAUSE OF ME.
I'M NOT...
MADDY'S DAD IS A GROWN-UP. THERE'S NOTHING WEIRD ABOUT IT.
NO, MOOMM...
COME ON, COME WITH ME.
HI, ANTHONY!
RACHEL! HOW ARE YOU?
BEAUTIFUL DAY, RIGHT?
DON'T YOU JUST LOVE OPENING DAY?
HI, LORI!
YOU'RE NOT IN UNIFORM, LORI...
AREN'T YOU PLAYING SOFTBALL THIS YEAR?
NO...
THAT'S TOO BAD. YOU'RE MISSING OUT.
I COACH MADDY AND THE METS EVERY YEAR. WE LOVE BALL SEASON.

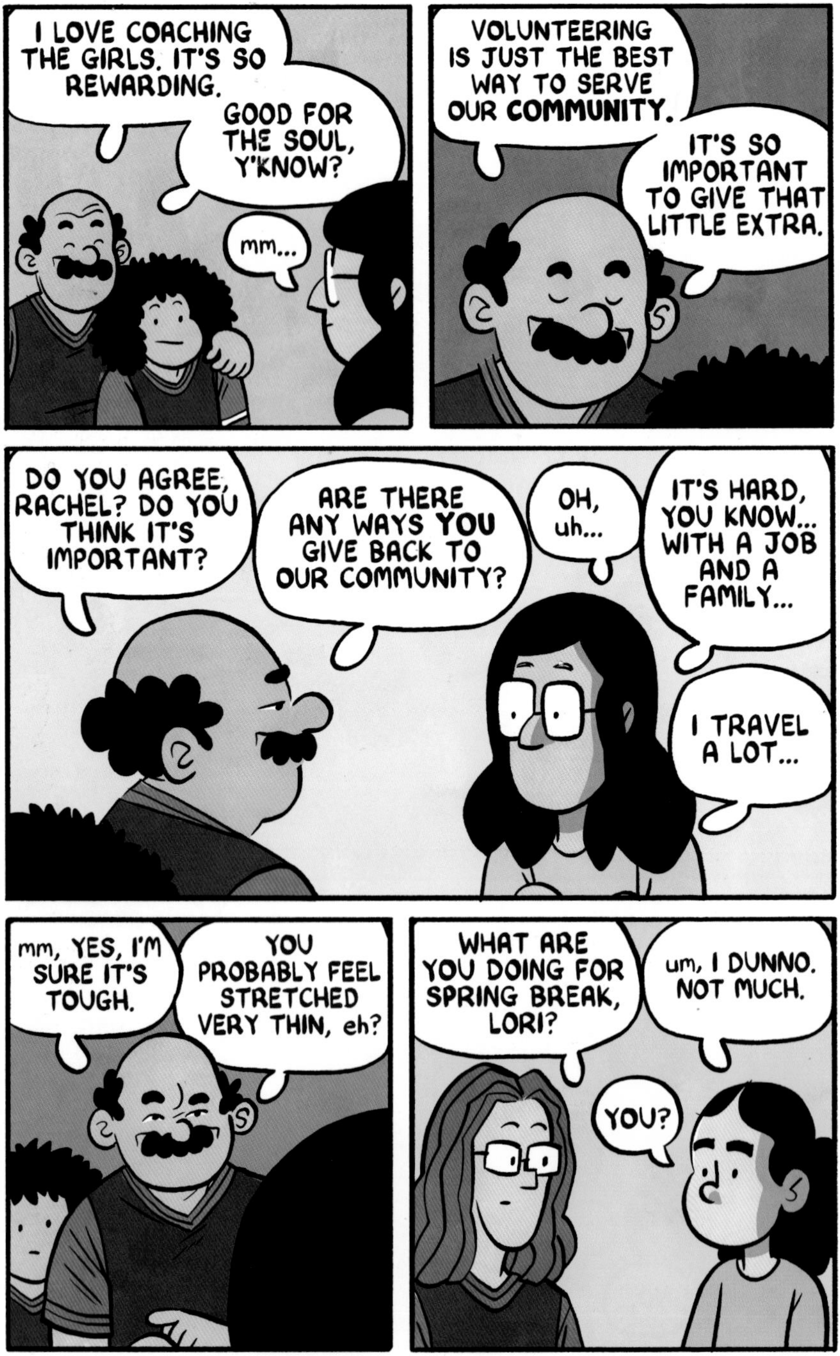
I LOVE COACHING THE GIRLS. IT'S SO REWARDING.
GOOD FOR THE SOUL, Y'KNOW?
mm...
VOLUNTEERING IS JUST THE BEST WAY TO SERVE OUR **COMMUNITY**.
IT'S SO IMPORTANT TO GIVE THAT LITTLE EXTRA.
DO YOU AGREE, RACHEL? DO YOU THINK IT'S IMPORTANT?
ARE THERE ANY WAYS **YOU** GIVE BACK TO OUR COMMUNITY?
OH, uh...
IT'S HARD, YOU KNOW... WITH A JOB AND A FAMILY...
I TRAVEL A LOT...
mm, YES, I'M SURE IT'S TOUGH.
YOU PROBABLY FEEL STRETCHED VERY THIN, eh?
WHAT ARE YOU DOING FOR SPRING BREAK, LORI?
um, I DUNNO. NOT MUCH.
YOU?

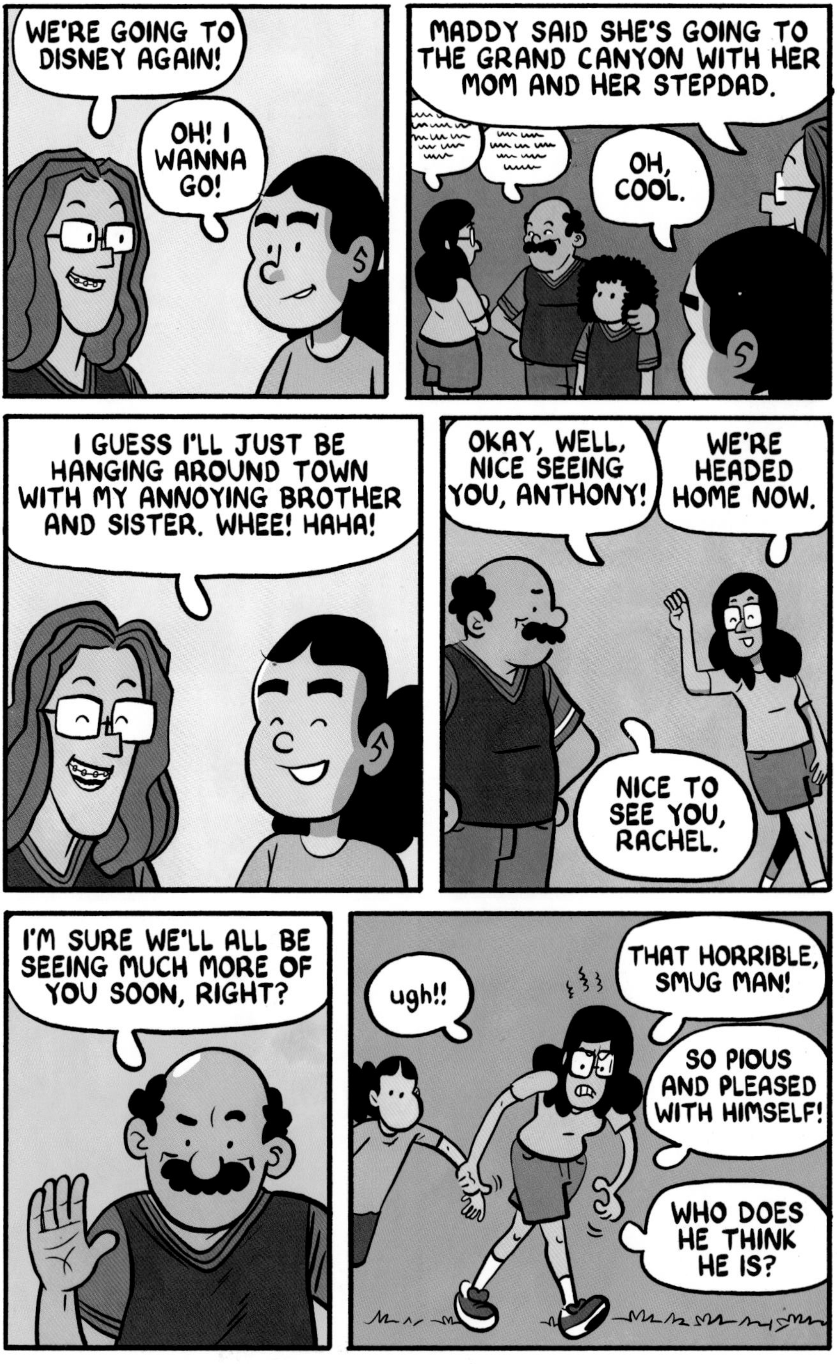
WE'RE GOING TO DISNEY AGAIN!
OH! I WANNA GO!
MADDY SAID SHE'S GOING TO THE GRAND CANYON WITH HER MOM AND HER STEPDAD.
OH, COOL.
I GUESS I'LL JUST BE HANGING AROUND TOWN WITH MY ANNOYING BROTHER AND SISTER. WHEE! HAHA!
OKAY, WELL, NICE SEEING YOU, ANTHONY!
WE'RE HEADED HOME NOW.
NICE TO SEE YOU, RACHEL.
I'M SURE WE'LL ALL BE SEEING MUCH MORE OF YOU SOON, RIGHT?
ugh!!
THAT HORRIBLE, SMUG MAN!
SO PIOUS AND PLEASED WITH HIMSELF!
WHO DOES HE THINK HE IS?

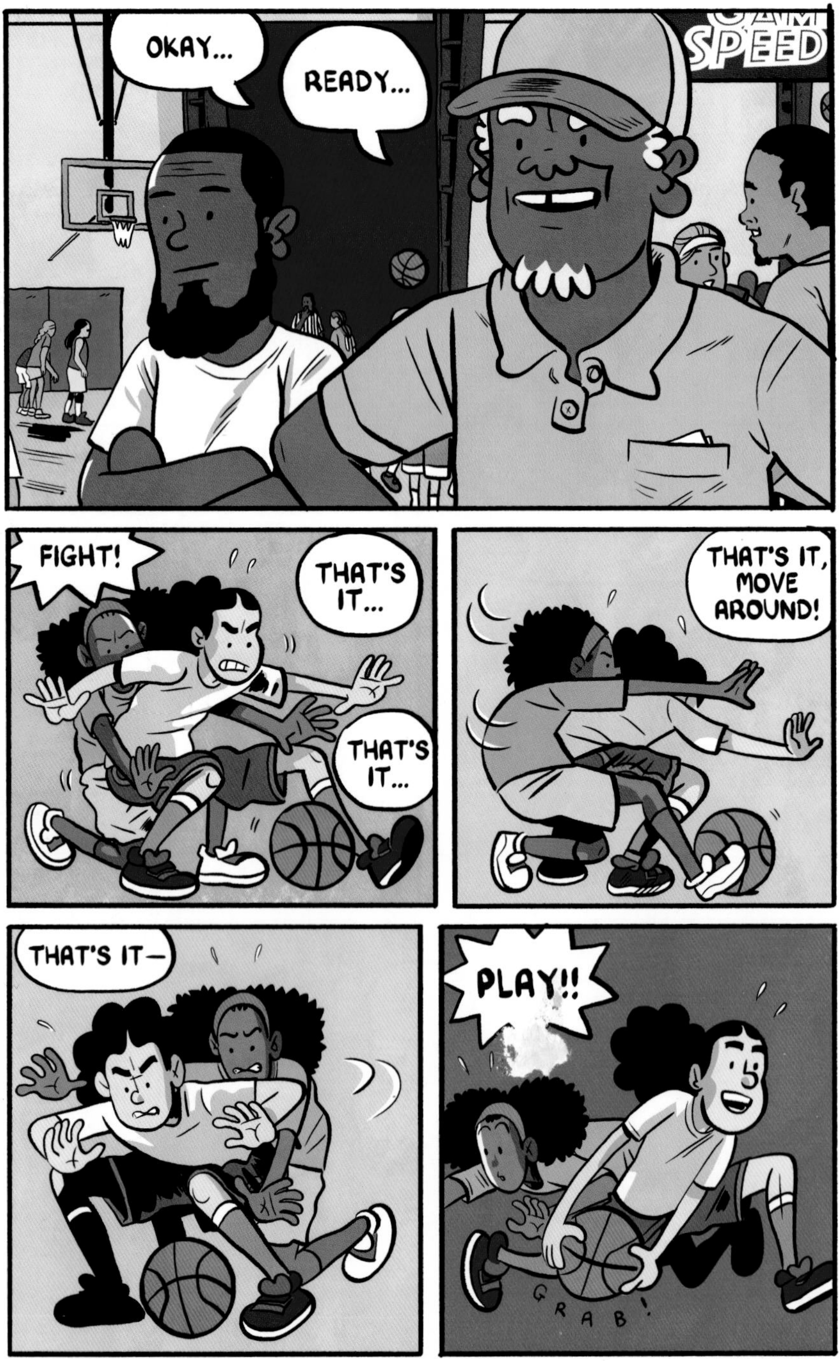
SPEED
OKAY...
READY...
FIGHT!
THAT'S IT...
THAT'S IT...
THAT'S IT, MOVE AROUND!
THAT'S IT—
PLAY!!
GRAB!

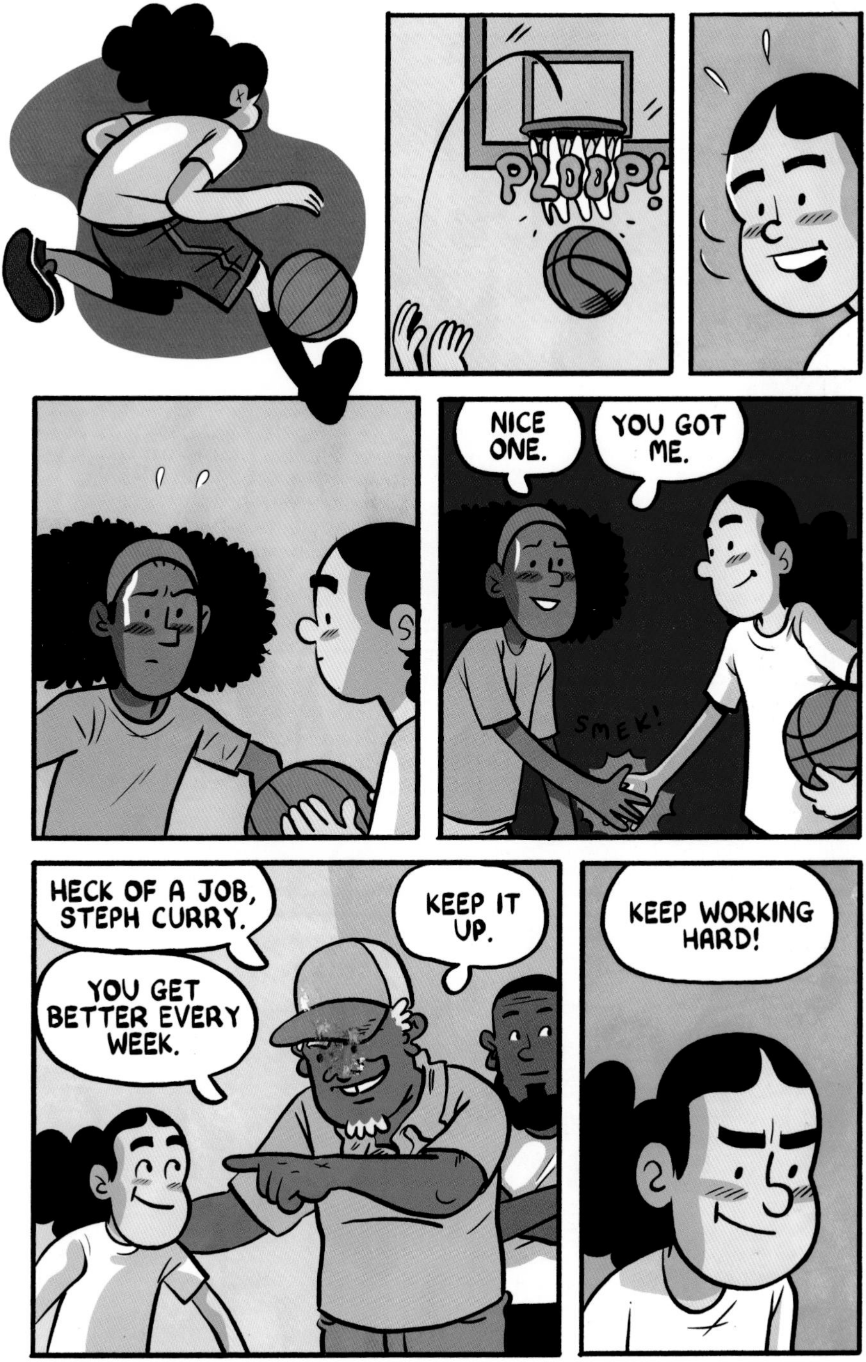
PLOOP!
NICE ONE.
YOU GOT ME.
SMEK!
HECK OF A JOB, STEPH CURRY.
YOU GET BETTER EVERY WEEK.
KEEP IT UP.
KEEP WORKING HARD!

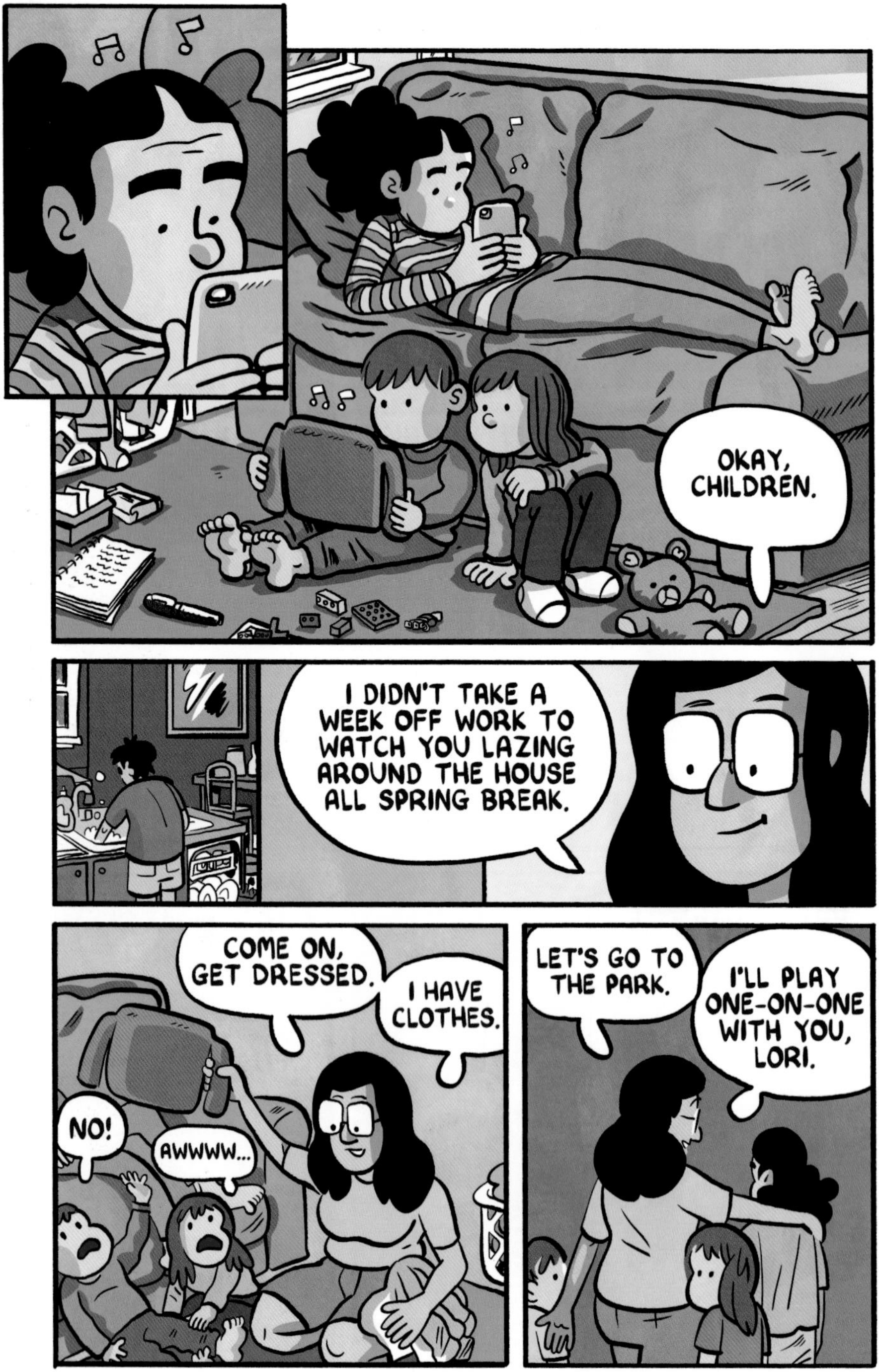
OKAY, CHILDREN.
I DIDN'T TAKE A WEEK OFF WORK TO WATCH YOU LAZING AROUND THE HOUSE ALL SPRING BREAK.
COME ON, GET DRESSED.
I HAVE CLOTHES.
NO!
AWWWW...
LET'S GO TO THE PARK.
I'LL PLAY ONE-ON-ONE WITH YOU, LORI.

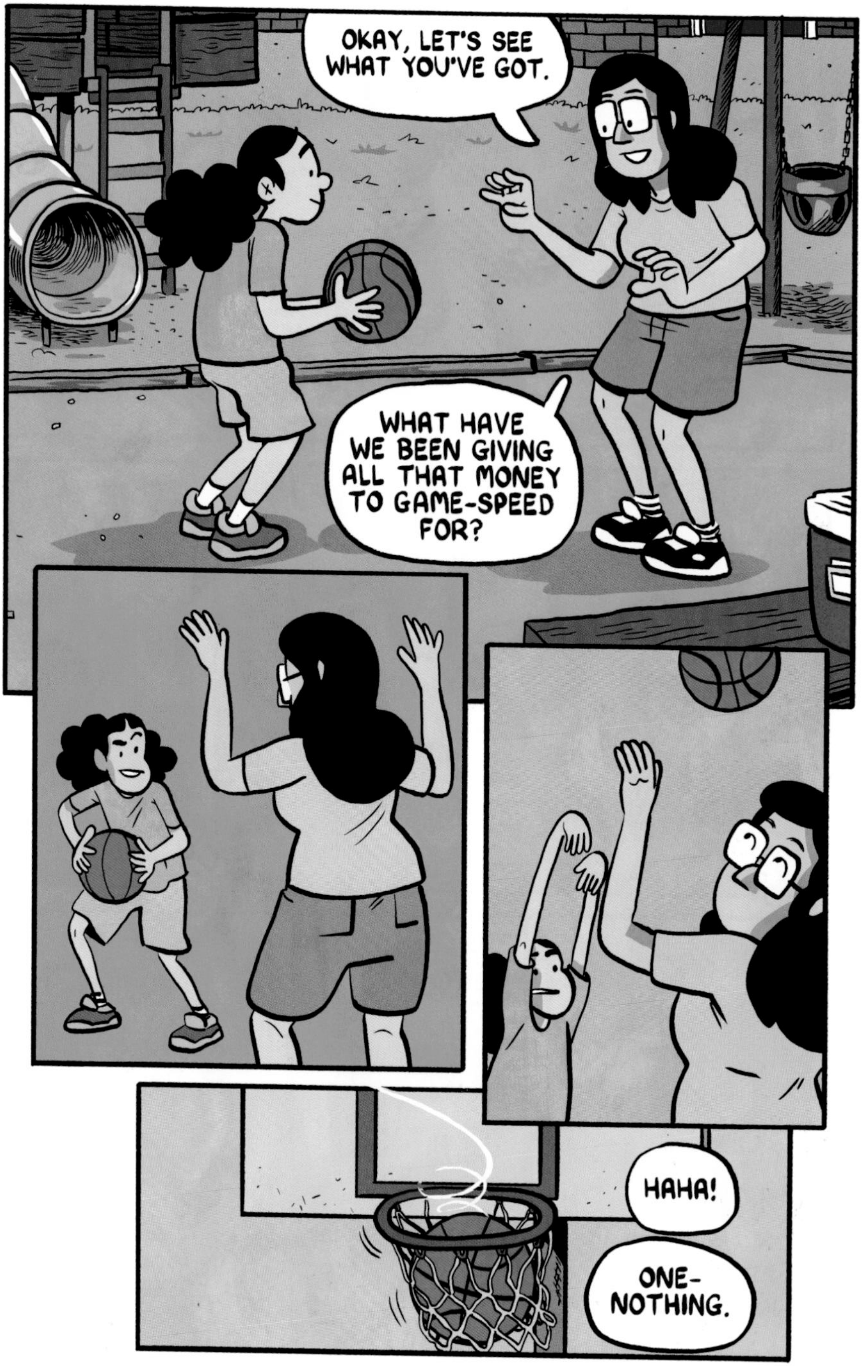
OKAY, LET'S SEE WHAT YOU'VE GOT.
WHAT HAVE WE BEEN GIVING ALL THAT MONEY TO GAME-SPEED FOR?
HAHA!
ONE-NOTHING.

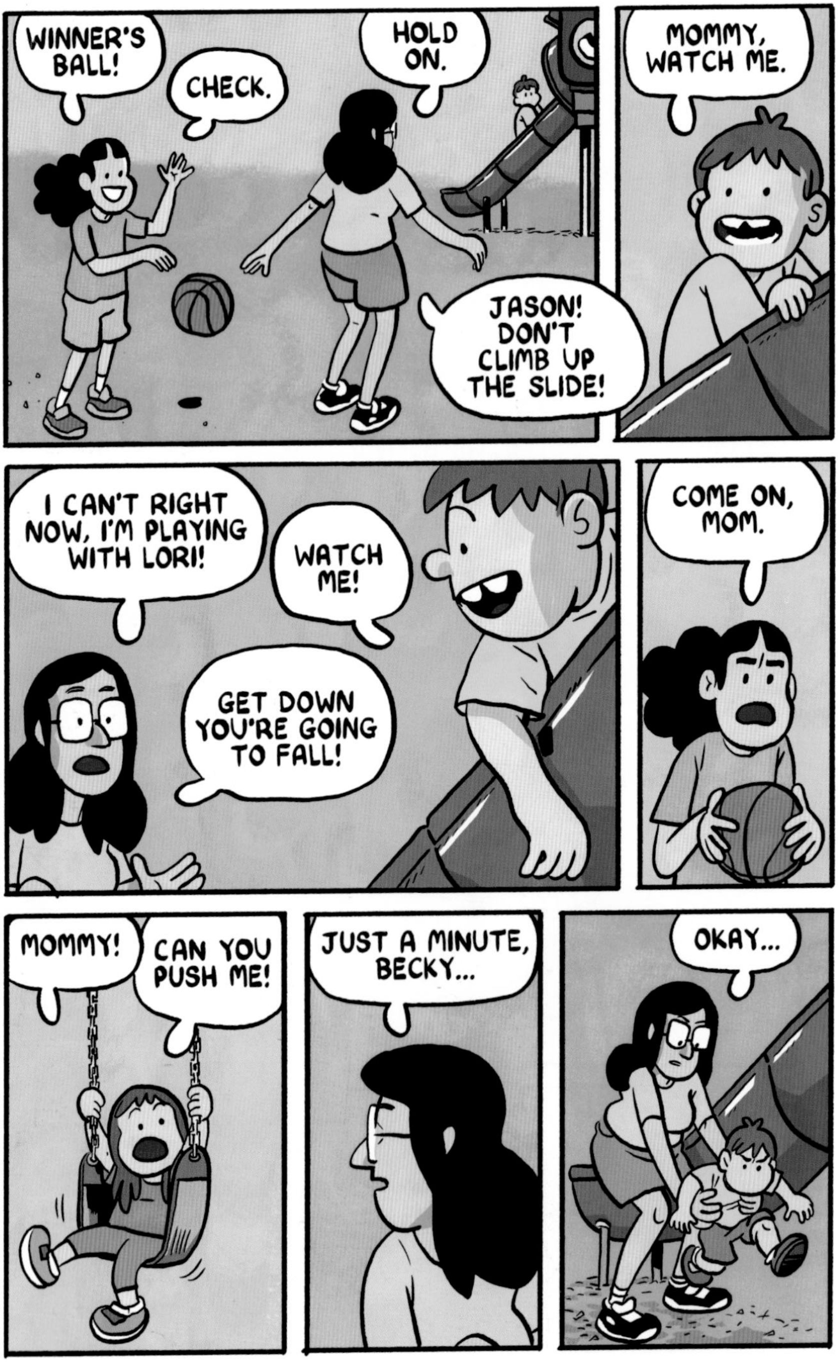
WINNER'S BALL!
CHECK.
HOLD ON.
JASON! DON'T CLIMB UP THE SLIDE!
MOMMY, WATCH ME.
I CAN'T RIGHT NOW, I'M PLAYING WITH LORI!
WATCH ME!
GET DOWN YOU'RE GOING TO FALL!
COME ON, MOM.
MOMMY!
CAN YOU PUSH ME!
JUST A MINUTE, BECKY...
OKAY...

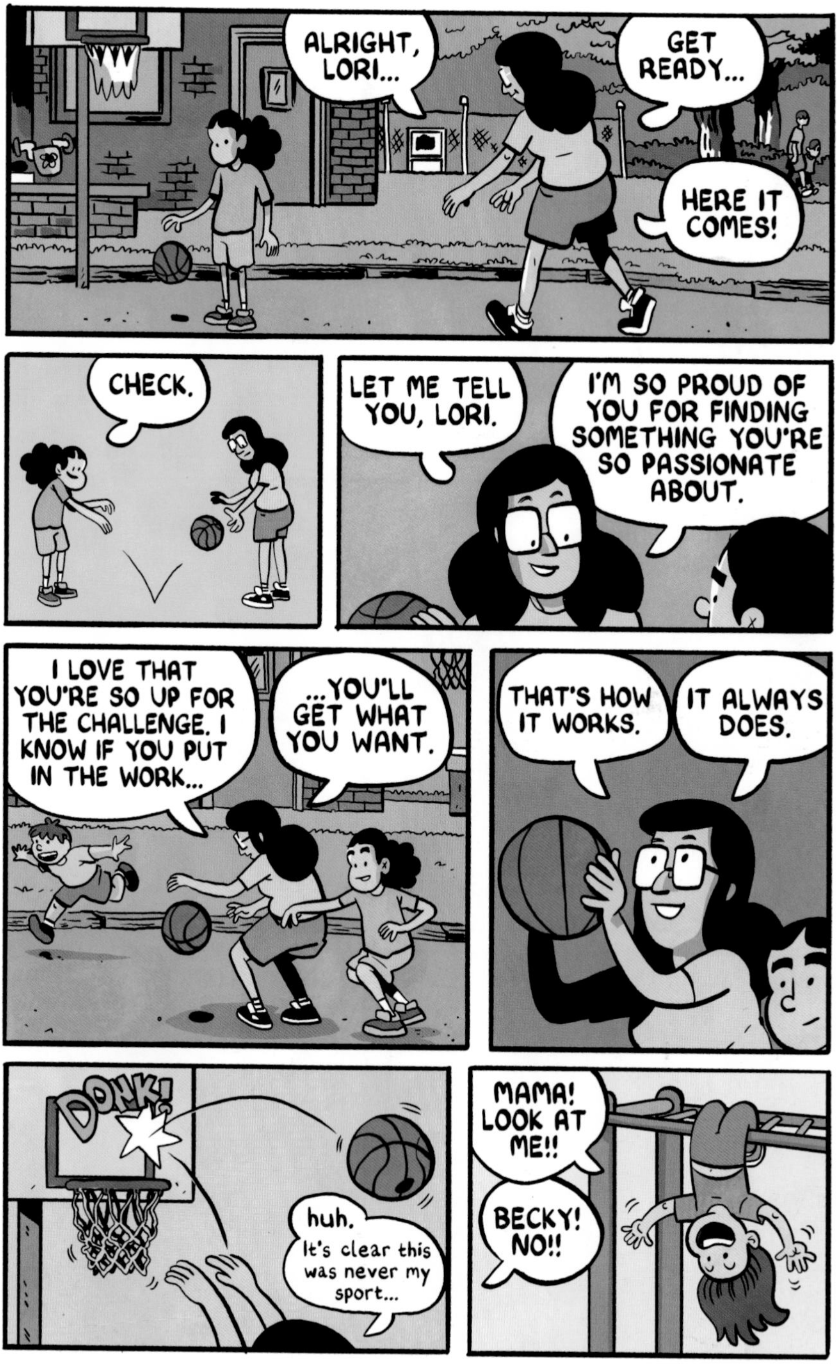
ALRIGHT, LORI...
GET READY...
HERE IT COMES!
CHECK.
LET ME TELL YOU, LORI.
I'M SO PROUD OF YOU FOR FINDING SOMETHING YOU'RE SO PASSIONATE ABOUT.
I LOVE THAT YOU'RE SO UP FOR THE CHALLENGE. I KNOW IF YOU PUT IN THE WORK...
...YOU'LL GET WHAT YOU WANT.
THAT'S HOW IT WORKS.
IT ALWAYS DOES.
DONK!
huh.
It's clear this was never my sport...
MAMA! LOOK AT ME!!
BECKY! NO!!

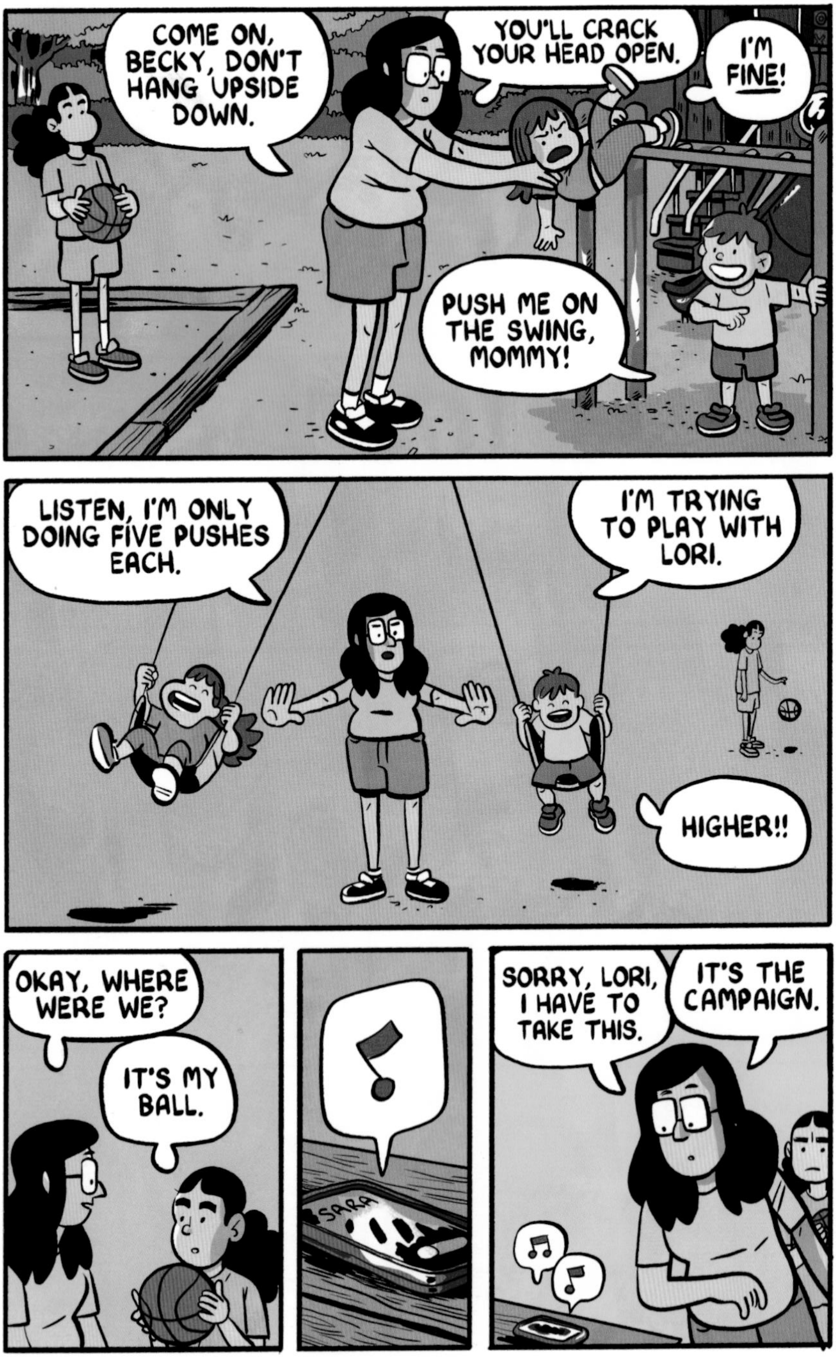
COME ON, BECKY, DON'T HANG UPSIDE DOWN.
YOU'LL CRACK YOUR HEAD OPEN.
I'M FINE!
PUSH ME ON THE SWING, MOMMY!
LISTEN, I'M ONLY DOING FIVE PUSHES EACH.
I'M TRYING TO PLAY WITH LORI.
HIGHER!!
OKAY, WHERE WERE WE?
IT'S MY BALL.
SARA
SORRY, LORI, I HAVE TO TAKE THIS.
IT'S THE CAMPAIGN.

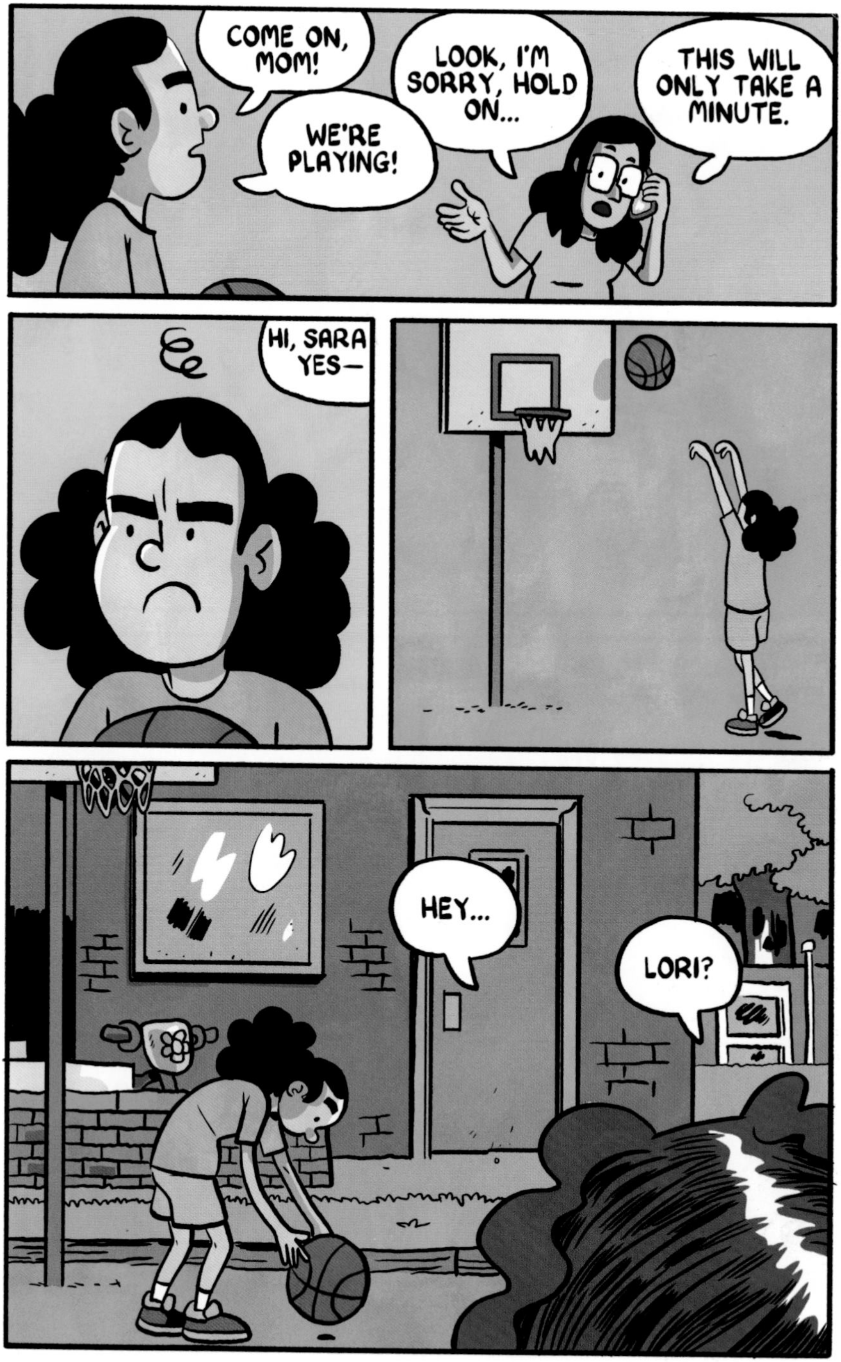
COME ON, MOM!
WE'RE PLAYING!
LOOK, I'M SORRY, HOLD ON...
THIS WILL ONLY TAKE A MINUTE.
HI, SARA YES—
HEY...
LORI?

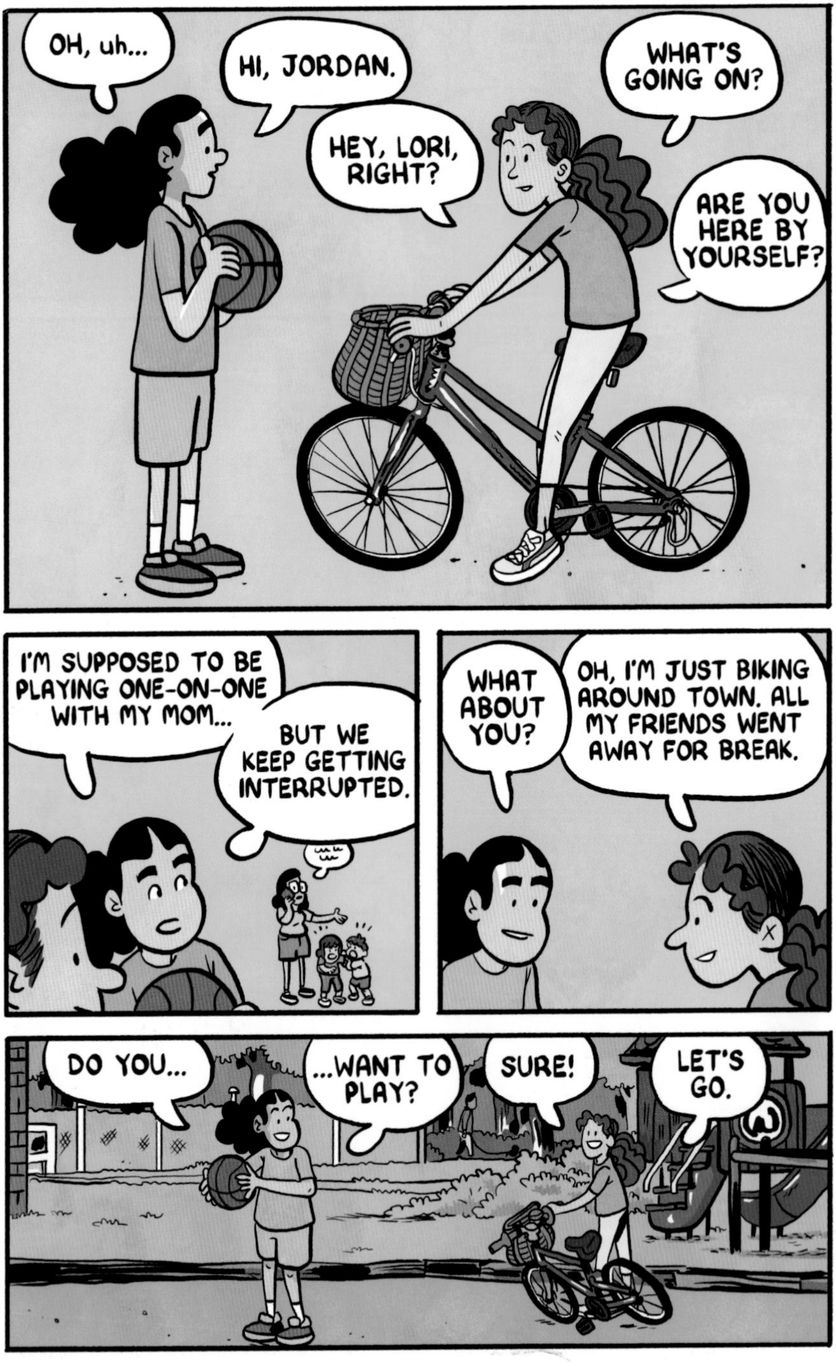
OH, uh...
HI, JORDAN.
HEY, LORI, RIGHT?
WHAT'S GOING ON?
ARE YOU HERE BY YOURSELF?
I'M SUPPOSED TO BE PLAYING ONE-ON-ONE WITH MY MOM...
BUT WE KEEP GETTING INTERRUPTED.
WHAT ABOUT YOU?
OH, I'M JUST BIKING AROUND TOWN. ALL MY FRIENDS WENT AWAY FOR BREAK.
DO YOU...
...WANT TO PLAY?
SURE!
LET'S GO.

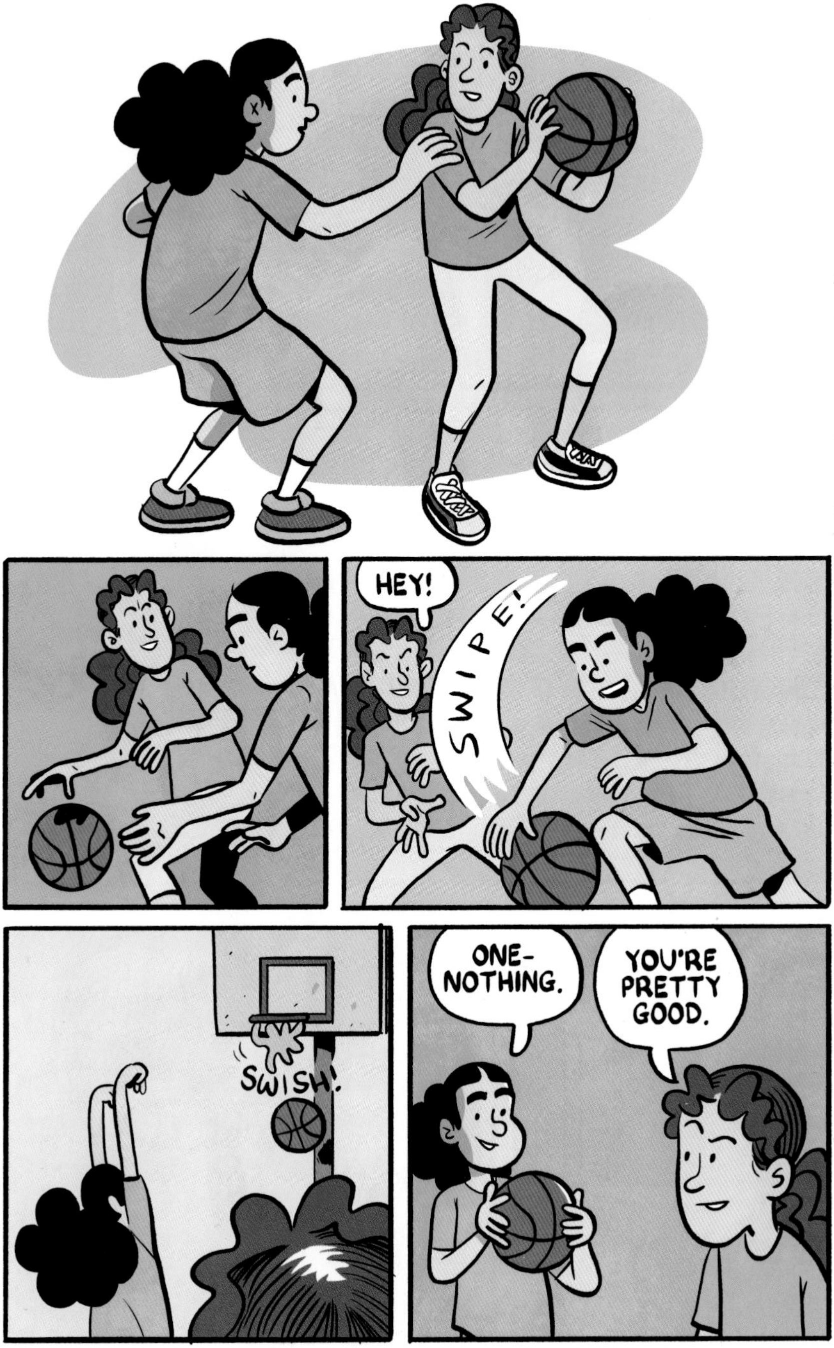
HEY!
SWIPE!
SWISH!
ONE-NOTHING.
YOU'RE PRETTY GOOD.

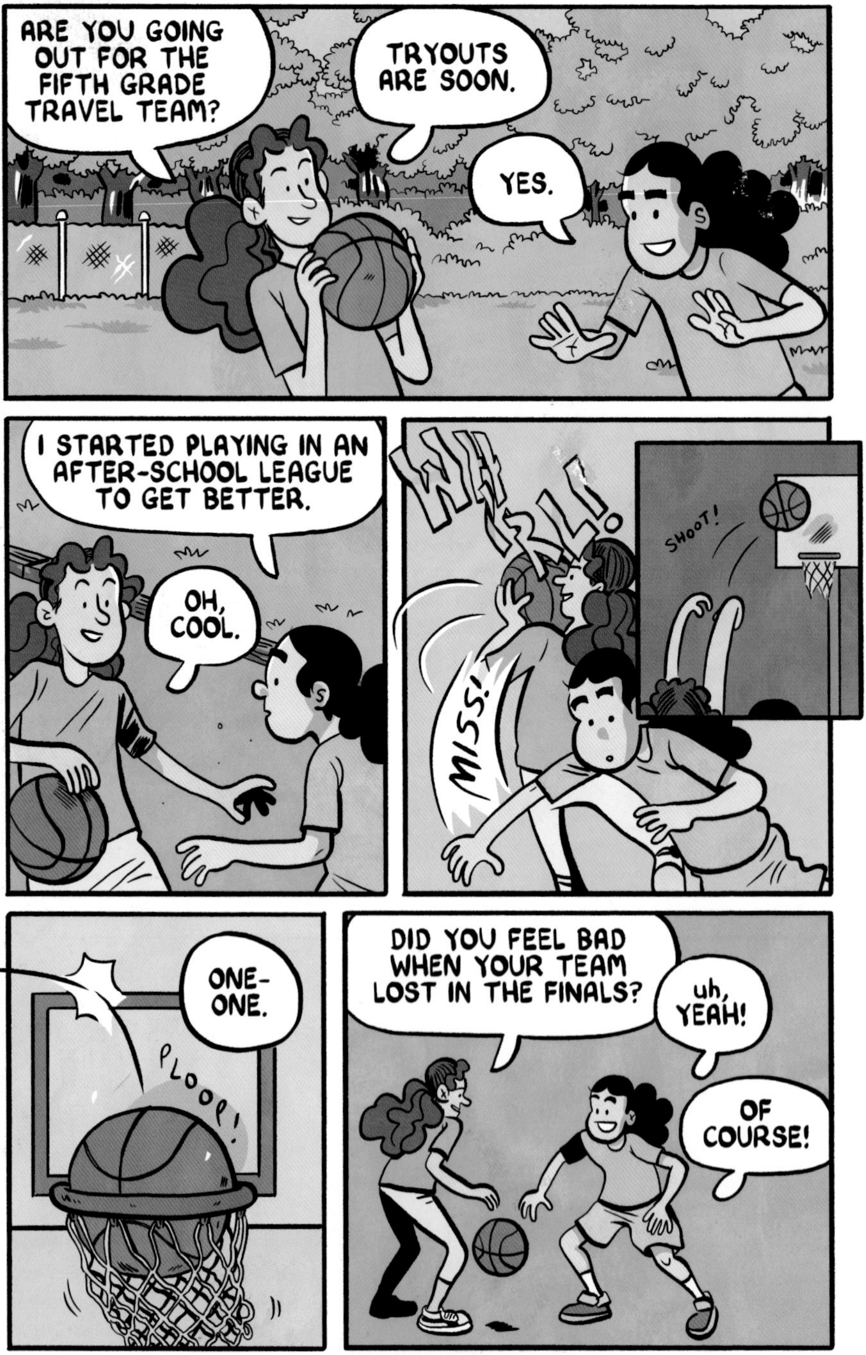
ARE YOU GOING OUT FOR THE FIFTH GRADE TRAVEL TEAM?
TRYOUTS ARE SOON.
YES.
I STARTED PLAYING IN AN AFTER-SCHOOL LEAGUE TO GET BETTER.
OH, COOL.
WHIRL!
SHOOT!
MISS!
ONE-ONE.
PLOOP!
DID YOU FEEL BAD WHEN YOUR TEAM LOST IN THE FINALS?
uh, YEAH!
OF COURSE!

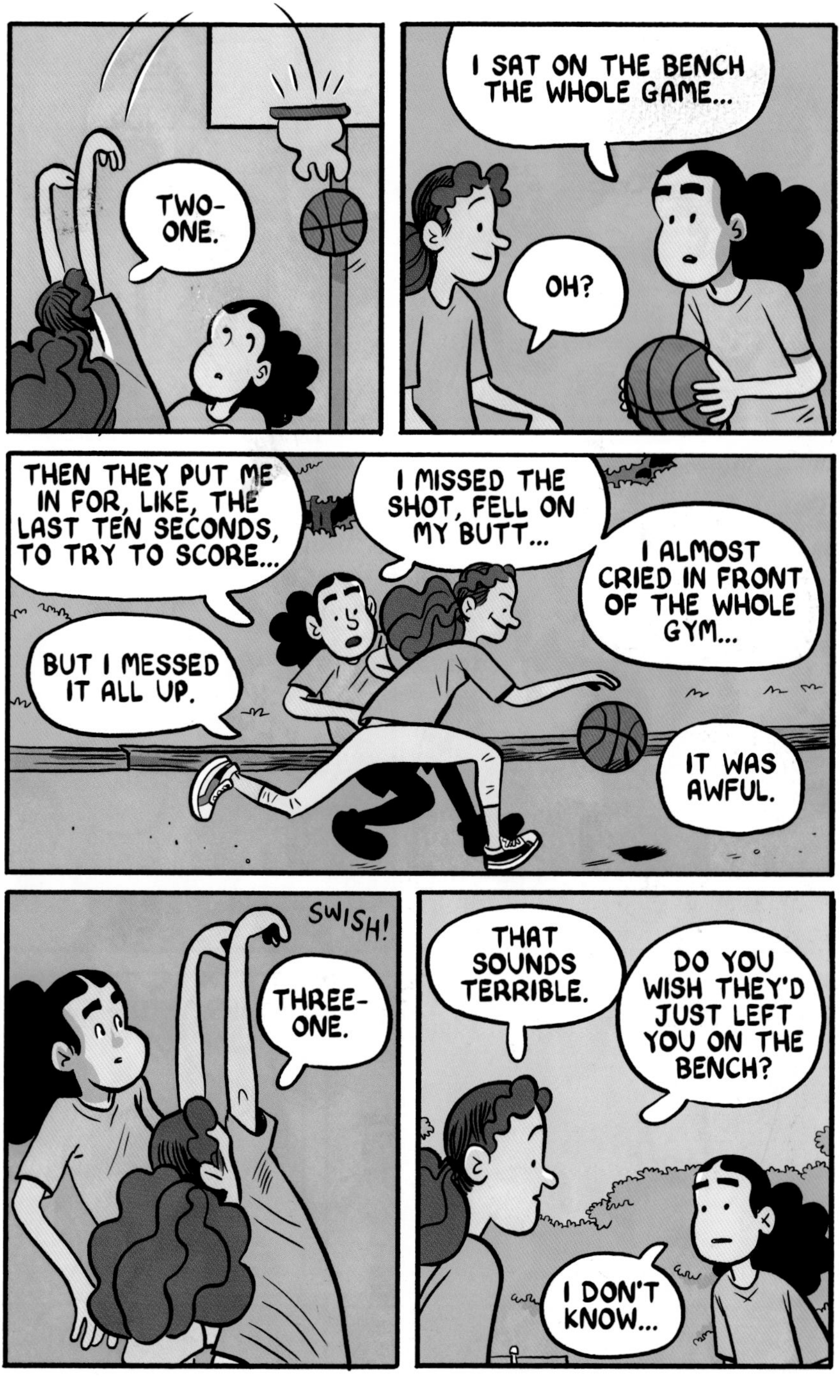
TWO-ONE.
I SAT ON THE BENCH THE WHOLE GAME...
OH?
THEN THEY PUT ME IN FOR, LIKE, THE LAST TEN SECONDS, TO TRY TO SCORE...
I MISSED THE SHOT, FELL ON MY BUTT...
I ALMOST CRIED IN FRONT OF THE WHOLE GYM...
BUT I MESSED IT ALL UP.
IT WAS AWFUL.
SWISH!
THREE-ONE.
THAT SOUNDS TERRIBLE.
DO YOU WISH THEY'D JUST LEFT YOU ON THE BENCH?
I DON'T KNOW...

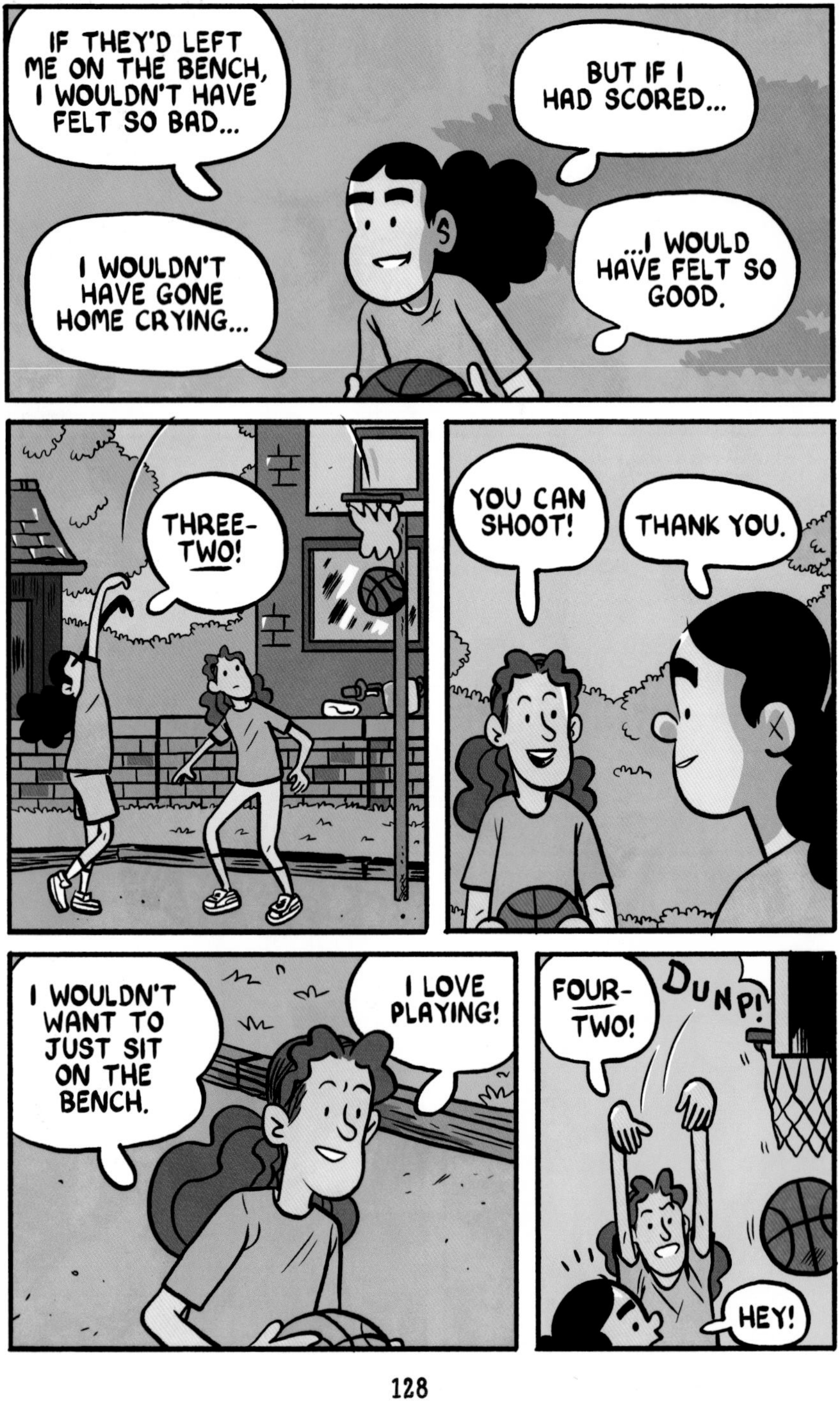
IF THEY'D LEFT ME ON THE BENCH, I WOULDN'T HAVE FELT SO BAD...
I WOULDN'T HAVE GONE HOME CRYING...
BUT IF I HAD SCORED...
...I WOULD HAVE FELT SO GOOD.
THREE-TWO!
YOU CAN SHOOT!
THANK YOU.
I WOULDN'T WANT TO JUST SIT ON THE BENCH.
I LOVE PLAYING!
FOUR-TWO!
DUNP!
HEY!

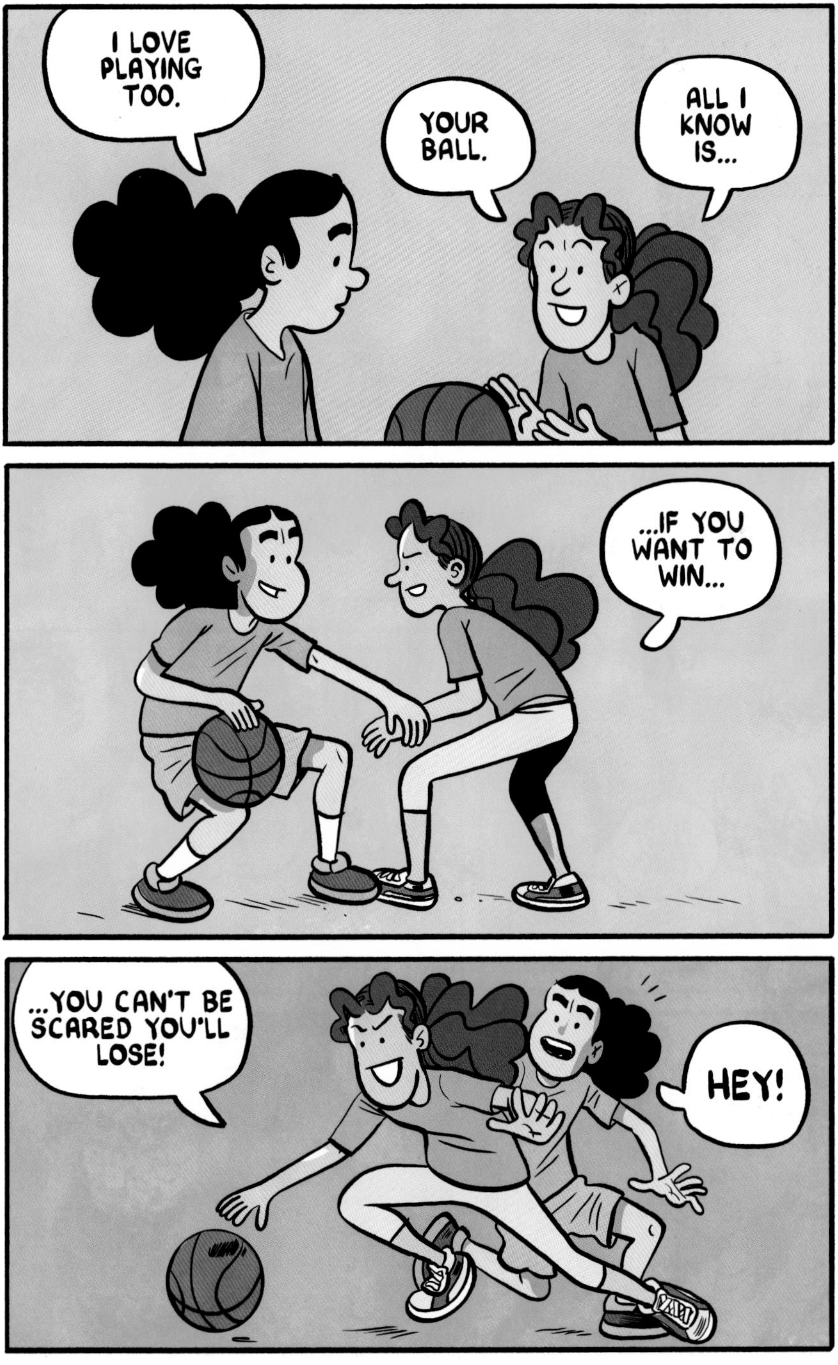
I LOVE PLAYING TOO.
ALL I KNOW IS...
YOUR BALL.
...IF YOU WANT TO WIN...
...YOU CAN'T BE SCARED YOU'LL LOSE!
HEY!

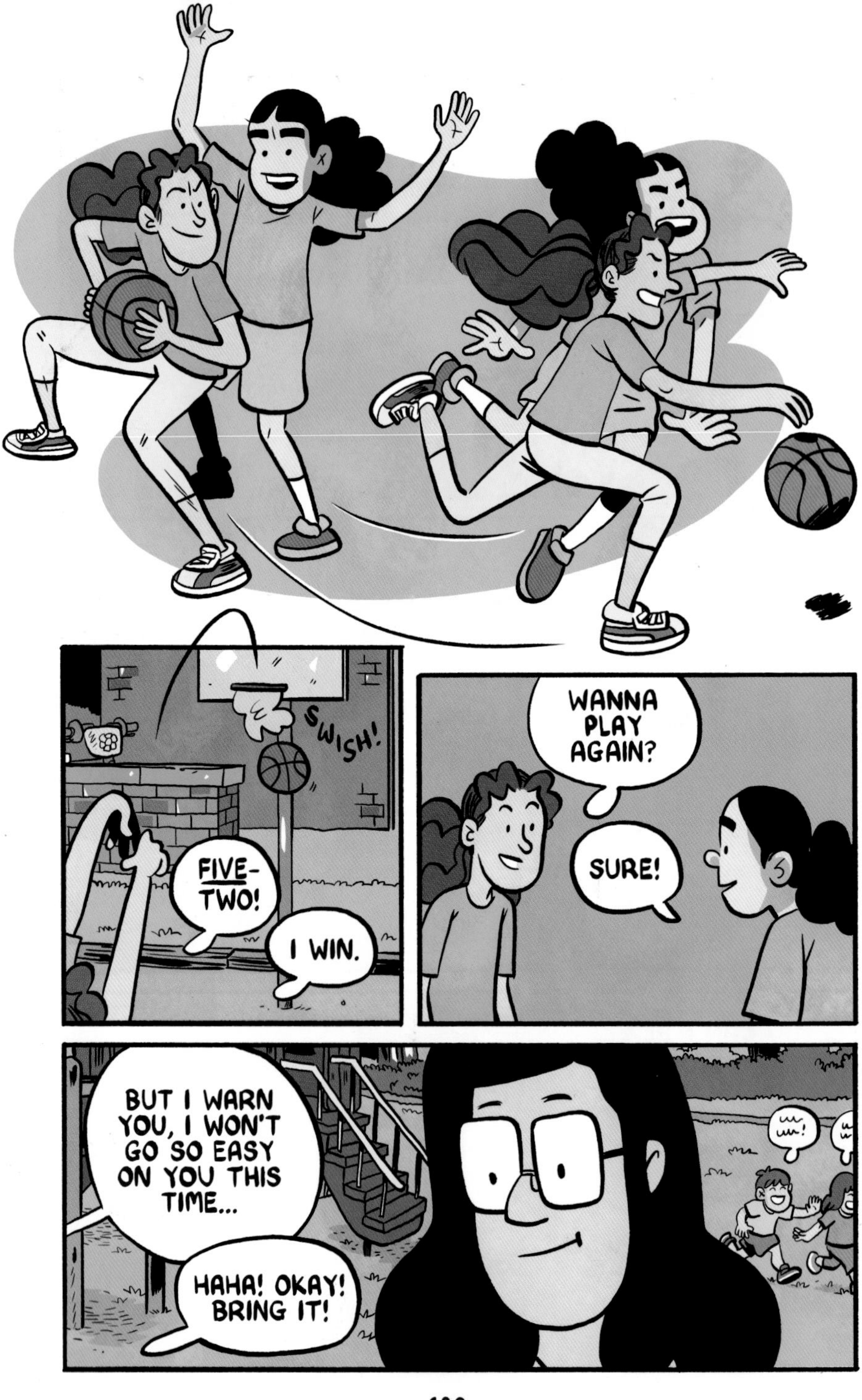
SWISH!
FIVE-TWO!
I WIN.
WANNA PLAY AGAIN?
SURE!
BUT I WARN YOU, I WON'T GO SO EASY ON YOU THIS TIME...
HAHA! OKAY! BRING IT!

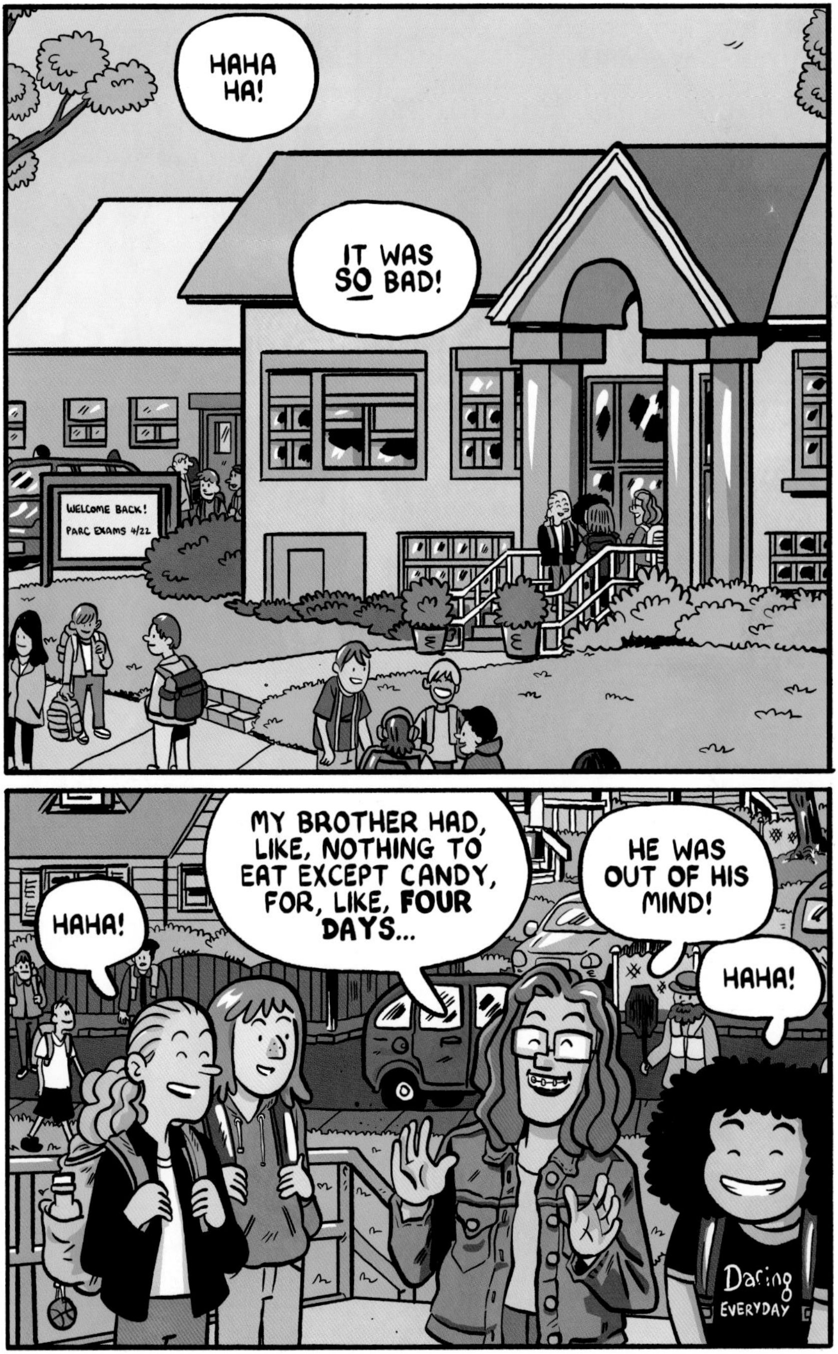
HAHA HA!
IT WAS SO BAD!
WELCOME BACK!
PARC EXAMS 4/22
HAHA!
MY BROTHER HAD, LIKE, NOTHING TO EAT EXCEPT CANDY, FOR, LIKE, **FOUR DAYS**...
HE WAS OUT OF HIS MIND!
HAHA!
Daring EVERYDAY

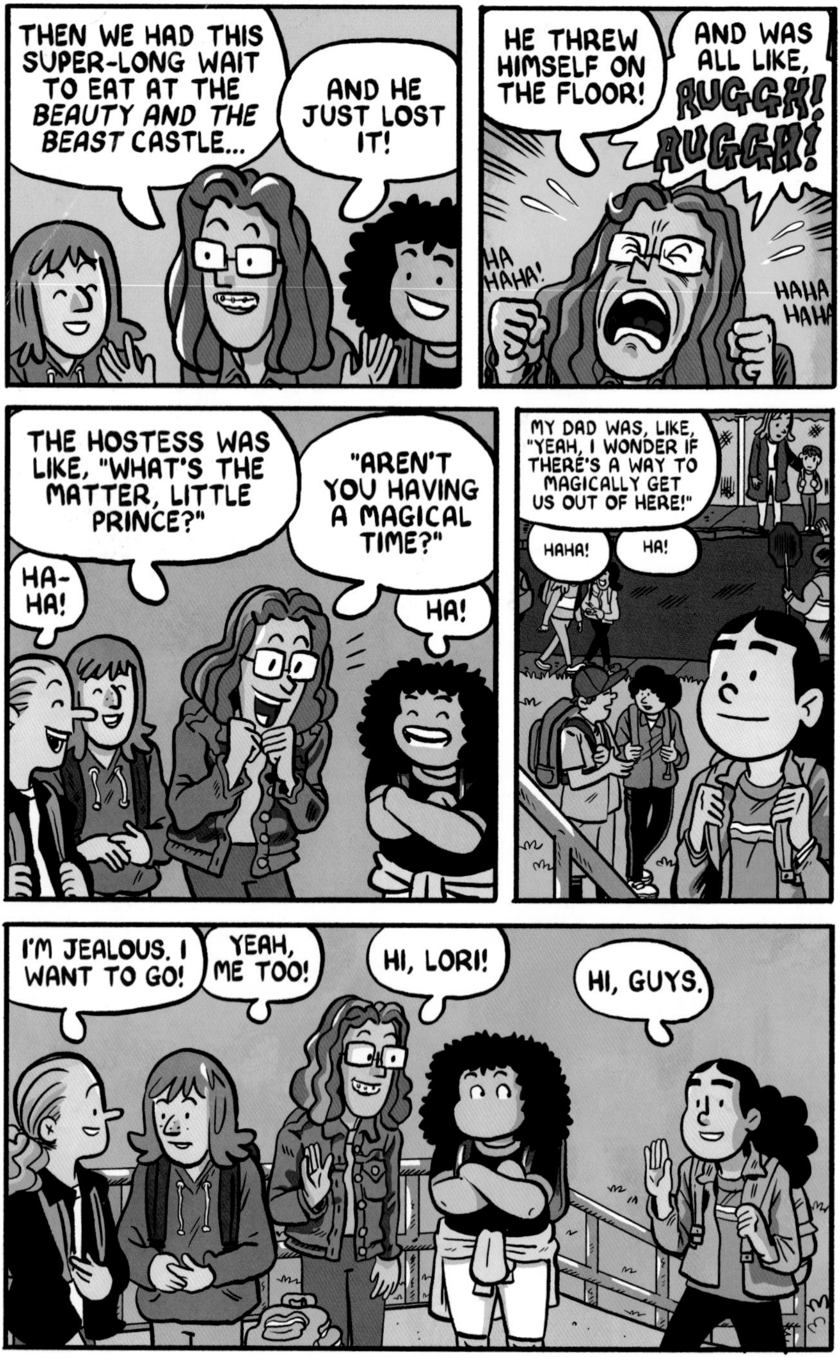
THEN WE HAD THIS SUPER-LONG WAIT TO EAT AT THE *BEAUTY AND THE BEAST* CASTLE...
AND HE JUST LOST IT!
HE THREW HIMSELF ON THE FLOOR!
AND WAS ALL LIKE, RUGGH! AUGGH!
HA HAHA!
HAHA HAHA
THE HOSTESS WAS LIKE, "WHAT'S THE MATTER, LITTLE PRINCE?"
"AREN'T YOU HAVING A MAGICAL TIME?"
HA-HA!
HA!
MY DAD WAS, LIKE, "YEAH, I WONDER IF THERE'S A WAY TO MAGICALLY GET US OUT OF HERE!"
HAHA!
HA!
I'M JEALOUS. I WANT TO GO!
YEAH, ME TOO!
HI, LORI!
HI, GUYS.

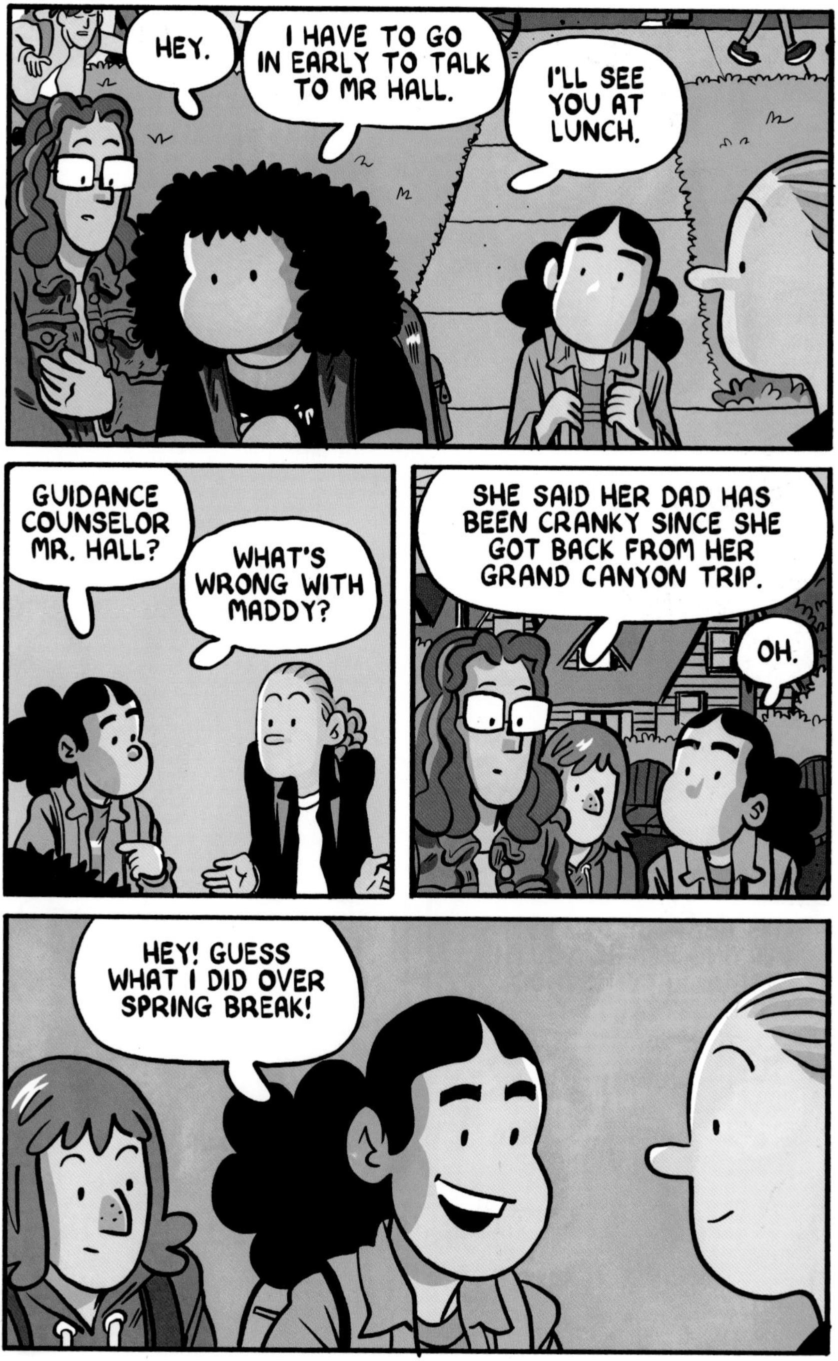
HEY.
I HAVE TO GO IN EARLY TO TALK TO MR HALL.
I'LL SEE YOU AT LUNCH.
GUIDANCE COUNSELOR MR. HALL?
WHAT'S WRONG WITH MADDY?
SHE SAID HER DAD HAS BEEN CRANKY SINCE SHE GOT BACK FROM HER GRAND CANYON TRIP.
OH.
HEY! GUESS WHAT I DID OVER SPRING BREAK!

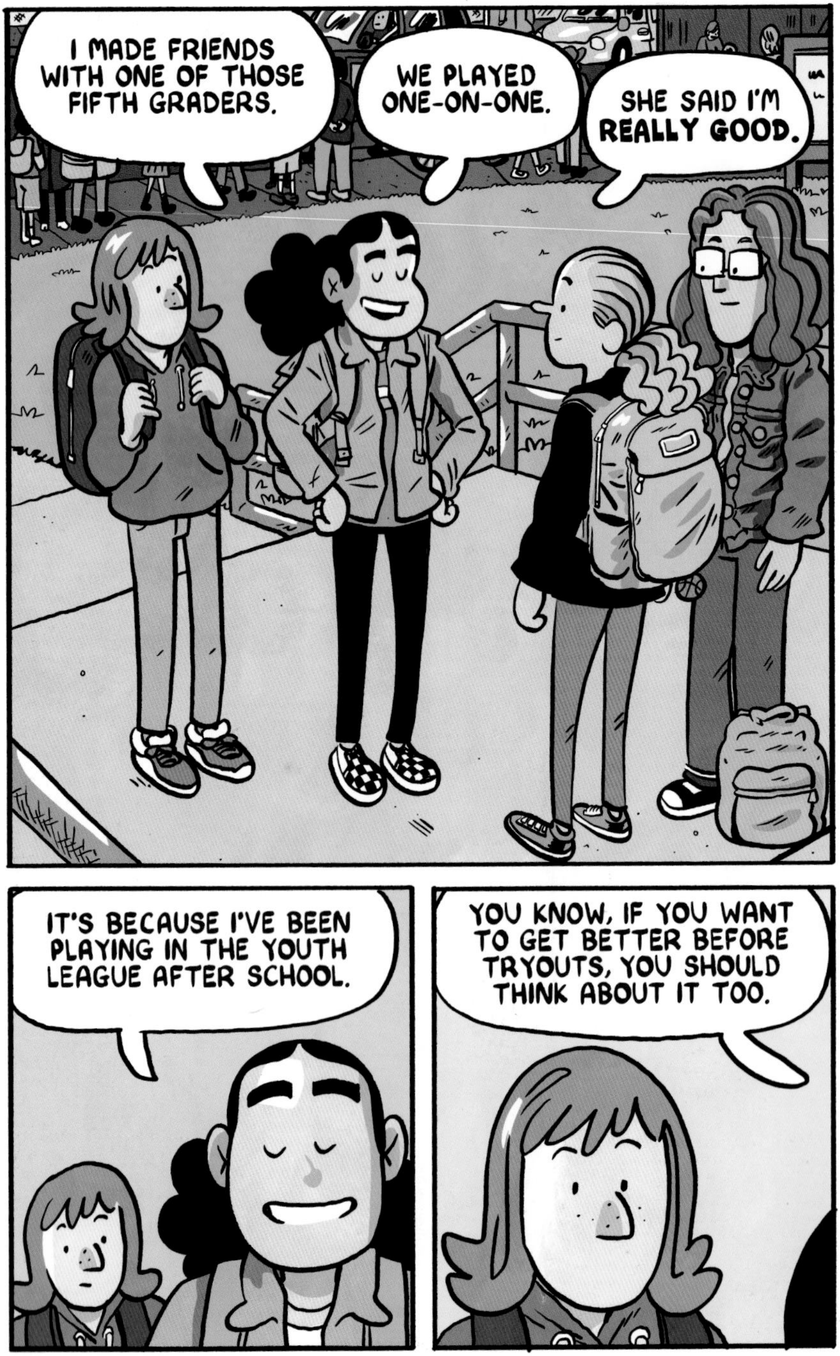
I MADE FRIENDS WITH ONE OF THOSE FIFTH GRADERS.
WE PLAYED ONE-ON-ONE.
SHE SAID I'M **REALLY GOOD.**
IT'S BECAUSE I'VE BEEN PLAYING IN THE YOUTH LEAGUE AFTER SCHOOL.
YOU KNOW, IF YOU WANT TO GET BETTER BEFORE TRYOUTS, YOU SHOULD THINK ABOUT IT TOO.

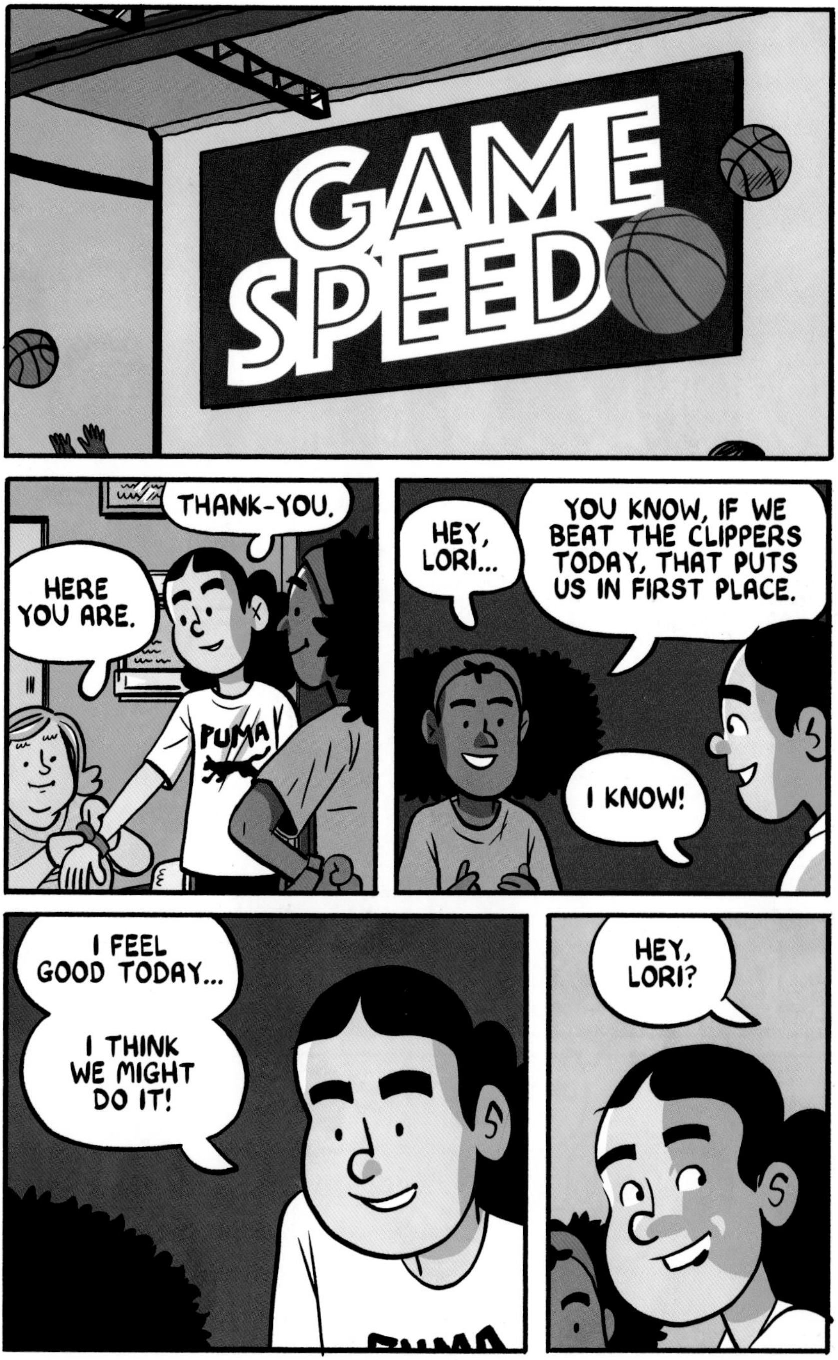
GAME SPEED
THANK-YOU.
HERE YOU ARE.
PUMA
HEY, LORI...
YOU KNOW, IF WE BEAT THE CLIPPERS TODAY, THAT PUTS US IN FIRST PLACE.
I KNOW!
I FEEL GOOD TODAY...
I THINK WE MIGHT DO IT!
HEY, LORI?

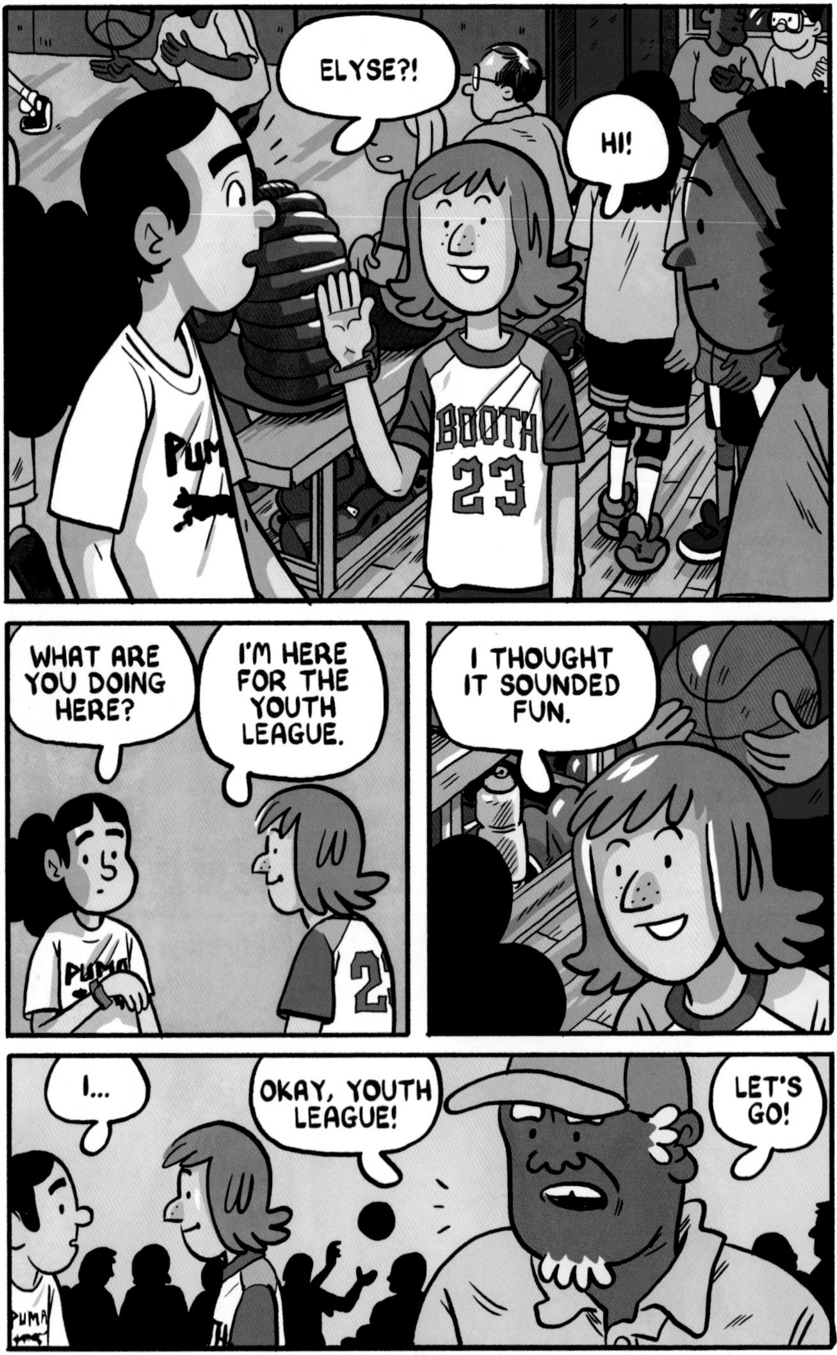
ELYSE?!
HI!
BOOTH 23
PUMA
WHAT ARE YOU DOING HERE?
I'M HERE FOR THE YOUTH LEAGUE.
I THOUGHT IT SOUNDED FUN.
I...
OKAY, YOUTH LEAGUE!
LET'S GO!

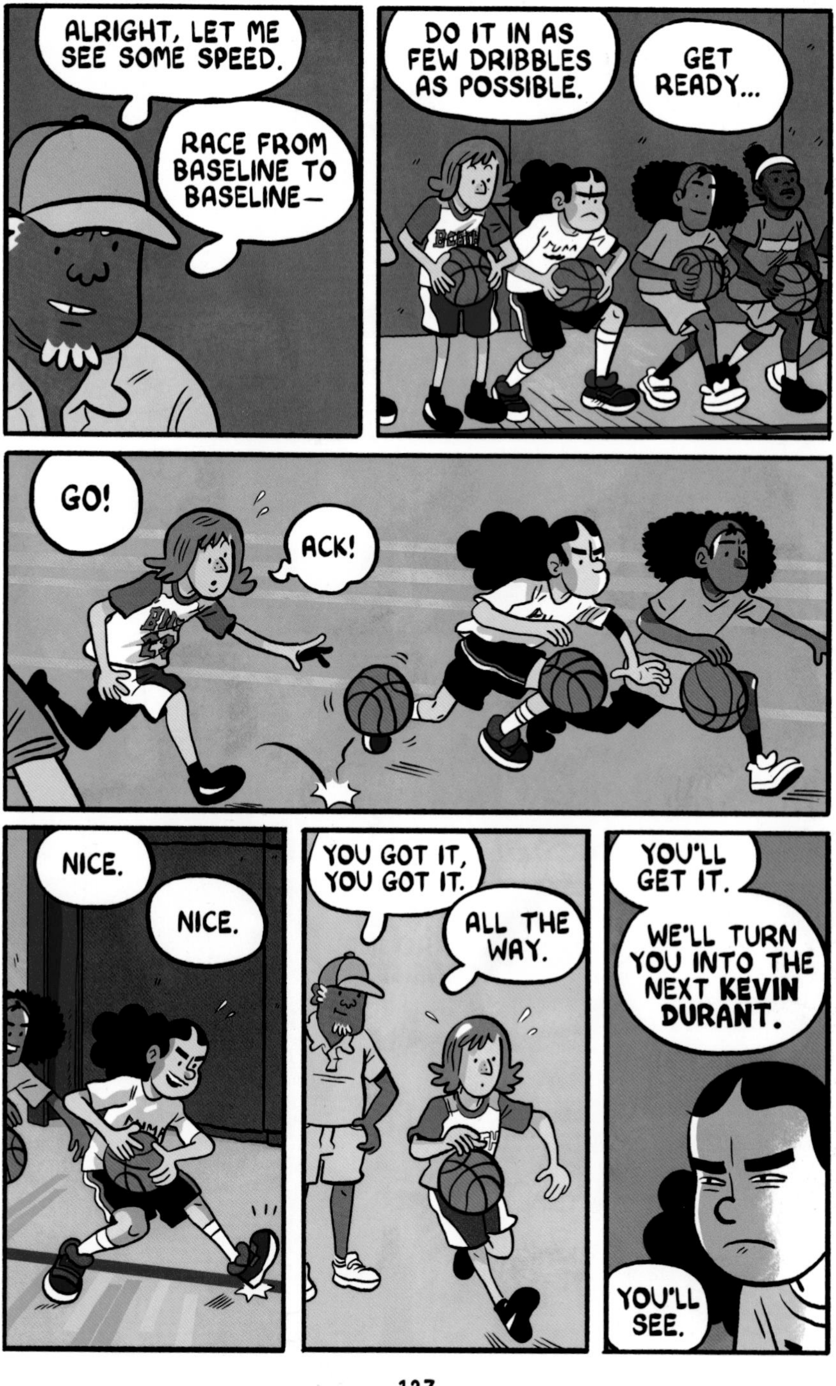
ALRIGHT, LET ME SEE SOME SPEED.
RACE FROM BASELINE TO BASELINE—
DO IT IN AS FEW DRIBBLES AS POSSIBLE.
GET READY...
GO!
ACK!
NICE.
NICE.
YOU GOT IT, YOU GOT IT.
ALL THE WAY.
YOU'LL GET IT.
WE'LL TURN YOU INTO THE NEXT **KEVIN DURANT**.
YOU'LL SEE.

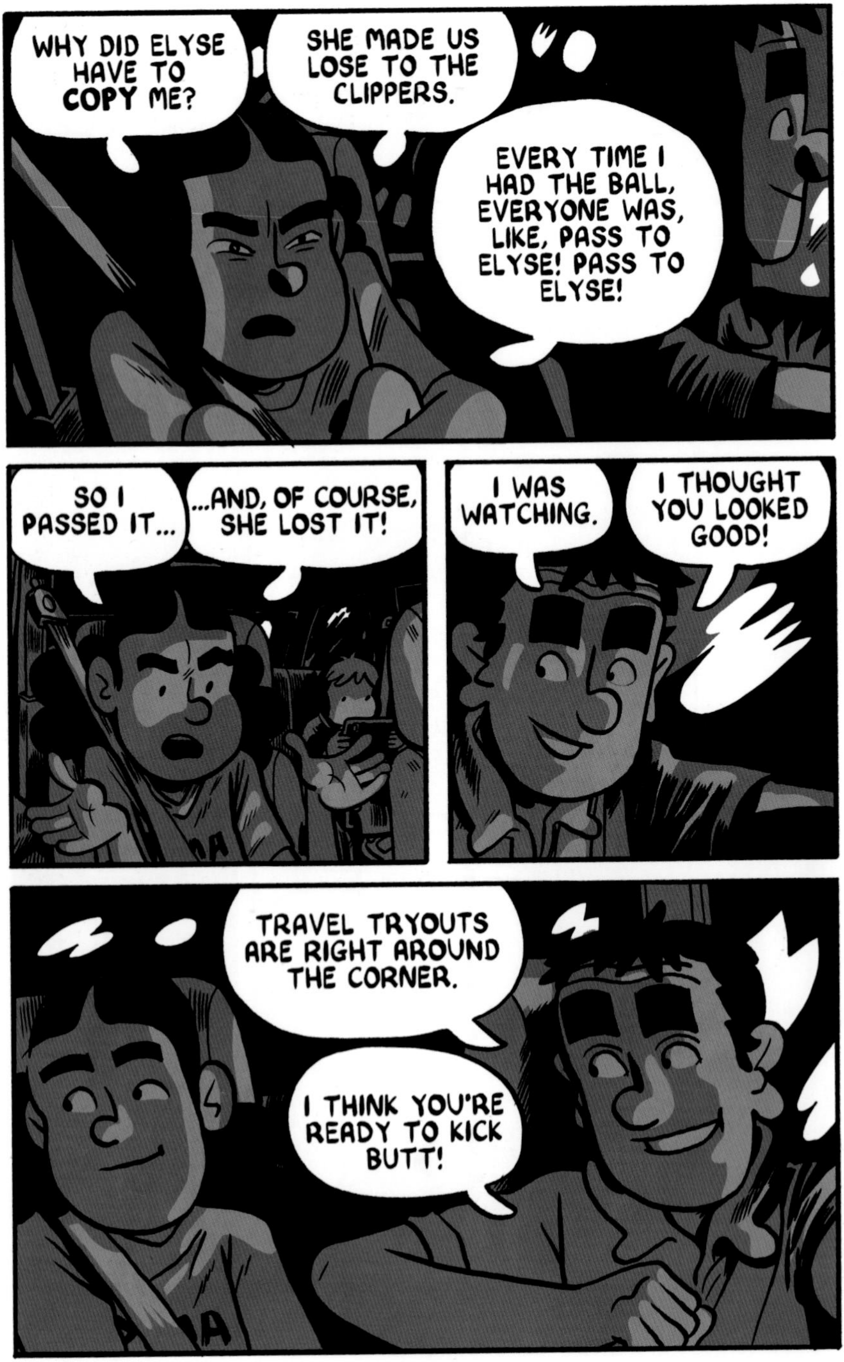
WHY DID ELYSE HAVE TO COPY ME?
SHE MADE US LOSE TO THE CLIPPERS.
EVERY TIME I HAD THE BALL, EVERYONE WAS, LIKE, PASS TO ELYSE! PASS TO ELYSE!
SO I PASSED IT...
...AND, OF COURSE, SHE LOST IT!
I WAS WATCHING.
I THOUGHT YOU LOOKED GOOD!
TRAVEL TRYOUTS ARE RIGHT AROUND THE CORNER.
I THINK YOU'RE READY TO KICK BUTT!

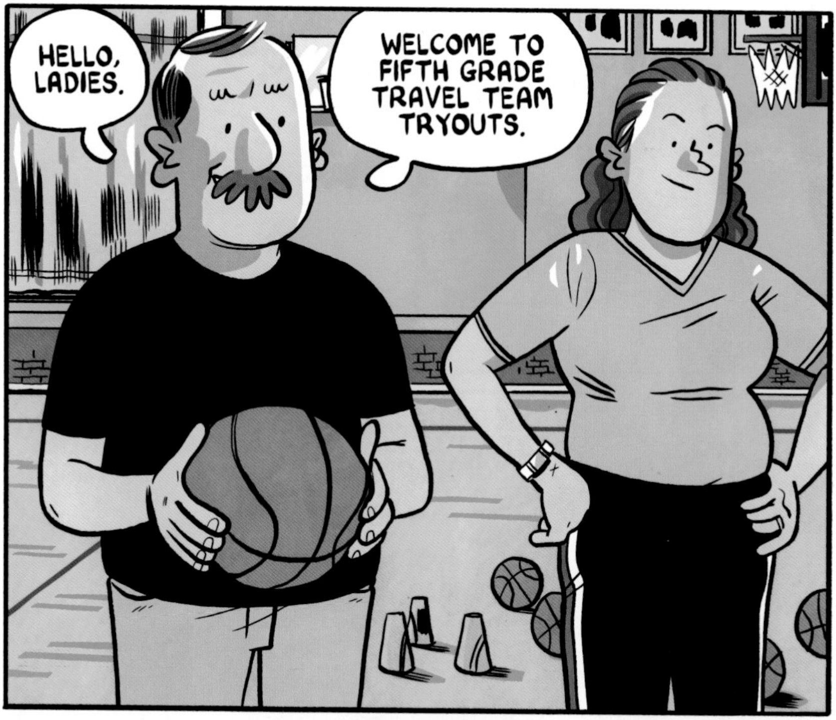
HELLO, LADIES.
WELCOME TO FIFTH GRADE TRAVEL TEAM TRYOUTS.

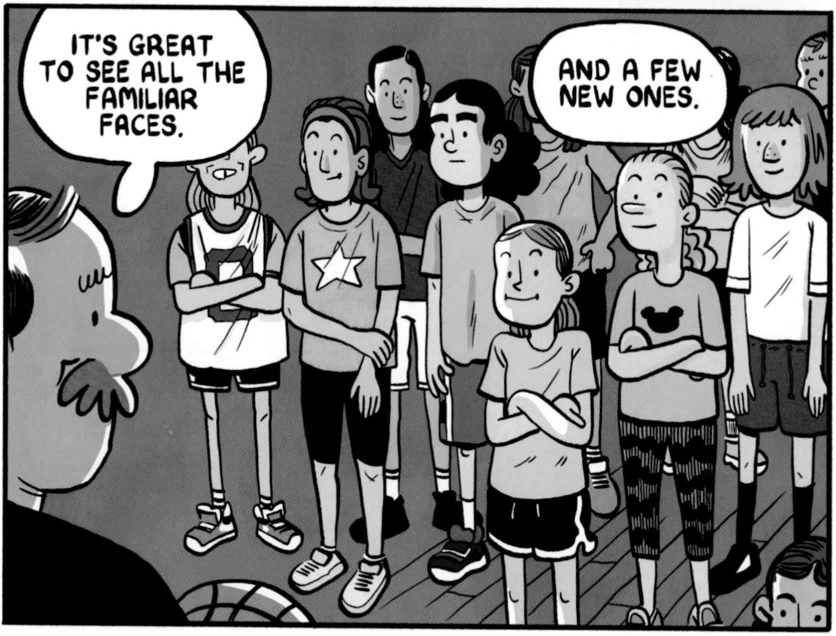
IT'S GREAT TO SEE ALL THE FAMILIAR FACES.
AND A FEW NEW ONES.

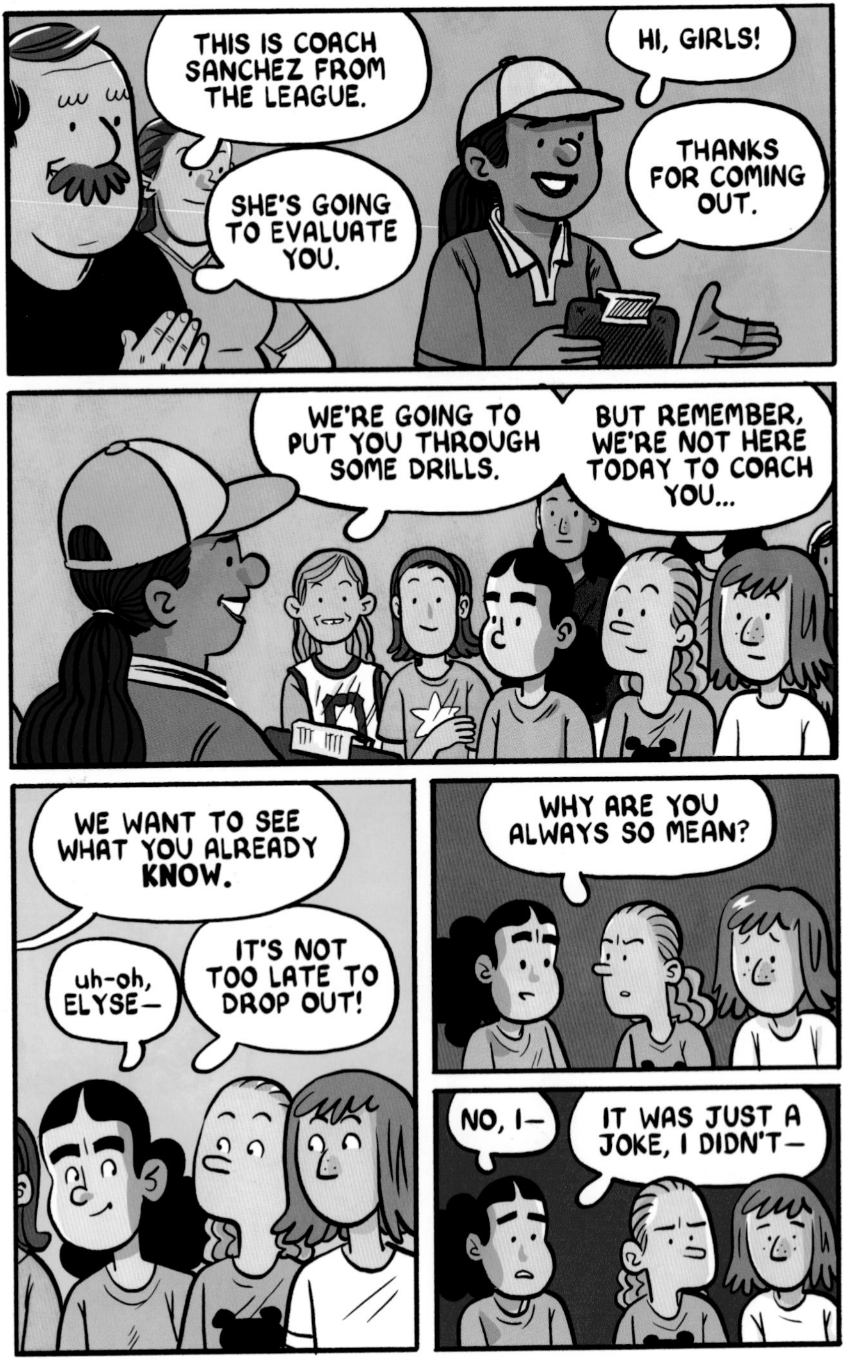
THIS IS COACH SANCHEZ FROM THE LEAGUE.
SHE'S GOING TO EVALUATE YOU.
HI, GIRLS!
THANKS FOR COMING OUT.
WE'RE GOING TO PUT YOU THROUGH SOME DRILLS.
BUT REMEMBER, WE'RE NOT HERE TODAY TO COACH YOU...
WE WANT TO SEE WHAT YOU ALREADY **KNOW.**
uh-oh, ELYSE—
IT'S NOT TOO LATE TO DROP OUT!
WHY ARE YOU ALWAYS SO MEAN?
NO, I—
IT WAS JUST A JOKE, I DIDN'T—

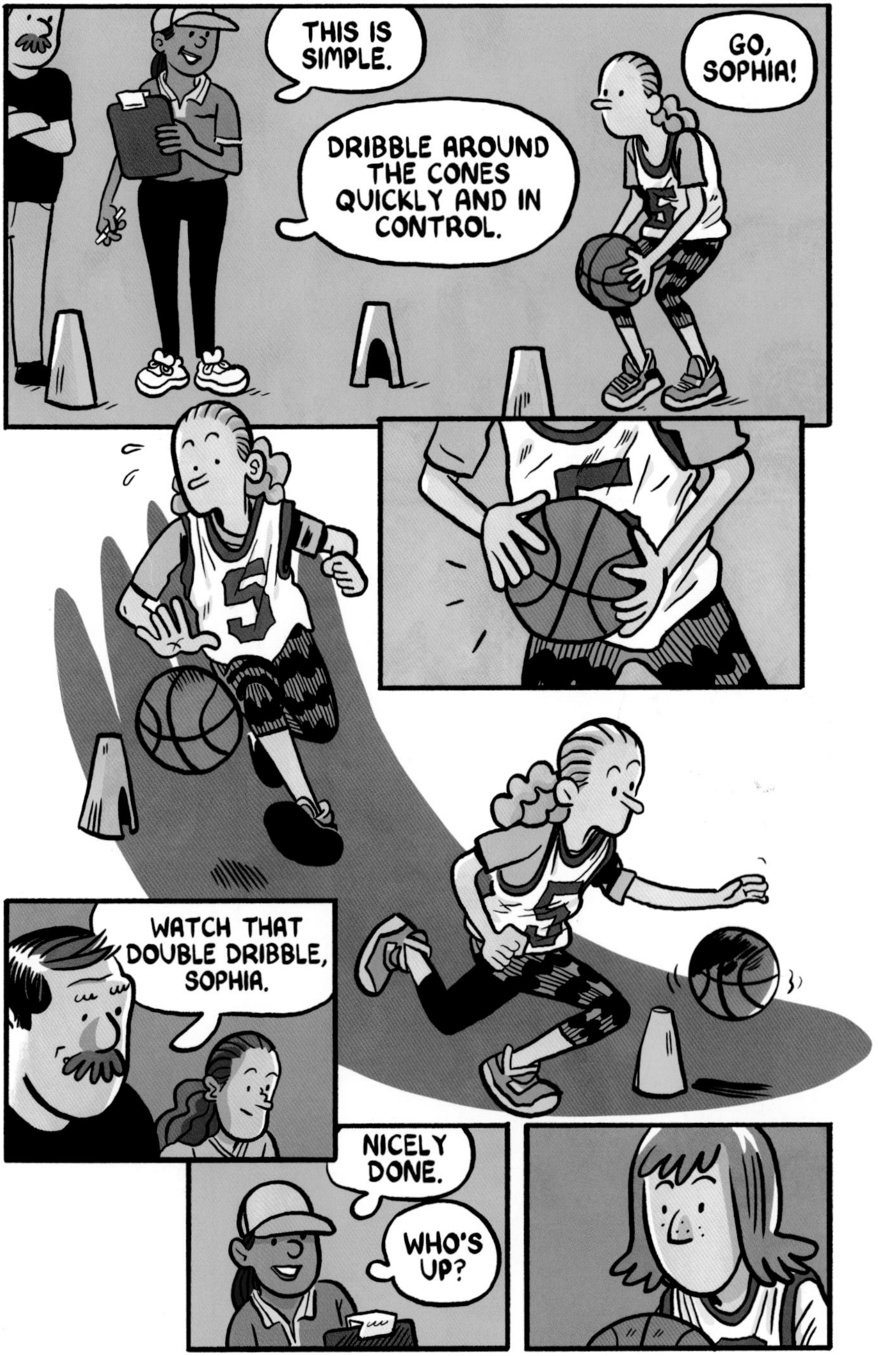
THIS IS SIMPLE.
DRIBBLE AROUND THE CONES QUICKLY AND IN CONTROL.
GO, SOPHIA!
WATCH THAT DOUBLE DRIBBLE, SOPHIA.
NICELY DONE.
WHO'S UP?

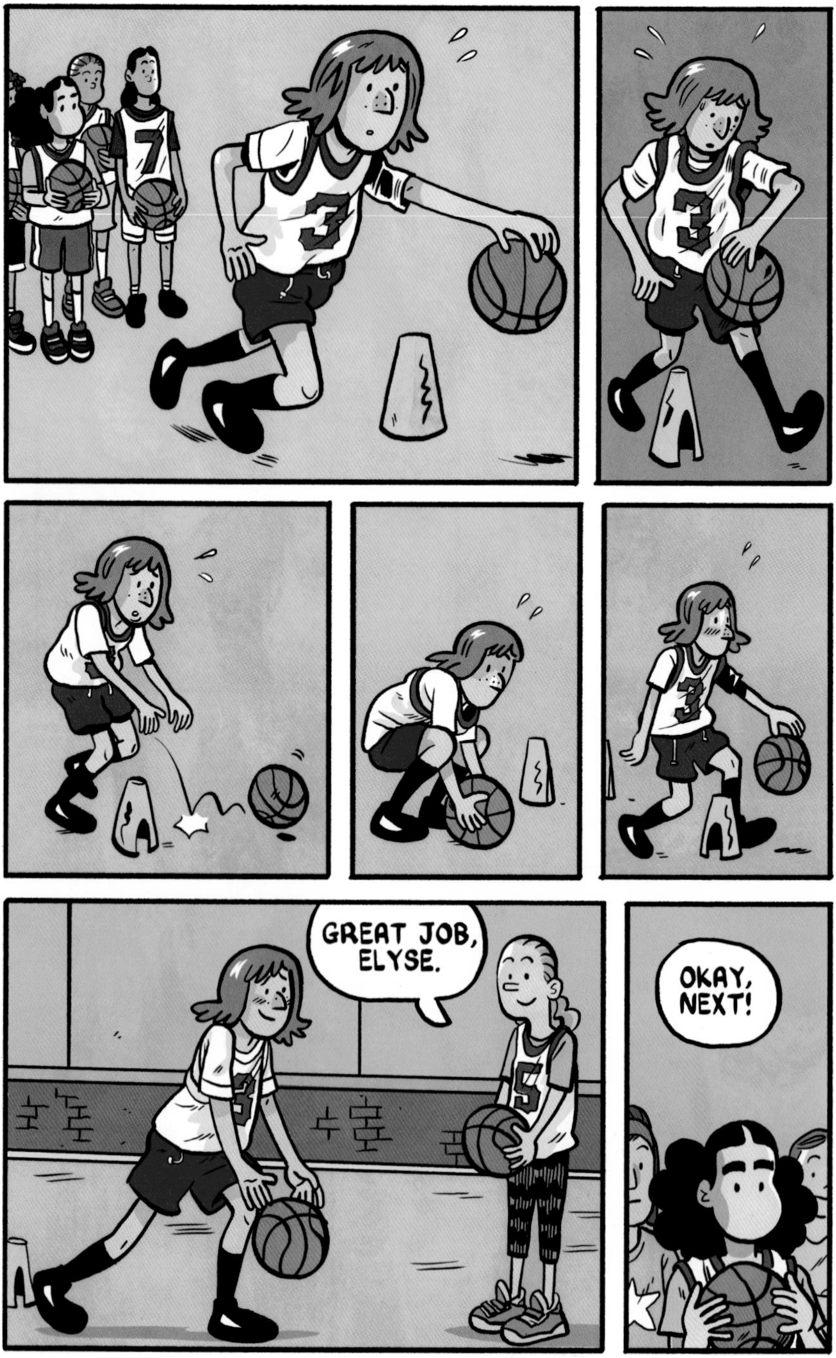
GREAT JOB, ELYSE.
OKAY, NEXT!

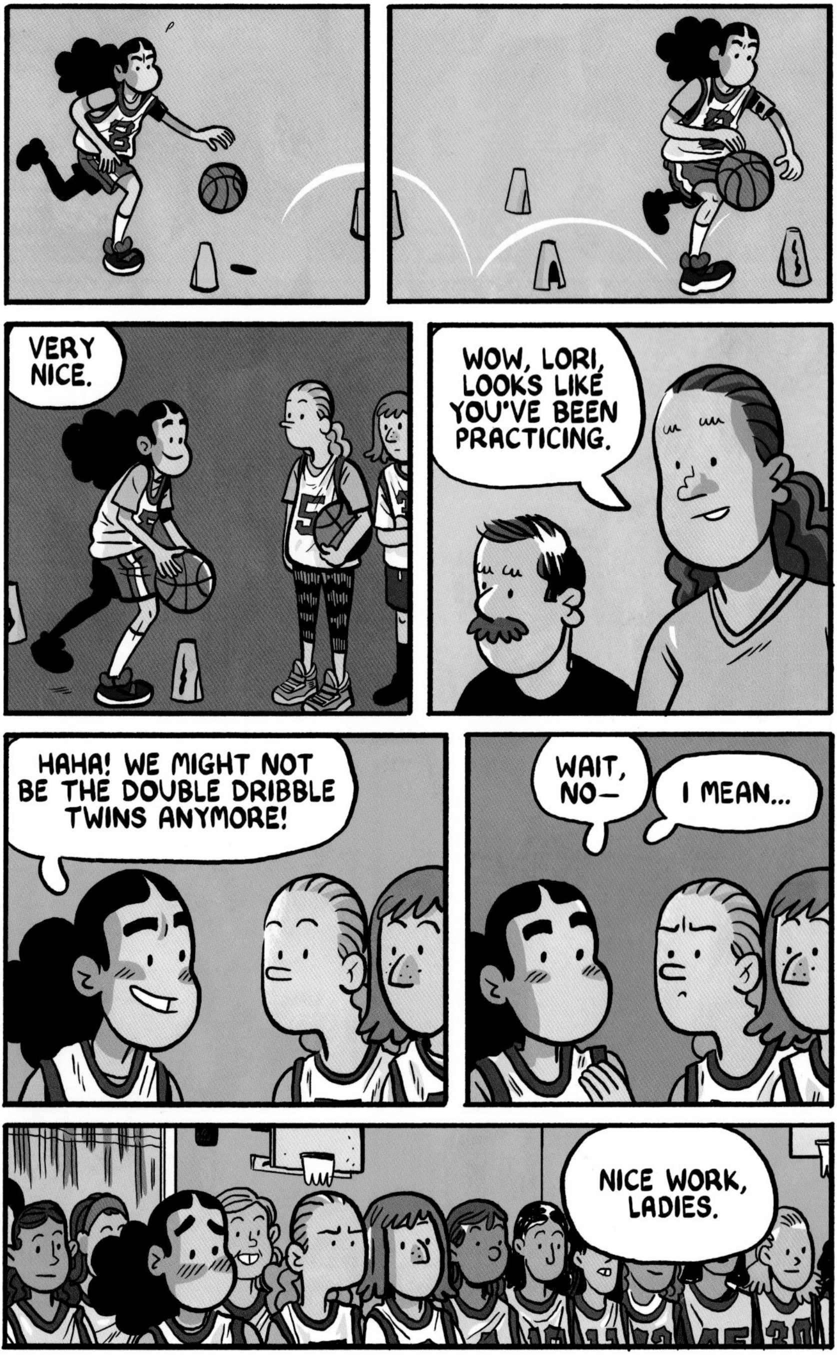
VERY NICE.
WOW, LORI, LOOKS LIKE YOU'VE BEEN PRACTICING.
HAHA! WE MIGHT NOT BE THE DOUBLE DRIBBLE TWINS ANYMORE!
WAIT, NO—
I MEAN...
NICE WORK, LADIES.

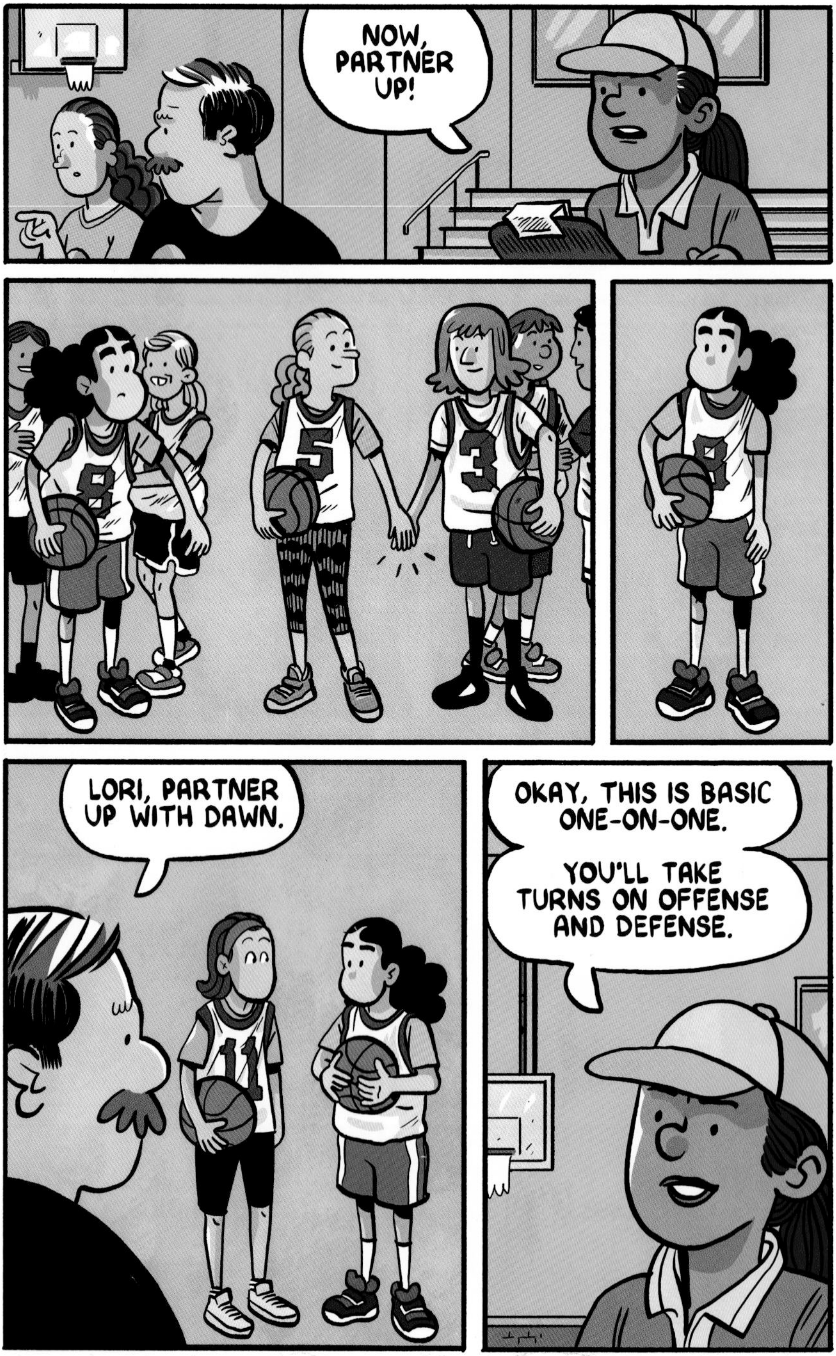
NOW, PARTNER UP!
LORI, PARTNER UP WITH DAWN.
OKAY, THIS IS BASIC ONE-ON-ONE.
YOU'LL TAKE TURNS ON OFFENSE AND DEFENSE.

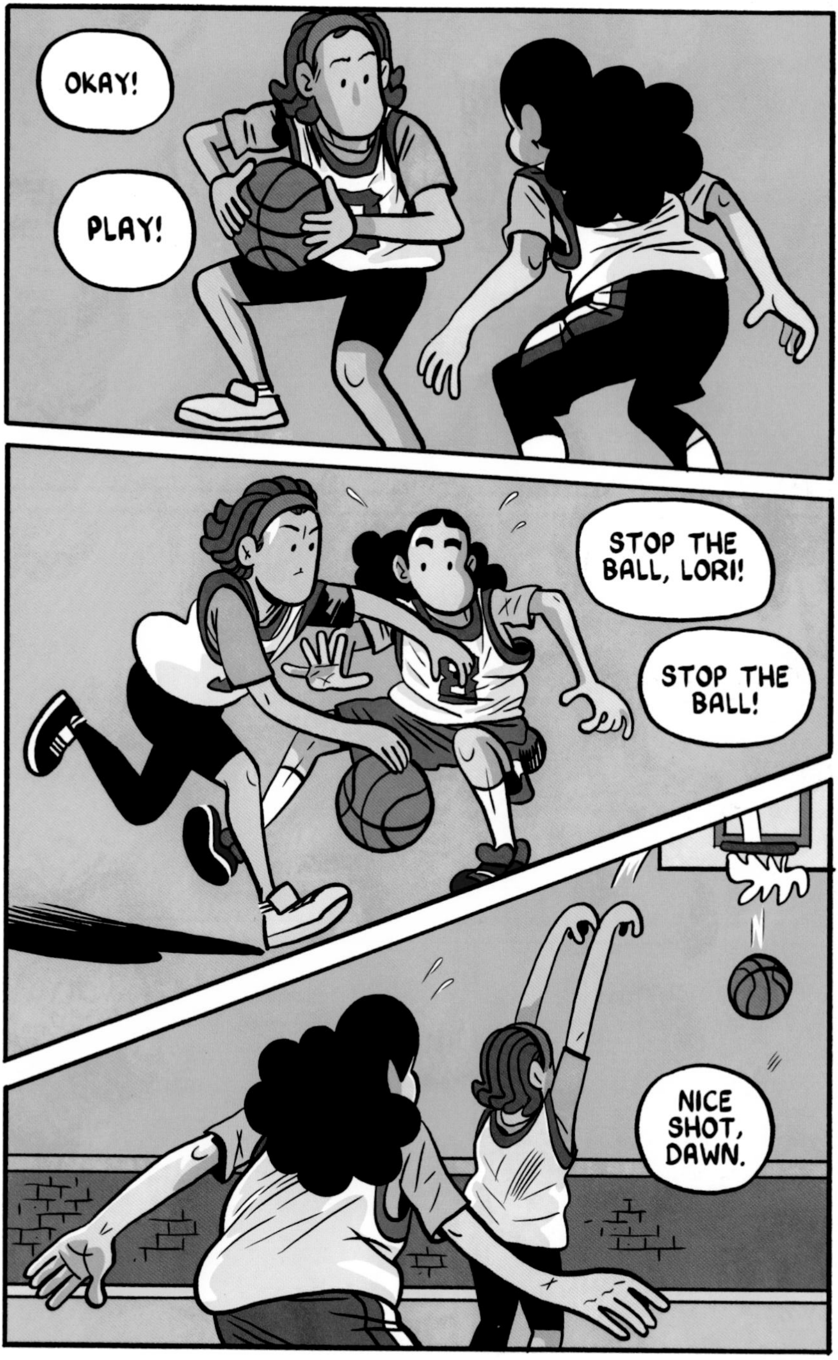
OKAY!
PLAY!
STOP THE BALL, LORI!
STOP THE BALL!
NICE SHOT, DAWN.

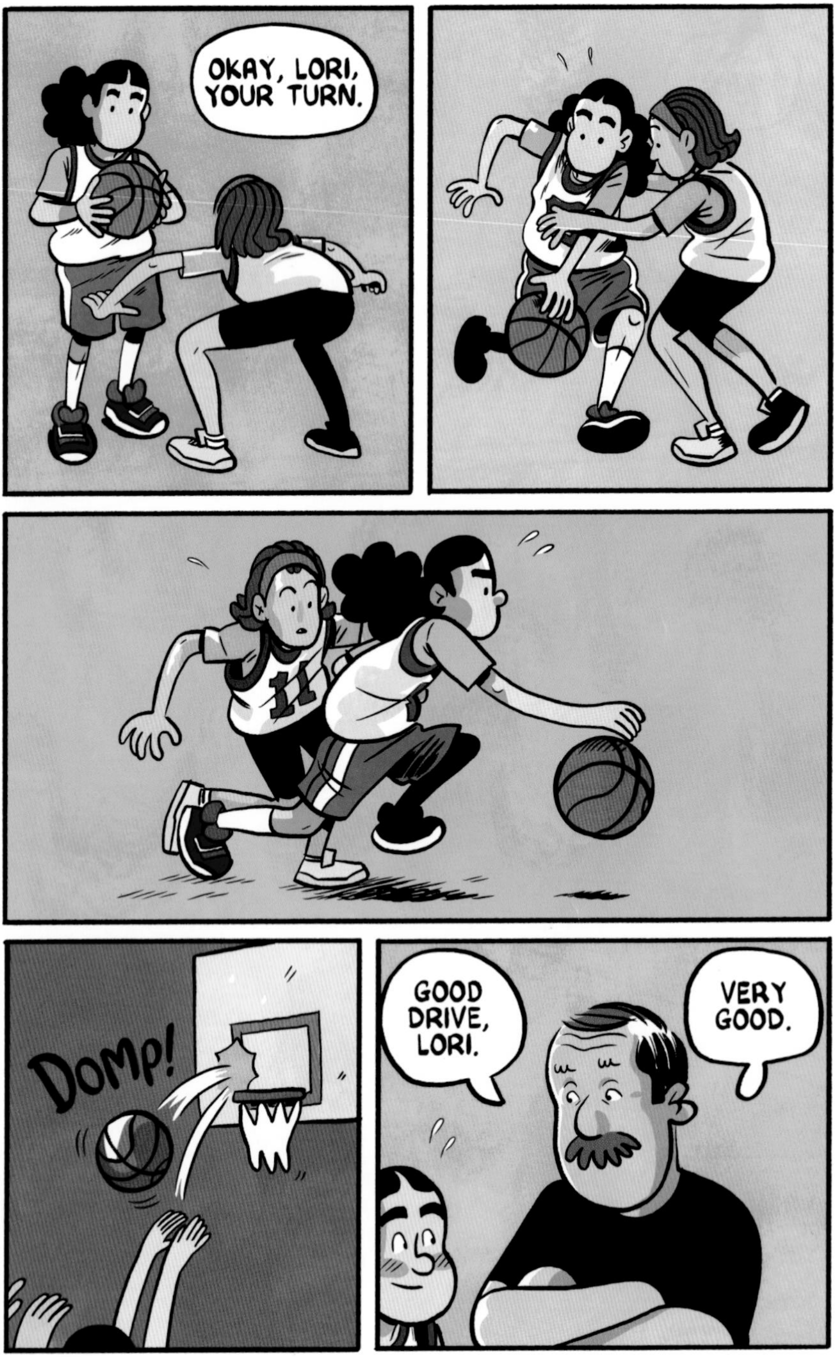
OKAY, LORI, YOUR TURN.
DOMP!
GOOD DRIVE, LORI.
VERY GOOD.

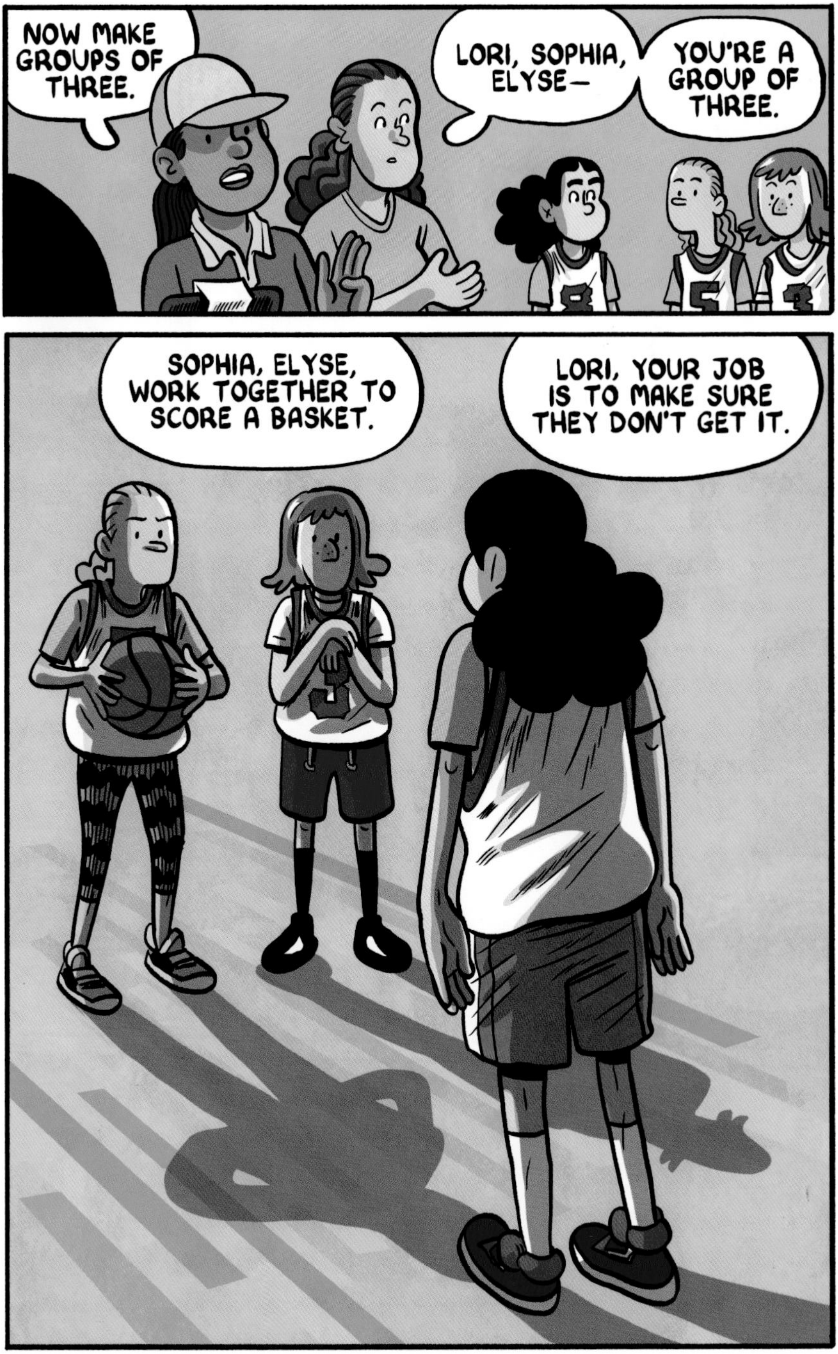
NOW MAKE GROUPS OF THREE.
LORI, SOPHIA, ELYSE—
YOU'RE A GROUP OF THREE.
SOPHIA, ELYSE, WORK TOGETHER TO SCORE A BASKET.
LORI, YOUR JOB IS TO MAKE SURE THEY DON'T GET IT.

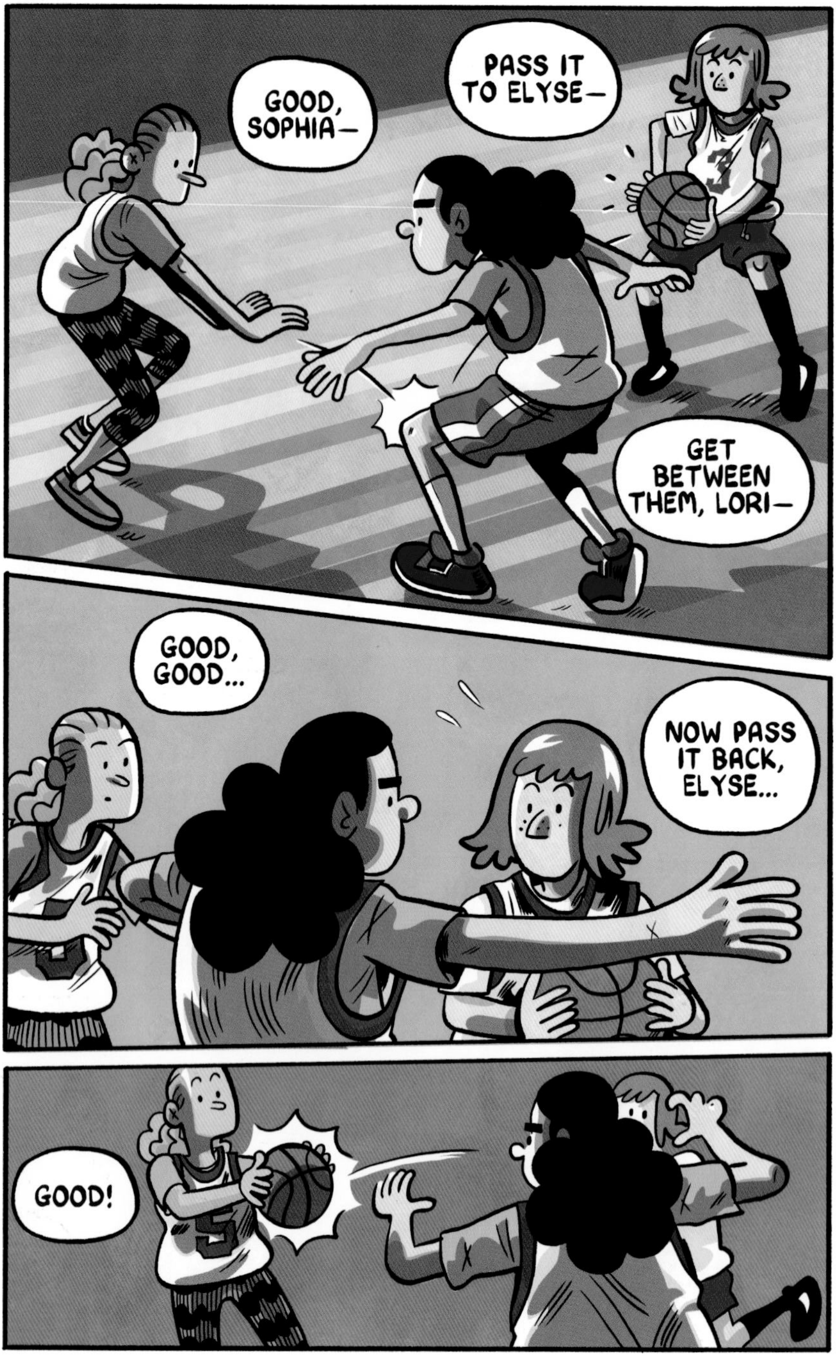
GOOD, SOPHIA—
PASS IT TO ELYSE—
GET BETWEEN THEM, LORI—
GOOD, GOOD...
NOW PASS IT BACK, ELYSE...
GOOD!

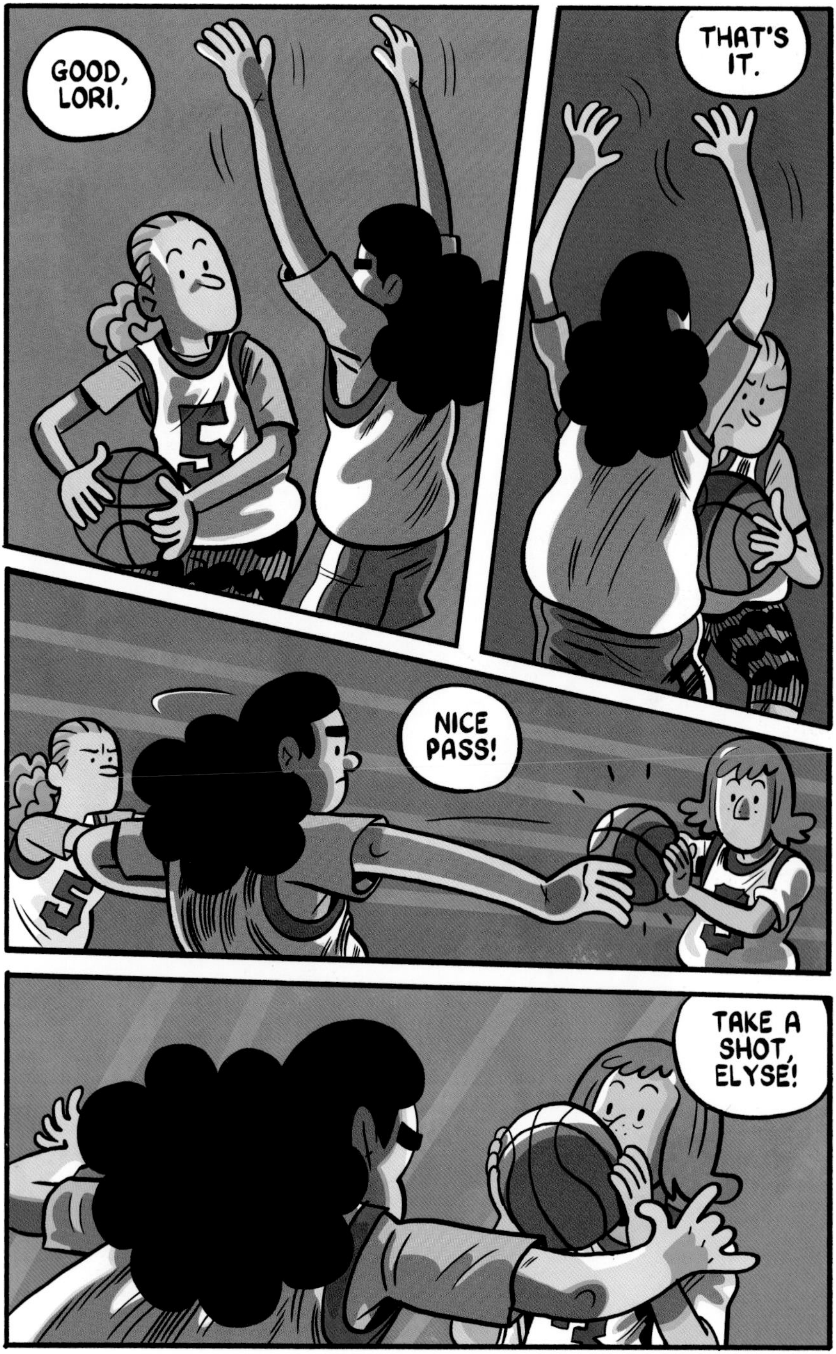
GOOD, LORI.
THAT'S IT.
NICE PASS!
TAKE A SHOT, ELYSE!

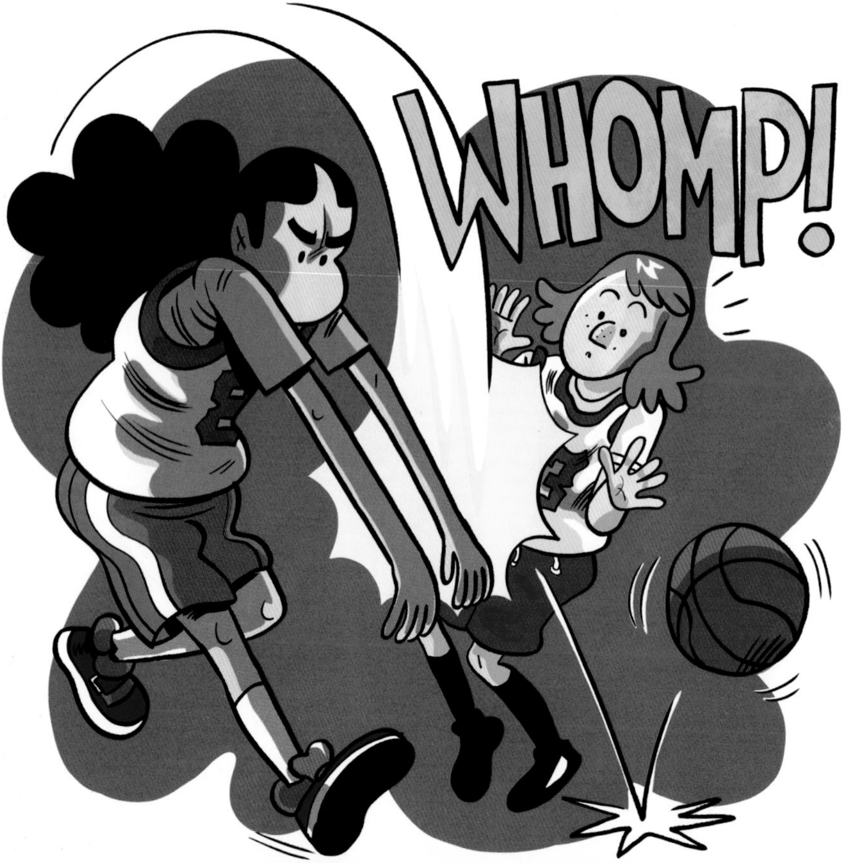
WHOMP!

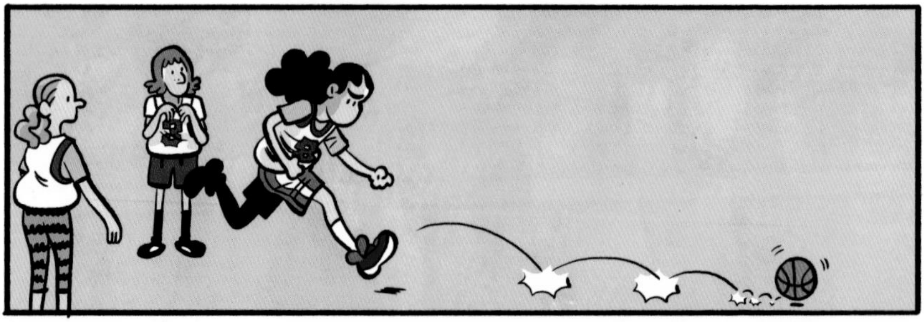

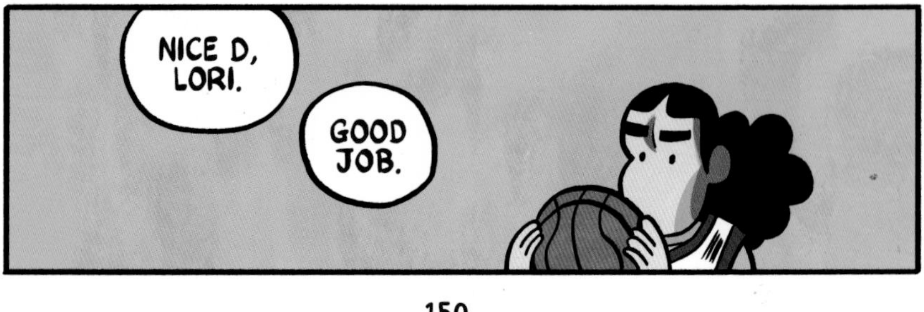
NICE D, LORI.
GOOD JOB.

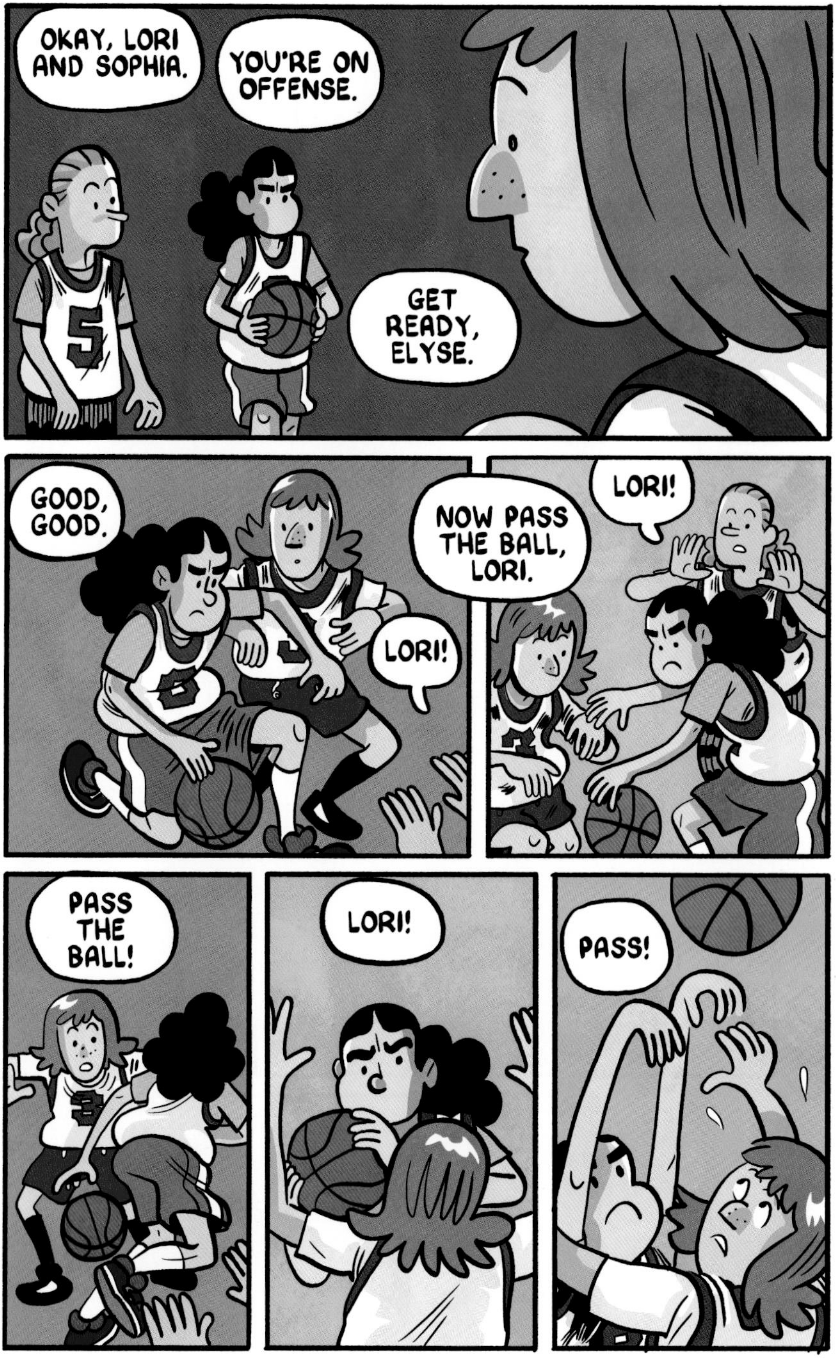
OKAY, LORI AND SOPHIA.
YOU'RE ON OFFENSE.
GET READY, ELYSE.
GOOD, GOOD.
LORI!
NOW PASS THE BALL, LORI.
LORI!
PASS THE BALL!
LORI!
PASS!

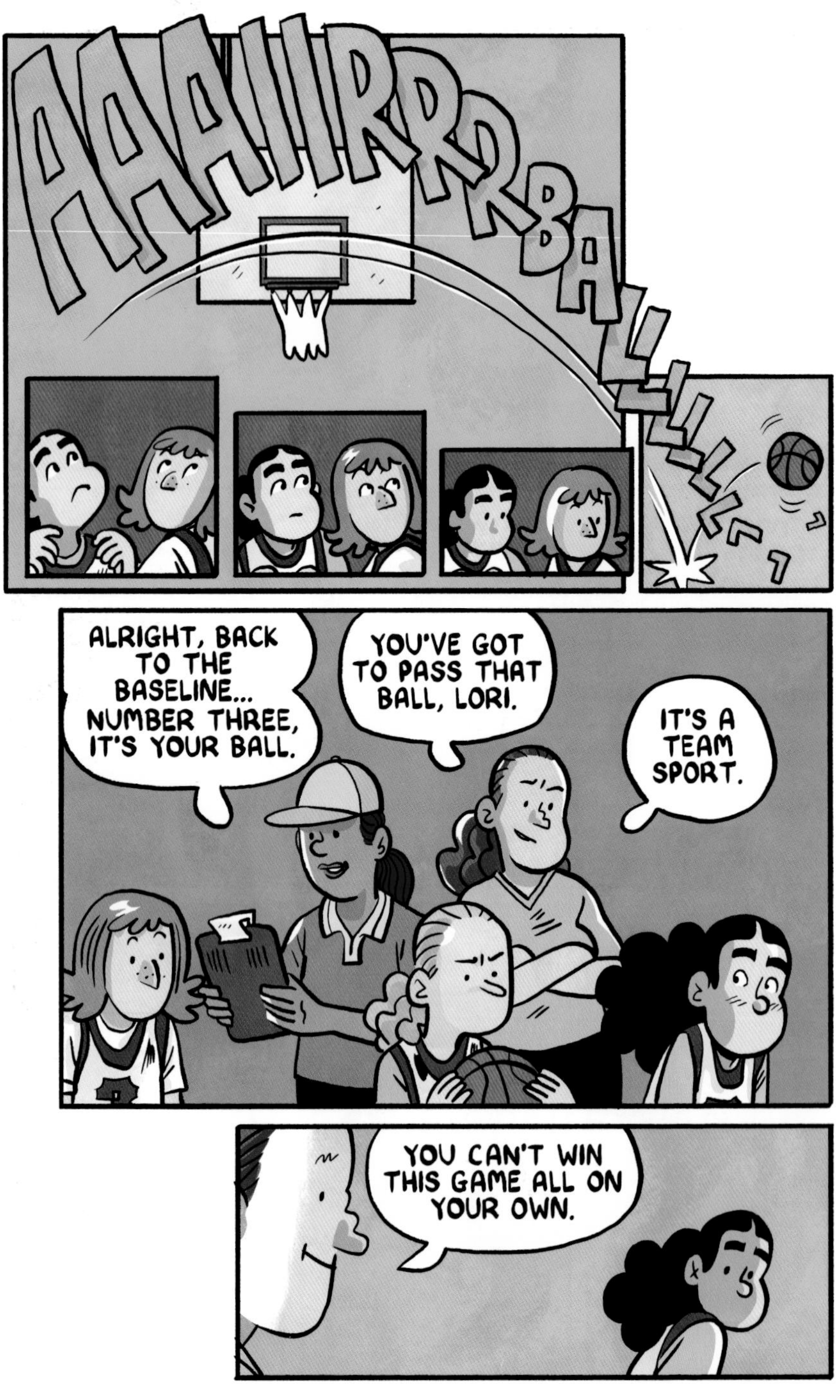
AAAIIIRRRBALLLLL
ALRIGHT, BACK TO THE BASELINE... NUMBER THREE, IT'S YOUR BALL.
YOU'VE GOT TO PASS THAT BALL, LORI.
IT'S A TEAM SPORT.
YOU CAN'T WIN THIS GAME ALL ON YOUR OWN.

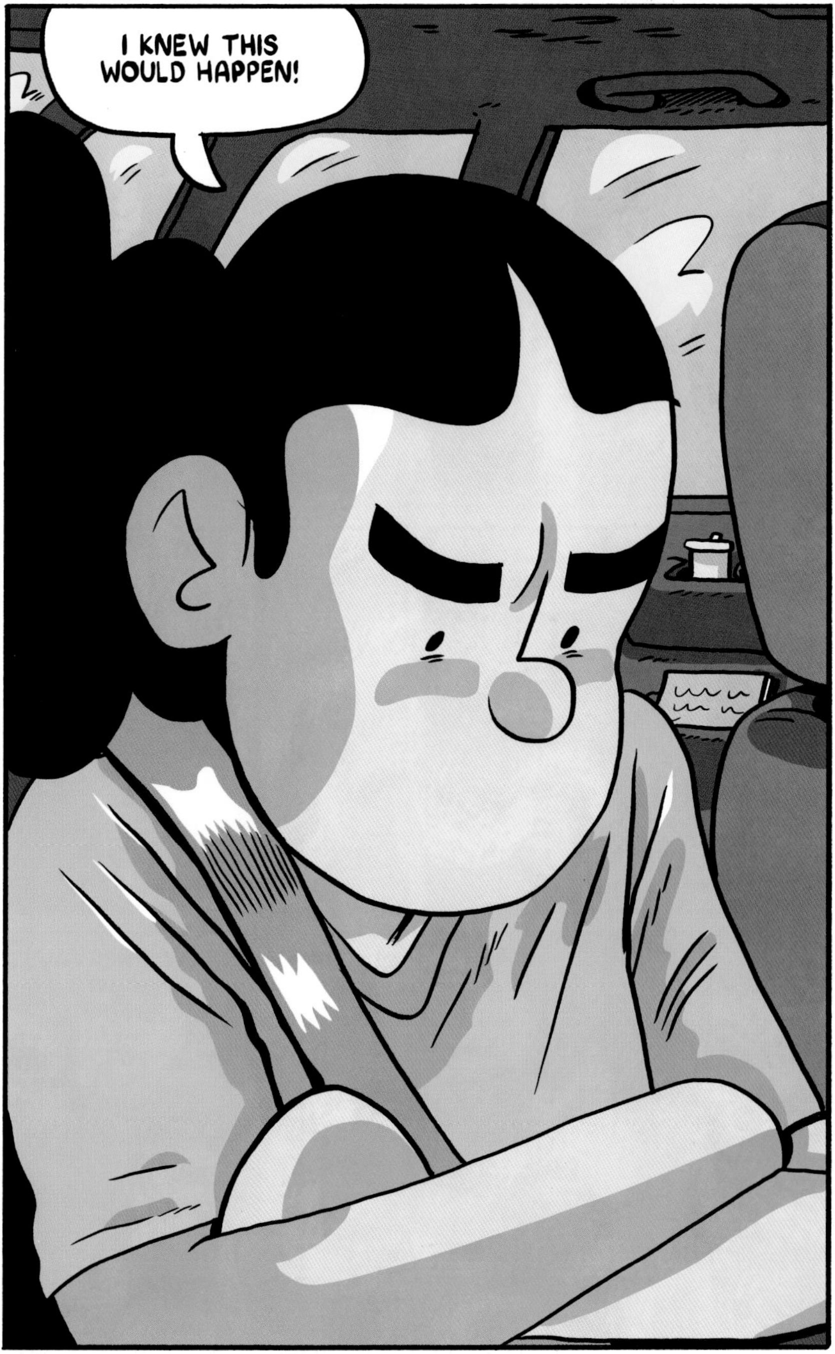
I KNEW THIS WOULD HAPPEN!

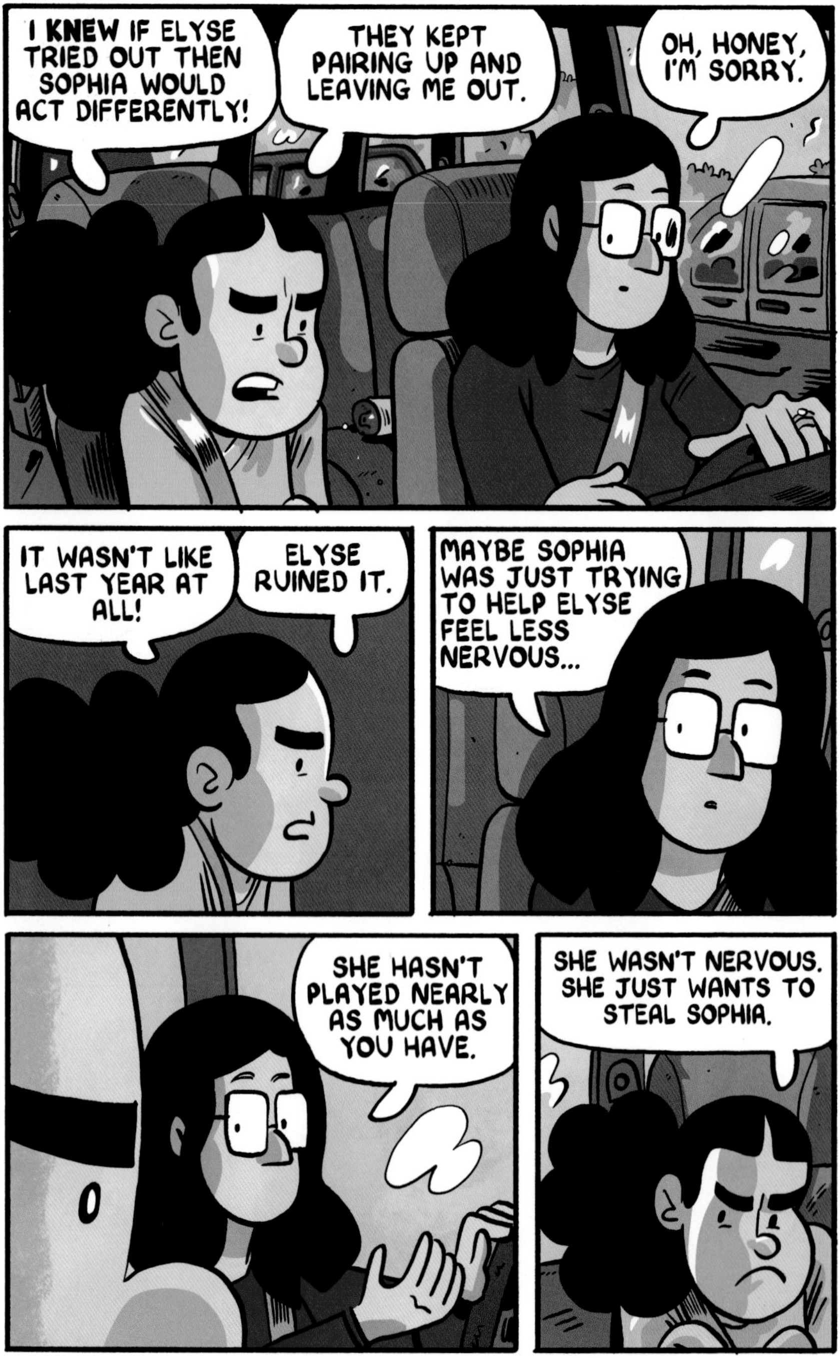
I KNEW IF ELYSE TRIED OUT THEN SOPHIA WOULD ACT DIFFERENTLY!
THEY KEPT PAIRING UP AND LEAVING ME OUT.
OH, HONEY, I'M SORRY.
IT WASN'T LIKE LAST YEAR AT ALL!
ELYSE RUINED IT.
MAYBE SOPHIA WAS JUST TRYING TO HELP ELYSE FEEL LESS NERVOUS...
SHE HASN'T PLAYED NEARLY AS MUCH AS YOU HAVE.
SHE WASN'T NERVOUS. SHE JUST WANTS TO STEAL SOPHIA.

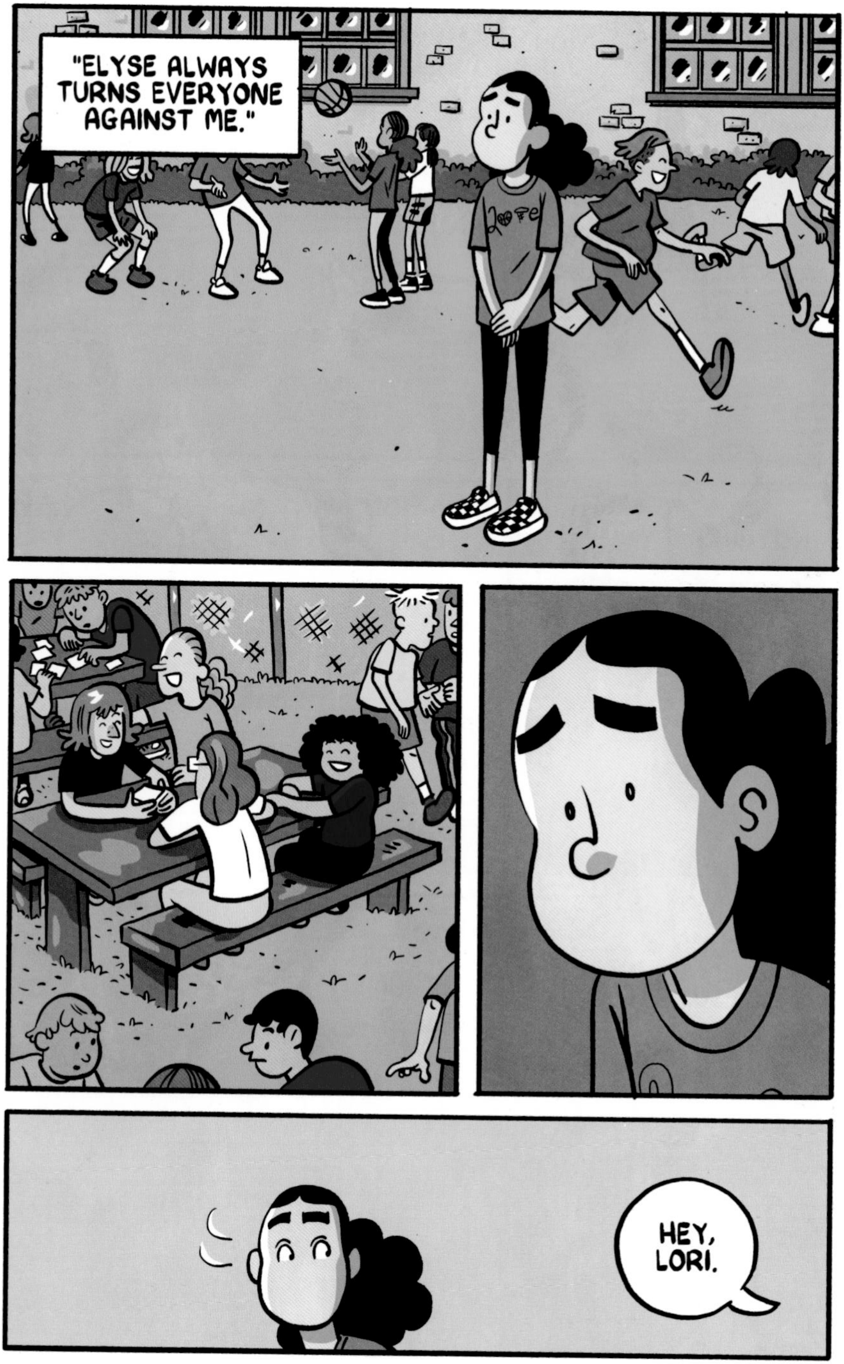
"ELYSE ALWAYS TURNS EVERYONE AGAINST ME."
HEY, LORI.

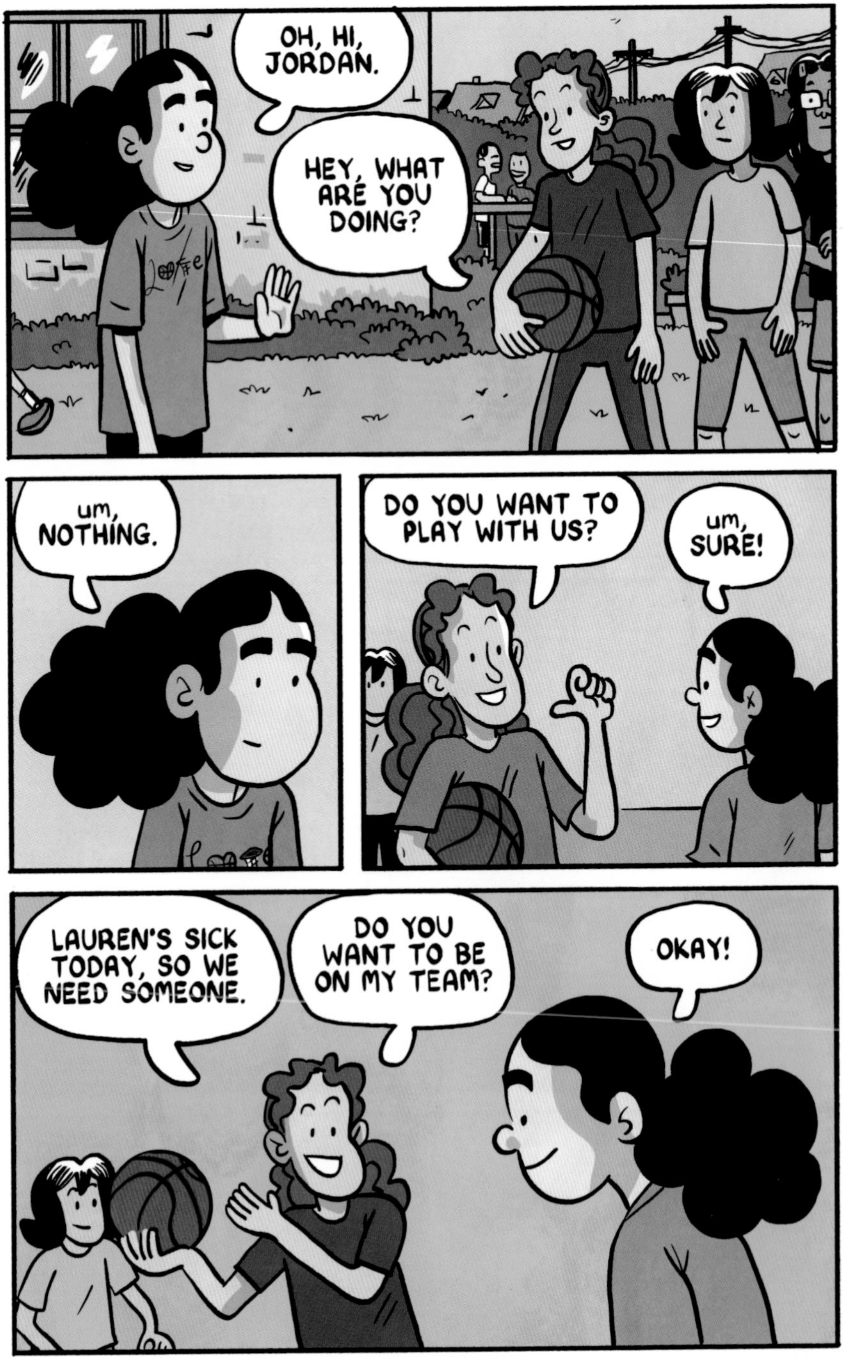
OH, HI, JORDAN.
HEY, WHAT ARE YOU DOING?
um, NOTHING.
DO YOU WANT TO PLAY WITH US?
um, SURE!
LAUREN'S SICK TODAY, SO WE NEED SOMEONE.
DO YOU WANT TO BE ON MY TEAM?
OKAY!

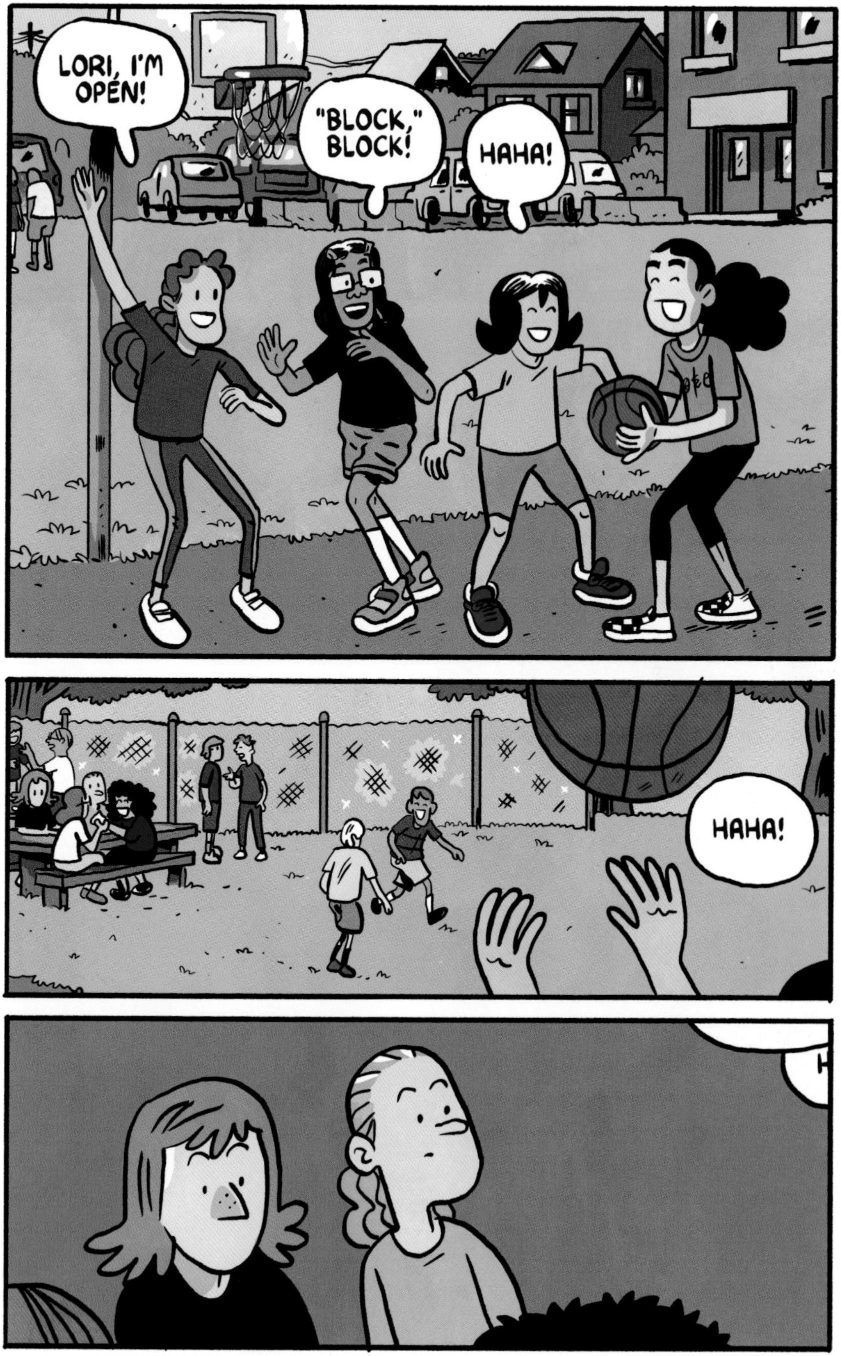
LORI, I'M OPEN!
"BLOCK," BLOCK!
HAHA!
HAHA!

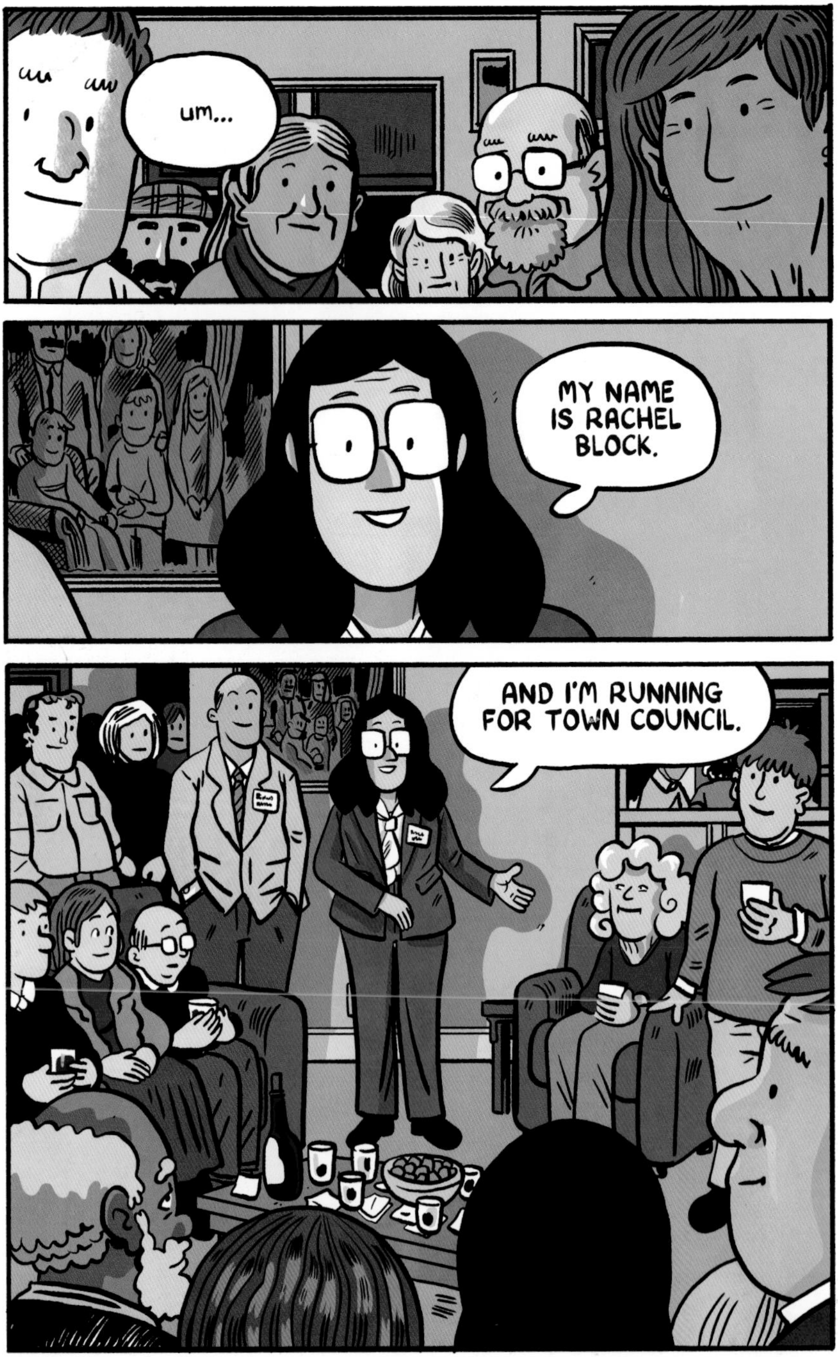
UM...
MY NAME IS RACHEL BLOCK.
AND I'M RUNNING FOR TOWN COUNCIL.

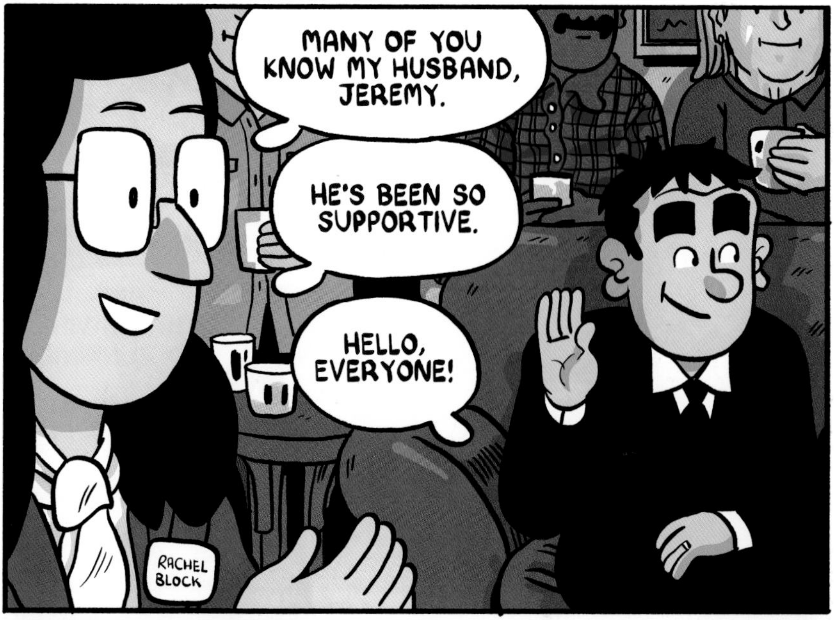
MANY OF YOU KNOW MY HUSBAND, JEREMY.
HE'S BEEN SO SUPPORTIVE.
HELLO, EVERYONE!
RACHEL BLOCK

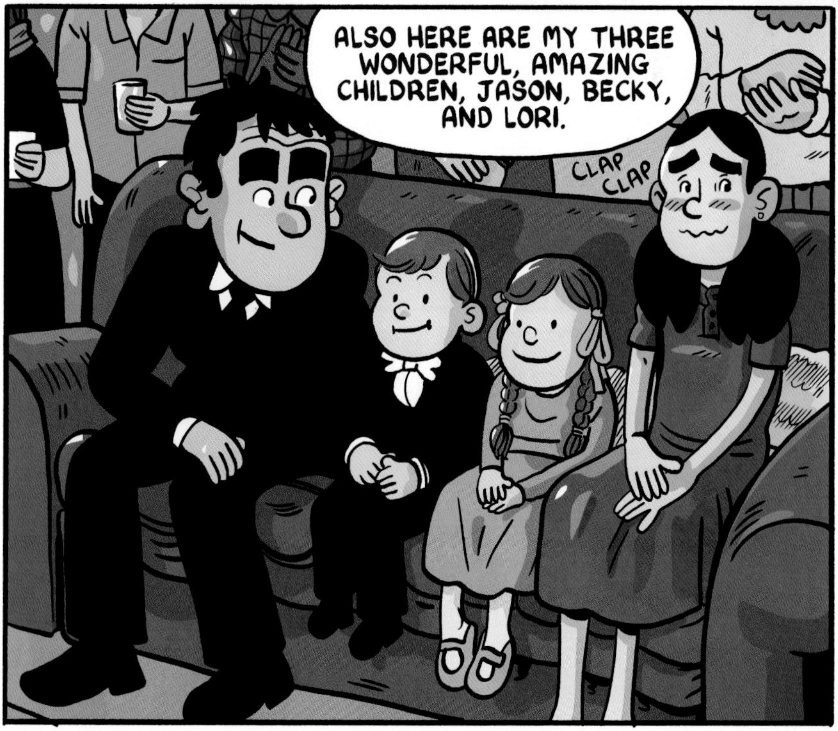
ALSO HERE ARE MY THREE WONDERFUL, AMAZING CHILDREN, JASON, BECKY, AND LORI.
CLAP CLAP

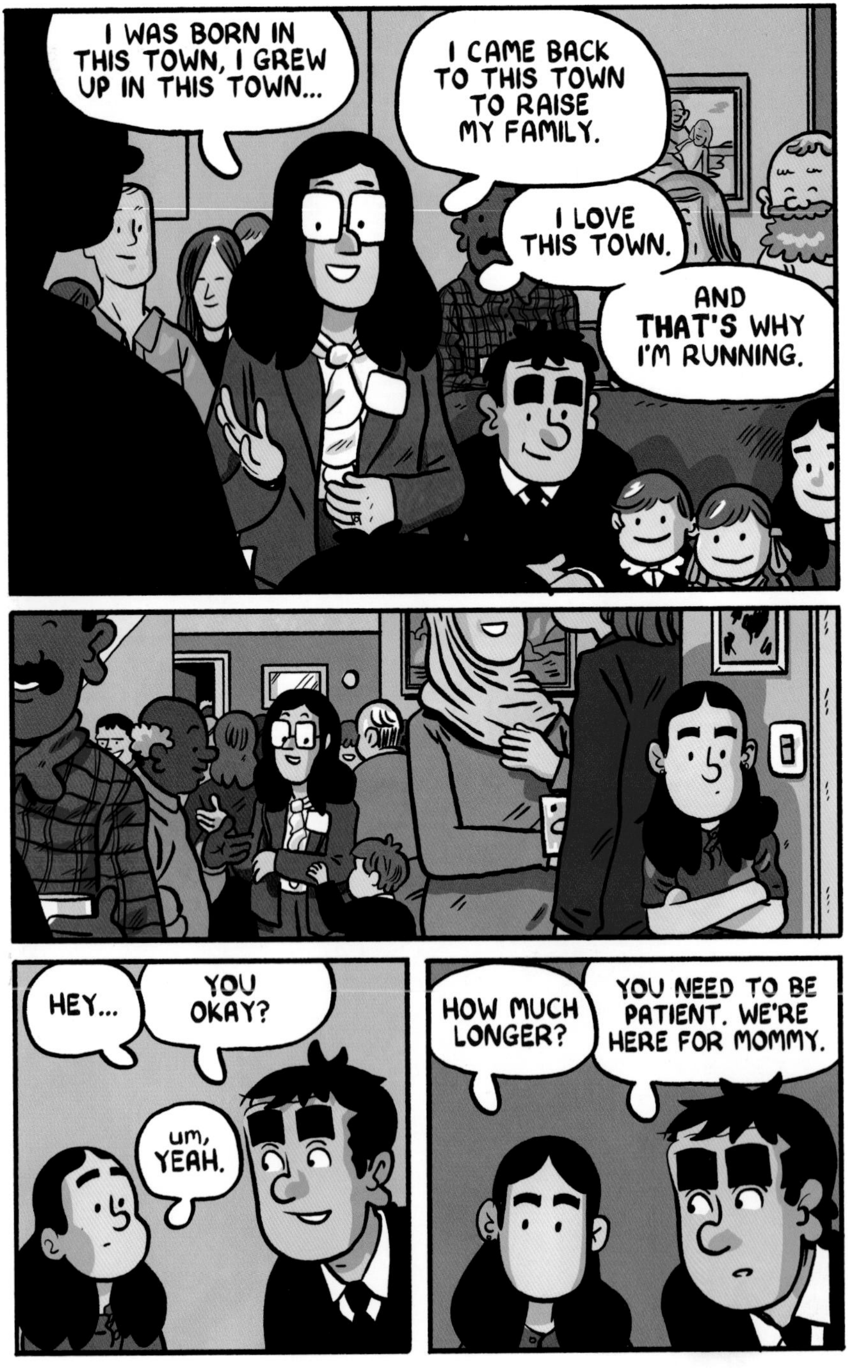
I WAS BORN IN THIS TOWN, I GREW UP IN THIS TOWN...
I CAME BACK TO THIS TOWN TO RAISE MY FAMILY.
I LOVE THIS TOWN.
AND THAT'S WHY I'M RUNNING.
HEY...
YOU OKAY?
um, YEAH.
HOW MUCH LONGER?
YOU NEED TO BE PATIENT. WE'RE HERE FOR MOMMY.

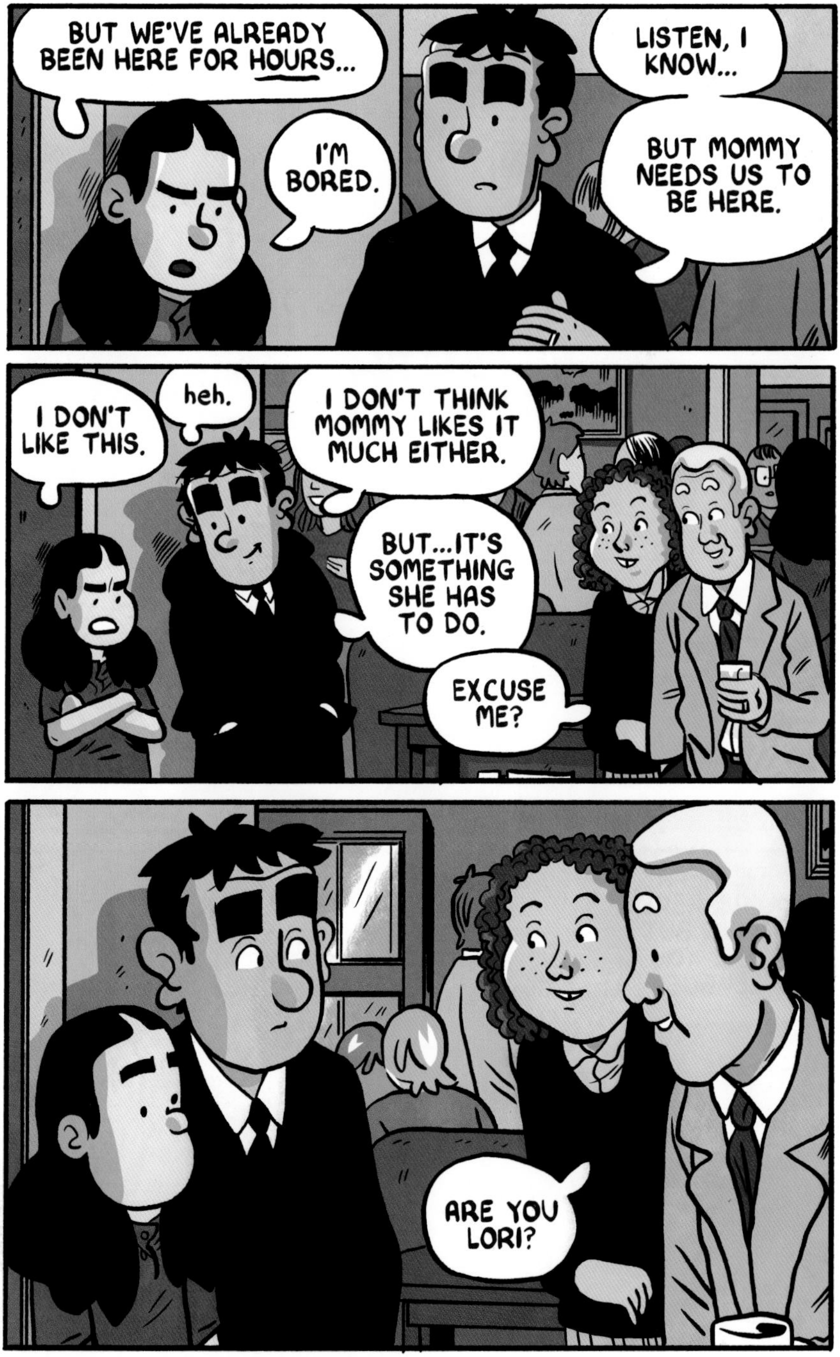
BUT WE'VE ALREADY BEEN HERE FOR HOURS...
I'M BORED.
LISTEN, I KNOW...
BUT MOMMY NEEDS US TO BE HERE.
I DON'T LIKE THIS.
heh.
I DON'T THINK MOMMY LIKES IT MUCH EITHER.
BUT...IT'S SOMETHING SHE HAS TO DO.
EXCUSE ME?
ARE YOU LORI?

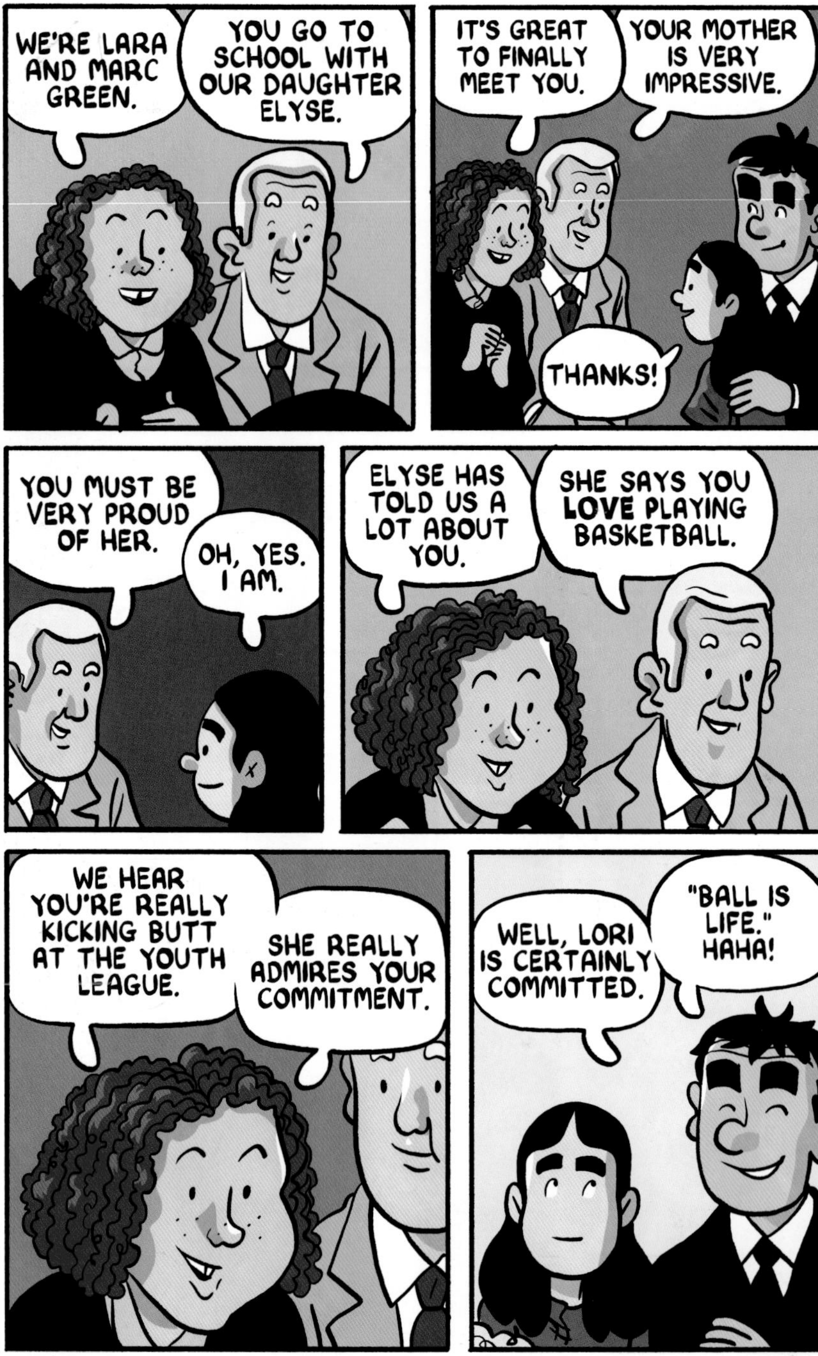

WE'RE LARA AND MARC GREEN.
YOU GO TO SCHOOL WITH OUR DAUGHTER ELYSE.
IT'S GREAT TO FINALLY MEET YOU.
YOUR MOTHER IS VERY IMPRESSIVE.
THANKS!
YOU MUST BE VERY PROUD OF HER.
OH, YES. I AM.
ELYSE HAS TOLD US A LOT ABOUT YOU.
SHE SAYS YOU **LOVE** PLAYING BASKETBALL.
WE HEAR YOU'RE REALLY KICKING BUTT AT THE YOUTH LEAGUE.
SHE REALLY ADMIRES YOUR COMMITMENT.
WELL, LORI IS CERTAINLY COMMITTED.
"BALL IS LIFE." HAHA!

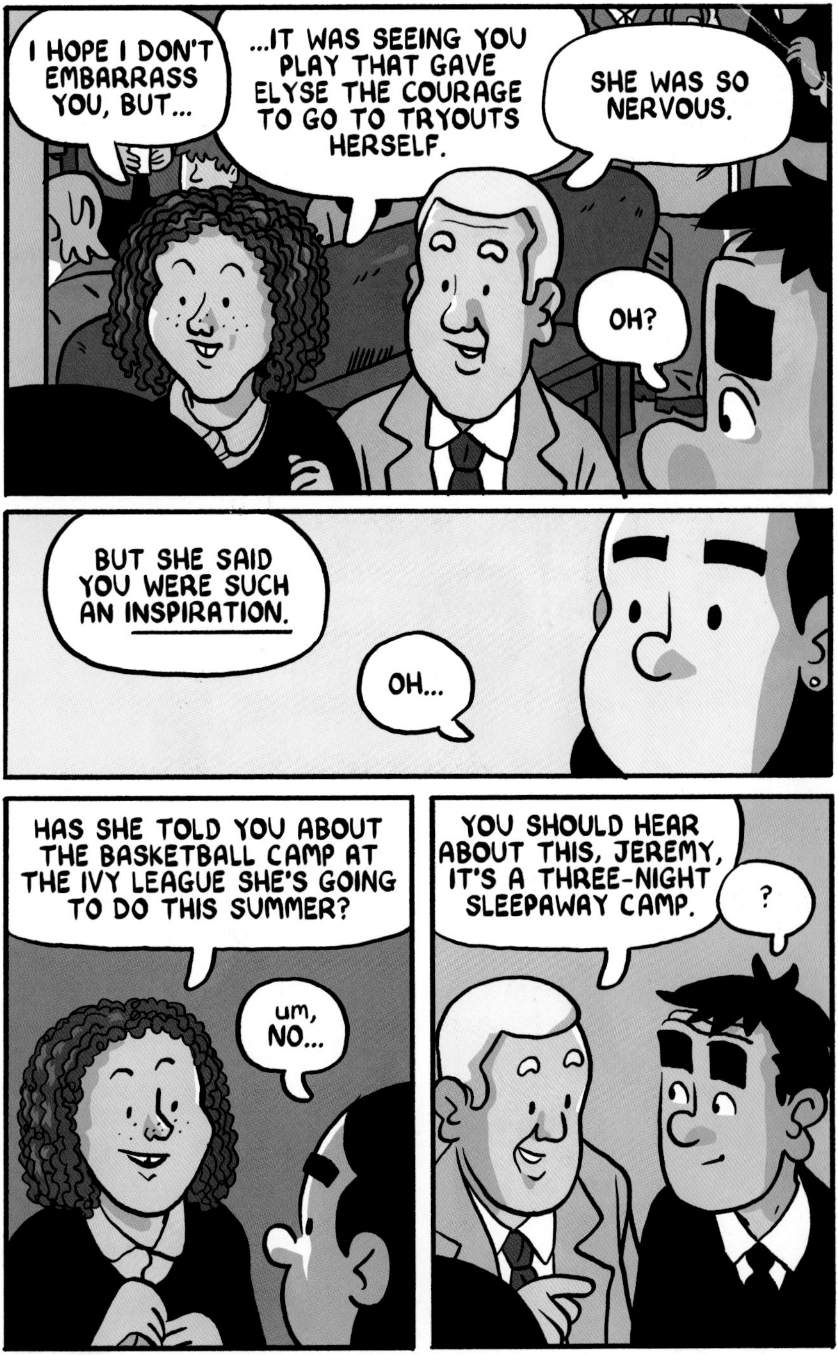
I HOPE I DON'T EMBARRASS YOU, BUT...
...IT WAS SEEING YOU PLAY THAT GAVE ELYSE THE COURAGE TO GO TO TRYOUTS HERSELF.
SHE WAS SO NERVOUS.
OH?
BUT SHE SAID YOU WERE SUCH AN INSPIRATION.
OH...
HAS SHE TOLD YOU ABOUT THE BASKETBALL CAMP AT THE IVY LEAGUE SHE'S GOING TO DO THIS SUMMER?
um, NO...
YOU SHOULD HEAR ABOUT THIS, JEREMY, IT'S A THREE-NIGHT SLEEPAWAY CAMP.
?

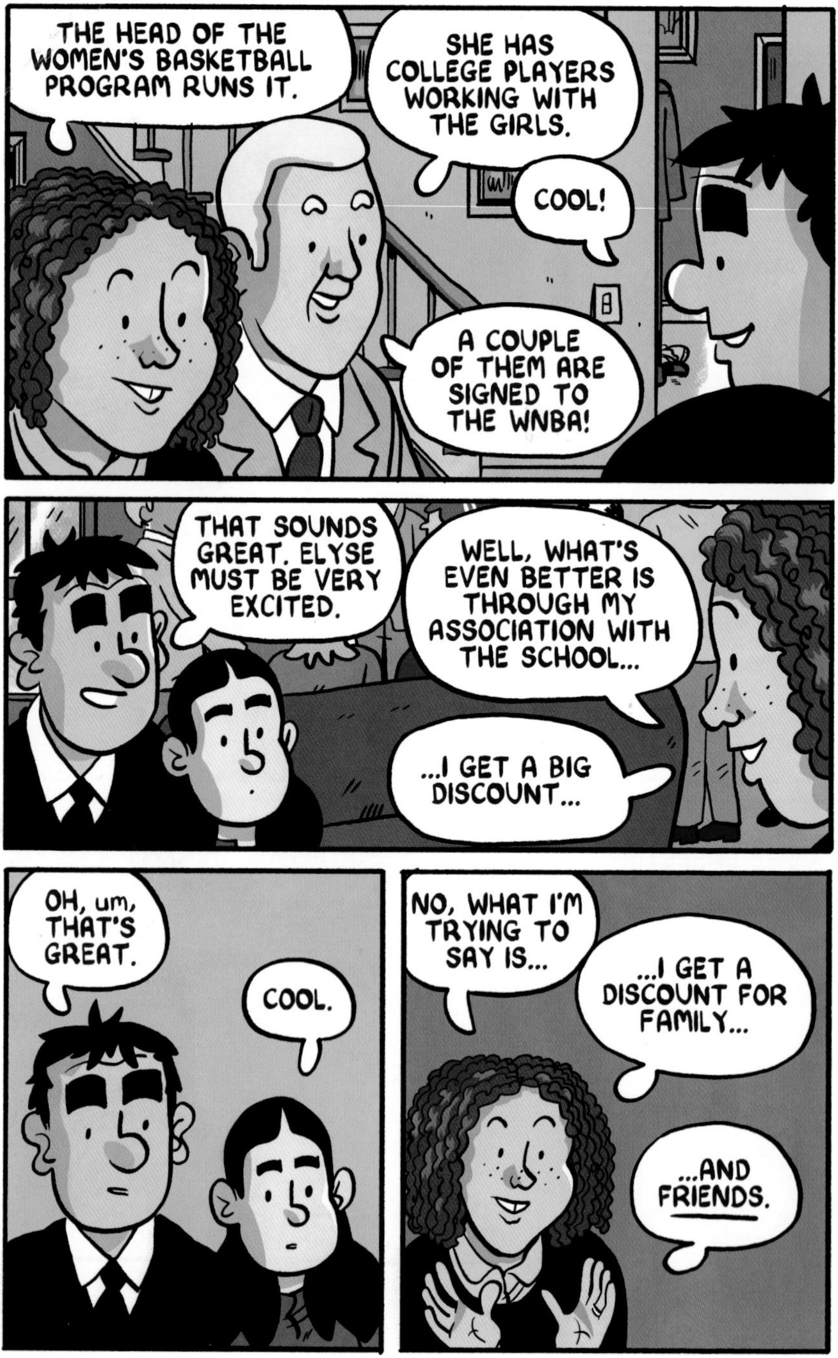
THE HEAD OF THE WOMEN'S BASKETBALL PROGRAM RUNS IT.
SHE HAS COLLEGE PLAYERS WORKING WITH THE GIRLS.
COOL!
A COUPLE OF THEM ARE SIGNED TO THE WNBA!
THAT SOUNDS GREAT. ELYSE MUST BE VERY EXCITED.
WELL, WHAT'S EVEN BETTER IS THROUGH MY ASSOCIATION WITH THE SCHOOL...
...I GET A BIG DISCOUNT...
OH, um, THAT'S GREAT.
COOL.
NO, WHAT I'M TRYING TO SAY IS...
...I GET A DISCOUNT FOR FAMILY...
...AND FRIENDS.

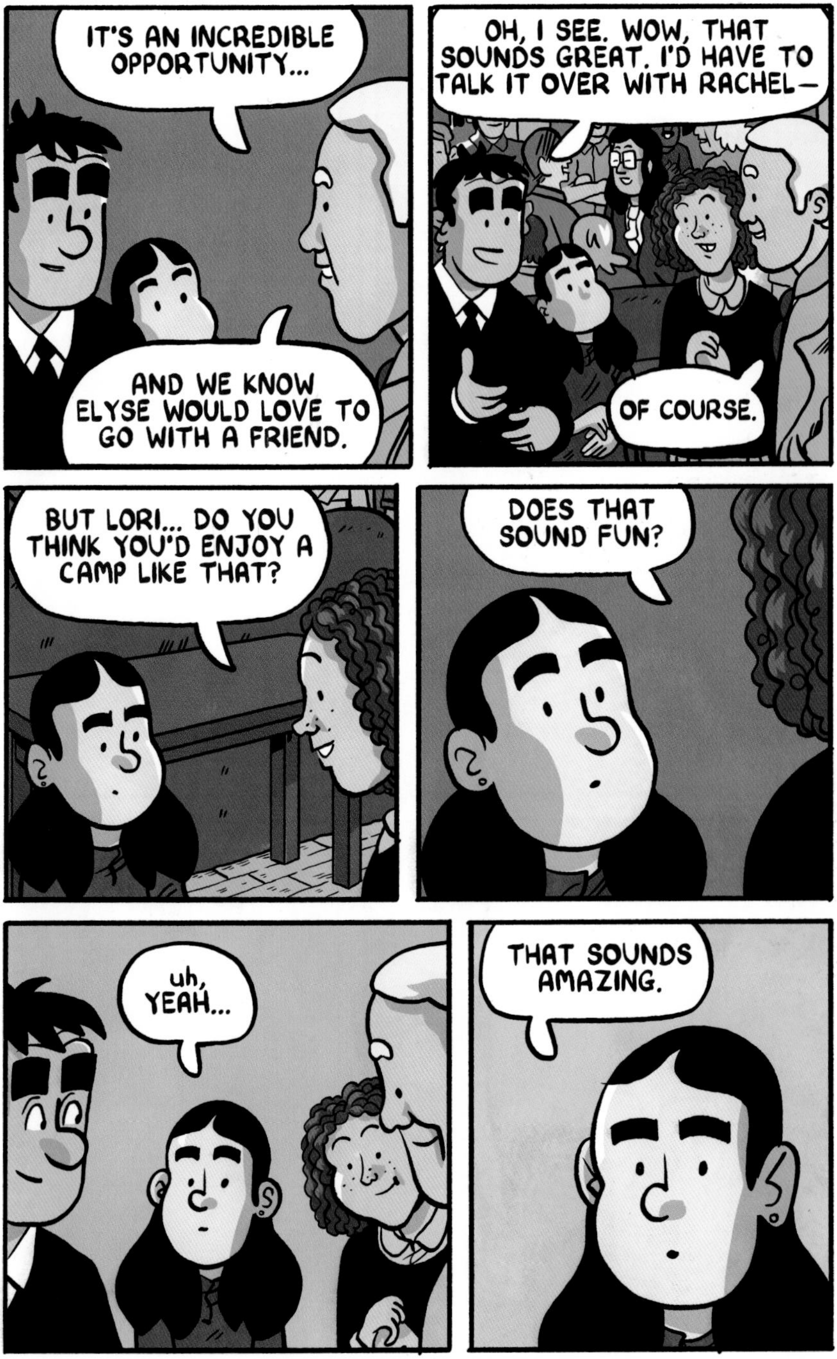
IT'S AN INCREDIBLE OPPORTUNITY...
AND WE KNOW ELYSE WOULD LOVE TO GO WITH A FRIEND.
OH, I SEE. WOW, THAT SOUNDS GREAT. I'D HAVE TO TALK IT OVER WITH RACHEL—
OF COURSE.
BUT LORI... DO YOU THINK YOU'D ENJOY A CAMP LIKE THAT?
DOES THAT SOUND FUN?
uh, YEAH...
THAT SOUNDS AMAZING.

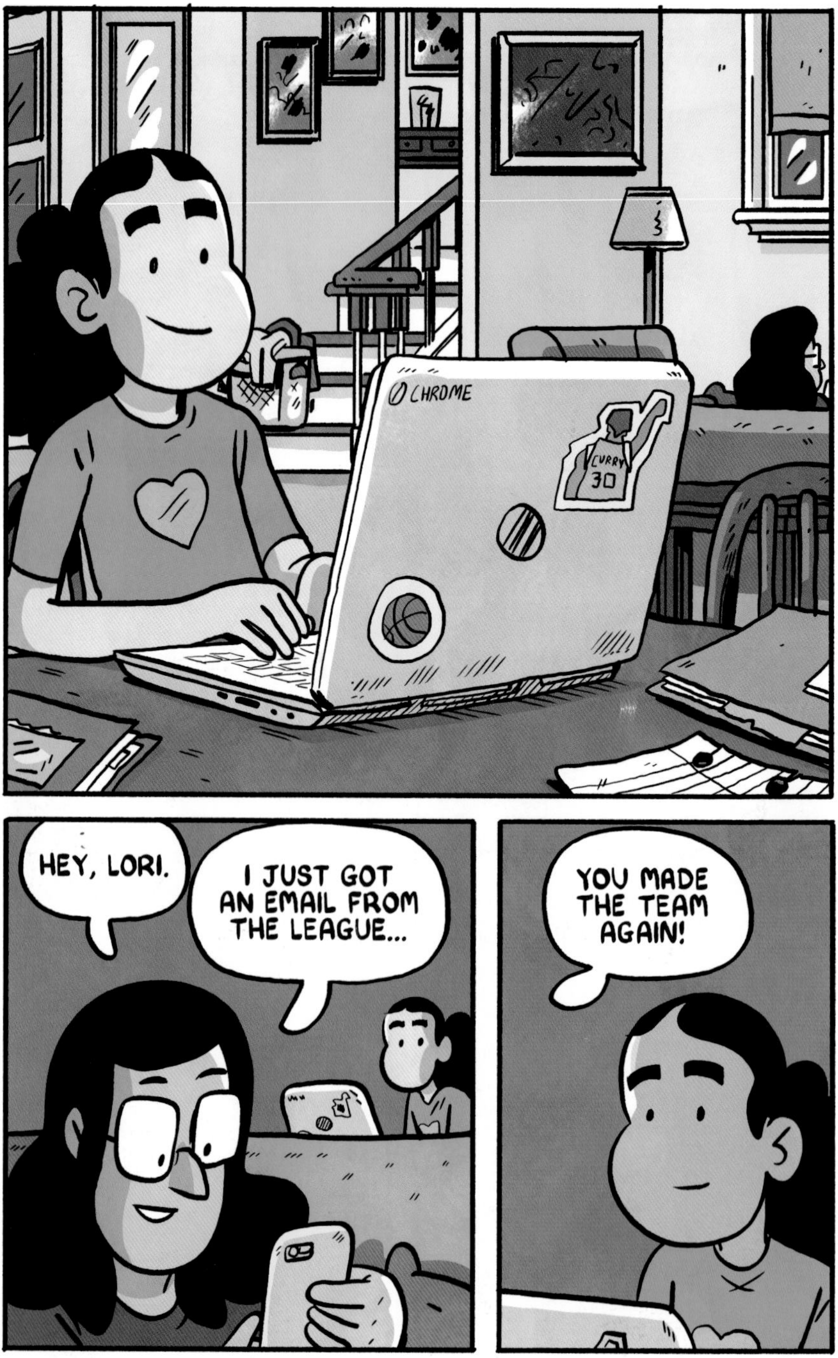
CHROME
CURRY 30
HEY, LORI.
I JUST GOT AN EMAIL FROM THE LEAGUE...
YOU MADE THE TEAM AGAIN!

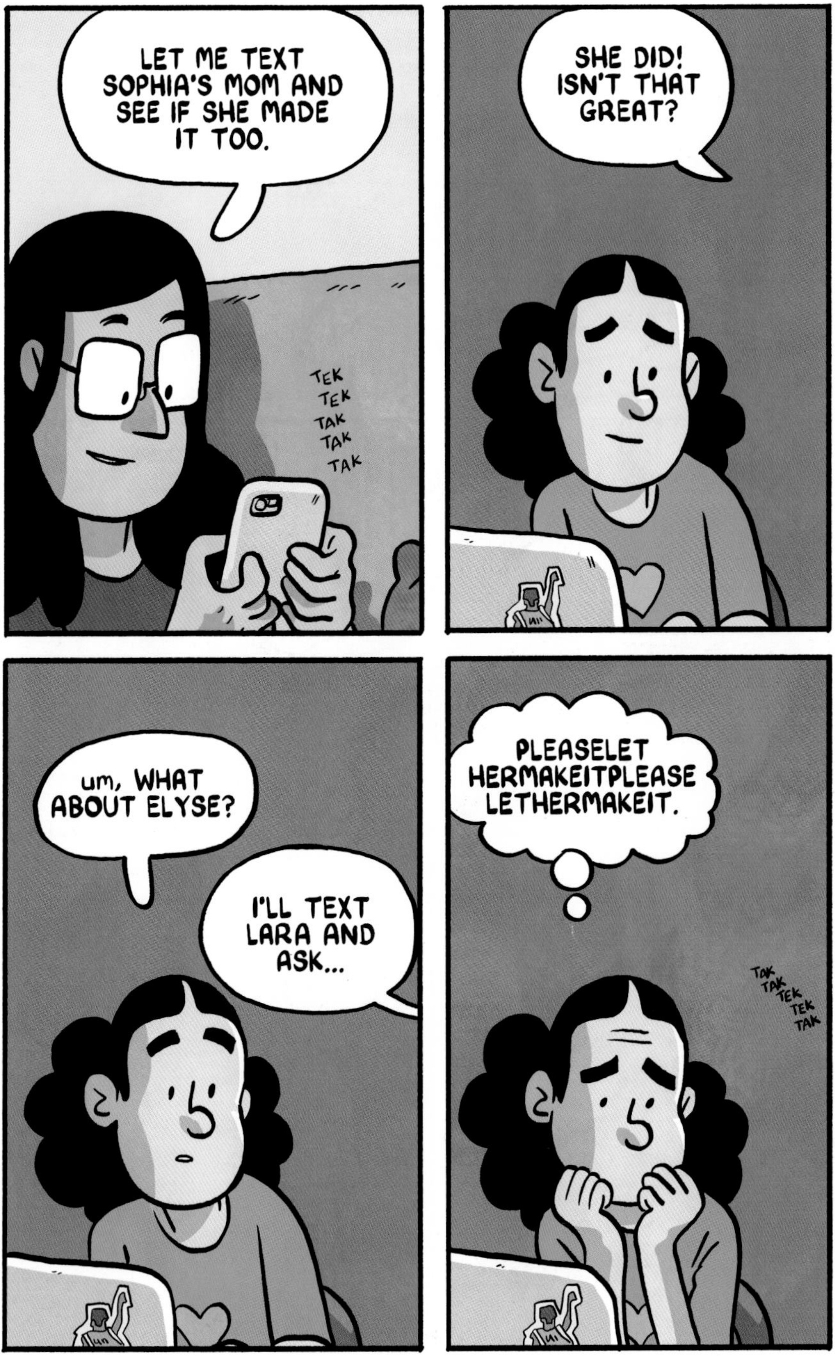
LET ME TEXT SOPHIA'S MOM AND SEE IF SHE MADE IT TOO.
TEK TEK TAK TAK TAK
SHE DID! ISN'T THAT GREAT?
um, WHAT ABOUT ELYSE?
I'LL TEXT LARA AND ASK...
PLEASELET HERMAKEITPLEASE LETHERMAKEIT.
TAK TAK TEK TEK TAK

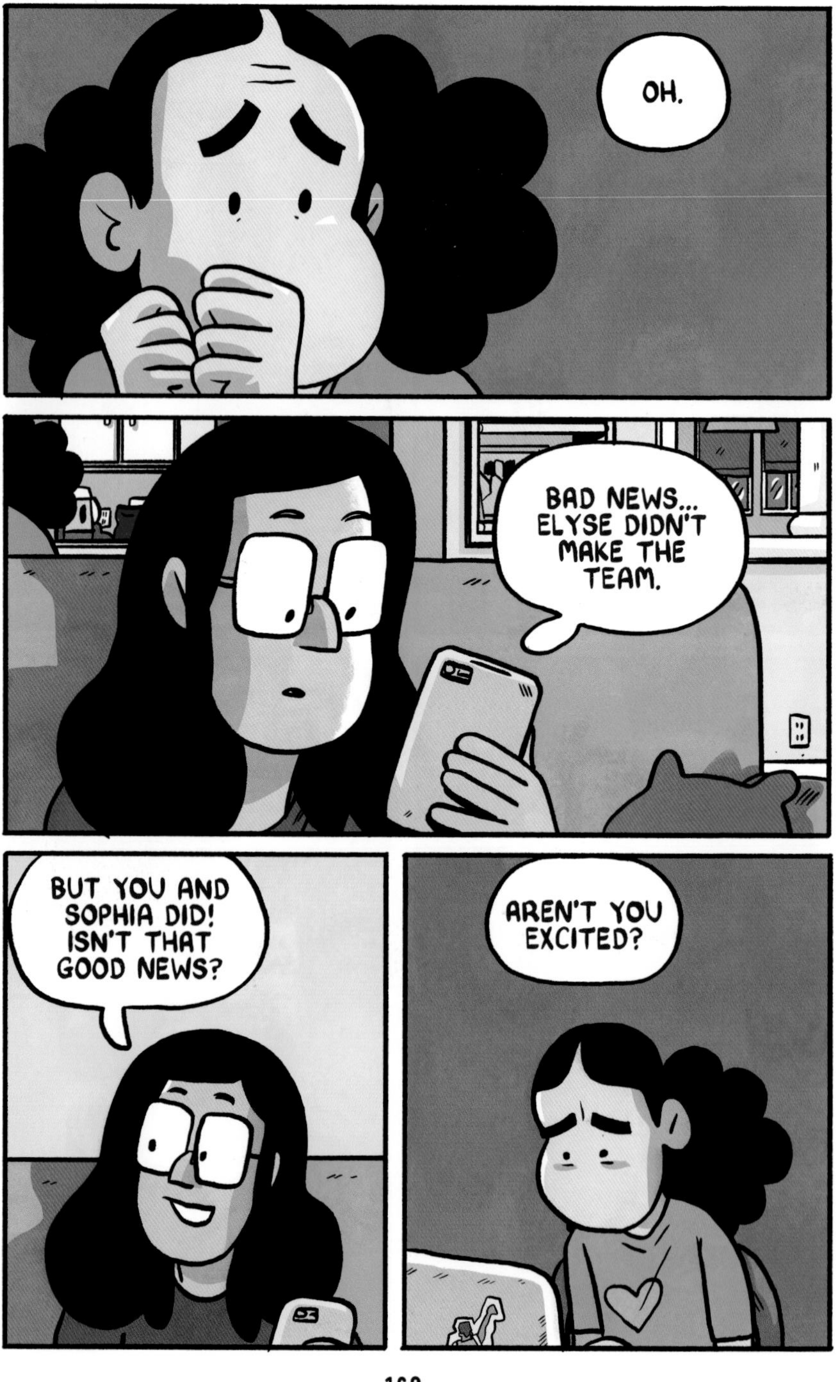
OH.
BAD NEWS... ELYSE DIDN'T MAKE THE TEAM.
BUT YOU AND SOPHIA DID! ISN'T THAT GOOD NEWS?
AREN'T YOU EXCITED?

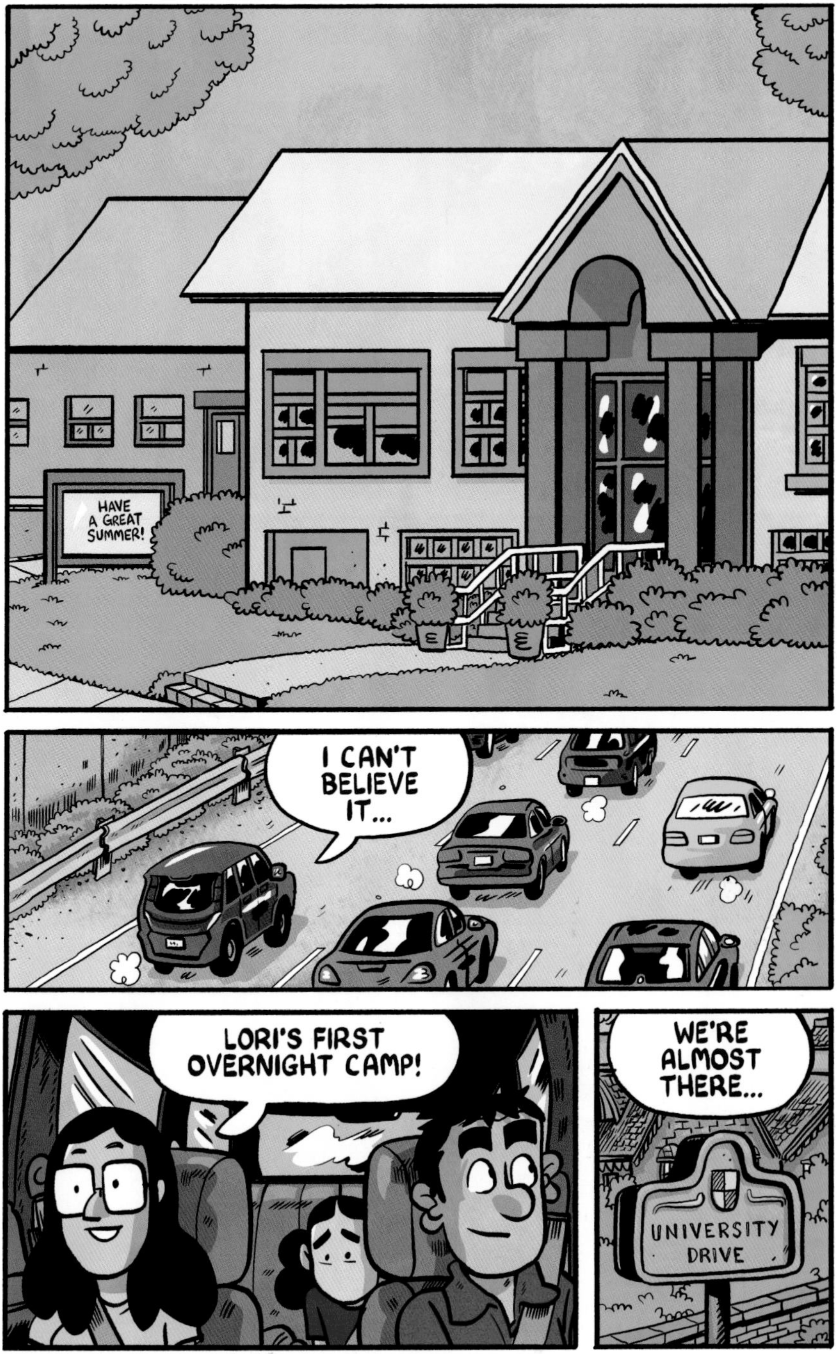
HAVE A GREAT SUMMER!
I CAN'T BELIEVE IT...
LORI'S FIRST OVERNIGHT CAMP!
WE'RE ALMOST THERE...
UNIVERSITY DRIVE

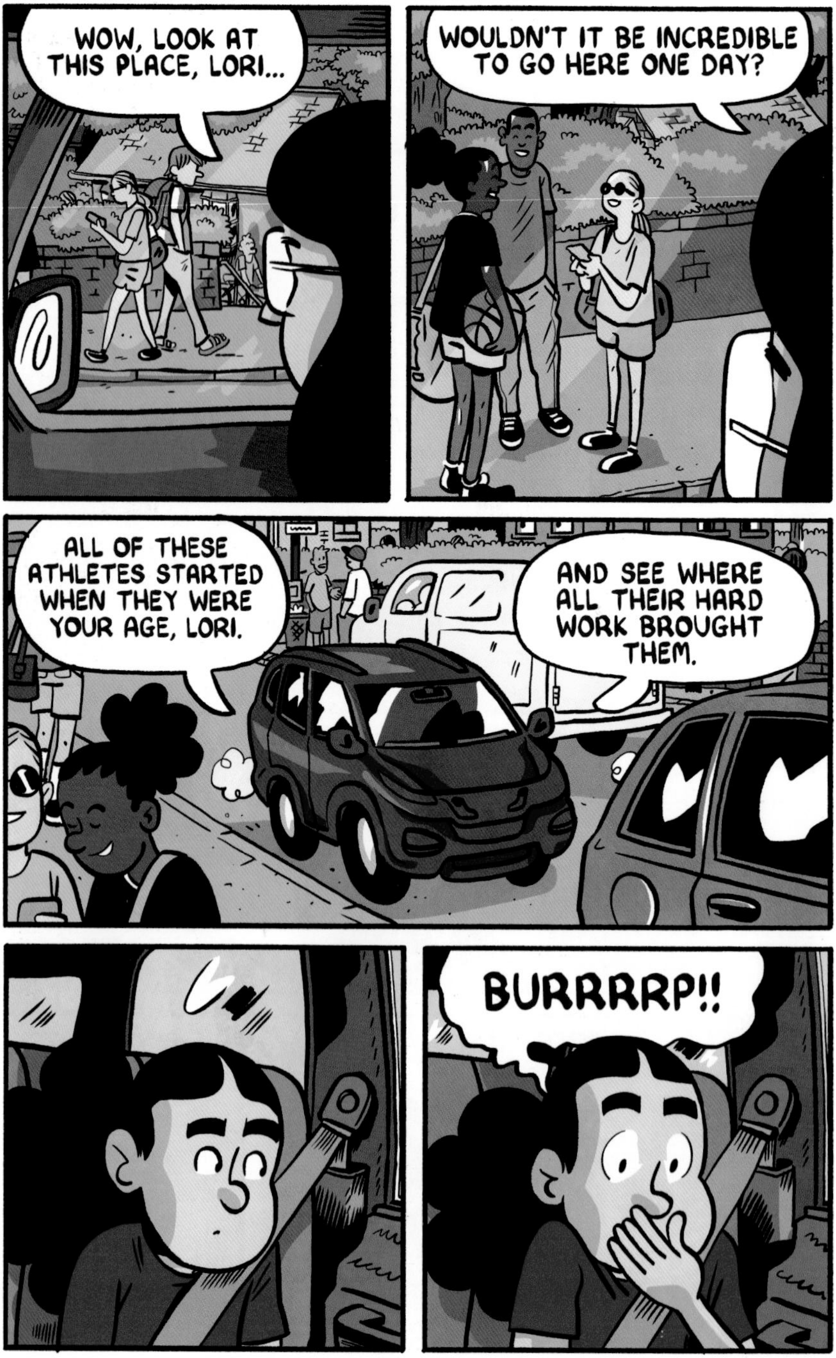
WOW, LOOK AT THIS PLACE, LORI...
WOULDN'T IT BE INCREDIBLE TO GO HERE ONE DAY?
ALL OF THESE ATHLETES STARTED WHEN THEY WERE YOUR AGE, LORI.
AND SEE WHERE ALL THEIR HARD WORK BROUGHT THEM.
BURRRRP!!

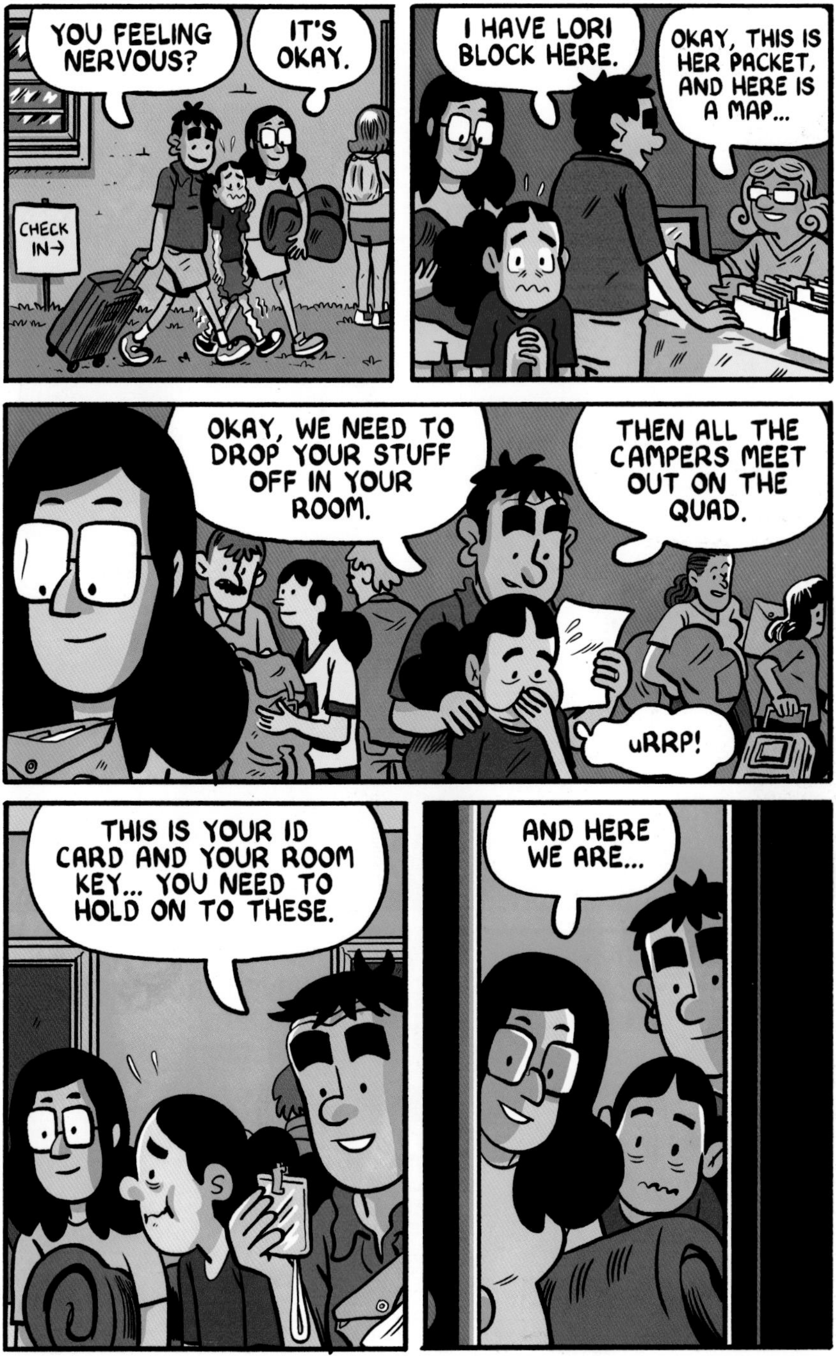
YOU FEELING NERVOUS?
IT'S OKAY.
CHECK IN→
I HAVE LORI BLOCK HERE.
OKAY, THIS IS HER PACKET, AND HERE IS A MAP...
OKAY, WE NEED TO DROP YOUR STUFF OFF IN YOUR ROOM.
THEN ALL THE CAMPERS MEET OUT ON THE QUAD.
uRRP!
THIS IS YOUR ID CARD AND YOUR ROOM KEY... YOU NEED TO HOLD ON TO THESE.
AND HERE WE ARE...

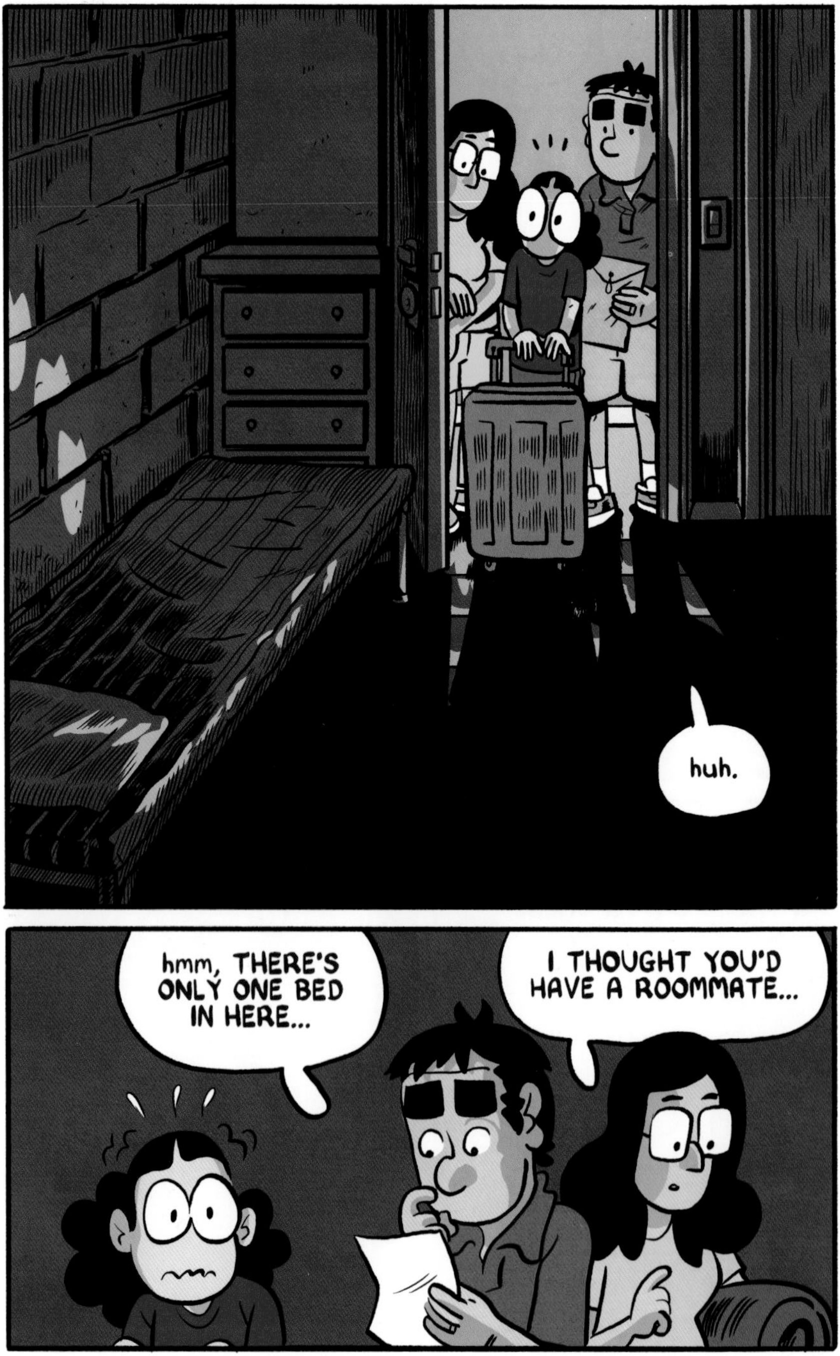
huh.
hmm, THERE'S ONLY ONE BED IN HERE...
I THOUGHT YOU'D HAVE A ROOMMATE...

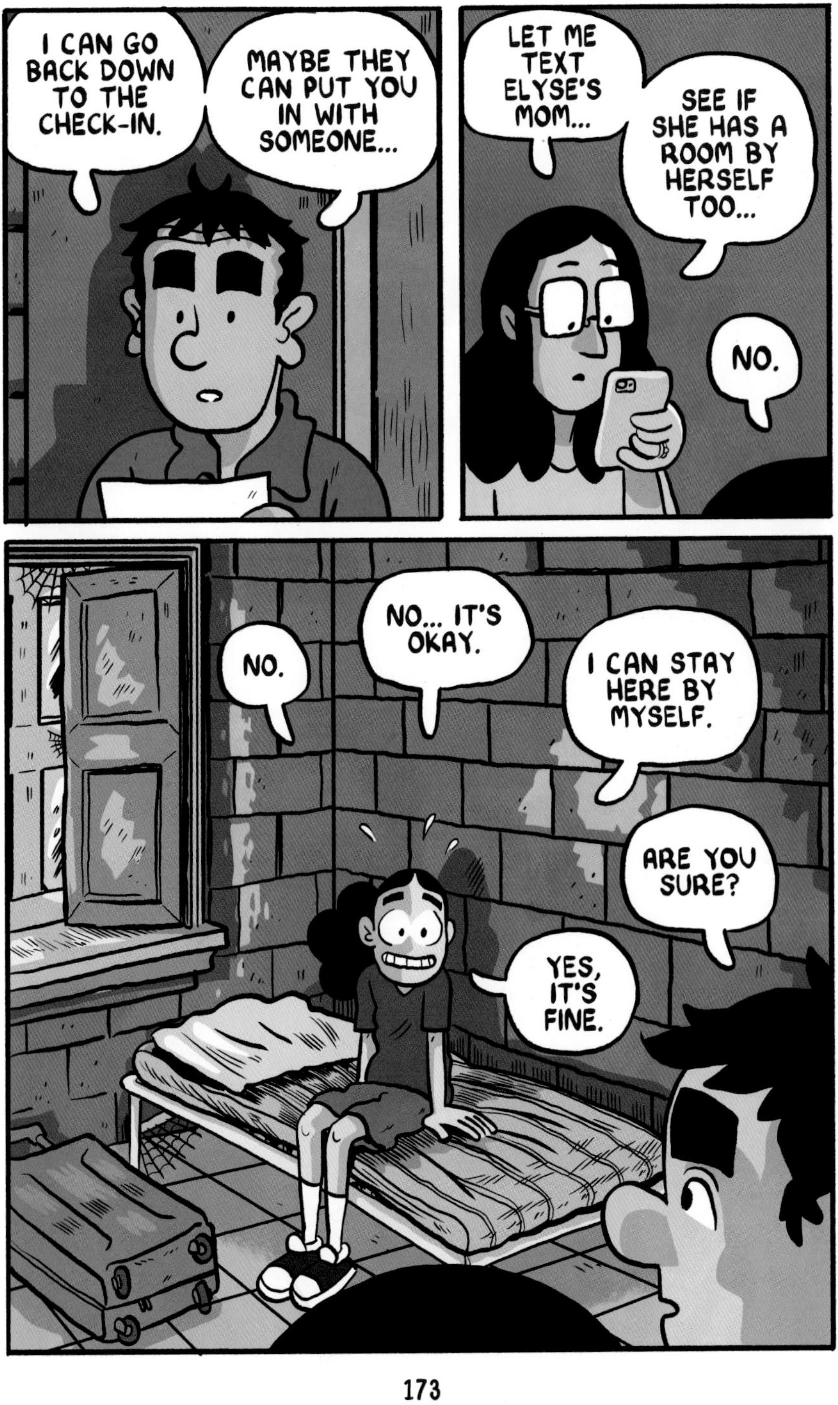
I CAN GO BACK DOWN TO THE CHECK-IN.
MAYBE THEY CAN PUT YOU IN WITH SOMEONE...
LET ME TEXT ELYSE'S MOM...
SEE IF SHE HAS A ROOM BY HERSELF TOO...
NO.
NO.
NO... IT'S OKAY.
I CAN STAY HERE BY MYSELF.
ARE YOU SURE?
YES, IT'S FINE.

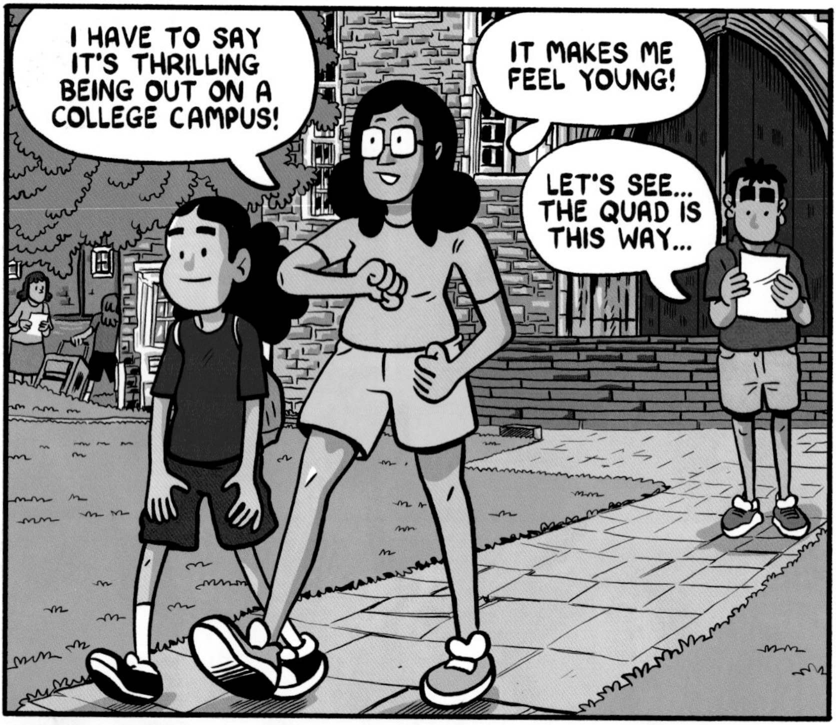
I HAVE TO SAY IT'S THRILLING BEING OUT ON A COLLEGE CAMPUS!
IT MAKES ME FEEL YOUNG!
LET'S SEE... THE QUAD IS THIS WAY...

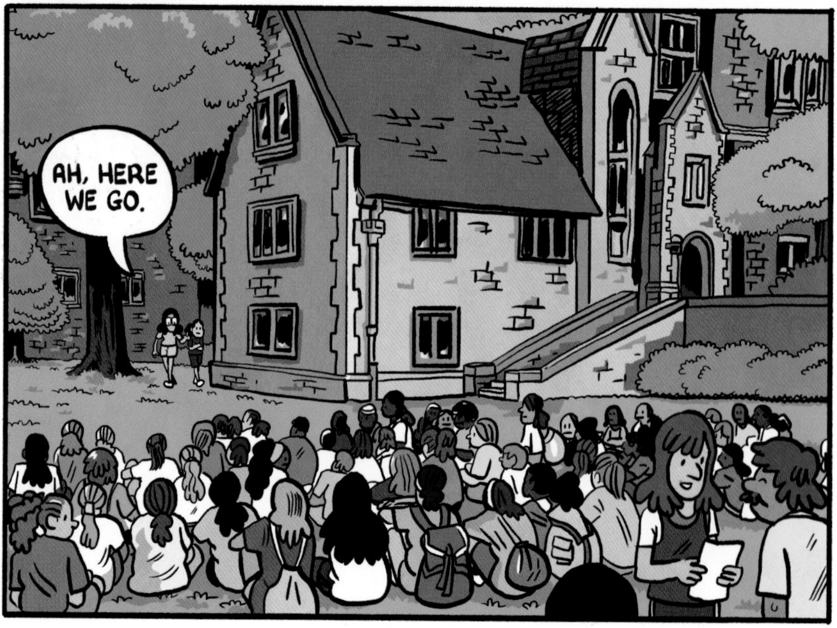
AH, HERE WE GO.

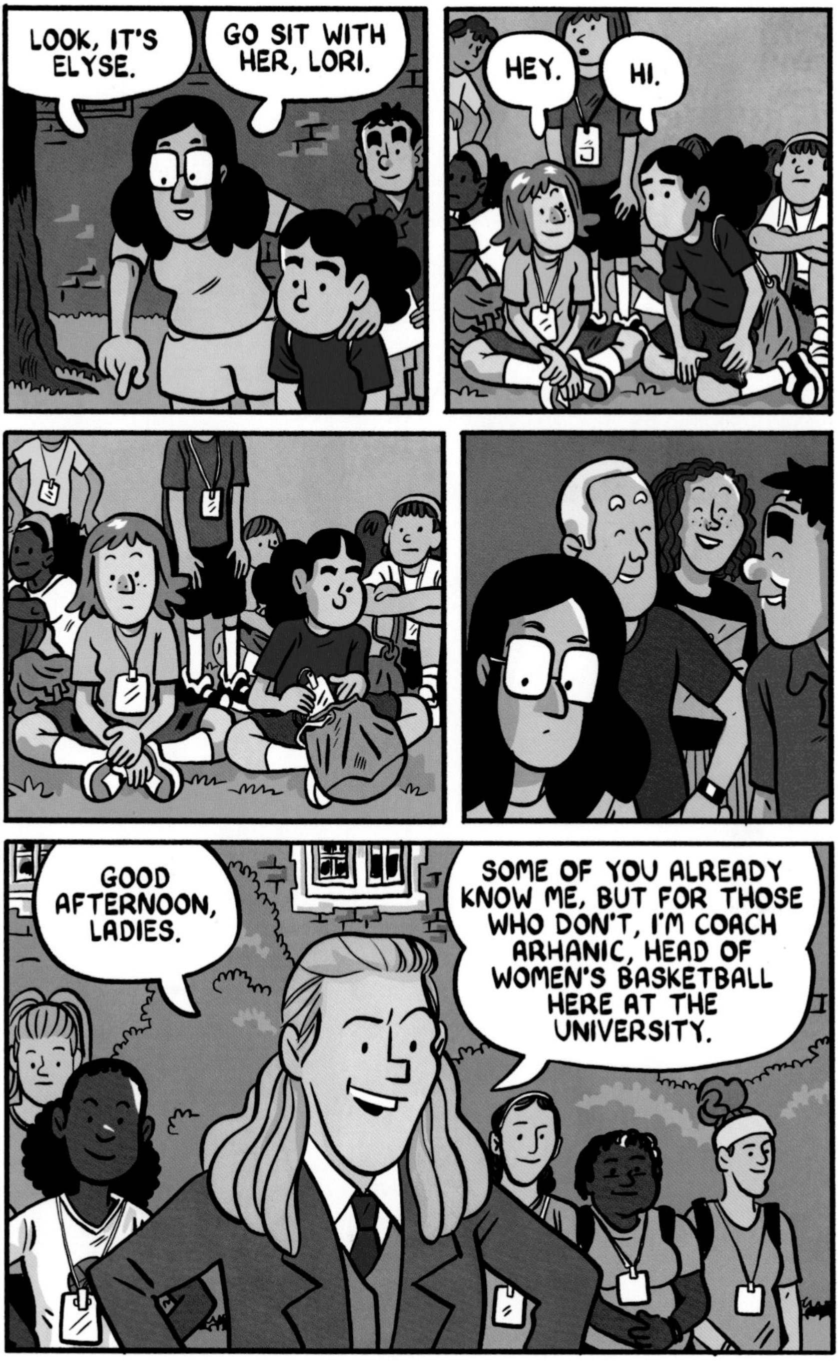
LOOK, IT'S ELYSE.
GO SIT WITH HER, LORI.
HEY.
HI.
GOOD AFTERNOON, LADIES.
SOME OF YOU ALREADY KNOW ME, BUT FOR THOSE WHO DON'T, I'M COACH ARHANIC, HEAD OF WOMEN'S BASKETBALL HERE AT THE UNIVERSITY.

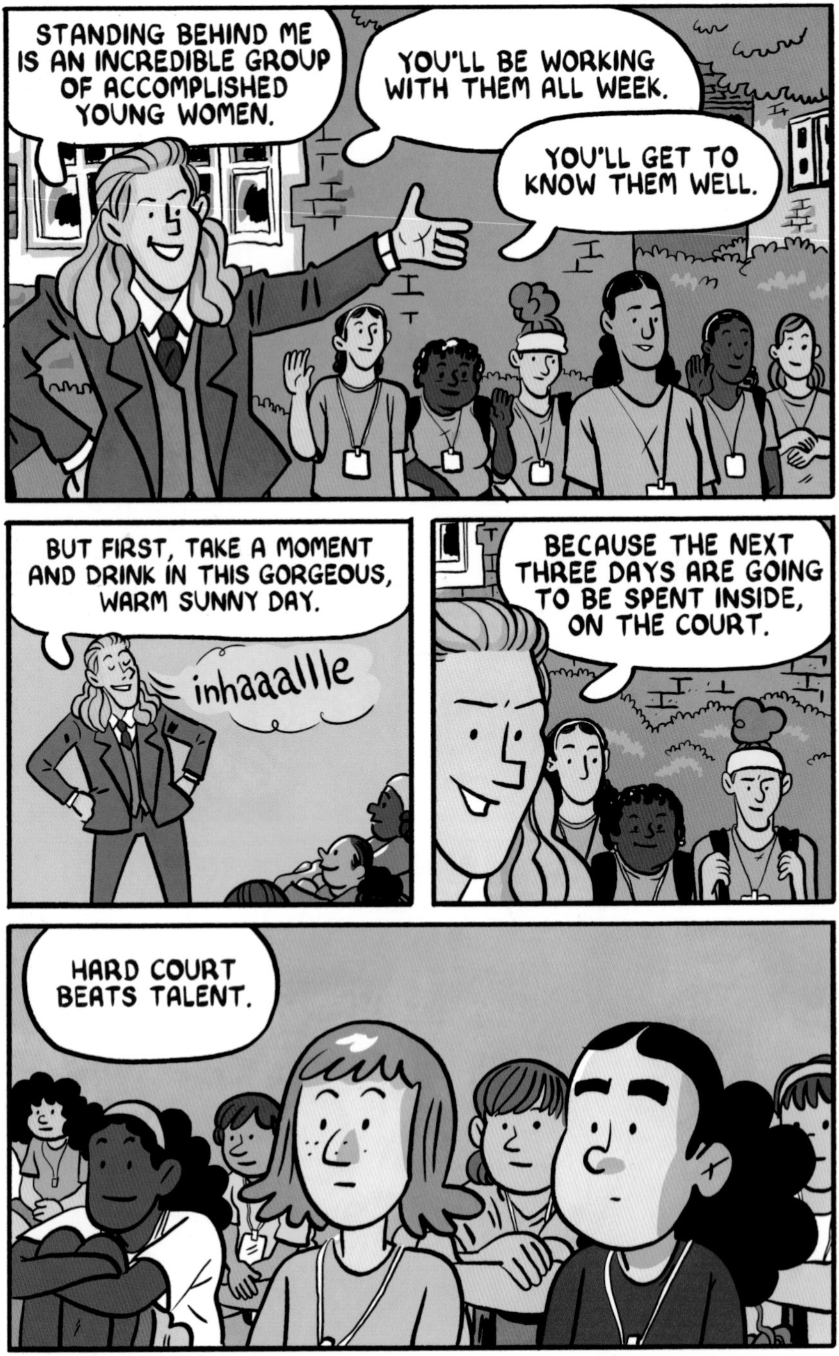
STANDING BEHIND ME IS AN INCREDIBLE GROUP OF ACCOMPLISHED YOUNG WOMEN.
YOU'LL BE WORKING WITH THEM ALL WEEK.
YOU'LL GET TO KNOW THEM WELL.
BUT FIRST, TAKE A MOMENT AND DRINK IN THIS GORGEOUS, WARM SUNNY DAY.
inhaaallle
BECAUSE THE NEXT THREE DAYS ARE GOING TO BE SPENT INSIDE, ON THE COURT.
HARD COURT BEATS TALENT.

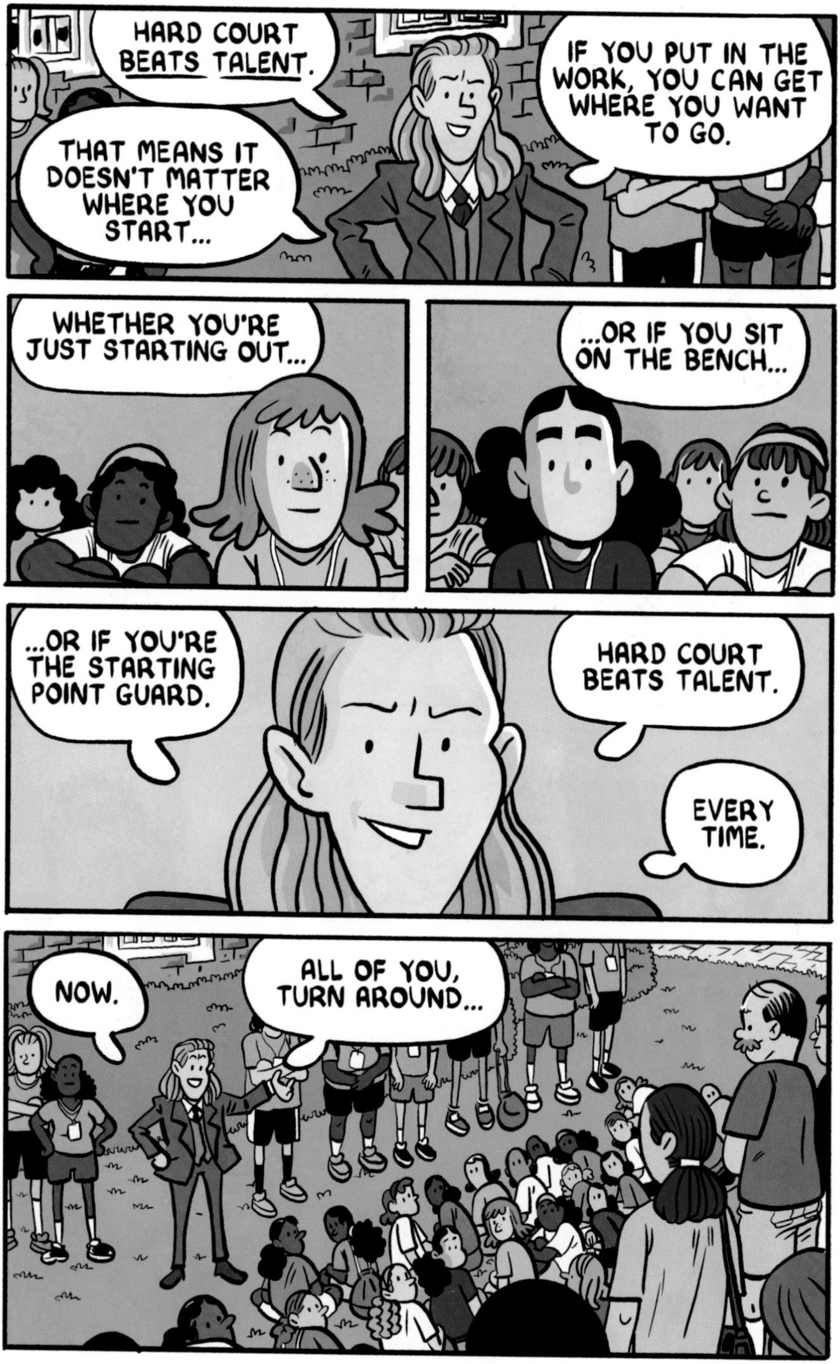
HARD COURT BEATS TALENT.
THAT MEANS IT DOESN'T MATTER WHERE YOU START...
IF YOU PUT IN THE WORK, YOU CAN GET WHERE YOU WANT TO GO.
WHETHER YOU'RE JUST STARTING OUT...
...OR IF YOU SIT ON THE BENCH...
...OR IF YOU'RE THE STARTING POINT GUARD.
HARD COURT BEATS TALENT.
EVERY TIME.
NOW.
ALL OF YOU, TURN AROUND...

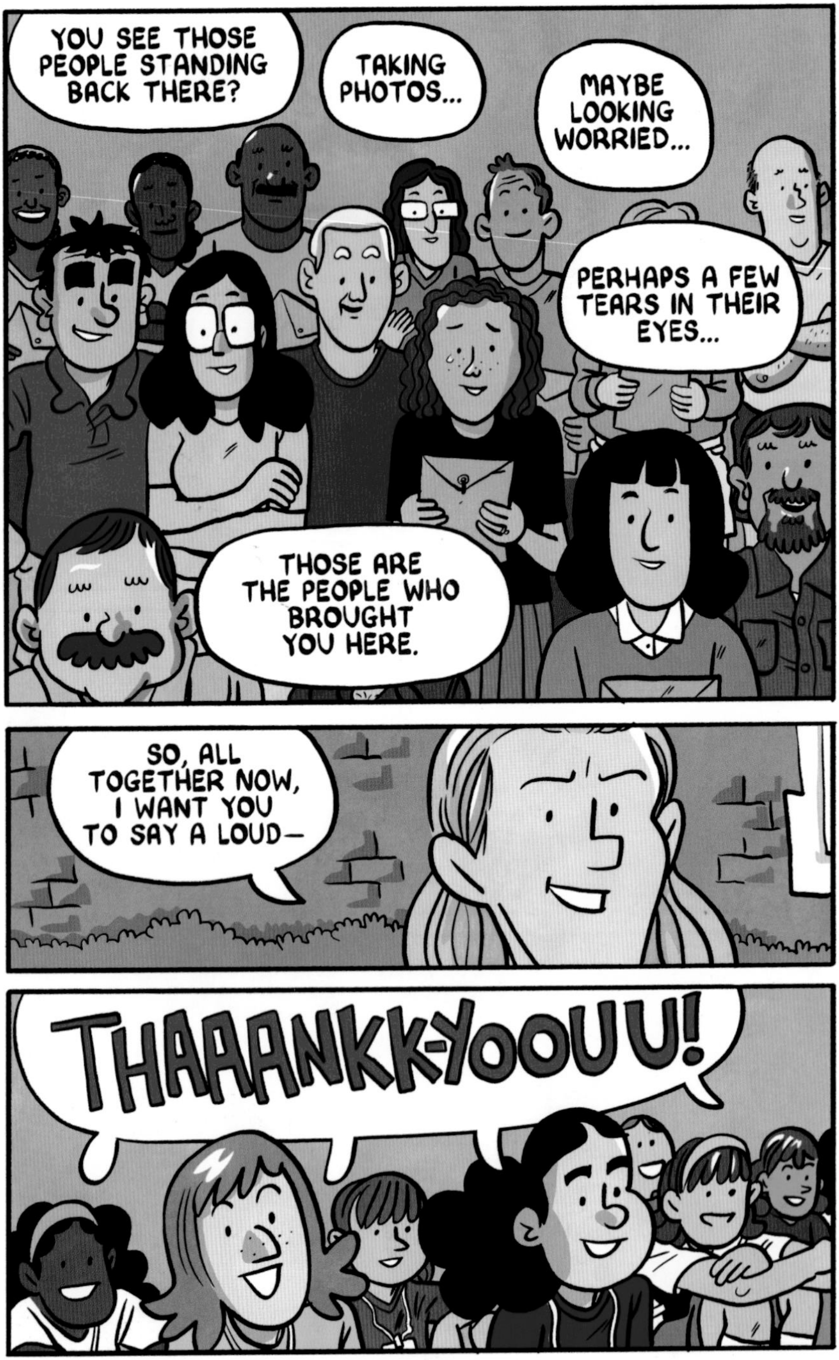
YOU SEE THOSE PEOPLE STANDING BACK THERE?
TAKING PHOTOS...
MAYBE LOOKING WORRIED...
PERHAPS A FEW TEARS IN THEIR EYES...
THOSE ARE THE PEOPLE WHO BROUGHT YOU HERE.
SO, ALL TOGETHER NOW, I WANT YOU TO SAY A LOUD—
THAAANKK-YOOUU!

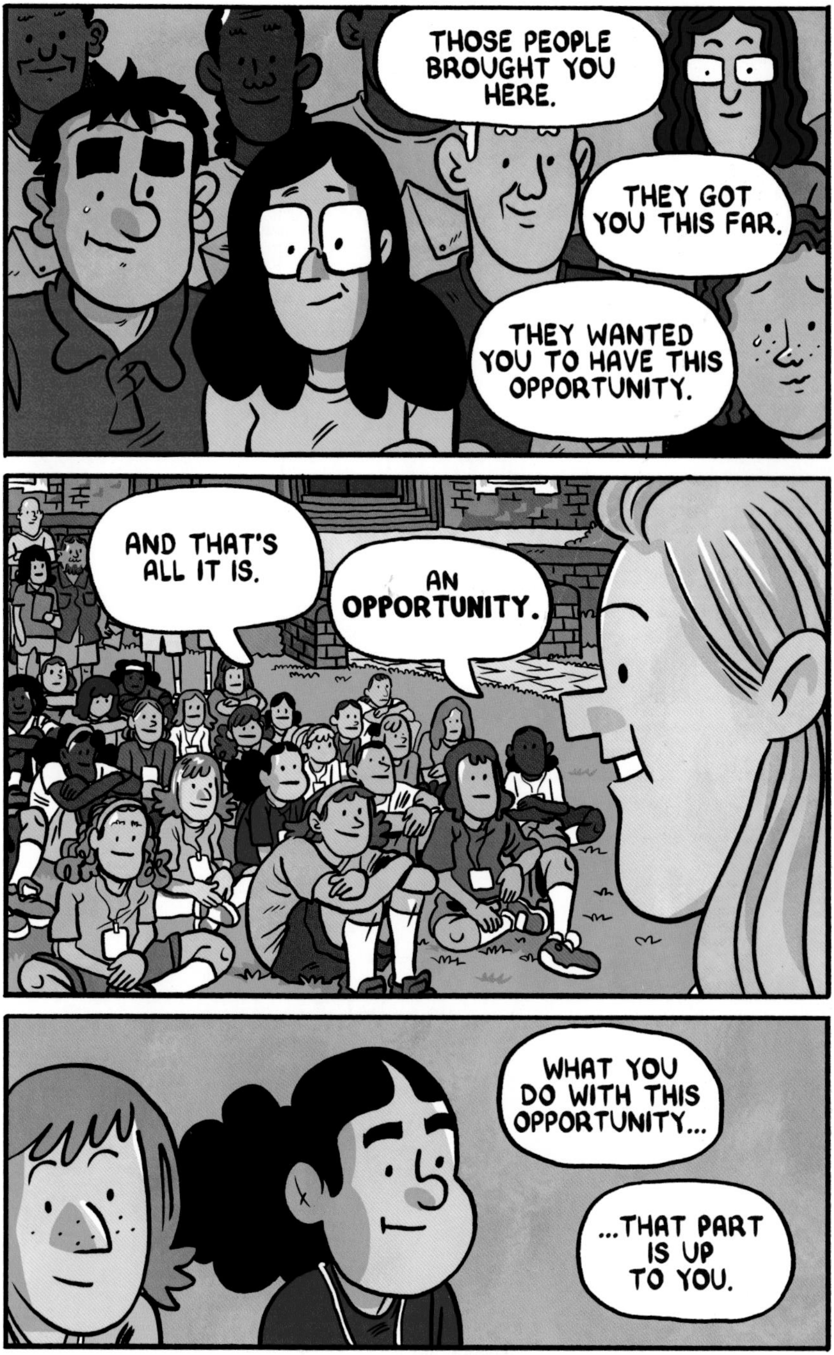
THOSE PEOPLE BROUGHT YOU HERE.
THEY GOT YOU THIS FAR.
THEY WANTED YOU TO HAVE THIS OPPORTUNITY.
AND THAT'S ALL IT IS.
AN OPPORTUNITY.
WHAT YOU DO WITH THIS OPPORTUNITY...
...THAT PART IS UP TO YOU.

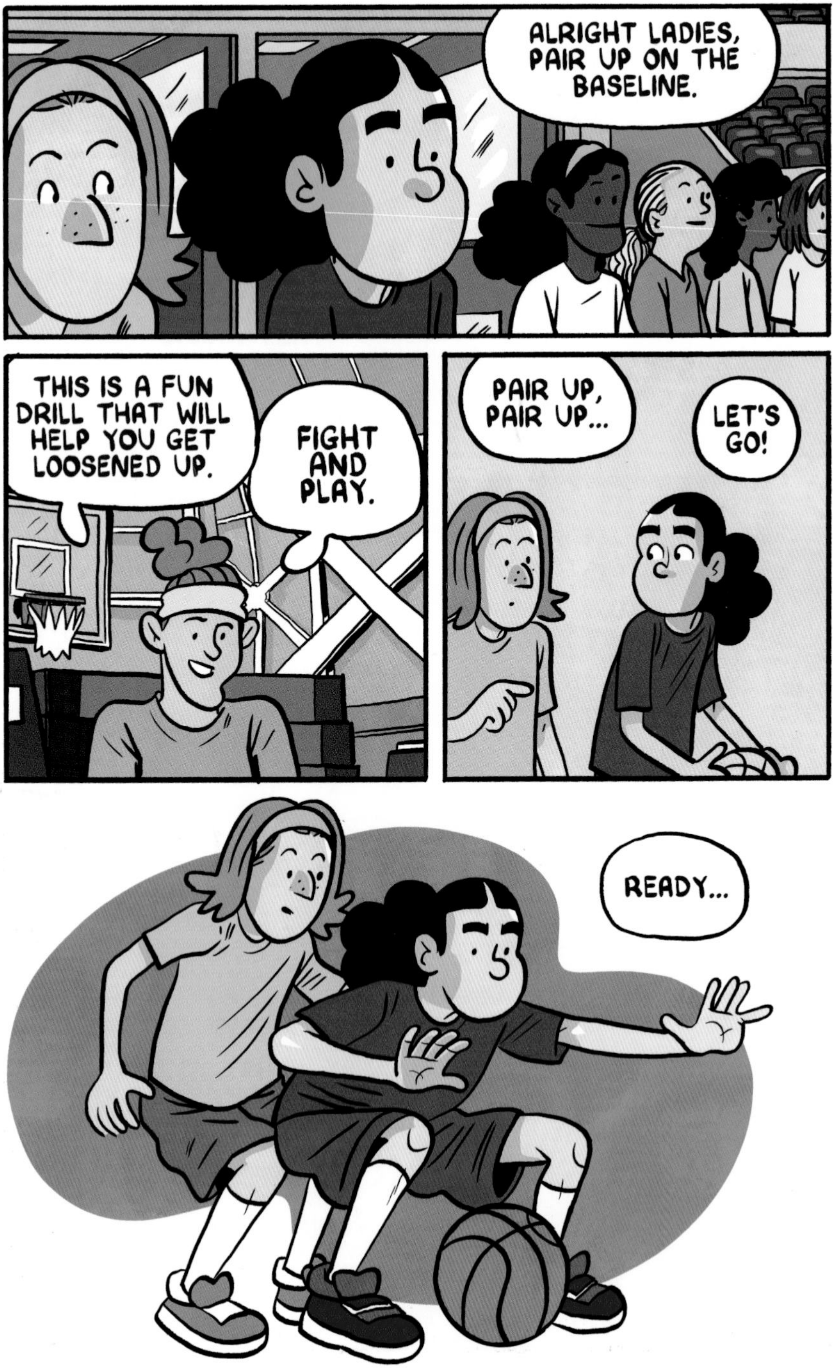
ALRIGHT LADIES, PAIR UP ON THE BASELINE.
THIS IS A FUN DRILL THAT WILL HELP YOU GET LOOSENED UP.
FIGHT AND PLAY.
PAIR UP, PAIR UP...
LET'S GO!
READY...

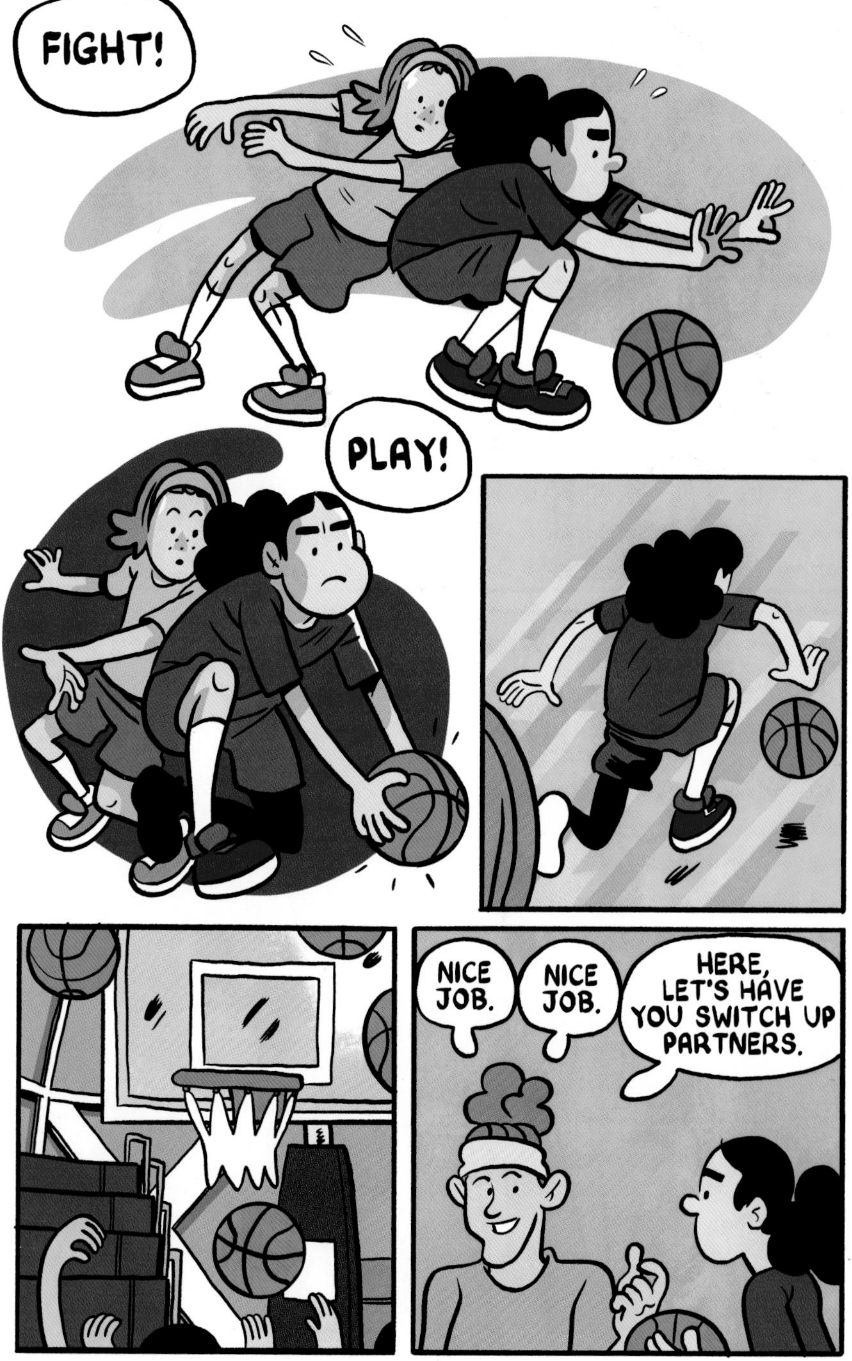
FIGHT!
PLAY!
NICE JOB.
NICE JOB.
HERE, LET'S HAVE YOU SWITCH UP PARTNERS.

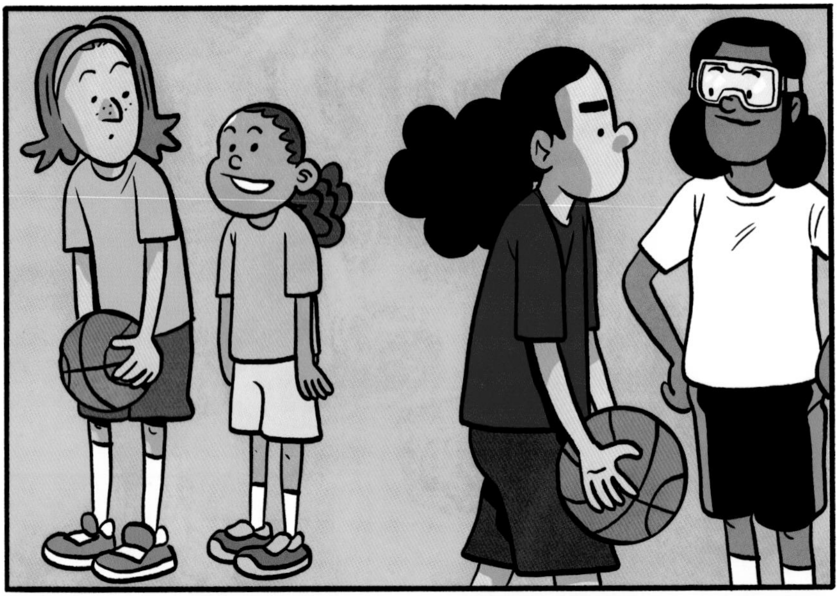

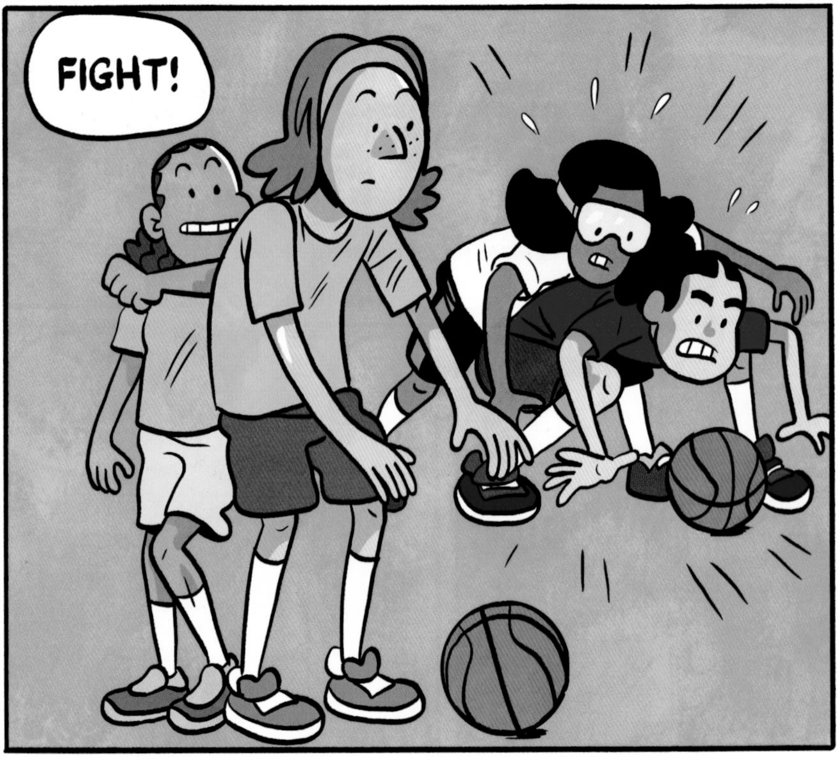
FIGHT!

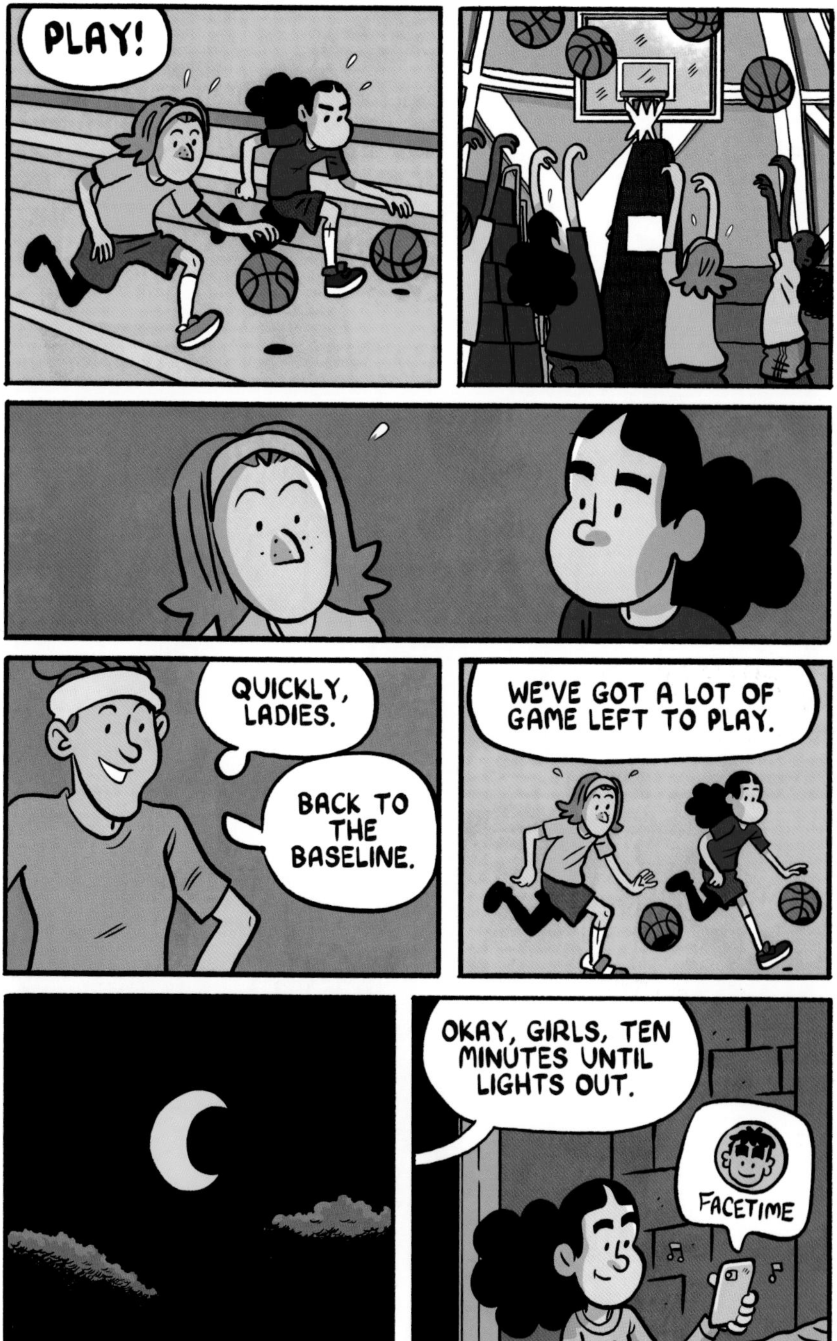
PLAY!
QUICKLY, LADIES.
BACK TO THE BASELINE.
WE'VE GOT A LOT OF GAME LEFT TO PLAY.
OKAY, GIRLS, TEN MINUTES UNTIL LIGHTS OUT.
FACETIME

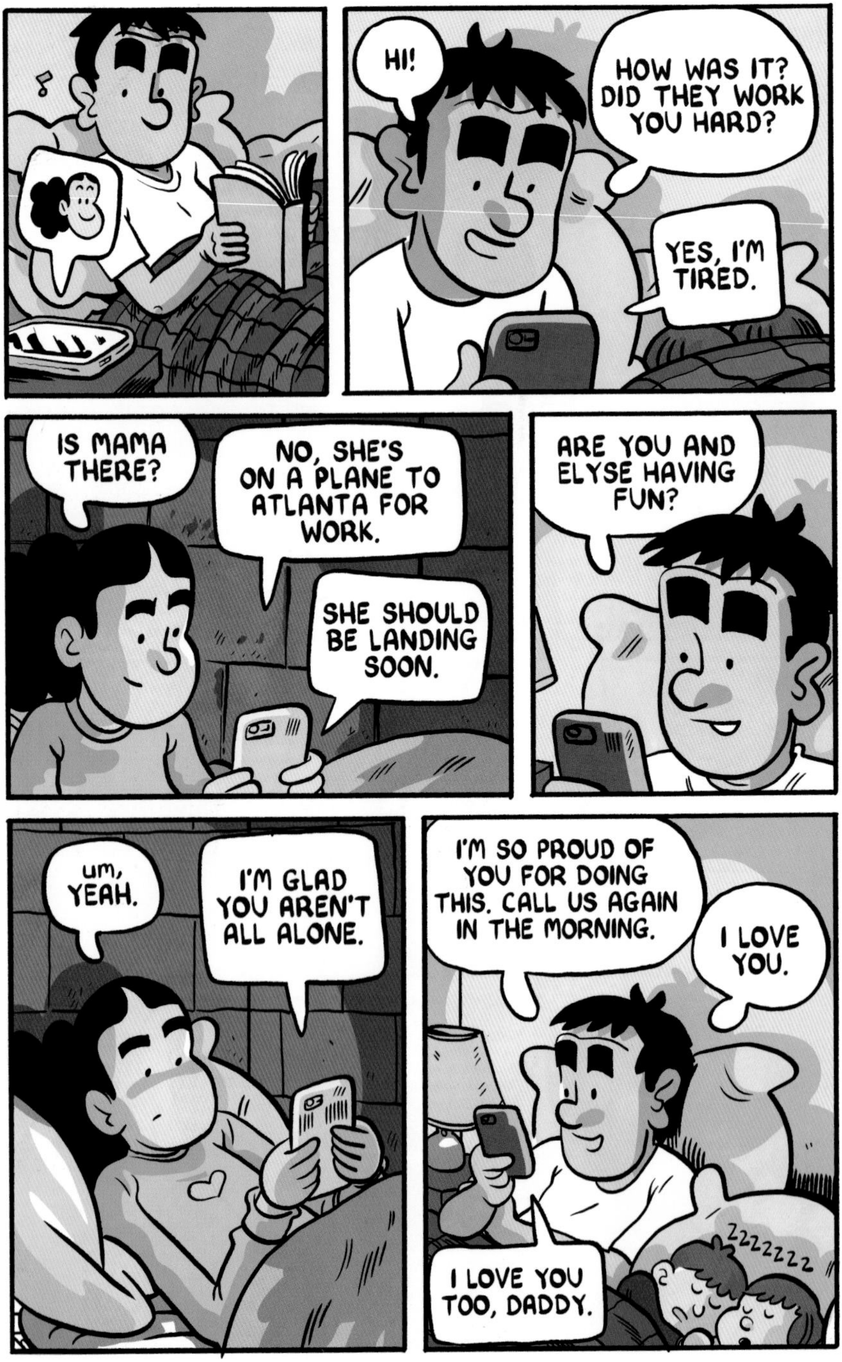
HI!
HOW WAS IT? DID THEY WORK YOU HARD?
YES, I'M TIRED.
IS MAMA THERE?
NO, SHE'S ON A PLANE TO ATLANTA FOR WORK.
SHE SHOULD BE LANDING SOON.
ARE YOU AND ELYSE HAVING FUN?
um, YEAH.
I'M GLAD YOU AREN'T ALL ALONE.
I'M SO PROUD OF YOU FOR DOING THIS. CALL US AGAIN IN THE MORNING.
I LOVE YOU.
I LOVE YOU TOO, DADDY.
ZZZZZZZ

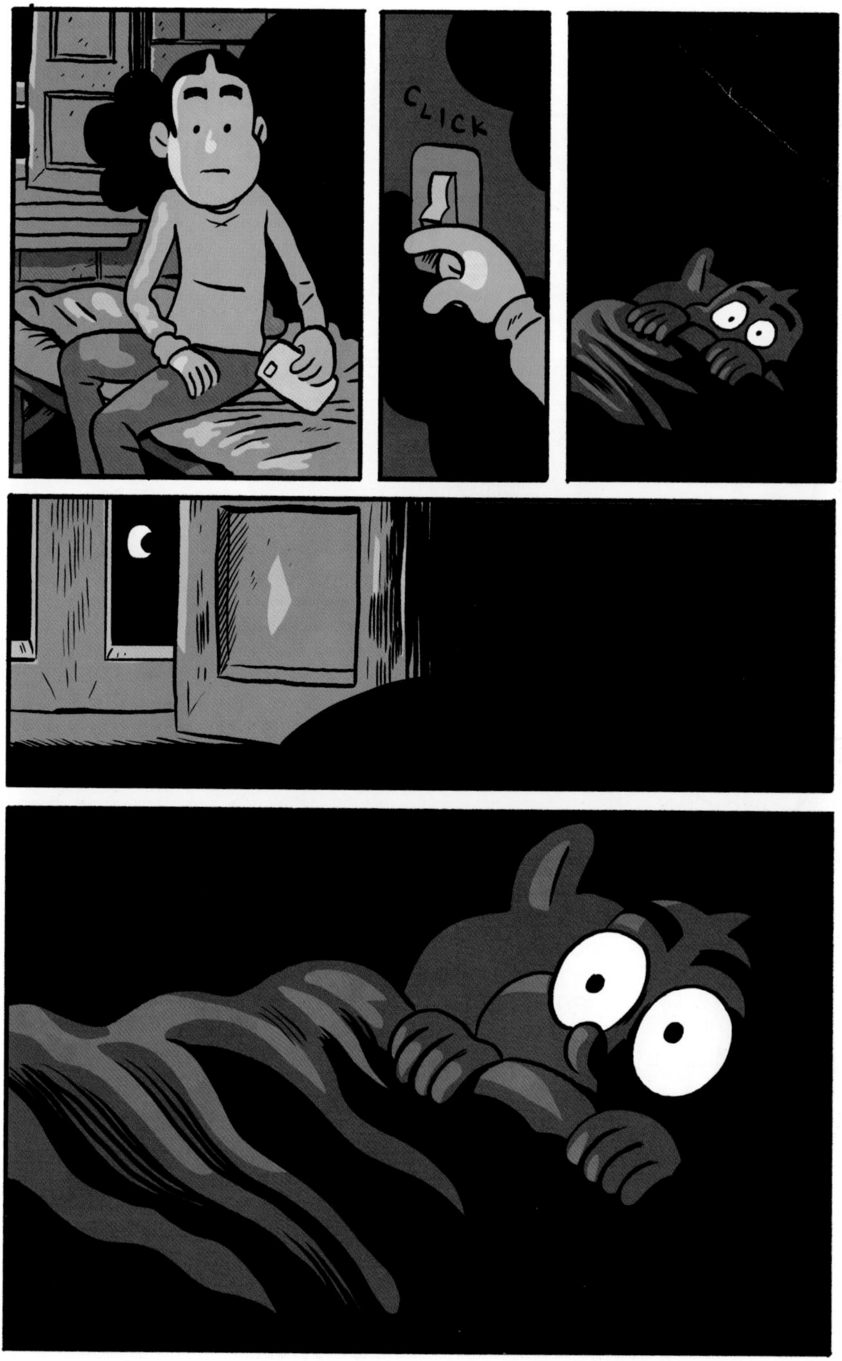
CLICK

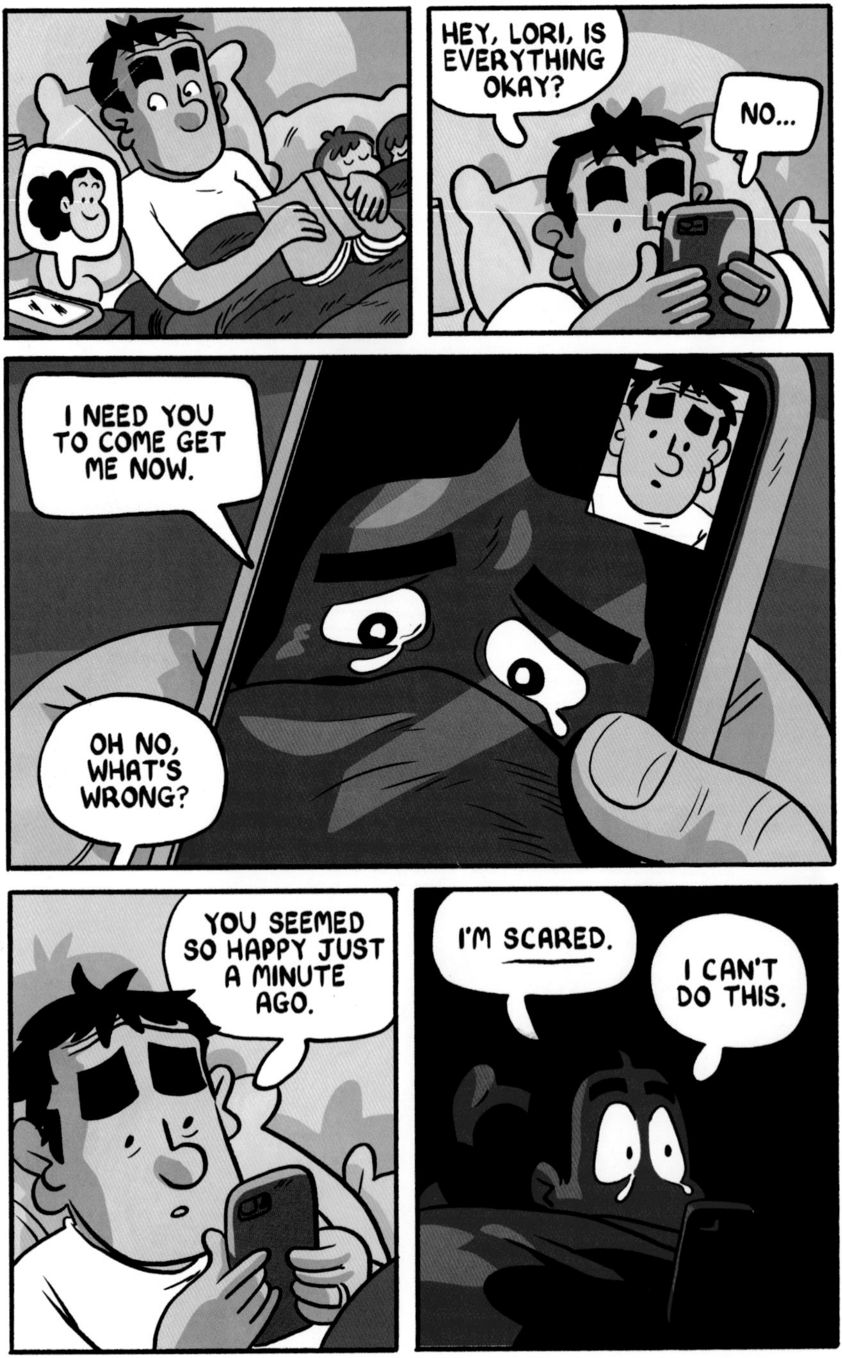
HEY, LORI, IS EVERYTHING OKAY?
NO...
I NEED YOU TO COME GET ME NOW.
OH NO, WHAT'S WRONG?
YOU SEEMED SO HAPPY JUST A MINUTE AGO.
I'M SCARED.
I CAN'T DO THIS.

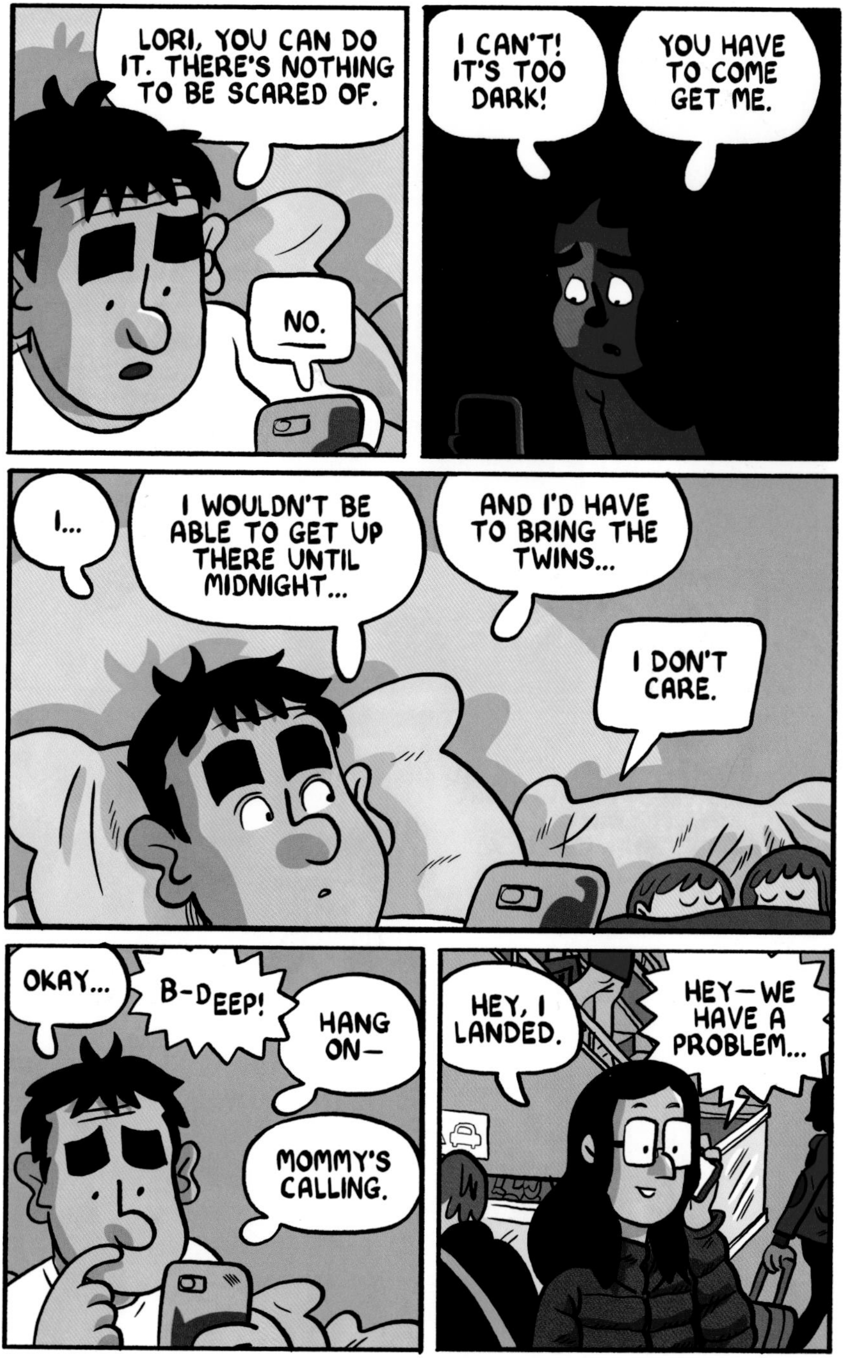
LORI, YOU CAN DO IT. THERE'S NOTHING TO BE SCARED OF.
NO.
I CAN'T! IT'S TOO DARK!
YOU HAVE TO COME GET ME.
I...
I WOULDN'T BE ABLE TO GET UP THERE UNTIL MIDNIGHT...
AND I'D HAVE TO BRING THE TWINS...
I DON'T CARE.
OKAY...
B-DEEP!
HANG ON—
MOMMY'S CALLING.
HEY, I LANDED.
HEY—WE HAVE A PROBLEM...

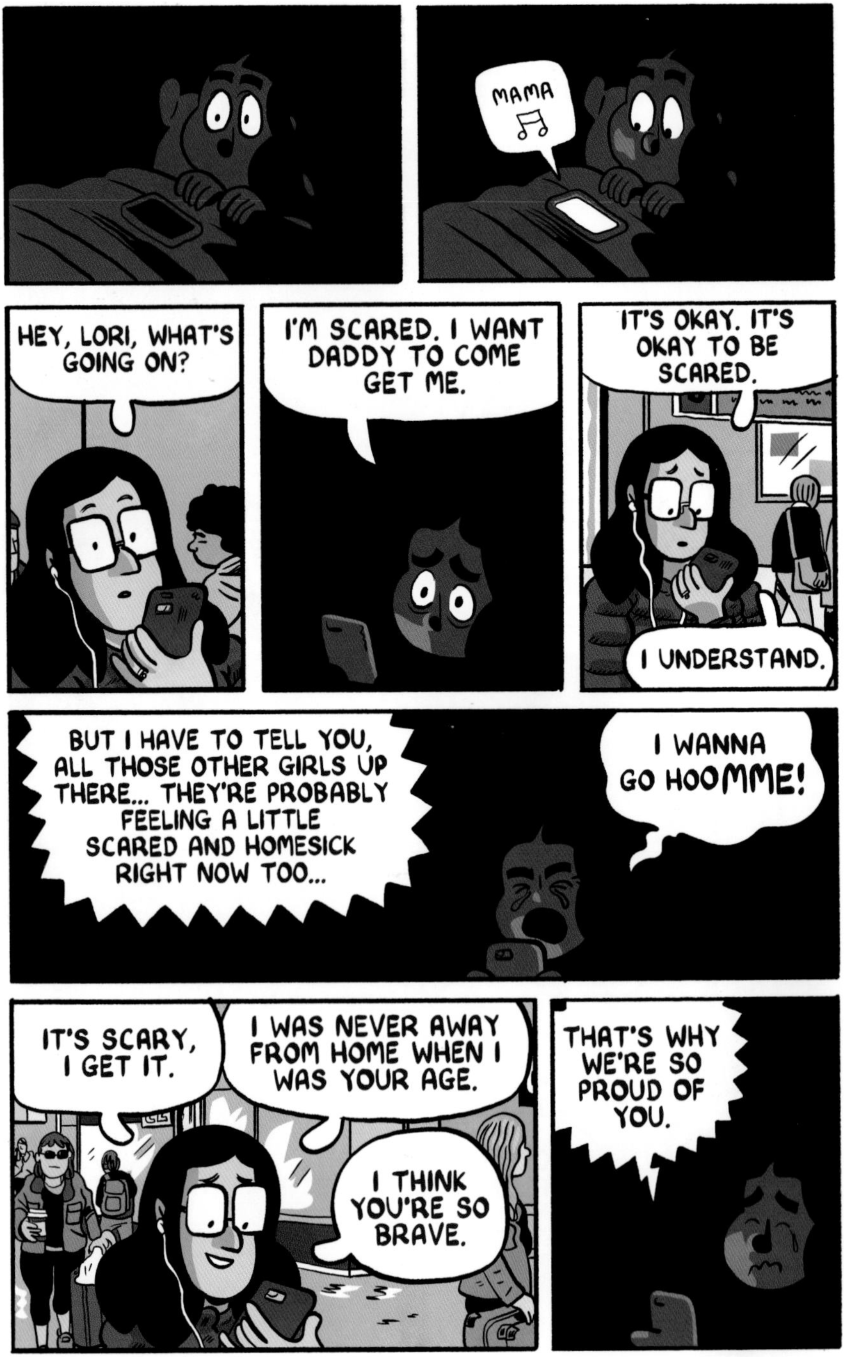
MAMA
HEY, LORI, WHAT'S GOING ON?
I'M SCARED. I WANT DADDY TO COME GET ME.
IT'S OKAY. IT'S OKAY TO BE SCARED.
I UNDERSTAND.
BUT I HAVE TO TELL YOU, ALL THOSE OTHER GIRLS UP THERE... THEY'RE PROBABLY FEELING A LITTLE SCARED AND HOMESICK RIGHT NOW TOO...
I WANNA GO HOOMME!
IT'S SCARY, I GET IT.
I WAS NEVER AWAY FROM HOME WHEN I WAS YOUR AGE.
I THINK YOU'RE SO BRAVE.
THAT'S WHY WE'RE SO PROUD OF YOU.

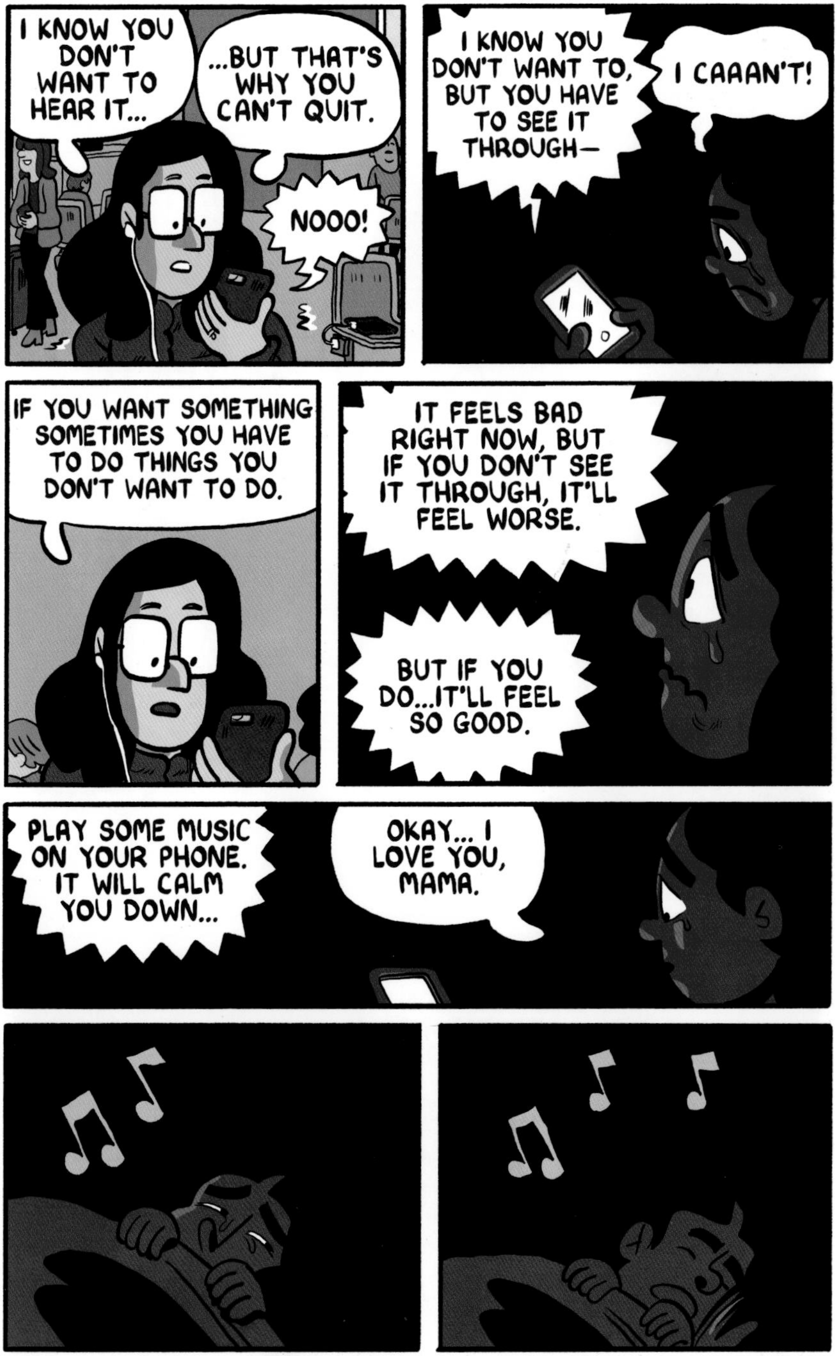
I KNOW YOU DON'T WANT TO HEAR IT...
...BUT THAT'S WHY YOU CAN'T QUIT.
NOOO!
I KNOW YOU DON'T WANT TO, BUT YOU HAVE TO SEE IT THROUGH—
I CAAAN'T!
IF YOU WANT SOMETHING SOMETIMES YOU HAVE TO DO THINGS YOU DON'T WANT TO DO.
IT FEELS BAD RIGHT NOW, BUT IF YOU DON'T SEE IT THROUGH, IT'LL FEEL WORSE.
BUT IF YOU DO...IT'LL FEEL SO GOOD.
PLAY SOME MUSIC ON YOUR PHONE. IT WILL CALM YOU DOWN...
OKAY... I LOVE YOU, MAMA.

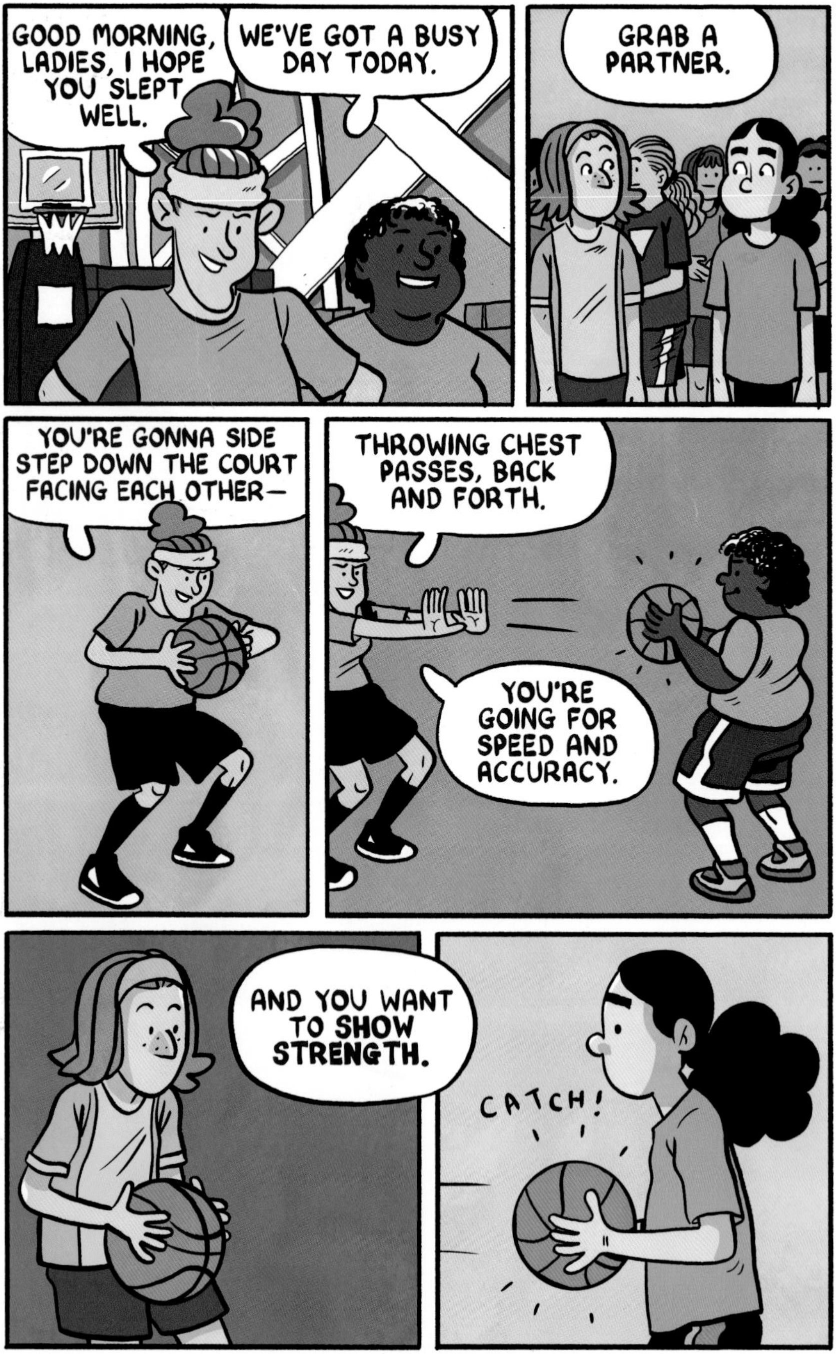
GOOD MORNING, LADIES, I HOPE YOU SLEPT WELL.
WE'VE GOT A BUSY DAY TODAY.
GRAB A PARTNER.
YOU'RE GONNA SIDE STEP DOWN THE COURT FACING EACH OTHER—
THROWING CHEST PASSES, BACK AND FORTH.
YOU'RE GOING FOR SPEED AND ACCURACY.
AND YOU WANT TO SHOW STRENGTH.
CATCH!

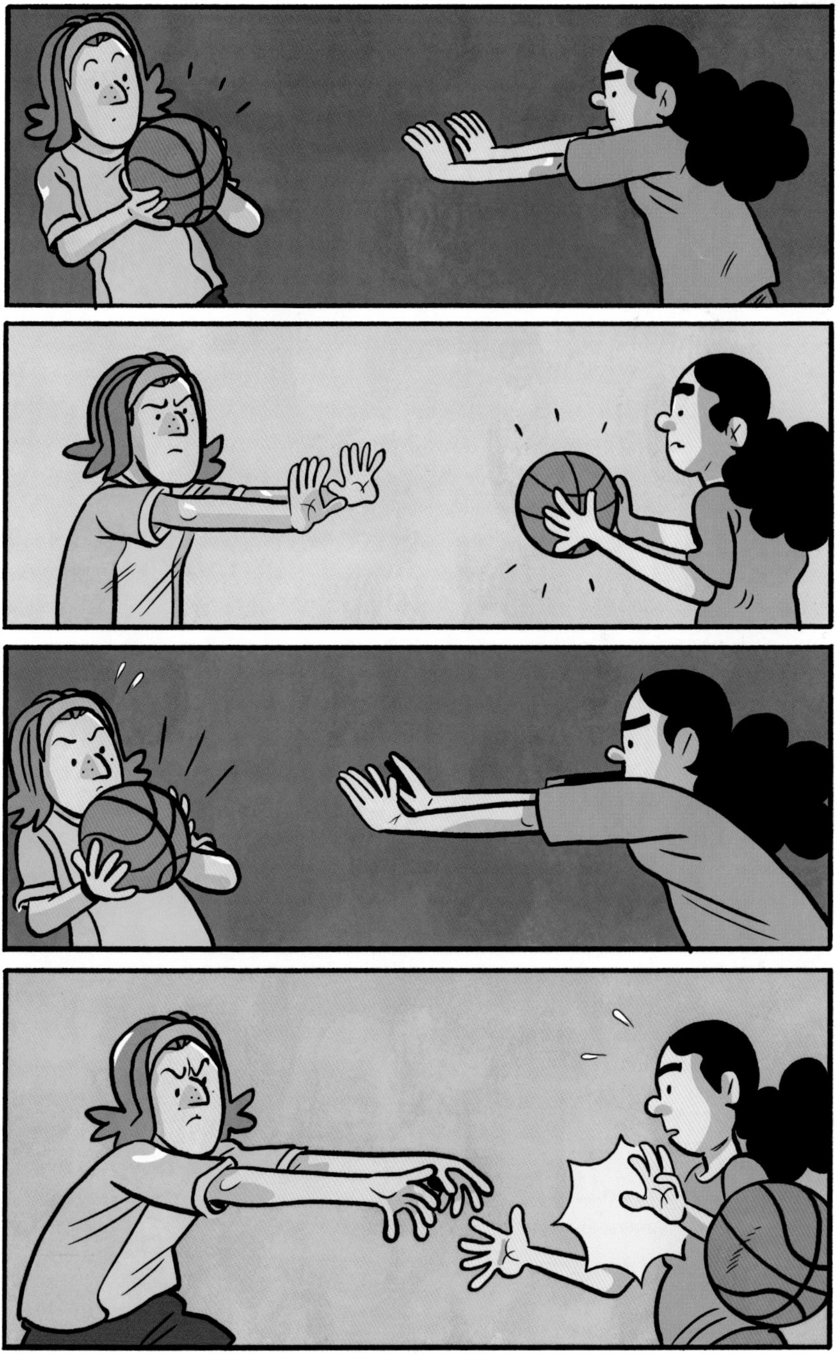

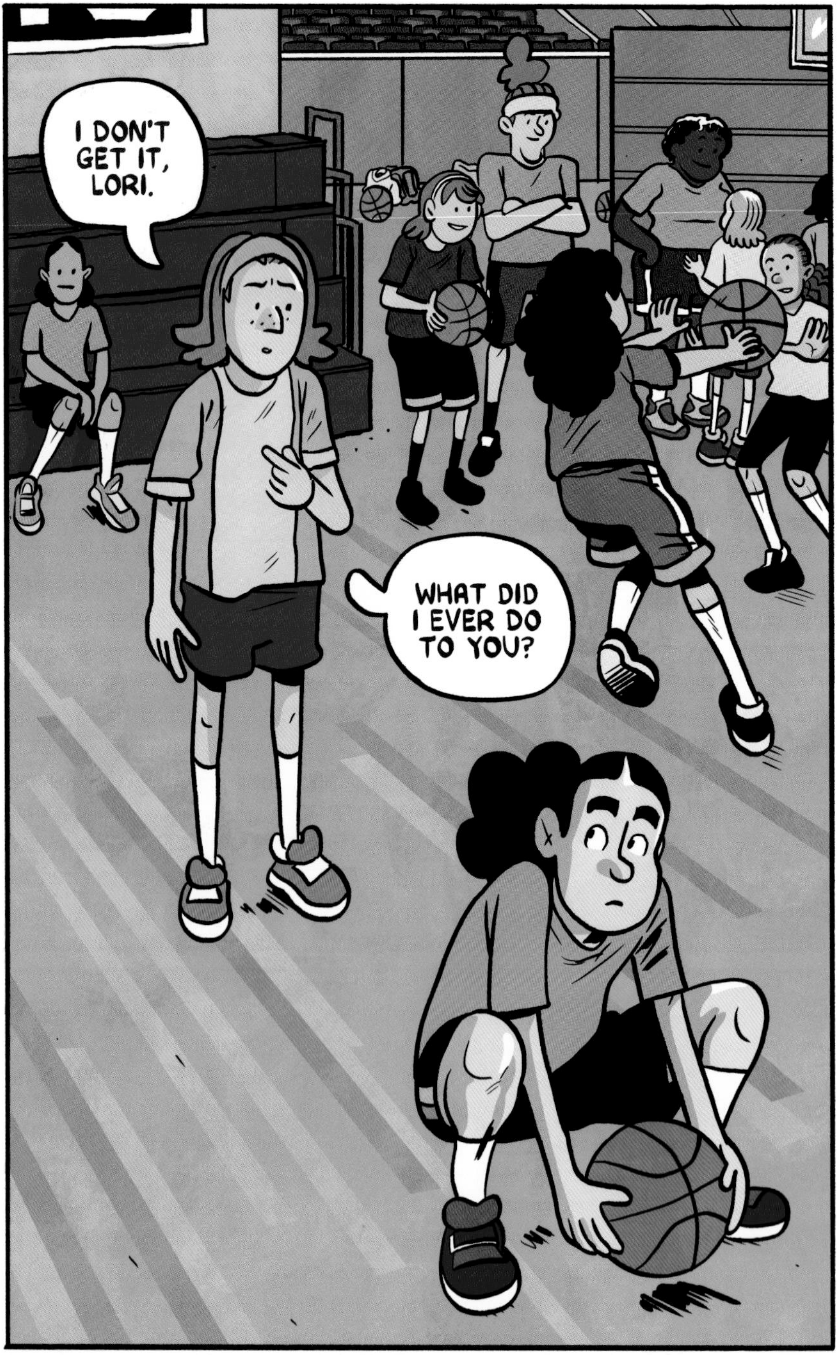
I DON'T GET IT, LORI.
WHAT DID I EVER DO TO YOU?

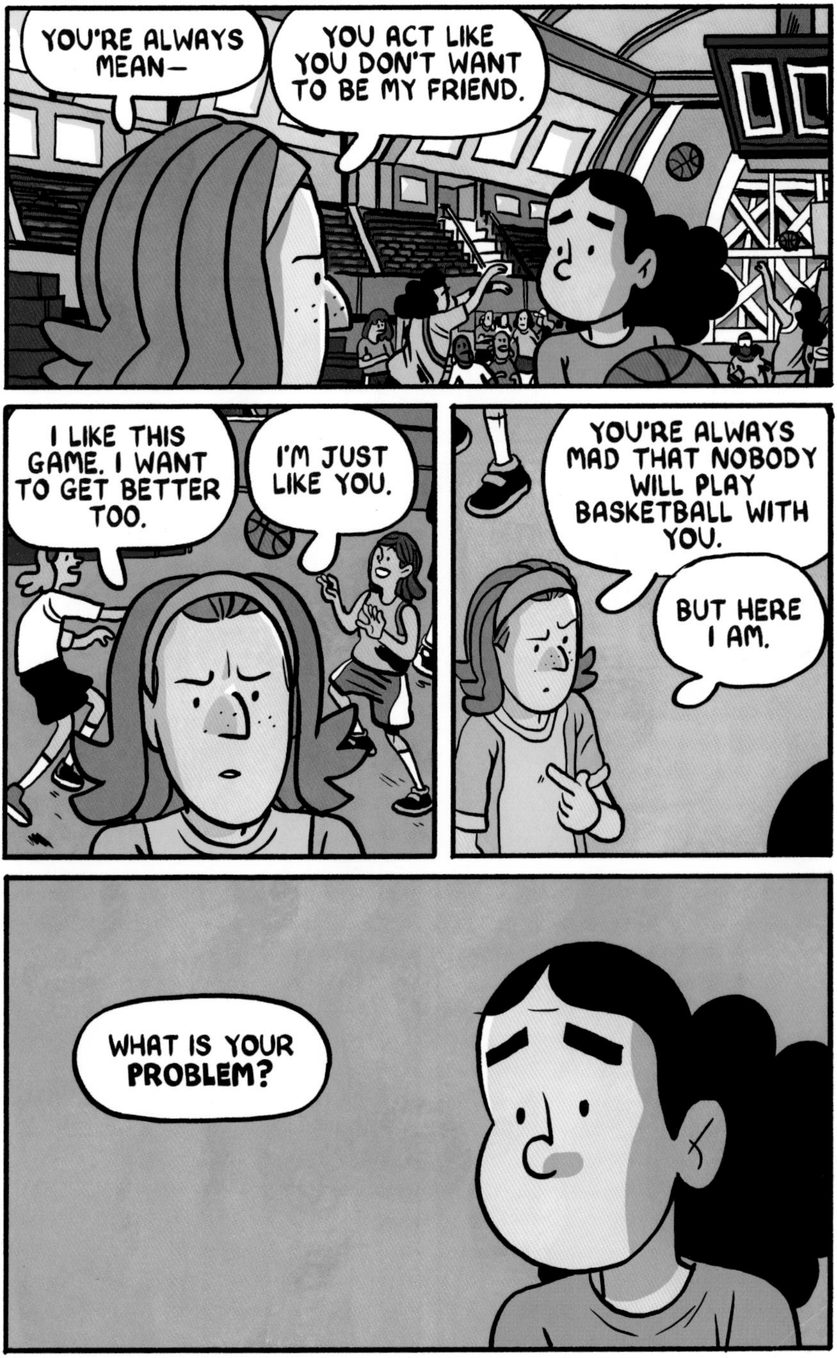
YOU'RE ALWAYS MEAN—
YOU ACT LIKE YOU DON'T WANT TO BE MY FRIEND.
I LIKE THIS GAME. I WANT TO GET BETTER TOO.
I'M JUST LIKE YOU.
YOU'RE ALWAYS MAD THAT NOBODY WILL PLAY BASKETBALL WITH YOU.
BUT HERE I AM.
WHAT IS YOUR **PROBLEM?**

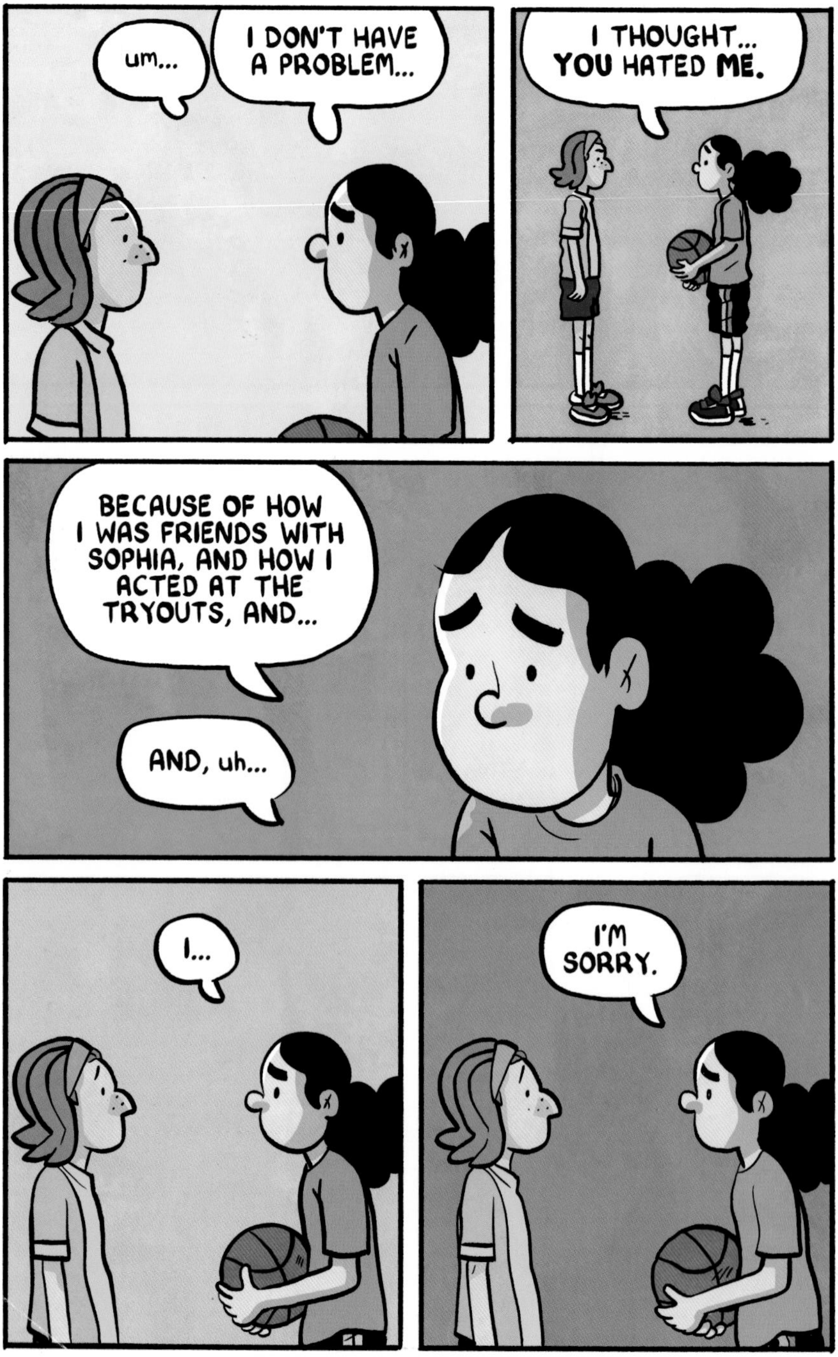
um...
I DON'T HAVE A PROBLEM...
I THOUGHT... YOU HATED ME.
BECAUSE OF HOW I WAS FRIENDS WITH SOPHIA, AND HOW I ACTED AT THE TRYOUTS, AND...
AND, uh...
I...
I'M SORRY.

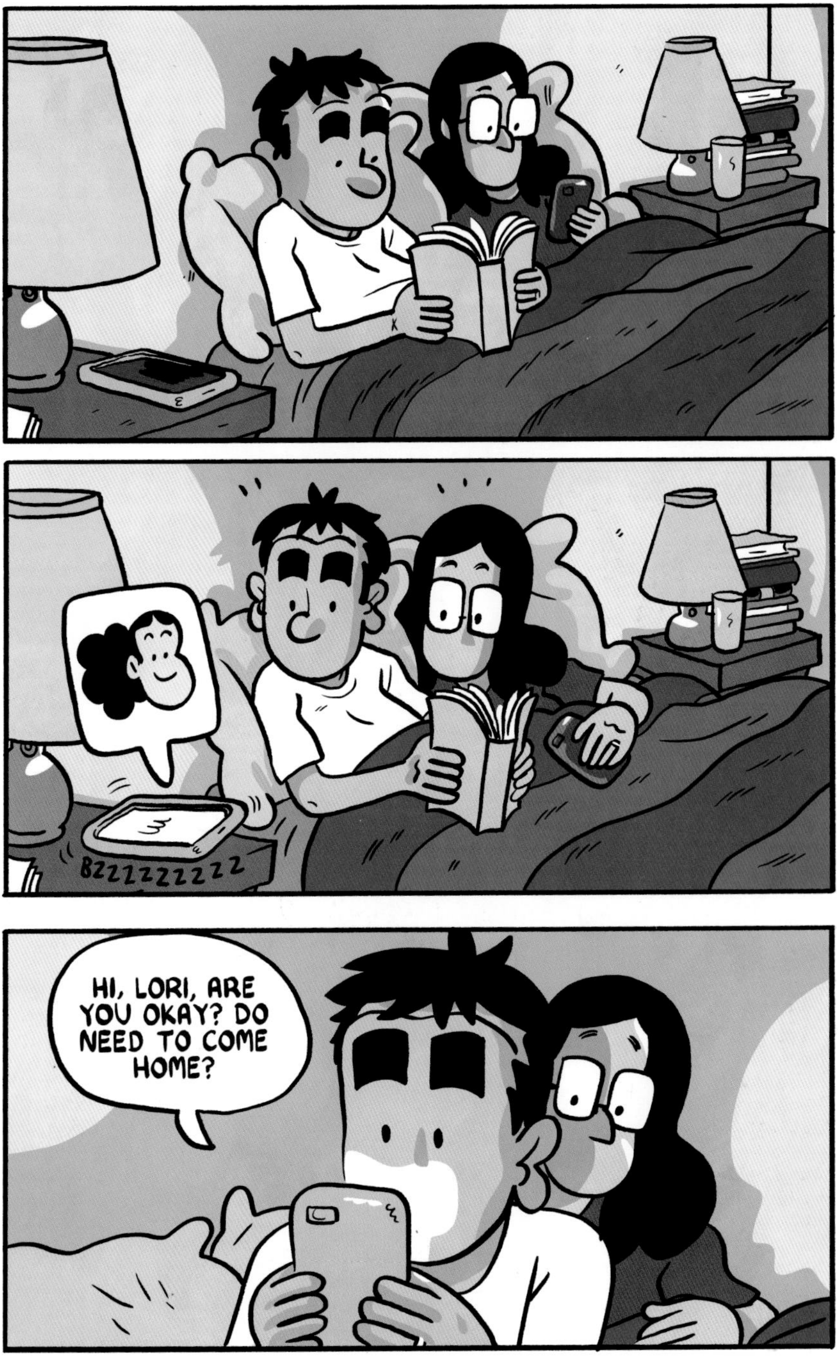
BZZZZZZZZZ
HI, LORI, ARE YOU OKAY? DO NEED TO COME HOME?

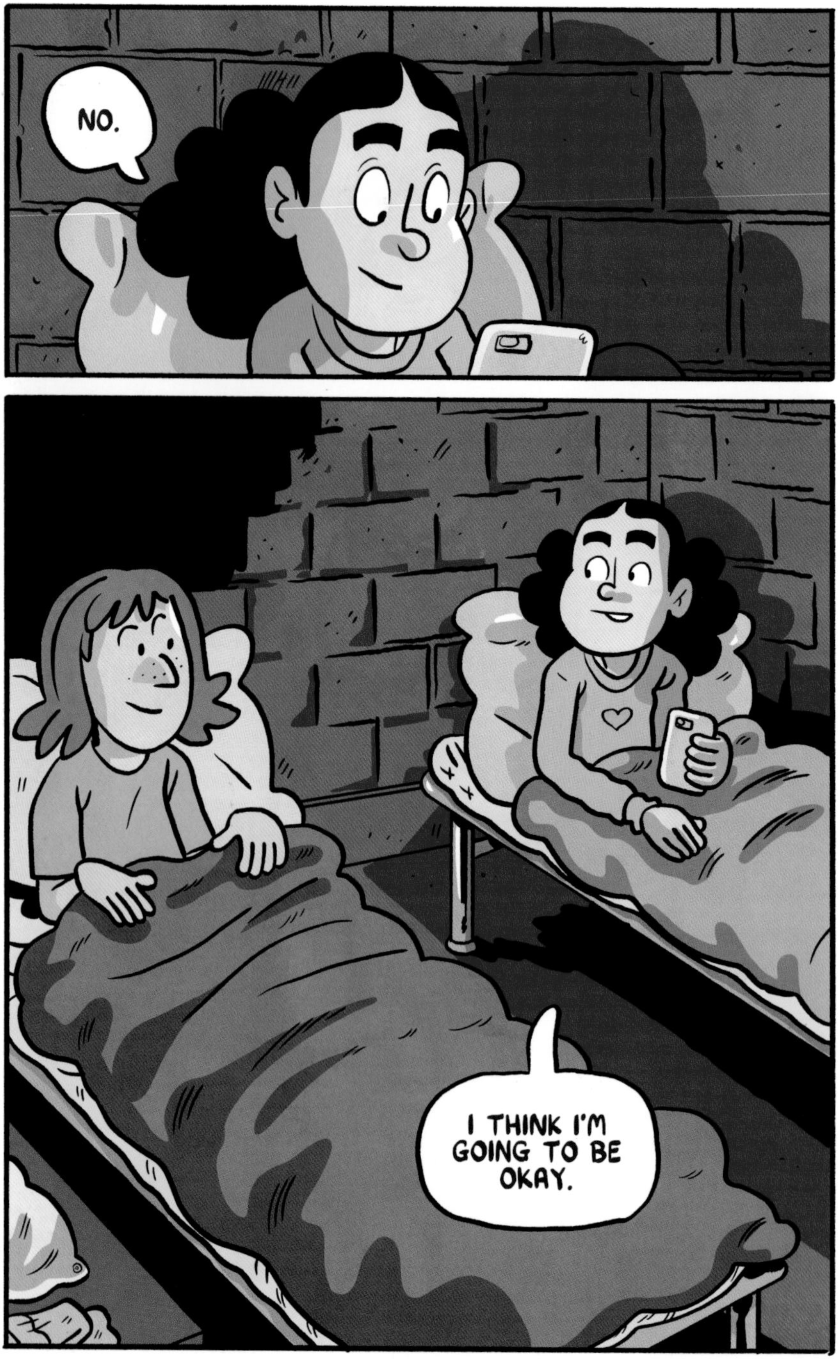
NO.
I THINK I'M GOING TO BE OKAY.

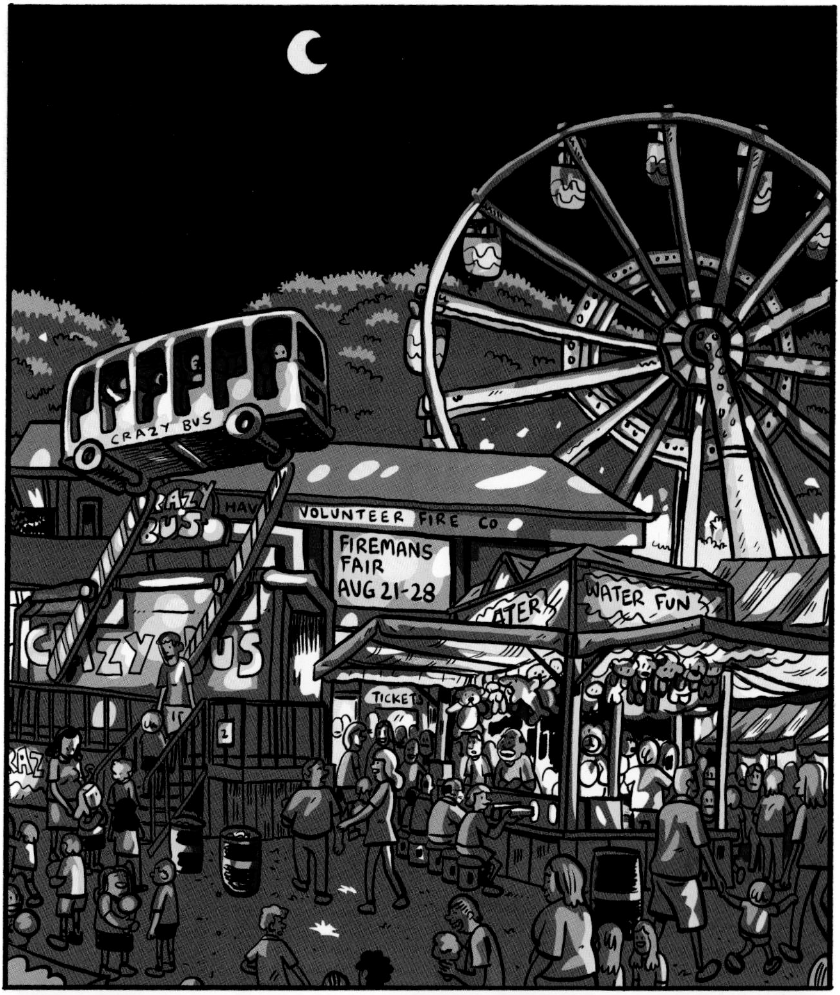
CRAZY BUS
HAV
VOLUNTEER FIRE CO.
FIREMANS FAIR AUG 21-28
WATER FUN
CRAZY BUS
TICKETS

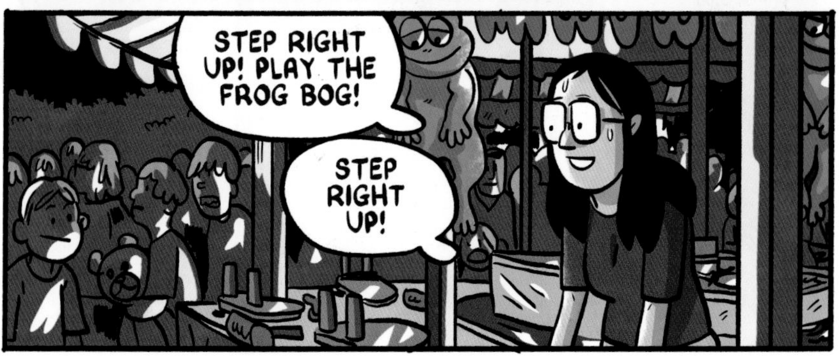
STEP RIGHT UP! PLAY THE FROG BOG!
STEP RIGHT UP!

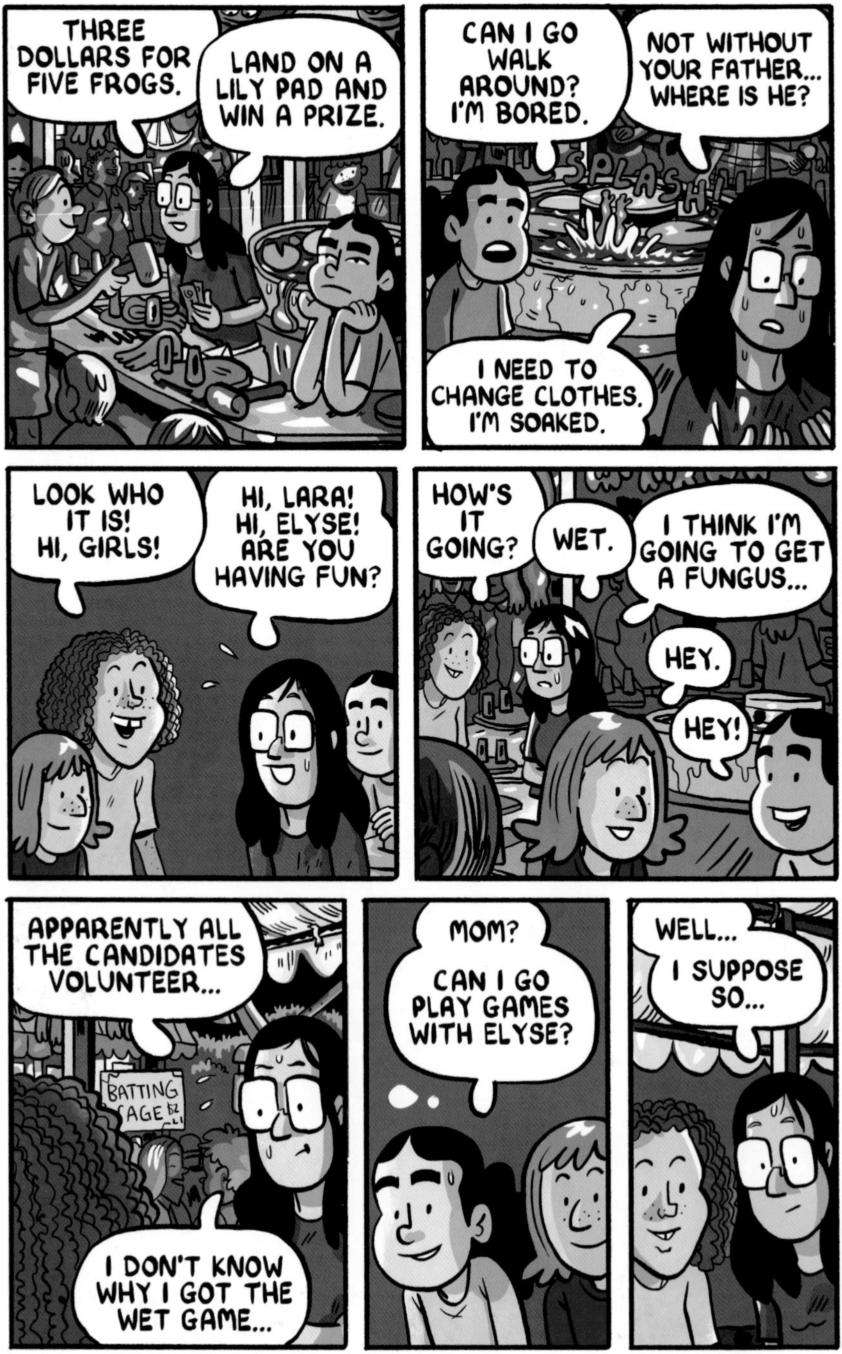
THREE DOLLARS FOR FIVE FROGS.
LAND ON A LILY PAD AND WIN A PRIZE.
CAN I GO WALK AROUND? I'M BORED.
NOT WITHOUT YOUR FATHER... WHERE IS HE?
SPLASH!
I NEED TO CHANGE CLOTHES. I'M SOAKED.
LOOK WHO IT IS! HI, GIRLS!
HI, LARA! HI, ELYSE! ARE YOU HAVING FUN?
HOW'S IT GOING?
WET.
I THINK I'M GOING TO GET A FUNGUS...
HEY.
HEY!
APPARENTLY ALL THE CANDIDATES VOLUNTEER...
BATTING CAGE
I DON'T KNOW WHY I GOT THE WET GAME...
MOM?
CAN I GO PLAY GAMES WITH ELYSE?
WELL...
I SUPPOSE SO...

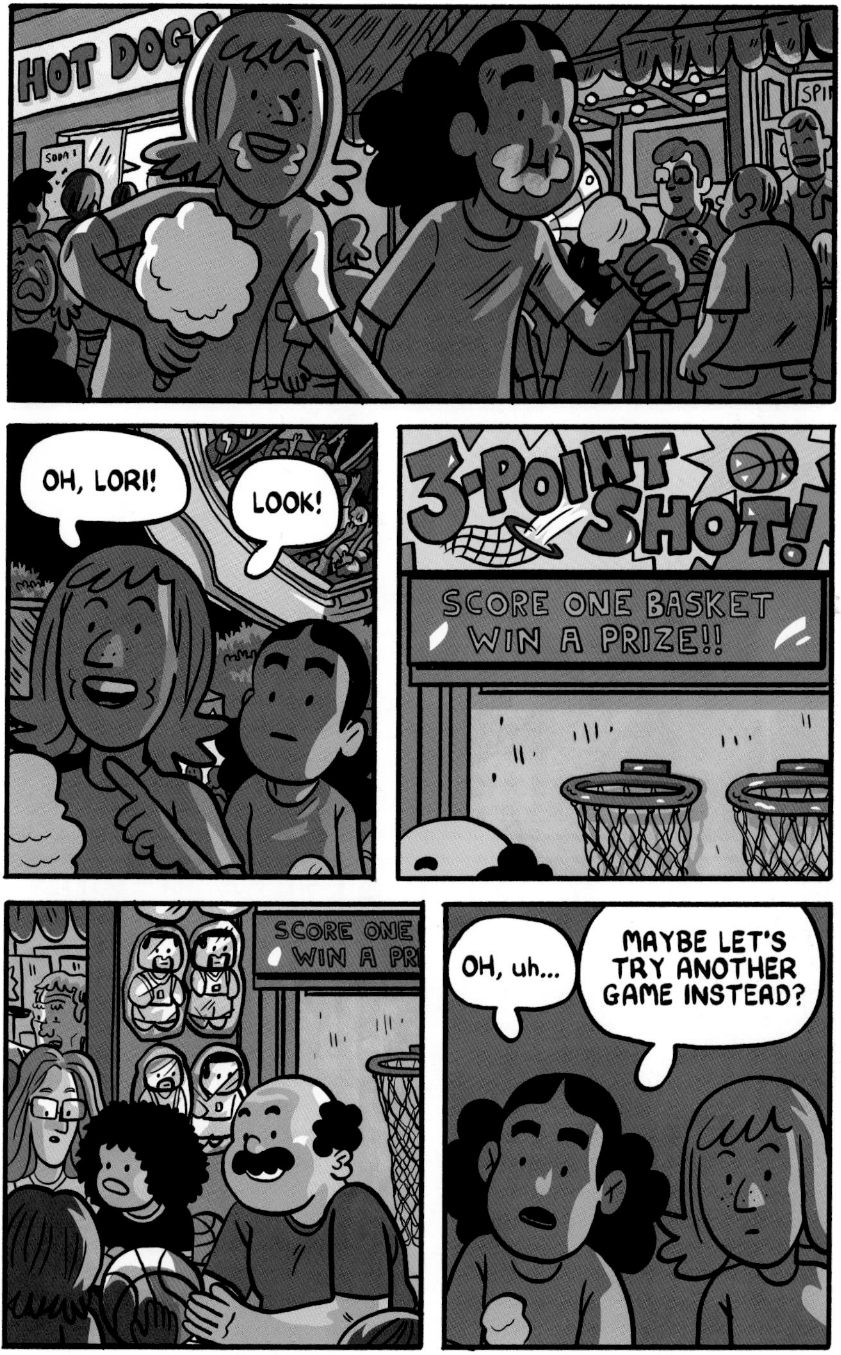
HOT DOGS
SODA
SPI
OH, LORI!
LOOK!
3-POINT SHOT!
SCORE ONE BASKET WIN A PRIZE!!
SCORE ONE
WIN A PR
OH, uh...
MAYBE LET'S TRY ANOTHER GAME INSTEAD?

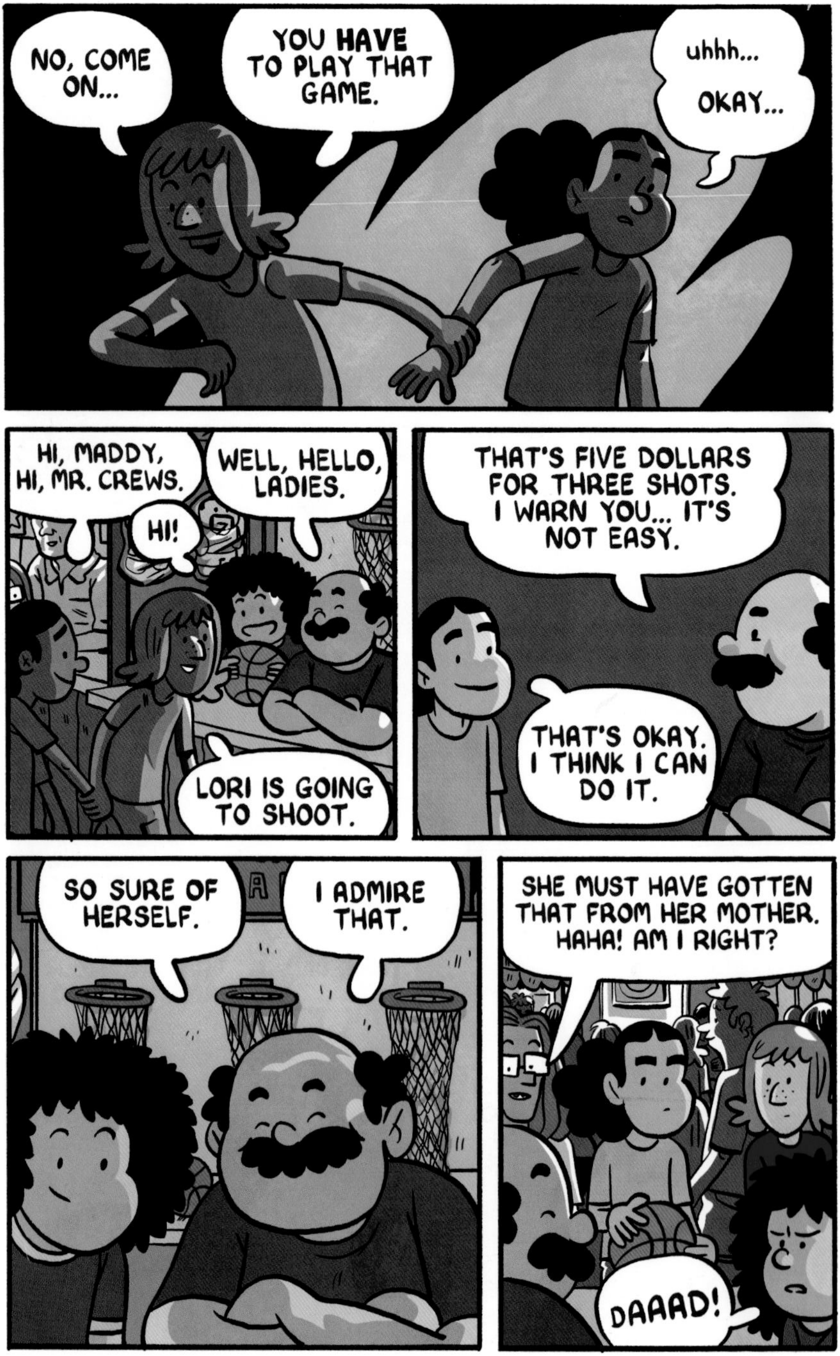
NO, COME ON...
YOU HAVE TO PLAY THAT GAME.
uhhh... OKAY...
HI, MADDY, HI, MR. CREWS.
HI!
WELL, HELLO, LADIES.
LORI IS GOING TO SHOOT.
THAT'S FIVE DOLLARS FOR THREE SHOTS. I WARN YOU... IT'S NOT EASY.
THAT'S OKAY. I THINK I CAN DO IT.
SO SURE OF HERSELF.
I ADMIRE THAT.
SHE MUST HAVE GOTTEN THAT FROM HER MOTHER. HAHA! AM I RIGHT?
DAAAD!

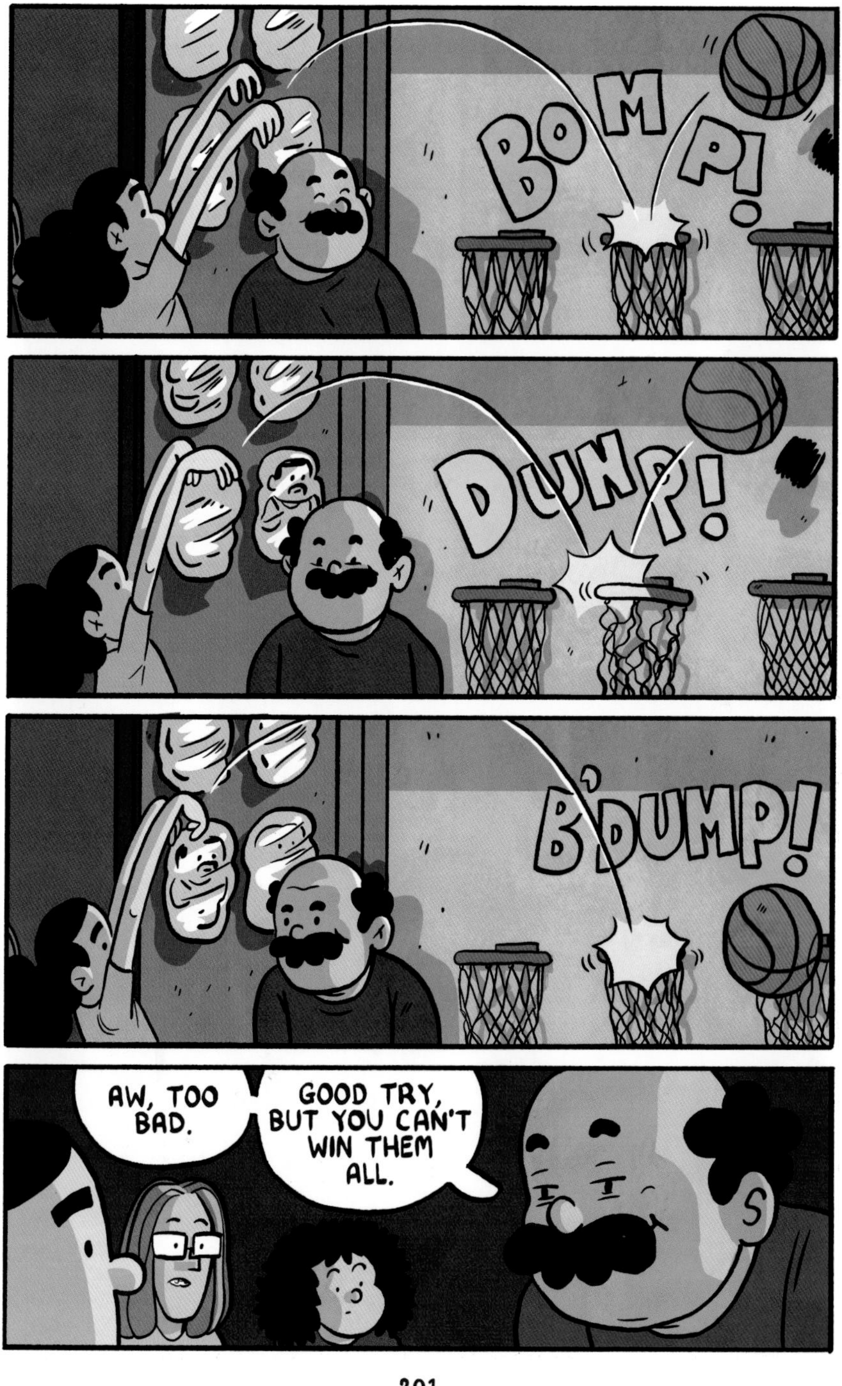
BOMP!
DUMP!
B'DUMP!
AW, TOO BAD.
GOOD TRY, BUT YOU CAN'T WIN THEM ALL.

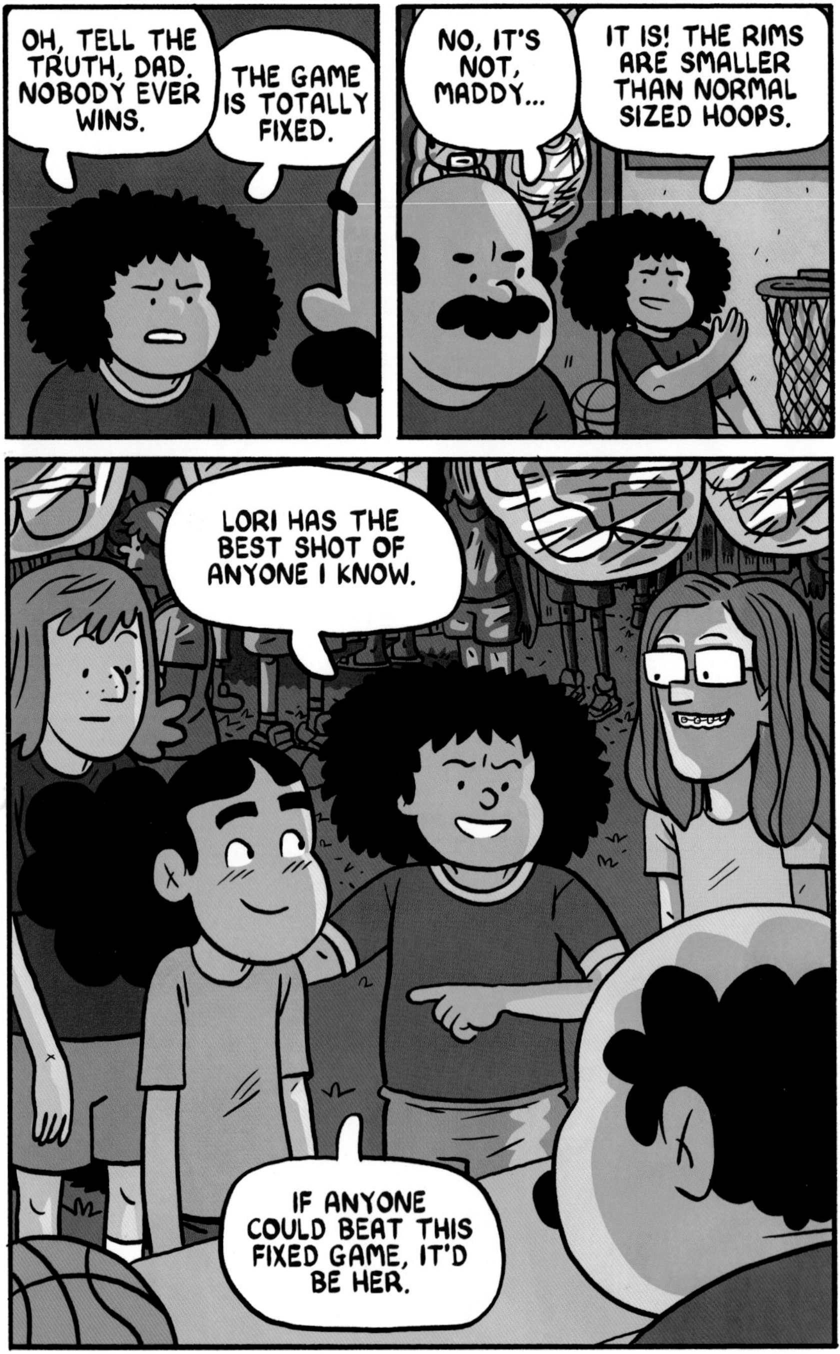
OH, TELL THE TRUTH, DAD. NOBODY EVER WINS.
THE GAME IS TOTALLY FIXED.
NO, IT'S NOT, MADDY...
IT IS! THE RIMS ARE SMALLER THAN NORMAL SIZED HOOPS.
LORI HAS THE BEST SHOT OF ANYONE I KNOW.
IF ANYONE COULD BEAT THIS FIXED GAME, IT'D BE HER.

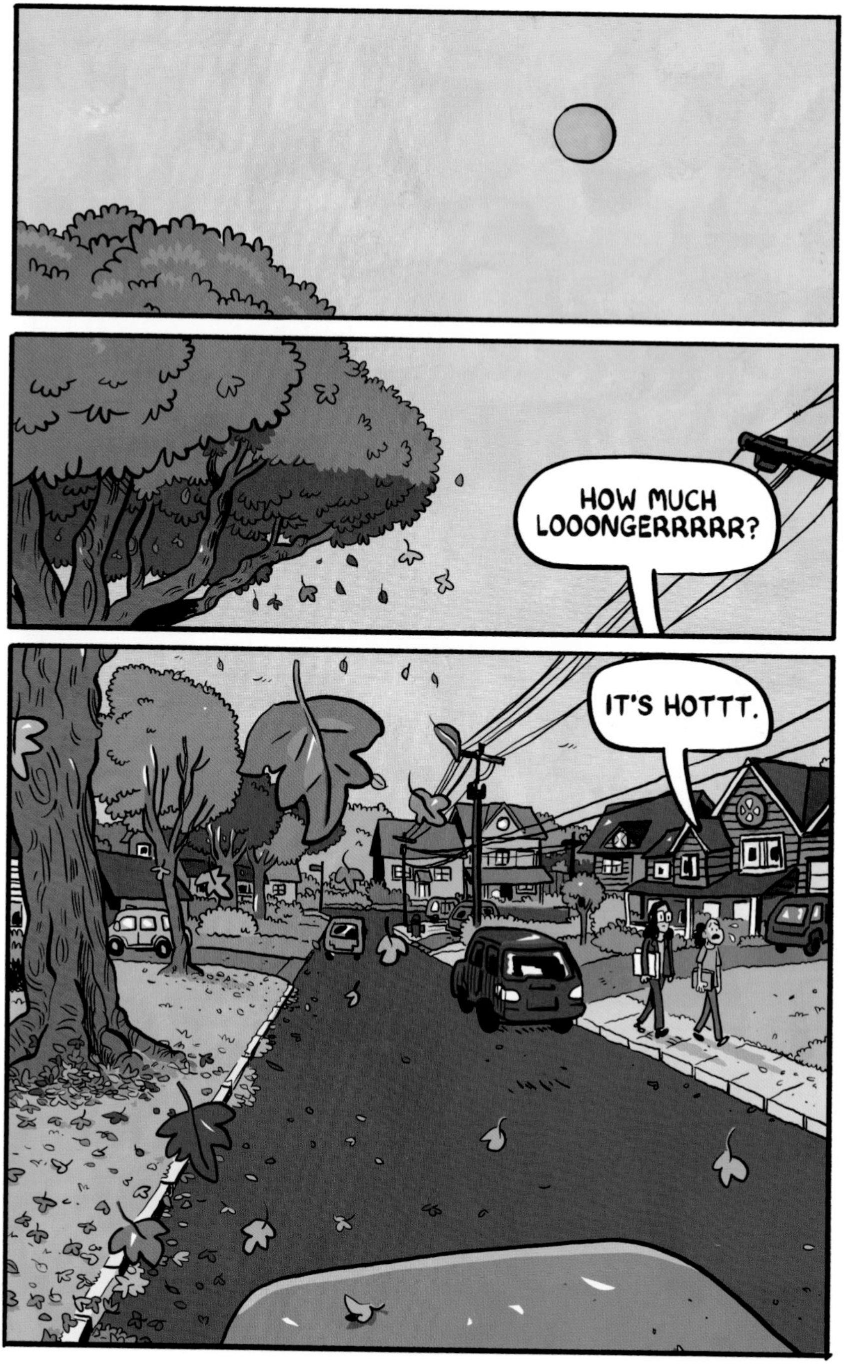
HOW MUCH LOOONGERRRRR?
IT'S HOTTT.

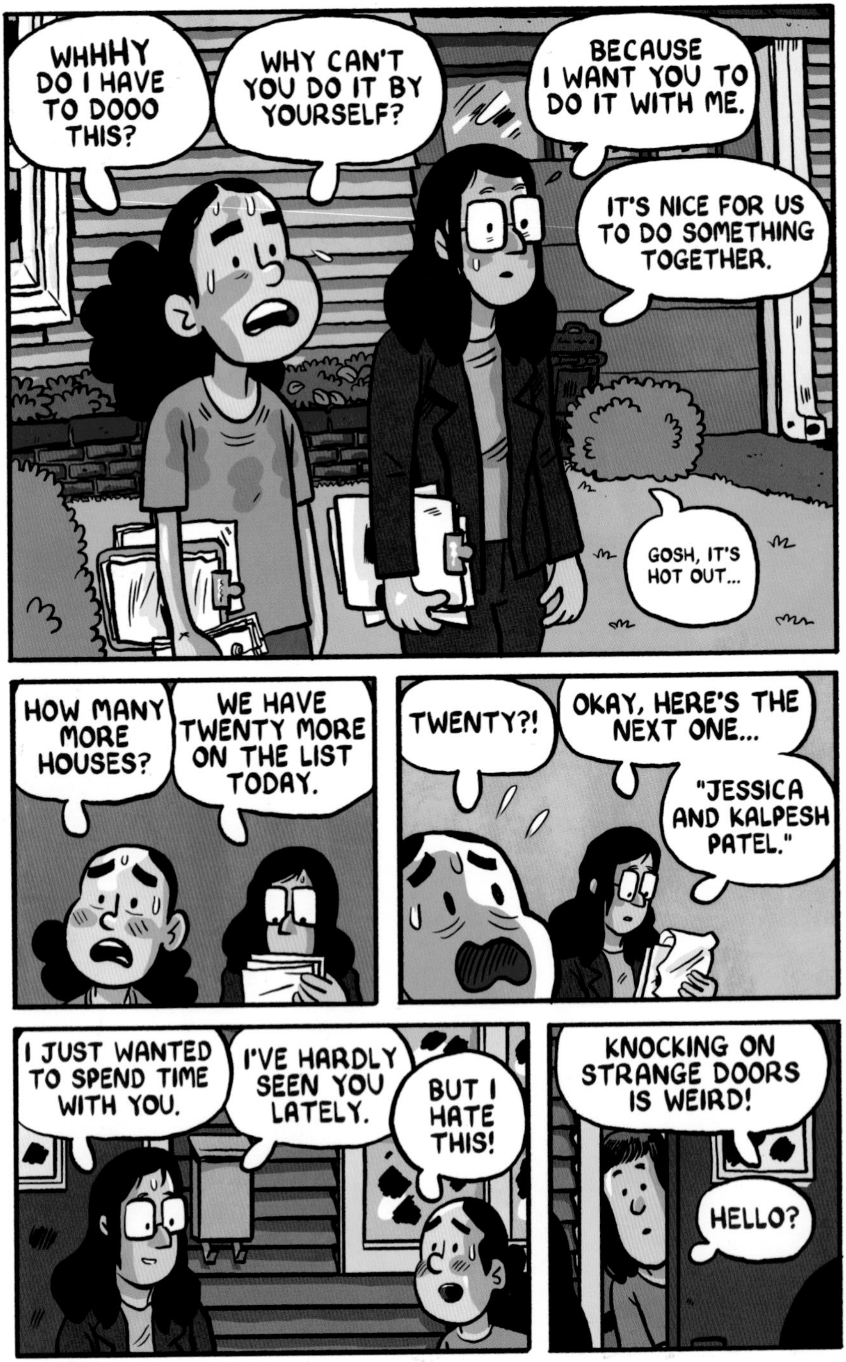
WHHHY DO I HAVE TO DOOO THIS?
WHY CAN'T YOU DO IT BY YOURSELF?
BECAUSE I WANT YOU TO DO IT WITH ME.
IT'S NICE FOR US TO DO SOMETHING TOGETHER.
GOSH, IT'S HOT OUT...
HOW MANY MORE HOUSES?
WE HAVE TWENTY MORE ON THE LIST TODAY.
TWENTY?!
OKAY, HERE'S THE NEXT ONE...
"JESSICA AND KALPESH PATEL."
I JUST WANTED TO SPEND TIME WITH YOU.
I'VE HARDLY SEEN YOU LATELY.
BUT I HATE THIS!
KNOCKING ON STRANGE DOORS IS WEIRD!
HELLO?

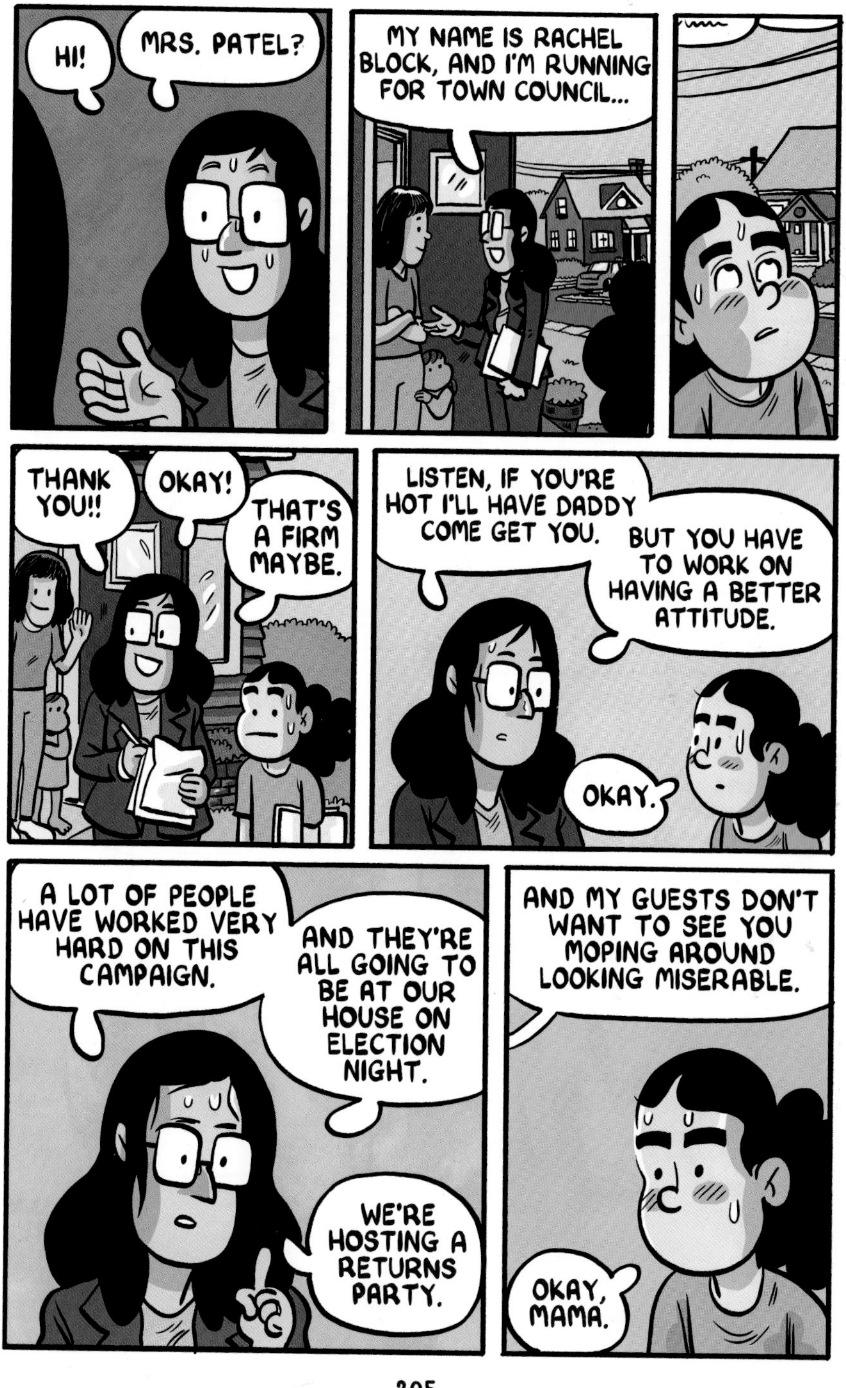
HI!
MRS. PATEL?
MY NAME IS RACHEL BLOCK, AND I'M RUNNING FOR TOWN COUNCIL...
THANK YOU!!
OKAY!
THAT'S A FIRM MAYBE.
LISTEN, IF YOU'RE HOT I'LL HAVE DADDY COME GET YOU.
BUT YOU HAVE TO WORK ON HAVING A BETTER ATTITUDE.
OKAY.
A LOT OF PEOPLE HAVE WORKED VERY HARD ON THIS CAMPAIGN.
AND THEY'RE ALL GOING TO BE AT OUR HOUSE ON ELECTION NIGHT.
WE'RE HOSTING A RETURNS PARTY.
AND MY GUESTS DON'T WANT TO SEE YOU MOPING AROUND LOOKING MISERABLE.
OKAY, MAMA.

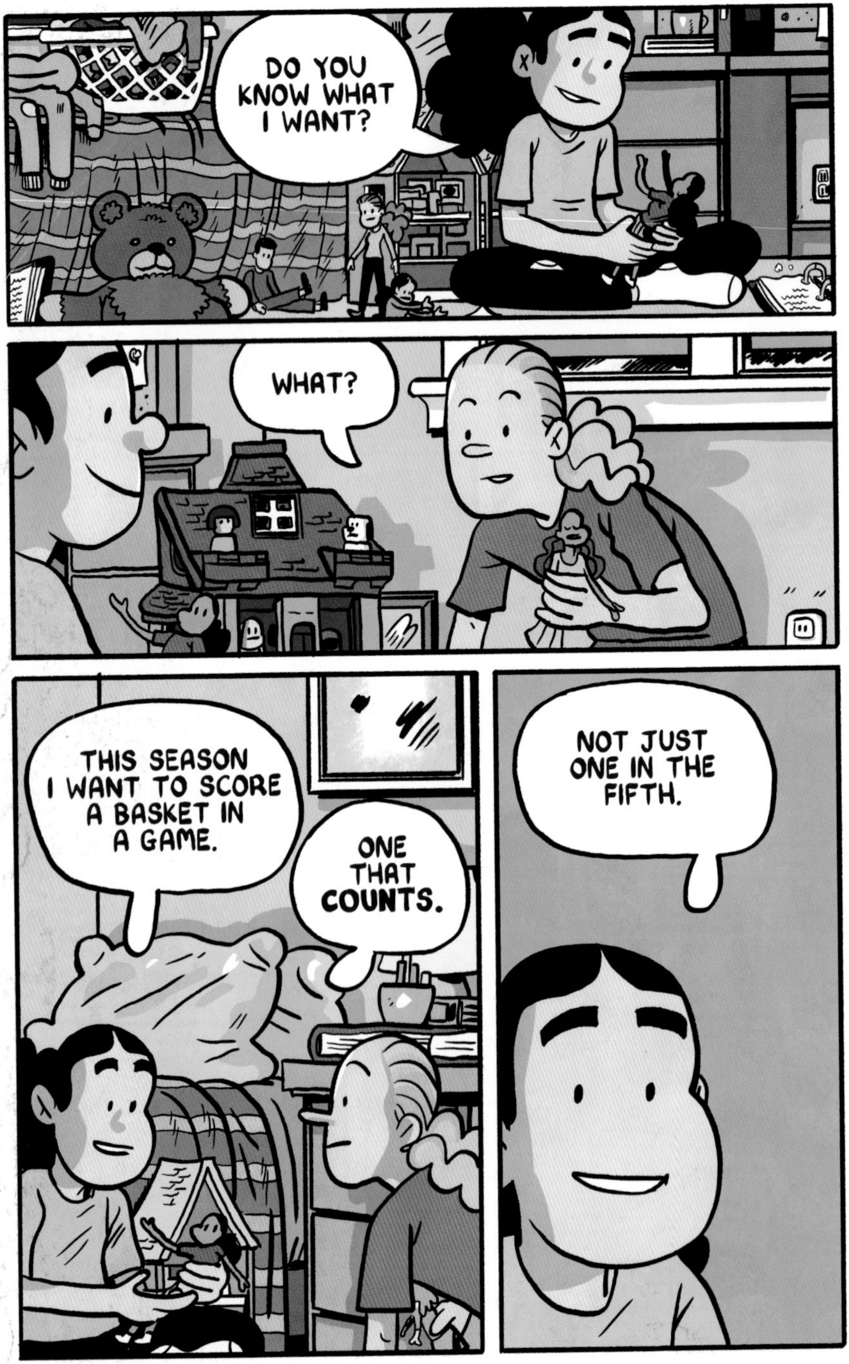
DO YOU KNOW WHAT I WANT?
WHAT?
THIS SEASON I WANT TO SCORE A BASKET IN A GAME.
ONE THAT **COUNTS.**
NOT JUST ONE IN THE FIFTH.

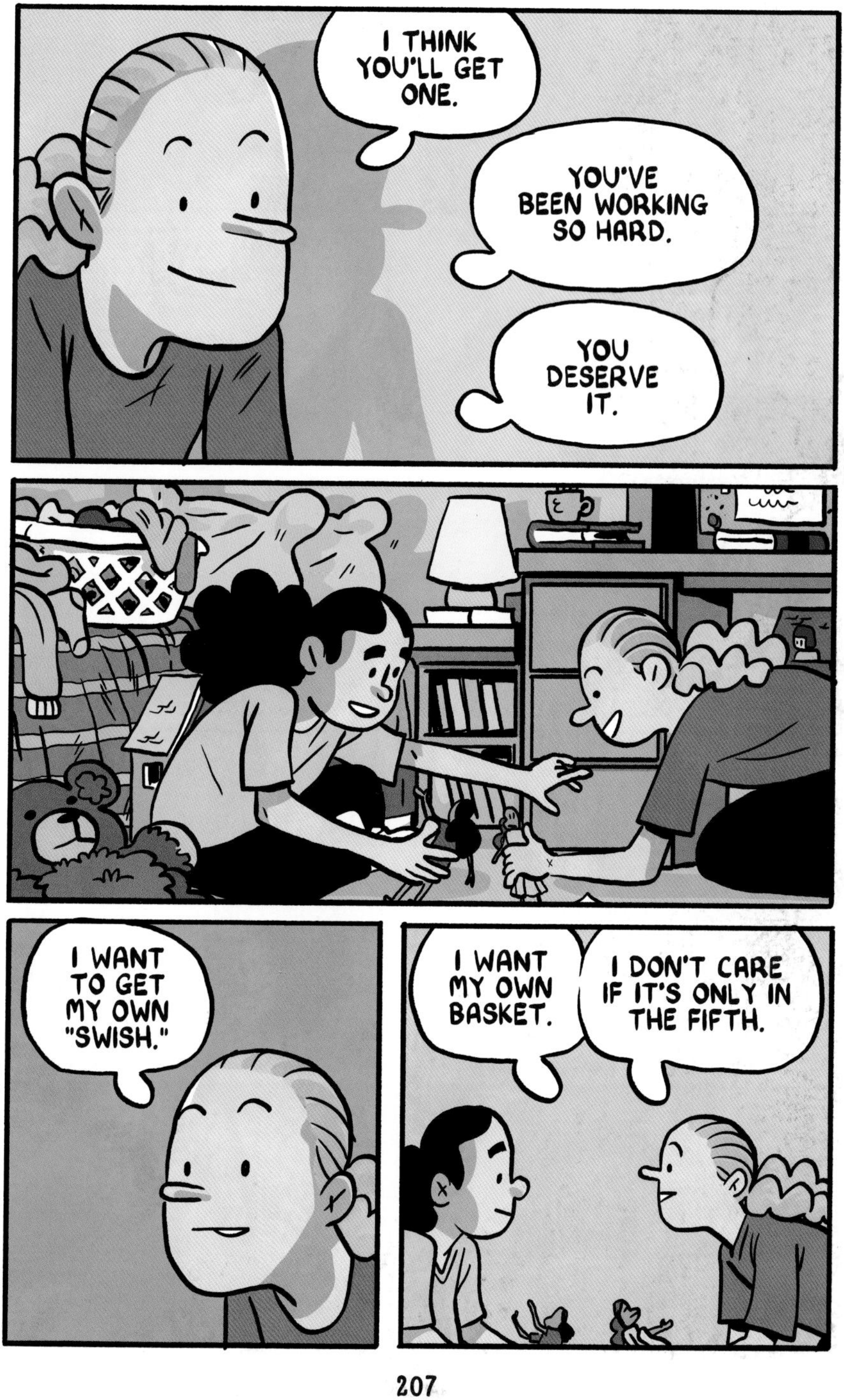
I THINK YOU'LL GET ONE.
YOU'VE BEEN WORKING SO HARD.
YOU DESERVE IT.
I WANT TO GET MY OWN "SWISH."
I WANT MY OWN BASKET.
I DON'T CARE IF IT'S ONLY IN THE FIFTH.

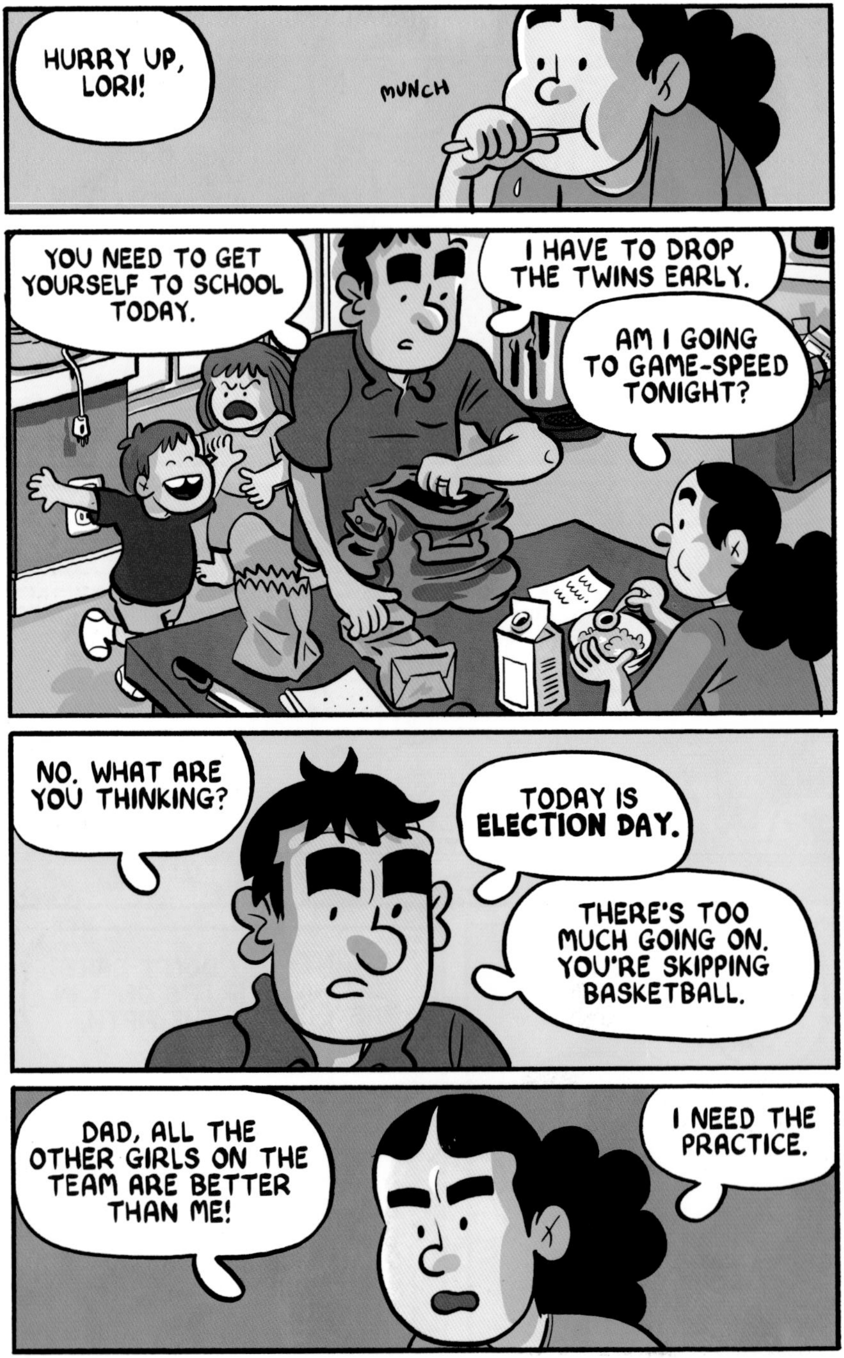
HURRY UP, LORI!
MUNCH
YOU NEED TO GET YOURSELF TO SCHOOL TODAY.
I HAVE TO DROP THE TWINS EARLY.
AM I GOING TO GAME-SPEED TONIGHT?
NO. WHAT ARE YOU THINKING?
TODAY IS ELECTION DAY.
THERE'S TOO MUCH GOING ON. YOU'RE SKIPPING BASKETBALL.
DAD, ALL THE OTHER GIRLS ON THE TEAM ARE BETTER THAN ME!
I NEED THE PRACTICE.

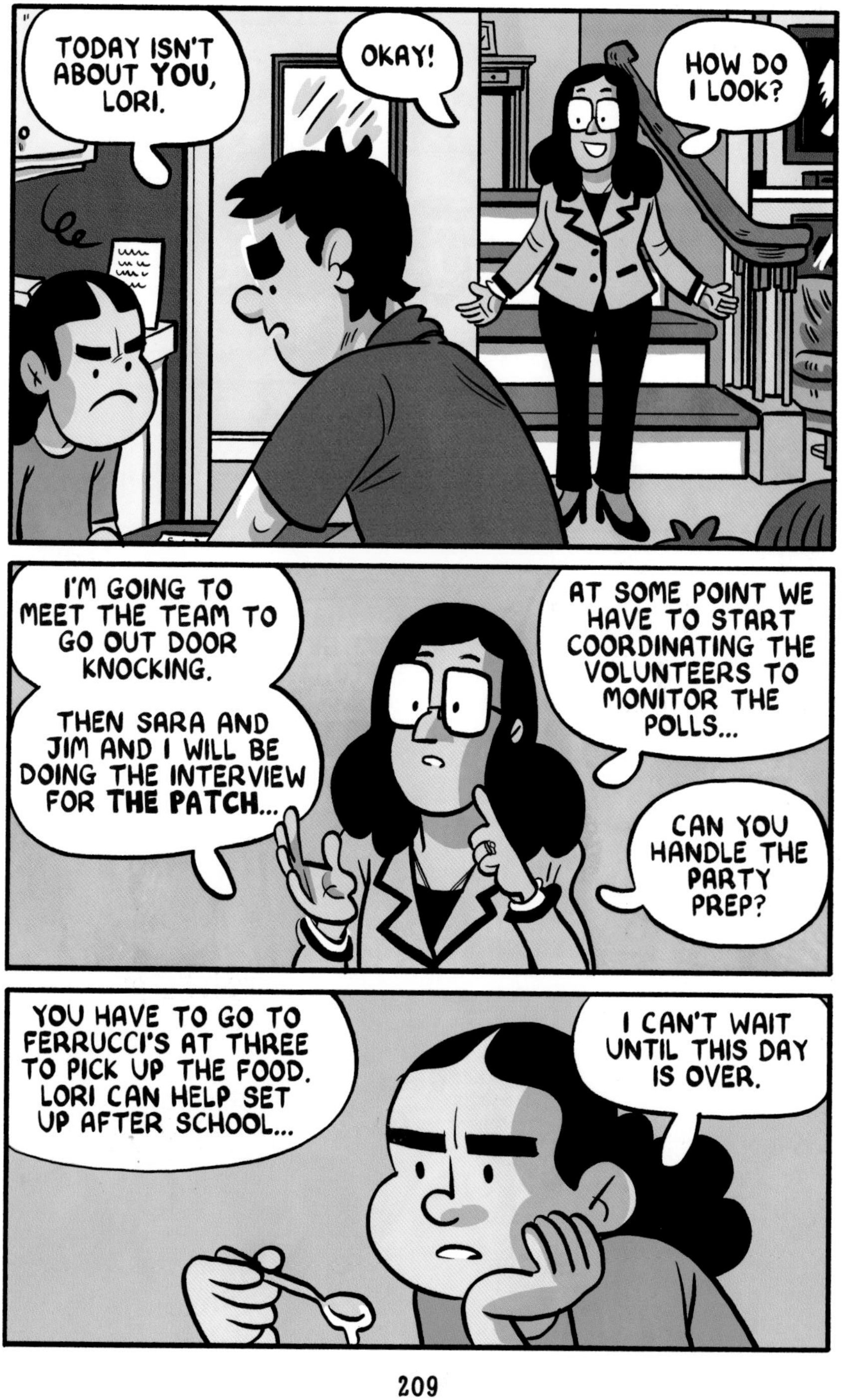
TODAY ISN'T ABOUT YOU, LORI.
OKAY!
HOW DO I LOOK?
I'M GOING TO MEET THE TEAM TO GO OUT DOOR KNOCKING.
THEN SARA AND JIM AND I WILL BE DOING THE INTERVIEW FOR THE PATCH...
AT SOME POINT WE HAVE TO START COORDINATING THE VOLUNTEERS TO MONITOR THE POLLS...
CAN YOU HANDLE THE PARTY PREP?
YOU HAVE TO GO TO FERRUCCI'S AT THREE TO PICK UP THE FOOD. LORI CAN HELP SET UP AFTER SCHOOL...
I CAN'T WAIT UNTIL THIS DAY IS OVER.

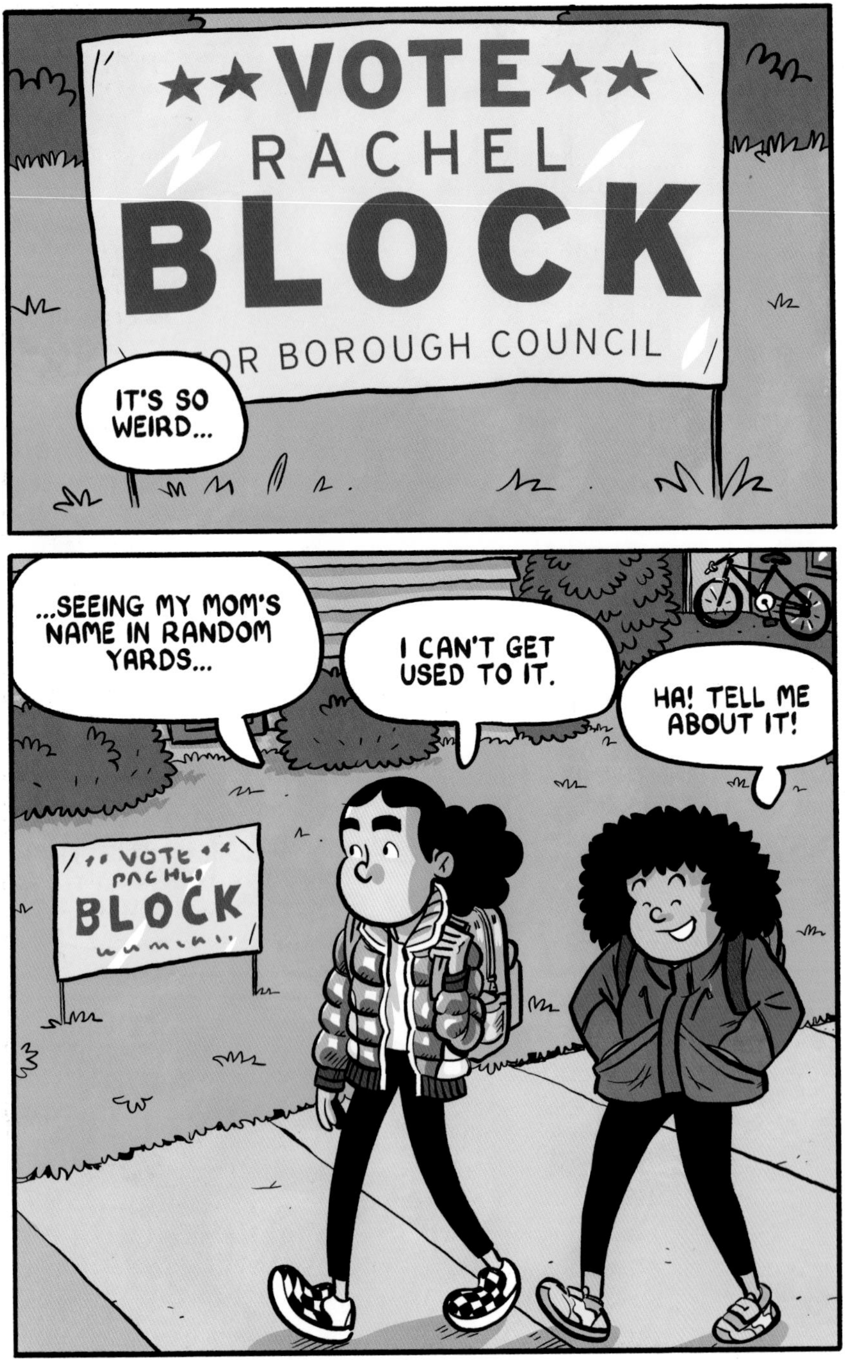
★★VOTE★★
RACHEL
BLOCK
FOR BOROUGH COUNCIL
IT'S SO WEIRD...
...SEEING MY MOM'S NAME IN RANDOM YARDS...
I CAN'T GET USED TO IT.
HA! TELL ME ABOUT IT!
VOTE
BLOCK

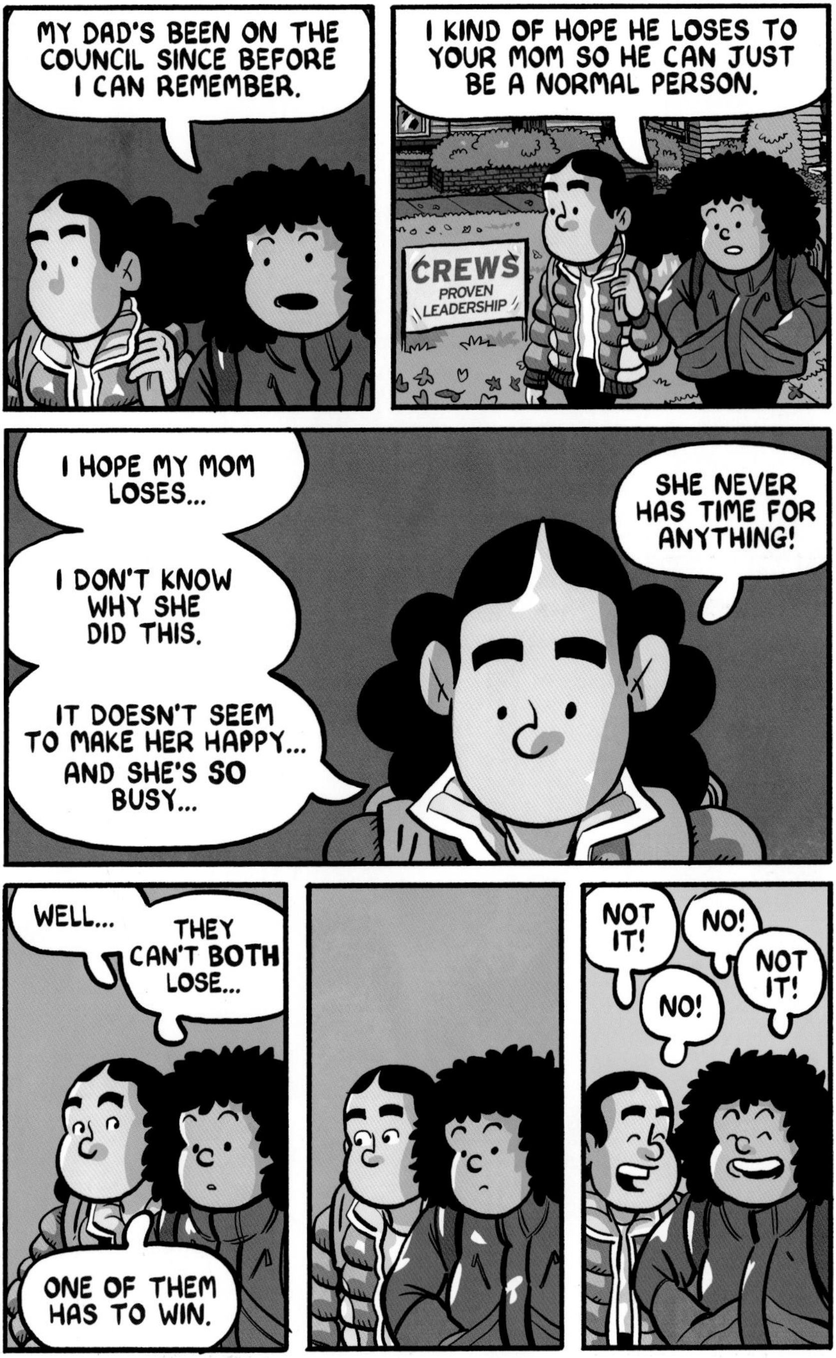

MY DAD'S BEEN ON THE COUNCIL SINCE BEFORE I CAN REMEMBER.
I KIND OF HOPE HE LOSES TO YOUR MOM SO HE CAN JUST BE A NORMAL PERSON.
CREWS
PROVEN LEADERSHIP
I HOPE MY MOM LOSES...
I DON'T KNOW WHY SHE DID THIS.
IT DOESN'T SEEM TO MAKE HER HAPPY... AND SHE'S SO BUSY...
SHE NEVER HAS TIME FOR ANYTHING!
WELL...
THEY CAN'T BOTH LOSE...
ONE OF THEM HAS TO WIN.
NOT IT!
NO!
NO!
NOT IT!

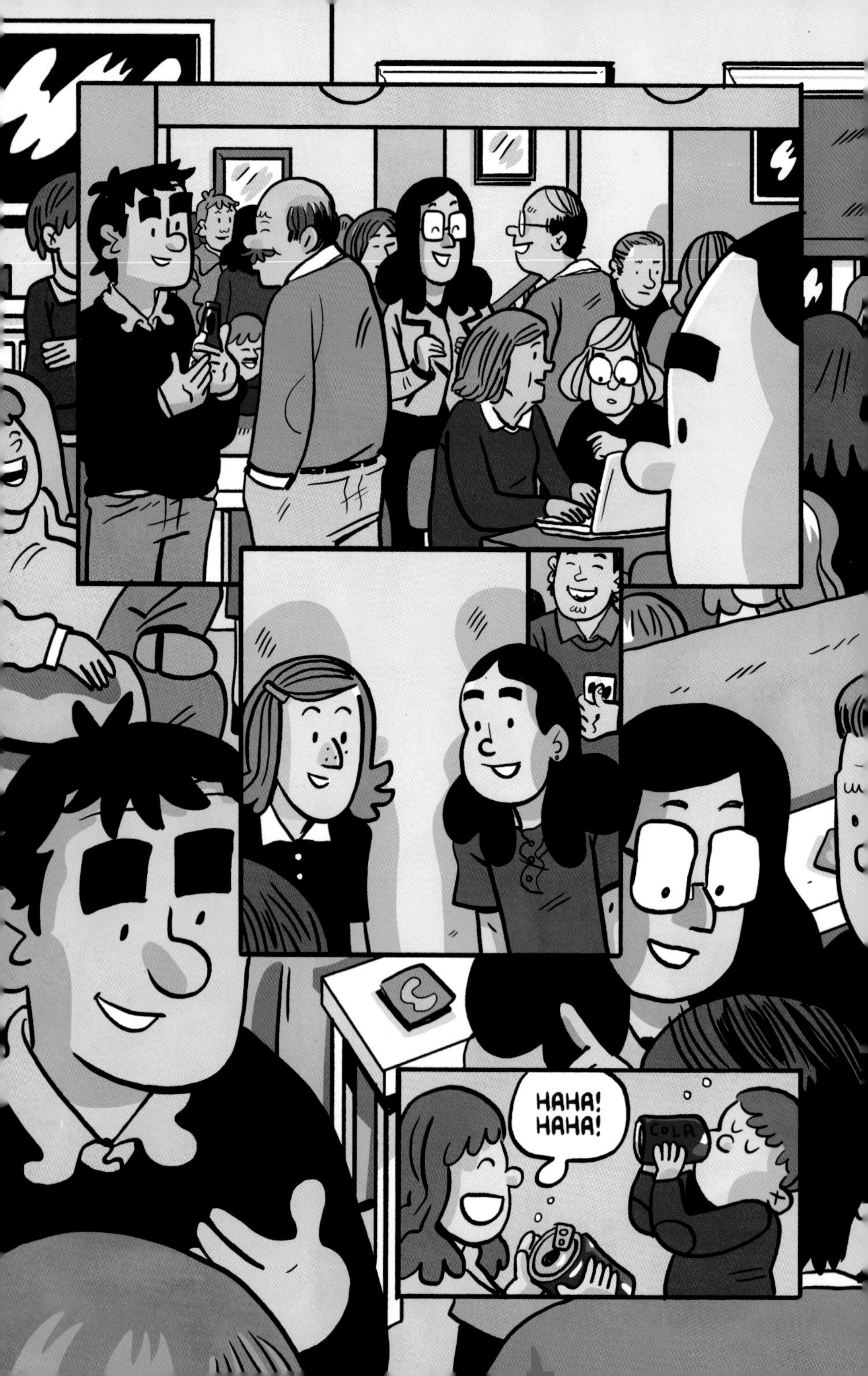
HAHA! HAHA!
COLA

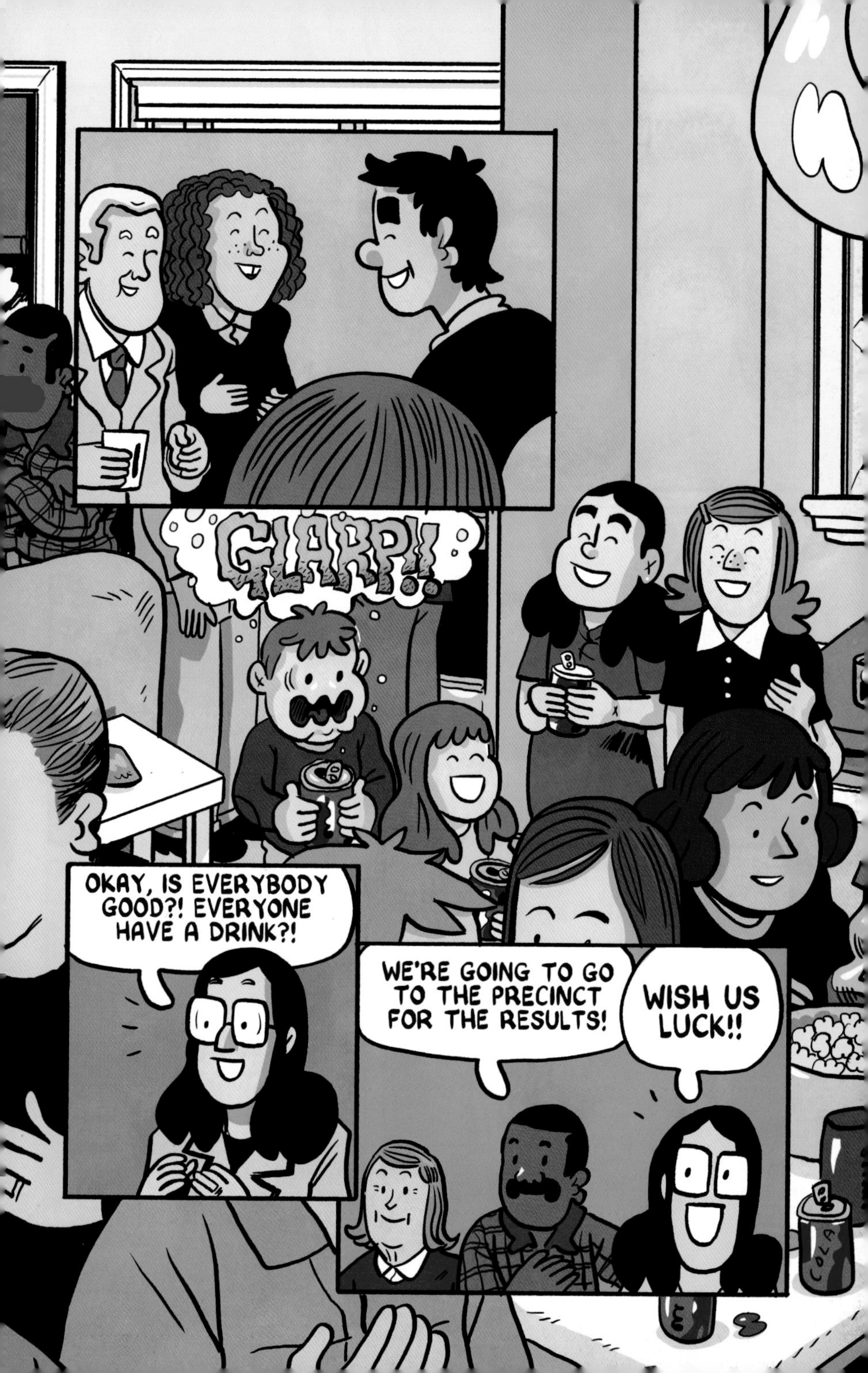
GLARP!!
OKAY, IS EVERYBODY GOOD?! EVERYONE HAVE A DRINK?!
WE'RE GOING TO GO TO THE PRECINCT FOR THE RESULTS!
WISH US LUCK!!
COLA

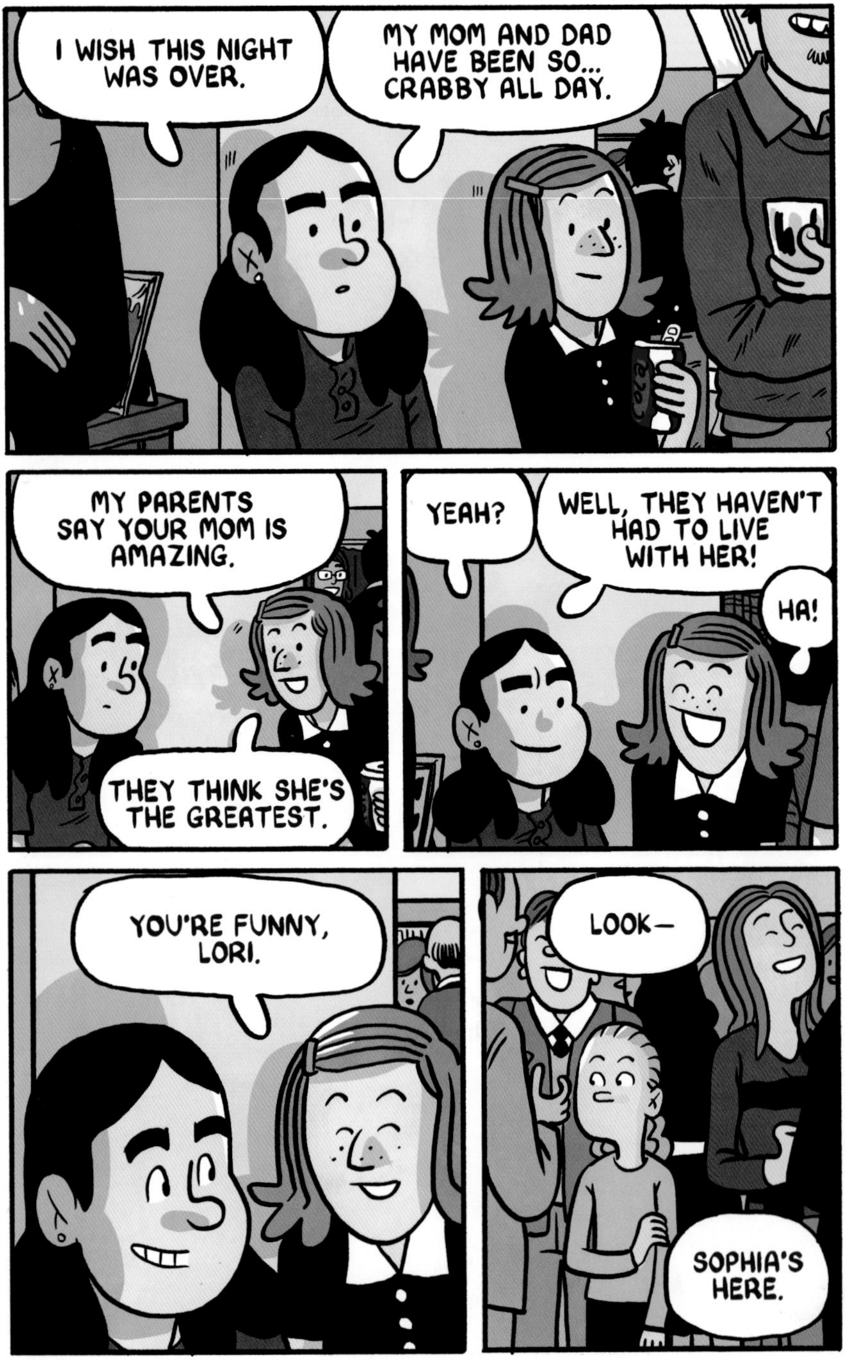
I WISH THIS NIGHT WAS OVER.
MY MOM AND DAD HAVE BEEN SO... CRABBY ALL DAY.
COLA
MY PARENTS SAY YOUR MOM IS AMAZING.
THEY THINK SHE'S THE GREATEST.
YEAH?
WELL, THEY HAVEN'T HAD TO LIVE WITH HER!
HA!
YOU'RE FUNNY, LORI.
LOOK—
SOPHIA'S HERE.

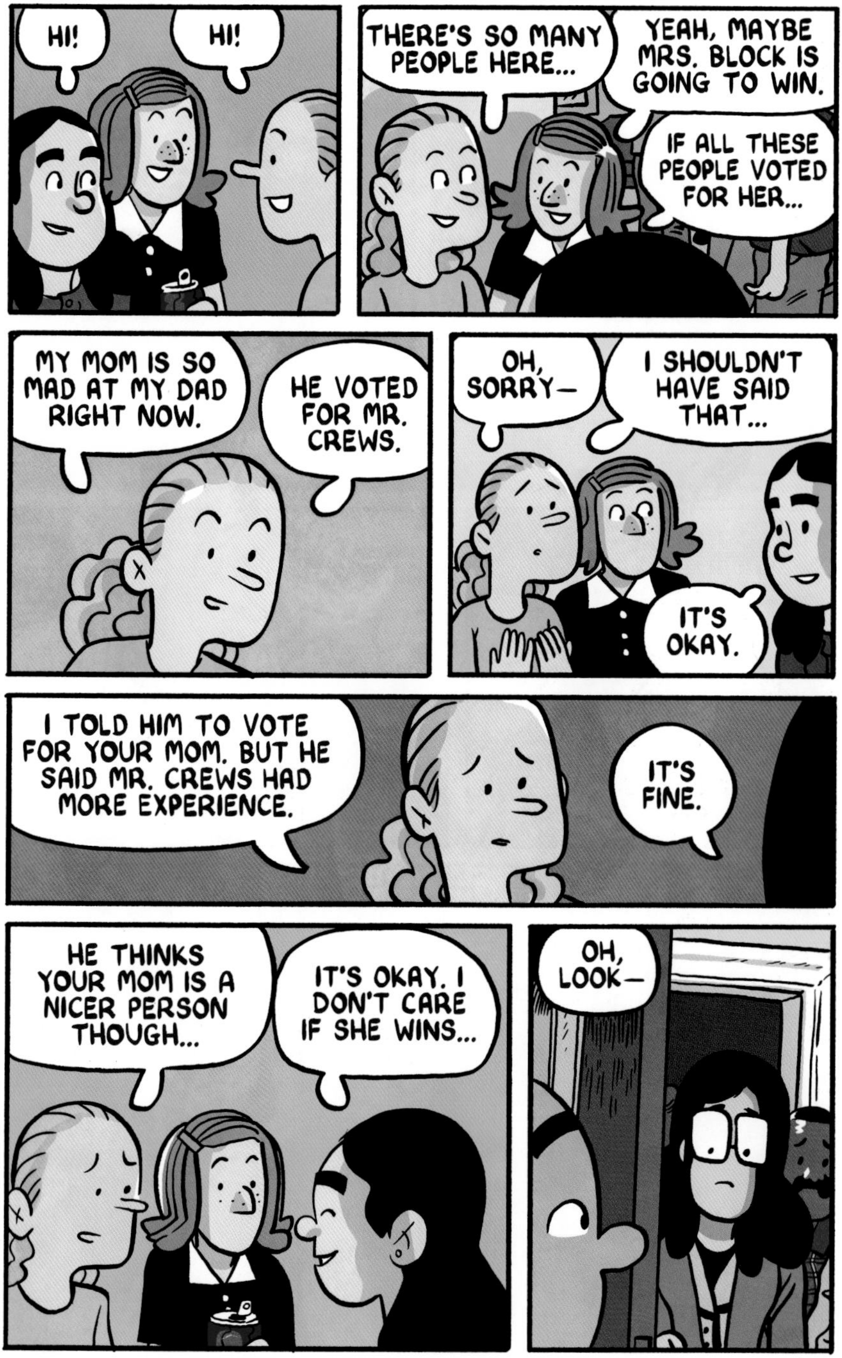
HI!
HI!
THERE'S SO MANY PEOPLE HERE...
YEAH, MAYBE MRS. BLOCK IS GOING TO WIN.
IF ALL THESE PEOPLE VOTED FOR HER...
MY MOM IS SO MAD AT MY DAD RIGHT NOW.
HE VOTED FOR MR. CREWS.
OH, SORRY—
I SHOULDN'T HAVE SAID THAT...
IT'S OKAY.
I TOLD HIM TO VOTE FOR YOUR MOM. BUT HE SAID MR. CREWS HAD MORE EXPERIENCE.
IT'S FINE.
HE THINKS YOUR MOM IS A NICER PERSON THOUGH...
IT'S OKAY. I DON'T CARE IF SHE WINS...
OH, LOOK—

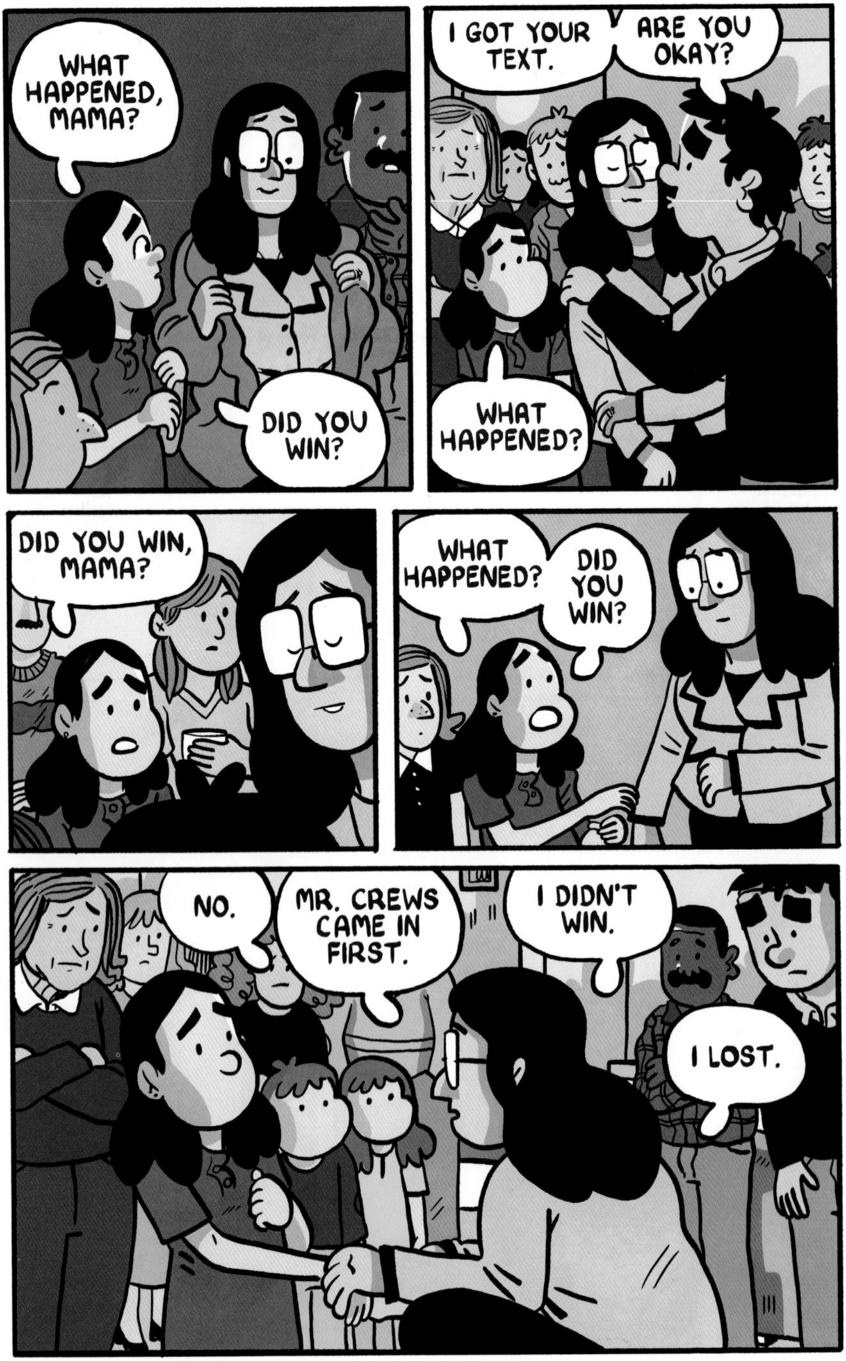
WHAT HAPPENED, MAMA?
DID YOU WIN?
I GOT YOUR TEXT.
ARE YOU OKAY?
WHAT HAPPENED?
DID YOU WIN, MAMA?
WHAT HAPPENED?
DID YOU WIN?
NO.
MR. CREWS CAME IN FIRST.
I DIDN'T WIN.
I LOST.

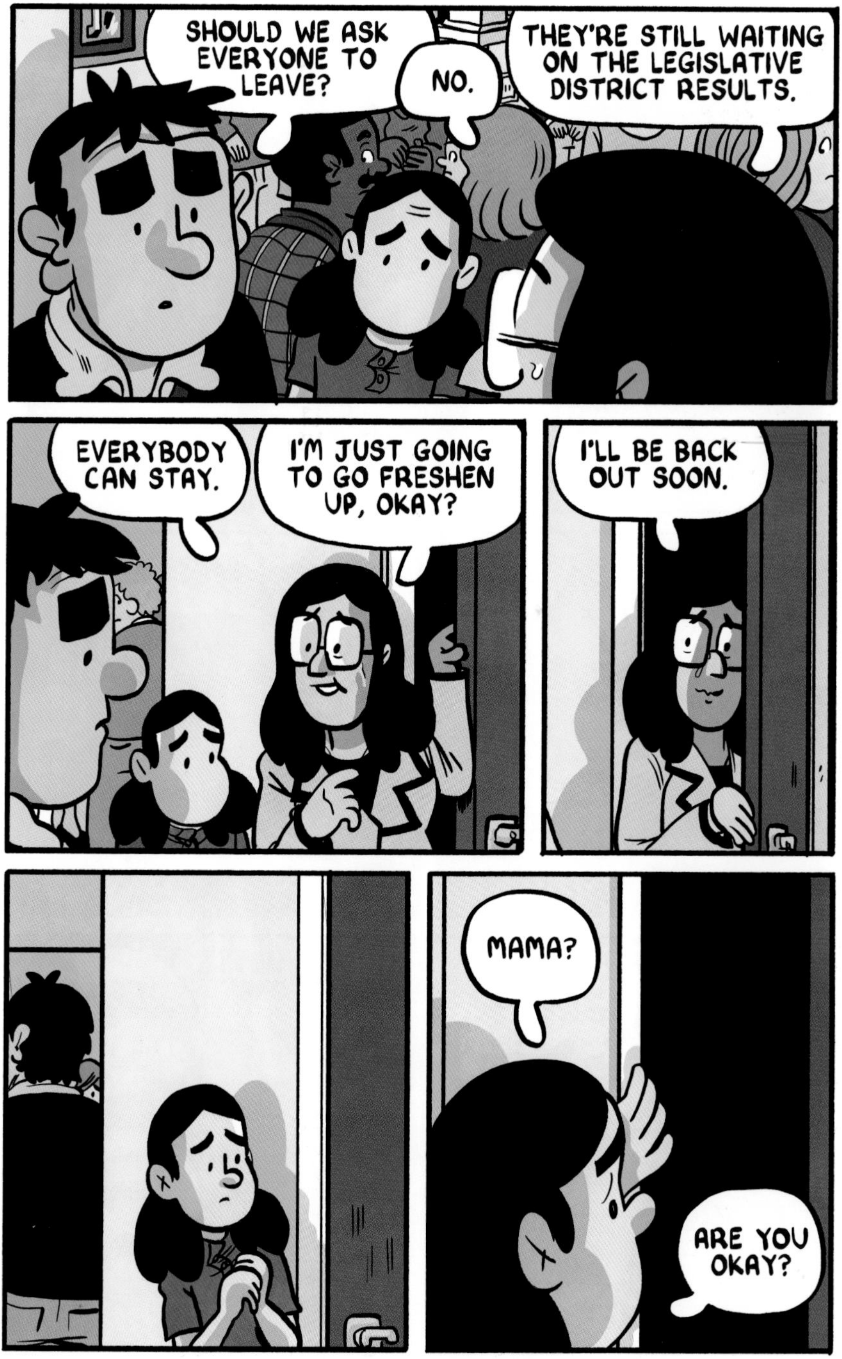
SHOULD WE ASK EVERYONE TO LEAVE?
NO.
THEY'RE STILL WAITING ON THE LEGISLATIVE DISTRICT RESULTS.
EVERYBODY CAN STAY.
I'M JUST GOING TO GO FRESHEN UP, OKAY?
I'LL BE BACK OUT SOON.
MAMA?
ARE YOU OKAY?

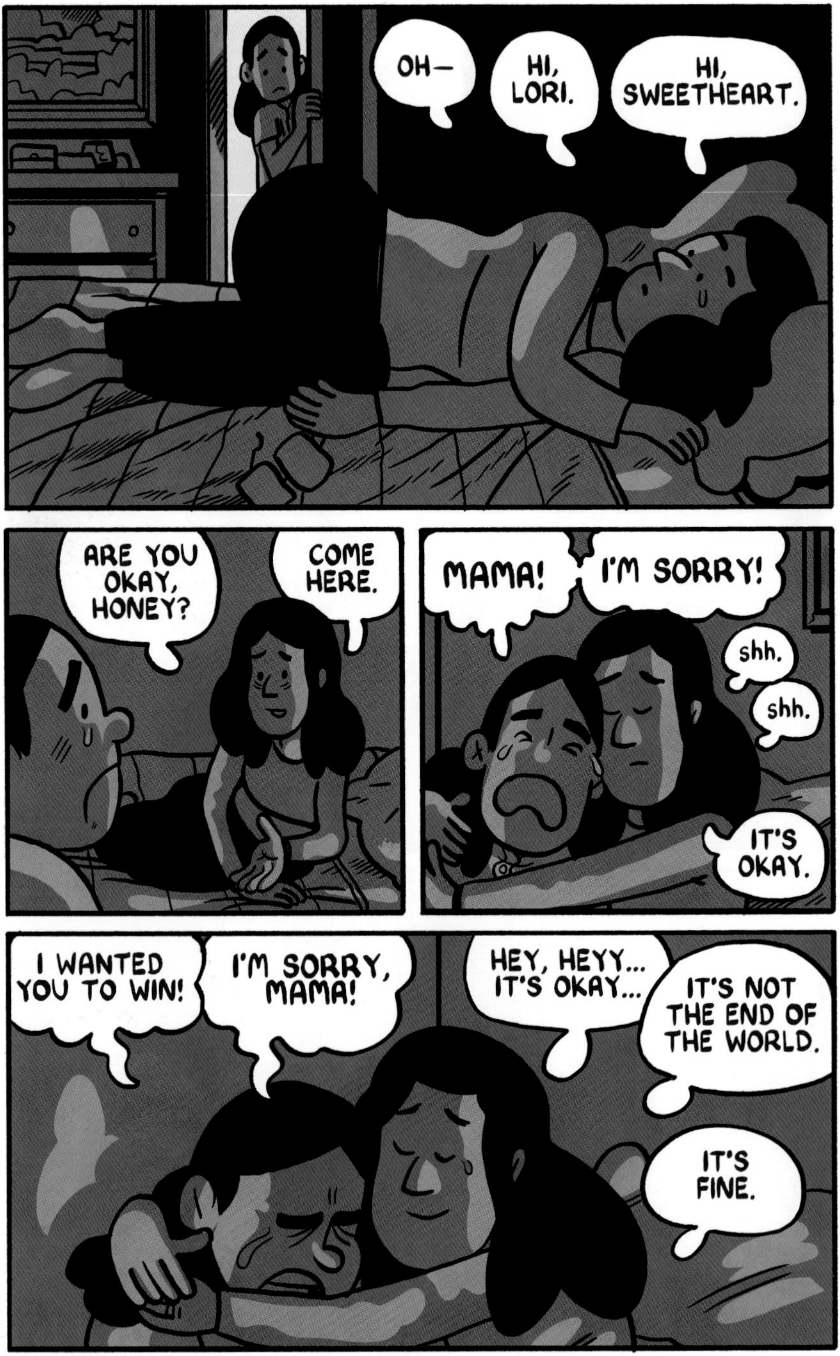
OH—
HI, LORI.
HI, SWEETHEART.
ARE YOU OKAY, HONEY?
COME HERE.
MAMA!
I'M SORRY!
shh.
shh.
IT'S OKAY.
I WANTED YOU TO WIN!
I'M SORRY, MAMA!
HEY, HEYY... IT'S OKAY...
IT'S NOT THE END OF THE WORLD.
IT'S FINE.

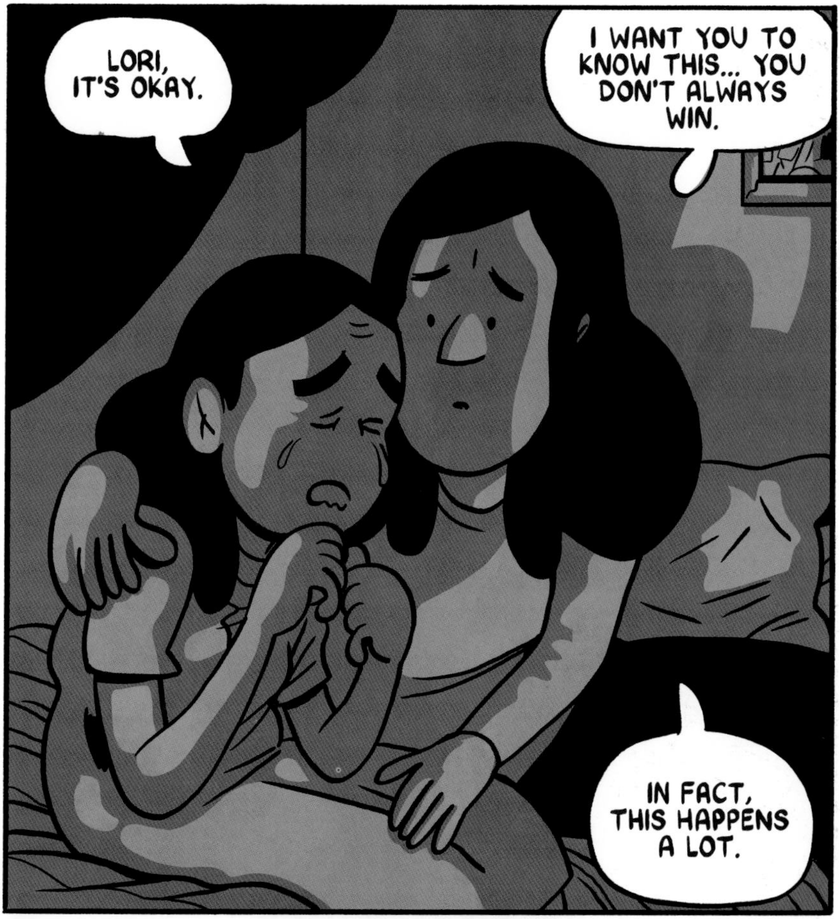
LORI, IT'S OKAY.
I WANT YOU TO KNOW THIS... YOU DON'T ALWAYS WIN.
IN FACT, THIS HAPPENS A LOT.

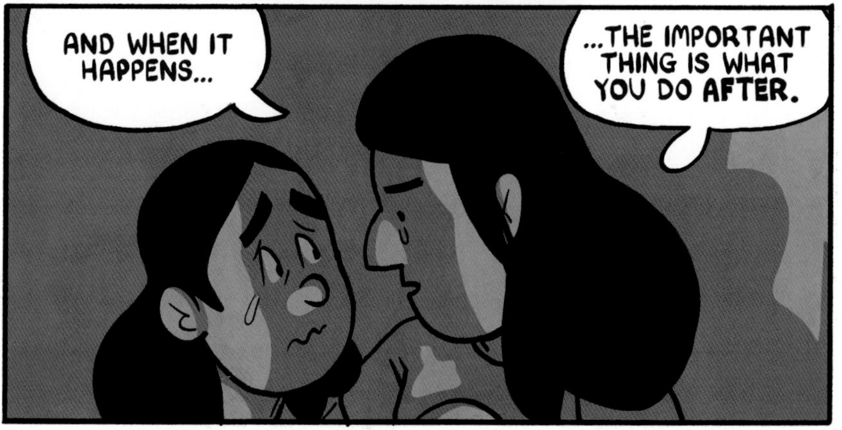
AND WHEN IT HAPPENS...
...THE IMPORTANT THING IS WHAT YOU DO AFTER.

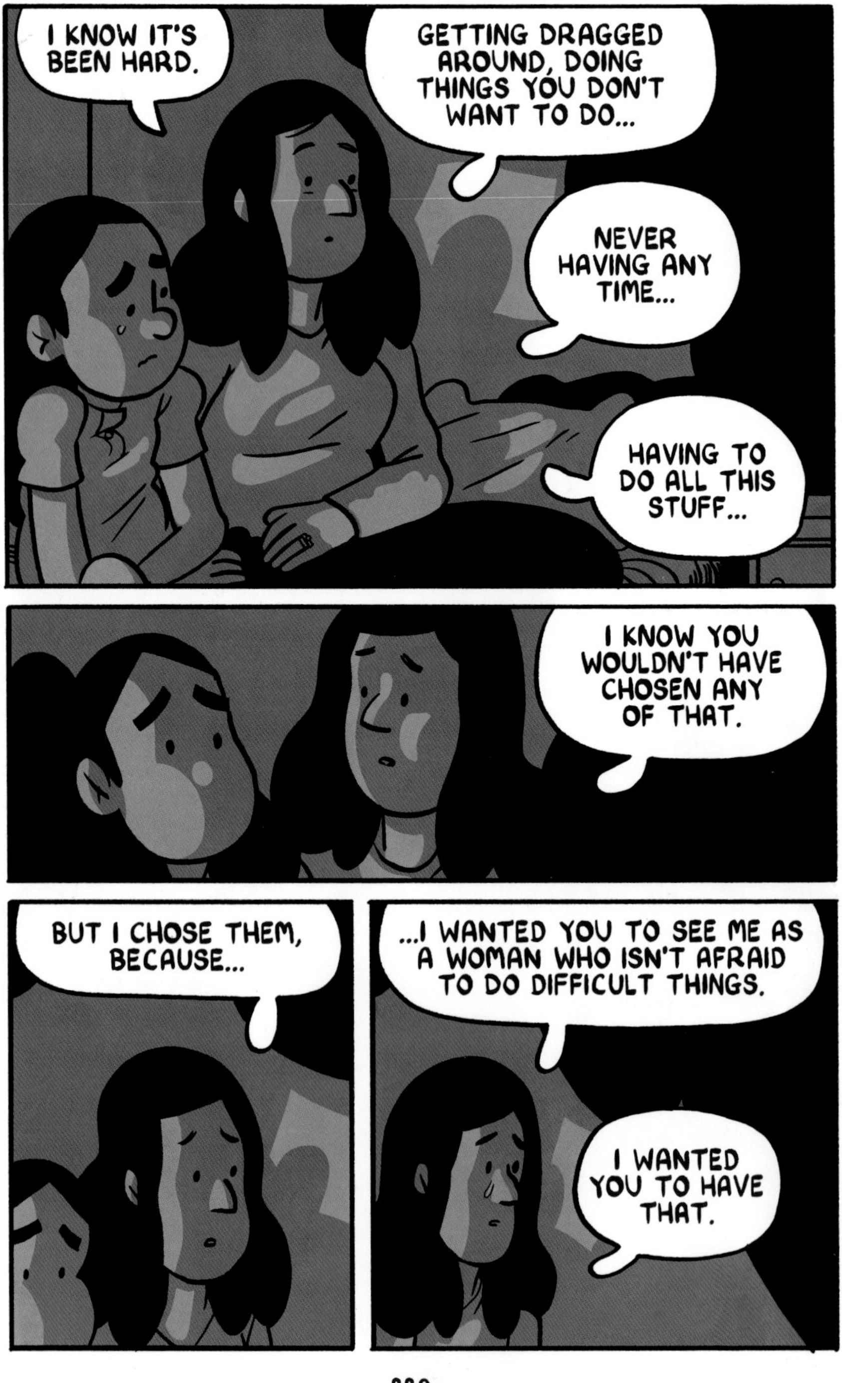
I KNOW IT'S BEEN HARD.
GETTING DRAGGED AROUND, DOING THINGS YOU DON'T WANT TO DO...
NEVER HAVING ANY TIME...
HAVING TO DO ALL THIS STUFF...
I KNOW YOU WOULDN'T HAVE CHOSEN ANY OF THAT.
BUT I CHOSE THEM, BECAUSE...
...I WANTED YOU TO SEE ME AS A WOMAN WHO ISN'T AFRAID TO DO DIFFICULT THINGS.
I WANTED YOU TO HAVE THAT.

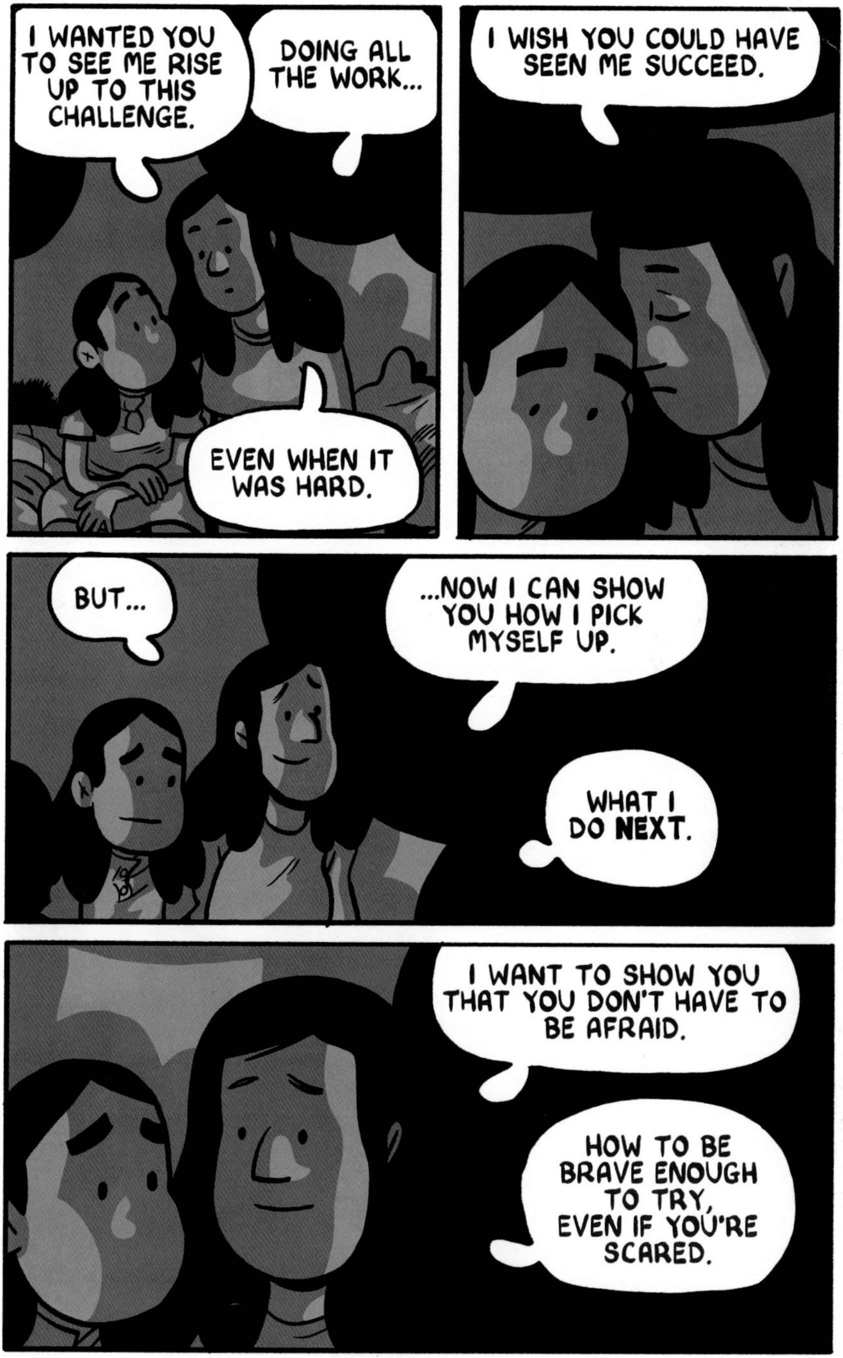
I WANTED YOU TO SEE ME RISE UP TO THIS CHALLENGE.
DOING ALL THE WORK...
EVEN WHEN IT WAS HARD.
I WISH YOU COULD HAVE SEEN ME SUCCEED.
BUT...
...NOW I CAN SHOW YOU HOW I PICK MYSELF UP.
WHAT I DO **NEXT**.
I WANT TO SHOW YOU THAT YOU DON'T HAVE TO BE AFRAID.
HOW TO BE BRAVE ENOUGH TO TRY, EVEN IF YOU'RE SCARED.

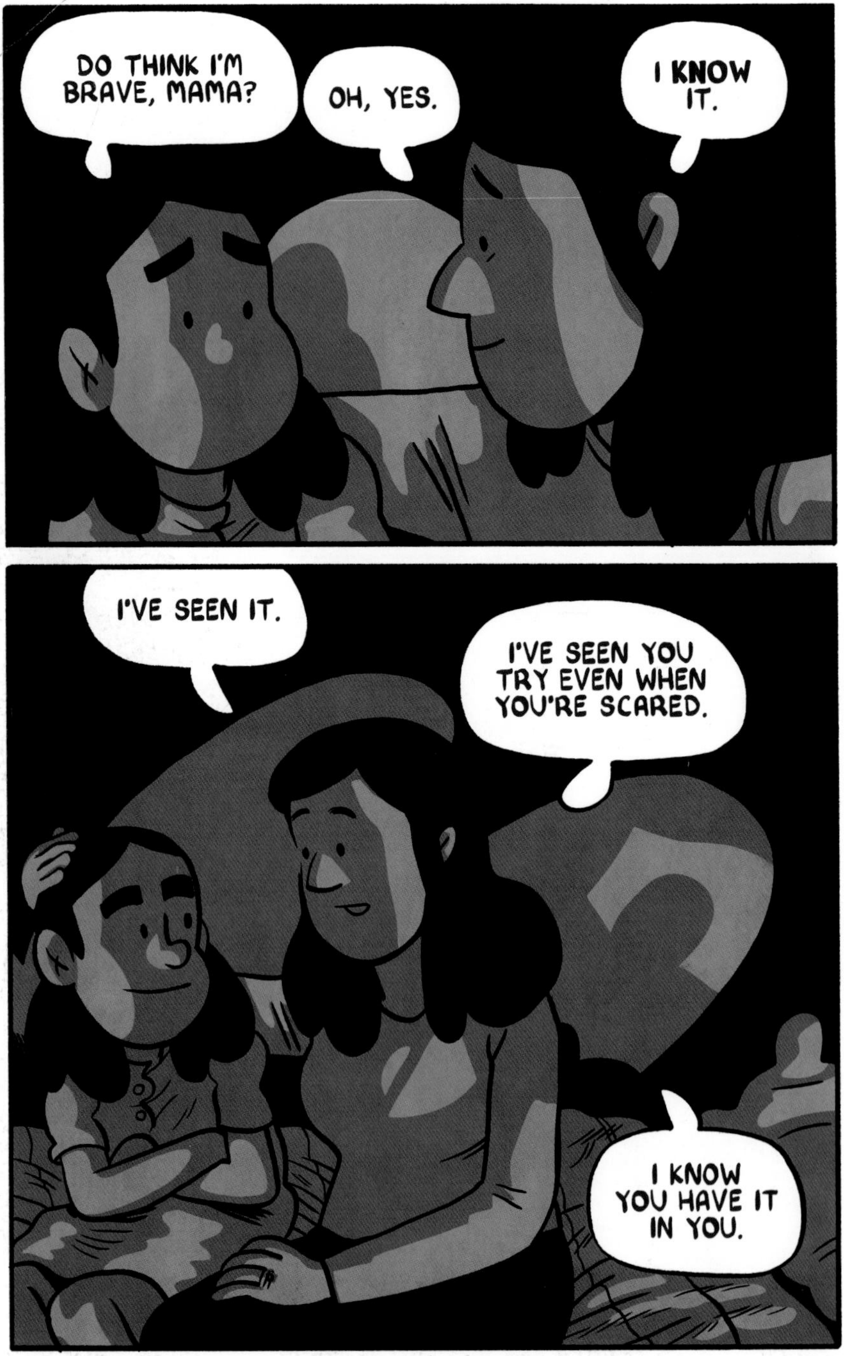
DO THINK I'M BRAVE, MAMA?
OH, YES.
I KNOW IT.
I'VE SEEN IT.
I'VE SEEN YOU TRY EVEN WHEN YOU'RE SCARED.
I KNOW YOU HAVE IT IN YOU.

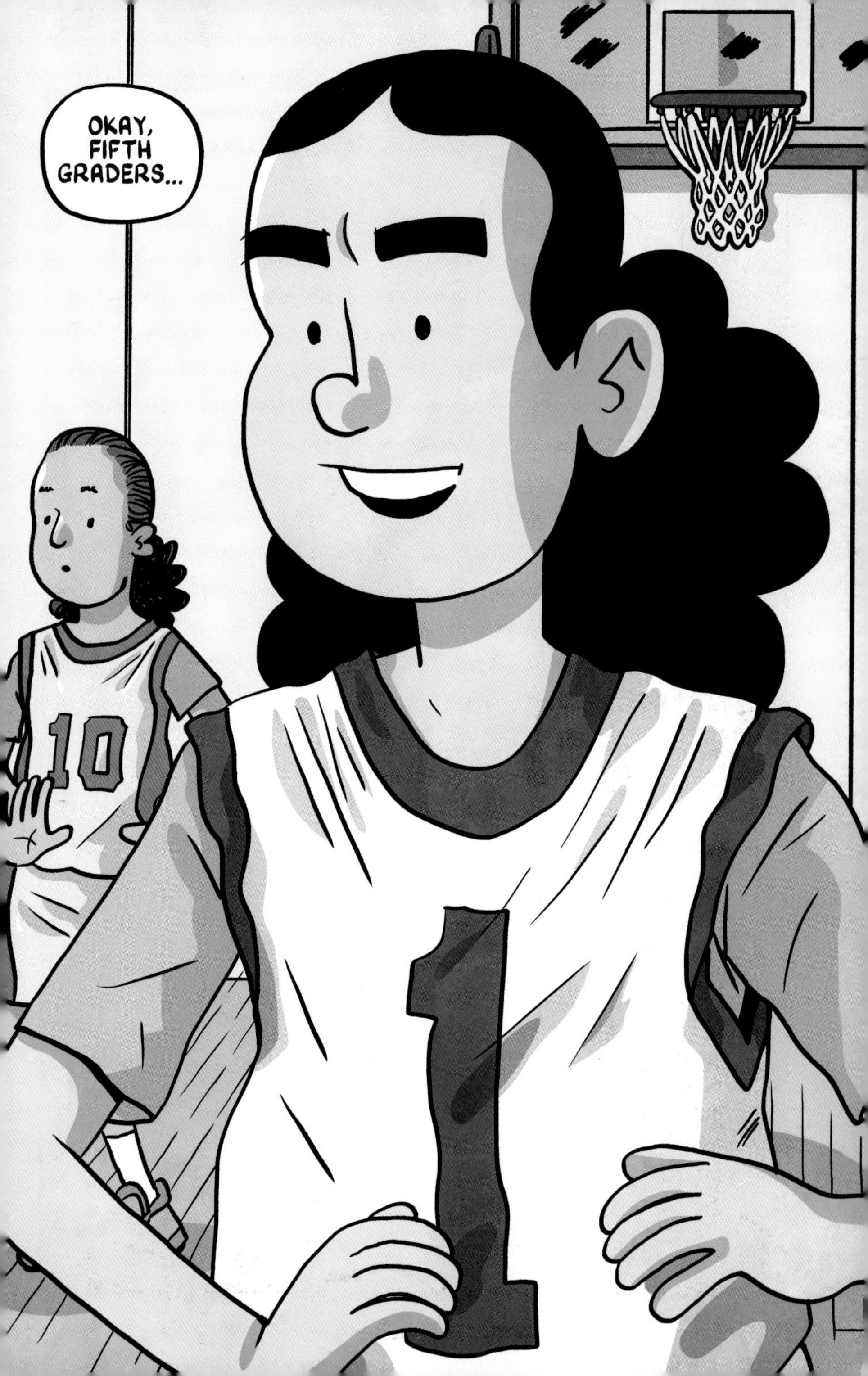
OKAY, FIFTH GRADERS...

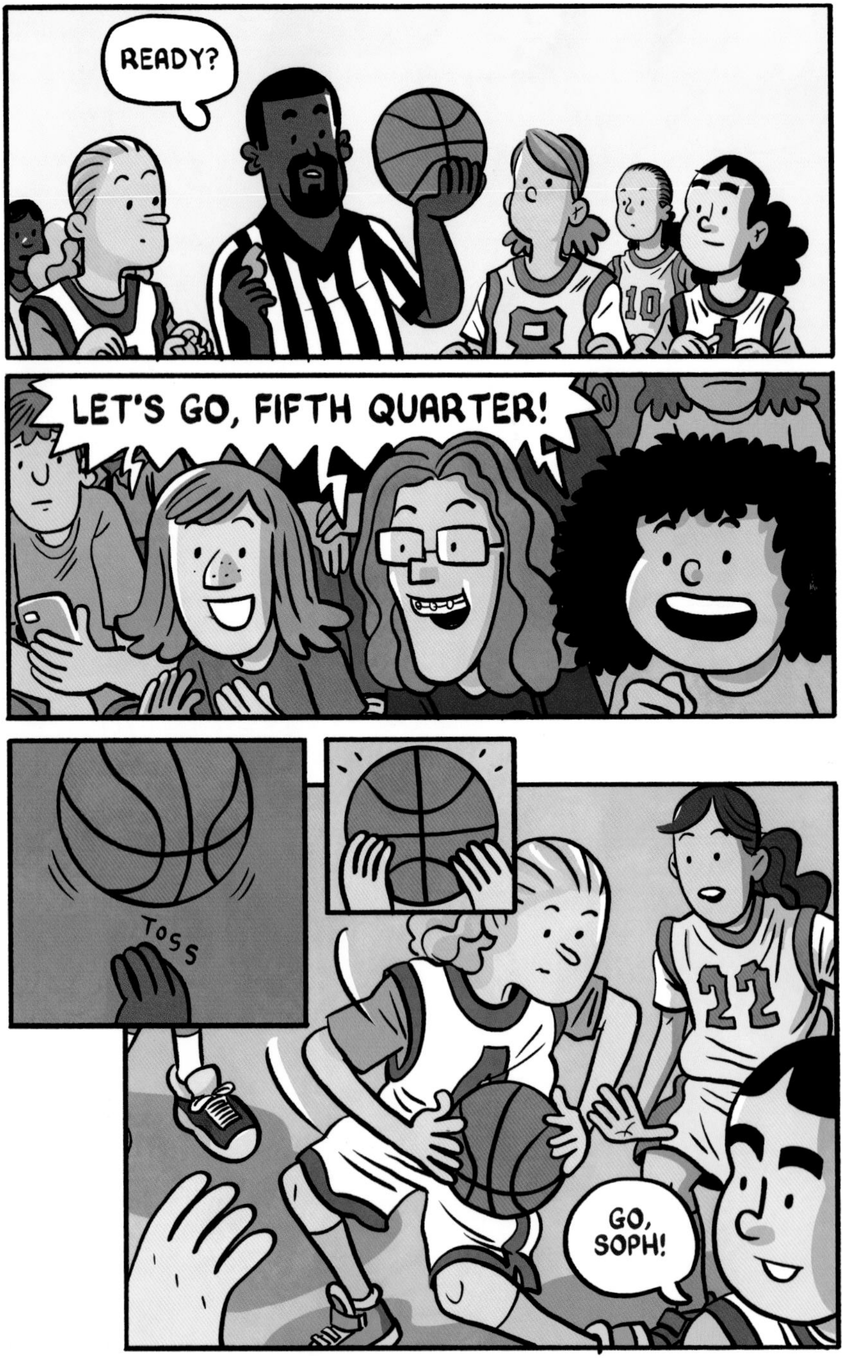
READY?
LET'S GO, FIFTH QUARTER!
TOSS
GO, SOPH!

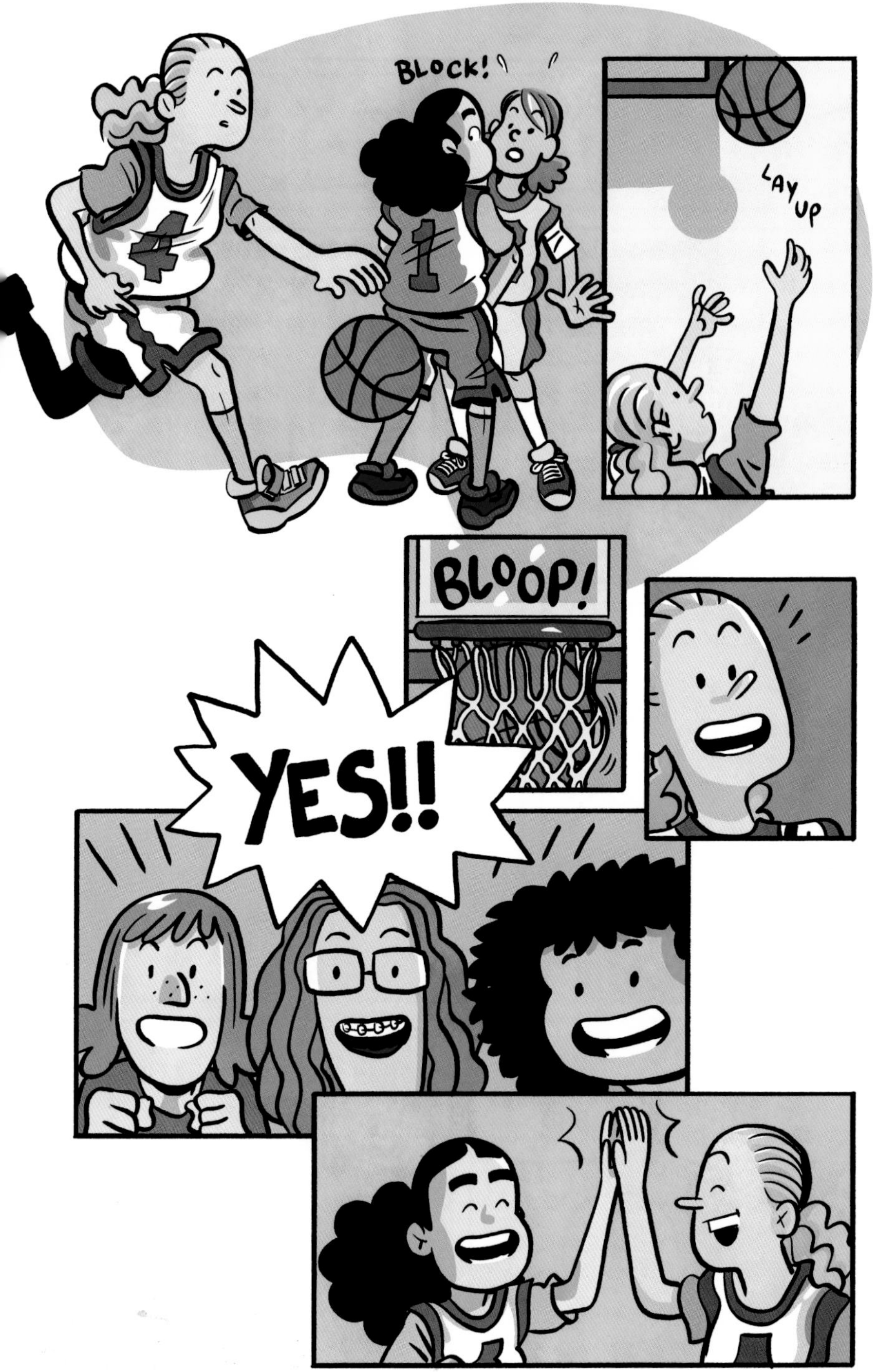
BLOCK!
LAYUP
BLOOP!
YES!!

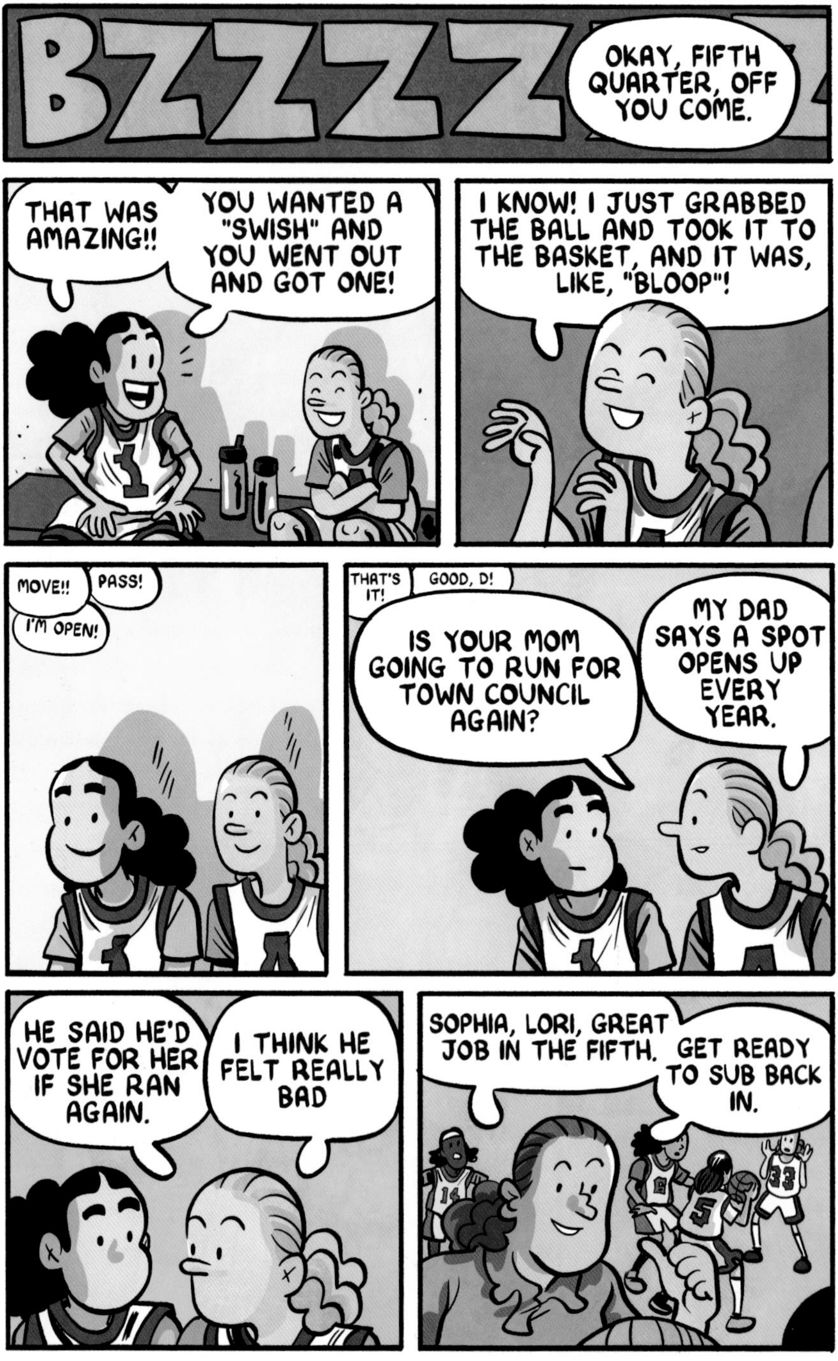
BZZZZ
OKAY, FIFTH QUARTER, OFF YOU COME.
THAT WAS AMAZING!!
YOU WANTED A "SWISH" AND YOU WENT OUT AND GOT ONE!
I KNOW! I JUST GRABBED THE BALL AND TOOK IT TO THE BASKET, AND IT WAS, LIKE, "BLOOP"!
MOVE!!
PASS!
I'M OPEN!
THAT'S IT!
GOOD, D!
IS YOUR MOM GOING TO RUN FOR TOWN COUNCIL AGAIN?
MY DAD SAYS A SPOT OPENS UP EVERY YEAR.
HE SAID HE'D VOTE FOR HER IF SHE RAN AGAIN.
I THINK HE FELT REALLY BAD
SOPHIA, LORI, GREAT JOB IN THE FIFTH.
GET READY TO SUB BACK IN.

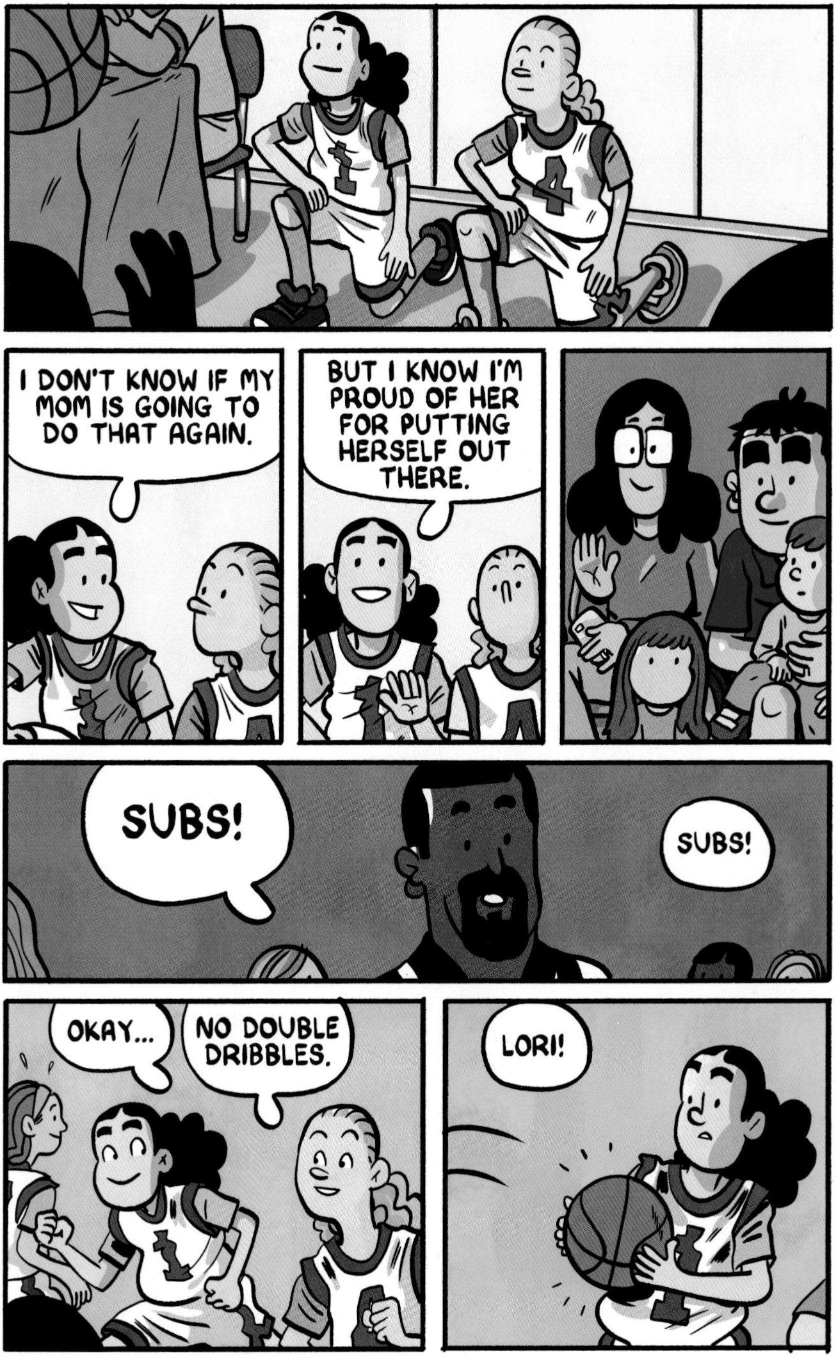
I DON'T KNOW IF MY MOM IS GOING TO DO THAT AGAIN.
BUT I KNOW I'M PROUD OF HER FOR PUTTING HERSELF OUT THERE.
SUBS!
SUBS!
OKAY...
NO DOUBLE DRIBBLES.
LORI!

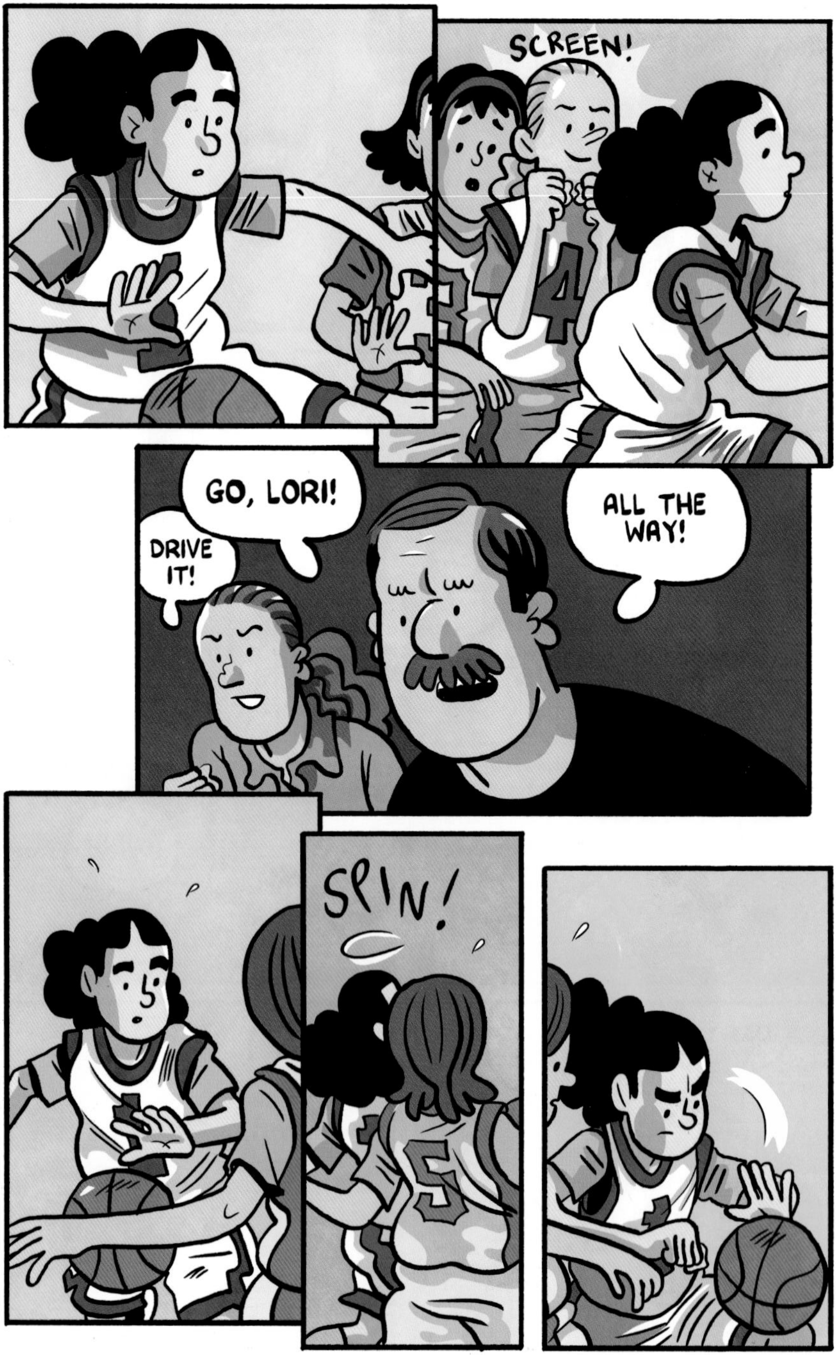
SCREEN!
GO, LORI!
DRIVE IT!
ALL THE WAY!
SPIN!

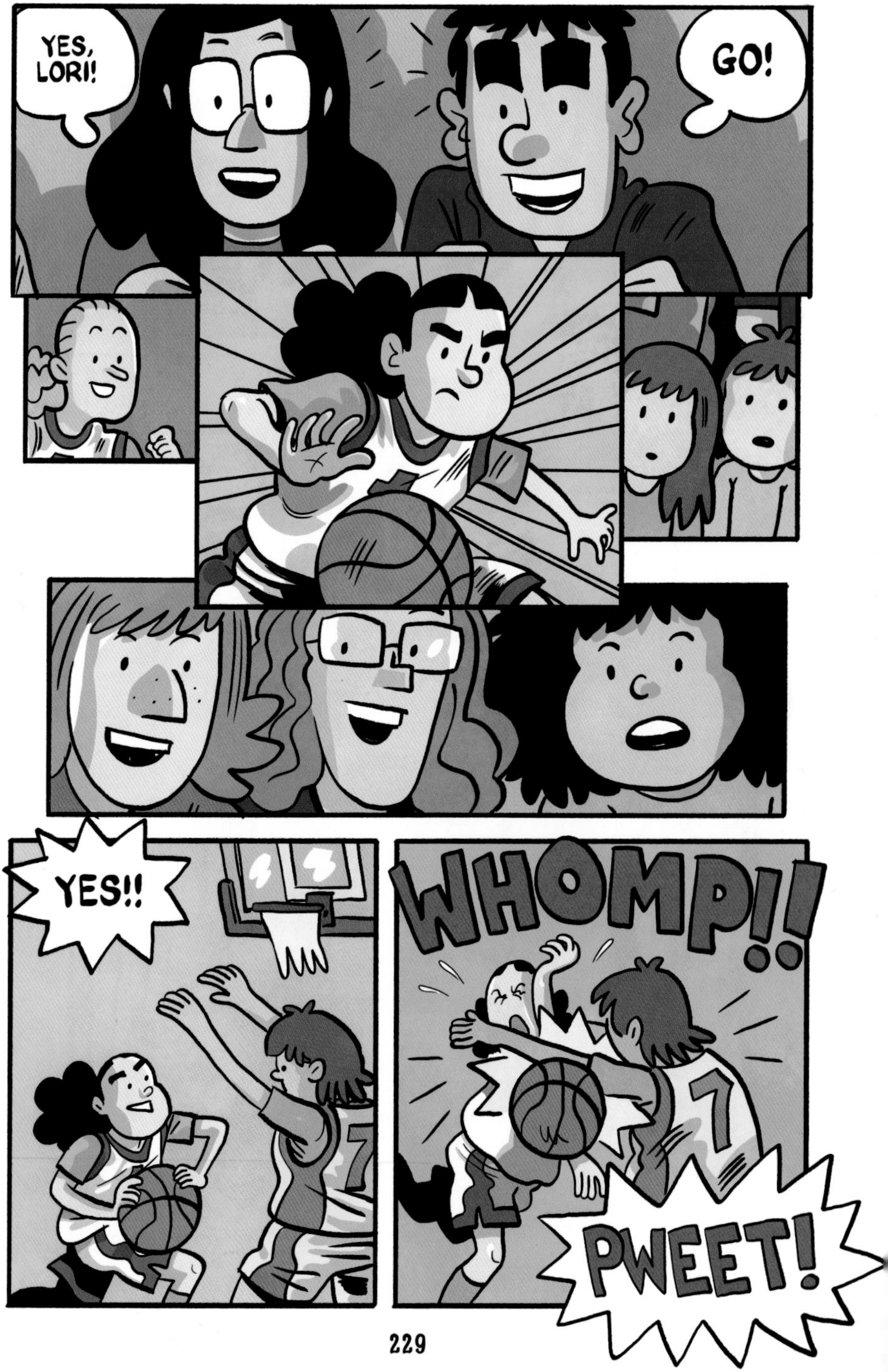
YES, LORI!
GO!
YES!!
WHOMP!!
PWEET!

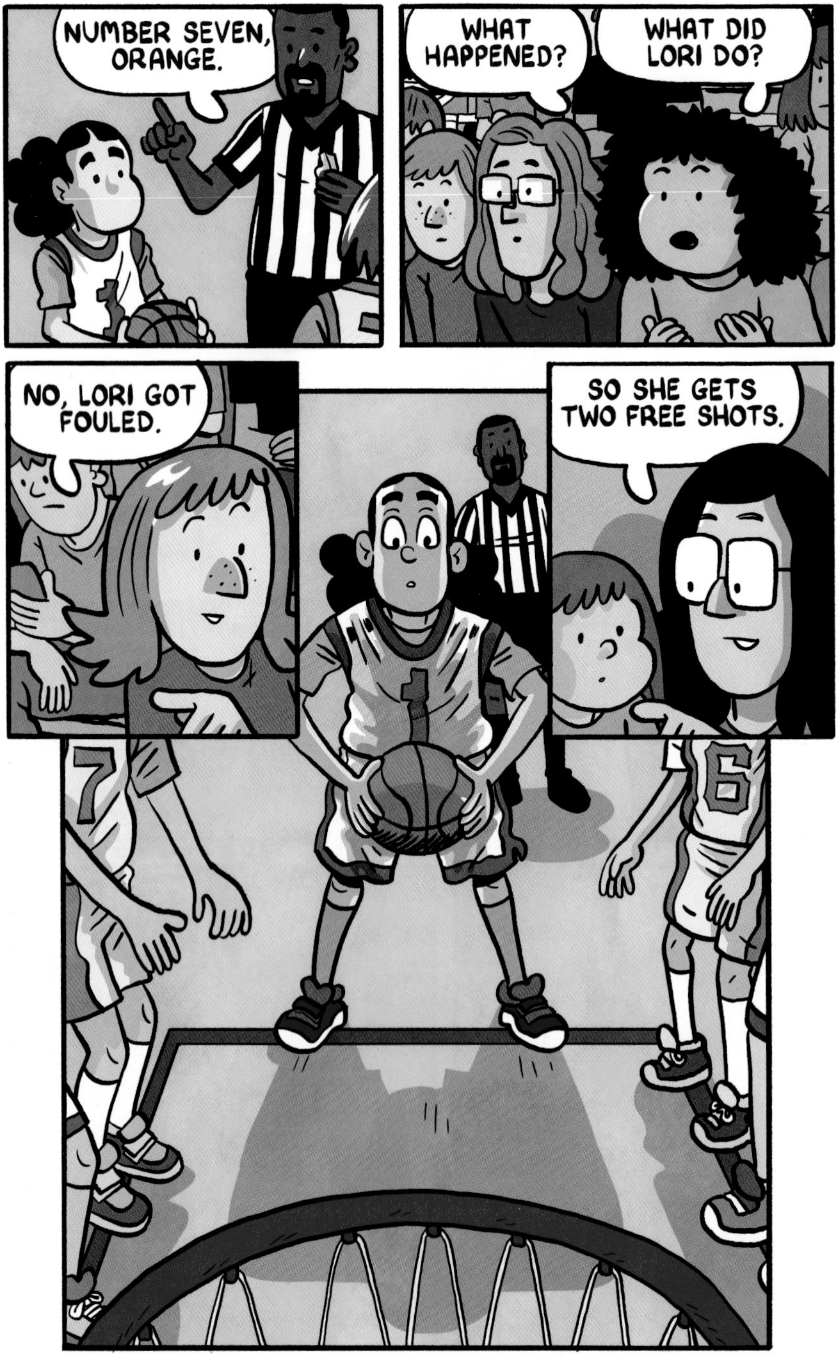
NUMBER SEVEN, ORANGE.
WHAT HAPPENED?
WHAT DID LORI DO?
NO, LORI GOT FOULED.
SO SHE GETS TWO FREE SHOTS.
7
6

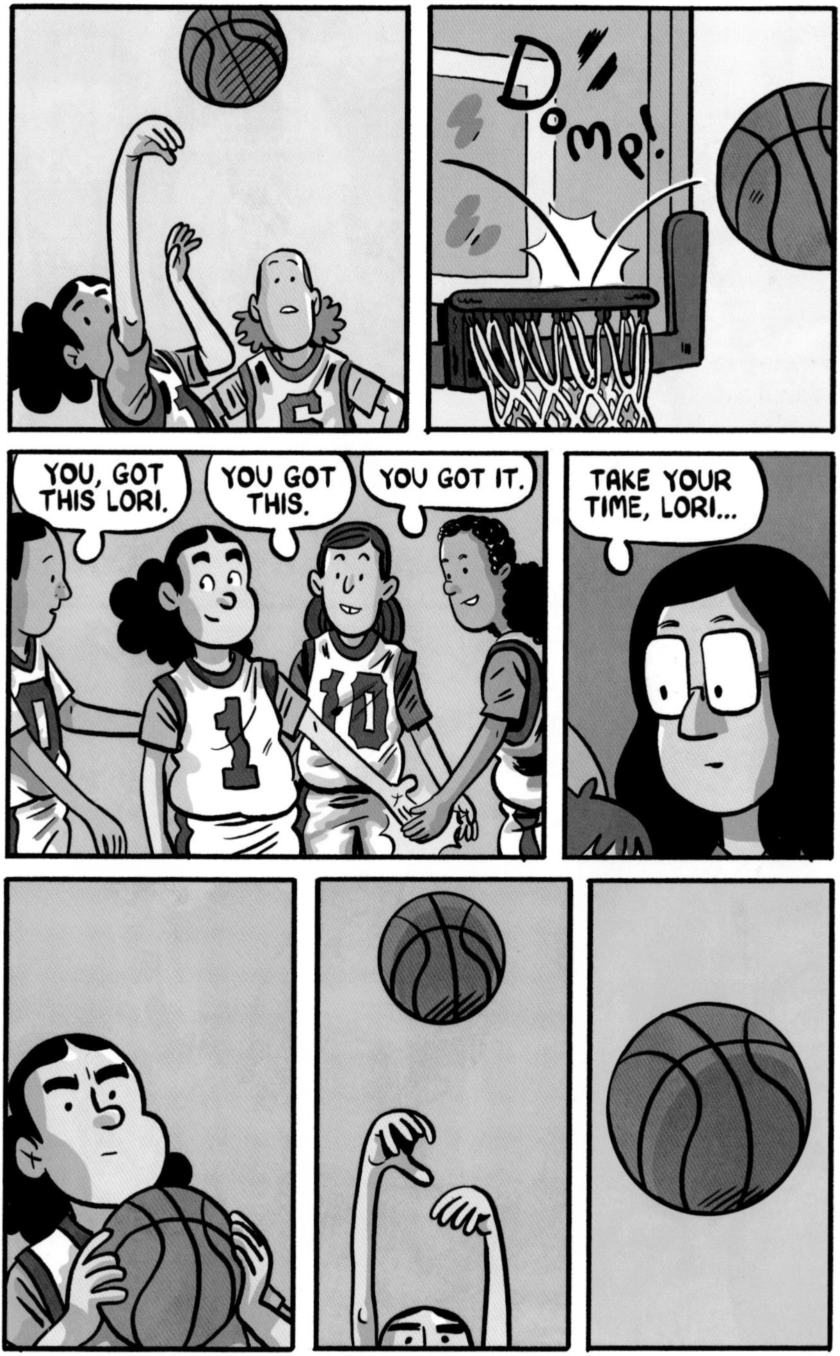
DOMP!
YOU, GOT THIS LORI.
YOU GOT THIS.
YOU GOT IT.
TAKE YOUR TIME, LORI...

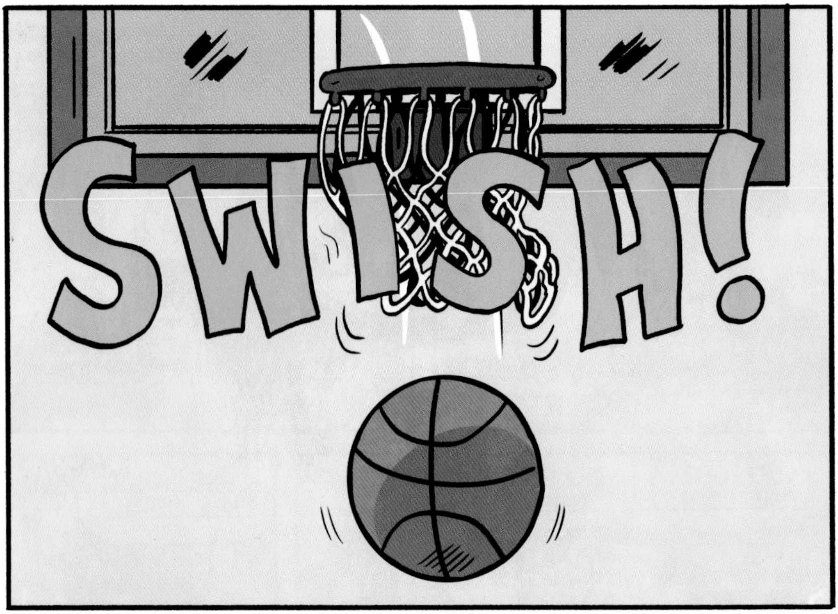
SWISH!

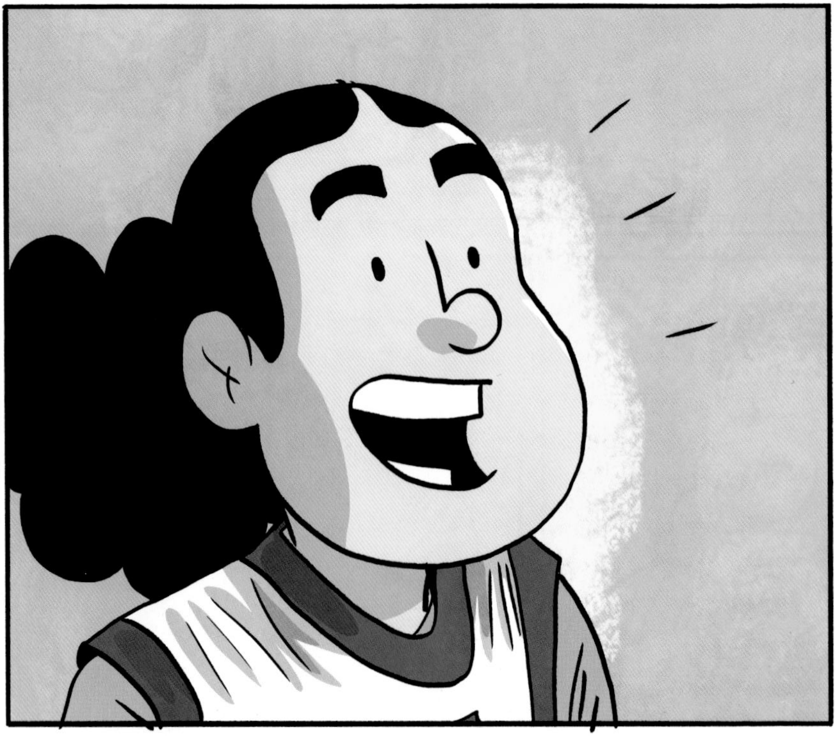

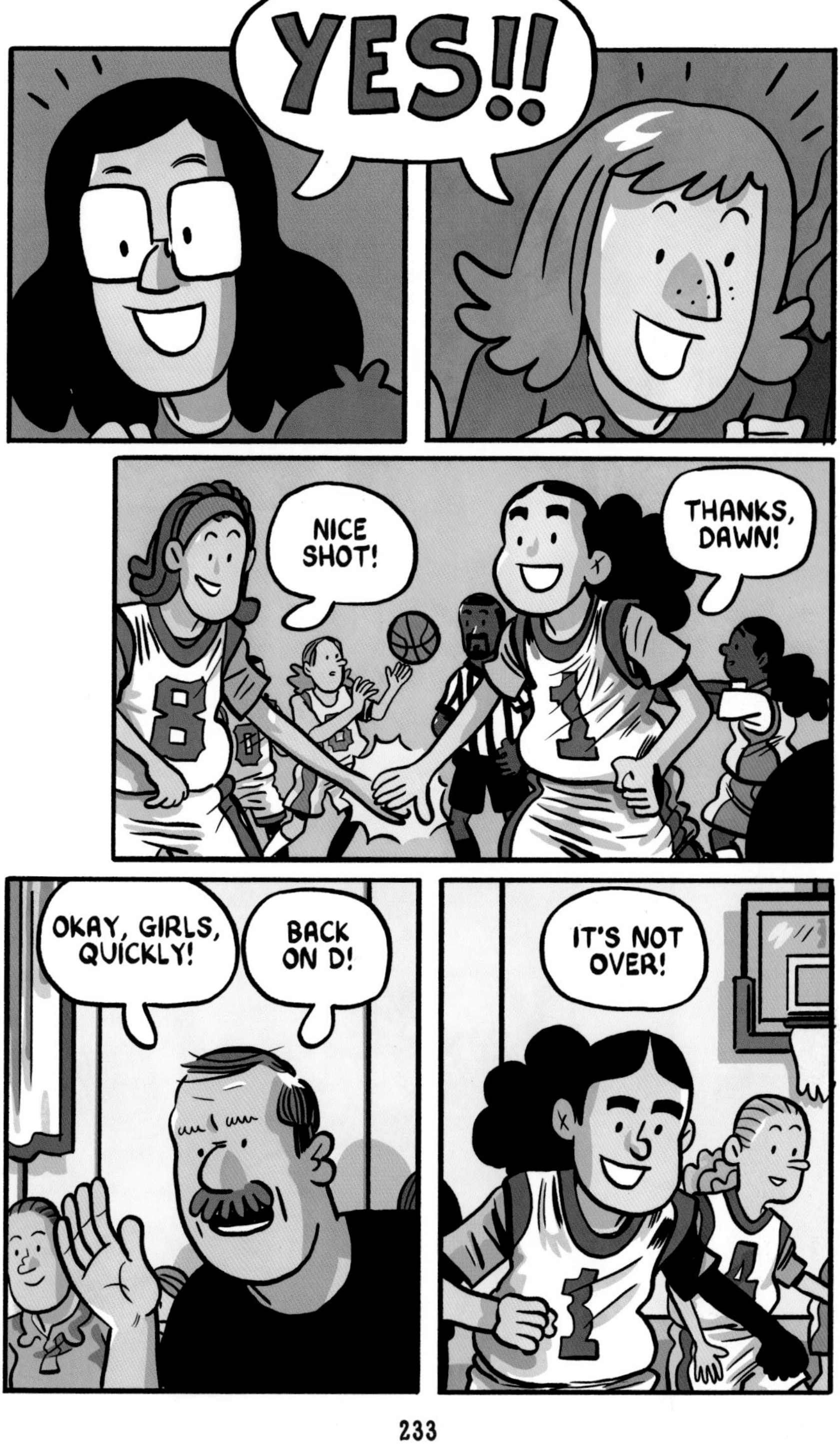
YES!!
NICE SHOT!
THANKS, DAWN!
OKAY, GIRLS, QUICKLY!
BACK ON D!
IT'S NOT OVER!

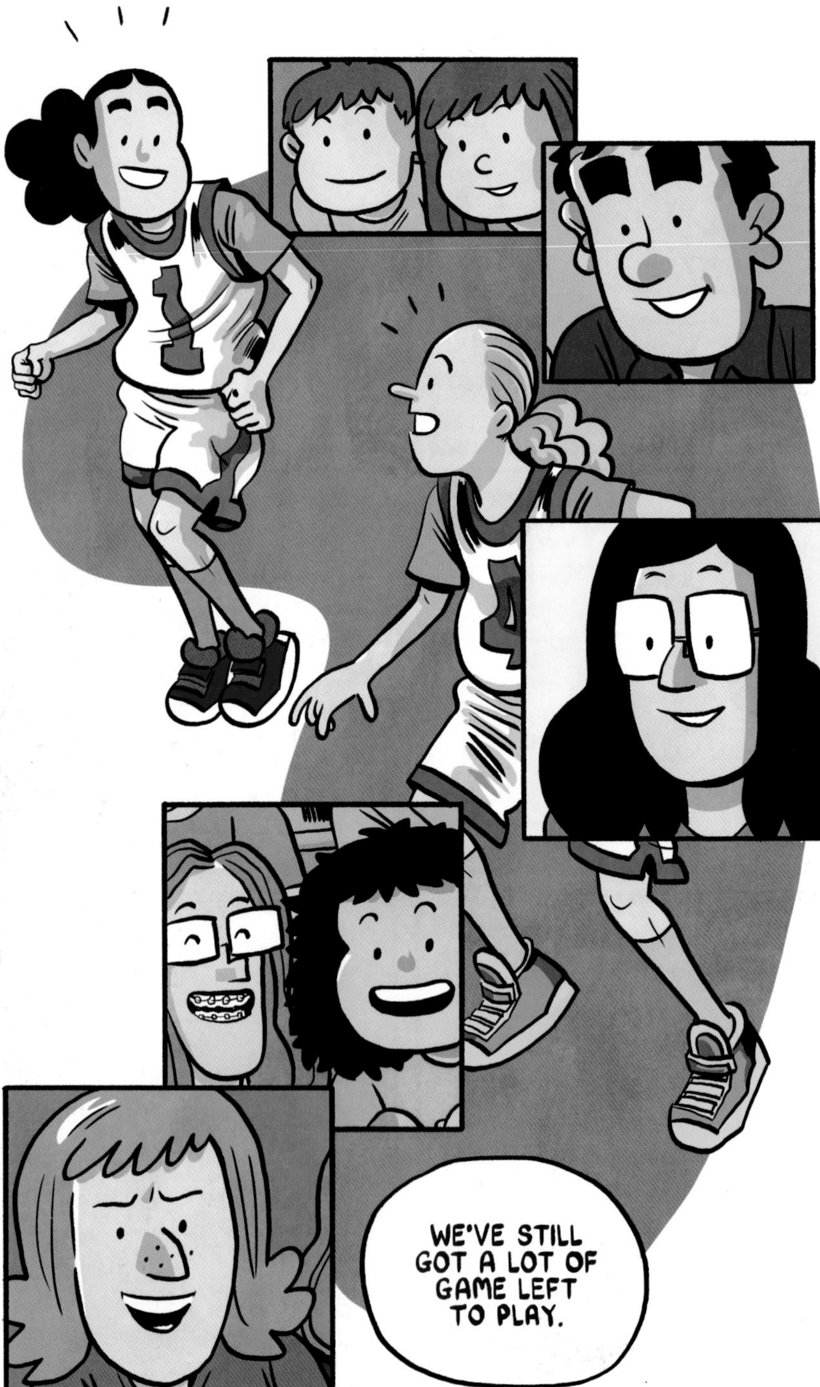
WE'VE STILL GOT A LOT OF GAME LEFT TO PLAY.

TO BE CONTINUED IN . . .

THE FIFTH QUARTER
HARD COURT

LIBERTY
9

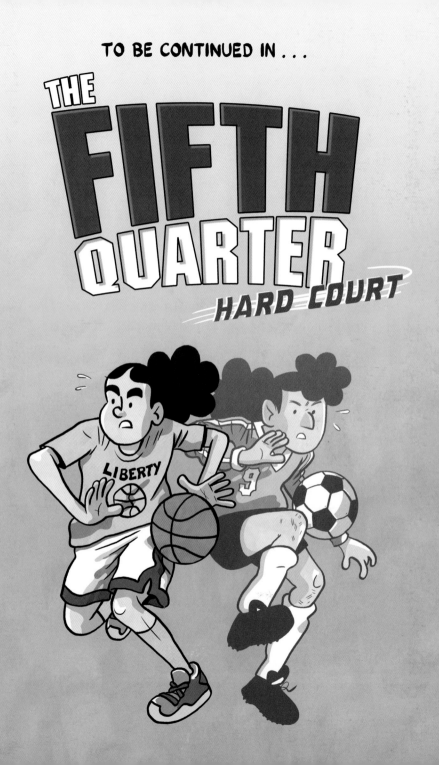

Acknowledgments

All of my love and gratitude to Aliza, Orli, and Ewan for their immense support and inspiration. Without you none of this would have been possible.

Thank-you to Greg Hunter, who provided the spark, Dan Kois, Hazel Newlevant, MariNaomi, Mark Siegel, and Gordon Warnock.

Special thanks to Jess Patel. Thanks also to Erin Howard, Liz DeBeer, Chris Rodriguez, Meghan Chrisner-Keefe, Michael McCue, and everybody willing to put themselves out there and run for something.

Thank-you to the coaches, Tiny Green, Jenny Liggio, Tracey Sabino and the incredible team at Hoop Group, Eugene Curran, John Reid, Jason Corrigan, and anybody who volunteers their time helping kids build confidence and get better.

Additional thanks to Brian Jensen, Zoe Arhanic, Annie Lachanski, and the talented players of the Lady Knights for their many exciting games.

© 2016 BY TED TERRANOVA

MIKE DAWSON is the author of several graphic novels and comics collections. His work has appeared in *The New Yorker, The Nib,* and *Slate,* and has been nominated for multiple Eisner and Ignatz Awards, as well as the *Slate* Cartoonists Studio Prize. He lives at the Jersey Shore with his wife and children. mikedawsoncomics.com